The Rising Star of Kimmie Coconut Tree

The Rising Star of Kimmie Coconut Tree

THOMAS STIMSON

The Rising Star of
Kimmie Coconut Tree

Copyright © 2024 – Thomas Stimson
ISBN: 978-1-965237-01-4

Cover by Roslyn McFarland

Contents

Dedication

With much love to my own Kimmie and her sisters.
You are the inspiration of this story's most important theme.

Prologue

Dear Reader,

Welcome to the story of our mother, Kimmie Pham Starbuckle. My name is Lois Starbuckle, oldest daughter and an author of biographies and historical fiction along with the television series "Who in the World is…" Of all the people I have researched, interviewed and written about, I have never delved into anything as personal as my family…until now.

As of this writing, my mother is in declining health and confined to a nursing home. Early last year as we were clearing out the Riverton family home in preparation for selling, I came across a box of notebooks in the back of a closet. Notebooks, I quickly discovered, to be a running diary of our mother's budding romance, first years of marriage, adaptation to life in America and the beginnings of a career that spanned nearly four decades.

None of us knew these diaries existed. Many of the stories she tells within its pages were new to us and others give depth and understanding to things we already knew, had heard or are in the public record. I have shared the diaries with family members and close friends who, in turn, have shared their stories and recollections of our mother's long and colorful life. The diaries brought back a flood of memories and many revelations that will be revealed within these pages.

If you are reading this book, you are either a fan of our parents or are at least familiar with their work. I have learned that sometimes the best stories are found in your own family, hidden by what is considered the ordinary and familiar to us, but far more interesting and enlightening to others.

So, with our mother's permission, we are publishing her diaries. The following pages have been translated from the original Vietnamese with the help of several family members and final approval given by our mother. The entries are either in their entirety or excerpted for brevity. I have added the recollections of my mother, brother and sisters and other surviving friends and family members to share our own views and context of the events presented.

We hope you will enjoy reading this as much as we enjoyed discovering the fascinating details of our parents' courtship, marriage and their seeds to stardom.

Lois Starbuckle – March 17, 2061

1999

Kimmie's Visitor From America

December 1st
Hello Dear My Diary,

It is 10 o'clock and I cannot sleep. I am nervous and excited about tomorrow as my American boyfriend is coming to see me for the first time. Tina said I should write a diary to make permanent memories of these times to come. I hope they will be good times and not bad times as I am not sure what to expect.

Tina said I should write in a diary in the same way as writing to a friend. I have never written a diary before, nor had any close friends, so I will take my sister's advice and make an introduction. Here it is: I am Pham Thi Kim. Family name is Pham, personal name Kim. I know this is different from how Western people present their names but that is our custom.

I like to be called Kimmie, but many people call me by another name, Cay Dua. My family and friends do not call me Cay Dua because it is not nice to my ears. It is vaguely clever, fits the way I look, but I don't like it and never have. I have not told Fred that I am a Cay Dua and I hope when he sees me, he will not run away. This is my biggest worry right now.

My boyfriend is Frederick Allen Starbuckle. Family name Starbuckle, personal name Frederick. He prefers that I call him 'Fred' but some of his friends call him 'Buck'. Fred is thirty-one years old (Year of the Monkey) and we share the same birthday of March 17th.

My auntie in America, Pham Giang, is the younger sister of my Ba, Pham Lo. Pham Giang was her old name before she married an American soldier. Now her married name is Greene and her American nickname is Ginger. I laughed and laughed after I learned enough English to understand that her name can be listed as Greene, Ginger.

Auntie has three children: two girls, Grace and Dorothy, and a boy Michael. The girls are married and Auntie has three grandchildren. Michael is studying business at a local university. Auntie knows Fred because they have a business relationship. She is the one who introduced us…or more correctly, introduced Fred to me.

Fred and I have been writing to each other for eleven months. I got his first letter on New Years Day 1999. Fred introduced himself to me in a short but very nice letter. I was nervous to write back but Me and Ba urged me to write and make a new friend.

At first, I wrote Fred only to please my parents and Auntie. I have never had a boyfriend and the only Western person I have known is Auntie's husband Paul. This has been a new experience for me, writing to a man far away and making a relationship.

Our friendship has become strong enough that he offered to come here and meet me in person. I am glad he asked, as I wish to meet him also. Can Fred be a real boyfriend if we have never met? I will find out very soon.

I am twenty-eight years old (Year of the Pig) and the youngest of four daughters. My father was not lucky enough to have a boy child, but he is kind and sweet to us and our mother. My father is a businessman, buying goods from factories and workshops in Vietnam and nearby countries, then reselling them to local and overseas buyers.

I have attended high school and college with a concentration in English language and business education. All my sisters have been to college in Vietnam or other countries, and we all speak one or more foreign languages.

Sister number one, Thao, went to college in Japan and speaks four other languages to enhance our business marketability. She helps Ba find buyers and negotiate deals, traveling throughout Asia with a special business visa that is difficult to get.

I have not travelled outside my homeland but sister number two, Trinh, she prefers Tina, lives in New York City and has been working for a prestigious Hong Kong bank since graduating from Columbia University. She speaks Mandarin and Cantonese as part of her job.

Sister number three, Thanh, lives in Riverton near Auntie Giang and owns a nail salon with her husband Vo. They have fraternal twin girls name Tam and Cam and they are very cute. I have not seen them since the girls were small.

I live with Ba, Me and Thao in Ho Chi Minh City. HCMC is the New York City of Vietnam and was called Saigon before Reunification. Even after twenty-five years, we still use the old name as much as the new one.

Fred says he lives alone and is not married. This is different from single people here who live with their parents until marriage, but Tina says it is very common for single Western children to live away from their parents…even expected! Tina lives with women roommates to save money on rent. My parents worry about her not being married or living with family members so as to avoid unhealthy influences from the immoral American culture.

My understanding is that Fred does not have a college education. This bothers us, but Auntie says Fred is very smart and makes good-sense business decisions without a degree. I am not so sure about this, but Auntie is, as my father likes to say, "sharp as a bamboo splinter" and my parents respect her judgement.

I have seen pictures of Fred. I think he is good-looking for a Western man. I sent pictures of myself to Fred but, because of the way I look, they are half-body shots and not with other people in the frame to show the comparison.

Still, I am sure he can see how different I am. Sometimes I am ashamed to be such a Cay Dua, but I cannot change this. I hope Fred is not scared or upset with how I look. The rest of my family are quite ordinary-looking.

I have written so much so I will try to sleep now. Fred's plane arrives tomorrow afternoon and I want to look and feel my best.

Hello Dear My Diary,

Now it is 2 o'clock and I still cannot sleep so I will try writing some more to make myself tired.

When I explained to Fred about our family business, he says he does a similar kind of business, but he calls it "Recycling". He gets things free or at low cost and sells them for a profit.

I get the impression that his business relationship with Auntie does not involve working in her stores and he does not have employees, a storefront or a business office where people can visit. Even so, he says he stays busy all day doing many different things. It sounds very different from our family's business with many dozens of employees, several warehouses and relationships with hundreds of business owners and brokers throughout Asia.

Fred says he is his own boss and can make time to visit me for six weeks during the Western holidays of Noel and New Year's. He must have a lot of money to not work his business for six weeks! Ba is giving me all six weeks off to have time with Fred because we think he wants to make a more serious relationship with me. I have never taken more than a few days off in a row except during the Tet holiday or the one time I was very sick.

His letters and emails are pleasant and he can be very funny sometimes. Fred says he wants a nice woman to spend a long time with. My English is good enough to understand he wants a wife and he makes this clear without saying it directly. When he sees me, maybe he will change his mind.

I don't know why he wants an Asian woman from far away when there are many pretty American women who will want a man like Fred, I am sure. I have to be careful and heed my family's impressions of our visitor. They are good judges of character as they have to be, in order to survive in our business for so long!

We have cleaned and polished everything to get ready for Fred's arrival. I hope he likes Vietnamese food because it is all we know how to cook. There are no American-style restaurants except in istrict One where the expats live.

There has been much discussion of where Fred will stay. For now, it has been decided that Ba will pay for one week at a nearby hotel and we will discuss the matter further after Fred arrives. That is, if Fred does not leave after seeing me.

I know I should not think like this about myself, but I never told Fred how I look…or how people treat me. If he likes me as much as I think he does, he will overlook the bad and accept my good traits.

We found it sad that Mama was so insecure about her looks and that she was all but convinced that her American boyfriend, whom she had not yet met in person, would leave soon after meeting her. When she re-read her old entries, Mama said she thought Fred might "flee like a South Vietnamese general during the Fall of Saigon.

Fred's Arrival

December 2
Dear My Diary,

We hired a taxi van to meet Fred at the Tan Son Nhat International airport. Me, Ba and Thao all came and we dressed extra nice for our visitor. I wore a long floral skirt and short sleeved white blouse with flat shoes as I do not own any high heels. Me said I will give a good first impression.

Fred spent a long time getting through customs. It can be like that for foreigners as the officers often hold people up, hoping for a gift to expedite the process. However, once out, he was easy to see over the tops of everyone's heads.

Fred saw me right away. "Kimmie? Kimmie!" and came over with two suitcases, a shoulder bag and a big toothy smile. He put down the bags and gave me a hug. I felt awkward as everyone nearby was looking at us and only my family have hugged me before. Me nudged my arm so I reached up and hugged him in return. His back is so broad and firm, not at all like hugging my parents or sisters.

I looked up at Fred. I can actually LOOK UP at Fred. This is a very different experience for me. Fred stepped back to get a full picture of me for his eyes. He smiled and said, "Wow! You look gorgeous!" I looked up the word in my dictionary later. "Gorgeous" means like "Beautiful".

I felt so shy and formal with Fred and maybe I acted too stiff, but I introduced father and mother and sister to Fred and Fred knew to say "Hello" and "Happy to be in Vietnam" in our language. His accent sounded funny to us but we are pleased that he tried. Perhaps Auntie taught him.

The hired taxi was nearby and Ba picked up one suitcase to help. He is a strong man, but I could see the strain on his face. Fred took it from Ba with ease. Ba muttered "I must be getting old."

Fred wore a short sleeve shirt and his muscles bulged to the edges of the fabric. He said the flight was long but pleasant with good food, "and seeing you in person was worth every hour in the air!". His smile and manner were relaxed as Fred tried to sweet-talk me. I don't know how I looked to Fred, but I felt a mixture of nervousness and excitement that he was really, finally here.

Many people were looking at us curiously as Fred is a full two meters tall. I am used to people staring at me, but with the two of us together I am sure they didn't know what to think, especially grouped with my typical-looking family.

Ba sat up front with the driver and Me and Thao took the back row. Fred and I sat in the middle where there is more leg-room. Fred wore thick khaki cargo trousers and a light blue button-down shirt with pinstripes and a white cotton undershirt beneath. Not a great combination for our hot, humid weather.

Fred has blue eyes and thick, curly yellow hair, so unlike anyone I have seen in person. He looked out the windows at everything as we drove through HCMC and not much on me. It must be very strange for Fred as the roads are crowded with bicycles, motorbikes, cyclos, taxis, big trucks and very few privately owned cars.

At one point, he tried to hold my hand but I took it away. We are new together and I am shy. Also, my family is right there looking at Fred but pretending not to look.

Thao asked Fred how Vietnam looks to him. He said "It's like being inside a Hollywood movie.

Back home is nothing like this."

Thao can speak English, but not so well as me. She also speaks Japanese, Korean and Canton Chinese with varying degrees of fluency. I don't think Fred can speak any of these languages.

When I told Fred that Vietnam is a very poor country, he observed that everybody looks like they are going somewhere or making business wherever they can. "Maybe they are poor, but they look very busy. There are lots of shops and people selling things on the streets!"

When we arrived at our home, other relatives had gathered and we made a welcome feast for Fred. Aunties and Uncles and Cousins from around HCMC were there to greet our American visitor as much out of curiosity as for the free food.

Fred said "hello" a lot, nodded, bowed and shook hands all around. Men put beers in Fred's hand and he would hold the bottle, make gestures and put the drink to his lips but the bottle always stayed full. The men did not notice it, but I did.

When the food was served, Fred asked if he could have the Orange Nehi the women and children were drinking. He drank several bottles of Nehi throughout the luncheon and no beer. Many men also offered cigarettes to Fred, but he politely refused.

Fred was the center of attention and some of the family spoke English to him as best they could. They would say nice things or ask questions and sometimes I helped with translating or explained the foods to Fred. We were surprised that he knew how to use chopsticks and proved to be adept with them.

Fred did not look tired despite the thirty-hour travel time. When I asked, Fred said he slept well on the plane. He looked at me many times and smiled and tried to make small talk, but we are so new together and suddenly he has many friendly strangers vying for his attention.

After everyone was gone and we could relax a little, Me told me, "Sit with Fred and be a good hostess." As she joined her sisters to clean up, Fred gave me a small stuffed deer with antlers and said his name is "Buck" like him. It is a Coming to Vietnam present for me. I feel bad that I did not think to get something for Fred's arrival.

I asked if he likes to be called Fred or Buck? He said Buck is an informal nickname and is based on the Starbuckle name, which now makes sense to me. "I would prefer you call me Fred," he said. "And you like to be called…?"

"Kimmie…just like in your letters."

"Your voice is very pretty," he said. No one has ever said that to me and I did not know what to say, so I just said "Thank you."

Our AC is not very strong, and Fred was perspiring heavily, but he did not complain. I asked if maybe he has some short pants to change into?

Fred brightened and said, "Good idea!". He reached for his thigh and unzipped his trouser legs from a hidden seam. I was surprised as the legs came right off and Fred folded and tucked them into the big cargo pockets of his shorts. His legs are as muscled as his arms and covered with yellow hair.

Thao came in for a few minutes to speak with us and, as she was leaving, Sister stood behind Fred winking and making two thumbs up. It was so unexpected that I giggled. When Fred asked what was funny, I was too shy to say what sister had done so I told him I just thought of a funny thing but it is not easy to translate.

Fred did not say anything about my being so different from the rest of the family. He is always smiling and saying complimentary things about me. I know he sees. Everyone can see. But Fred is too nice to say.

Ba came in and we made preparations to go to the hotel, a half kilometer from our house. It is a small hotel, but clean, and we know the owners. Our car is too small to take all the baggage, so we took one suitcase and a smaller bag and left the other suitcase at home.

Mr. Chau was surprised to see how tall Fred is…I thought he was going to fall on his bottom! He made apologies for not having a big enough bed but he still showed us a room. It has one bed and we can see Fred will not fit in it at all.

Fred asked for a room with two beds. The room is larger and Fred easily moved the second bed in front of the first to make an upside-down 'T'. Now the bed is long enough for Fred to be comfortable. Fred made a presentation with his hands and said, "Ta Da!"

Mr. Chau said Fred is very clever to think this way. He brought an extra table for the luggage and showed Fred everything in the room: Color TV, air conditioner, shower and chest for clothes. It is not a fancy hotel, but it is near our home. We hope Fred does not think us poor for it.

Ba took out some cash to pay for the room and Fred said "No, please. I have money," and he pulled out a credit card.

I said, "Put away your money and we will talk about this later." Fred looked disappointed and said he is not tired. I said, "I wish to spend more time with you too, but my family is tired so please relax in the hotel and watch TV."

I asked Mr. Chau to check on Fred and, if he is hungry, get some foods for him and we will pay. He asked, "What kind of foods does he eat? And how much?" He eyed Fred curiously, as though estimating how much our food bill will go up this month.

"Fred just ate twelve kinds of Vietnamese foods today and did not complain one time, so most anything will be fine. Just add it to the bill."

Mr. Chau laughed and said "If your Fred likes our food so much, he will be a good Vietnamese husband!"

Fred thanked us for the hotel room and was glad to meet so many of our family. Fred tried to say goodnight by kissing me on the cheek, but I pulled away, shaking his hand and letting him know I will come back in the morning. I felt bad to refuse his kiss, but Fred just smiled and said, "I can't wait."

When we got home, Fred's other suitcase was in my room and Thao was looking inside. She said "Ooh! Fred has lady clothes inside. Do you think he will wear them for you?"

Thao knows well enough that Auntie often ships me clothes and shoes from America. I am so tired but very, very happy. Fred said nothing about the way I look except words like Beautiful and Pretty and Gorgeous. Fred is too polite to say what everyone else sees.

Fred Learns a New Word

December 3, 1999
Dear My Diary,

I slept too long this morning and hoped Fred would not be upset with me. As Thao joined me on the walk to the hotel, the neighborhood children called out to us "Hello Miss Thao! Hello Miss Kim Cay Dua!" They were very excited this morning. "We see Foreigner Cay Dua! Do you know the Foreigner Cay Dua? He's in that shop over there!"

We went into the bakery and Fred was buying some pastries. The shop owner was boxing them up and waved at us. All his family had come out to see the American visitor.

Fred turned around and gave us a big smile. "I was just getting some breakfast things for the family. I wanted to surprise you by coming to your house first, but many of the houses here look so much alike, I was afraid I might get lost." The baker could not take credit cards and Fred has no Dong yet so we paid for the foods and started home.

The children ran around us, waving and saying "Cay Dua! Two Cay Dua!" Fred said back "Cay Dua to you! Cay Dua!" I am embarrassed because Fred does not know what they are saying.

"Everybody says 'Cay Dua'. Is that a greeting like 'Good Morning'?" I shook my head.

Thao laughed and said "It means…" and I elbowed her, making a "no" face. She said in English, "He will know anyway. Fred, 'Cay Dua' means 'coconut tree'."

"It means what?"

"Co-co-nut tree!"

Fred laughed, "Why do they call out Coconut Tree? What does that mean?"

Thao shook her head and explained. "You very tall. Kimmie very tall. You both very tall like coconut trees."

Fred laughed again and said, "That's so cute! That's really too funny."

I did not laugh. I have been called Cay Dua all my life. There is no 'really too funny' about it, but I will not tell Fred this. His mood is very happy. My mood is not. I must stop now, My Diary.

My Ong Noi

Dear My Diary,

After a breakfast of pastries and sweetened Vietnamese coffee, Fred gave a satisfied burp and patted his belly. I wonder if this is what Fred normally eats for breakfast? For us, it is soup or a hot noodle dish, but I liked what we had this morning as something different.

As I cleaned up, Fred went to the wall where our family pictures are hung. Some are from when we are children. I am the tall girl in almost every picture except in my youngest years. Another photo is of Sister Trinh's graduation from Columbia University in New York and one of our current favorites is a studio portrait of Thao and her family, the twins were seven years old and their wide smiles are missing baby teeth.

I saw Fred studying an old photo of a big family group in central Vietnam. Everybody is about the same size to each other but in the middle is a very tall, serious-looking man. He is two meters tall, maybe more. Fred showed great interest in the picture, so I joined him.

"This is a picture of Ba's Ong Noi, his grandfather, my great grandfather and others of our family. Ong Noi's parents, siblings, children and so on."

Fred pointed to a small person in front "Is this Ong Noi?" I laughed and said no, that is a boy! He said "How about this one? No, this one!"

With my finger, I circled the very tall man, "That is our Ong Noi."

I could tell Fred was making some fun with me. "Oh yes, that was going to be my next guess!"

I explained how Ong Noi was the leader of his village, a very strong and successful farmer of animals. Also, he was the only member of our family who has been so tall until me.

Fred smiled and said, "So, you were the big winner of the genetic lottery!"

It took me a short time to understand his meaning. Then, most unfortunately for Fred, all the years of being stared at, teased and shunned by men as a possible marriage partner caused my emotions to boil over. "No, I am NOT the big winner of the genetic lottery. I am the big LOSER of the genetic lottery!"

Fred looked hurt and as soon as I said it, I was very sorry to have bitten his ears. I know now he meant it as a compliment, but I could not feel it as a compliment.

"Oh, Kimmie! I'm sorry if my words made you upset, I truly am. But do you really believe what you just said?" His face turned soft. "You are a winner to me."

I put my head down in shame and my heart came out of my mouth. "No man wants to marry me. They say I am too tall, too ugly and have too much education. They say I am an unlucky woman and will make giant babies. Maybe you also think I am too tall and are just being nice to me!"

His eyes grew wide in surprise, then Fred put his arms around me and my emotions came out in tears. He held me close and said quietly in my ear, "Shh. It's okay. It's all right." I heard Thao and Me come from the kitchen, then go back in. They saw me with Fred and left us alone. It is not the first time they have seen me like this.

Fred asked softly, "Have you dated men who told you these terrible things?"

I shook my head. "I have not dated a man before," I admitted. "You are my first boyfriend."

He looked surprised, "Oh, I did not know that. But have other people told you these things? About being too tall? Too ugly?"

I nodded. "People on the street sometimes, or workers in our business. I hear them when I walk by or when they think I do not hear them."

After a time, Fred asked "You okay now?" I nodded. He said "First, yes you are tall. That is the way you are made and not something you can help. Second, do you have a mirror? A tall one?"

I took Fred to our dressing area where we have a full-length mirror bought especially for me. Fred stood behind me, his face over my shoulder, and we looked into the reflective surface together.

"Do you know what I see?" he asked. "I see a very beautiful woman in front of me. Your face has a smooth, oval shape." Fred traced the frame of my face with his long fingers.

"You have beautiful eyes, a shapely nose and a very pretty smile with straight white teeth…and cute dimples." He put his fingertips on my cheeks. I smiled at his nice words and gentle manner.

"See?" Fred continued, "I knew the pretty smile was in there somewhere! Your body is not thin and not fat. You have the feminine curves many women dream to have." He lightly followed my curves with his hands. It tickled.

"As far as being unlucky, I don't believe that is true. After all, I feel very lucky to have found such a beautiful, smart and nice woman to be my friend. I can't wait to learn more about you and your wonderful family."

Fred turned me around and looked into my eyes. "Do you believe me?"

I turned shy and said, "I don't know."

"Well, I *do* know. I will not lie to you. And I hope by knowing me, you will feel lucky too."

"Yes," I say softly.

He lifted my chin so I have to look into his blue eyes. "Good," he said, and hugged me deeply.

I heard Me's footsteps out of the open door and know she is looking in. When she saw Fred is being good to me, her footsteps retreated. Fred kissed my forehead and held me more.

I whispered to Fred "I do not like to be called Cay Dua."

I felt him smile against my cheek. "May I call you Sweetheart?"

"Yes, Fred, you can call me Sweetheart."

Later, I asked Fred if he knew I was so tall before he came to Vietnam?

He said "Of course!" Auntie had told him from the beginning and Fred had also met and talked with Thanh and Tina. They told him many things about me and how we might be a good match. They had also warned Fred how sensitive I am about my height so that is why Fred never brought it up.

Fred asked, "Do you remember when I asked you how tall you are?"

I said "Yes, I told you my skin is tall enough to fit my bones."

Fred had liked my answer and wrote back, "Me too!"

I told him I thought he was saying to me that he is very tall, but I was not all the way sure. Now I know!

Fred opened the suitcase he left here yesterday and said, "Ginger gave me some clothes to bring. At first, I thought they were for me, but then I saw that they were not my style," as he held a bra up to his chest. I blushed and snatched it away from him. Fred is so naughty!

Lois: The picture of Ong Noi is a treasured heirloom in our homes. We each have a copy to remind us of where we came from and how randomly life can hand us a challenge. We have heard the stories of how Mama and Dad first came together but to hear it fresh from her, and the pain and embarrassment she felt being called names over her height...this was not brought up very much, if at all, in their recollections to us.

Grace Nguyen: I was a newlywed when my mother and Fred became business partners. He was a very good-looking man in those days, always dressed in worn jeans, T-shirts or flannels and work-boots while driving one or another of his old trucks. He looked like a male model dressed to be a construction worker, or at least that's how I saw him.

We weren't so sure about him at first. Fred appeared broke, or close to it, but he was always cheerful, polite and respectful. I think that is what attracted Mom to him as a possible partner. And he was unfailingly honest. Fred never tried to take advantage of the partnership with my mother and often came up with great deals on equipment and other things she needed for the business.

Fred also introduced Mom to Bobby and Robbie who really helped her manage and grow her business and investments. Eventually we all ended up as clients of B and R. In return, Mom introduced Fred to Cousin Kim and, well, the rest is history, isn't it?

Dear My Diary,

Today Fred wanted to exchange currency, so Thao took $500 from Fred to exchange for VN Dong as some money changers are happy to cheat an inexperienced foreigner. When Thao arrived home, she showed Fred the rate of just over 15,000 VN Dong per dollar and the total was more than 7,500,000 Dong.

Fred was very surprised at the big bundle of cash, but a good dinner is less than 30,000 dong. I explained to Fred that incomes here are very low at about 100 USD per month for the average worker.

"Does this mean that for less than $100 I can be a millionaire?"

"Yes, but only in Vietnam I think."

He laughed and said, "I had no idea being a multi-millionaire was so easy here!"

December 6
Dear My Diary,

Fred and I have no problem finding things to talk about and today, he asked me about the jobs we have with the company. Our company is Pham Lo International Trading Company and Ba is the owner and President.

Me is the Office Manager and co-president. My oldest Sister Thao is the Director of Marketing and Sales, Phung is the Director of Finance and Accounting and I am the Director of the Domestic Labor Force.

"You're a Director? I didn't know that. I'm impressed!" Fred said, with admiration.

It only means that I am in charge of workers in our warehouse, but if he is impressed, I won't spoil it with the details.

Fred asked if Phung is another sibling so I explained Nguyen Phung has a business degree from Berkeley University in California and is the son of one of Ba's closest friends. He returned to Vietnam after college instead of getting a job in America. Phung is very smart and helps make our business more profitable. He comes to our home often to discuss business matters, but we all know that some of his business is with Sister Thao. They work closely together on many projects, but we can also see the chemistry they have with each other.

When I brought up how Ba, Me, Thao and Phung often fly to other parts of Asia, Fred asked "And how many countries have you been to?

I am ashamed to admit, not even one. Even my mother has been outside the country. He asked, "Why? Are you afraid to fly?"

I said no and pointed to my legs. "I am too long and cannot fit in the seats."

Fred made a sad face and said "Me too. I can't fit in the airplane seats either."

"Then, how did you sit on the airplane to Vietnam when you are even taller than me?"

"I had to stand up all the time and hold a strap, like on the public bus." Fred stood and pantomimed how he hangs on to the handle and bounces around.

I know better, but he is comical to show me this way of traveling. I giggled "No, you didn't!"

"You are right. Actually, I have to lie down in the aisle. When people want to use the toilet, they have to climb over me. 'Excuse me! Xin loi! Excuse me!'" Fred rolled around on the floor like people are scooting past him. "Food cart, please move!"

I laughed so much that even now my sides are still hurting. "No, no! How do you really fit in the airplane seat?"

"If I have to fly, I use Business or First Class. I am not going to wreck my legs sitting in Coach. So, how do you like being the Director of the Labor Force?" Fred asked, changing the subject.

"It is okay," I admitted. "I spend most of my time on the work floor as I am a strong worker and fast and can do many jobs including driving trucks and forklifts. But the workers do not respect me because I am the owner's daughter and too timid. They make fun of me when Ba is not around, and do not work so fast as we need sometimes."

Fred's face got soft. He said workers need to have a firm guide, not too hard or they might quit, but not so soft either. Then Fred asked me "Do you have back pains?"

"No, my back always feels fine."

"I ask because you tend to slouch" and Fred demonstrated with his own back and neck. I am ashamed that he brought this up, as do my parents. I think it is a natural action for me as I want to look less tall. Less Cay Dua.

"There are many studies that prove tall people get more respect and make more money than shorter people. You must show more confidence in yourself and that show of confidence will get more respect from others. And to do that you need to make a habit of standing up straight."

Fred took me to the big mirror and, turning to the side, made his back very straight and had me do the same. Then he gently pulled my shoulders back and prodded me here and there. It is not easy for me to do this as I have been slumping for a long time.

One benefit I saw right away in making my back straighter, is how it makes my breasts look bigger. It felt strange and made me a bit shy, also. Fred was encouraging in how much better I looked just doing this simple thing.

Fred said "Mary, I need you on the forklift and get those boxes over here!" He said this in a firm but not angry voice, then asked me to repeat his words this way. I did and he said to do it again with a little more force. I did it again and he said that sounded better.

"Now say it in Vietnamese, like to a worker," and I do. He asked "How did it feel?"

"I like the way I sound," I admitted. "My voice sounds stronger when I stand up straight."

"See? What did I tell you? Now, work on making this a habit that wherever you go in the house, the street or at work, work on keeping your spine straight, shoulders back, look directly at who you talk with and speak firmly. Nicely but firmly." And he said all of this in the same manner…nicely but firmly.

As we practiced, I pretended to give orders. "Tuan, I need to see you in my office!" "Huang, this is not a dating service, back to work!" and so on. It is fun to do this at home, but I wondered out loud how it will be in the warehouse?

Fred assured me that it will work, but also it will take time for workers to get used to the new Kimmie. And one last thing Fred instructed: "Do not let them call you anything but your given name."

I thought of another order to give. I stood up straight, shoulders back, looked directly into his eyes and said firmly, "Fred, come to my office and kiss me!"

His eyes got big, "Yes Ma'am!" Fred ran over like an eager employee and, taking my body into his muscled arms, his sky-blue eyes became soft with desire and I closed my own as Fred gave me my first romantic kiss.

Fred and I made dinner together. He may be a good cook at home, but needs my direction because he does not know our style of cooking. When the family came home from work, Fred poked my back a little and I made it straighter. It is not easy to stay straight constantly, but I tried. Ba watched me closely but said nothing. Soon we all sat down to eat and Fred, sitting across from me, made a subtle reminder move.

Finally, Me said, "Kimmie, is there something different about you?"

"I don't know Me, what do you mean?"

"I am not sure, but something is different. You have a new lipstick?"

"No, Me."

"New clothing?"

"No, Me."

"Did Fred give you a ring?"

"No!"

Then Thao said, "I think Kim looks taller. Did Fred give you some growing herbs?"

Ba said, "Kimmie is not making herself look smaller anymore. She is making her back straight to look taller. I am right, yes?"

"Yes Ba, you are right."

"How does it make you feel?"

I do feel better, and Fred says it will give me confidence."

Ba looked at Fred and grunted in English, "You good man, Fred."

Fred smiled and thanked Ba. I told him later about the conversation and how Fred had impressed the family to help me be better.

Fred asked, when I said No! so suddenly, if Me asked if we were kissing. I blushed and said "No!" again. But I did not tell Fred what Me asked either. It is too soon for this kind of talking.

Frankie: There was a part where Mom said some men did not want her because she "has too much education". It was never addressed again in the diary so I asked her about that. She said men of her culture preferred ignorant and uneducated women so they could be manipulated and cowed more easily. Most men in Vietnam at that time did not have college degrees so marrying a woman with a higher level of education would make her husband look weaker in the eyes of others in the same way many men feel emasculated if their wife earns more money or has a more important work title than they have.

Lois: I didn't know what to expect for their first kiss but knowing Mama and Dad, I would have thought it to be more romantic. And to imagine Mama being so mousy, insecure and easily disrespected by the workers is not something any of us can imagine from the woman we grew up with. No wonder she was always telling us to stand up straight and show confidence…she got it from Dad!

Kim: I remember my first kiss. Yes, I ordered Fred to my pretend office to kiss me. I was trying to be funny and just blurted it out. He was trying to make me feel better about myself and it was working. And deep down, yes, I wanted to be kissed. Fred leaned me back a bit and hesitated just a moment, to be sure of my intention. I kept my eyes closed and my heart was racing. Then he kissed me. It was brief, but sweet. I still pull up that moment now and again, because it was so special. You really do never forget your first kiss.

Fred's Family

December 7th, 1999

Dear My Diary,

Now I am learning so much more about Fred than when we were writing to each other from far away. I already knew many things from his letters, but it is the little details I am getting now that are so important to really, truly understand someone.

His parents are Franklin and Margaret, but they are called Frank and Maggie. He has an older brother Barney, but he changed his name from Barney Starbuckle to Bernard Bartlett and prefers to go by Bernie. Bernie is married to Bernice but she is called Bunny. It is very confusing…I feel like no one wants to keep their original name! Then I remembered that sister Trinh is "Tina" and Aunt Giang is "Ginger" and Thanh is called "Tammy" by her customers. I guess my family is not so different from Fred's at all. Even my city has two different names!

I asked "Why did your brother change both his first and last name? Is this common?"

Fred agreed that it is not common for Americans to change both their names. "Barney always hated his birth name and wanted something that sounded more professional as a lawyer."

"Barney must be very rich if he is a lawyer."

Fred made a face and said this: "You know how many people are considered smart because they are at or near the top of their high school or college class? Like the top five or ten percent?"

I said, "Yes, Tina was in the top five percent at Columbia University." I hoped it did not sound like I was bragging.

"And you know that for every top five percent, there is a bottom five percent, right?"

"I have never thought of it that way before."

"Well, Barney was at the bottom five percent of his law school class. And it wasn't even a very good school. That's my brother." I didn't know what to say to this so I just nodded. Fred was definitely not bragging.

I asked Fred if he has been to college? He said he went for a while, took a handful of classes he found useful for his business, then quit. "I'm what you call 'self-taught', I do okay for myself and I'm happy with the way things are."

"Do you make more money than your brother?"

He shrugged, "Not if you ask Barney."

I am not sure what that means, but it does not answer my question. I am finding that Fred does not have a close relationship with his brother, and he avoids talking about his personal finances. I thought Americans like to boast about their money and possessions, but maybe Fred is different. Or maybe he does not have enough to boast about.

Happily, Fred changed the topic to teach me American measures. We calculated Fred is fully two meters tall or, as he says, "six foot eight" and I am 1.88 meters tall or "six foot two". He is 100 kilos in weight or 220 pounds while I am 73 kilos or 160 pounds. I sound so much bigger in pounds!

Throughout the diaries, Mama refers to Uncle Barney as either Bernie or Barney with no particular preference or reason for using one or the other. Growing up, he was always Uncle Barney to us. Same goes with Bernice/Bunny, Trinh/Tina and Giang/Ginger. Oddly enough, she always refers to her sister Thanh by her given name, never Tammy. The next part helps fill in some of our grandparents' backstory.

The Story of Ba

December 10
Dear My Diary,

This afternoon was very special. After lunch, Ba told Fred the story of our family, a story we all know well. I told Fred some things about us in our emails, but this is really Ba's story to tell. By sharing our past and present to Fred, he will understand where we come from and what kind of people we are. If Fred has any intention of joining our family, then he needs to hear this, and this is our story:

Ba grew up very poor in Saigon with many brothers and sisters. We do not have free public education so much of Ba's education was learned from others who had the time and willingness to teach and he taught himself French, the second language of Vietnam as the French were in control of our country at the time.

Ba and his brothers were always looking for things to sell or trade to feed their family. By developing a talent for bartering and speaking French, Ba made friends with local officials and helped them get specialty items they wanted for their families. In return, Ba was introduced to other people of influence and from there, his business kept growing.

Ba gained the attention and respect of the right people who made arrangements for this savvy trader to take university classes at no charge and earn certificates for business knowledge. During this time, his circle of contacts grew to where he could buy goods from other provinces, then other countries as he stretched his business ties even further. His brothers and other traders they trusted worked alongside Ba to build and strengthen their network.

Eventually, the French gave up control of Vietnam and Ba was hired by the new, democratic government to broker purchases of necessary supplies and to sell government commodities to local and overseas buyers. All during the war years, Ba earned great prestige as a primary middleman between the South Vietnamese government and many private companies.

One of the government secretaries at the purchasing office was smart and resourceful, helping Ba make new contacts and smoothing relations with difficult officials. He married her and, in time, she quit her job to start a family and help Ba with his private trading business from their home. This is my mother, Nguyen Thi Mai.

When Reunification occurred in 1975, Ba lost his job and, like many citizens, was imprisoned because he had been part of the old government.

But Hanoi is over eleven hundred kilometers from Saigon and the government needed to quickly set up offices throughout their newly doubled nation. During the war, American bombing missions had caused enormous damage to roads, railways and ports. This made it difficult and expensive to transport supplies from Hanoi and officials did not have good supply contacts in the South. Word got around and Ba was soon released from the re-education camp and was put to work for the new government.

The post-war years came with great economic struggles for everyone, but Ba not only helped the new government rebuild, but did plenty of side deals for his own business. Growing up, we all learned how to seek out opportunities, make bargains and follow up to be sure we were not being cheated, and that we were not cheating others.

Ba brought home 'gifts', kickbacks, leftover inventory and government confiscated goods he purchased and we sold from our home and the local marketplaces. We were able to buy two adjoining houses and Ba broke down the separating walls so we could have more room for our family and storing inventory.

Eventually, warehouses and trucks were purchased, trade routes were established and this is how all of Ba's children, and many family members have gone to college and are continuing to make successful lives for themselves and their families. Some work for us, but many others are independent business owners in Vietnam, Australia, France, Hong Kong, Canada and America.

One of Ba's most important contributions to the business was doing for others what French officials did for him: he has paid for, collected contributions for or found sponsors for the higher educations of certain loyal employees or their children. Many of these people are now key members of management here and abroad to make our business more competitive. Ba is a strong believer in higher education, as we all are.

Phung explained that he went to Berkeley, partly with scholarship money and partly with help from Ba and other sponsors. He did this with a promise to return to Vietnam and help make our country grow stronger.

Fred listened closely the whole time and let Ba talk while Phung or I interpreted. When the story was done, Fred said many admiring things to Ba and said my father sounded like himself, but "super-charged". Ba smiled and nodded. He likes the term "supercharged".

Ba told Fred that one of the reasons Auntie Giang introduced me to him is that Fred reminded her of her successful brother doing similar kinds of work. It surprised me to hear that! I thought she only asked Fred to make friends with me because we are both very tall. I wonder if Ba sees Fred as the son he could have had?

The Emergency

December 15
Dear My Diary,

Such a long, busy day today, and Fred made a big impression! We had a large order scheduled to ship out this evening with much to prepare. As we were having breakfast with Fred, Ba got a call from the warehouse that some of the workers showed up late and very drunk. They were making a mess, arguing with other workers and getting us behind schedule.

I explained the situation and told Fred to stay home with Mother while I go to the warehouse with Father and Thao. Fred refused to stay and insisted, "I can help. I will go with you."

We all went down in two cars, plus two neighbors who had the day off from work. Ba called the warehouse to call for more workers to come in.

We discussed what to do with Fred as he does not speak or understand Vietnamese and decided it was best for him to pack boxes. I told him three different things we are packing and how many of each thing go in the boxes. He repeated it exactly and understood.

I took Fred to the packing area and introduced him to the workers. "This is my friend Fred. He will help with packing."

Someone said, "Her AMERICAN boyfriend!" and another called out "Our Coconut Tree has found a foreign coconut tree!" and everyone laughed.

"Hey!" and everyone turned to the visitor. Fred smiled nicely and wagged his finger at them. "Khong Cay Dua!" He pointed to himself and said "Fred!". He pointed to me and said "Kim!" Fred shook his finger again, "Khong Cay Dua! Okay?"

I was shocked!

Everyone went quiet and their mouths became like marketplace fish. Fred gave me a small sign so I made my back straight and tall, took a deep breath and said in a firm voice, "Fred is our guest and he wants to help us be successful today. He understands more Vietnamese than he speaks so be careful you do not offend him. And from now on, I am Kim. Not Coconut Tree. Not Walking Bamboo. Not Head in Clouds. We have much work to do and we will bring in lunch for everyone. Now, let's get to work! Thank you!"

Suddenly shamed, workers were looking down saying "Xin Loi, Xin Loi" and "I did not know he understands Vietnamese". Fred smiled and nodded at everything. I went to Fred, pointed to the bins of packaged shirts and said to him in Vietnamese "Six stacks of ten shirts each per box, Okay?" He smiled and nodded. He repeated the instructions back to me in English with fingers showing "6" and "10". The workers again had their mouths falling open. Of course, we had already discussed the packing details in the car but the workers did not know this.

I helped Ba organize the other workers and get trucks ready for loading. Thao made calls and let the ship know the goods were coming later than expected. I worked the forklift to load trucks with pallets of finished goods.

Later in the day, I helped deliver soup and French bread sandwiches to workers with hot tea and bottles of cold water. Fred had his shirt off and wearing just a sleeveless undershirt. His muscles shined with sweat in the muggy air. I think some of the women hurt their eyes looking sidewise at him. The workers said Fred moved fast like a machine once he got used to the tasks.

The team leader said when the crew had finished with shirts, they showed Fred how to pack dishware with thick paper layers between. Fred and I had also discussed this in the car so, of course, they told him in Vietnamese, and he showed them as I said. They were amazed when Fred smiled, nodded, then went straight to work.

Thank goodness we got the entire shipment to the boat and loaded before the scheduled departure time. Ba fired the men who came to work drunk and hired our neighbors who had come to help.

After telling Fred about this, he told Ba, "Good employees make a big difference."

Ba smiled and thanked Fred for his help today. It meant a lot to all of us. Fred said he was happy to help and also to see how our company looks. He said, "What happened today shows that you are a good businessman and Kim is a skilled manager."

We were all very tired and it was too late to cook anything. We invited Phung and the neighbor men to dine with us. Back at the hotel, I told Fred that he shocked me when he said "No Coconut Tree" to the workers, but I am glad he did. I explained how, later in the day, some of the workers came and made apologies about calling me names. They said it was just joking around but there will be no more name jokes at my expense. I accepted their apologies and told the workers not to let this happen again.

After Fred had spoken up, I knew to put on the act of confidence as he had taught me. I could feel the power coming out and it made me feel better about myself. There was a new change in me and I explained all this to Fred.

Fred shrugged and said, "It was nothing."

I took Fred in my arms and rewarded him with soft kisses that he returned with equal tenderness. I whispered in his ear, "It was not nothing…it was everything."

Lois: I checked with the family and no one had heard this story before. I read the entry to Mama and she smiled that soft smile of hers. "I could not believe how easily I lied to those workers. You know, I do not like to lie, but your father helped put them in their places and made the day a success."

She then added, "Yes, Fred made me look very good that day. I got no more trouble from any of them the rest of the time I worked at the warehouse. It was a small but very important moment that affected the rest of my life, including how I felt about your father. I did not tell him until much later, but that was the day he earned my heart."

The Starbuckle Name

I learned an interesting story today when I asked Fred what kind of name 'Starbuckle' is. I was thinking about it last night and when my mind pulled apart his name, it is 'star buckle' like on a belt. It had not occurred to me before, so I asked Fred about his family's name.

"The story is that one of my ancestors from the eighteen somethings, his name was Stanislav, worked on sailing ships trading goods all over Europe and Africa. He loved the sea and studying the stars on clear nights. One of his favorites was Orion the Hunter. Orion is easy to spot by the three stars in a short, straight line representing the hunter's belt.

"He was so enamored by the belt of stars that he had a large buckle made by a silversmith in the shape of a star and had a wide leather belt tooled with his favorite constellations all along its length. He wore it everywhere. He was so proud of this prized possession and, burdened with a Slavic name that was difficult to pronounce or spell, that when he landed on Ellis Island and officials asked his name, he pointed to his belt and they wrote down 'Starbuckle'."

When I started asking more questions about Stanislav, Fred added, "I don't know how true the story is, or whatever happened to Stanislav or his belt, if it ever existed. All I know is that's the story that has been passed down over the last few generations. It's as good a story and explanation as any other, and that's why I named my company The Orion Group...as a tribute to the Starbuckle story."

The next time it is very dark out, I will have Fred show me Orion the Hunter and his belt.

Dealbreaker?

December 17, 1999

Dear My Diary,

One of our biggest concerns about Fred is that he does not have a college degree. Having an education is an expectation in my family and not something to be taken lightly. Today, at our family's request, Phung came to our home to ask Fred about this for our knowledge and understanding.

Ba began that all his daughters have college degrees, his second oldest daughter in New York, Tina, has an MBA from Columbia University and Phung got his Masters from Berkeley. Ba rubbed his thumb and fingers together. "Muuuch money!" he emphasized. How is it that Fred does not have a degree? Was it for lack of money?

Fred began by complimenting Ba for having all the children go to college. "I know college is very important, and one of the reasons I am attracted to Kimmie is how smart she is." Then explained how he has taken selected classes like accounting, marketing and computer skills to help him work smarter in his recycling business and has been making his own money since the age of ten. "As far as I'm concerned, college classes have been helpful, but a full degree isn't necessary for a self-employed person like me."

"Have any of your immediate family been to college?"

"Pops learned the auto repair business from his father, my mom started university but left to marry Pops and my brother is the only one with a degree in my immediate family."

"His brother is a lawyer," I added helpfully.

"Ah, very good. Yes."

"If you marry and have children, would you allow them to go to college?"

Fred replied, "Of course!"

"Could you *afford* to send them to college" Ba asked, rubbing thumb and fingers again, smiling.

Fred smiled back and stated confidently "Absolutely."

I can see Ba and Phung are not wholly convinced, but they smiled and nodded at Fred to indicate this topic is over for now.

I only hope Fred's words are true.

Frankie: There were lots of different conversations and topics discussed between Dad and various family members during his six-week visit. One of them did not find its way into Mom's diary, but has been told to us by Dad and Phung at different times and changes very little in the telling. It goes like this:

Phung: So, Fred, do you play basketball?

Fred: Funny you should ask. The top three questions I get are How tall are you? How's the weather up there? and Do you play basketball? My answers are six feet eight, always sunny and no.

Phung: You don't play basketball? Really?

Fred: I don't play or watch any sports.

Phung: Why not?

Fred: Never had any interest in sports and don't understand the point of them. It's boring. They do the same things over and over again. Throwing balls, kicking balls, hitting balls with sticks.

Kimmie: I thought men like to play games with balls?

Fred: Some more than others

Phung: (chokes on his beer)

Fred's Parents

Dear My Diary,

I asked Fred about his parents as he does not talk about them much. From our emails, I know that his grandfather, George Starbuckle, once owned a car and truck repair business that he renamed Starbuckle and Sons Auto and Truck Repair because the business was expected to go to his sons Franklin, Grant and Jackson. The boys worked for their father during high school and were to take over as partners.

Frank's brothers were sent to fight the war in my country and both died here. Frank, the youngest, was left to take over the garage and was very successful with it. Fred helped with buying and selling used vehicles and parts but neither he, nor his brother Barney, were interested in learning to be mechanics or garage owners.

However, Frank does not have the business anymore "due to financial hardships beyond his control" as Fred told me, with no further details about how he lost the business, his home and his savings. Frank was too young to retire so he now works managing another garage as well as buying and reselling cars and auto parts to get back some of what he lost.

Mother Margaret works in one of the secondhand stores that Fred does business with. She was a housewife until the bad financial thing happened, so her income also helps to pay the bills.

Fred has not told me what this bad financial thing is and, although curious, I do not want to ask too much. Fred's face gets dark when he talks about it. I asked if Fred could have helped his parents when they had the problem. He said "I wish I could have, but it was bigger than all of us."

Fred has other family in and around Riverton, mostly on his mother's side, but Fred is not close to any of them. Fred's childhood friends are Bobby and Robbie. Bobby and Robbie's parents are close friends and they all grew up in the same neighborhood.

When Fred talks about them, it is like Bobby and Robbie are one person or brothers, but they are just best friends. Now they own an accounting firm that belonged to Bobby's father until he retired. Both friends went to the same college to get their business and accounting degrees.

Bobby and Robbie are skilled at their jobs and are growing the business. Fred says he trusts them "one thousand percent" as they keep his books, do his taxes and help him grow his business.

I asked Fred, "If you trust Bobby and Robbie one thousand percent, how much do you trust your brother?"

"One percent."

I'm sorry I asked, but I am not surprised either. Fred speaks of his friends in a more brotherly tone than he does of Barney.

Although Mama and Dad emailed each other a lot, based on her diary entries, it doesn't seem she knew a lot about Dad's family and some of the dynamics. When I asked her about it, she said she had learned some things from the emails, but it was much easier to get the details in person so she could see and hear the way the answers were given rather than just reading them. Then she could judge better the truthfulness of what was being told to her. She didn't want to be fooled!

The next entries are pretty long and detailed about Dad, Ong Noi and Phung discussing Dad's business and his frugal lifestyle. Whereas Mama's family bought and sold things on an international scale, Dad was more locally based. Here are some telling bits:

To help us understand Fred's business life better, we had Phung help us as his English is so much better than ours. He introduced the subject one evening by casually saying he understood Fred was in the recycling business.

"Yes, this is true."

"What kind of recycling? Steel? Glass? Paper? Aluminum?"

"More like furniture, tools, books, toys, jewelry."

"Do you own the recycling business with Ba's sister?"

"Ginger has convenience stores selling gas, foods, drinks and tobacco."

"How are the businesses are related?"

"They are not, but I recycle my profits into other investments, like Ginger's stores."

Phung asked, "Is there so much profit in recycling that you can do this level of investing?"

"There can be, if you work it right."

Phung pointed out that Fred wears GnG brand shoes. Fred looked a bit annoyed, like he has heard this many times before. "I prefer them."

I asked about GnG and Phung explained they are one of the largest discount retail chains in America. It used to be called Granny and Grampy's but was later shortened to GnG. I had not heard of them before.

"Why not wear Apollo, Hi-Style or Fast Forward brands that are popular in America?"

"I'm not going to pay top dollar for a name when I can get a perfectly decent pair of sneakers for twenty or less. Saving money is making money, after all."

Now I am worried what Fred will think as I wear name-brand shoes that Auntie sends me from America. My feet are so long that people call them *sampans.* Perhaps Fred will think I am too expensive to keep as a wife. This is something I must consider and speak with him about. Actually, he sounds a lot like my father…Ba does not follow fashion trends either.

Phung asked Fred if he has heard of the book 'Blue Collar Millionaire'. "You remind me of the people interviewed in the book. They tend to have their own businesses, very ordinary sorts of businesses, and live well below their means. Wealthy, but not flashy."

Fred said "Well, I don't know about the 'wealthy' part, but flashy, I admit I am not."

Phung laughed, "I think we are all in the same boat with you." He glanced at me and the look in Phung's eyes said he knows new things about my American boyfriend.

They also discussed health insurance with Dad, who admitted he did not carry any because he is in good health and does not feel a need to pay far more for insurance than he was paying out of pocket. Having lived in America, Phung understood how important health insurance is in a country that does not have universal coverage as many other developed nations have.

This was a concern to Mama and her family. If Dad could not afford health insurance, what would that mean to her and the children they might have if someone got sick or injured? Dad grudgingly agreed to shop for health insurance, but said he preferred to pay for just what was needed. Dad got a good grilling over that day!

Is Fred a Fraud?

December 19, 1999
Dear My Diary,

Oh, my! I am so weirded out that I must get this off my chest.

Fred and I were sitting on the couch and he looks *especially* handsome. As I admired his blonde, curly locks, I said to him, "You have wonderfully thick hair. I could run my fingers through it all day long."

And Fred said, "This? This is not my real hair," and he pulled off his wig! Fred is as bald as a monk! I am shocked but I say nothing. After all, no one is perfect.

I concentrated my attention further down. "I love your very blue eyes. They are the color of the sky."

And Fred said, "My eyes? They are not blue!" He reaches in and takes out blue contact lenses! Fred's eyes are as brown as mine. I am shocked again but still I don't say anything. Colored contacts are common these days.

Fred is smiling that big smile that makes me feel so happy and warm. "You have such wonderful teeth. They are like perfect pearls."

Fred grinned widely and said, "These?" He grasped his teeth and pulled out a full set of dentures and smiled again, showing bared gums. Ugh! Again, I say nothing. At least he saves money on visits to the dentist. I look down his body some more.

I cannot be wrong this time. I said, "Your legs are very muscled and strong with fine blonde hairs all over."

Fred said, "My legs?" and he reached down and yanked off both his legs!

I screamed and screamed and screamed until Me and Thao were shaking my shoulders in a panic "Wake up, Kimmie! Wake up!"

Oh, such a nightmare I had! I hope Fred is not a fake man like he was in my dream.

Dear My Diary,

I had difficulty getting back to sleep after my nightmare. I was still thinking about it as Fred helped me make lunch. As we ate and talked, he flattered me with many nice compliments. I can't help but pay particular attention to his blonde hair, blue eyes, straight white teeth and well-muscled arms and legs. He is so perfect looking. Was my dream trying to tell me something?

We sat on the couch together and no one else was home, just like in the dream. I am a little scared but I smiled and said, "You have very beautiful hair." He smiled back and said, "Thank you!"

I reached over and gently tugged his hair. "Is it real?"

He took my hand and let me pull different parts of his scalp. "All real!" he said.

I gazed into his eyes. "I love your beautiful blue eyes. They are like a summer sky." He said that is very sweet of me to say so.

"I hear some people wear contact lenses to change their eye color. Do you?"

He laughed and shook his head. "No contact lenses and no glasses."

Fred smiled and I said, "Your teeth are like strings of perfect pearls."

"Yes, I am very lucky for them."

"Do you wear man-made teeth?"

He smiled even bigger and shook his head. Fred opened his mouth and tugged his teeth up and down. They didn't come out.

Fred was amused at my questions, like I am playing a game. "Anything else?"

I am feeling shy now, but I have to ask. "Your legs have big strong muscles and nice hairs." I stroke a thigh as I would a cat. His flesh is firm and warm.

Fred offered, "If you don't believe they are real, I can pull my pants down and you can see how real they are!"

This made me blush very strongly and I shook my head. He began to stand up to make his point, but I pulled him back down, embarrassed that he might actually do it…and kind of hoping he would.

Fred kissed my nose and said, "You are a funny girl, Kim. You make me laugh."

I read these entries the first time, with understandable shock. Then, I read it again and again thinking I had heard or seen this story before. I asked around and found that my sister Sang had heard the story from Mama during an overseas flight. Sang shared it with Lang who, in turn, shared the story with a writer friend who had used it in the comedy film "Dating Nightmares". No wonder it sounded familiar!

Love Spies and The Golden Ticket

December 20, 1999
Dear My Diary.

Thao and I were making lunch in the kitchen as Phung and Fred talked in the parlor. Me and Ba are out visiting family, so it is just the four of us at home. It's a very relaxing day.

Thao had secretly put a baby monitor in a corner, and we had the speaker with us with the volume turned down low. We can hear the men, but they cannot hear us listening to them. We are like Love Spies on our boyfriends. I did not feel right to do this, but sister said it will be fun. "Maybe they will tell secrets on themselves."

Fred asked Phung "With an MBA from Berkley, why didn't you stay and take a high paying job there?"

Phung explained, "I made a promise to my sponsors that I would return home to give back to my people, help others get better educations and create new jobs to build up our economy."

Then Phung told a story I had not heard before: When Saigon fell in 1975, thousands of citizens attempted to escape to North America, Australia, and Europe "…and Mr. Pham had the opportunity to leave with his whole family to the United States. He had, what you would call, The Golden Ticket to get out and start a new life. He would have been given money, housing, and other assistance from the US government."

However, Ba's English was limited, and by having such a large enterprise here, Ba's thinking was that the bad times would not last long before going up again and he could help rebuild Vietnam by doing what he does best.

"Mr. Pham was a real inspiration for me to come home and help our own people because instead of fleeing for the safety of America, he stayed and risked his family on an uncertain future."

I had never heard that Ba had a Golden Ticket to leave Vietnam for a new life in America. I can't remember ever hearing this story growing up! This Golden Ticket would have been very valuable. Of course, Ba is wealthy now and we have a nice life, but would it have been better in America? Or worse? I guess we will never know.

I spoke to Thao later and she said she knew about the offer made to Ba. She was old enough to remember our parents discussing whether to go to America or not. Once the decision was made, they never discussed it again…they just moved forward and did their best. I can't believe neither of my parents ever told me this story before. And I learn like this!

Getting to Know Each Other

Dear My Diary,

I often wonder why Fred, did not bring or wear any new or stylish clothes. Most of what he wears looks ordinary, and they generally fit well, but I would have expected better when a man flies across the ocean to visit a woman he hopes to marry.

I am afraid to ask him about it as I don't know if his wardrobe is a personal style or only what he can afford. Some of my relatives make unkind and demeaning comments about his clothing when they visit.

Fred has told us that he gets most of his clothes free through his business, or at discount stores and either does not know, or care about, fashionable name brands. Meanwhile, Auntie Giang sends me clothing in the specialty larger sizes because finding my size of almost anything is difficult here and many of my clothes must be made by local tailors. I fear Fred won't let me buy the clothing I want in America, or worse, that he cannot afford them.

I feel ashamed to think like this as it feels like a petty issue…and it would be if I were a normal-sized woman. But I am not normal-sized, either here or in the West. If Fred is serious about marriage, as we believe he is, I need to know what to expect from him and he needs to know what to expect from me. After all, he is not normal-size either, so he should understand.

Finally, I got the courage to ask Fred about his clothes buying habits. As before, he patiently told me that nearly everything he wears comes from auctions. "Every time I buy auction goods, the first thing I do is see if there are any clothes my size that are in good condition. Once everything else is sold, the clothes become free. Nearly everything I have has been owned by someone else. But don't worry, you can be assured that all the food I buy is new and not used." That made me laugh, but I still worry too.

Emboldened by his frankness, I asked "If I come to Riverton, is that what I will have to do for the clothes I need? Buy used blouses and skirts and jeans? And shoes?"

He smiled gently and took my hands in his. "Look Kimmie, I know that for many people, buying and wearing used clothes falls somewhere between "uncomfortable" and "disgusting". I know I am different from most in this respect. I have done the same kind of buying for myself for a long time. It is my habit, my way of doing things. Many Americans will not buy used clothes unless they must. However, many others will, especially if they enjoy finding some style they really like at a bargain. That's a big part of how I make my living…selling used clothes and stuff.

"I knew I would probably have this conversation with you and I am prepared to put your mind at ease. I know it is hard to find clothes for someone as long and lovely as you and I have no problem with you purchasing new clothes. I like your taste and you always look terrific in my eyes."

"Please do not be offended by my question, but can you afford to buy the new clothes I will need, assuming I do not have such expensive tastes?"

He smiled indulgently, "What better person than you to spend my money on? I will be happy to buy all the new clothes you need. I promise."

"Oftentimes I use local tailors to make things I need and I can sew my own clothes on a machine.

However, my home-sewn clothes do not look skillfully made, so mostly I make around-the-house and bed-time clothes."

"I can't wait to see you in bed-time clothes," he said with a wink. I blushed and we changed topics.

Fred complimented me on my short, boyish hairstyle and I told him it is easier to dry and style than long hair. I did not tell Fred the real reason for the "garcon" cut is, because of my height. Sometimes when I go out in public, I find it easier to get by, by dressing as a man.

I prepare by wrapping a long bandage tight around my chest to make it flatter, and donning a loose shirt to hang outside my trousers to make my womanly hips less noticeable. I don't use makeup, wear a wide-brimmed hat to hide my facial features and speak in a lower voice if I must talk.

In this manner, I attract less attention from men who want to stare and make rude suggestions to me. It also helps me when I drive a company truck to other provinces for pickups and deliveries. Men do not pay attention to other men who drive trucks, but they will if the driver is a woman. My method does not always work, but most times it does.

Of course, I do not do this at work or in my local area as everyone knows me. I am not happy about having to do this because I like being a woman, but I do it for my own protection. I wonder if I will have to do this in America? I am too shy to tell Fred about dressing as a man. Maybe he would laugh at me…or want to see me dressed like him.

This is another side of Mama she never discussed with us. When I asked her about the cross-dressing, Mama said she thought it would be too weird to talk to us about dressing as a man to avoid unwanted attention. It wasn't even her own idea! Auntie Trinh had employed the same technique herself in New York City for much the same reasons…avoiding unwanted male attention.

December 22
Dear My Diary,

I have been thinking much about Fred and his history with other women. Fred has never talked about dating other people or having a serious girlfriend, but I feel he must have had some because he is so handsome and a genuinely nice man. On top of that, he has no bad habits that I can see like drinking alcohol, smoking tobacco or using bad language. To use one of Fred's phrases, "What's not to like?"

I am too shy to ask and not sure how to approach the subject. I feel it is an important matter to discuss, but what if Fred answers that it is none of my business? It is common knowledge that unmarried Western men and women sleep with each other…a lot! Sometimes they do not even know each other's name and have, what are called, one-night stands. What if Fred has been married before or has children that he does not talk about? I don't know. I worry sometimes what kind of secrets he is keeping from me…or is he? It is hard to trust men.

I asked Thao her idea and she agreed I should ask directly. Her advice is to try to understand his attitude about romantic and sexual relations and not be afraid if he refuses to answer me. "If he is a good man, he will be open and tell you the truth."

Sister cautioned me not to ask how many women he has slept with, or who, but do ask about prior marriages, children, serious relationships like did he have a fiancé before? Thao said to be direct but in a soft style, and if I don't understand the answer, ask again until it is clear.

I feel better now. I know Phung has eyes for Thao, and she with him, but they do not date openly. I can see it in the way they talk to each other and every time Phung comes to our home, he tries to see if Thao is here too. Working together at the warehouse, it is natural, I think, that they become close. Maybe one day Phung will be my brother?

Dear My Diary,

I talked with Fred today about his past dating history. I was very nervous doing so because he has never asked me about boyfriends. First, I began with how I have never dated any man before. Men in my country do not want a woman much taller than themselves. Fred said this attitude is common in the West too. Women prefer men at least the same size or taller than them.

"Sometimes men make me feel bad by saying crude things like they want me to come to bed with them as they have never had such a tall lover before." I was uncomfortable to be so frank, but Fred nodded and agreed that "Men like that are everywhere and it makes the rest of us nice guys look bad."

When I asked Fred if he has done a lot of dating, he said "No, I'm not a dating kind of guy."

"Why? You are a good-looking man, I think, and very nice and easy to talk to."

He thanked me for my kind words and explained how he stays busy with work all the time. "It's what I like to do as I find it fun and interesting. Most women do not, but I think you will. At least, I hope so."

This is the first time Fred has hinted that he would like me to join his business, and I have heard enough from Fred about what he does, to believe what he does may very well be fun and interesting. At least to me…and certainly not with many females.

Fred said he finds many people boring and shallow. He only knows about sport teams, TV shows, movies and other pop culture things around him as it relates to his business of buying and selling, and not because he has any personal interest in them. He just likes to focus on making money and helping others with it.

He also admitted that because his clothes, home and cars are not new or stylish, many women call him "cheap" while he prefers the term "frugal".

"What is 'frugal' and how is it different from 'cheap'?"

He thought a minute and said "When I buy a genuine diamond ring for my girl, negotiate the price and get it at a discount, I am being 'frugal'. When I buy a crystal ring for my girl and tell her it's a genuine diamond, I am being 'cheap'…and a liar."

But I needed to hear more about Fred's love life. "Did you not want a girlfriend before?"

"Well, sure! Of course! When I see people holding hands, talking and playing with their children, it looks really nice. But in reality, and I don't know why it is, either the woman I am with spends time gossiping about people I don't know, complaining about the most trivial, fixable things, or listing all the stuff they have or want to buy if they had the money." Fred smiled wistfully. "I say I don't like complainers, and here I am, doing just that. Sorry, Kimmie."

"Well, be careful Fred, because I am a boring woman. No drinking or dancing or doing wild things. Mostly I work and stay home with my parents and do a lot of reading and watching movies. Besides, I am too embarrassed with how I look to go out and socialize. Too much staring. And I want to know, will people stare and say rude things to me in America as they do here?"

Fred was sympathetic, but honest with me. "On the good side, many American women, especially the younger generation, are taller than most people I see here of either gender so you won't stand out quite so much. As far as people saying rude things, well, most folks behave themselves and mind their own business…at least that's how it is in the Midwest.

"The trick is to look and act confident and people will think twice before being rude to you…but mostly people are nice.

I took a deep breath and asked my really important question: "Fred, do you have any children?"

He laughed at the suddenness of my inquiry. "NO! I don't even date. I've never had a serious girlfriend until you came along."

"Men don't need a girlfriend to make a baby," I reminded him. "Just a one-night standing intercourse with a stranger can make a baby."

Fred nodded, acknowledging the universal truth of my words, then he made a serious face and his voice went lower, even though no one else was in the house. "Kim, I could never have had a baby with anyone."

I am surprised he said such a thing! "Why not? Is something wrong with you? Can you not have children?"

He smiled and said gently, "I have never been with a woman like that."

It took me a minute for my mind to understand his meaning. "Never?"

He shook his head. "Never. Not even a, what did you call it? A one-night standing intercourse."

I blurted out, "But you are an American!" then realized how wrong that sounds.

Fred laid his hand over mine and said "Not all American men act like dogs with women. Some do not have sexual relations before marriage for religious or moral reasons. I do not want to make a baby before marriage and do not want a woman to trap me into marriage. Like they say, 'the best defense is a good offense'."

I am not sure what that means, but it sounds like "Stay out until you are ready to go in."

He patted my hand and said in the sweetest voice, "I hope to share my body with you when the time is right."

My face felt as red as a stop sign when I said "I hope so too".

It looks like we have one more thing in common. I am not sure I believe him 100%, but I feel he is sincere. If he is, Fred is a very, very good man to catch.

Back in the day, this would have been called "TMI" or Too Much Information. Especially hearing this from your own parents. But it is sweet to know that neither of them had a tawdry or complicated sexual past. And believe me, Mama talked A LOT about keeping ourselves chaste until marriage. Even Frankie wasn't spared.

After speaking to everyone, it sounds like most of us held off a lot longer than most people we know and knew. So, I guess Mama's words worked their magic on us. At the same time, we are pleased by how much she pressed Dad to give up information and keep checking to see if his stories changed.

When Did You Fall in Love with Me?

December 23, 1999
Dear My Diary,

This morning, Ba sent me to the warehouse to help Thao. I agreed but was not happy about it. I explained this to Fred who was perfectly fine and said I should help the family. He would spend time exploring the neighborhood. I reminded him to be careful as some people are not very nice.

"Look at me! You think anyone will make trouble with this?" flexing his arms and making the muscles jump up and down. "Or this?" and he made his chest muscles jump like something inside him was alive. This took me by surprise and I burst out laughing. Fred said, "Good! I made you laugh." We kissed goodbye and I knew Fred would be just fine.

At the warehouse, I helped with office work and made sure some trucks got loaded. It was a slow day, being so close to Noel, and they didn't really need my help. Later Thao sent me home and I thought 'What a waste of time!'

Fred was sipping milk from a coconut and, with no one else home, it gave me the opportunity to ask Fred something I was thinking about at work. "When did you know you had fallen in love with me?"

He thought a moment and said, "Good question…it happened gradually, I think. There wasn't an 'Ah ha!' moment for me. You know, the more we wrote and learned about each other, the more I found myself talking with you in the truck. I would tell you where we were going or things about my life. Sometimes it was about fun things I had seen in the news or I would explain things about American culture you might not know. Later, I would write some of these things I talked about with Imagine You and share them with Real You.

"I never take vacations or do things for fun, but over time I found myself going to a park or a local event and see other couples out and about. I imagined you by my side, walking with me, holding my hand, and talking about whatever was on our minds. It was a nice feeling, to have your spirit with me and relax on a pretty day, doing fun things. My hope was to make this kind of feeling come true. I'm getting tired of being alone and that's why I am here with you now."

I can't remember exactly everything Fred said but I wrote it down as how I remember it. Then I asked, "You never take a holiday?"

"Oh, I went on vacations with my family as a boy, but not as an adult. Any trips I made was for business and I would look for fun things to do only if it fit within the timeframe of what I was doing there. You know…even this vacation is for business".

That surprised me! "This is a business vacation? I am business to you?"

Fred gave me a warm smile and said, "The best kind of business…business of the heart."

I asked, "Are you sure?" in what I hoped was a teasing kind of way.

He put his hand on his chest. "With all my heart to you." Then he added, "And what about you? When did you feel I might be Mr. Right?"

"As we came to know each other better, I felt pulled into your life little by little. I felt we were becoming friends and after a couple of months, I began looking for your letters and emails and pictures every morning and evening. I was very happy when I got them and a bit sad when I did not.

"Then, there was one special letter in the post I will never forget because you wrote it by hand. You said you wanted to have a deeper friendship with me and asked me to be your special girl and not just a pen-pal anymore. The letter was dated July 5th."

"Yeah, that was a special holiday for me," Fred said. "I attended the annual July 4th Festival with music and fireworks and lots to see and do. It was the first time I had been there since I was a boy. You were next to me, in my mind, to dance, eat carnival foods and watch fireworks bursting over the lake. Then I took you home and we cuddled until we fell asleep in each other's arms."

Fred's letter touched my heart and made my feelings stronger for him. That he is no longer a male friend, but a real boyfriend. The feelings I had for Fred matched the feelings he had for me.

I read and re-read the letter, trying to put myself into Fred's day at the park. After thinking about this for a time, I found some heavy paper and set to work on making a card. On the front I drew grass and trees and a bridge crossing a river. On one side of the bridge is a boy saying, "Will you be my friend?" and on the other side is a girl who says "Yes, very much!". Opening the card, the boy and girl are in the middle of the bridge and holding hands. Fireworks burst in the sky behind them with my message: "Yes, I very much want to be your Special Girl. Kimmie"

I confessed that it took three tries to get the pictures just the way I wanted.

"Your card really touched my heart. Truth be told, I keep it in a special place and look at it often."

Now we know how and when we fell in love with each other.

Believe it or not, Dad kept that picture, sealed in clear plastic, in a locked desk drawer with other of his most prized possessions. Mama has it still, and looks at it when she is missing Dad.

Kimmie: His letter touched my heart to know how close he felt to me. We had been writing back and forth for about six months and I enjoyed his communications, but I wasn't expecting to get such a heartfelt letter as this one. It was a bit of a shock to me! However, once I thought about his feelings, I realized that I also had similar feelings for Fred...talking with him in my head, coming up with things to write about later and having daydreams about him. I am not much at drawing, but I was very proud of that piece.

Our First Real Date and a Christmas Surprise

Dec 24, 1999
Dear My Diary,

Yesterday Fred asked me if there is some place special to go and do in Ho Chi Minh City? I said there are many nice hotels and restaurants, some place like that? He suggested a nice park or a fun public place and I thought of Dam Sen Park. "It is across the city, but I can drive us there." Fred said it sounded good and asked that we dress up nice. I agreed but was not sure why we need to dress nice to go to a park.

After lunch today, Fred went back to the hotel and I put on a dress and some make up. I can't do much with my hair as it is so short, but I tried to style it up with some gel and put on one of my better earrings. I do not have many nice things to wear because I have so few occasions to dress up outside of family weddings and Lunar New Year, but I am pleased that Fred wanted to take me out.

Fred was waiting in the tiny lobby of the hotel. He wore pinstriped trousers I have not seen before and an ironed dress shirt with shiny shoes. His hair looked extra curly and puffed up. Very handsome! Because many Catholics are staying home to prepare for Noel and it is a school day, few people were at the park…mostly families with small children.

Our mood lightened once we were inside. My eyes were happy to see colorful flowers and small trees everywhere, along with rides, games of chance and food stalls. The air smells fresh by the man-made rivers that flow throughout and fountains that spray water and turns the air misty.

Holding hands, we walked around and made small talk. Fred bought a bag of popcorn for us to share and he reminded me that when he was young, he sold popcorn for extra money. The popcorn is lightly sugared and Fred says he has not had this kind of sweet popcorn before. It is very good. I feel very good.

It dawned on me that we are on our first real date. The kind of first date I have seen in movies but never had for myself. Dressed up. A pretty place. Holding hands. In love.

I looked over at Fred and squeezed his hand. His eyes crinkled as he looked back, squeezed my hand in return and grinned. Perfect!

As we got near the Big Wheel ride, I excused myself to use the toilet. When I came out, Fred was using his hands to communicate with the ride operator. I asked Fred if he needed my help, and he looked a little guilty saying he just asked a question about the Big Wheel. The operator smiled and gave a thumbs up. Fred presented me with two tickets to the Big Wheel and said, "Come on, this will be fun!"

I felt nervous about the ride going so high, and said as much, but Fred insisted, "Don't be afraid! I'm right here with you." The operator encouraged me, saying it is very safe with a full view at the top.

The cars are shaped like hot air balloons and as the wheel creaked slowly higher and higher, the park spread out below us. Dam Sen covers many hectares and the Big Wheel is its focal point. I can see why Fred wanted a ride. The wheel came down and back up again. At its highest point, the Big Wheel came to a halt and the car swayed in midair. I started to panic…why is it stopped?

Fred gently turned my face to his and said in English "Kimmie, when I am with you, I feel like I am on top of the world. You have many qualities I am looking for in a friend, a partner, and most importantly, in a wife." Then, more slowly, in Vietnamese: "Pham Thi Kim, will you accept this ring as a promise of marriage to me?" He held out a small blue box in his very large hand. By now, my heart had risen into my throat. Opening the box with shaking fingers, a diamond ring sparkled in the afternoon light.

Not only was I surprised by Fred's proposal in the Big Wheel, but that he proposed in my language! I started to respond in Vietnamese, then quickly switched, "Oh, Fred! You are a wonderful man and now my best friend. I accept this ring and I do promise to marry you. Yes! Very much, yes!"

He put the ring on my finger, and we hugged and kissed. "Merry Christmas, Sweetheart." Fred said to me. "Anh yu Em."

"Em yu Anh," I returned. The three most special words two people can tell each other. "Merry Christmas to you, my darling."

Fred called out the window, "Oi!" and the Big Wheel started back down. Now I understand! He made a plan with the operator while I was gone. We went around two more times and stopped. The old man had an ear-to-ear grin to match mine when we got out. I showed him the ring and Fred gave him some money. The operator accepted the bills with both hands and gave us another thumbs up sign. "Number One!" he said in English. "Cam on!" Then to me in Vietnamese, "Big happiness to you both!"

After that, my heart was so filled with emotion that I do not remember much else but a lot of holding hands and walking and enjoying each other's quiet company.

When we arrived home, the family was sitting down to dinner with Phung. Me said "You both look very happy!"

Thao said, "And very dressed up!"

Phung said, "Merry Christmas, Fred!"

And Fred answered "Yes, it is!"

Facing the family, my new emotions came rushing back and I blurted out, "Fred asked me to marry him!" Thao screamed and came to hug us. Then everyone gathered around, hugged and gave their congratulations. I showed off the ring and everyone agreed that it is beautiful. Really, it is a little loose, but that can be fixed.

Me and Thao set extra bowls as they were not expecting us to be home for dinner. I could not eat very much because I was too excited and happy. I expected Fred might propose to me while he was here, but I did not know when. I should have expected it when Fred asked us to dress up for the park. Also, because it is Christmas Eve, a special time for Westerners. And now it will always be a special time for me!

Frankie: We have heard this story so many times and have ridden the Ferris Wheel a few times before they tore it down. Dad was always looking for romantic ways to show his love to Mom, but this was definitely one of the better ones he pulled off.

Kimmie: I do not know which was the bigger surprise, Fred proposing at the top of the Ferris Wheel or asking me in Vietnamese! He had Aunt Giang write the words phonetically and teach him until he had the pronunciation just right, then he kept practicing at the hotel so when the time was right, it would sound perfect...and it was!

First Christmas

December 24, 1999
Dear My Diary,

After dinner, I spoke to Ba and Me alone while Phung and Fred talked in the parlor. I felt bad for not asking permission before saying "yes" to Fred's proposal of marriage and hoped I did not offend them by doing so. I apologized to my parents for not asking first.

They asked me how I felt about Fred?

"He is the same kind of man I had been exchanging letters and emails with: nice, respectful, funny and he gives me feelings of confidence." Then I shared the story of the day Fred came to work with us and told the workers in Vietnamese to call me Kim and not Cay Dua and how he reminded me to straighten my back and speak firmly and with confidence to the workers.

I also explained that I more fully understand how he runs his business and that every day is different for him. It is not a boring office job and is honest work I can help with.

Fred does not have a good relationship with his brother but very much loves his parents. Moreover, he likes our family and wants to be part of us. Maybe I cannot find such a good man like him in Vietnam and he makes me feel attractive and loved. I said "yes" to him because I felt he is the right man for me, and I hope they understand this.

Ba explained that when he sent me to the warehouse yesterday, it was not because he needed me there, but because Fred wanted to meet with Ba, Me and Phung in private to ask their blessing for my hand in marriage.

Ba went on to explain that the family does have some concerns about the life Fred leads. "We agree that Fred is a nice man. He is cheerful, agreeable, respectful, worked very hard at the warehouse, makes no complaints that we have heard and has his amusing moments.

"But daughter, your boyfriend, your fiancé, your future husband, has no steady job. He has no health insurance, no college degree and seems to do what he wants. We cannot accurately tell how much money Fred has, or is making, and if he can support a family adequately. There is no dishonor in being poor, but if he is, you do not have to settle for that and we will not subsidize it.

"Honestly, my child, he may say he runs a recycling business, and that sounds very nice and proper in a business marketing context, but in reality, Fred comes across as a glorified junk peddler. Phung told us 'By calling what he does a recycling business is like putting lipstick on a pig. The pig may look prettier, but it's still a pig.'"

Those last words hurt my ears and tears threatened to show themselves. Of course, I understand enough of his business to know that he is not on the same level as my parents. Fred is small and local while my family's business is international. Fred does not brag about how much he makes but speaks of the passion for what he does and the people in his life.

Perhaps he exaggerates his skill or ability to make money from other people's castoffs, but I do not think he is so poor either. Ba's words were harsh…but maybe he knows more than I do. If Fred is so bad, I do not think my parents would accept him as part of our family and refuse the marriage proposal. As these thoughts swirled in my mind, Ba continued to speak.

"But on the good side, he is a business partner with my sister and maybe other people. Giang speaks highly of Fred…enough to recommend him to you, and to us. She knows him better than we do.

"When I went to pay for the second week of Fred's hotel stay, Mr. Chau would not take my money because Fred had already paid several weeks ahead and had negotiated with him for a lower, long-term price by paying with US cash. Chau is also exceedingly pleased with Fred's cleanliness and respectful, friendly behavior."

Me said, "An act like that carries the weight of his character. We were surprised, and impressed, he did such a thing and never brought it up to us."

This is the first time I have heard about Fred making a deal for his room without our help. Another good surprise. Most importantly, the family sees Fred's influence on me and how I have changed in such a short time. My parents said they have never seen me more confident or happier.

Me said, "In the past, dark clouds always followed you around. Now, every day, you glow like the morning sun. The clouds are nowhere to be found."

Despite their concerns about his financial stability, Ba and Me agree that Fred looks like a good match for me. And as a precaution, since I will be living in the same city as Auntie and Sister Thanh, if something goes wrong with the marriage or if Fred is treating me badly, my family will be nearby to help.

That's my parents for you: "We expect you to live happily ever after, but if that doesn't work out, here's a Plan B".

"One last thing, Daughter," Me said gently. "May we have a closer look at your lovely ring?"

I held my hand out to show them, and my mother removed the ring from its new home. Ba brought out a small electronic device I know well and have seen them use many times. My heart sank at what they might learn about Fred at this very moment…was he Frugal? Or was he Cheap?

Ba touched the tip of the jewelry tester to the band in several places, watching numeric figures on the small display that I could not see from my angle. Then he adjusted a knob and checked the largest facet of the stone, a stone larger than I had expected to receive from Fred. Ba's face was impassive. "Crystal. Definitely crystal…a diamond crystal," he said at last.

My breath let out and Me gave Ba's arm a push, "Lo! Don't tease the poor girl."

"And eighteen carat band. Very nice way to show his love to you," he said, placing the band back on my finger. "Sorry not to trust Fred, but you know how it is."

During dinner, Me and Thao confessed that before he came to Vietnam, they expected Fred would propose and had already planned for an engagement party without telling me. As most Vietnamese are Buddhist, like my family, they do not celebrate the Noel holiday and this makes it a slow period for caterers, photographers and suchlike until Lunar New Year when there is much more demand. Me had shopped vendors during her work hours so to have a good selection to choose from.

Thao said "Why not have the party on New Year's Eve? It's in one week and on the weekend."

When I said that the timing is awfully fast, she pointed out that it will be two celebrations in one: Millennium New Year and our engagement, so it will be a very lucky day to make the engagement party.

I had to catch Fred up as everyone was speaking in Vietnamese and asked his feelings about having a party on December 31st to announce our engagement to family and close friends. "It will be a ceremony and luncheon to make good wishes for our future."

Fred loved the idea and said he looked forward to meeting more of my family and friends. "Aaaand! This will also mark one year since we made our introductions to each other, so actually a third celebration!"

We called Auntie Giang to let her know of our engagement and I thanked her for introducing us and how Fred has honored me with his kindness and good cheer since his arrival.

Fred also spoke to Auntie, addressing her in the formal Vietnamese way as I taught him because this is a special call. He thanked her for introducing me to him and how I am such a "great gal" and "gorgeous" and "sweet as sugar pie". He told Auntie he can never thank her enough and this is his best Christmas ever.

Then Ba took over the phone and told his sister how much Fred has influenced me in the short time he has been here and that we, as a family, have had many long talks to get to know each other better. "The whole family is very happy to have Fred as our newest member." He said the last part in English for Fred's ears and Fred cannot smile big enough.

Fred made the final call to his parents to share our good news, keeping the speaker on so we could all hear them, and his parents sounded so happy with our news. Father Frank said Fred had only good things to say about me before he came to Vietnam and even more since he has been here.

Maggie welcomed me to the Starbuckle family and hoped that I will be happy with Fred for a very long time. I thanked them for their good wishes and Fred told them we would have an official engagement ceremony on New Year's Eve. They wished they could be here for that and hoped to see pictures soon.

Fred admitted afterward that he calls his parents every few days to let them know how it is going between us. This is the first time I have spoken to his parents and I am a little unhappy that he waited so long to let me speak with them. I think Fred was being cautious not to share too much in case I turned out to be a disappointment, or said no to his proposal.

"Mom and Pops trust my judgement, but they were a little nervous about this, as you live so far away, and I've never had a serious girlfriend before."

"That's okay," I reassured him. "My parents felt the same way."

We have so many things in common!

We have heard this story so many times and to read about it at the time it happened is so touching. Mama has been asked many times in interviews about how Dad proposed to her and she loves to say "At the top of a Ferris Wheel!" which always leads to a surprised reaction and more questions.

Their first kiss might not have been exactly romantic, but Dad had his idea to make the proposal memorable. Dad has also told us how our grandparents Ong Ngoai, Ba Ngoai and Phung asked him a LOT of questions before they would agree to the proposal. He said they were unfailingly nice and polite, but firm and insistent.

Dad said he wasn't so sure they would allow the marriage at all based on his unorthodox way of earning a living. But in the end, Dad's kindness to Mama, his clean habits and that she had a way out of the marriage by way of Aunties Ginger and Thanh got him the approval of the family. Sounds like he got grilled by everyone before he could pop the question!

December 25, 1999
Dear My Diary,

This is my very first Christmas celebration! Fred made decorations for our home and bought a small, pre-decorated tree from a neighborhood vendor.

For someone who prides himself on being frugal, Fred gave us surprisingly nice gifts: a laptop computer that I can use at home and is able to be connected to the internet, a beautiful bracelet with snowflake bangles to celebrate our wintertime engagement and two lovely dresses with modest necklines. The fabric is light and the style and colors please me very much. Fred did not say so, but I think Auntie Giang helped him pick out the clothes as she knows my size and tastes.

Fred gave Ba a nice big wallet with a chain attached so it can connect to a beltloop or pocket. It has the logo of a popular motorcycle company and is large enough to accept VN Dong. I have seen tourists carry these kinds of wallets…tourists who look like they could have been former soldiers.

Me got a necklace of pretty beads and an old Chinese coin as a pendant, the kind with a hole in the center. I think Fred does not know that China controlled Vietnam for over one thousand years and we have little love of that country except as a trading partner. Oops! But the necklace will look good with some of Me's outfits.

Thao got a portable CD player with headphones and extra batteries. She has two others but did not say so to Fred. He was kind to bring gifts for all of us.

He gave Phung two bottles of ManScents cologne: Broiled Steak and Sea Breeze. Phung calls this "Surf and Turf" and Fred liked his clever joke.

Fred likes to say he buys used things for himself, but all the Christmas gifts he gave are clearly new. I had wondered if Fred would be giving us used things as gifts but it looks like I overestimated his frugality. Thank goodness!

I gave Fred a high-quality set of men's products made in Vietnam that we sell to overseas buyers: belt, wallet, coin purse and key chain. The wallet, coin purse and key chain I had specially made with our birth symbols to show our being together. The Monkey's arm is draped over the shoulders of the Pig and their heads lean in to each other. I explained the symbolism of the design and Fred was touched by the thoughtfulness of my gifts.

The last thing I gave Fred is a set of portrait photos I had taken in October, just after he made plans to visit me. I did this especially for Fred and I hope he likes it. The studio did all the make-up, hairstyling and posing me in front of different backgrounds.

I wore my three best outfits including an ao dai that I use for special occasions. The photo shoot was pricey and I think I look a bit silly in some of the poses, but I figured that if Fred can accept my height and the way I look, then maybe he will look at them with love eyes while we are apart.

I gave Fred the pictures in private as I am too self-conscious to share them with the family. Fred expressed great happiness as we sat together looking at the different photos. I felt shy but very satisfied at his obvious pleasure. Sometimes I copied a pose, tilting my head with cheek in hand and blinking at Fred quickly like women do in the movies. Then Fred made a funny pose of his own, crossing his eyes, flaring his nostrils and puffing out his cheeks. He is so funny and makes me feel comfortable with myself. I think I have found my true soul friend.

Sang Starbuckle: Dad was an investor in ManScents for a few years. Despite the novel premise that men would want to smell like steak, beer, wood smoke, cut lumber, scotch whiskey and the seashore, the product never took off with the public and it was one of Dad's few business failures. He sold off the remaining inventory through Ubiddit, marketing them as "rare" and "collectable" novelty men's fragrances.

Lois: Mama mentions sometimes about Catholics, especially in relation to religious holidays. Most Vietnamese are Buddhist with a small percentage of Christians, the vast majority of whom are Catholic from the prior influences of the French. She was not aware that there were many other denominations of the Christian faith and it took her time to not automatically identify everyone as Catholic.

As for the studio pictures, we still have some of them. Glamorous yet modest, even corny, she posed with much more makeup than Mama was used to having at the time. And yes, the poses are a hoot!

The Engagement Party

Dear My Diary,

I spent the morning contacting family and friends for the engagement party with Me and Thao. Many had met Fred when he arrived and we have had numerous visitors since then, curious to see my American boyfriend. I am not sure who they want to see more, me or Fred!

We made our decision on a hotel party room not far from the house and fancy enough. We visited the venue and Fred likes it so much that he tried to give me $1000 to help pay for the party. "My family has money and this party is for us," I hissed. "It's very nice of you to offer, but I think my parents would be insulted." I told Fred he could pay for our wedding and he agreed with a big smile.

Me and her sisters made the final arrangements with the hotel and monks from our temple will conduct the ceremony. It will be less formal than a wedding because my family and friends will not see me marry in America. I explained all this to Fred with Phung.

Phung will stand next to Fred to translate the words spoken and make sure Fred knows what to do. Fred said, "I could not ask for a better man to be next to me than Anh Phung."

Phung smiled and clapped Fred on the back in agreement. It was amusing to see how high Phung had to reach for the middle of Fred's back. Forget about high fives!

I must admit here that, before Fred came, Me had taken me to the tailor to update my current measurements on file and pick fabrics for the engagement ao dai in case Fred proposed. The day after Christmas, we went straight to the tailor, and told her my good news, gave a deposit, verified the fabrics and styling and she went right to work on it.

The Vietnamese Ao Dai (pronounced "ow yai" and translates as "long shirt") is a traditional outfit that symbolizes beauty and elegance. It consists of loose trousers with a closely-tailored long-sleeved tunic that drapes the trousers front and back.

The ao dai is most often worn for special occasions or in certain work settings, particularly in public areas such as banks, public offices, restaurants and hotels. It is sometimes worn with a conical straw hat or an open-topped crown tipped upward to enhance the wearers' face.

Fred showed me the suit he would be wearing for the engagement ceremony, and it looks, well, kind of worn. I asked if we could go shopping for a new suit? He grudgingly agreed so I took Fred to the heart of District One where many expats live and shop. I know Fred could not possibly find a suit in the VN shops and it would take too long to be made by a tailor.

Phung recommended two European-owned shops that specialize in fine men's clothing where we found a beautiful blue suit to match his eyes and splurged on new shirts and ties. Fred will wear the new belt I gave him for good luck and his dress-up shoes will work fine.

The store tailor made some alterations while we had lunch in a nearby British-pub style restaurant, then we window-shopped for a bit longer. Many people looked at us, but now I do not care if they stare. I have a man who loves me and makes me feel special.

I put my arm in his like I see people do in the movies and it felt so romantic. Fred looked down at my smiling face, patted my arm and smiled back at me. I felt like melty ice cream. Now I know why people love to be in love.

Translated from the December 27, 1999 edition of Tuoi Tre: "Pham Lo and Nguyen Thi Mai, owners of Pham Lo International Trading Company, officially announce the engagement of their youngest daughter Pham Thi Kim to American businessman Fred Erick Star Buc Kle of Riverton, a suburb of Chicago, United States of America. A formal engagement ceremony and reception is to take place on 31 December, 1999.

Lang Starbuckle-Kitsap: I asked Mama why they said Riverton was a suburb of Chicago when it is hundreds of miles away and in a different state? She said that most Vietnamese know only a few US cities like Los Angeles, New York, Chicago, and Washington DC. It was easier and more prestigious to say "suburb of Chicago" than to get more specific about a small city in the Midwest.

Trang Starbuckle-Clark: Mom was embarrassed at how badly the newspaper had butchered Dad's name. She figured it happened when one of the uncles had been trying to spell Dad's name over the phone and repeated it over and over to get it right.

Because the Vietnamese language consists almost entirely of one syllable words, and the way Uncle was spelling it in blocks of letters, that is how it came out in the article, as separate names. And since it was not a Vietnamese name, the person taking down the information did not question the accuracy of the spelling. It was also spelled that way on the video and engagement cards. Dad would laugh about it whenever he or someone brought up the incident. He said it made him more Vietnamese to have his name spelled that way.

The Engagement Ceremony

December 31, 1999
Dear My Diary,

Too emotional to sleep but we leave for Dalat in a few hours and I will be doing all the driving. I want to get everything down while it is still fresh so I can remember the details of this day for all my life.

The ceremony was very magical for me. Family members from the city and nearby provinces, along with friends from childhood, college and some select business associates and key employees of our company attended. Nearly a hundred and fifty in all. Most have known me a long time, if not my entire life. How many of them thought the shy Coconut Tree would ever marry? And with a foreigner? Not many, I'll wager.

The ballroom was very dressed up with colorful tablecloths, balloons, flowers, good luck banners and streamers everywhere. In front of the stage, chairs were lined up in orderly rows for people to watch the ceremony before moving to the tables for lunch.

A ceremonial altar is centered on the stage with potted trees, large flower arrangements, tall pyramids of oranges, pomelo, dragon fruit and a gong. Monks guided us to the altar where Ba, Me and Thao stood with me and Phung accompanied Fred along with a brother and sister-in-law of Me who acted as representatives of Fred's parents.

Phung stood directly next to Fred to quietly translate, give directions, and help him understand the ceremony. In order to do this, Phung stood on a cloth-covered box so that Fred would not have to lean to one side like bamboo in a strong wind.

For a brief moment, the usual dreadful sensation I feel in public is enhanced by the height of the stage and the seating of our guests below. I used to be the only very tall person in any group. Now I have a partner I can share that feeling with, like being a part of each other. The feeling of dread evaporates and I gaze at the man who loves me: handsome Frederick Starbuckle. He meets my eye, gives a soft smile, a wink and a small nod. I look down modestly but my heart reaches out to him.

The reverie is interrupted by a struck gong that brings me back to the here and now as the monks chant prayers. The Thay spoke about the importance of marriage: of sharing our lives and being responsible for each other equally during times of happiness and hardship, good times and bad times; To thank our ancestors for all they made of us and to share those qualities with future generations; To make peace with each other after a fight and not show our bad sides to anyone but to keep a good face with all.

Another monk poured tea into small cups. I present a teacup with both hands to the couple acting as Fred's parents and they take a sip. Fred does the same with my parents. This shows respect to the elder in-laws and thanks them for allowing their good wishes to come to us.

Now, I give a cup of tea to Fred to sip and he does the same for me to show respect to each other as we are to serve and share with each other the whole of our lives.

Me and Thao put diamond earrings and a blue sapphire necklace on me…engagement gifts from Fred. Then he put the diamond ring back on my finger to make the engagement official and kissed my hand in a gentlemanly manner.

Soon, the gong sounds again, and Thay presents us as a couple who makes their promise to marry and announces our names. We bowed to each other, a kiss on each cheek, a turn and a bow to our friends and family.

As we walk down the stage steps arm in arm and make our way to the head table, everyone applauded us for a very long time. I don't know why it lasted so long but it made me feel very humble. I am not used to feeling this way…to be the center of attention in a genuinely positive setting.

To many, I was Kimmie Cay Dua, someone they could tease and make fun with. Now I am Pham Thi Kim, engaged to marry an American businessman and become Kim Pham Starbuckle.

No longer am I a too tall awkward girl with long arms and big feet. I feel confident, graceful and am proud to stand tall with my man. When Fred looks at me, his beaming face tells me everything I need to know.

Today, I am the happiest I have ever been. I never want this feeling to go away.

Lois: The first time I read this, and I speak collectively for my siblings on this, was wow! What a turning point for Mama. She saw her life click up a big notch and felt hopeful for the future.

Phung and Thao had let Dad know that earrings and a necklace were important gifts to be given at the ceremony and Mama was completely unaware of what he would give her. She has worn these pieces on many occasions over the years as a constant reminder of the love and generous attentions of her first and only love.

Phung took Dad on his motorbike to a good jewelry store for the purchases and it was the first time he had ridden on a scooter in Saigon traffic. Dad said he was laughing non-stop as the traffic was so wild and Phung was a skillful driver. He claimed that that was the time he started getting gray hairs! Phung has told us he was nervous about Dad riding on the back as he is so much heavier than his normal passengers, but everything turned out fine.

The reception lasted for hours and Mama got many thousands of dollars in Lucky Money from their guests. It was made to understand from our grandparents' invitation that the couple would be getting married in America so there would be no formal wedding in Vietnam. The guests then treated this information as a way to show their good wishes, pre-wedding, to the lucky couple

The guests would hand their red envelopes to Mama with both hands while making their congratulations to the couple and then she would hand the envelope off to Thao for safekeeping. We are not sure if Dad knew what was in the envelopes at the time, or if he even gave it any thought, but the funds were put into a special account for Mama. More on that later.

For Mama, the reception was the first time she had kissed a man in public and the first time she had ever danced. At other events like weddings and parties, Mama was too self-conscious to draw attention to herself by dancing and neither of them had ever been one of the "let's go to a club and dance" kind of people. Dad had probably danced before, but it was not something they ever did regularly. If they looked awkward or inexperienced when they danced, Mama never heard about it and Dad would not have cared.

2000

Holiday in Dalat

January 4th
Dear My Diary,

Woo! Fred and I arrived home last night from our engagement trip and I feel strangely worn out and yet energized, so it is time to write. Dalat was fun and relaxing but before we left, Me and Ba were very concerned that Fred would try to bed me before our marriage time.

Fred had already promised to respect me, making it clear that he has not been with a woman as I have not been with a man. He said, "If I break this sacred promise to you, how could you trust me in the future? You couldn't and you shouldn't, so I won't and that's that." And that is what makes Fred very special to me.

I explained all this to my parents, but I think they do not believe Fred has never bedded a woman before. They trust me and hopes he keeps his promise.

I did not tell Fred this story but as we drove to Dalat, he told me that Ba had taken him aside and made it very, very clear to be perfectly respectful to me or he would hurt Fred's "two best friends".

I was shocked my father would say this. "Ba threatened to hurt Bobby and Robbie?"

Fred laughed. "Not THOSE two best friends, THESE two best friends!" pointing at his lap.

Oh, yes, that sounds like Ba.

Three or four times a year I drive a company truck to various provinces and pick up handicrafts and manufactured goods for our business while delivering items the shop owners have ordered such as raw materials, electronics, fabrics, specialty foods, medicines and imported cosmetics.

I have favorite restaurants and hotels where I stay each time, so I am known to many business owners throughout the region. Dalat is in the highlands of Vietnam, several hours from HCMC, but this time we drove a family car and took the most direct route. Also different about this trip? I did not dress like a man!

Fred offered to drive but I declined and told Fred he can drive me around Riverton when I come. That led to talking about our future married life in America. It was a great way to pass the time.

I asked Fred if he likes Phung, as he has spent so much time this last month speaking and running errands with him.

"Oh, yes," Fred said happily. "I've learned many things about you and your family from Phung."

"What kinds of things about me?"

Fred rolled his eyes and said "Oh, I forgot now!" then laughed and winked at me. Fred certainly likes to tease.

Also, surprise! Fred likes Vietnamese pop music. He does not understand the words, but he says he enjoys the way the singers express themselves with their voice.

And we had so much fun on our engagement night! After the reception was finished, the hotel manager offered us a special invitation to their New Year's Eve roof top garden party where we could watch the Year 2000 fireworks show. We went back to the hotel in the early evening after showering, changing clothes and doing some last-minute packing.

We had not eaten since the engagement luncheon and there were several buffet tables laden with wonderful foods, so we had our fill of whatever we wanted. Despite the bars serving exotic cocktails, Fred would only drink the soft drinks and fruit juices available. He let me know that if I wanted something stronger, that was okay with him, but I followed Fred's way as I have never cared for alcohol either.

We kissed at midnight with everyone. I mean, I only kissed Fred, not everyone! There was a live pop group performing and we enjoyed dancing to the music. I have never really danced before, so we just moved our arms and legs and did different things. It was fun.

During the slow songs, I felt shy with Fred among all these strangers, but we put our arms around each other and moved slowly to the rhythm of the music. Fred stroked my back and it felt so nice. Sometimes I put my head on his shoulder or we looked into each other's eyes. It was a beautiful time for us. Like a movie scene with the colored lights around us and many couples dancing, but at the same time we are alone on the dance floor and the camera is circling us, round and round.

We took a taxi home after 2 o'clock. Sooo romantic! It was too late to go back to his hotel, so Fred slept on the long sofa in our living room just this one time.

As we climbed into the highlands, we passed coffee plantations and small farms growing the kinds of fruits and vegetables that do not grow well in the hot, humid lowlands. Dalat is cooler than Saigon with many pine trees and a big lake in the middle of the city. It is a popular place for honeymooning couples which is what we are…almost!

After leaving home in the early morning, we stopped for a picnic lunch in Bao Loc and visited the famous Dambri Waterfall. Fred took some photos of the area and our meal. Afterward, he had me stand next to him and, with the camera at the end of his long arm, he videoed us smiling and waving with the waterfalls behind us. Such a lovely time!

We got to Dalat in the early afternoon. Stopping at my regular hotel, the owner was surprised to see me on New Year Day, with no truck and dressed in feminine attire. Then she saw the ring on my hand and made many congratulations. She asked to see my husband, so I brought Fred in, who had to duck through the doorway.

"You found a man you can look up to!" she blurted and spoke to Fred in English, "You very lucky man! Very lucky!" Fred smiled and bowed and said "Cam on! Thank you! Yes, I am! Cam on!"

She gave us a big room with one bed. I was going to ask for two beds, but now I am too embarrassed not to correct her at the beginning and say that we are only engaged, not married, so we accepted the room. She was so happy for me that she would not accept payment and made it like a wedding gift to us because my family has done business with her for so many years.

I explained to Fred what happened with the owner, so Fred offered to sleep on the floor or in the overstuffed chair. I said, "You do not have to do that, we will just cut the bed in half!" He laughed so much at my joke, and it pleased me. It felt nice to make a good joke in a foreign language.

I told Fred we will go out to a special place now, so we need to take showers and get dressed in nice clothes. I took Fred to the well-known park Thung Lung Tinh Yeu (Valley of Love). I have never been there before as when I come on business, I felt it would be silly to come by myself. Like going to a children's film without a little one in tow.

However, with my future husband, it is a perfect reason to go! I have heard many things about Valley of Love from other workers and it is so beautiful! A large park with flower arrangements, bonsai trees, a lake, and many lovely things to see.

Today is our first anniversary of when we started writing to each other as well as the day after our engagement party. This will always be our very special time as a couple: Christmas engagement and New Year's to begin our relations.

It is not common in Vietnam to see men and women holding hands in public or kissing as they do in the West, but it was very common here. "The Valley of Love" says it all. I took Fred's hand as I saw others do and Fred swelled a bit with pride that I did so. We walked and rode the shuttle bus and talked of many things.

We had dinner at the lakeview restaurant, then walked along the shore to a spot where no one was about, and it was here Fred gave me a long, romantic kiss. He expressed how much he loves me, and the park is such a wonderful romantic place. What a special New Year Day this has been!

That night we cuddled in bed together for the first time. I wore new, colorful silk pajamas that Thao bought as a honeymoon gift. We spent much time kissing and hugging and sweet talking before falling asleep in my lover's arms. Such a luxury…

The next day we got up late and walked around the city, ate breakfast in a café and then went to some crafting places that sell goods to tourists and to my family's business. Fred wanted to see the famous Dalat crafts and get some souvenirs for family and friends.

At each place, the workers recognized me and when the owner or general manager came out, they made a show of congratulating me, sprinkling in many compliments and good luck wishes.

At some stores they gave us one or two things as a wedding gift and Fred paid for the rest. I do not bargain with them as I know the prices they charged are similar to the wholesale prices we pay. It was very sweet of them, and everyone made me feel very proud to have Fred by my side.

Fred said some polite and simple things in Vietnamese, and he was praised for his language and accent, even though I know it sounded clumsy to their ears. Everyone was very happy to see me in feminine clothes and light make-up, saying how pretty I look. I think if I was a normal size woman, they might not recognize me in dress-up clothes but because I am so tall, well…it's hard to miss me! Fred purchased many gifts and I bought some to give his parents and brother/sister-in-law.

After lunch we visited the Crazy House Hotel to see the artistically strange rooms and then on to the Summer Palace of the last Emperor of Vietnam, Bao Dai. He was removed from power in 1945 by Ho Chi Minh. I told Fred the emperor's birth name was Nguyen Phuc Vinh Thuy and he was the 13th Nguyen of the emperors' dynasty, which is why so many Vietnamese people have the family name of Nguyen, as an honor to the royal family. From there, we drove to the top of Lang Biang to look down on Dalat and the surrounding province. It has very pretty views and we took pictures of each other, and other tourists took pictures of us.

There is a restaurant in the middle of Dalat that sits on a wooden platform over the lake. Now that New Year's is over, there are not many people in the restaurant so we got a table at the picture window and watched the sun set over the water. Dinner was delicious and we held hands under the table, which I find quietly romantic.

When we returned to the hotel, the owner had us come to her living quarters attached to the hotel office. We had coffee and sweets with her and her husband and we visited for an hour. I told her I will probably come back one or two more times for business before getting a visa to go to America. They wished us much good luck.

On our last day, we went to another Palace of a Vietnamese emperor, which is more like a park, nicer than the other palace and is well preserved. On the way home, we visited some other waterfalls and took more pictures. The weather held up beautifully for us, and I am so glad, as Dalat is known for its rainy climate as much as it is for their coffee and crafts.

Frankie: Our family has been to Vietnam many times over the years. One year, when we kids were in our early teens, the family went on a trip to Dalat. It is, much cooler, greener and more rural than Ho Chi Minh City. Mom and Dad could not stop holding hands and reminding each other of this place or that street. It was a very special time for them and for us. I don't think I had seen them so happy in a long time. After speaking to Mom about it, she said that trip gave their relationship a much-needed boost…what with their careers taking them away from each other so much and spending less quality time together.

While driving home, I confessed to Fred about how I dress when I go to Dalat and other towns to pick up deliveries and the reasons why. I told him the people in Dalat were as surprised to see me dressed as a woman as my showing up with a foreign fiancé.

Fred said "Of course they were surprised. I would've been surprised if I was used to seeing you dressed as a workman. Now that they can see the real you, they are as happy as me!

"By the way, now that our engagement is official, I brought the K1 fiancé visa paperwork, and we will need to fill them out before I leave. I want to make sure that all your information is perfectly correct and I will need some passport photos for the form."

Fred's words make me feel one step closer to being his wife in Riverton. He is so thoughtful to bring the paperwork with him!

Then Fred got more serious and said, "So, um, Kimmie. Speaking of paperwork, I hate to bring this up, but we need to talk about something important…" and I felt an "uh-oh" in my stomach.

He said he loves me very, very much and trusts me with everything 1000%, "…but to protect myself and you and your family from any possible…um, issues that we can't resolve, I need you to agree to sign a pre-nuptial agreement." He did not sound happy to bring this up and I am not happy to hear it, but I let him continue.

Fred explained that he sees my family has good money, property and income and Fred also has his own incomes and businesses. The PreNup, as he calls it, will protect my family by keeping separate any money and property I bring to the marriage and any of the same things Fred has. That way, if something happens and one or both of us decide to divorce, what we bring into the marriage will not be affected or taken by the other. "Please understand, Kimmie, this is as much for you as it is for me, and God forbid we should ever get to the point where we need to use it."

Does Fred think I am rolling around in cash? That I am personally wealthy? I don't have any money or property. I have worked for Me and Ba all my life. They paid for my schooling, they feed and clothe me and give me pocket money.

Part of me understands what Fred means and part of me thinks he does not trust me even as he says he does. I know if something is not good about our marriage, I will try to fix it. If it can't be fixed, then I will go back to Vietnam and take nothing from Fred. Nothing.

I am not the kind of woman to take everything or half of everything from a man. I read and hear of these things all the time: One person will trick or lie their way into a marriage and, once it is legal and they have had their fun, they file for divorce and demand repayment.

It makes me sick that people are greedy enough to do this. I could not and I will not. Does Fred think I am this kind of woman? I hope not. But if so, I should end this engagement now and send Fred back home with his diamond ring and other things he gave me.

All of this and more went through my head as I drove through the countryside past farms and villages. I think I was too quiet after Fred stopped talking. He gently asked if I understood and I nodded. Fred said he will not ask me to make this big decision until I can discuss it with my family.

I nodded again, feeling numb. Ba will know what to do. He always knows what is best. After some thought, I think Fred is right to ask me to sign a PreNup if it protects both of us...all of us. If it was only for him, he would not emphasize me and my family so much.

After we came home, Me ask me how was the trip? I said it was fun and relaxing and Fred was a good boy. I thanked her for letting me do this trip and trusting Fred. I cannot lie to my mother and she can see that I am telling the truth. She smiled, gave me a hug and said she was very happy for us, but the house was so quiet while I was gone. It was funny she should say this as I am the quiet daughter!

January 5, 2000
Dear My Diary,

Fred spent the evening in his hotel room while we discussed the idea of doing a prenuptial agreement with Fred. Phung came to the house and Tina was on speakerphone since both are very familiar in areas related to American and Western customs and ways of life.

Tina said many of her coworkers and managers have these agreements with their spouses due to the high rate of divorce in America. They often have their own retirement accounts, inherited money or trust funds and they try to keep these separate. This is much like how Fred explained it to me.

I reminded everyone that I do not have money to bring into the marriage and if something bad happens, and we divorce, I do not want any of his money or property. That keeps it simple.

Tina said this is a noble attitude but what people say today and what they do tomorrow can change. "What if Fred says something like 'Kimmie is not as I expected. I took a lot of time and money to bring her to America and now we have a bad marriage. I want re-payment for my time and trouble.' Then what do you do?

"Also, let's say you build up savings and investments and after five years, the marriage falls apart…don't you think you should get half of what you two built up together, or the money you accumulated from jobs that you worked or the house you built equity in? It's not being greedy, it's being fair. And if terms are laid out in the agreement, it makes things that much easier, if not less painful, to part ways."

As much as I would prefer to step away from a bad marriage with nothing, Tina's reasons for the prenup make a lot of sense. Everyone agrees that Fred is a very nice and respectable man, but money can make people do unsavory things. Best of all, Fred brought this to us as his own idea.

The decision was made to ask Fred for his proposed paperwork so we can look it over, discuss it further, have it reviewed by our family attorney and make an educated decision.

I feel so strange to have this as part of my engagement. I think this is something only rich people do…or people not certain of their heart.

Mama said her family's estimation of Dad went up a lot as he was the one to bring up the pre-nuptial agreement first. It also indicated that he might have more money and property to lose than they first thought, which they did not think was very much if he was buying and selling other people's castoffs. Having Trinh and Phung's knowledge in this area and agreeing that this was a smart move for both families lent even more weight to the matter.

January 11
Dear My Diary,

Today we got the pictures and videos from the engagement party along with our childhood pictures that were included in the montage and photos from our time together before the engagement.

Such a beautiful job they did with the romantic music and special effects. The ceremony made me emotional again as the videographer stood near Fred part of the time to catch Phung's translations.

We had ordered video cassettes for ourselves, and family and Fred will take home for himself, his parents, my sisters, and Auntie Giang. We watched them together after lunch, then again with the whole family in the evening. It felt like being engaged all over again!

Lang: It was in early January when, at the urging of his future father-in-law, Dad showed the family how Ubiddit works and described the pros and cons of selling goods online. Ubiddit was one of the earliest auction websites and Dad was highly skilled with its features.

Dad demonstrated its virtues by having a selling contest: Ong Ngoi and Dad each picked five different things from the company warehouse, Dad photographed and listed each item and both picked their own starting bid for a seven-day auction.

At the end of the week, all but two items sold and some of the final bids impressed Grandfather, seeing how he could turn this into a new income stream. Selling in bulk was more efficient, volume-wise, but if multiples of the same product could be sold using the "Grab it Now!" price or auctioned individually using a template, it could produce healthier profit margins over the long term.

After a year or two of experimentation, the company hired a handful of young workers proficient in English and computer skills to crank out Ubiddit auctions, selling a wide variety of attractive and pricey items and earning commissions along the way. This would eventually lead to online catalogs and various iterations of an online store that continues to this day.

January 14
Dear My Diary,

We have agreed to move forward with the Prenuptial Agreement. Our lawyers have gone over the documents that Fred brought with him and advised us that this contract might not be 100% perfectly legal in the United States or Vietnam and different laws may or may not be consistent with how the prenup is worded. Other than that, it was decided that if our family agree to all parts of the document, then it should be signed with lawyers and a notary present. Phung and one of our lawyers will be a witness to everything.

The pre-nup will be considered as, in Fred's words, a Gentlemen's Agreement, meaning that although it may not be 100% valid in either country, we agree to follow the terms and spirit of the document. With that, I have learned that nearly all of Fred's money and business interests are listed under The Orion Group, LLC to protect his assets. I don't think anyone would do this if their money and property were meager in nature.

January 16, 2000
Dear My Diary,

I am a romantic rebel! It was Fred's last day and night with us before going home to Riverton. My parents took time off from work and we all went to the park where Fred asked me to marry him. It was a nice time, but the better term is what they call "bittersweet". We rode the Ferris Wheel, but the man who worked as operator last time was not there today.

Fred talked about how he has become used to some of the things he first thought very strange in Vietnam like all the motorbikes speeding through the streets, vendors everywhere busy earning money and the many interesting foods and marketplaces to explore.

Fred told Me and Ba what good parents and businesspeople they are, and he is proud to have them for his own second parents. Ba reciprocated Fred's sentiments in English, telling him he is a good son, and we are very proud to have him in our family too.

Me nodded and held Fred's hand very tight, saying "I am too proud Fred", and "My Son". She almost never speaks English, so this was very special for him. Fred hugged her small shoulders and said, "Cam on nhieu lam, Me. Cam on."

We went to dinner at the Rex Hotel, the most famous hotel in Saigon where Thao and Phung joined us. Phung has become like a son to my parents and a brother to us. Maybe he will be a real brother one day…it looks like this to me. I had a hard time holding my emotions in check when I think, after six weeks, Fred will be gone to America. But I am happy to know that in a year I will follow him to be his wife.

When we got home, I packed a few things in my big purse and told parents I will take Fred back to his hotel and spend time with him for our last night. They said to be good and be careful. I said I will. And I meant it. I really meant it.

We walked the short distance from my home to the hotel, hand in hand, heart in heart. No one was at the desk, so we went directly to Fred's room for our last private time together.

Fred said he wanted to wash up as we were out all day in the hot weather. He took a shower, and I was ashamed I did not think to do the same at home before coming. I was in such a rush. 'That's okay,' I thought. 'I will shower here.'

Fred came out with only a pair of shorts on and brushing his teeth. Big muscles. Blonde curly hair. The sky-blue eyes I often see in my dreams. This is the last I will see of him for a long time. I showered and brushed my teeth. My heart is pounding. I peeked out and Fred is laying on the bed, relaxing with his eyes closed and a smile on his lips. He is still in shorts and nothing else. I made a bold decision.

When I opened the bathroom door, Fred looked up and his eyes got big, mouth falling open. I can almost see his heart racing in his chest. "Oh…Kimmie!" is all he can say. I matched his outfit…a pair of shorts only. He got up and came to me. We kissed like we have never kissed before.

"I am your woman, and you are my man. You deserve a special last night with me. We just need to keep our special promise to each other."

We spent the night kissing and touching and holding. Fred taught me how to release his pent-up desires and I taught him mine.

There was very little talking. We have talked enough. And we kept our special promise.

I had planned to go home that night. My parents expected the same, but we fell asleep in each other's arms. When I woke up, the early sun was peeping from behind the curtains. I started to panic, then I thought, 'I am almost a married woman! I deserve to do this. I did nothing shameful.' But my parents…

Fred saw me to the street and the hotel owner tried not to pay attention to us as we said good-bye. I told Fred we will pick him up later for lunch, then go to the airport.

Entering the house, Ba and Me did not look happy and focused on their breakfast soup. Thao smirk-smiled without meeting my eyes. She knows better than to make some joke when our parents look like this.

I said, "good morning" and Ba grunted. Me went to the kitchen to make a soup bowl for me. They avoided looking at me. I felt part proud of my action and part ashamed because what my family is thinking I did.

When Me put down my bowl and took her seat, I sat too. I have to say something. I took a deep breath and said quietly, "I spent the night with Fred. He is my fiancé and this was his last night in Vietnam. We did nothing wrong to bring shame to my family." Ba turn red but only nodded. Thao looked like she wanted to ask me many questions but knew to keep silent. This is a serious issue for my parents.

Me said, "As you tell us this, we believe you. We are not happy you did this, but we understand. You are a woman and still you are our youngest child. And he is American. Americans do not have a good record of holding themselves back with romance."

"Fred and I held back our deep desires. We did nothing wrong. Watch my belly and believe my words. Do not hold Fred at fault for what happened last night. I meant to come home, but we fell deeply asleep and that is why I am here now. For this I am sorry if I made you worry. But I am not sorry for last night."

Ba's face was very red. He got up from the table and said "We will not discuss this anymore or with anyone. What is done is done," and he stalked to his room. Me took the empty bowls to the kitchen in silence.

Thao let out a big breath. "Did you really NOT do it?" she whispered.

I wanted to ask her if she "does NOT do it" with Phung, but I could not. I just pointed to my tummy and said "Watch".

It's hard to imagine a twenty-eight-year-old woman, even in the year 2000, having to defend her reputation for spending the night with her fiancé. Mama was not an exception. That's just how many Asian women were raised to be back then. Mama said at that time, due to Western influences from the media, more and more young people were living and sleeping together without marriage, but it was still on a very small scale compared to what was going on in the United States and Europe.

Fred Goes Home

Dear My Diary,

I feel so empty tonight. We had lunch at Fred's hotel and everyone was quieter than usual. Fred knows my parents are not happy with us and asked if we were in trouble with them?

I said a little, but they also understand he was a good man to me. I said they are sad to see him go, as I am. I thanked Fred for being such a big influence on me and making me feel pretty and special.

"You ARE pretty and special. And you make me feel special too. My first impressions of you from our letters and emails was even better in person. Kimmie, I am very glad that I came to meet you."

I know it will be a long time before I see him again. Everyone tells me it takes most of a year to get the K1 Fiancé visa before I can go to America and marry Fred. This is Fred's first time travelling overseas and he said he will come back to get me.

I told him most people I know, including sister Thanh, came to America by themselves. "It costs too much to come back for a few days to get me."

"Coming back for you and making sure you get to Riverton safely will show your family my respect…and gives us more time together."

"You don't have to do that," I assured him. "But if you do, that would be wonderful to have your company on the long flight to America."

Fred smiled, "Then it's a date!"

Fred can't wait to introduce me to his family and friends and show me his home and city. "I hope you will like it. VERY different from Saigon!"

Fred promised to file the visa paperwork as soon as he gets back.

I said, "Don't forget about me!"

"I can't forget such an unforgettable lady."

At the airport, many family members came to see Fred for the last time. Uncles and aunts and cousins all like my handsome American boyfriend…no, Fiancé. I will soon become an American wife and maybe I will fit in better with United States culture than I do in my own country. I think there are many tall women in America, but I am the only one here most people can see.

We took pictures with different family members to make lasting memories and keep from leaving each other. All the men made a show of giving Fred strong, masculine handshakes and many women gave him shy, awkward hugs.

Fred gave Ba a big handshake and then picked up Me for a kiss on the cheek. No one was more surprised than my mother! She laughed and blushed in good humor.

I am too shy to kiss Fred in front of so many people, so I let him kiss my cheek and I did the same in return.

"Anh yu Em" he whispered in my ear.

"Em yu Anh" I whisper back.

He took his three suitcases inside, one more than he came with, waved one last time to everyone and blew me a kiss. Then the doors closed behind him. Through the windows, we saw him go through the security desk and soon he was gone. No one can go inside the airport without a valid ticket.

I pray the next time I come here I will have a valid ticket. A Golden Ticket to America.

Fred Shares the News

January 18, 2000
Dear My Diary,

Fred called me to say he got home safely and did not forget about me. He told me this was his biggest adventure ever and will try to get me to America as soon as he can. I know it will be many months before I will have the chance, but I appreciate his enthusiasm.

Fred's family cannot wait to hear about all the things he did in Vietnam. I hope he does not tell them everything we did! I am still thinking much about our last night together and how good it felt to be with a lover.

He will start back to work right away, but by being in my country, Fred sees America in a very different light. He does not know how it will affect his business, but it truly affected the way he sees how different we live from Americans. Especially how hard we work without government assistance to pay those who cannot. He is very touched by the experience and is honored to be my man.

His words affect me deeply. He does not think of my country as being so poor with money but as so rich with strong people. I can move in my life with more confidence next to a man I respect so much.

I told him he honors me, and my country, with these words and I can't wait to join him and show how hard I can work. We wished each other a good night and sweet dreams.

Mama told us she was a very different person when Dad left Vietnam than the way she was six weeks before. She came to know how it felt to be truly in love. She saw Dad become accepted by her family by the many ways he treated Mama and everyone around him. Dad's flattery to her was hard to accept at first, given the way Mama thought of herself and how others treated her. But his words and feelings were genuine and over time she came to accept, and eventually believe, the flattery, compliments, and kind words. And so, she should have! Mama was beautiful in her 20's and is still very lovely to this day.

Sunday, Jan 21
Dear My Diary,

I got an email from Auntie Giang saying Fred and his parents spent last night with her family at her favorite restaurant. Fred brought pictures and videos including the engagement videos to share along with gifts for everyone, to say "thank you" for introducing us.

Auntie is very touched by his thoughtful words and gifts and said Fred's parents were warm and friendly. They exchanged phone numbers and email addresses to keep in touch. I so wish I had been there for it!

Dear My Diary,

Frank and Maggie emailed me today for the first time! They said they have not seen Fred so happy in a long time now that he has me in his life. They admitted they had not been sure of his early interest in me, but since his return, and after meeting with Auntie and her family, Fred's parents understand better the kind of people I come from. They want very much to meet me in person and join the Starbuckle family as their new daughter.

I thanked them for their kind words and encouragement, adding that my parents have accepted Fred as a new son with the desire to one day meet his parents and share many happy times.

They responded to my email with pictures of themselves and Auntie together at the restaurant. A very happy family!

Grandma and Grandpa Starbuckle loved to tell us about the time they met Mama's different relatives in Riverton. Getting to know their future daughter-in-law by way of her sister, aunt and cousins, especially as they are all Vietnamese, was a bit of a culture shock for them but they took it all in stride. Dad was so happy and excited to share information of his new family and the country they live in that it became a big topic of family conversations for weeks after he returned.

January 31, 2000
Dear My Diary,

I feel different since going back to work. It has been two weeks since Fred left and although my family has said nothing, I feel an unspoken obligation to make up the lost time. My family gave me the most special gift of quality time with our American guest and for this, I am compensating with extra time of my own. There is plenty to do as Tet is upon us and many shipping containers are being loaded, unloaded, or transferred every week through our warehouses and the work keeps my loneliness at a distance.

Since Fred came to help, the whole company knows I have an American boyfriend. Even those who did not work that day heard about Fred and "how well he understands Vietnamese". I do not correct them, of course. That is my own secret! The best part? No more Kimmie Cay Dua. Not one time!

I use the lessons from Fred to be more in control of the working area. I try to balance 'nice' with 'firm', keeping the workers busy and not letting them give me one of their many excuses about why they do not work so hard. I keep my back straight and no more slumping.

Because of this, I feel a change with the workers toward me. Not in a bad way, but less informal than before. Thao mentioned to me last night that she sees the change and it is a good one. I am acting more like a manager and less like the half nervous and half unsure woman of last year.

I am touched by my sister's words. What she says, I feel it also. Fred had told me the workers are not my friends, they don't care so much about me as I am a boss and daughter of the owners. However, it does not mean I cannot be nice with them, especially if it helps get the work done. It is a delicate balance that can be developed over time. My sister is very like Fred in this way, and I appreciate her so much!

Dear My Diary,

Fred emails me almost every day. He sends pictures of our visit and tells me what they mean to him. At the Valley of Love, we made a funny pose with a woman employee wearing a giant heart costume. We both leaned over her head to kiss each other while she is making a big surprise face with hands on her cheeks. Fred added a caption "I just Love to be in Love! Don't you Love to be in Love?"

In another photo, Fred had set the timer on his camera and we positioned ourselves on some steps. Just before the camera clicked, he picked me up suddenly in his arms, like they do in the movies. I was not expecting his action, so the surprise on my face was very real when the shutter clicked. No one has ever picked me up before and it was so easy for him too! Fred is so strong, I have confidence that he can carry my heart forever!

Every day I look forward to seeing what Fred will send me next. I respond by telling him about my day and how I hope to be a big help with his business. Phung has given me some of his Berkeley business textbooks to read and help me understand the American way of doing business. Much of it looks familiar to me as the way we run our company and from the business classes I took in college. Still, it is interesting to find some differences and techniques that I have forgotten or did not know before.

Year of the Dragon

Feb 5, 2000
Dear My Diary,

I miss Fred as he cannot be here for our first Lunar New Year as a couple. I went to our local temple before and after work to burn incense and make prayers. I pray for my marriage to be long and happy and for Fred to be as loving a husband into old age as he is with me now. I want to make Fred happy and hope I do not embarrass him with my ignorance. Speaking of ignorance, I realized today that I must learn more about where I will be living and what kinds of things are there.

I looked around and remembered how bare the temple was when I was a little girl. Now it is very bright, filled with color, large statues and shiny gongs. Monks hand out oranges, lucky money envelopes and sweets to those who come.

I realize now that much of this came about from my family and the many families working for us who give donations of money, gold and materials to build and decorate the temple as well as giving food, clothes and medicines to the poor. As Phung told Fred, there are people upstream and downstream who benefit from our successful business.

Fred has told me that he does not go to any Christian church, but he donates to hospitals, schools, neighborhoods, and homeless people places. I feel like we have much in common to help our home cities as well as how we do our business. This is a good sign to me. I made my last prayer for good health to Fred and his family and to keep me in his heart.

One of the many things Dad and Mama's family shared was the gift of giving to those less fortunate. It's an important feature of well-rounded families, wealthy or not, and it is a trait all of us have continued throughout our lives. Dad may not have been a practicing Christian, but his values and way of living crossed all religious, economic, and social levels and he did a lot of good for a lot of people, same as our Pham families.

A Banh Bao in the Steamer Basket?

February 7, 2000
Dear My Diary,

I am so scared. I think Fred did something bad to me and now I have an appointment to see a private doctor.

This morning, I was feeling poorly and nauseous and said so to Thao.

"Nauseous? So soon after Fred is gone?"

I told her it was probably something I ate or gas pains and Thao, with a little smile on her lips said, "Or maybe you have a banh bao in the steamer basket?"

"Are you saying I have a baby in me? That is impossible and please don't say that again," I snapped at her. "Not even as a joke."

"You spent nights with him. You cannot deny that, can you?" she reminded me.

"I am still a virgin," I hissed back, not wanting parents to hear. "There is no banh bao anywhere!"

Thao held up her palms in surrender. "I believe you. But I also know how heavily you sleep. What's to say lover boy didn't make a sneaky in you while you slept? A little premarital taste of heaven?"

Another wave of nausea hit me the same time as her disgusting suggestion. "No! Fred would never do such a thing as he…he is a virgin too!"

I can't believe I said such a private detail out loud. I should cut my tongue out for that. Thao scoffed, "Did he tell you that? And you believed him?" She shook her head "My poor naïve little sister! Since you believe so strongly that you are not pregnant," Thao reached under some towels, took out a long, slender box and handed it to me, "then take the test."

My mouth was hanging open, I am sure, wondering why in the world she is keeping pregnancy tests hidden in our bathroom. But of course…Phung.

To prove to her I am not with child, I tore open the box, got the test out of its wrapping and started to use it when Thao grabbed the test back, "What are you doing?"

"I am putting it in my mouth. That's how it works, right? Like a thermometer?"

There was laughter in her eyes but patience in her voice when she showed me what to do. Minutes later, the laughter was replaced by genuine sympathy and pain when the test showed positive.

The Dreaded Question Answered

February 7, 2000
Dear My Diary,

Thao knows a private woman doctor not associated with our family. Our family doctor will certainly report something like this to my parents and I will be in deeper trouble than anything any of my sisters have ever done.

As we are closed this week for Tet, I do not have to go to work and I am feeling awful in my bowels and in my heart. Thao and I begged off from visiting family for today as I am clearly not looking well and Thao offered to keep me company until "the flu bug" passes.

Thao can be mean to me sometimes, but I can see she is as scared as I am. After all, it could happen to her, too.

If there is a baby, it will be born before I can go to America. Then what? If I tell Fred about the baby, will he deny it, accept it or just disappear as so many men do when given inconvenient news?

Even if Fred accepts the baby, how can I accept Fred if he did a sneaky to me while I slept? Probably he has not been a virgin for a long time. How STUPID I am! My family's status will be stained as well. It's not like I can go away and hide…I am the most visible woman in Vietnam!

Thao said this doctor has ways to make the baby go away before it shows in my belly and no one will have to know…not Fred and not our parents. How does my sister know these things?

I have to stop writing now. I am too depressed and confused and hurt beyond belief.

Dear My Diary,

At the doctor's office, the nurse had me fill out forms and I answered everything honestly, hoping this would not come back to my parents. After I turned in the papers, neither of us spoke. Only the tick tick tick of the office clock breaks the silence of our personal thoughts.

The nurse reviewed the answers and asked some of the same questions again, "When did you last have sexual relations?"

"I have not knowingly had sexual relations, but I slept in the same bed with my fiancé just over three weeks ago."

She asked when I had my last moon time and I said it stopped five days ago.

She glanced sharply at me, "Are you sure?"

"Positive."

"Then you are not pregnant."

Thao told her that I took the test and it showed positive. It was a good thing we brought it with us, wrapped in a plastic bag with the testing box and instructions. The nurse took everything and went away.

About twenty minutes later, the doctor came in and we made our introductions. She said the test we used is a brand that has a poor accuracy record of less than eighty percent. Based on the answers I provided, the test gave a false positive. She explained that by having my moon time well after possible relations, I could not be pregnant.

I took another test at the office and it was negative. After Thao spoke privately to the doctor about me, as I was too shy to ask her myself, the doctor gave me a physical exam and verified I am still intact. No sneakies. No babies. No broken promises.

Thanks to Buddha! Thao has proven herself to be as ignorant as I am! Such a weight has been lifted from our shoulders and sister could not be sorrier for starting this whole stupid mess.

I have learned another way of being cheap: buying the lowest-priced pregnancy test. Troi oi!

Lois: We spoke to Mama about this and she shook her head at the long-unspoken memory. "Thao and I swore each other to everlasting secrecy and never discussed it again. I never told a soul. Not even to your father…and believe me, I kept very little from him.

"But I will say this, Thao and I became much closer after that. I always had the feeling that if she had been having relations with Phung prior to that day, that she stopped right then and there after what happened to me. I was never more terrified in my life until the time of your birth.

"And one more thing…even after all these years, I still cringe anytime I hear or read the word 'sneaky'."

February 10
Dear My Diary,

I looked up information on the computer about where I will be living. Riverton is a city of about 300,000 people on the Missouri River. It has a Coast Guard and Army base, a shipping center with big warehouses for river trade and is intersected by two main highways. There are also some colleges and several major companies in the metropolitan area.

Riverton covers a large area with many smaller towns around it and the land appears to be mostly flat. Not so very different from where I live but much smaller in size and population. Ho Chi Minh City has over seven million people and more coming from the provinces all the time.

I see that Riverton gets snow in the winter too…brrr! I have never seen snow in real life and don't know if I will like it. Trinh and Thanh get snow where they live and they seem to like it only if they stay inside and watch out the windows! Much of this information Fred has told me before, but it is good to remind myself and verify what he has told me. I will email Thanh to get more information about her city and what I should know about it.

Again, we were surprised that Mama did not research where her American boyfriend lived and what it was like before she accepted him. Mama said Dad had told her things about Riverton and the area, but once it hit home that she would be moving there one day, it became more important to soak up the necessary information.

Thanh said Fred came and had dinner with her family. They talked much of Vietnam and me and what Fred did here. Thanh is very pleased with how Fred spoke about his time with our family and said it is clear that he is very much in love with me. He brought some small presents for nieces Tam and Cam from us and they are very excited about their new Uncle Fred.

Valentine's Day

February 14
Dear My Diary,

Today is the American holiday Valentine's Day. Yesterday I got a pretty card from Fred for this occasion. I am ashamed as I did not know so much about this day, so I had not sent him a card too. I am sure I have seen Western movies about this day but forgot.

I emailed him back to say "Happy Valentine's Day" too with a picture of me making kiss lips at him. Last year we did not do Valentine's Day because I did not know about the holiday and Fred did not know me so well as to consider me his "sweetheart". We were still very new to each other. Not now, of course! Maybe next year we will be together for this holiday. I hope so!

March 1, 2000
Dear My Diary,

Today I sent my Fred a birthday card purchased from one of the downtown stores that cater to expats. I got some fashion magazines for myself and Thao as a treat.

I hope Fred remembers my birthday because he and I share the same day. Is this a lucky thing? I think so. I like to think of when he celebrated birthdays as a little boy and there is a little girl across the world also having a birthday that he will meet one day.

I made a poem inside the card:

There was a boy, there was a girl
Living far across the world
They did not know of each other
One had sisters, the other a brother
Many years must go by
Before the boy would go and fly
Far across the ocean blue
To say these words: "I love you".

I don't know if he will like the poem, but I spent three days to make it sound right to me. I feel special to make and write this to Fred. For the signature, I put on some lipstick and pressed the card to my lips to make a special love signature.

Chuc Mung Sinh Nhat to Us!

March 17, 2000
Dear My Diary,

When I got home from work, there was a birthday card and letter from Fred. He sent it on March 1st…the same day I sent his card! His sweet message said he cannot wait for me to celebrate our next birthday with him in person. The card has lots of green, four-leaf flowers call "clovers" and a cute message.

I understand March 17th is a holiday called Saint Patrick Day and it is a fun day for people to be Irish, even if they are not. I find it very interesting for lovers to share the same birthday, even if not the same year. Today I am 29 and Fred is 32. We are kind of old, but not so old, I think. Especially when I think how Trinh and Thao are older than me and both are not married yet.

There is a VHS tape in Fred's package, but I did not look at it yet because I also got a letter from the consulate. It is either a routine follow-up or it may be bad news. I think maybe this is not a good birthday letter.

I held my breath and opened the envelope. It says I have an appointment at the US Consulate office April 4, 2000, 11:00 regarding the application for my K1 visa.

This is not possible! I read it three times to be sure my eyes are not tricking me. It has only been two months since Fred left Vietnam to make the application…how can I have an appointment letter? Someone must have sent this to me as a mean joke to get my hopes up, only to have them dashed when the truth is revealed.

I read the letter again and studied it carefully. It is printed on heavy paper with a raised seal on the letterhead. It looks as official as the wording in the letter. The instructions say to bring this letter, official identification, proof of relationship to the applicant (Fred), passport photographs and other items.

My hands were shaking when I brought the Consulate letter to Thao. She read it over and jumped up and down saying "Kimmie, this is great news! How wonderful for you!"

I asked her if she thinks it is a mistake? That this is too soon to get the appointment?

She agreed it is very fast and could not explain why this is so, but it looks real and I should do what it says.

I called Fred to wish him a happy birthday, followed up with news of the letter. He is very happy to hear about the appointment and have I looked at the VHS tape yet? When I said, "not yet" he asked me to please watch it and bring it to the interview with me. I will understand why when I see it.

I shared my worry with Fred that this letter came far too soon and was not expecting to see it until late in the year.

Fred said, "Maybe this is a secret birthday wish coming true?"

I answered, "Maybe so. It looks official so I will go, of course!"

Fred said he really likes my poem and is very touched by it, especially my "signature", causing me to blush. We finished by saying "I love you" to each other…me in English and he in Vietnamese. How romantic!

At dinner, my parents were pleased by all the happy news I shared with them and agreed this is a special birthday for me. We do not customarily celebrate birthdays as we see done in other cultures, but we went out after dinner to a café for dessert and boba tea. There was much talk of the April 4th appointment at the consulate.

I expressed my concern once again, this time to my parents, about the timing of the letter and the possibility that it is a practical joke being played upon me.

Ba said, "I have seen enough documents from the US Consulate to fill a room full of filing cabinets. You have no worries, daughter, but to decide what to wear to your appointment."

When we got home, I loaded the VHS tape and sat with my family to watch the whole thing. I quietly cried in my chair to watch Fred and our family members make many hellos and good wishes. In the tape, Fred included pieces of video from his visit: He with members of my family, us together in Dalat, at the engagement party and in my home. Fred showed many parts of our lives in the tape to show we are a real couple to each other and our families. I could not ask for a better birthday gift this year or any year.

Over the years that VHS tape was transferred to DVD and various computer and video formats. Every time we watch it, Mama has tears and gets emotional. She and Dad would cuddle up and he would wrap her in his long arms.

They would stop the video at different spots and reminisce about this person or that place or some event. The transfers did not always hold up well and for their 25th anniversary, we all chipped in to have the original VHS tape electronically cleaned up and enhanced, then transferred to the most current media format. It was a top-notch job and they could not thank us enough for the gift.

K1 Visa Interview

April 4, 2000

Dear My Diary,

Ba brought me to the Consulate in his car as I am too distracted to drive. He made sure I had all my documents and wished me luck.

After going through security, I approached a Vietnamese receptionist dressed in a blue ao dai with her consulate badge on a lanyard. She reviewed my letter and identification and had me sit until called.

I have a large bag with me containing handwritten letters from Fred and his family, some pictures of us during his visit and the special VHS tape Fred made for me. I brought more than what the consulate asked for because we all know that sometimes people pay to arrange fake marriages with foreigners and then divorce their spouse but stay on as a permanent resident. I dressed in my best business clothes and Thao helped me with makeup. I want to give a "best first impression".

Mr. Sawyer came to the reception area with my file folder. When I stood up, he bumped back a little in surprise but said nothing. He is tall, but I am taller. Mr. Sawyer smiled, shook my hand and led me to an interview room with an interpreter. He asked me if I wanted the interpreter and I said no, I am confident with my English. She stayed anyway in case she was needed.

Mr. Sawyer asked questions like how did I know Fred? Did I ever meet him in person? How long have we known each other? I showed Mr. Sawyer letters and postmarked envelopes from Riverton, pictures of Fred with me and my family at home and in the botanical garden where we had a picnic.

He asked me what is Fred's birthday? What color are his eyes? Do I know what Fred does for work?

I said "Fred is the owner of a recycling business. He buys new and used things at low prices, then uses the profits to buy more inventory. My father operates a similar kind of business, but on a much larger scale."

He asked me if anyone has offered me money or gifts to marry Fred? I know he is asking if I am doing this for money and not love. I said "No one has offered or given me money, gifts or property to encourage me to marry Fred Starbuckle. The biggest thing Fred has given me is his heart." Mr. Sawyer and the interpreter smiled at my answer. I knew I had said the right thing.

He looked carefully at some paperwork in his file. I can see it is not a letter but some forms with a large "1040" printed in one corner. I do not know what 1040 is but he is studying the papers carefully.

Mr. Sawyer asked me if I know how much Fred makes for income? I got a funny feeling about his question. Maybe Fred makes so little and this will be a problem? He never told me how much he makes, and I don't want to lie, so I admit I do not know and now I feel foolish for not knowing such a basic and important thing.

To counter this, I told Mr. Sawyer that when I had asked Fred if he can make a comfortable home for me and our children and pay for college and doctors and dentists and a house, he told me that will be no problem and I believe Fred to be honest about this. My hands started to shake in my lap, and I forced them to be still. This is not the time.

Mr. Sawyer's eyebrows went up at my answer, but he smiled and said, "Yes, I don't think that will be a problem for Mr. Starbuckle." He closed the folder and asked me do I know what his family thinks of Fred marrying an Asian woman? Do they know this and is there perhaps some problems I will be facing? I see the meeting room has a TV and VCR in a corner near the interpreter. I smiled, pulled the videotape out of my bag, and said I have something that may help.

The interpreter set up everything and after a moment, Fred came on the screen. He smiles brightly, says Hi! to me and my family and welcome to Riverton! He said he wants to introduce his family in person before I come. His parents, Frank and Maggie, come to the camera and wave and smile and say nice things. Barney and Bunny are next to say hi and hope to see you soon and welcome to the family. I have them stop the tape and show a picture of Fred with his parents, Barney and Bunny all together at a picnic table by a lake.

Then we start again, and my sisters and two nieces jump in from each side of the camera shouting "Kim, Oi!" and waving and say they can't wait to see me again and to please hurry. I show Mr. Sawyer pictures of my family portrait from a few years ago and point out Thanh and Trinh so he can see they are my family. Mr. Sawyer stops the tape before it gets to the part where we are together in Dalat and my home.

Mr. Sawyer said that was enough and thanked me for coming. Then he said the most special words to me: "Congratulations! I am approving your application, and your visa will be ready in two weeks to pick up." He walked me back to the reception area. I can't feel the floor. I am floating. I shake Mr. Sawyer's hand and thank him for his time and gave a little bow. He bowed back and I stepped outside into the brilliant sunshine.

I found Ba leaning against the car door with arms crossed and a little smile played across his face when he saw me.

"I am accepted! I got the visa, Ba, I got the visa!" Then my emotions broke free, and I cried happy tears before I can get into the car.

He said "I knew you would get it. Mother and I made many prayers for you and Fred."

I tried to get my emotions under control, but it is hard. I said, "I was nervous when they asked me about Fred's money. Maybe there is a problem, I don't know, but they said they did not think it would be a problem, so it must be all right." I told Ba about the video, and he said that was a smart thing to bring.

I can't wait to call Fred and tell him the big news. We went to the office, and I called his home phone as it is night-time in Riverton.

Fred answered on the second ring and asked, "Did you get it?"

"I did!"

"Woo-woo!" and we talked some more. I thanked Fred for the tape as it showed his seriousness about me and his family's acceptance. I asked when does he want me to come to Riverton?

He said, "I will pick you up right now!"

So sweet! I let him know the visa will be ready in two weeks and I need time to prepare. I mentioned that I am nervous to fly to America by myself, but Fred reassured me, saying "Do not think twice about that. I will come get you myself!"

Now Fred must get another travel visa and plane tickets and things. I teased him by saying, "I hope your house is clean!"

And he came back with, "Who said I live in a house?" Always making jokes!

What to Bring? What to Leave?

April 5, 2000
Dear My Diary,

I am so light-headed today that I can barely focus on my duties. I am sure some of the workers notice something different, but I am not about to tell them. They will learn soon enough. I do not know when Fred can be here, but he insists on escorting me to America and that means getting tickets and another travel visa plus taking more time off from work and more expenses for him. Fred doesn't have to do that for me.

I am trying to figure out what I will bring to my new home. I don't own much…clothes, books, CD's, video tapes and a few pieces of jewelry. Almost everything I have belongs to my parents or are from my young girl times and I can't take furniture or anything big with me. I finally decided to take mostly clothes, shoes, accessories, and gifts for my American and Vietnamese family members. Most anything else I can get in America.

I have a large binder of printed emails from Fred, so I read through our early ones…how we introduced ourselves and started getting to know each other. Then I found the one where Fred asked to be "more than just an email pal". He asked me if I was willing to consider him as my boyfriend…to make a more serious relationship.

I remember how it made me think, "How do I feel about this man I have never met? Do I want to take a chance with him?" I decided I had nothing to lose if I said "yes". He is very nice and shared funny things with me. Fred often asked about my life and opinions on various things. Most importantly, he was still very far away and there was a chance he might get tired of me, never visit, and have no chance of breaking my heart.

Now I am going to America because I said "yes" to him: Yes to be his email pal, Yes to be his girlfriend, and now Yes to be his wife. Sadly, the binder is too bulky and heavy so I will leave it here and perhaps bring it back another time. I wonder when that will be?

When I look at my life of twenty-nine years and realize I own almost nothing, it saddens me. I live with my parents, just like most single women here. I don't read much anymore, do not hang out with groups of friends to party, smoke or drink like the other young people and have never had an interest in collecting or buying things "just to have".

And it is hard to build up savings because our inflation rate is so high. To keep money in the bank would be worth next to nothing within a few years. For that reason, I give my extra money to Me to buy food or use it for our business, even though I know they do not need it. I do not need it either.

Now I feel like a failure. I did not feel this way before because money and men were not important in my life. But now, when I want to bring something to America and show my value to Fred, I have nothing for my pockets. Sigh!

I pick up the stuffed deer Buck, kiss his black nose and put it in my suitcase. He is cute and reminds me of happy times with Fred.

It hurts to read this entry as Mama felt she had no value. This is not the woman who raised us. She has often described herself in interviews as having been "a moth that turned into a butterfly". I guess Dad saw the butterfly within the moth.

Today Thao took me to a different doctor to get BC pills. I can't even say the real words in my mind, it is so embarrassing. So adult. Thao talked to the doctor like she has done this before. The doctor asked me about my cycles, then told us which pills to get and how to use them and what to change if I have some side effects.

I am glad sister went with me as I do not know what to ask or how and maybe I won't understand the details. But I understand. I asked Thao how she knows so much to ask the doctor? She said, "I've read about it and talked with woman friends." Hmm.

Getting the Visa

April 20, 2000
Dear My Diary,

Today I got the paperwork that will change my life forever…my fiancé visa. The American Consulate called me two days ago and I took time from work to pick it up. I presented my identification card and appointment letter from the consulate and the woman retrieved the visa from a large safe. She checked everything carefully and had me do the same before smiling and congratulating me.

She reminded me that once I land in the United States, I will have ninety days to get married before the visa expires. If the visa expires without a legal marriage, I am required to leave the United States and do I understand everything? I say I do. Then she wished me good luck and I was out the door.

I called Fred from the company office and left a message for him as to what happened. Later, I got an email from him that only said "Woooo-hoooo!" It made me laugh to see just his singular expression of happiness.

I showed the visa to my family at dinner and Ba made a photocopy for our records. It is becoming very real now. My face stares back solemnly from the K1 visa. I did not smile in this picture. Maybe it is a bad luck sign? I know I do not smile a lot as people often tell me this. Me told me she has never seen me smile so much as when Fred was visiting. What she said made me smile. I told myself to smile for the green card picture.

Sister Thanh called to congratulate me on getting the K1 visa. When she got hers, she had to fly by herself to America with heavy suitcases and a limited English vocabulary. I remember what happened when she got her visa and began packing. She had so many things she wanted to take but not enough room. Our parents sent more boxes of things, at great expense, after she complained of the high cost of clothing in America and how little she had to wear.

She has always been a very stylish woman and spent all her money on clothes, cosmetics, shoes and purses. That is why she is a successful nail salon owner…she dresses to impress. Thanh is surprised to hear that Fred will come get me and openly wished Vo had not been so cheap so he could carry more suitcases for her. "I hope your marriage will be better than mine," she said in parting.

Later, I thought about her words and wonder what she meant? Does she have a bad marriage to Vo? Is something wrong with her husband or is she just bored with him? I cannot worry about this right now, but it was nice that she called. We almost never talk except when she visits here, which is rarely.

Ticket to Ride

April 23, 2000
Dear My Diary,

Fred has the plane tickets now. Round trip for him, one way for me, a visitor visa for him and a Fiancé visa for me. Fred will be in Vietnam for one week, so I need to make sure that I have all my packing done and say my good-byes to family and friends. I don't know when I will be back to see everyone again.

I am a little nervous to make this big move to America, but I will not be alone in my adjustment: Fred is always pleasant and easy to be with; his parents sound friendly and want to make me welcome; even his brother and sister-in-law look very nice in the video and, of course, I have my sister, Aunt Giang and their families close by. Lots of people to help me if I need it, and to visit with if I don't.

I straighten my back, take a deep breath and give myself a boost of confidence. My life in America will be my first big adventure. Me likes to say, "A good attitude brings good luck." I believe this is true. I pray it is true.

Dad always had such a great attitude and Mama did too, but she needed help sometimes when things got bumpy. They both taught us how good attitudes, smiles, kind words and deeds can bring good luck in many forms. We have all been witness to people with chips on their shoulders, axes to grind and clouds over their heads who attract trouble and headaches to themselves and others, then blame their troubles on everything but themselves. Our parents were never those people.

Kimmie: I was so happy and so nervous about moving to America. I had every confidence that Fred would treat me well but I was not sure I could adjust to such a new living environment. My sister Trinh did very well in New York, but Thanh had a rough time of it in her first years. I learned about this later after I moved to Riverton, and we had become closer, but it was not something she had shared with our family.

Dear My Diary,

Maggie called me today to say she and Frank are looking forward to meeting me in two weeks. I said the same to her as well. She said if I need anything or want to talk as woman to woman, she will be there for me as my American mother and friend. I said I appreciate her kindness and am sure I will ask her advice as needed.

My things are packed in two big suitcases, and I have more clothes set on a table as Fred said he was bringing an extra bag for me. I do not have any clothes for cold and snowy weather as we are a tropical country so, in anticipation of this, Ba and Me got me some pretty sweaters, knitted hats, gloves and a good sheep's wool coat from factories they do business with. I hope it will be enough!

Fred Starbuckle Returns to The Tall One

May 16, 2000
Dear My Diary,

I met Fred at the airport by myself as family is busy working and they had taken time to meet Fred on his first visit but this time I am solo. I drove the family car, but it was hard to find a parking space as people mostly come and go to the airport by taxi. Once I found a place to park, they charged a very high fee. I think in America there are so many cars that people do not pay for parking at the airport or other places.

When Fred came up to me, he said "Hey, Stranger!"

I do not know why he called me Stranger, but he was smiling so I said, "You look Stranger too!" And Fred laughed heartily at my joke.

He said, "I won't be a Stranger for long if you give me a kiss!" That made me shy as there were many people nearby and some are looking at us, but we made a quick kiss on the lips. He is my fiancé and I should not care what other people are thinking.

This time, we are letting Fred stay in our house since he has proven himself to be a respectful man. Moreover, in five days I will leave with him to America so we will have more time with my family before we leave. The neighbors have seen Fred before and know who he is so they will not say anything to the local police, I think. The Police do not like foreigners staying in private homes but my family is well-known and respected so they will not say anything to us.

Fred brought two suitcases, but they are empty, and an overnight bag with most of his clothes for the trip. I asked why there is so little in the suitcases? He said they are both for MY things, not his.

Ba had got some new suitcases from one of his suppliers as a wedding gift, no charge. Ba knows many people like this and I think maybe the talk goes like: "My youngest daughter is getting married. That's right, the tall one. To an American. Oh, yes, he is very tall too. NBA tall. They are a good match that way."

I am always "The Tall One" to my family. Perhaps it is better than being known as "The Horse-Faced One" or "The One Who Talks Too Much". So now I will have four suitcases and two smaller bags to bring.

When the family came home from work, Fred gave Ba a good handshake, then a hug, then he hugged Me and Thao. When he made a move to hug Phung, Phung put up his hands and said, "I'm good!". Fred laughed and shook his hand instead. I think hugging is much more common in America than it is in Asia. I will try to get used to it.

We went out for dinner to celebrate Fred's return and talk about the plans for the next few days. I have been invited to some going away parties and, of course, Fred is invited too. One at work, one with my college friends and another with all the family from around the HCMC area. We told all this to Fred and he just grinned and said, "The more the merrier!" He always has such a good mood!

And Just in Case...

May 21, 2000
Dear My Diary,

After so many parties, so many gifts and numerous wishes from everyone, I am very tired…and yet I can't sleep. One week ago, I did not have much to bring to America except clothing and a few personal items. Now I have packs of dried shrimp and fish for cooking, beautiful sets of chopsticks, jewelry boxes (maybe they hope I will fill it with a rich husbands' gifts?), along with necklaces and earrings, bracelets and anklets, fancy moisturizing creams and other nice things.

Everyone was so kind and showered me with lovely wishes for a long and happy marriage with many babies to follow. This is what makes me so tired. I am not used to being around so much social activity, but I also appreciate my friends and family.

Being tired and unable to sleep reminds me of the first time I began writing this diary. Fred was coming to Vietnam and I was as nervous then as I am now, yet it is different because tonight is my last night in Vietnam. I believe I will be fine in America and Fred will be good to me and his family will like me. I really believe this. My parents, I think, not so much. Here is why:

Last night after Fred went to bed, Ba, Me and Thao sat with me at the dining table. Me gave me a thick envelope and I opened it. It was stuffed with fifty- and hundred-dollar bills. I asked what this is for?

Me explained this is almost $5,000 in Lucky Money from our guests at the engagement party. It is mine for shopping new clothes or jewelry or anything I want to start my new life in America. It is my money to do as I want.

I said, "But half is Fred's money too, yes? It was OUR engagement party."

Me nodded and said this is true. If I want to share it with Fred, that is my decision. The family just thought I might want or need things that Fred can't give me right away as we start our new life. She turned to Ba, "Lo?"

Ba gave me another, larger envelope. This also had cash, but much more: $10,000 USD. Ba said, speaking on behalf of the family, that they like Fred very much and believe he will be a good husband to me and that my life will be a happy one. They also know I love Fred and believe I will do everything to fit into my new American life.

"BUT sometimes things in life go wrong. There is a chance that Fred is bad. Or maybe you will not like life in America. Or some other thing will happen that makes you want, or need, to leave Fred and come home. If so, this will help you get a plane ticket or a place to stay for a time."

Ba scared me. I asked, "Do you know something about Fred? Some secret I do not know?"

Me said, "Do not let your Ba frighten you. If we knew something bad about Fred or have big unanswered questions or doubts, we would have told you and stopped everything before now. Think of this as a kind of insurance. First, you have your sisters and your Auntie and cousins. They are the first ones to call or run to if you have the need. This money will give you a way out without having to ask others."

I asked, "Are you sure everything is okay with Fred?" Everyone assured me they are very, very happy with Fred, but I need to have a Plan B, "just in case".

Ba said, "I never go into a business deal without two backup plans, no matter how confident I am it will go the way I expect. You have a backup plan now. Contact family with money to survive. We hope you never need it." Me and Thao echoed his sentiment and we put the money away for safe keeping.

Before I forget, there was one more thing: Today, we had a small going away party for me at home. Phung asked me to the kitchen, away from Fred who was telling stories in the parlor. He gave me a wrapped gift to open. It is a book called "The Blue-Collar Millionaire". The book sounded familiar, and I said so. He reminded me of the long afternoon talk we had with Fred the first time he was here, and Ba wanted to know many things about Fred and how he makes his business.

When listening to what Fred had to say, Phung thought of this book he had recently read and the people it talked about. He said, "I think you will find this a very interesting read. You might learn some new things."

I asked what kind of things? He shrugged his shoulders. "Whatever there is to learn."

I don't like it when Phung talks like a mystery monk. I thanked him for the book and asked him if he will be the next one to marry into the family? He gave me a big smile and lifted his shoulders again. "Kay serah serah". I think it is a foreign phrase but I do not know the meaning. I took the gift to my room and added it to my luggage.

Good night, Dear My Diary! I leave for America tomorrow!!

It was years before Mama learned that "que sera, sera" means "whatever will be, will be" from a song she heard in a movie. I don't think Mama expected so many parties and get-togethers as what went on that week.

There was a surprise party at the warehouse with the workers she managed, a group of fellow Alumni from the HCMC Pedagogical University for a going-away party, and gifts from neighbors and local merchants of all sorts.

Mama had told all of us the story about the $10,000 many times, to make sure we understood how important it is to have a "Plan B" and even a "Plan C" if things don't work out. This story has helped us many times over the years in a variety of situations.

Kimmie: It took a lot of reassuring from my family to convince me that they did not really believe the marriage would fail or that Fred would not be a good husband to me. Their intention for the escape money was well-meant but it still planted seeds of doubt in my mind.

However, I did think The Blue-Collar Millionaire book was an odd choice as Phung's going away gift. Not like the cooking, home decorating and family planning books I had gotten from others. I chalked it up to Phung being a man of little imagination. Years later, his gift would become the most memorable of any I received that week.

Coming to America

May 23, 2000
Dear My Diary,

What a busy bee time it has been! We went to Tan Son Nhat airport with a small army of family and friends to see us off with lots of hugging and kissing, taking pictures and more than a few tears.

Me gave me motion-sickness pills, "Remember to call when you get to America!"

Ba said, "Remember to go to Auntie if Fred gives you trouble!"

Sister said, "Remember to take your birth control pills!" as everyone laughed. Ugh! I am glad Fred does not understand Vietnamese.

This is my first time flying and the first time I have been inside the airport. No one is allowed inside without a valid ticket and we went through customs with no problems. Fred only has a large carry-on for himself, and the four full-size suitcases contain over eighty kilos of belongings for my new life in America at no extra charge. Fred is smart that way.

It would have been a lot more weight and a much higher cost if Fred had not put a stop to a common practice. As we were making our goodbyes, I had a lot of friends and family pushing things on me to bring to America. But they were not for me: I was to send the items on to other people. When I showed Fred everything and what it was for, he told me, "We are not a delivery service. That's what the post office is for."

He made it clear that anything we took for others, was taking away space for my new life. Fred said I could blame him for saying "no" to them. I am not sorry he stood up to them for me. I hate saying no to others because they might think less of me. In this way, Fred is braver than me.

We were seated in First Class and Fred was right about the leg room. I peeked into Coach and the seats are so much smaller. Our seats are leather and wide, three pairs across, not the 3/4/3 pattern I saw in Coach. Fred let me have the window seat so I could see everything.

Takeoff was very exciting and scary but after a while, it became relaxing. I looked out the window as Ho Chi Minh City fell away and became the Pacific Ocean, flying East to get to the West. I miss my family already.

Fred diverted my attention with American coins, how they look, their values and who is on the fronts and backs. Fred and I also practiced converting Metric and American measures. The American style of measurements is very strange and confusing. Not like the simple metric system where everything is based on the powers of ten. Fred says he wishes America was on the metric system as even his own people often get confused by how many ounces are in a pound or cups in a quart. The measurements are like a foreign language to me.

We had a choice of Asian or Western style dinner and breakfast. I tried the chicken breast stuffed with greens, salad with lettuce, boiled egg slices and tomatoes, steamed carrots and a bread roll with butter. It was different and I liked it.

We had sparkling juice and pretended it was champagne, toasting each other for a new life. Fred said he is not a bad cook at home, but I will have to be my own judge of his edible efforts.

It is hard to sleep as I am so excited, but I napped off and on and caught up my diary entries. Fred and I talked sometimes and were quiet other times. He held my hand a lot under the blankets. It was nice to look at the big ocean below, but I miss my family too.

We arrived in Los Angeles and went through customs and immigration. Fred was next to me the whole time as a woman stamped my passport and welcomed me to America. We had lunch at the airport and waited about three hours to get on the plane for Riverton.

I felt a strong mix between being tired and excited to be in Los Angeles. I wanted to see the city, but Fred said it was not a good idea to leave the airport.

We spent many long hours flying across the ocean, but it is still Sunday. Fred said it was because we flew across the International Date Line so instead of becoming Monday, it stayed as Sunday.   This is becoming a very long day!

When we got off the plane in Riverton, there was such a big crowd of people to see us! Auntie Giang, both my sisters, Fred's parents and brother and sister-in-law, cousins and nieces. Flowers and balloons welcoming me to America. I got very emotional as I was not expecting this, and Fred kept it as a surprise for me.

After lots of hugging and kissing my family and meeting my in-laws-to-be, Fred and his brother retrieved our luggage and we took a chartered bus to a Vietnamese restaurant for a Welcome-to-America lunch. There was a private party room in back and we ate many Asian and American dishes, talking about the flight and how very happy I am to be here.

Back at that time, the security measures as we take for granted today were not yet in place. Before the hijackings of September 11th, 2001 airports were open to anyone to come in and see friends and family onto or coming off airplanes right at the gates. We hardly know anybody who was around at that time, it was so long ago.

I was touched that Sister Tina flew in from New York to greet me. She is staying with Thanh's family. Thanh said if I need a job, she can have me help at the Pretty Happy Nail Salon and I thanked her for the offer.

Tina said the first thing I need to do is get settled into my new home and learn how Fred wants me to be with him. She said living with a man is very different from living with parents. I wonder how she knows this? It is all very new to me.

Family asked if we have a wedding date set yet? I said no but will let them know when we decide. Because my visa is good for only three months from today, we need to make some decisions soon.

I asked Barney and Bernice how they like the Vietnamese food and Barney made a sour face, saying "My name is BER-nie, not BAR-ney." I had forgotten that he had changed his name and Fred always speaks of his brother as Barney.

Then I remembered that Bernice likes to be called by her nickname. I apologized to brother and sister and promised to remember to call them Bernie and Rabbit. Suddenly there was much laughter and Bernie said, "She called you a rabbit!"

Fred and his parents were laughing too. Fred explained that Bernice's nickname is "Bunny" which is like saying "cute rabbit", so I was partly right. I was so very embarrassed, but Bunny came over, hugged my shoulders and said, "I like you already!"

Fred added, "Don't worry about it, Sweetheart. That was a cute mistake. No harm done."

Bernie said, "Couldn't you find someone closer to home?"

Fred and his parents made dark faces at Bernie. Bunny gave him a little slap on the side of his head as she sat down and whispered loudly, "Be nice!"

After lunch we went to his parents' house. The whole home is on one floor, not like the tall narrow homes in Vietnam. During the drive, I could feel exhaustion catching up with me.

Fred let me call Me and Ba from the house phone. It was the middle of the night but Me said to call anytime. I did and she sounded wide awake. I told her about the flight and how so many family members came to meet me at the airport and the lunch we just had.

Me cried and said the house is not the same since I am gone. I said I miss her and Ba and sister too and I will call later to speak some more. As I hung up, someone said "Can't wait to see your new home?" I turned and Bernie was there. "I hope you like the smell of old grease," and he walked away without further explanation.

'What a puzzling thing to say', I thought.

At the same time, I realized how much shorter Bernie is to Fred and their parents. Even Maggie and Bunny are taller than Bernie. Then I thought, 'Well, I am taller than anyone in my family. It is not so different to be the shortest.' Is that what makes Bernie so sour? If it is, then I know the feeling.

Fred offered to take me home. He looked the way I felt, so I said, "Yes, please. This is too exhausting for me." It was so much fun, especially with the children running about, but also so much talking, switching between two languages, answering Maggie in Vietnamese…twice!

We said our good-byes and I promised to meet my sisters tomorrow for lunch. Tina is here for three more days before flying back.

Fred moved the suitcases to an old van and we left. Soon we are in a run-down looking area with warehouses and small factories. Fred pulled up to a large brick building. The sign said, "Starbuckle and Sons Garage and Repair Service." White letters on a black background trimmed with white. Just after the name is an illustration of a looped belt with a star placed where the clasp would go. Star Buckle. Just like Fred explained! Then I thought, 'Didn't Fred say his father lost the car repair business?'

Fred unlocked the gate and we drove in, then he pushed a button on the visor. A tall, wide door rose slowly up and up and Fred drove in. I asked what is this place? He said, "You will see." The door closed behind us and inside are several cars and trucks parked along the walls on either side of the entrance. Then Fred announced it was time for the "nickel tour".

Fred clicked some switches, and everything went bright. Near the trucks are large tables, wheeled bins and rolls of tags and stickers. Just beyond those is a windowed office area, big enough for three or four workers. I think the garage would have used this for the manager and support staff. I could see several computer screens and what looks like a photo studio set-up with partitions and lights. There are many sets of shelves and racks in neat rows across the ground floor level.

The walls are old brick and the floor is concrete with fresh gray paint. It smells like old cars and machinery. I understood now that this is Fred's work area for his business, but couldn't this wait until tomorrow? I wanted to go to his house as I am so tired, but I was polite and said it was all very interesting.

Fred took our luggage and put them near the wall and suddenly big doors opened from the middle like a giant mouth. It is a cargo elevator! We have one like this at Ba's warehouse. We put our things inside, Fred closed the doors and we went up. It was such a mystery to me as to what he is doing. As the doors opened, Fred turned on the lights.

A spacious room several meters high with parlor and kitchen areas combined spread out before us. Splashes of bright colors here and there gave the room a modern look. As Fred took my coat to hang it up…Surprise! Mannequin hands poked out from the wall with their palms up to take our coats and hats. Very strange but whimsical. The ceiling is covered with tiny colored lights that give off a cheerful glow.

Fred showed me around and now I understood what Barney was saying to me. Fred lives in his father's old business building and he never told me. The kitchen has a big gas stove and oven, the long refrigerator has clear glass doors to see everything inside, not like any household refrigerator I have ever seen. There is a work island in the kitchen with a wheel overhead. Pots and fry pans and long handled spoons hang from hooks…and it turns, too!

We went farther back to see the sleeping quarters. One bedroom is larger and kind of fancy with its own bathroom and a large closet. Fred told me he had the bed custom-made extra-long for the two of us. The other two bedrooms are smaller and not as decorated and they have a full bathroom between them. The upstairs office is more modern and tidier than the downstairs office.

Then we went up another level to the roof top. There are greenhouses full of different vegetables and herbs Fred grows to eat. He said they used to store cars on the roof when there were too many for the garage and outside, which is why the elevator goes to the roof.

Fred asked how I like my new home? I said it is very different from what I was expecting, but honestly, I'm not sure what to think. He explained that before he came to see me the first time, the living space was very plain, wide open and did not have much privacy.

After I emailed him that I was interested in having a more serious relationship, he had Bunny help him design and decorate what he hoped would be "our" new home. He did much of the work himself and hired builder friends for the difficult parts. It sounds like he was very confident that I would say "yes" to him!

Fred showed me the smaller bedroom where he will sleep and I will have the big room with its own bath until we are properly married. He made it clear that he intends to keep his special promise to me even as we live together.

I locked the door and scrubbed myself clean from so many hours of traveling. After I dressed, Fred served up warm chamomile tea for two to help with falling asleep, then we kissed and said goodnight. Despite my weariness and the tea, I could not sleep. Probably because it is a big, strange room and very quiet, not like in Saigon where city noises constantly bleed their way through the walls. I heard Fred using the other shower and humming to himself until he laid down on his squeaky bed.

Finally, I got brave and went to the next room. I knocked softly on his door and asked, "Are you asleep? I'm lonely and want to sleep next to you." He said okay, and I went to him. He held me in his strong arms and soon made soft sleeping sounds…then I fell asleep too.

What a surprise to find herself NOT living in a house. Remember, Dad had asked Mama at one point "Who said I live in a house?" She thought it was one of his little jokes. It also made clear Uncle Barney's remark about the smell of old grease. Not what she was expecting at all.

We don't know why he did not tell her about the garage being his home except maybe he did not want to scare her off before she got to Riverton. Also, it kind of explains why Dad could not get a girlfriend, if they saw where, and how, he lived.

The glass-fronted refrigerator Mama described in the kitchen was actually a commercial store cooler Dad had found in one of the storage lockers he had purchased. He liked that it was easy to see what was in the fridge without having to open the door.

We grew up playing all over that garage. It was a great place for hide and seek, we learned about growing vegetables and Frankie broke one of the hands thinking he could hang from it. We also got to play with a lot of retro toys that were being sold and learned a lot of history from other items the folks collected and Dad shared stories with us. Lots of great memories from the garage.

All Night Shopping Store

May 24, 2000
Dear My Diary,

When I awoke, Fred's eyes were open and watching me. I became shy and said, "Am I so bad to come to you?" He smiled and said, "No, Sweetheart. Nothing happened and it is natural to be lonely and scared in a new place. I'm glad that you did."

He asked if I was hungry and I said, "a little". It was after two in the morning and very quiet outside. Fred turned on the lights in the parlor and it was so very pretty with twinkle lights like stars all over the ceiling. Fred calls them Christmas lights and he put them up to create a soft atmosphere.

He made vegetable soup from a can and baked some little breads called biscuits. It is not Pho, but it did make the hunger go away.

Fred told me to get dressed so we can get some groceries. I argued that it is too early for stores to be open…isn't it? He said he knows a place and smiled. We took a small van to the GnG store he often talks about.

I have heard about supermarkets, but this is the first one I have seen. It is like one of our marketplaces, but without the stalls and individual sellers. Food and shoes and clothes and medicines and toys and furniture…I cannot tell all the things they sell. There is so much, and the store is so quiet! I never knew American stores are open all night!

Only a few people were shopping but many workers were putting things on shelves and cleaning the floors. We got fresh fruits and vegetables, meats, rice, canned food and some other things.

Fred says he tries to cook with fresh ingredients from his rooftop garden when he can, but often he is so busy that he uses canned and frozen prepared foods to make meals faster. There are so many things to see and ask about!

Oh! When we got some chicken eggs, I looked and looked and could not find what I wanted. I asked Fred who said to speak to the man over there. I asked the worker who looked at me strangely.

At first, I thought he was surprised to see such a tall Asian woman before him or maybe my accent is so strong that he does not understand me. Then he said "Duck eggs? No, we never have duck eggs here. I did not know people eat them."

I turned to Fred who was hiding a smile behind his hand. I was upset and asked him why he did not tell me American stores do not sell duck eggs? He acted innocent and said, "Well, we both learned something today!"

Fred used a credit card to pay for our groceries. When we were back in the van, I asked about this. I have read that many Americans use credit cards and they frequently put people in too much debt. I hear about this all the time. That is why, in my country, we only use cash.

Fred said, "If you can't control your money, your money will control you." He explained that he always pays the monthly bill in full and on time. By doing this, he pays no interest and gets refunded two percent of all the money he spends with the credit card. "This is one of my multiple streams of income. I get paid by the bank for using their money."

Fred asked me if I have any money to put into a new bank account? I shared the nice news, "We got $5000 of Lucky Money from our engagement party! Parents gave it to me before we flew out. It was in the red envelopes guests were putting in the basket at the reception."

He laughed and said he thought it was just congratulation cards. "Lucky for us, I was wrong!"

I offered to give Fred half the money, but he thanked me, said "no" and that I should use it for myself for anything I want. "I got lucky getting you to say 'yes' to me!"

So sweet of him to say! I did not tell him that my family also told me to spend it on myself…how funny!

I have decided that most of the cash will go into a new bank account and I did not tell Fred about the Plan B money from my parents. For my parents' peace of mind, I will keep this secret from him and find a hiding place for it. With such a large building, a hiding place should be easy to find.

We will go to his bank this week and start a new individual account. I feel good about this because from the women at work, I hear that most men, given the chance, will take their woman's money and spend it on themselves. Fred does not want even a dollar from me!

We put the groceries away and had coffee and toasted bread with cinnamon inside, like a breakfast dessert. Then Fred gave me "The five-dollar tour". Last night it was the nickel tour and now it is the full tour.

In the guest bathroom there are several shelves full of products like in a store or for a very big family. So many different brands and kinds of toiletries and cleaning supplies. I asked why does he have so many kinds of similar things?

Fred laughed and said "This is the price I pay for buying other people's things. Most people won't buy partially used bottles or packages of toiletries, so I use them for myself and give some to the folks."

Fred admitted that he had moved all these things to this bathroom so the main bathroom is tidy and nice for me. I observed, "You have many months of supplies," and he said, "More like many years!"

We took the stairs down one level to the floor between the garage and living spaces. When it was still a working garage, the second floor held inventory, supplies and machines to make and refurbish parts. Now Fred uses the space for storing goods not to be sold right away.

He explained that when the selling side is slow, he buys and stores more things and then sells when the demand is higher, "Like the way squirrels store nuts for winter." I don't know what that means exactly, but I will ask sisters later. Maybe they will know.

In the garage, Fred showed me his system: He unloads the truck and sorts things onto large tables near the office into "sell now", "sell later", "donate", "keep for self" and "trash". Trash goes into one of two dumpsters…garbage and recycling.

Then he tried to explain more about how things work for selling and donating but there were too many details for my travel-tired mind to grasp, and I said as much. Fred apologized for all the shop-talk and took me back upstairs.

Before I arrived, Fred had installed a telecom system so we can talk between floors. That way, if he is on the first floor and I am on the third, I do not have to come all the way down or yell down the stairs with a question. So much to learn!

We took a rest and Fred gave me time to put away my clothes and personal things. I put the family pictures on a shelf so I can see everyone when I am lonely. Next to that, I put the book Phung gave me as a going-away present. I don't know when I will have a chance to read it, but it will be a reminder for me.

The sun is up now, and I promised sisters I would meet them for lunch. Maybe Fred will not want to go because it will be all girl-talk in Vietnamese. Meanwhile, I made a list of things I need to get and will ask Fred later to help me with that. Enough writing for now. Fred set an alarm clock so I can take a nap and not be late for my luncheon date.

Lunch with my Family

May 24
Dear My Diary,

Jet lag is so tiring. Now it is late night in Saigon and my body says it is time to sleep but the clock says it is time for lunch. Fred took me to the Golden Waterfall Restaurant to meet sisters, Auntie, and cousins. He came inside to have tea and say hello to everyone before leaving to make phone calls and run errands. He promised to come back in two hours.

Everyone asked me what it is like to live in the garage? I said it is very big and mostly used for his business, but the living space is clean and open and modern looking like in a magazine. I described the freight elevator and steps going to all four levels and about the roof with greenhouses full of vegetables and tables and chairs for entertaining.

They wanted to know when we will invite them to a rooftop party? They had fun teasing me, but I am sure Fred will allow for this. I still need to ask as it is not my house. I have difficulty calling the garage a house, but it is Fred's home.

Auntie said she will take me to a store called Tree Top Gals where she gets much of my clothing. No need for a tailor to make my clothes except if I want something very specific. There are other stores that have tall sizes, but the actual shopping is mostly done through catalogs.

Tina works for a large Asian banking firm selling investment products to companies and wealthy families. She is fluent in several languages and her English is so clear that she sounds very American to me. I am sure I sound very immigrant to everyone else.

Thanh said Fred and I should come with her and Vo to the local casino and play with them. I have never been to a casino but have seen them in movies. It sounds very glamourous and exciting to win big money. I saw Auntie pointedly avoiding this subject with us. I think she does not approve but I will talk to Fred about it later. It sounds fun and will be a good way to get to know my brother-in-law better.

My cousins talked a lot about their children, and it made me wonder again if Fred and I will make very tall children. Maggie, Frank and Fred are all taller than most people I have seen here so far, and Fred says much of his family "runs tall" as well.

I have asked Fred why Barney is so short, and he said sometimes that happens in families, just like I am especially tall and that height is not the only thing Barney is short in. I asked what he meant by that, and Fred just said "morals". I understood his meaning after I looked up the word in my dictionary. Yes, not a good thing to be short in.

We are not thinking of having children yet, but the family is teasing me that I will be pregnant soon. I am too shy to answer them back and I have not even told Fred about the birth control pills.

We sat at a circular table with a revolving tray in the center and took turns helping ourselves to different dishes. Time went quickly with much laughing, learning and getting different impressions of American life from the family.

Thanh came to Riverton after meeting Vo through an ad in one of the many Saigon matchmaking newspapers. Vo's family fled Saigon when he was a boy in 1975 and stayed for a time in a Philippine refugee camp before a Christian church sponsored Vo's family to settle here.

As most refugees settled in California, Seattle and Texas where it was either warm like Vietnam or had a large Asian community, Vo could not find a nice VN girl in Riverton to marry so he and Thanh had a long-distance relationship like I had with Fred. Thanh looks happy to me and they have their own business and two sweet girls.

Auntie married an American army officer during the war and came here to live. Because of bad warfare chemicals, her husband got sick with cancer and died, leaving her with insurance money, a military pension and a paid house for her and three school-age children.

Instead of doing nothing, she went to work in a small store as a cashier, then assistant manager, then store manager, all the while saving and investing her husband's insurance and pension money.

She found a store to buy in a good location and bargained with the owner but still did not have enough to buy it. Fred was a regular customer buying fuel and drinks but never tobacco or alcohol. Auntie notices these kinds of things and as they talked, she told of her dreams to own her own store.

Fred and Auntie checked out the store she liked and Fred offered to put in some money to help her and share the profits. Then Fred went to the owner and negotiated a better price along with having some much-needed repairs done before they signed the contract.

Now auntie has three stores and is looking for a fourth and Fred is a partner in all of them. Fred helps find things free or at a discount like shelves, refrigerators, cleaning supplies and printer paper. If she gets rid of something, Fred sells it and they reinvest the money back into the business.

And even though Fred is part-owner of the stores, he still pays full price for everything to keep the books honest. She also thinks he does it to reduce the temptation of employees who think they can get things free if Fred does.

Auntie asked how I like Fred so far? I said it is so new here and there is much to learn but Fred is nice and respectful of me. I told her about the duck egg incident this morning and she laughed, saying she will show me the best Asian markets to get the foods I want.

Auntie advised it will be most helpful in the marriage if I can enjoy Western foods along with my husband because some Asians do not like to eat Western foods and with an American husband, that can be a problem for meal-planning. I told her that so far, the Western foods are different but interesting and Fred enjoys VN foods too, so I expect to have some of both in our home.

Auntie was happy to hear this and said when I am ready, she will help us with the wedding plans. We only have three months, and I don't know how much planning Fred has done yet, so we need to talk.

Auntie and cousins also asked if I am going to keep Pham as my name or change it to Starbuckle? Go the Eastern way or Western way? I admitted we have not talked about this detail yet. Auntie's last name is Greene as are my cousins because she adopted her husband's name at marriage. Thanh kept Pham as her married name. What will I do?

Dorothy "Dot" Kahn: I remember Cousin Kimmie's first weeks in Riverton, especially the welcome luncheon we had for her at the Golden Waterfall. She was so different from her sisters! Whereas Thanh was outspoken, brash and a little too earthy for some people's tastes and Trinh was more cosmopolitan and cultured with a clipped manner of speaking from having lived in New York for so long, Kimmie carried a kind of quiet grace about her.

She was striking to look at with a well-proportioned body that was neither slender nor stocky, a long, angular face with prominent cheek bones that were softened by gentle eyes and dimples on either side of full lips. Her voice was almost musical and her laughter was soft and genuine.

Her sleeveless blouse revealed taut, well-muscled arms and I remember thinking, 'Wow, she must really hit the gym and work out a lot.' When I mentioned this to my mother, she said, "Those are not gym muscles. Kimmie earned those the old-fashioned way, through pure hard work. She had the most physically demanding job of anyone in her family, but I've never heard her complain or express regrets about it. It's one of the main reasons I thought Kim would make a good match with Fred. She is not shy to get her hands dirty and would not complain if she did."

Fred came back and made small talk with us before we left for the bank. There may be a small problem about opening the account as I do not have a Social Security number yet. Fred said I will get it once I marry and apply for the Green Card.

Instead, the bank manager used my passport and visa information to open the account for me. Fred did not want to be on the account, even after I asked him, saying "It's your money, it should be your account."

I deposited $4,500 and changed the rest into smaller bills. I have signed my first paperwork in America! I will get an ATM card and some checks in the mail soon and Fred will show me how to use them. I found the bank employees here to be friendly and helpful, unlike the arrogant attitudes of the bankers back home.

Fred gave me a notebook and pen to start making notes of things I want to remember or lists of things I need. Fred is always making lists, recording ideas, people's names and information, appointments, and such. Fred has an appointment book, an accounting book for all his buying, selling and miles he travels and an address/phone book for the many people he knows and does business with.

We drove around Riverton and Fred showed me this place and that area. We stopped by the house he and Barney grew up in. It is in an older neighborhood with large homes and big trees along the street. It looked very charming. I did not ask why his parents do not live there anymore because it is part of the painful thing he does not like to talk about.

We went to different neighborhoods, then the riverfront where there are many warehouses, ships and Coast Guard boats, very much like Ho Chi Minh City's port where my family lives and works.

The streets are so different here - no motorbikes and few bicycles anywhere, just cars and trucks staying in their own lanes and not honking their horns all the time. It is the opposite of Saigon.

Fred said it will take time for me to learn the area and to get around by myself but for now we will work together. I asked Fred when do we start working? He said "Tomorrow." Oh, so soon!

Tonight, we will meet Robbie and Bobby for dinner at their home. I have heard so much about them that I can't wait to see what they are really like.

We went back to the garage and Fred pulled out some clothes to try on. He asked me to change out of my nice clothes and put on work jeans and a shirt, then put on the coveralls he handed me. He has a few kinds and colors for me to try and find the ones that are the right size and comfortable enough.

I asked, "You want me to wear this to dinner tonight?"

"Sure, if you want to."

I made a joke but now am not sure if Fred is making a joke back or is saying it is okay to wear them to dinner? I found three coveralls that fit well. They smell freshly washed. One has the name "Earl" stitched over the pocket. It is clean, anyway.

I went to the kitchen and Fred was seasoning fresh chicken pieces, a beef roast and pork ribs. I ask what is all this food for? I thought we were going out for dinner. He said it's for the rest of the week's meals. Prepare now, cook later. Fred uses fresh herbs, tomatoes and onions from the roof garden and it all look so good! Most VN men will not cook so I am very lucky, I think.

I will take a nap before we have a late dinner with Fred's best friends. I plan to wear a long skirt and blouse to dinner, NOT the coveralls!

Must stop now. So much to tell but not so much time for writing.

Thomas Stimson

Bobby and Robbie

Dear My Diary,

Robbie and Bobby are so funny! I remember Fred had told me they all met in kindergarten and have been best friends ever since.

B&R live together on the top floor of the building they own in downtown Riverton. No driving to work, just go down in the elevator, much like us, but they don't live in a garage. Well, there is a parking garage but that is two floors below street level and offices on eight floors, three of which are for the B&R Group and the rest are rented to other businesses.

B&R live in the penthouse with big windows to see the entire city. The ground floor has a security desk, some shops and eateries. Fred showed me a directory on the wall and said we will be visiting this business a lot too, pointing at RPR Management. RPR stands for Riverton Property Rental but everyone calls it "Ripper".

We went into one of the shops and bought a bottle of wine as a gift, then Fred got the special elevator key from security to go up to the penthouse. Our hosts are warm and friendly men with Bobby being the taller and thinner of the two with a full head of hair against Robbie's shorter, pudgier frame with less hair on top and a big moustache that curls up at the ends.

We shook hands and they told me how lovely I look and asked how do I like America so far? I said I have been here only one day and a half and so busy meeting family and learning about my new home and city.

Bobby asked me if I wanted some wine, juice or a soft drink? I looked to Fred for a cue, and he said, 'the usual' so I asked for 'the usual' too.

Bobby then asked, "And what is *your* usual?" I did not know what to ask for and had just repeated what Fred had said, so I pushed on with, "Whatever Fred is having."

He smiled and I knew he caught me in a language trap. Bobby poured two drinks of a golden color with a strong taste of ginger. I later learned this is called Ginger Ale. Bobbie and Robbie drank the red wine we brought and complimented the taste.

B&R asked many things about my family and told how much they like Auntie Ginger, how sweet she is and the way she has grown her business so much. Robbie's father had started the CPA firm many years ago and both men found they had an interest in accounting but each works at their own specialized area.

Bobby is more about promoting the business, getting new customers and streamlining the technology side while Robbie is 'the brains of the operation', an expert CPA who runs the business and personnel side.

Fred told me later that Robbie inherited the business two years ago from his father when his parents retired to Hawaii. The business was already doing very well and they have made it grow even more after taking it over. Very hard-working men!

They have a servant man or butler in their home sand I could hear him working in the kitchen before he came out with drinks, and later, our dinners. I wonder if it is common for people to have servants in America? I had not heard this from Auntie or sisters.

We ate small, very tender steaks wrapped with bacon, roast vegetables with rice, salad and tomato soup while our hosts told stories about Fred selling things in school like toothpicks soaked with mint and cinnamon oils until the teacher made him stop. Then buying and selling sport cards from gum packages until the teacher made him stop. Then little toy cars until the teacher made him stop. So many things Fred was selling and buying from other students, and all ended with 'until the teacher made him stop.'.

"And he's STILL buying and selling things!" said Robbie.

"And no one tells him to stop!" said Bobby.

Then Robbie asked me, "Are YOU going to tell him to stop?"

"Oh, no!" I said, "I never tell Fred to stop!"

And they laughed and laughed so hard when I said this, tears were coming from their eyes. I don't know why. Fred smiled and laughed and his face got kind of red.

He told me later that it sounded kind of like a naughty thing, the way I said it, but I didn't mean for it to sound like that. He said it is no problem and they don't think anything bad about me. They are good friends and like me very much.

I asked them "Do you live together here?" They said yes, so I asked what will happen if one of you gets married, then who will move out? They looked at each other from the sides of their eyes and smiled.

Robbie said, "I don't think there is any danger of that," and he patted Bobby's hand. Then I understood the nature of their friendship. Fred did not tell me about this relationship between them. I looked at Fred and he winked at me as if to say, "It's okay, Babe". This is America. I have heard about this kind of thing, but it is the first time I have ever seen it.

It was late when we left. Bobbie and Robbie gave us both hugs and said again "Welcome to Riverton" and "don't beat a stranger" and "we will see you again soon". I told Fred I think they like me, and he said, "What's not to like?"

Such a long two days with so many things to do and people to meet that I know and didn't know before. And so many times I made people laugh too. This does not happen to me in Vietnam, to be so funny.

I don't know if I am looking like a foolish immigrant or if they find me witty and charming. Fred never looks unhappy with me so I will think to the positive side.

After we got home, I called Me and Ba as it is morning in Vietnam. We spoke a short time, maybe ten minutes, as I am sure it is very expensive for international calling. I told them about my big day to meet new people and see new places. I said I am happy but miss them to see all the interesting things in America with me. They said to have fun and be good and do what Fred asks of me. I said I will.

Trang: Mom must have been so excited AND exhausted after all that visiting, jet lag and learning how to work things in her new home. It was the first time she met an openly gay couple (how American!) who happened to be childhood friends of Dad. Bobby was not in the picture while we were growing up but Robbie was such a sweet, funny man who gave a lot of support to the gay and immigrant communities in our region. Our family had always stayed close with him and we kids considered Robbie to be like a favorite uncle. We miss him a lot.

Frankie: Mom liked the phrase "Don't beat a stranger" but did not know what it meant.Later, after she said it a couple of times to other people in front of Dad, and was greeted with polite laughter, Dad asked her why she was saying it? She said it was what Bobbie or Robbie had told her. Dad corrected her, "They said, 'Don't BE a stranger.'" She was kind of embarrassed about that but took it with the humor one must have when speaking in a language not your own. Later, she would use it as a humorous and memorable way of saying "good-bye", especially to newer people she was having a good time with.

Earning and Spending

May 25, 2000
Dear My Diary,

Woke up this morning at seven and Fred was already out of bed. He was not in the kitchen or bathroom, so I pushed every button on the Telecomm, calling out "Fred! Where are you?"

"Right below you, Morning Glory!" he answered from the second floor. He was preparing for our first day of work together. "I'll be up soon."

I walked down and Fred was putting big plastic totes on rolling metal racks. He explained that before 10 o'clock we will leave to visit the resale stores he does business with to trade out merchandise and collect his share on products that have already sold.

When I was having lunch yesterday, he had called all seven resale stores and got orders for what they are low on. I find his inventory system is well-organized and easy to understand. He could not fill all their needs today but packed what was available.

We had breakfast and Fred made sandwiches and bags of fruit for later. He said it will be a short workday as we are just doing the resale stores, picking up from the university donation boxes and putting out flyers. I wondered what he meant by "flyers" but did not ask.

With Fred, I have learned that if I do not ask, he will tell me soon enough. I can tell he is happy to have someone to talk with in this huge, quiet building and likes to explain what he is doing and why. I welcome the chatter…it helps with my English and gives me the chance to learn more about Fred and his world.

Kimmie: My parents were quiet people and mostly spoke to each other and us about work or family related matters. Fred was much more talkative and enjoyed making little jokes, compliments, and teases, always looking to get a smile or a laugh from me. He was also very affectionate physically, starving to catch up on years of being alone. I was not accustomed to the attention he lavished on me…but his sweet nature and gentle kindness soon reaped great rewards for both of us.

Fred reminded me that today is Tina's last day so we will have dinner at his parents' home tonight and to please invite sisters and other family members.

Once we were in the truck, Fred announced, "Let's go make some money!" and he kissed me. It was a funny and unexpected thing to say and it made me excited to make some money too!

It took about five hours to do everything. Fred introduced me to everyone as his fiancé so the owners and managers chit-chatted with me and talked shop with Fred.

Fred has an organized system with the totes and has a good idea of what and how much to bring to the stores. Some stores are higher or lower end than others. Some things that could not sell at one store he would take back and leave with another store for a chance to sell.

On the front seat of the truck, Fred has a stack of advertisements with his cell number along the bottom and cuts in between them. He quickly stops at different supermarkets, gas stations and other places that have community bulletin boards. His ads offer to "buy collections and estates of all kinds, fair offers made." Others say "Will clear out any or all areas of your home or business, from basement to attic. Fair prices offered." The places where he puts the ads follows the same driving route as the resale stores. Very efficient.

Then we went to three different colleges and loaded the truck with everything from Fred's donation boxes. One was so full, there were donations piled outside.

Mama went into great detail in this part of her diary about how it was all done, so she could go back and review it later to refresh her memory. One of the main jobs of going to the resale stores was bringing in what was needed plus anything Dad thought was exceptional enough for the stores to resell, quickly negotiate a price for the lot, balancing that against unsold/unwanted items from the store Dad might want to sell elsewhere. Goods were often exchanged between one store and another until they either sold or were liquidated through other venues.

With the ads, Dad would just as often get information about things other people had for sale and would contact them to see if it was something he could make a quick profit on.

We came back with the truck mostly full, took well-earned showers and relaxed before going to Frank and Maggie's house. We will unload the truck tomorrow.

Fred made over $3000 in cash and wrote in his books each place and plus or minus the amount from each store. Then Fred did something I was not expecting: He gave me $1524, exactly half of the cash he made that day and said, "Congratulations on your first payday!"

Apparently, it is my share of the profits for the day. I argued that it was his money and he should keep it but Fred came back with how I worked hard like he did, so I get half.

I asked, "What about the Pre-nup?"

"That is for the money we have before we get married."

"Ah! But we are not married yet, so this is still your money." I realized at that moment that this is our first argument about money…money he wants to give me rather than take from me. I can't believe what I am doing...I am working the wrong angle!

Fred made a sly look, "So, you don't want the money?" and waved the cash in my face.

I took the opportunity and snatched the money from his hand, "Yes, I want the money, even if we are not married yet!" and we laughed and kissed.

Fred asked how long it would take for me to earn that much money with my parents? I didn't know how to answer him and am ashamed to admit that my parents did not give me a regular salary so I quickly made up, "Six months."

"See that? Six months of pay in just a few hours. You will be rich in no time!"

I asked Fred about a wedding date and what kind of plan does he have so far?

"I've given this a lot of thought and we have two ways to do this:

"The first is to make a small legal marriage at City Hall to start the paperwork for your green card, then have a larger, formal ceremony with friends and family to celebrate.

"Or, we can wait and do the whole thing in early August."

Fred has family in and around Riverton he will invite, along with a few friends and those who are part of his business circle. I only have a few other relatives around the US I have not seen yet and will need to contact to see if they wish to come.

Fred confessed that he is afraid if we do marry right away, I might find that I don't like him, or Riverton, or his business, or I will be too homesick and want to go back to Vietnam. If so, then I might want to divorce him and that would be more complicated than if we are not married at all. He also felt that it would be dishonest, in a way, to make a legal ceremony now, then do a bigger wedding later when we are already married.

Fred has picked out a place for the wedding called a chapel, but it is not a church. We can do a combined Vietnamese/American type wedding so both sides can have some familiar customs and we can show our cultural mix.

"What do you think, Babe? Legal now and formal later, or the whole thing at once?"

I like the chapel idea and asked how many people he thinks we will invite? He said maybe one hundred. Family members and some business partners like Robbie and Bobby and their families and other people. One hundred does not sound like a lot but when I think about family members we have together and some extras, one hundred to one hundred twenty-five sounds about right.

Considering the options presented me, I thought about the time I have spent with Fred so far: six weeks in person during the winter holidays and just a few days in Riverton plus over a year writing to each other.

Fred works hard, has clean habits and treats making money like a game rather than a chore. He is sweet, funny and makes me feel more confident about myself than I ever have before.

It is easy to see that Fred is more successful than many other people with higher levels of education. I can't tell how much money he has, but by being part owner of several businesses and a three-story business building, he is not a poor man.

I stare at Fred until our eyes meet and I have his attention. I looked deeply into his blue eyes and said, "Fred, I have my decision. I love you very much and I like what I see of your life here. You do not live like most Americans, but that makes you more interesting to me. I cannot see myself going back to Vietnam unless you are my husband and we go together.

"You make me feel normal, not like a cay dua. I want to marry you and have one wedding in front of family and friends. We can take our time to know each other better and make our wedding plans together. That is my wish."

"Perfect! Mine too."

We sealed our agreement with a long, warm kiss.

Big Shopping Day

Friday May 26
Dear My Diary,

This morning, we brought Tina to the garage before driving her to the airport. Fred made a special "Happy Breakfast" for us. For each plate, he made two eggs fried only on the bottom so the yellow is very bright on top, two sausage links over them, one whole peeled banana below the eggs and a large strawberry in the middle so it stands pointy end up. It looks like a face with eyebrows, eyes, nose and smiling mouth…so funny to look at! And very good to eat!!

This was one of Dad's signature meals for guests and special occasions. Sometimes the eyes were pancakes instead of eggs or bacon strips instead of the banana. You get the idea…he made a happy face out of the food. Sometimes he did it with other meals but usually it was with breakfast foods. Most of us took up the practice with our own spouses, kids and grandchildren. It's a nice tradition!

We had a wonderful visit last night at Frank and Maggie's home. Tina is so happy to see me in America and said she had a very good impression of Fred when she met him last November.

When I related the story of Fred working with us at the warehouse and how the workers were amazed that he "knows" Vietnamese, Tina laughed so hard that I ended up telling the entire story again to the rest of the family, this time in English for the benefit of Fred's parents.

Fred added in his own parts as well and it was great fun. Even Cam and Tam had fun wagging their fingers at us, saying "Khong Cay Dua! Khong Cay Dua! That's Aunt Kimmie! That's Uncle Fred! Khong Cay Dua!"

We tried speaking English in deference to my American hosts but sometimes we slipped back into our own language. The parents either did not notice or care if we did this. This will be the last time for all of us to be together until my wedding, so we made the most of what we had.

Frank and Maggie made a point to tell me how nice my family is, and they are so happy to have me as their new daughter. I am very pleased to hear this and feel more relaxed knowing my new parents and sisters and other family are giving me the support I need for my new life in America.

Today was a busy day for shopping, so after dropping Tina at the airport with lots of hugs and a few tears, we went to the telephone company Fred uses to get my own cell phone. Now I can speak to sisters whenever I want!

After getting the cell phone (a bright red one that was on sale), we picked up Auntie and went to three different Asian stores for groceries and specific kitchenware I will need. Fred came so he can see where each store is located and learn my preferences.

I annoyed Fred as I kept asking, "May I buy this? Can I have that?"

Finally, he said, "Please don't ask, just buy what you want."

Auntie laughed and said, "You better hold him to that, Kim, especially at the jewelry store!"

Auntie paid for everything anyway and Fred noticed too late. He smiled and shook his finger at Auntie, but she claimed it is good luck that she does this for me. I don't think we have this kind of good luck custom in Vietnam, but Fred does not know that. It makes Auntie happy to buy things for me.

I did not tell Auntie that Fred has given me my first wages for working with him. I put the new money with the money my parents gave me and will consider what to do with it later.

Next stop was the Vietnamese tailor Thuy, who has made some things for me through Auntie and was very excited to meet me in person. Thuy said she can make many kinds of clothes including Ao Dais for weddings and special occasions.

Except for my wedding, I don't think I will have many events to wear traditional VN clothes. I thanked her but did not say I have already brought my wedding Ao Dai from the homeland. We took her card and I put her phone number in my new cell.

We went downtown to Tree Top Gals in the historic part of Riverton where old warehouses and factories have been turned into shops, nightclubs, restaurants and apartments.

Auntie gets many of my clothes here and the shop is very stylish. The owner is Hilaire, about my height and with an air of confidence I hope to cultivate. She said it was so nice to finally meet me and how do I like America so far and etc. I learned that she helped start the women's basketball program at Riverton University many years ago and is in the University and State Sports Hall of Fame (two places) so I think she is kind of famous.

Tree Top Gals catered to women five feet eight and taller. The Riverton location was Hilaire's first and only store in 2000, but over time, as a certain local person gained celebrity status, she was able to parlay that friendship into more locations. More on that later…

They have a variety of styles and prices but I am not sure what I need at the moment, so I did not buy anything today. I need to sort out my own wardrobe and check with Thanh and Tina of what I might need for the colder seasons before doing any clothes shopping. I brought winter clothes from home, but don't know if they will be warm enough for winter here. Fred enjoyed looking around and making small-talk with the owner and staff.

Best of all, they have shoes, including the kind Auntie sends me. Hilaire said they can special order many things from catalogs and she has contacts in the fashion world to find specialty items for her customers.

Auntie took us to a late lunch at one of the restaurants in the historic area called "One-Eyed Jacks". Very interesting decorations from the old riverboat times and the waitstaff dressed in costumes of the same era. Fred explained the name is a playing card term, and not the name of the half-blind restaurant owner, which caused the waitress to giggle.

Late in the afternoon we picked up parents and, with Auntie Giang, we visited Hilltop Chapel. It is such a lovely area with grassy fields on a hill overlooking the Missouri River.

The manager of the chapel is Abe, short for Abraham, like the President. They can do outdoor or indoor weddings, and both kinds will have the river in the background so the guests can see us marry with a beautiful backdrop.

It is the same with the reception hall, lined with floor to ceiling windows and stunning views of the river. The chapel is far enough away from the Riverton industrial areas but close enough to be a short, pretty drive for the guests.

Abe said they do several Asian weddings each year, but this will be their first Vietnamese-style wedding and if we tell him what we want, he can get the things we need. Auntie said she knows where to get what we need and asked me if I wanted her to perform the VN part of the ceremony?

I asked Auntie if she can represent my parents who cannot come to the US to see me marry? She said she can do both and wants very much to honor me by performing the ceremony. Abe offered up several people on staff who can perform the American part and make everything official for the marriage license.

I like the chapel on the hill very much and it pains me that my parents and sister cannot be here to see me marry. It is very difficult to get a tourist visa to the U.S.

Abe said nine or ten weeks out is very short notice for a wedding but Fred explained about the Fiancé visa and how important it is to have the wedding before the end of summer.

The manager studied his computer and said both venues for weddings are booked every Saturday in July and August but if we want a Sunday, he can do August 13th for the indoor chapel and is that okay? We saw the formal wedding garden which I really like, but it is not available.

Fred explained August 13th is within the visa deadline, everyone will be off from work and if we do the ceremony at noontime, we can spend some hours with our friends and family.

We gave Abraham an estimate of 150 guests at the very most, but we need to make a detailed list also. He was surprised that we do not have a completed guest list yet, so we explained that I just got here a few days ago. Abe said, "Just a few days? Oh my! Your English is so good!"

We made a general plan and Fred put down a deposit to hold the chapel. We will take some menus home and make an appointment very soon to decide on foods, drinks, seating style and other details.

Later, I realized this was the only place we visited and I don't know of any other choices to make. I don't know if the cost is reasonable or expensive or if the food will be fresh. I do hope everything goes well.

Such a very busy day today and I am exhausted. It was so great to spend the day with Auntie and she knows so much about everything I need. I don't think Fred could have done as good a job as Auntie did with tailors, food stores and wedding chapels by himself.

But Fred made up for it by making dinner with left over pork rib meat and vegetables, stir-fried with noodles and sauce. So good to have a man cook!

Trang: The Hilltop Chapel is still in business and two of us have gotten married there. They have done major renovations and upgrades over the years and doesn't look anything like the wedding pictures from 2000. It's nice to go there for picnics or attending social events. Dad got lucky to get any kind of date for a summer wedding! I am sure he had a Plan B but it was never mentioned in the diary and Mama doesn't remember, even if Dad had told her. It was a long time ago, after all.

Kimmie: Later that day, Fred and I laughed over Abraham's comment, upon learning I had been in the US just a few days, "Your English is so good!" as though I had stepped off the plane barely able to say Hello and Thank you. I had been learning English since I was a child but did not bother to tell him that. He was the first one to make that comment to me, but he would not be the last.

Bad Luck Groomsmen?

Monday May 29
Dear My Diary,

Over the weekend, we made a list of guests for the wedding and, more importantly, who will accompany us at the altar. The selections were easy: My sisters Thanh and Tina and Fred's' best friends Bobby and Robbie.

I have seen pictures of weddings with many bridesmaids and groomsmen alongside the marrying couple, but this is a small wedding and I do not know many people here. When I asked Fred why he does not have his brother in the wedding party, he just gave me a look that said I should know better than to ask.

I asked Fred if it is bad luck for Bobby and Robbie to be in our wedding party? He looked puzzled, "Why would they be bad luck? Because they are accountants?" I could tell he was kidding about the last part…but he was not smiling either.

Now I feel embarrassed to have asked as they are his closest friends but pushed on anyway. "Because they are not a normal couple."

Fred looked hurt and I felt terrible to have said it at all. Fred is clearly offended and was holding his feelings in check. "Do you really think they will bring bad luck to us? To our marriage?"

Ashamed, I made myself small and said, "I don't know."

Fred took a deep breath, "They may not be a couple in the traditional sense, man and woman sense, but they have been together longer than many legally married couples.

"They love each other, are good men and respected citizens. I have no doubt they would have married a long time ago if the law would allow for it.

"And one more thing Kimmie, you should know that they have brought me good luck not only in business, but in love as well. Bobby and Robbie have earned their place by my side."

I feel foolish and ashamed of asking such a thing now. I know they are good men and when one patted the others' hand at the time of my visit, I could see the tenderness between them.

Fred is right and I wanted to make things smooth between us, so I said, "I am sorry, my love. I did not mean to offend you or your friends. In our culture, this kind of relationship is not considered normal or proper. People can go to jail for this."

"Being gay is not considered normal or proper to many Americans, and even in this country people have gone to jail for being the way they are, but attitudes are slowly changing and becoming more accepted." Fred looked easier after getting this off his chest and I agreed to keep the wedding party as is.

We made our final headcount of 150 attendees which leaves us some room for any last-minute guests. As Fred likes to say, "The more the merrier!"

Kimmie: I had picked up on the words "brought me good luck…in love as well," but after the bit of tension we had with each other, I was afraid to ask Fred what he had meant by that. I would learn weeks later how true those words were.

My First Auctions

Tuesday May 30
Dear My Diary,

Today I went to my first auctions. In preparation, Fred went over the rules the night before and let me know what to expect. We dressed in jeans, work shirts and comfortable shoes but also brought coveralls and steel-toe boots in case we win any lockers and need to load the truck along with a thick roll of cash tucked into the breast pocket of his flannel shirt. Apparently, auction sales do not accept credit cards.

Mama wrote a lot of details about the locker auctions from here so she could go back to review and remind herself of different details. I left in a few of the highlights…

Fred has a shopping list for the resale shops but tends to concentrate on buying lockers with "promise". That is, things he can re-sell quickly and profitably.

We ate a big breakfast and packed food and drinks in the truck while Fred put a very big bird called a turkey into the oven at low heat, saying it will cook all day and be ready when we get home. Then, when we were ready to leave, we said in unison, "Let's go make some money!" and kissed. This is our new habit to make good luck for the day!

Every time Dad went on a business trip or to a meeting or working any kind of job, before leaving the house or car, he would always say "Let's go make some money!" and they would kiss, or if it was us kids, would do a high five or yell "Ka-Ching!"

One of the auctions we attended had a locker with a strong, familiar smell. Fred wrote to me "Cat P" but I shook my head and shrugged, not understanding the term. He added more letters "Cat Pee" and I still did not understand "Pee".

Then he made a quick sketch: the back half of a cat with its tail straight up and spray coming out. I laughed suddenly in recognition and people turned to look at us. Now I understand this slang of "Pee = Urine". hat locker did not sell, and people complained "No wonder they left everything there." Fred said the property manager will have to take it all to the dump.

We went to three different storage facilities with the same auction company, won four units and paid $200 total, with one of them containing a free-standing full-length mirror we can use at home, costing us only ten dollars. As Fred likes to say, "Saving money is earning money."

We had lunch in the truck before sorting and loading everything. Sandwiches, fruits and tea. Simple, filling and delicious! Fred just puts tea bags and sugar into large bottles at home and by lunchtime, it is ready to drink.

We put on coveralls, gloves, and boots, got the crash cart out and quickly went through the boxes and bags, sorting by Trash, Treasure, Keep and Donate, then loading them into the truck.

He is very quick to decide which is what and, for my education, he made a running commentary of everything he was doing and why. Fred has been doing this for about twenty years so he knows best what will sell, what won't and how to get the best prices in the shortest amount of time.

I asked Fred how he does this all by himself as some lockers are full to the ceiling. He said, "The same way you eat an elephant, Sweetheart, one bite at a time." We used the dollies for large items and stacks of boxes. Fred is right…Americans do leave a lot of things to waste.

During our slow times, we reviewed the catering menus and packages offered but not many things suit the traditional VN wedding style. Fred called the chapel, and they said the packages are one way to go, but they are flexible about customizing the ceremony and reception. The reception will be the easy part and Auntie can get the ceremony part done through her own contacts.

After we finished the lockers, we went home, left everything in the truck and got the turkey out of the oven. It was very nice and brown with lots of juices and bones to make soup later.

Fred made rice and salad while I showered. After dinner, we unloaded both trucks, the one we used today and the one we filled up five days ago, throwing bags of trash into the dumpster, and sorting the rest into different piles to be worked more thoroughly tomorrow.

Dear My Diary,

I am learning that Fred does not sleep much at all, just four to five hours each night while I sleep longer and more heavily than him. Fred and I go to bed holding, hugging and kissing each other and when I wake up, he is either downstairs putting things on Ubiddit, packing items that sold or doing research.

He likes to make breakfast for me like sweetened coffee, American foods like pancakes, waffles or fried eggs with different pork meats or foreign foods like French Toast and English Muffins with fruit jelly. If I wake up early enough, I make an Asian-style breakfast for Fred to surprise him. He likes my cooking style and I like his.

Fred's' kitchen equipment is not like what I see in other people's homes. Much of it is stainless steel restaurant equipment that is sturdy and made to last forever. He said many restaurants open, then fail in their first years so this is Fred's way of recycling some of the equipment he finds.

That is an important point with Fred about what he wants to keep…things must be useful and potentially last for decades. Hmm…I wonder if that is how he thinks of me? Useful and will potentially last for decades? I find it a funny thought. I can think of Fred in the same way, of course. Better that way than to be used for a short time, then thrown away or left ignored until someone else comes along looking for a bargain.

Fred says the most common things he gets from lockers or people clearing out their homes is clothing. Americans go through a LOT of clothes! The most desirable clothes go through Ubiddit and Free Post, the worst go in the trash. Then, depending on brands and quality, the remaining clothes move through the resale stores or flea markets, many children's clothes are donated to the local school districts and homeless shelters along with unused toiletries, linens and similar necessaries to help poor families. Fred says he gets tax breaks for doing this and it is good for the community.

Now I understand better how Fred helps not only make money for himself, but also helps other people who cannot help themselves. He does not look to make a profit with every single item.

In the back area of the ground floor where Fred keeps items for active selling, I found a shelf full of name-brand shoes, the kind he has a disdain of purchasing for himself. Some are still new in their boxes and all tagged with Ubiddit auction codes. I considered taking a picture of them and emailing it to Phung to show him what Fred has, but chose against it. If Fred did not feel a need to tell Phung about it during their shoe conversation, then I won't either. It feels petty to do so.

We met with Auntie today along with a Vietnamese mother and son whose family runs a restaurant that offers catering. They brought samples of food to try for the reception.

Fred and I already decided that a sit-down dinner will be more costly, and some people might not want some of the culturally different foods, so if we have a buffet, guests can pick and choose what they want, fewer servers will be needed, everyone gets exactly what they want and there will be more mingling between guests.

We chose spring rolls, crab soup, grilled pork with vegetables, sliced roast duck, fruit salad bowls with mango, dragon fruit, Asian pear and sweetened coconut strings…very pretty to look at! This will be combined with an equal number of dishes through the chapel's catering service.

Fred Scares Me!

Dear My Diary,

Fred scared me nearly to death! This morning he was preparing for tonight's dinner and asked me for the big pot in the end cabinet. He kept pointing at the last cabinet, below the counter and next to the window. He said to hurry as he needs it right now.

I opened the door and something big and hairy jumped out at me. Its mouth was wide open and making GRRRROOWWR sounds. I screamed and fell back to get out of its way. As I kept scrambling backwards on my bottom, the animal stayed inside the cabinet making its loud roars.

Fred just laughed and laughed. When he finally came over to help me up, I hit Fred on the arm to show him how funny I thought it was not. My heart was beating so fast! Fred rubbed his arm and said, "I deserved that!"

The animal is a model bear head with a mouth that opens and closes. When you open the door, a spring or piston pushes the head out of the door and makes the growling sounds electronically.

If you close the door, the head goes back in and stops making noise. Fred found it years ago at a shut-down carnival and when Bunny helped him design the home, he found a way to put the bear into the cabinet as a joke for visitors and snooping guests. He apologized many times, but he kept laughing at the way I tried to get away from the bear. Hmm!

Mama said the first time Frankie showed me the bear, he had told me there was a big bag of candy behind the door. Of course, as a toddler, I was eager to get my little hands on a lot of candy. She said I cried and screamed for a long time, in part due to fright, and in part because there was no candy.

After that, I screamed and laughed every time I opened the door for a quick scare. Eventually we wore out the bear and it no longer worked by the time our younger sisters were old enough to play that trick on. We just told them it was a real bear that Dad had shot outside the garage and to be careful because bears still lived in the neighborhood...we were so mean!

Casino Night

Saturday June 3
Dear My Diary,

Thanh invited us to the casino for a fun night. I asked Fred to come along as I have never been to a casino before. Fred said he does not gamble and did not want to go but I cajoled him into it, saying I wanted to see how it looks and have my best man with me. Fred smiled and said, "How can I argue with that?"

We met up at Thanh and Vo's house and they had hired a babysitter for the twins. Thanh complained how they have trouble getting babysitters as they always quit. She often hires teen girls who come to the nail salon because they work cheap.

Cam and Tam were very excited to see us and we played for a bit, with Fred giving them big lifts into the air.

The babysitter is a mid-teen girl and did not look very happy. Thanh told her we would be back at eleven or twelve and to make sure the girls have their dinner. We left in T&V's auto which is an expensive model and Thanh likes to talk about it to everyone.

The casino is very noisy with lots of lights and musical sounds and people playing machines. Vo and Thanh know many people here. They wave, say Hi!, shake hands, make jokes with their friends and introduce me as their "baby sister" and everyone laughs. Of course, I am the baby sister, but one who towers over my "big sister", so it gets a harmless laugh, and everyone is in a good mood.

Vo headed to the card games and invited Fred to join him. Fred played 21 to be polite and Thanh played as well, telling me it was okay to watch because I do not know how to play the game.

Fred bought chips for $100 and Thanh and Vo bought $200 each. Fred bet $5 each time but sister and brother bet $20 each time. Vo told Fred to put more money down so he could win more, and Fred nodded and smiled but kept making $5 bets. Sometimes they won and sometimes not.

I would see Fred win a bit, then he put two chips down. If he lost, then back to one chip. Then Fred did something interesting. He won one, put down two chips, won again and put down four chips. When he won again, he took away the extra chips and kept four to play again. Fred did this four more times: bet four chips, win the hand, take the extra chips away and bet another four. Twice Fred got 21 and won extra money. Vo and Thanh cheered him on, saying Fred is very lucky, very lucky.

After several wins in a row, Fred lost four chips on one bet, got up and took all the chips he won, asking me if I wanted to play? I said, "I don't know how," and he smiled.

Vo asked Fred "Where are you going? You are on fire, brother…keep your winning streak going!" Fred smiled and thanked brother and sister for playing with him. Vo begged, "Stay and win more money! You very lucky!" Fred waved and we went to the cashier. Fred got back $265, $100 seed money and $165 in winnings.

I asked Fred why he would not play more? Vo is very unhappy now that Fred walked away. Fred said "If I had kept playing, it is guaranteed that I would lose all the winnings back to the casino. That is the way it works most of the time. I would rather quit while I'm ahead. After all, I have Lady Luck with me tonight." Then he squeezed my hand and put it into his back pocket. Fred is very sweet to me!

Thanh came to me and said, "Let's play the slots." Fred gave me $50 for playing and Sister showed me how it works. Lots of people around us are playing. Some look very old and sick. Sometimes coins come out with lights flashing and music playing to show that we won but mostly it is losing money. There is no skill to the slots, just put in money and push a button. It is boring, too.

Thanh told me she and Vo go on a Date Night every Saturday after a busy day at the Happy Pretty Nail Salon. They have fun and she encourages women to come to the salon by putting her business card on their machines.

Many people do not look like they are having fun like I see on the advertising signs. Happy, excited, pretty people on the signs, bored sick-looking people in real life. It is kind of depressing.

Fred wandered back and forth to watch me and Thanh play and speak to us, then go to watch Vo play. As always, people look and stare at me, especially men. One came over and tried to ask me questions, saying he likes tall women.

Thanh said, "Go away, she is my sister."

He said, "You are not her sister, short-stack. Mind your own business."

Then Fred walked up behind him and said, "Can I help you?"

The man turned around and I can see he will say something rude, but then he looked way up at Fred and said "I, I, I was just asking where the men's room is?"

Fred replied, "Why are you asking them? They are not men!" and the fool quickly ran off. We laughed at his "I, I, I...

Vo is drinking cocktails and smoking many cigarettes. I saw Fred with a cocktail too. I asked what he is drinking, and he gave me a taste. There is no alcohol, but it looks like a cocktail. He was trying to fit in for Vo and Thanh but I can see Fred is bored too.

Fred had me hold his drink while he used the men's room. While he was gone, Thanh told me when I am ready to have children, to sign up for free food from the state. Something called Snap. "I've been getting it since the twin's birth. Free food and another program for free milk and cheese. You sign up and they just give it to you. No paying back!"

Fred came back with Vo, out of breath with excitement. He gathered us around him and said, "I can't believe what just happened to me in the bathroom. This is the greatest casino I have ever been in!"

We asked, "What? What happened?"

He looked around and lowered his voice, "You're not going to believe this, but I was in the restroom, minding my own business, right?" He looked around again, "And when I finished, I flushed the urinal, and all this came out!" Fred pulled a fistful of coins out of his pocket and showed them to us. "I won a jackpot from the urinal! Can you believe it?" The coins were all wet and he pushed them towards me. I touched them and then fully realized what Fred was saying as Vo and Thanh burst out laughing.

I jerked my hand away in disgust. "You pee-peed on the money?"

My family laughed even harder as Fred put the money back in his pocket. "No sweetheart, that was a joke. The coins are clean." Then it was my turn to laugh as Thanh teased me about being so gullible.

I gave Fred a not-too-hard punch on the arm and he hugged me in return. "I thought of the joke while I was in the restroom, bought a roll of quarters and wet them in the sink to make it more realistic."

Vo high-fived Fred and Thanh said "I almost believed you, Brother. Aaalmost," stretching out the first syllable. I must admit, it was pretty clever.

Finally, we went home early because I think we are too dull for sister and brother. Thanh drove as Vo drunkenly complained in VN that Fred is too scared to win big money. When we got to Thanh's house, she asked me to pay the babysitter and she will pay me later.

The girls whined about being very hungry, and Vo snapped at them, "You eat too much!" Sister and brother went to change and when I asked the girls what they had for dinner, they said "nothing".

I found very little food in the refrigerator, and nothing prepared. Fred asked the babysitter what the girls had for dinner, and she said no food was left for them.

She also said she babysat last Saturday, and they did not pay her for that time either. The girl said, "I keep going to the salon after school to get paid, but they send me away, saying they are too busy and will pay me later."

Fred looked disgusted at me and shook his head. He paid the girl $25 for each of the two nights she worked and $10 more for her troubles trying to collect.

Fred told her, "Let me give you some advice: if someone does not pay you the first time, you don't work for them a second time."

Fred went to his truck and brought back some healthy snack foods and bottled juices he always carries. The poor girls ate everything so quickly that it hurt my heart to see them like this. No wonder they are so thin. I wonder where all the free food is Thanh gets from the state?

Vo did not come out of the bedroom as he had passed out. Thanh thanked us for coming and she had a good time talking with me. She told Fred that he is very lucky with cards and if he plays more, he will be rich soon. Fred just smiled and thanked her for inviting us.

At home, Fred confided to me that he saw Vo spend maybe $1000 or more at the card game but was not sure as he spent time with me too. He said he saw Vo make some foolish bets and lost many hands, especially after drinking alcohol.

I said I feel bad that Tam and Cam are so small for their age, especially compared to American children and now we see why. Fred says many babysitters have quit because they are not paid for their services and that is a kind of cheating.

I shared an idea with Fred, and he likes it: "I will ask Thanh if we can babysit Cam and Tam on their date night so I can get to know the girls better and they can have fun with us.

"We will feed them good foods and play games and teach them things. They can learn better English with you and sister will make no more problems with other babysitters."

I confided to Fred that I don't want sister to spend so much money on gambling, but Fred said they are adults and making their own decisions. But if we can help the girls, then that will be a good thing. I told Fred that he will be a good Ba when we have children. He said I will be a good Me and am already a very good Auntie.

Mama learned later that although Dad did not spend time in casinos, he had learned to play Blackjack with a computer game and it taught tips and tricks of increasing the odds of winning like the 1-2-4 method of betting and then walking away after finishing a winning streak. That was how he was able to make and keep his winnings that night. Dad had discipline and a real aversion to gambling. He would say things like "The best way to win at a casino is to come to the buffet really hungry." And "The best way to not lose your money at gambling is to not play in the first place."

Where's the Television?

Monday, June 5
Dear My Diary,

Thanh was telling me about the different TV shows she and her family like to watch and then asked what TV shows we enjoy? I had to admit that we do not watch television as we are so busy with work, planning the wedding and learning about each other, adding, "We spend a lot of time talking to each other."

Sister winked, "Of course! Talking!" I know she thinks I mean "making love" and she is trying to be playful, but her insinuation is not comfortable for me, so I don't say any more. "Television is a good way to listen to English, practice the way Americans talk and learn what is going on in this crazy country."

I looked around our living spaces and cannot find any TV set. How odd I have not noticed this before! When Fred returned from an errand, I asked him where is his TV?

"Kimmie, how long have you been living here?"

"Almost one month."

"And is this the first time you noticed there was no television here?"

"Yes."

"And that is because I am so fun and interesting to be around that you don't need another form of entertainment?" Fred fluttered his eyes at me and I can see he is having fun so I said, "No."

He pouted and said, "If I am no longer fun and interesting to be around, I guess we have to get a TV!"

I explained how television will help me with English listening, speaking and comprehension skills, as well as learning what is going on in Riverton and America, by watching the news and talk shows.

Fred agreed that those are good reasons for having a TV and when we find a good one at auction or through other methods, we will put it in our home.

"Why can't we just buy one at a store today?

To which he answered, "What is the fun in that?"

Ring Shopping

Thursday June 8
Dear My Diary,

This morning, Fred looked unhappy and said he knows that maybe I think badly of him for getting everything, or almost everything, second hand and how it must make me feel. "I don't want second-hand things for you in your new life."

"Too late, Fred. I already have a second hand." I showed Fred my left 'first hand' and my right 'second hand'. "See?" and I wiggled my fingers at him. He laughed heartily and said yes, he sees.

I know he thinks I feel some shame for taking used items when I could have new, so I tried to make a joke of it. I appreciate the fact that he will not force me to wear second-hand clothing, but it might not be such a bad thing either…I have already found some really cool fashions for myself!

Then, to add to what he was saying, Fred announced that he wants to take me ring shopping. "Whatever you want." Auntie Giang's words echoed in my ear, and I laughed inwardly.

"Don't worry, my love," I assured him, "I will not break your bank."

To that, he comically wiped his brow and said, "Whew!"

Then I asked, "Don't you want to surprise me with a ring like last time?"

"Nowadays, couples usually shop for rings together."

"Will you get a ring too?"

"Of course! I need something to keep the other women away."

I retorted, "Some women are attracted to married men and try to take them away for their own!"

"That is true, but I will not let that happen because you are strong enough to kick my butt!"

"Ah," I said, in a wise-woman voice. "You know my secret of how to keep a man!"

We laughed and kissed as it is fun making this kind of teasing talk. Fred added that he will have my engagement ring adjusted so it will fit better. I am glad because I have been using a thick bandage around the palm side of my ring to keep it from slipping off.

We went to several jewelry stores and had lunch downtown with Robbie so Fred and he could talk some business. Robbie paid some attention to me and asked how I like Riverton so far and is Fred behaving himself with me?

I said, "Riverton is very nice, and I like everything so far…even Fred." I said the last part to make them laugh and it worked! I normally do not make jokes like this back home, but Fred's constant cheerfulness is infectious. It makes me want to share my good cheer with him and his people. So far, it is working.

Robbie said, "If this big lug gets out of line, just let me know and I will have the IRS pay him a special visit!"

Fred reminded Robbie, "Just don't forget who is doing my taxes before you make that call!" It was good-natured banter and I feel more included here than I did with other groups back home.

By the end of the day, I found five different rings that I like and am embarrassed that I can't make up my mind on one or another. The selections are overwhelming.

With each ring I liked, Fred took digital pictures that we can look over and study later at our leisure. Fred said he can be satisfied with a plain gold band but what he really wants is something different because *I* am different and not an ordinary woman.

He found two rings he likes and took pictures. Each photo has a special digital number, and it was written down in a book with the name of the jewelry store and address, so we know which is what.

As frugal as Dad was, he knew when to buy new and when to wait for a deal. Ring = New and TV = Deal. He taught us these lessons too, so we didn't wind up looking shabby when we needed to look sharp and know when to spend on quality vs. getting something "good enough to do the job".

Babysitting the Twins

Saturday June 10
Dear My Diary,

Thanh and Vo are happy to have us babysit Cam and Tam, especially as we are doing it for free. The girls were very excited about the garage, exploring everywhere and when they found the Jumping Bear "Grrowr!" the twins screamed and opened and closed the door again and again.

Fred made grilled pork chops with the rooftop barbecue, along with baby potatoes and fresh salad, showing the girls how we grow our food in the greenhouses. He pulled a big green plant out of the dirt to show them the cluster of potatoes at the bottom and let the girls pick them off for their dinner.

They also helped cut different kinds of fresh greens for their salad and pick the fruits they wanted blended for their dinner drinks. Everything was so new and exciting that they happily ate and drank all that was put in front of them.

After dinner, Fred let the girls pretend to drive the different trucks he has and make motor noises with them and turn the wheels. They never asked where our TV is.

When they were worn out, we put the twins on a bed with warm blankets and they looked like sleeping angels. Fred agreed that this was a good idea and was fun for all of us. He wondered out loud what we will do when we have work to get done on some Saturdays and I told Fred that he can do the business things by himself and I will care for the girls. He said, "Ah, just like old times!"

But we both agree that the girls are better off with us on Saturdays than to go hungry and be cared by, or uncared by, different babysitters all the time and no one knows what is going on at the home. We will not tell sister this directly, but we think the girls will be better for it.

Thanh thanked us very much for taking care of the twins and they will do something nice for us later. I will say nothing to Ba and Me about this. I do not want them to worry, but I do worry about Thanh and the girls.

After they left, I asked Fred "When we have children, is it true the state will give us money for food?"

Fred looked puzzled. "No. Why would the state give us money for food?"

I explained what Thanh had told me and when I said the word "Snap", Fred's eyes widened in understanding.

"Ahh, SNAP! Okay, yes, that is a government program that gives free food to people who live on very low incomes. I mean, really low incomes."

"Thanh has been getting it since the girls were born, but they hardly have any food in the house."

"I don't know where the food money is going, but people who can toss away a thousand bucks a week at the casino don't qualify for government aid. We certainly don't qualify."

My heart sank. "Are you saying Thanh and Vo are cheating the government?"

"I'm saying, we don't qualify for food stamps, SNAP, free milk and cheese or anything else. If your sister somehow qualifies, then fine. If not, someone's going to be in big trouble when they get found out."

"Fred, are you going to tell the authorities?"

"Not me," assured Fred. "I'm not getting caught up in any more drama than I can help."

Cam: We had such a great time with Aunt Kimmie and Uncle Fred. No offense to my parents but they weren't very good cooks and for a long time we did not have much in the house. At the garage, we played games, ate garden fresh foods, learned cool stuff, played with retro toys they had for sale and there was tons of room to run around.

Sometimes our parents did not come get us until the next morning, after we had Uncle Fred's Happy Breakfast and fresh juice that we helped make. Aunt Kimmie had us teach her American slang stuff until Uncle Fred heard some of the "slang" and said it was too adult for little kids to know or repeat. Oops!

Wedding Outfits

Wednesday June 14
Dear My Diary,

Everyone has accepted their roles for the wedding party. Cam and Tam will be flower girls. I did this to give the girls something special to do and I hope by doing so, it will bring us luck for children in the future.

We want everyone to wear ao dais and I sent pictures to the men so they can see what theirs will look like. Everyone has agreed to wear them so I spoke with Thuy at her shop and she and her workers will make them for us after getting the measurements.

Trinh has already had her measurements taken during my first days here and Thanh already uses Thuy so that is covered as well. Auntie already has several fancy ao dai for special occasions so she will not need another.

We met Bobby and Robbie at the shop and it is a very long process with many parts of the body to be measured for an accurate fit. Bobby complained that his tailor does not take so many measurements for his suits and Robbie said, "And look how they fit on you."

I think he was making a funny insult, not a serious one. They have their own kind of love talking as Fred and I have ours. Thuy did not say much to them but worked very quickly and called out the numbers to a helper who kept track of everything on a pre-made chart.

After Bobby and Robbie left, Fred and I had our own measurement taken and made color and fabric selections for everyone's costumes. Later this week, the girls will have theirs done and we will pay for everything. I feel good to get this important step out of the way.

Thuy has everyone's phone numbers for fittings and adjustments. I had brought a wedding ao dai from home but Fred and I decided to make matching wedding outfits so I will not wear the one from Saigon. It seems like a waste, but Fred likes the idea. "After all," he said, "we will only get married once!"

Buzzy Brew

Dear My Diary,

I see many people in Riverton carry paper cups of coffee or getting coffee from small shops and stands. There are a variety of different coffee shops around town, but Buzzy Brew is predominant among them. Their logo is that of a steamy coffee cup with a happy looking bee standing up over the cup. It is a very cute logo.

Bunny took me to a Buzzy Brew for coffee the other morning. She asked me what kind of drink I want and I do not know. The menu is written in English, but also like in another language with many strange names for the products. I felt so lost and ignorant.

I asked if they have Vietnamese-style coffee? Bunny didn't know and asked the counter-girl, but nobody knew how to make it. It is strong and made with thick, sweetened milk but I did not try to explain. Maybe it would sound strange to them. I don't know.

Bunny asked "How about if I order for you? Is that okay?" I let her because I had no idea.

And the prices are so high…between $3 and $6 for a single cup of coffee! Bunny ordered two different drinks and let me taste both with a spoon, then I picked one I like better (less sweet) and we sat with our coffees and bread treats. Over $15 for this little bit of food and drink. We had a nice chat…but I feel bad.

When I told Fred about my experience at Buzzy Brew, he said "When we make coffee at home, it is less than ten cents per cup without milk or flavorings, but Buzzy Brew and other shops sell the same coffee for not less than $2.75.

"The shops make huge profits and people are happy to pay the prices to be trendy. Some customers buy several drinks each day. Crazy, huh?"

"Do you ever drink the shop coffees?"

"If someone else is paying, yes. Otherwise, no."

Frankie: Buzzy Brew got its start in Riverton by the Wysocki brothers in the 1980's. It was a hipster coffee bar selling obscure varieties from different parts of the globe and an international menu of ways to serve them.

The brothers picked up on the growing trend of California wineries to educate their customer base and create an aura of exclusivity, even to the point of having "coffee tastings" to select (i.e., highly influential and popular) customers who would then spread the word.

One shop led to two, then three and soon Buzzy Brew had become a staple in the Midwest with other states clamoring for their own stores until they went public.

Fred asked, "Do you know what I really like about Buzzy Brew?" He smiled and said "I don't spend money on the coffee, but I enjoy the flavor of the company. I find the company to be *very* tasty!" He licked his lips and winked in a very knowing way, then changed the subject and would not discuss it further. He is teasing me with a juicy secret he does not want to share. The same as Phung did to me about the book! Are all men like this?

Frankie: Dad had a LOT of pet peeves when it came to money wasters and often wrote articles to that effect for a variety of outlets. Mama and Dad only bought BB drinks if they had to meet someone for business there and then they used it as a tax deduction. Mom would learn more about Dad's interest in Buzzy Brew later on...

Dissolving Debt

Saturday June 17
Dear My Diary,

Yesterday I watched Fred teach an eager crowd of about one hundred and fifty people his Dissolving Debt seminar at the Riverton Library's main auditorium. He does it as a public service to educate people about the dangers of too much debt and how to manage their money better.

Fred has workbooks printed and he brings boxes of books from different authors who write about budgets, getting out of debt, money management, living frugally and similar topics. He collects the books from auctions and resale stores and then sets them aside for his quarterly classes.

As people came in, many with their Buzzy Brew drinks in hand, I handed out the workbooks along with numbered tickets and greeted everyone while Fred made the final adjustments to the computer slide-show and audio system.

Fred greeted some of the people as they are returning students, oftentimes with friends or family members to share what they have learned from Fred. Others come back for a refresher.

The class runs from nine until noon and once the seats were well-filled, Fred had me sit in the audience to watch, listen and learn. The Dissolving Debt class is full of information…too much to talk about here, but much of it is common sense.

I have heard that in wealthy countries it is very easy to get into debt and many people do not manage their money well, causing big problems for themselves, their families and sometimes for their employers.

At the end of each hour, there is a five-minute break and Fred announces, "I will call out numbers from the tickets you were given. If you have that number, you can come up and pick out a book from these boxes," and he pointed to the boxes lined up on folding tables.

He quickly called out ten numbers from the tickets he drew out of a coffee can and people came up with their matching ticket and selected the book they wanted. At the end of the seminar, everyone else is welcome to come up and get a book of their choice until the boxes were empty. Fred reminded the attendees that they can also get books like these right here in the library or buy them at local thrift shops for much less than new.

I think this information is a very good thing to teach people…but in my opinion, it should not be necessary. I can see the big difference in our cultures: We in Vietnam think Americans are rich because everyone can have a car or a nice TV or many new clothes with seemingly little effort. However, I can see now that much of this wealth comes at the cost of high interest rates and other fees. In Vietnam, we must pay cash for everything, including our homes and cars. Personal loans are rare or at prohibitively high rates.

After the seminar, we walked over to the B&R building, but we did not visit our friends. Instead, Fred introduced me to Hazel and Holly. They own the Ripper business Fred sometimes speaks about.

RPR or Riverton Property Rentals is owned by Hazel and Holly, sisters in their fifties and very nice. It seems like everyone Fred knows is very nice, friendly and successful. They asked me how I like Riverton and such questions I get asked frequently now. Fred discussed some business things with them for a few minutes, and then we left.

Later I asked Fred for their last names so I can remember them better. He said "Wood". They are not married, or not now anyway, and they have kept their family name.

Later, I put their names together in my head and started laughing and laughing. Fred asked what is so funny?

"Is the older sister's name really Holly Wood? Like Hollywood in California?"

Fred looked serious, "Yes, of course. Is there something wrong with that?"

I looked closely at Fred, then saw the spark in his eyes that said he knows exactly why I am laughing. "Yes, that is very much their real names, Kimmie. Hazel Wood and Holly Wood. And their mother's name was spell F-Y-R-E."

Fyre Wood, Fire Wood! I said "Really?"

Fred smiled and said no, he made that one up. That Fred!

In the afternoon, we made a final pick for the rings. They will be a matching pair consisting of a yellow gold band with two woven lines of white gold on a black enamel background creating an Infinity symbol to show how our love goes on and on forever and is never ending. I like this symbol and it is a pretty design.

The jeweler cut a small segment out of my engagement ring and now it fits perfectly. The jeweler has to special order the rings and they should arrive in about three weeks.

For someone as frugal as Fred claims to be, he looks happy to spend money on me. He did not want plain gold wedding bands, he did not want a simple "town hall" wedding and he does not want our wedding party to pay for their own outfits.

I do not think my family would have expected this from Fred, with Ba calling him "a glorified junk peddler". Those words upset me at the time. Now I wish Ba and Me could see with their own eyes how much Fred is spending for our wedding.

Flea City Market

Saturday June 24
Dear My Diary,

I am getting to know my way around Riverton more and more. Where places are, how to get there, and lots of little details. As we drive around, Fred often pulls over to grab things that have been left out on the sidewalks or along the roadway that can be resold or recycled for cash.

He often gets phone calls, and we dash off to a different part of town to purchase a collection or buy unwanted inventory from a store for pennies on the dollar or go through an attic or basement full of things that need to be gone. People call him looking for a specific something or other or he calls collectors to say he came across some good thing or another they might want. Every day is different.

For example, today we went to Flea City Market. Now I understand it is "flea" like the insect and not "flee" like to run away. Neither word makes sense for a market but that is what it is called. The flea market is much like Vietnamese markets with tables and spaces for rent. It is only open Friday to Sunday and on holiday Mondays.

Everyone seems to know Fred as "Buck" as he sells here on an irregular basis. He introduced me to many sellers and buyers, and we chatted briefly here and there. People asked me the usual questions except about my height, which is refreshing, but "the look" is always on their faces.

I got some Asian spices from The Sugar and Spice Lady and Fred bought a big box of obsolete video games from an older couple who were selling them for $1 each but Fred told me that most are worth $15 to $20 so he negotiated for less by buying the entire collection including the game systems and paying cash. "Churn and earn" as Fred likes to say.

Before I came to Riverton, Fred had set up computers and a desk for me on the first floor to help with Ubiddit, FreePost and other kinds of online selling. Now it is time for "learning and earning". He has me researching current prices of things Fred does not have a good knowledge of, packing sold items and printing shipping labels.

I found a cute pair of silver earrings with butterflies set in semi-precious stones, among things we are selling. I asked Fred if I could have them "for a while" and then we can sell them when I am tired of them. He hesitated at first, then smiled. "Oh, why not! Sure. Go ahead and wear them. They are pretty nice, aren't they?"

Fred doesn't want to say 'no' to me, I can tell, but I won't keep them for long.

Thomas Stimson

Selling at the Flea Market

Monday July 3
Dear My Diary,

We set up at Flea City last weekend as the weather was rainy, taking most of the video games and systems he bought the previous week along with a van-load of assorted items and small furniture pieces that have not sold at the resale stores. Fred has already listed the most valuable of the old games on Ubiddit and the rest we will sell for $10 each, with Fred saying, "Let's throw this stuff against the wall and see what sticks." It's a funny saying and I think it means Fred is giving a last chance for these things to sell.

We got four tables and displayed things in like groups with clothing racks behind us and larger items under the tables for easy access. We cleaned up what we could to make them more attractive to buyers.

There were LOTS of people at the flea market because of the rain and the aisles were crowded with shoppers. Many vendors have permanent tables and have much the same inventory all the time, but Fred comes out only sometimes, so for many people, we have "new" things to look at and the tables were crowded with browsers and buyers.

Fred gave me a general idea of the prices, and most are tagged, but he reminded me to let people bargain if they want, and adding, "I don't want to bring any of this stuff home." Living and working all my life in a family where bargaining is in our blood, I had no problem working this way. It was so much fun!

I think many people came over to look at me more closely while pretending to look at our things. No matter. We chatted up customers, sold most of what we brought and what was left over, we sold to another vendor for a little money.

In the end, we made over $3,000 and Fred gave me half. He always gives me half of what we make, and I put the extra cash into my new bank account. I hid the $10,000 emergency money in a small metal box in the roof garden behind some old pots. Hope the mice don't get to it!

Fred has never asked me what I did with the Lucky Money. I spent a little, but since we have nearly everything we need and Fred buys most of the rest, there is little reason to spend it.

I am not sure what to do with the extra money but will keep saving it for now. I did not have money in Vietnam, but the way I see how Fred uses his profits, it makes me want to grow my money too. Then I can repay my parents for the $10,000 they gave me. Me and Ba will be proud of me for this, I think.

American Independence Day

July 5th
Dear My Diary,

Independence Day was busy and fun! The rain had stopped, and Fred and I hosted a Fourth of July party on our rooftop yesterday. Fred's parents, Thanh and her family, Bobby and Robbie and some other friends of Fred's came over. We made a big salad with all the ingredients coming from the rooftop garden: three kinds of lettuce, carrots, tomatoes, spinach, cucumbers, and other plants I do not yet know the names of.

We ate pulled-pork sandwiches, the meat simmered in a seasoned sauce and served on hamburger buns. Some people brought other foods like noodle salad, desserts, and whole corn to roast on the grill. Such a feast!

We invited Thanh and her family to see the fireworks at Riverside Central Park. They are shot over the lake, and it is very pretty. It surprised me when sister said they have never done this before. Fred said, "the more the merrier!" so we left in the van about 7pm and everyone else went home or to other places.

The park was full of people with many vendors selling foods, arts and crafts, toys or playing games for prizes. I saw an Asian family selling Vietnamese French bread sandwiches, but we were too full to eat any more. I saw hot dogs, barbequed ribs, different kinds of fried foods and many things I do not know names of yet. There was a stage with bands playing popular songs and people were dancing wherever they happened to be.

The girls got their faces painted at one booth, with Cam getting a butterfly on her cheek and Tam with a fairy girl on her arm. Such a cute thing to do!

"I like your earrings," Thanh said. "You get those from Vietnam?"

"No, they were in a box of jewelry we were sorting to sell. They were cute, so I decided to wear them."

"Fred buys jewelry to sell? I thought he only buys junk."

I don't know if sister means to be insulting or it just comes naturally to her like the forked tongue of a snake. I kept my own tongue in check to keep from poisoning our evening together. "He buys all kinds of things, jewelry included. This is silver but there were also some gold pieces as well that we already put up for sale," I bragged a bit. Thanh went quiet for a moment, then changed topics.

Fred told me that last July he walked around the park like this and wanted very much to have me there with him, holding hands and having a nice time. Now his wish has come true. And mine too! Holding hands with my lover in a beautiful park with many nice people around.

At ten o'clock, it was dark enough and the fireworks flew into the sky over the little island in the lake. Marching music and the American national anthem played, filling my heart with pride. Lots of people "Ooohed!" and "Ahhhed!" and we put Cam and Tam on our shoulders to see the fireworks better over the crowd.

After one hour of the most beautiful fireworks, it is all over. The girls are tired and sleepy, so we carried them back to the van. It took a long time to get out of the traffic jam, but we got sister home and put the girls to bed. Sweet little angels.

Vo and Thanh thanked us very much for taking them out and spending the day with us. I am feeling closer to my sister and her family each week and Fred made all this happen. I gave a special "thank you" to him when we got home.

They still do the 4th of July party and fireworks at the park but now they charge a nominal fee and the fireworks show is about 20 minutes long, but Mama and Dad went every year they could, just to relive the memory of their first months together. We took Mama in a wheelchair last year and she just glowed with happiness, mixed with a tinge of sorrow that Dad could not be there with her.

Honeymoon Choices

July 7th
Dear My Diary,

Fred has given me choices of where to go for our Honeymoon. He offered up Los Angeles to see Hollywood and the possibility of glimpsing movie stars or Las Vegas for the big name shows and glitzy entertainment available. There is also New Orleans for jazzy music and the historic French Quarter, but I picked New York City. That was the easiest choice because it is one of the most famous cities in the world and best of all, Tina lives there, so she can show us around!

Bobby and Robbie have offered to pay the airfare and hotel as their wedding gift to us. Since we chose New York, they threw in tickets to the Broadway musical "Love Takes a Chance". There is a hit song from the show they play on the radio and I can't wait to see it! I thanked them many times for such a generous early wedding gift to us. They looked very shy and pleased and that made them even more endearing in my eyes.

Tina shares a small apartment with three other women from work so staying with her is not possible. We are going through a travel agent to find a nice hotel in Manhattan near all the popular places at a reasonable price. Tina will try to carve out some time with us, but she has already taken so many vacation days to see my arrival, attend the wedding, etc. She can see us only in the evenings and on weekends.

I have made a list of things I wish to see and do: The Statue of Liberty, Twin Towers and Empire State Building, see at least one Broadway show (I have never seen a professional play before), Times Square, ride on the subway, eat a New York hot dog and a giant pretzel from a street vendor, Central Park (but I am afraid to be robbed there, I hear this happens a lot), Rockefeller Center for ice skating. I am sure there are many other things to see and do but I cannot think of any more right now.

I asked Fred how long we will stay in NYC? He said maybe ten days so we can have enough time to see what we want and visit with Tina as we can.

For so many days in a big city like this, I am worried about the expense and said as much. He said, "I think I can swing that cat." I am not sure what cat he will swing but it sounds like, "Don't worry about the money".

We decided to go very early on the Friday after the wedding and spend two weekends, coming back late Sunday. That way we get to spend quality time with Tina and have lots of time to explore and do the things we want day and night.

The travel agent also got us a package of discount tickets to many popular places, so we don't have to pay full price. Fred and the travel agent have made a good plan for us. I am so excited!

Because my sisters and I are so close, I want Fred to try being closer to his brother. I know the family has problems with Barney but maybe things can change with effort on both sides. "Forgive and Forget" as they say here. To that end, Bunny and I arranged to have dinner at their home on Friday night. Wish us luck!

Trouble with Barney

Monday July 10
Dear My Diary,

I am in big trouble! Maybe I will be arrested!! Maybe the INS will deport me!!!

Fred insists that nothing will happen, but I am not so sure. I am still shaking just thinking about it. I hope writing it down will settle my nerves. Here is what happened:

The dinner I hoped would bring Fred and Barney closer together was a big disaster. It was the first time I have been to Barney and Bunny's house, which is not so big or fancy as I thought the house of a lawyer would be. Bunny answered the door looking very stylish and Barney was splayed on the couch, ignoring us while drinking beer and watching a sporting game on TV.

Bunny made Barney get up to greet us and he did so reluctantly. We all said "Hi" and Bunny gave each of us a quick hug. Barney just stood there with his attention on the TV. I am glad he did not try to hug me.

Trying to make polite conversation, I asked what kind of sport he was watching? Barney said, "Baseball. It's an AMERICAN sport." I said I have heard of baseball but had not seen it before. Barney pointed at the TV, "Well, there it is!" He was being very rude, so we moved to the kitchen.

Bunny was making a dish called Pot Roast with potatoes and vegetables and beef roast in the oven and it smelled delicious. She was cooking rice in a pot on the stove, not in a rice cooker like we do at home. She said she hoped that I like her dinner and I assured her that it will be fine. She showed us around the house and their small back yard.

While touring the house, the fridge door opened and Bunny called out, "I hope you are not getting another beer!"

Barney yelled back, "Don't get your hopes up!"

I went back to the living room to see how baseball was played while Fred and Bunny talked about people they know and I don't know. Barney said, "The butcher shop did not have your favorite meat."

I did not fully understand his comment, so I asked him what he meant. He spoke slowly, "They did not have fresh dog meat at the butcher shop. Dog is your favorite meat, isn't it?"

Now I understood Barney was saying 'dog' as an insult, so I pretended that he said a similar word. I said, "Yes, hog is my favorite meat. The butcher shop did not have hog? How odd!" I was proud of my little rhyme, but Barney ignored it.

"Dog! Dog! You know," and he made barking sounds. He was funny but looked mean while doing it.

"I thought you said 'hog'," and made a pig-squeal but I was so mad that it came out louder than I intended.

Fred and Bunny ran from the kitchen, "What happened? What happened?"

Barney said "Nothing," and looked down like a little boy caught in a lie.

I explained, "We were showing each other how to make animal sounds. Mine is a scared pig." Barney looked surprised and Bunny and Fred laughed.

"That was really good!" complimented Fred and Bunny added, "I thought one of Bernie's friends had showed up!"

During dinner, Barney told big stories about himself: what kind of law case he won, or sporting game that he gambled on and won. When he got to the best part of the story, he would say, "And that was the cherry on top!" I do not understand the expression, and no one explained it to me.

Now, Barney seems more relaxed and keeps looking at me when telling his stories. Maybe it's the beer talking. I am sure Bunny and Fred have heard these stories before and this is Barney's way of impressing me about how smart or successful he is.

Whenever Bunny or I tried to turn the topic to something else, Barney would get annoyed and say things like, "Who cares?" or "What's that got to do with anything?" or "That reminds me of the time I…" It was all about Barney or nothing at all.

After dinner, Bunny told Fred that her car is making strange noises but Barney keeps saying that nothing is wrong so they went outside to see if Fred can find the problem.

I started clearing the dinner table and Barney, I thought, came over to help. Instead, he stood close to me and leaned his body into mine. His breath was as sour as the words he was about to say.

"Do you know how you got your visa so fast?" I shook my head. "It's a fake. Fred does not make enough money to qualify, so he got another lawyer to dummy up your paperwork."

My heart started beating faster. I shook my head again, involuntarily. I have been to the US Consulate, did the interview and passed. I do not believe Barney, but a small part of me questioned what actually happened. My stomach tightened and I got scared.

Barney sensed my fear, my hesitation. "I can prove it. I can have you arrested…deported. Fred will go to jail for a long time." Like a snake, Barney hissed, "I can make things right for you…no deportation…no arrests…if you are extra, extra nice to your brother Bernie." Then he squeezed my bottom.

Stomping hard on Barney's foot, I threw back my elbow into his smug face to get him away from me. Fast and hard. The way my sisters taught me years ago when I was quickly looking older than my tender years. I screamed "No! You lie!"

Barney screamed too, but in pain, "You bitch!" and "I will call the police! I will call the INS!"

Fred rushed in, "What's going on now?"

Bunny was right behind as Barney kneeled, holding one hand over his eye and other hand to against a wall to steady himself. "She attacked me for no reason! She's crazy! I'm pressing charges!"

Fred asked me what happened, but I was scared and upset by all the commotion and what I had just done. Out of instinct. Out of self-protection. I shook my head, "No! No! I don't want to tell!"

"What did Barney do? I need to know Kimmie!"

Then everything spilled out of my mouth. "He says my fiancé visa is fake. If I sleep with him, he will fix everything. Then he made a big pinch here," I said, pointing to the spot where he touched me. "I did not believe him, and he was scaring me, so I hit him to make him go away."

"What? You lying bitch!"

"Barney, is that true?"

Barney said, "No way! She is lying! She's crazy! Nuts!"

Then Fred did something I was not expecting. He smiled and gave his hand to Barney, pulling him up gently from the floor, but I could see Fred was keeping a strong grip on Barney's hand. "Are you okay?"

"Hell no, she attacked me for no reason!"

"My little Kimmie?"

"Yes, your goddamn giant Kimmie. Didn't you hear? The freak admits it!"

I know the word 'freak'. That hurt more than Barney's clumsy attempt to bed me.

"Which eye did she hit?"

"My right." The eye was quickly swelling, and blood was oozing from his nose.

"Hurt pretty bad?" Fred sounded more concerned for his brother than he did for me. I could not believe what I was seeing and hearing.

"Hell, yes it hurts! She assaulted me!"

While still holding his brother's hand in a firm grip, Fred punched Barney's left eye and knocked him down again! "Don't you EVER touch Kimmie again! Go ahead and call the cops on both of us if it makes you feel better." I have never seen Fred angry but there was fury in his eyes. Clearly, he had feigned empathy to get revenge.

Barney screamed louder, blood running down his face. Bunny still stood in the doorway, never saying a word.

Fred said, "Come on Kim, let's go home. He won't call anyone." Then to Bunny in a gentle tone, "As always, it was a lovely meal. Come by the house sometime…without him," as Fred jerked his thumb towards Barney, writhing on the floor, yelling and cursing at us all. "We will let ourselves out."

As the front door latched shut, Bunny yelled, "You jerk! Why did you have to do that? Kimmie's such a nice…" then I heard another "smack" and Barney howled again.

We got in the truck and drove home, my body shaking with fear and adrenaline. "Bernie is a lawyer. He will call the police! He will call the INS and make big trouble for us."

Fred assured me that Barney won't tell anyone. "Your papers are all in order and perfectly legal. The police and judges won't believe him anyway."

"Why?"

"Barney has a reputation for being a liar and a troublemaker. They will believe you and I over him any day."

Trang: One of the family stories often told about Uncle Barney happened during a traffic safety promotion by the Riverton City Police Department in conjunction with Westside Mall. The mall had donated one hundred $50 gift cards to be given out by police officers who witnessed drivers doing something good or safe. It was promoted on the TV, radio and newspapers and it was clear at least one person did not hear about it.

Barney was driving through a residential neighborhood and stopped for some children waiting on a corner to cross the street. They crossed safely and Barney moved on. An officer parked nearby saw this and decided to give out a gift card.

The policeman pulled Barney over and before he could begin to explain what was going on, Barney started yelling at the officer. He had done nothing wrong! This was police harassment! He was going to sue the city, the department and the officer! I want your badge number! Do you know who I am?!

Barney went on and on, never letting the officer get a word in.

It ended with Barney being charged with "Abuse of a Public Servant", given a Breathalyzer test (passed) and jailed until Aunt Bernice could bail him out. After his hearing, he was awarded the $50 gift card he had earned and had to pay over $500 in fines and court costs.

Stories like these were almost always told to us for the lesson they contained and not to make fun of the person involved. In this case, the lesson was to respect authority figures and say, "Yes Sir" and "No Ma'am" and "I'm sorry, I did not know that was against the rules. I will not do that again." And always, <u>always</u> let the authority figure do the talking first.

Fred gave me a lot of special attention that night, soothing and comforting me. I had really hoped that the four of us could have a nice dinner discussion and perhaps make some progress to healing whatever problems lay between Barney, Fred and their parents.

But since that did not work, I kept thinking about what Barney had said to me. Now I wanted to be absolutely certain about the origins of my visa and I was tired of not getting a straight answer.

"Fred? Many people I know who got the K1 visa says it takes almost a year to process. I got the interview in two months, and on our birthday. How did you manage that if it is not a fake?"

Fred simply said, "That is the magic of Robbie and Bobby. Getting it on our birthday was more of a coincidence…a very happy coincidence."

Fred smiled and changed the subject, "I still can't get over what happened tonight. How did sweet Kimmie get to be a butt-kicking Beast from the East?"

I explained that as I grew so fast as a child, many men thought I was much older than my very young age and it made for attracting problems. My sisters had all learned to protect themselves and it was especially important for me. When men are rude to us, we act first to ignore them. But if they get too physical or we feel endangered, we use some martial art techniques to shock them with pain, then to get away.

Fred said a bully will run away from someone showing more courage than himself and he does not think Barney will want to make any trouble with me now. I am not a shy mouse but a fierce tiger. "If you have to do such a thing again, just do it and I will back you up 100%. No one has a right to touch your body if you do not want it…not even me."

I told Fred he is always welcome to touch me. He thanked me for saying so, but added "Just the same, you did the right thing tonight."

Still, I am nervous about the police coming for me and Fred.

I checked around and nobody had heard this story before. With some trepidation, I called Aunt Bernice at the retirement center where she lives, told her about the diaries and related the story to her.

"It's been a long time since I thought about that dinner. Barney was a real shit in those days and your mother was so nice and wholesome. I really wanted to be close to Kimmie, but Barney didn't make it easy."

The way Dad handled the situation was nothing less than admirable…and exactly what we would have expected him to do. Our parents always backed us up if we got into trouble, as long as we told them the truth of whatever happened.

As for truthfulness, Barney got along with Truth as easily as he got along with everyone else. More on that to come…

Barney Was Not the First

July 11th, 2000

Dear My Diary,

After what happened with Barney, it brought back memories of a time from my college days when another man touched me in a bad way. I decided to tell Fred, as my best friend should know.

When we were alone and relaxed, I told Fred of the day one of my college instructors kept me after class to talk about my grades. I thought my work in his class was above average, so this news concerned me.

He spoke softly, not with the cold manner he normally employed in class. He said my work was below standards and I was in danger of failing and possibly being removed from the program, which I found hard to believe.

With these words, he began touching my hair, which was long at the time, and saying he can fix the grades to my advantage if I will be extra nice to him. His hands moved to the end of my tresses and came to rest on my breasts.

As soon as I realized what he was doing, I swung my hands quickly in front of me and clapped his ears…hard! He fell back onto the desks, scraping and clattering into a jumble with the corner of one striking his forehead.

The teacher started breathing heavily like a fish out of water, hands fumbling in a shirt pocket for an inhaler and blood dripping from his ears. Frightened, I thought he might die in front of me, so I fled the classroom.

At the warehouse, I told my parents everything and how I feared going back to school to see the teacher again. Ba's face became like stone, leaving the office, getting into his car, and driving away as Me made every effort to comfort me.

When Ba came home for dinner, he told me to go back to school tomorrow, that I am not in trouble and will not be bothered again. I did not question my father. His face was not so much like stone now, but he was not in the mood for talking, either.

When I returned to school, the male teachers avoided eye contact with me and when I went to the bad teacher's classroom, there was a different instructor…a female. I never saw the bad teacher again. He had been fired and I learned later that both his eardrums were broken, and his wife filed for divorce after learning why he was dismissed.

Fred never said a word during my confession. When I finished, I asked Fred what he thought?

"The only person who did not do the right thing was the teacher…even his wife was smart enough to get away from him. And it also sounds very much like the other night."

"That is why I remembered the teacher after so many years. I feel like we both did the right thing too, just like my father and I."

Fred held my face in his large hands, looked into my eyes and said, "If you ever have a problem, a concern or a worry, you can tell me anything...anything at all." Then he smiled and added, "But if you need to kick someone's butt that's doing you wrong, just do it and let them know who the boss of your body is."

"Now you know a story that only my parents and sisters know about me. Oh yes, and the teacher!" I cuddled up closer and whispered in Fred's ear, "Thank you for being such a best friend. Tonight, you can be the boss of my body."

I could feel his grin grow against my cheek as he replied, "And you can be the boss of mine."

Mama's size and strength were to her advantage, as well as her father's influence in getting the teacher fired. Who knows how often that teacher had gotten away with his despicable behavior? Mama and Dad made sure we all took martial arts and self-defense classes growing up for just these kinds of incidents...even Frankie.

Dear My Diary,

I asked Fred what "cherry on top" means? He explained that with a fancy dessert, sometimes they put whipped cream and a bright red cherry on top to add extra eye-appeal. The "cherry on top", as part of a story, just means "and here is the best part". But this time, in Barney's case, it was "here is the worst part."

I never thought I would ever see Fred hit anyone as he is so patient and easy-going. I asked Fred "Could you ever get so angry that you would hit me?"

"What I did was a BIG exception to what I would normally do, and I did it because he laid hands on you. Sweetheart, I cannot imagine any reason to ever hit you, even if you hit me first. Even if you broke my heart," and he put his hands over his heart and made puppy eyes at me. I laughed, but then Barney's words came back to me again and I needed to have an answer to my question.

"Fred, how did I get my K1 visa so fast? It was too fast, and Barney seemed to know something about this. But why? Please tell me the truth."

Fred put up his hands as if to surrender, "Okay, okay, let's get your question answered," and took out his cell phone. He made a call and got Robbie on the line asking if he had a minute to talk. Then, "Kimmie has a question for you," and handed me the phone. I was not expecting this and did not know what to say but Fred encouraged me to ask him the question.

After the hellos and how-are-yous, I explained my concerns about the K1 visa, finishing with, "If it is true that it was your magic to make this happen, then I thank you so very much, but can you explain, please, how this magic happened?"

Robbie explained that they have a client who works in a high position at the regional INS office. When B&R learned Fred was applying for a fiancé visa, they spoke to this person for a small favor and he put me at the top of the list for review. That is all. "Yes, it was very fast, but your visa is perfectly legal and you have nothing to worry about. Does that make you feel better?"

I said it does and thanked Bobby again for being such good friend to me. He laughed and said he is happy to be my friend too.

Fred's words of a few weeks ago came back to me: "Bobby and Robbie have brought me good luck not only in business, but in love as well." Now I understand what he meant, and it made me more ashamed that I feared bad luck for having gay groomsmen at our wedding. They most certainly earned a place in my heart today!

Dear My Diary,

Bunny called and apologized about the other night. She hopes that we can still be friends and sisters and wants to come to the wedding, but not with her husband. "I've been thinking long and hard about splitting from him after what he did to you. I don't know for sure if he really sleeps with other women or if he was just trying to scare you. Either way, it was a shitty thing to do and I'm glad you taught his ass a lesson."

I did not know what to say to all of this, so I said I was busy and hung up. I was not busy, but I do know that I would not have to "think long and hard" about staying with a man who made threats and sexual advances to anyone, especially a sibling's partner. That decision is simple. I would rather go back to Vietnam and remain single for the rest of my life than to be with any man like that.

I talked to Fred after calming down and thinking it over some more. Fred said he really likes Bunny but if we invite her to wedding, Barney will likely come and make trouble. I had thought the same thing would prefer to avoid problems on our special day. Yet another thing we can agree on.

I got an "I'm sorry" card in the mail from Bunny. She apologized again and is very proud how I stood up to Bernie and showed that I wouldn't take any bull from him. She finished by saying that she hoped we can still be friends and sisters, but if not, she will understand.

I spoke to Fred about what I can say to Bunny. I want to be her friend and sister, but I do not want to be near Barney anymore. Fred explained how Bunny comes from a poor family and she married Barney for the income and prestige of his job. "If they split, she's afraid of winding up with someone even worse, or being alone which she hates more than being married to a loser." Fred helped me how to say what I am thinking and I called Bunny.

I explained to her how very upset I am with Barney's behavior and afraid that if I invite her to the wedding, Barney will come and make problems for us. "You are a very nice woman and I do want to be your friend and sister, but I must protect myself, my family, and my special day."

She was quiet for a moment, then said, "I can respect that. Barney ruined our wedding day too." She did not explain further and I do not want to know. Bunny finished with, "Well, see you around sometime," and hung up. I hope she is not too mad with me, but I will not change my mind, either.

Mulchables

Sunday, July 23
Dear My Diary,

Last week, a man called Fred to tear down an old barn on his property that is getting saggy and dangerous. After looking things over, Fred charged $10,000 including hauling the wood away as part of the fee.

The barn is two stories high with rafters, stalls and lofts. The dump fees would be astronomical! "What are you going to do with all the wood?" I asked.

Fred winked, "You, my little helper, are going to see another area of my recycling world very soon." We each drove the largest of his moving trucks and Fred towed a rented one-man lift to the farm.

We arrived at dawn with plenty of food and drinks and started with our customary, "Let's go make some money!" and a kiss. First, we cleared out old equipment and trash, culling lanterns, tools, saddles and other resellable things out of the pile and setting them aside.

This is the first time I have worn so much safety equipment…hard hat, safety glasses, leather gloves, steel-toed boots, and earplugs. Fred took the lift to the eaves and, with a chainsaw, began cutting away the wall planks while I was inside breaking apart ground-floor animal stalls with a crowbar and sledge. As Fred stripped one area away, he would back up the lift and do another section, leaving a trail of lumber on the ground.

We stacked the lumber into the trucks as efficiently as possible and, at one point Fred, panting with exertion, said, "Would have been a lot faster with a can of gas and some matches." Too funny!

When the trucks were completely full, Fred kept cutting and I kept stacking until 3pm when Fred called someone and said we would "be there in about a half hour to unload".

We went to a company call Mulchables where they make two kinds of products: Mulch, made from a combination of shredded wood, leaves, grass clippings, paper and coffee grounds. The other product is Recyclogs, logs for campfires and fireplaces, made with the same ingredients and bound together with paste made from wastepaper. No man-made chemicals are added to either product.

Fred gives the wood to Mulchables, pays no dumping fee, and it helps the environment. The company contracts with local governments, landscaping firms, paper recyclers, farms and coffee shops to take in raw materials that will stay out of the landfills. I think this is a very nice thing to do, and clever too! We went back to the barn and worked until nearly dark.

It took a full week to complete the tear down. The best part was, after the walls were stripped up to the eaves, Fred chain-sawed deep notches in each of the exterior supports, tied chains from the corner posts to both trucks and then we pulled from opposite directions. What fun!

We are now $10,000 richer. Once the last load of lumber was taken off, we drove the trucks to another part of the building and a forklift loaded pallets of fifty-pound bags into the trucks while Fred signed some papers. As we left, I asked "Where are we going?"

Fred smiled and said, "A part of town you haven't seen yet."

We pulled up to a big garden between sets of apartment buildings. The garden took up the space of maybe two house lots. The sign in front said, "Roosevelt Community Garden sponsored by Feed the Neighbors and The Orion Group".

Fred explained that this piece of land, in an undesirable part of town, had a lot of taxes owed on it, so Fred bought the land from the city very cheap and started a community action group called Feed the Neighbors.

He raises money, provides mulch, tools, and other necessities so neighbors can work together for fun, exercise, education and, of course, much needed fresh food. The mulch we brought was donated by Mulchables who will get a tax benefit, as will Fred for donating the wood, plus free advertising and the good feeling of helping others.

There are five community gardens managed by a committee of volunteers, including Fred who began the project. Each garden is in a different part of town where the need is greatest. The residents get professional planning and help from volunteer gardening experts to make their gardens as productive as possible.

We unloaded a pallet of mulch into a storage shed and residents came out to help. They chatted with us and we toured their gardens. The mulch will conserve water today, protect plants through the winter and feed the soil in the spring.

I am always learning new things about my husband! We visited the other four community gardens and dropped off a pallet of mulch at each. People were so happy to Fred and called him "Mr. Buck" and me "Mrs. Buck". It was so much fun and made me feel even more proud of my man and what he does.

At the last garden, a family named Carter had us in for dinner with most of the food coming from their garden. It was so delicious and the family very welcoming. I was comfortable in their home, though humble with not a lot of things inside.

I do not know a lot about gardening except for what we do at the garage, but Fred was very knowledgeable and he shared some of this with the family and stories about how we met and how wonderful Vietnam is. Such a fulfilling day!

Feed the Neighbors now has over 150 community gardens throughout the state. Frankie is on the Board of Directors, as Dad had been for many years. Mulchables long ago stopped making Recyclogs due to environmental concerns of greenhouse gasses, but they are one of the country's largest producers of mulch and soil products with over 20 processing centers in the US and Canada. And yes, Dad was an original investor and the family has always had a stake in the business. One of the Multiple Streams of Income we all share.

Cam and Tam's Visits

July 30
Dear My Diary,

Tina can't wait for us to come to New York, so she sent us brochures and maps of the city to look over. It's fun to make my dream plans for everything I want to see with Fred.

On Saturday we had the girls over while their parents went to the casino. Thanh stopped asking me to come gambling with them as we are too boring. Or maybe she likes that we are free babysitters. I don't care. The casino was not as I had imagined and we like having the twins over and playing with them.

We teach them simple cooking skills like slicing bananas, peeling garlic and onions, breaking open peapods and stirring things together. I show them how some foods go better with others, like ginger and pork or shrimp with tomatoes and pineapple for soup. They eat everything I make, and so does Fred! I think the twins are gaining weight and have more color to their cheeks.

Part of what Fred teaches in Dissolving Debt is a section called "Cooking is Not Rocket Science", meaning it is not necessary to buy convenience or take-out foods and that cooking can be simple, cheap, healthy, and nutritious. He finds and gives out cookbooks at his classes that specialize in quick-to-prepare meals from scratch. I have two of them now and I use the recipes with Cam and Tam to make our Saturday night dinners. It makes the girls so proud to say they helped!

The twins also assist in the gardens and Fred lets them play with some of the toys and games he gets before putting them on Ubiddit. We take them to playgrounds, for exercise and playing with other children. By taking care of my nieces, I can see how it will be to have our own children…to teach and play and make fun things happen.

Thanh has told me that the twins could not speak English when they started school, even though they were born here, because the parents talked all the time in Vietnamese and were lazy to teach the children English.

The first year was hard for the girls but now they speak very clear English, better than me! I speak to them all the time in English so I can practice to make perfect. Yes, that's the term…Practice Makes Perfect.

Sometimes they correct me on grammar and the pronunciation of words and sounds that Fred does not bother with anymore. I have asked him to please correct my English if I make mistakes so I do not sound so immigrant. Fred says he does not want to criticize my English, but I let him know that I will not bite his ears for correcting me.

Fred is also good with the girls. I know he has not been around children very much in the past but has been getting more time with Tam and Cam and their cousins in recent weeks. I think this is good training for him to be a Ba one day. And for me too!

Friday August 4
Dear My Diary,

The wedding clothes are made and fitted for everyone, we got most of the RSVP's back and those we did not get, Fred or I will call, depending on whose family or friends they are. Almost everyone we invited will be coming and I have not heard from Bunny in a while. I hope she is all right.

We have been busy working, gardening and finalizing details for the wedding. Auntie has arranged the music and entertainment as our wedding gift, so no need to think about that. The chapel will fix things up nice based on the packages we purchased through them, so there is not a lot for Fred and I to do.

Thanh and Vo are having their Date Night so we took Cam and Tam for a special treat. We are not sure if the girls will think this is boring or not, but we took them to the Friday Night Auctions on the western edge of the city. Like the name says, the company holds auctions every Friday night and many people come to buy, sell and visit.

Fred used his auction voice to make the girls laugh and show how it will be. We told them to behave and not to call out bids for fun as it is a business and grown-ups will not like pretend bidding. Instead, they can watch and make guesses about how much something will sell for before they start the bidding, like a game.

We brought snacks and fruit juices and looked over the many tables of things to sell before the start of the auction. The girls made fun chit-chat about some of the pretty things for sale and the old toys and what is this? And why would someone want that?

The girls found a set of books and dolls called The Twins Club. Fred said it was a popular series of books for 8-12 yr olds from the 1970's. Several sets of twins in a small town make a club and have adventures. The set includes dolls for all the characters and twelve books. Fred also found some things to bid on and wrote them in his notebook.

When the book and doll set came up for bidding, I asked the girls if they wanted it and they said "yes, please!", so I bid for the girls until I won. There were two other people bidding against me, but I wanted it for the girls, even if I paid a little too much. For me, the value will be in the girl's enjoyment more than someone else making a profit.

When the auctioneer called SOLD! the girls jumped up and down in excitement and people around us smiled and applauded for their happiness. Fred bought three things to re-sell and we all had a good time. The girls spent the rest of the evening at home imitating the fast auctioneer-talk, then "SOLD"!

Thanh and Vo will be very annoyed with their daughters talking silly and yelling SOLD! for the next few days. Too bad! That is the fun of being children.

When we got back to the garage, we had dessert and I let Cam and Tam read me the first chapter of first Twins Club book. It's a nice story and they are good readers. Fred said the more reading a child does, the better it will help them in school. I know this is true.

We all had a good time and the girls are asleep now. It looks like they are spending the night as it is after one o'clock, and still no parents…

The VIG's

Wednesday August 9
Dear My Diary,

Fred announced that we must go to airport today and he wants me to dress nice. I asked, "Who is coming?" It is four days before the wedding and most of the out-of-town guests are driving, not flying.

He said we are picking up some VIG's. I asked what is a VIG? Fred said "Very Important Guest" but would not tell me who.

I cannot think of who it will be. We have a guest list and I think I know where everybody is coming from. Tina is arriving tomorrow from New York so I asked Fred if Tina is coming early? He would not say. What is it about men and mysteries? Men ARE a mystery!

Fred borrowed Bernie's expensive sedan as we have no nice vehicles and I think it must be a very special guest if we are using this car. Bernie is out of town so Bunny let Fred use his car but not to say anything to his brother. I wonder if Fred knows some famous musician to play at our wedding as I can't imagine who or what else it could be.

I felt the ache again of not having my parents here this weekend to see me married. I think we all thought I would stay single forever while living in Vietnam. Now I will marry such a very nice man but I had to leave my homeland to do it. I guess we can't have everything.

We parked the car and went in to find the flight from Seattle. I don't know anyone in Seattle and Fred would not tell me more. As we walked to the gate, I thought I saw my cousin Grace but Fred pushed me to hurry along.

We found the gate and when the door opened, lots of people were streaming out. Suddenly, I felt my heart stop and I am not believing what my eyes see. A woman who looks like my sister Thao, then I saw Me and Ba behind her. My family!

They saw me and waved their arms as we ran together for much hugging and kissing. Fred made the best surprise for me…I would not have expected this to happen in one hundred years!

I learned later that before Fred left Vietnam with me, he made some plans with Ba and Me to come for the wedding, and later worked with an immigration attorney in Riverton to apply for their tourist visas. Tourist visas from Vietnam are difficult to get unless you are very rich or know someone with influence. My parents fit both categories and everyone managed to keep this a big secret from me.

When we headed back to the airport entrance, Auntie and cousins, Thanh and family and Frank and Maggie came to us from nearby tables. They had wanted me to have the special surprise first, before making their own greetings second. It is almost like when I came to America just a few weeks ago.

We went out for lunch at an American style restaurant to show my family what it is like, then we took them to one of best hotels in Riverton where Fred had rented a suite of rooms for them with a view of the river and downtown. They will be staying ten days before going back. I asked why not longer?

Ba said they can't leave the business alone for too long. Phung is taking care of things and he is very good, but ten days will be enough time to see where I live and visit with my new American family.

Thomas Stimson

Remembering my first hours in America, I said, "I hope you like the smell of old trucks!"

Kimmie: Your father could not have given me a better wedding present than to have my parents and sister come to our wedding. It was a deep desire of mine and he made the wish come true. At that time, Vietnam was very reluctant to issue tourist visas as they were afraid our citizens would seek asylum and not return.

Between Fred's help from an immigration lawyer and my parents having a large company and other assets worth a great deal of money, it was not difficult for the tourist visa to be approved. Fred was always so good to my family…and they loved him very much in return.

Reuniting with My Family

Thursday, August 10
Dear My Diary,

Today my parents asked to spend time with me, without Fred, so they may speak freely in Vietnamese. Having not seen Me and Ba for almost three months, it makes sense to do this, so I asked Fred if this is okay?

"Sure! I understand your family wants to have some catch-up time, so go ahead and have fun with them. Give them my love!" Fred is so sweet and knows when to give me space and when I need closeness. Besides, I don't want him to know about the special gift in my purse.

Trinh and Thao picked me up in a rental mini-van and when I entered the hotel suite, Me and Ba were having coffee, pastries, and fruit from room service, so we helped ourselves to the cart and sat for a chat. Parents looked well-rested, in good health, and ready to go out exploring, which pleased me. It is like a dream they are here, and I can't stop smiling.

They asked me how I like life in America and with Fred? I said, "Fred is a happy man and always finding the sunshine in a situation, even when things are not going well. I have met many of his friends and business associates and all appear to be clean and honest people."

Ba nodded thoughtfully at this and Me asked, "So, Fred has many friends?"

"Well, I don't know about close friends, but many are more like acquaintances or known casually. Often people approach us on the street or at stores and want to talk to Fred, say hello, chat for a few minutes. Sometimes he makes appointments right there to look at things they are selling or take orders for something they want to buy. I feel like Fred has done some business or charity work with most of Riverton!"

Ba chuckled and observed, "Your fiancé grew up here and is not a man to be missed easily in a crowd…much like one of my children," he said. "People remember a man like Fred, whether it be a good experience or bad. Sounds like Fred has a history of good experiences with people. Can't go wrong with that!"

"I agree, Ba. We both work hard, and I am learning so much about his business affairs. He makes sure we have fun things to do, so it balances the work…but the work can be fun too!" and I told them about the barn and Mulchables. They liked the story of hard work combined with social responsibility and charity.

"That's why you look so tanned and buff!" Thao said, "It's like you have this glow about you."

I flexed my arms, "Who needs a gym when I have Fred as a workout partner?" I stood up and mimicked picking up boxes and tossing them into an imaginary truck. "In the sun, in the rain, indoors, outdoors. I don't mind it at all."

Ba shifted in his chair and said, "That all sounds wonderful, Kim. We are glad you found happiness with Fred and your new life here. Now, we have some family business to discuss…"

But I interrupted him, saying "Please Ba, before we start with family business, I have something I want to give you." Ba looked annoyed at being interrupted but he gave a small wave of his hand to say, 'All right, you go first.'

I took a deep breath and said, "You gave me some money before I left Vietnam. Emergency money in case Fred was bad to me. Well, Fred makes many kinds of business deals and when we do something together, and makes some money from it, he always gives me half because we are partners in business now. So, with deepest respect, I want you to have this."

With my head bowed, I handed my parents a small square envelope with both hands. Inside is a card to let them know how much I love them and what good things I have in my new life. Me read it out loud and everyone nodded and smiled.

Then I handed over the thick, red envelope containing the $10,000 they gave me in Vietnam. "I have more than $10,000 of earned money now and I want to give this back to you. Thank you for the concern you showed for my well-being as I begin a new life in America. I do not need this now. If I need to leave America, I can do so with my own money."

Me and Ba looked in silence at the money, then at sisters. I think I saw Trinh make a small shoulder shrug from the side of my eye but am not quite sure. Me had a tear come out, then a tissue to clear it.

Ba composed himself and said "You have done well in your short time here. I am glad our new son is so good to his future wife like this. Many men will hide their money from the wife…"

Me added, "…and the wife hides money from husband too!" and we all laughed as it is very true. "Do you hide money from me?"

She gave him an innocent look, "Not me, Lo. I never do such a thing!" and we laughed again. I like it when they speak in loving teases. It reminds me of my time with Fred. So funny and sweet.

Ba and Me then gave the money back to me, hugged me and said it is mine forever. It was never a loan, so now I can use it to invest or spend how I want. I asked, "Are you sure?"

My parents smiled and said "Yes, very sure." Like the money is nothing but a coin to them.

I asked Ba what kind of family business did he wish to discuss with me? His face started to say one thing, then he appeared to change his mind, saying, "We want very much to see how beautiful Riverton is. Can you give us a tour?"

This does not sound like family business, but I said, "Of course! I know how to get to some nice places for you to see."

We took Tina's rental and drove around Riverton where my parents admired all the open spaces and so many large, leafy trees everywhere. We stopped at The Treasure Hut where Maggie works, and she was happily surprised to see us all walk in.

I explained how this is one of the stores we do business with. Everyone looked around and admired the interesting merchandise. Me and sisters bought some small things as gifts for family members at home and Ba found a vintage Saturn Sports shirt his size, back when they used to put shoe prints going around Saturn's ring.

I explained to Ba that Saturn had stopped making that logo design in the early 1980's and are very collectable now. When Ba asked how I knew this, I admitted that Fred told me. He tapped my forehead with his finger and said, "Sounds like someone is learning a lot of useful information for the family business," and bought the shirt.

We drove through downtown and I pointed out the building Bobby and Robbie work and live in, then on to Riverside Central Park to walk around the lake path. Children fed ducks and people held hands or enjoyed picnics on the lawn.

Older boys and girls raced remote control-boats around the island in the middle of lake where birds make their nests and raise their little families. Maybe one day Fred and I will make picnics here with our own little family? I hope so.

The sun is warm, and I feel better to walk and speak with my family freely in my mother tongue. Thao said the warehouse workers and neighbors ask about me and are told I am happy in America and everyone passes their good wishes on to me. I am pleased to hear this. I called Fred to say we are coming home.

I drove back to the garage and Fred met us with open arms. "Me! Ba! Sisters! Welcome to our little home!" Of course, my family had heard of the garage but I think it looks far larger than from what I have told them. Tina has been here but the look on our parents faces…priceless! Ba pointed out the Starbuckle and Sons sign to Me.

We took everyone to the living area and gave them a tour. I know our home is a bit avant-garde to my parents, seeing mannequin hands poking out of the wall to take coats and twinkle lights all over the ceiling. Fred was playing VN pop music over the speakers and making fresh fruit blender drinks for everyone, served in fancy tall glasses.

He placed chilled plates of fruit and avocado salad with shrimp and crab meat, on waiter's trays as we went up to see the gardens and sit under patio umbrellas.

We made small talk and later I showed everyone how we do our business in the lower floors of the building. Ba grunted in admiration and Thao said this is a great way to work from home.

Everything looks so different to my parents as it looked so strange to me when first I came here. I am still learning things every day but I am getting comfortable in how things are in Fred's world.

I wonder if I should keep the secret from Fred about my money? Sometimes I feel Fred does not tell me everything about his business affairs. Maybe they are not bad things, but the door is not all the way open, either. Like about Buzzy Brew being a tasty company, even though he does not buy their products…what does that mean?

Whenever I think about the money Fred gives me for working with him, and now the extra money from my family, I am reminded of a phrase Fred likes to use: Multiple Streams of Income.

I'm taking notes on the way it works for Fred. Now I need to think of ways to make my own streams of income, beyond taking what Fred pays me.

After lunch, Fred drove everyone to the chapel for a sneak preview. Family is very impressed with our location and the scenic river views from the hilltop. There was a business conference in session today and Abraham was not available, but another helper showed us where everything will be and how it will look. They also printed out some copies of our reception menu to show parents how it is a mix of Asian and American dishes. "Something for everyone!" as Fred likes to say.

With my parents and Thao here, I don't think my wedding could be any more special. I just hope Barney does not decide to make it worse…

Bachelorette Party

Dear My Diary,

I will be writing this whenever I can for the next several days between activities with Fred, family, and friends so that I do not forget any details about my wonderful wedding time…and a couple of surprises!

In the week leading up to our special day, there was a flurry of errands and last-minute details to attend to. My sisters were disappointed at my not having a bridal shower or bachelorette party and I explained that I hardly know anyone here, but they said, "You know US!" and sister Thanh took over the party planning.

On Friday, all four of us and Me went to the riverboat casino with Fred, Ba, Vo and the twins for their Friday night seafood buffet. Everyone dressed up and we got a big table to make our feasting. So many wonderful dishes including lobster, different kinds of crab, shrimp and fish dishes and other local favorites.

We made toasts to each other with sparkling cider drinks and the girls pretended they were getting drunk until Thanh told them to stop a little more sharply than I thought was necessary.

Afterward, Fred took the men and children to a local amusement park so the real bachelorette party could begin. Vo had wanted to stay and gamble, but Thanh chased him off saying, "Spend time with your family, instead of your cards!"

We had such a time doing things I normally never, ever do…like drinking margaritas and singing karaoke (in English!) on a dare from Thao. I'm sure I was awful because some people kept yelling, "You SUCK!", but Tina pointed out the same group was harassing nearly all the other singers. Then I didn't feel so bad…but I probably did suck.

Sisters gave me gifts of lingerie, necklaces and earrings, Me gave me a book on pregnancy and baby care, (hint! hint!) and Thanh told the absolute dirtiest stories I have ever heard! Our mother finally put a stop to it as we were all laughing so hard that people were staring. I think this is what they do to pass the slow times at the salon…sharing dirty jokes, stories, and gossip.

I have no idea when I got home but Me drove us under Thanh's directions as she was the only one who was sober. I don't think I have ever had such a loose time with my mother, who, for the night, was more my equal than my mother. In fact, I can't remember having had such a fun time in all my years back home.

Now I know what a hangover feels like…I felt queasy on Saturday morning but was better after aspirin and ginger ale, Fred's own idea. Luckily, I did not get sick in the car, or anywhere else, and we are not getting married today…that would have been very embarrassing! Fred was more amused at my condition than upset and was glad we had a good time.

There was something new in the living room I had not noticed when I came home last night. I must have been pretty well out of it not to see the giant television box that sat in the corner of the living room.

Ba had seen that we have no TV and insisted on buying one for us as a wedding gift, so Fred took everyone to VideoWorld for the largest television they had in stock and brought it home in the van. It is not hooked up yet, but there it sits with a built-in VCR and one of the new video disc players that just came out.

Once they settled the TV in the parlor, the girls got to practice their dancing skills and tumbling tricks while Fred showed off some of our latest acquisitions to Ba and Vo.

Out of curiosity, and a little guilt, I asked Fred if he felt bad not to have his brother at the wedding. He said, "Not at all. In this instance, the more is NOT the merrier," and said no more about it. I feel bad that Bunny will not be there, but that is also for the best.

On Saturday night, Fred gave me a wedding gift. He presented me with a square red velvet box and said, "Here is something to remind us of our first times together." Inside was a gold necklace with a pendant of two cay dua leaning and crossing over each other. I can see they are coconut trees because there are little clusters at the base of the leaves.

He pulled out another box, blue velvet this time, saying, "And this is your wedding gift to me." My "gift" to Fred was a matching necklace and pendant! He asked me to wear the necklace as part of my wedding outfit, and he will do the same. Of course, I agreed, but I felt ignorant not to know that couples give each other a wedding gift.

Fred explained the story behind the pendants: after I had successfully completed my visa interview, he took a pile of scrap gold jewelry he had been saving and took it to a skilled jeweler he does business with. Fred explained what he wanted, the jeweler came up with the design and made the pendants from some of the scrap and took the rest in on trade for the chains and labor. That's my man!

I am pleased with Fred's choice of wedding gift because only he and my family will know the real meaning behind it.

As I think about it, I am not so upset these days about being called Cay Dua…my pain about that is lessened. Nobody here makes fun of my height and I see many women much taller than most women back home, which means I do not stand out *quite* so much.

Thomas Stimson

Our Wedding Day

After waking up early with the morning light streaming through the curtains, Fred and I had some special pleasure time to be relaxed for later in the day and to remind each other of our love and commitment this day will seal. We still kept our special promise to each other, but it wasn't easy!

We all gathered in my parent's hotel suite, having breakfast with the family and coordinating the morning's preparations. Thanh had all her employees come to the hotel to do my hair, sisters, the twins and both mother's hair and make-up this morning.

I'm sure Maggie felt left out as so much Vietnamese was being spoken, but at my suggestion, everyone made some effort to bring her into the conversations with stories and questions to her about her own wedding day. I could tell she appreciated the effort we made to include her in our happy girl-talk.

My hair has grown out since coming here and Me said it makes me look more mature and feminine. I feel that way also. No more garcon cut for me. No need.

At one point, Thanh asked, "What time is the limo taking us to the wedding?"

"What limo?"

"You don't have a limo?" Thanh responded incredulously, her eyes getting wide.

"We want to ride in a limo!" the twins chimed in.

"I don't think we have a limo. Fred and I never talked about hiring one."

Thanh put her hands on her hips as everyone turned to look at us, "How are we supposed to arrive at the chapel? In our cars? Minivans?" Then she sneered, "Your work truck?"

Everything had been so pleasant until now…and on this day of all days. My face grew hot at Thanh's words and as I groped for something juicy to say, Thao stepped in. Using her no-nonsense manager's tone, she instructed, "Kimmie, call Fred to learn his plans and Trinh, please contact the hotel concierge for a limo service we can hire. Your English is better than mine."

As Trinh called the front desk using the room phone, I called the garage where the men were getting dressed. Fred answered on the fourth ring and I repeated Thanh's question, "What time is the limo picking us up to go to the wedding?"

There was silence, then Fred responded, sounding confused, "What limo?" His voice was clear through the receiver and Thanh spat out one word, "Men!", as she snapped a credit card down in front of Trinh to pay for the transportation and going back to work on Me's hair.

At the chapel, my parents, Vo and Thao sat with our cousins in the front rows on the left side and Fred's parents were joined by some of their siblings on the right. The boys and girls look so sweet in their dress up clothes. There are three entrances to the main aisle from the back…right side for the groom and attendants, left side for the bride and her people and the double doors for the guests in the center.

The two limousines that brought everyone are in the parking lot nearest the chapel where everyone can see them. White for the ladies and black for the men. The men were a little late as the limo driver had trouble believing she was picking up a wedding party from the part of town where we live. She probably thought the address was wrong. I would have.

Trinh was able to secure them on two-hour's notice, and Thanh said this would be her treat! Most of us have never been in a limo and it was such a luxury. I will have to ask Fred why he did not order limos for us. Thanh made it sound like the most obvious thing in the world to have for a wedding.

At noon, the chapel bells chimed to alert guests that the ceremony was about to start. The music began playing and, from the back, our fathers approached the altar in slow, measured steps.

In unison, they lit each of the large candles, then ignited joss sticks and placed them in the central sand bowl, bowing in prayer. This is something new for Frank, but he and Ba had practiced yesterday and he did very well.

Next, Bobby and Robbie walked slowly down the aisle in their man-style ao dais with small, close-fitting hats. As they stepped in unison, a man's voice sang the first verses of a popular Vietnamese duet, then sang the next lyrics in English. I recognized the voice but could not think of the name. I did not plan for this music and the recording was very clear and rich.

When Fred completed the group at the altar, it was time for Trinh and Thanh to join them. A different singer took over, doing her part in the same style…Vietnamese lyrics first, then English, as my sisters matched steps down the aisle.

Each pair of attendants have different colored ao dais to match their partner, so from the outside spots Thanh and Bobby are in green, Trinh and Robbie in blue. The fabrics are a shiny satin and almost glow in the diffused lighting.

Now the singer's names dawn on me. They are a popular Vietnamese couple who immigrated to the US. The sound system is so clear that their singing calms me as I am about to join Fred at the altar.

The twins go before me, side by side in their sunshine-yellow ao dai's and matching hair-ribbons, dropping flower petals and smiling shyly as cameras take their pictures. They are so pleased to be a part of our wedding and this pleases me too.

As I am about to step off, I took a deep breath and slowly let it out. I am nervous, but not too much. I glanced around the chapel. No Bernice and no Bernie. There are many faces I am not familiar with on both sides of the chapel: Fred's relatives, business partners and my distant cousins, known better to Auntie Giang and my parents than to me.

Some people are wearing tinted eyeglasses, but one black-haired woman stood out by wearing a floppy hat and large-framed sunglasses even though we are inside. Like someone in a movie who is trying to disguise themselves but, in doing so, becomes the most obvious person in the room.

I drew myself up straight, shoulders back, chest out and followed Cam and Tam down the aisle. The duet has stopped and a keyboard plays the familiar "Wedding March" as we planned, just like I have heard in so many romantic films.

Fred stood at the front with the big, gentle smile I love so much. I smiled back, not too big, but enough to show pride in my appearance and not let the mask of heavy make-up crack apart as I feel it might.

As I took my place next to Fred, he gave me a little wink and smile. Our ao dai's are red with gold patterns and trim, flowers for me and intricate Asian-styled designs for him. My hair has small fresh flowers at the top where the crown is open and we are both wearing our cay dua necklaces.

Auntie is presiding at the altar and did the entire ceremony in English for the comfort of our American families and friends. Most of our Vietnamese guests are long-time residents, so they understand as well. Auntie looked like a Queen, with the kind of presence that makes everyone sit up and pay attention.

She started with a little history about us: How Fred and I lived so far from each other until being introduced, our journey from email pen pals, to friends, and finally, finding true love. When Fred made the journey around world to visit my family, his kindness and sweet soul won my heart and that of my family. (I am trying to remember all the parts of Auntie's speech. I hope I did not forget anything!)

Then she described how my good nature and hard work in the family business has made me a good and kind person, pursuing ways to better myself with education and language skills. That we have many interests in common and found each other from far away is the miracle of the power of love.

The altar has two large metal bowls and a box between them. Bobby and Thanh moved to the altar and removed the red decorative covers from the bowls. One has a beautiful display of fresh fruits and the other, a bottle of brandy and box of sweets.

The center box was then uncovered by Robbie and Trinh to reveal a beautiful cake with our names on it, the date, and decorated with flowers. Cam asked, "Can we have the cake now?" and there was some polite laughter from our guests. I think everyone wants some cake now! Vo hushed her and Me gave her a little hug.

Auntie asked Fred's parents up to the altar. I poured tea into two small cups and Fred and I said some words of thanks for their blessing of the marriage. We presented the cups to Frank and Maggie as a sign of respect and bowed our heads slightly. They took a sip and returned the cups. Then my parents approached the altar and Fred poured two more cups of tea and repeated the steps.

Lastly, I poured one cup of tea and handed it to Fred who took a drink, then brought the cup to my lips and I drank also to show how we will share our lives together.

Fred's parents said a few words to accept me as their daughter and then my parents did the same. Ba and Me had practiced the words I wrote for them and Me sounded very good, but I know she was shy and nervous in front of so many native English speakers. I am proud of Me and Ba for trying.

As the conclusion to Auntie's part of the ceremony, she directed her next words to us: "Fred, Kim has traveled far and given up a wonderful life in her homeland to be with you. Give Kim the utmost respect as husband and friend. Show her the love, compassion and understanding she needs to be her best with you in the new country she has adopted."

"Kim, I know you to be a kind and gentle woman with good morals and who conducts herself with care at home and work. Please carry these traits into your new life as wife and friend. Be patient with Fred in all things and learn the ways to make your marriage happy and strong."

As Auntie completed her part, Abraham stepped in for the rest of the ceremony. As he did so, from each side of the stage came the two singers. It was not a recording after all!

We all stood together, Fred and I in the center, the singers on either side of us and finishing the song they had started as we had walked down the aisle. A song of first love, last love, together love, forever love. A perfect wedding song!

Abraham did the next part as I asked. Maybe it is silly, but I have seen so many Western romantic movies that I long ago learned by heart all the things they say during weddings like 'For richer or poorer, in sickness and in health" and "You may now kiss the bride." With this background, I had told Abraham that I wanted "all the trimmings" for this part of the ceremony. He said to me, "You got it!"

And did we get it! Me was softly crying as Abraham made a beautiful wedding speech. Before we exchanged rings, we did another Vietnamese tradition: Fred gave me diamond earrings that he had picked out himself.

This was the first time I had seen them and, as my mother helped put them on, people near the front gasped and murmured. The stones were larger than I expected and, for a brief moment, I thought they might not be real.

We exchanged rings while saying "I do" to all the vows and promises to love and cherish till death do us part. FINALLY Abraham said, "You may now kiss the bride!" Fred and I had practiced how to kiss in front of everyone…not too tiny like a peck, but not so much like the "get a room" kind of kiss either. I heard the children giggling as they played the music that says it is time to go back up the aisle and to the reception.

The Reception

We had planned to change into formal Western-style clothes for the reception but decided to keep the ao dais on as an unusual and special treat for our American guests.

Auntie Giang brought the singing couple to meet us alone, before we went out to greet our guests. They both have the same name: Hao Ho. The wife is more formally known as Ho Thi Hao and the husband is simply Ho Hao, in the same way Chris or Pat can be used for men or women.

Their stage name is H2Ho and they have many hit songs in the Vietnamese language. Their two English-language cross-over songs, "Love is Like a River" and "Two Hearts, One Soul", the song they sang during our ceremony, are both played regularly on pop-music stations.

They came to Riverton just to sing at my wedding. I cannot believe it! The Hao's blessed us with many good wishes for a strong marriage, as many healthy children as we want and a long life together. She wore many sparkly bracelets and rings and he has a large diamond on his right pinkie finger.

As we chatted with the Haos, Fred was called away by his father to attend to a problem of some kind. We spent a few more minutes talking before Fred came back and apologized for stepping away.

I will tell Fred the full story later of how this talented couple came to the US to start their lives over. Today, the Haos work regularly in casinos and nightclubs, have hit songs in three languages and are popular enough to have their own VidLive channel. They are a very inspirational couple to me and I told them so. Fred was gracious with his thanks to them for coming and making our wedding a very special one.

As our guests filed into the reception hall, we got in line to greet them: Fred, me, our parents, Bobby and Robbie, Thanh and Trinh and the twins while the Haos sang light pop songs on stage and the photo/videographers captured all the activities.

There are many people I do not know, and I have not met any of Fred's extended family before today, but he introduced a number of uncles, aunts and cousins who live mostly on the outskirts of Riverton and the surrounding counties.

Their manner of dress and attitudes appear different from that of Fred's parents, much like the way people of the provinces differ from the citizens of the city. I am sure I can't remember all their names and titles, but the same probably goes for Fred and my extended family.

Some people asked where Barney and Bunny are? We simply said that they were not able to make it and nothing else. Some guests said, "What a shame, and on your wedding day too!" and others had relieved looks on their faces.

After all the guests were in, we got some food and sat at the head table. The chapel's food was quite delicious and Auntie's caterer did a great job as well. I am still a little uncomfortable with handling knives and forks, but I did not drop anything in my lap as I do at home sometimes.

Bobby and Robbie started the toasts with the story they told me the first day I met them, about how Fred kept bringing in things to sell to his classmates until the teacher told him to stop. I was afraid they were going to ask me again, in front of all these people, if I was going to ask Fred to stop. Instead, it finished up like this:

"And he's STILL buying and selling things!" said Robbie,

"And no one tells him to stop!" said Bobby,

"Will *we* ever tell him to stop?" asked Robbie.

"Not on your life!" said Bobby "Because that is what makes Fred such a success at what he does."

"And when we met Kimmie…dear delightful Kimmie…we could see she will never tell him to stop doing what he does best or mess with his success."

"In fact," added Bobby, "rumor has it that Fred has gotten even better at what he does, now that he has someone who can match him in brains…"

"And surpass him in beauty!" concluded Robbie, creating laughter and applause from the guests.

I overheard a few people from both families complain of the dry bar, but it was our decision not to serve alcohol. As Fred told me while we were planning the reception, "If folks can't enjoy themselves at a family event without alcohol, then they have bigger issues than I can solve."

Along with the usual selection of soft drinks, juices, coffee and tea, Fred had had several cases of Fierce Five drinks brought in as something unique to serve. The cans are very colorful and I saw many of the younger guests drinking it, so it must be popular with the teens.

After we got some nourishment, the Haos slowed the tempo and lowered the volume as we visited each table with the videographer to meet our guests. They took the microphone, said some nice wishes to us and we thanked them for coming.

Caterers brought out the big green mint cake and we made a short speech to thank everyone for coming and supporting us. We cut the cake and fed each other a bit, another romantic thing I had wanted to do, but some people started chanting "Mash it! Mash it!"

I do not know what it means to "mash it" and Fred shook his head at the guests. He told me later that sometimes the couple will make a messy pushing of the wedding cake into each other's faces. Ick! I do not like the sound of this tradition and Fred said he would not do such a thing to me. It is not nice.

The Haos came back to the stage and announced that it is time for the newlywed's first dance as a couple. As both of us are inexperienced dancers, Frank and Maggie offered to teach us the waltz so we could look our best and be confident on this most special day. It is a very beautiful dance and easy to do. Frank and Maggie used to go dancing as teens and young adults but limit their dancing these days to special occasions at home.

After they showed us, Fred and I practiced at home and on the roof, even among the plants in the greenhouses! After we danced for a couple of minutes, and Fred had dipped me to the "ooh's and aah's of the guests, Fred took Me and I took Ba in my arms to continue the waltz. Ba was a very smooth dance partner.

"Ba, I did not know you could waltz."

"I'm sure there are many things you don't know about me, daughter," he said mysteriously. "When we were young and in love, we did many things that we don't do now…but we are still very much in love," and Ba squeezed my hand in a loving gesture. "We are very pleased that you have found love, also."

Then Frank and Maggie took my parents' place. Other guests joined us on the dance floor and soon we were all dancing. I was not expecting this, as I do not know any other kinds of dancing but, like we did on New Year's Eve, we moved our arms and legs freely to the music and had fun!

The Haos picked up the tempo with faster-paced pop music and everyone was having a good time. Cam and Tam came to us and we all danced together. Fred danced with all his new sisters, as well as doing a dance-off with Brother Vo…too funny! (Vo won…he is a very good dancer). Fred describes his own dancing style as "a scarecrow in the wind". I need to look up what "scarecrow" means.

I did not see Bobby and Robbie dance with each other but I did see them dancing with their mothers, our mothers, my sisters and other female guests. They looked quite comfortable on the dance floor and had switched hats to be funny, with the different color combinations.

I never saw the woman in the big hat and sunglasses at the reception. Maybe she was there but had taken off the glasses and hat. There were so many new faces for me at our party, it was hard to keep track of who was who, sometimes.

Such a special day! All my sisters are here, my parents are here, my American parents are very kind and sweet to me. It could not have been a better day.

Six o'clock was our time to finish with the reception room, so I gave the Haos my email address and big hugs for making this day so special. I made a heartfelt thank you to Auntie Giang for inviting them to perform for us.

The wife told me that I am very lucky to find a man like Fred. She said "I can see the love light in his eyes when he looks at you." I turned and found Fred gazing at me lovingly, just like she said.

Later, Fred told me that Auntie had hired the Haos through an agency, at great personal expense, as they are the most popular Vietnamese singers living in America. Along with doing the ceremony, this was her wedding gift to us. I am touched to the bottom of my soul by this gift…it was a very beautiful experience.

I felt bad for what I said to Fred earlier, about his friends possibly bringing bad luck to us, so I gave my warmest thanks to Bobby and Robbie for all their help with my family's visas, for being part of our special day and that they are my best American friends. Impulsively, I kissed both on the cheek. Robbie turned to Fred, saying, 'She's a keeper!" and Fred laughed, "Don't I know it!"

The last goodbyes of the day were to my parents and Thao. I said there are no words to describe what I feel to have them here today, the most special of days, and see my new life with Fred in his homeland. I feel like such a different person here and I am quickly growing comfortable with Riverton.

My mother told me, "All good things will come when you have a good man by your side."

Ba said, "She knows what she is talking about!" They smiled warmly at each other and kissed. It is rare to see my parents kiss, but this is a rare time for us too.

Auntie told us to go and have a good time tonight and she will pack our gifts up so we can get them later. Most of the family took the white limo back to the hotel while Fred and I took the other back to the garage.

Outside the main door, our smallest van was covered in ribbons, balloons, good wishes in two languages and cans tied to the back with strings. Fred said, "Get in…we have one more stop to make."

Wedding Night Love Nest

We left the garage and drove to the Royal Arms Hotel. It's not the same hotel as where my parents are staying, but still VERY fancy.

When we pulled up, Fred gave the doorman the truck keys saying, in a very serious tone, "Be careful with it. Last time I was here it got all messed up like this," waving his arm around at all the dents and scratches.

The valet just said, "Yes, sir." We are still in our fancy wedding clothes and driving a truck older than the valet. I don't think he got the joke.

"Fred, are we staying here tonight?"

His eyebrows shot up, "Would you prefer we stay at the garage for our wedding night?"

Actually, I thought we would, but this is much better! As we checked in, several people in the lobby looked at us with curious eyes.

Then I thought of something. "Fred, we did not bring any clothes for changing!" Fred assured me that he had already taken care of that detail.

A woman in uniform showed us to the room and held the door as Fred picked me up and carried me over the threshold like they do in the movies. SO romantic!

The bellhop showed us all the room features and next to the bed are two brand-new overnight bags. Fred gave her some tip money and she said, "Thank you, sir. And may I say, your ao dais are quite striking!" She surprised me…I did not think Americans knew what an ao dai is!

The Honeymoon Suite is very luxurious with a balcony that overlooks Riverside Central Park and its lake with the island. The heady smell of roses led me to the bridal chamber and before me are thousands of rose petals covering the enormous bed like a blanket.

Fred came up from behind and took me in his arms. "Was today everything you hoped for?"

"More than anything I can think of, with many happy surprises."

Then I remembered something. "Fred, you gave me a wedding gift. I feel bad that I did not get you one."

Fred cupped my face in his large hands, piercing blue eyes gazing into mine, and gave me a soft smile, "YOU are my wedding gift, Sweetheart."

Lois: Mama and Dad wore their Cay Dua necklaces from time to time, especially on anniversaries or other meaningful occasions. We have all met the Haos when we were children, but they were quite old by then and winding down their show-business career. I don't have strong memories of them, but Frankie said he never saw them without a smile. Maybe it was a conditioned part of their act, but I was always under the impression that they were just truly happy people who loved doing what they did, despite whatever obstacles life tossed in their path.

Kimmie: When Saigon fell in 1975, the Haos were very outspoken against the Communist government and they faced the difficult choice of escaping the country or spending time in re-education camps. They fled Vietnam with their children and as many valuables as they could carry to start a new life in

America.

Although they were a popular singing couple in Southeast Asia, the Haos were unknown in the West and very few Vietnamese people lived in America at that time. They swallowed their pride and did what they had to do, working at low level jobs while learning as much English as they could.

But they did not give up entertaining. They wrote new songs, rehearsed old routines, created new ones and performed wherever homesick Vietnamese were gathering, often just for tips and selling homemade records and tapes to feed their family and getting their name out to the public.

The Haos riches-to-rags-to-riches story, along with their unfailingly optimistic outlook on life, were among the reasons I was able to accept what I cannot change and change my way of thinking to bring peace and happiness to my heart. Fred certainly had that impact on me from our first times together, but the real-life examples I could find, like the Haos, boosted my efforts as well.

Trang Starbuckle: One of our parents favorite wedding stories was when they were driving from the garage to the hotel and got pulled over by a police officer. The truck was festooned with TP streamers, balloons, funny messages, and a trail of rattling cans. The policeman asked, "Do you know how noisy you were driving?"

(Dad) "No, I don't. How noisy was I driving?"

"You were 20 decibels over the limit. I am going to have to give you a ticket for disturbing the peace and another for not inviting me to your wedding."

Mom was upset about being pulled over on their wedding day and puzzled why the officer expected to be at their wedding? Dad introduced the officer to Mom as Dustin "Dusty" Almond, an old friend from high school who had recognized Dad's truck and pulled them over to give Dad a hard time. When they had made their good-byes, Dad had said "What a nut!"

Later, Mom saw a candy bar with almonds and pieced together Dad's "joke" about his friend "Almond" and "What a nut!"

The Morning After

Monday, August 20, 2000
Dear My Diary,

Oh, my…What a night! We were both a little nervous at first, but we took our time and Fred was gentle, sweet and kind with me, as I with him. We did not get much sleep after we understood what all the fuss is about!

The multi-colored array of rose petals that blanketed the top of the king-sized bed was soft and velvety, richly scented and it was all very romantic…at the beginning.

As things warmed up between us, the petals began sticking. First, it was a petal or two here and there, then little clumps that we gently blew off our lover, trying to add some sexiness to the foreplay. Soon, romantic turned to comical, and then distracting. Finally, we pulled the covers off, scattering petals everywhere, and spent the rest of our love-time either under, or on top of, the silky sheets of the marital bed.

We took breakfast in the main dining room, and it was quite a feast with chef-prepared omelets, waffles topped with warm fruit compotes, pastries, and a coffee bar like they have at Buzzy Brew, but without the long line.

Afterwards, we strolled to Central Park and walked around the lake, relaxing and reflecting on the last twenty-four hours. I hope the birth control pills are working...I have been taking them every day since Thao bought them for me in Vietnam.

As an added precaution, Fred wore a "raincoat" each time we did it…and I did not know a man can do it so many times! I thought we would only do it once.

At the park, we held hands as mist rose from the warm water, kissing the cool morning air like a lover. It is the perfect time to walk here, before the day heats up. There are people jogging around the lake and a young Asian man is setting up his food stand. The sign says, "Anh Hai the Sandwich Guy". I think he is the same one we saw at the July 4th celebration.

I told Fred how I had heard bits of conversations from my family to different guests and it reminded me of Fred's early amazement at how eager the people of Vietnam were to make business. Here is what I heard from Thanh: "A model? No, Kim is not a model, but I can make *you* look like a model. Here is a card for my salon… Trinh: "Cell phone sales and apparel factories are exploding across Southeast Asia right now. I can get you into some lucrative IPO's before they take off.… Ba: "My new son-in-law introduced us to Ubiddit a few months ago and since then, we have increased our revenues over three percent just from Ubiddit sales. Yes, true!"

Which reminds me, at the reception, I was asked several times by members of Fred's extended family or business associates if I were a model. I just said, "No, I help Fred with his business." This is not the first time I have been asked about being a model, but just a very few times here and never in Vietnam.

I am too tall to be a model, I think. Especially for Asian fashions. Who will buy clothes designed for someone my height when most of the women are so petite? It does not make sense to me, but I know to take these questions as a compliment, as they are asked in sincerity with no hint of meanness.

Arriving back at the hotel, I saw the woman who showed us to the room last night. I had a question for her but was too shy to ask. When I told Fred what I wanted to know, he said, "Just ask her, she will not bite!" So, I asked her how she knew about ao dais? She told me that her aunt-in-law is Thuy the tailor! She is married to a Vietnamese man and wore an ao dai at her wedding also. Mystery solved!

Lois: Even though Mama has been dressed by some of the most famous designers in the world, Thuy was Mama's tailor for a lot of her special outfits and business suits during her early years until Thuy retired. Mama and Dad were very loyal to those who did a good job for them and talked them up at every opportunity so they could get additional business.

Back in the room, we made pleasures and showered together one last time before checking out and going to Auntie's house in the early afternoon. When we arrived, my parents and sister were there, finishing lunch. They greeted us warmly and asked how we slept? I said we slept very well and a long time, but their knowing smiles indicated otherwise. They tried to feed us lunch, but we settled for tea and leftover desserts from the wedding.

As we packed the gifts into our van, I noticed there were fewer boxes than envelopes. I pointed this out to Fred who said it is becoming more common to give gift cards or money because, like it is with many couples, our home is already ours and furnished with dishes, linens, furniture, and such in the styles we like. It is easier to give a gift card or check and let the couple pick out exactly what they want.

When we got home, Fred cleared the big dining table and we sorted envelopes to one side and boxes to the other, then went through the gifts, boxes first. Fred wrote down who gave us what so we can personalize our thank-you cards back to the givers.

We got flower vases, a juicing machine, prettily patterned dishware, fancy table and bed linens, a bread making machine (Fred has one but it is old and doesn't work well), beautiful wine glasses and similar items.

The envelopes had beautiful cards with sweet things to say to us and inside is either a check or gift card from one or another of the better stores in Riverton. Several have pairs of gift cards for Tree Top Gals and The Paul Bunyan Shop.

Among the wrapped gifts, I found one from Bunny. She was not there, so I wonder how her gift came in without being mailed? It's a mobile art piece to hang from the ceiling with different beautiful birds that move delicately around in the gently moving air of the home. The card gave the usual good wishes and signed only as "Bernice Bartlett".

When I asked Fred how he thinks Bunny's gift got to the wedding, he looked uncomfortable, took a deep breath, and said, "She brought it herself. Bernice was at the wedding."

My mouth must have fallen open because he hurriedly continued, "I saw her car pull into the parking lot and I went outside to head off any problems. Bunny had told Barney she was going out of town to visit her family for the day. Now, that normally means visiting her mother in Norwood, but she didn't specify to Barney *who* exactly she was visiting or where out of town, because we are family and the wedding is being held out of town, so she didn't lie to him."

I was surprised to hear this and that Fred had kept this from me. "What if Barney had followed her here?" I asked.

"When she goes out of town like that, Barney takes advantage of his time alone to do whatever it is that she doesn't like him doing around her…God knows what that might be…so Bernice knew she was safe on that point."

"But why didn't she stay and come to the reception? Say hello to everyone?" But even as I said it, I knew the reason.

"After what happened, and promising us that she wouldn't come, Bernice was afraid you would be mad if you knew she was there. Also, she tried to disguise herself and not talk to anyone in case Barney found out about it later."

Then I had a flash, "Was she wearing really large sunglasses and a big hat?"

"And a black wig. Hiding in plain sight, yeah, that was her."

Sounds like Bunny had a good plan…and I'm glad she was able to witness our big day, even if I didn't know it then. I feel better knowing this now…and that Fred did not lie about what happened, as he could have done to protect her, in case I got angry about Bunny breaking her promise.

Thomas Stimson

Precious Family Time

Dear My Diary,

Between the wedding and leaving for the Honeymoon, we spent most of our time with my family. Tina flew back to New York late Sunday night with our own flight scheduled to see her again in a few days, but Ba and Me do not have that luxury.

I know my parents treasure the time they have with their children, especially those of us who have flown so far from the nest. But with everyone working, it is hard to go to Vietnam for more than a few days or a week, which is not worth all the travel time and expenses involved.

We took Ba, Me, Thao, and the twins on a drive to the state capital where we toured the government buildings and the Veterans Memorial Garden honoring those who died fighting in all the wars since statehood.

We found the names of Grant Starbuckle and Jackson Starbuckle under the "Vietnam Conflict" heading, took pictures and left two bouquets of flowers in their memory. Fred never knew them, of course, but that does not make them any less important to honor their lives.

Fred said his father comes to the memorial from time to time to leave flowers and "talk" to his brothers as well as at their gravesites in Riverton. I explained much of this to my family and taught the girls the importance of showing respect to the dead.

One morning, for fun, we showed Ba exactly what we do. He helped us pack the truck and went on our rounds to the resale stores, making deliveries and picking up unsold items as well as visiting the campus donation boxes which are slow during the summer.

I think Ba had fun doing this for the exercise and seeing all the different stores. He better understands at least part of what we do now. There are no auctions this week and Fred did not have ads out soliciting offers to buy collections, so Ba missed out on those parts of what we do. I also let Me go through the costume jewelry we have set aside for selling and gave her whatever pieces she fancied.

Every day, we took the family, including the twins and Auntie Giang, to Riverside Central Park for walking and talking and snacking on Vietnamese banh mi sandwiches from Anh Hai the Sandwich Guy. We time our visits to arrive as he opens and be the first customers.

We spoke to the owner, a young man in his early twenties, who explained that he sells sandwiches at the park during the warm months to earn money for college and help his family. His name is not really Anh Hai, but he uses that name to rhyme with "Sandwich Guy". We wished him good luck adding that his sandwiches remind us of home.

My parents asked me about the garage and the fact that the signage says "Starbuckle and Sons". They had understood from me that Frank had lost the business somehow and, if that was the case, how did Fred come to have the building?

I had to admit that I do not know the answer to that. I explained that when Fred was visiting us, he told me something really terrible happened financially that caused Frank and Maggie to lose their home, business and savings. Whatever happened is so painful that Fred has not and will not discuss it with me and I am not willing to bring up the subject, so as not to upset him.

I understand my parent's curiosity, for I was taken aback when I first arrived at the garage and saw the sign. I feel like he will tell me when the time is right, but I have been in America three months, and he never even hinted at why he lives in the family's old business building if his father had "lost" it.

Now I wonder if Fred was the cause of the financial hardship and, if he was, how did he get the building? And why are his parents on such good terms with Fred? I can't think about this right now…there must be a logical reason.

Cam and Tam love their grandparents and have many things to say and show them as we walk. They feed the ducks and play in the playground and frequently hug and hold hands with us. My parents admire how easily the girls change between English and Vietnamese with good accents in both languages.

And it was through the twins that I had learned why Fred was called away from me at the wedding reception:

The girls and I were playing on the monkey bars (I like the name 'monkey bars') and the older adults were talking among themselves on a nearby bench when I asked them how they liked riding in the limousine?

Tam: That was so cool!

Cam: Yeah, I felt like a movie star!

Tam: A hip-hop star! Bling City!

Cam: Glad we didn't have to walk back!

Tam: Yeah, that would have been a looong walk back!

Cam: Like, a hundred miles, or something.

Me: But we didn't walk back. Everyone rode back.

Cam: We almost had to walk home…

Tam: …in the hot sun!

Me: Why would we have to walk back?

Tam: Mommy's credit card was broken…

Cam: …again!

Me, puzzled: Mommy's credit card was broken?

Tam: Yeah, sometimes the credit card is broken, and she yells at Daddy that it's his fault.

Cam: The drivers said they had to be paid or they would leave without us…

Tam: …and they wouldn't take any more of Mommy's credit cards, so Daddy got Uncle Fred to fix it.

Me: Your daddy got Uncle Fred to fix the credit card? (I did not like where this was going).

Tam: Yeah, Daddy was afraid to ask Grandpa or Elder Auntie and Mommy said not to bother you, so he got Grandpa Frank to get Uncle Fred.

Cam (to Tam): Did you see how much money he pulled out of his pocket?

Tam: Oh my gosh! Aunt Kimmie, do you know how much money Uncle Fred has?

I know Fred carries large amounts of cash with him in case he finds a good deal and needs to make it happen right away. It's always been his habit, but I didn't know he was carrying his roll at the wedding.

Me: No…do you?

Both: Over one thousand dollars! (Said with giggles and loud enough to catch the attention of my parents and Auntie, who glanced over briefly, then went back to their gossiping)

Cam: Uncle Fred gave them hundred-dollar bills…

Tam: …ten of them! Then he gave the drivers another hundred dollars…

Cam: …each!

Me: What did the drivers say?

Cam: Oh, they were real happy after that. They called their boss on the phone and said everything was okay now…

Tam: …and Uncle Fred talked to the boss and apologized and thanked them for working with him.

I can imagine my sister getting upset and making things worse with the drivers, then Fred smoothing things over and calming everyone down, taking care of the bill and giving extra to the drivers who were in the middle of this. I saw it all in my head and it made perfect sense.

Me: That was very nice of Uncle Fred, don't you think?

Cam: Mommy and Daddy said "Sorry" to Uncle Fred and thanked him for helping us.

Tam: Then Mommy said (and they both clapped their hands over their mouths)

Me: What?

Both: We forgot…we weren't supposed to tell you what happened!

Cam: Mind eraser! Mind eraser! (both made motions around my head to 'erase' what they had just told me.)

Tam: Do you remember what we were just talking about?

Me, playing along: About how much fun the monkey bars are? Of course!

Auntie visited my parents frequently at the hotel or with us in the park, sometimes with grandchildren in tow. Once, when I was running errands, she took them to Tree Top Gals to see where she had been getting my clothes all these years and introducing them to Hilaire and the staff. I can only imagine what that was like!

But it was good for the older generation to reconnect after so long of not seeing each other. Auntie is talking about getting a seasonal second home in Vung Tau, the beach resort not far from Ho Chi Minh City, as she nears retirement. She does not want to have to deal with snow and ice and will either sell her businesses or let someone else manage them.

On Wednesday, we met Bunny for lunch so she could meet my family. She told them how I am a wonderful sister and has fun hanging out with me. My family was pleased to hear this but were not clear as to why she and Bernie did not come to the wedding.

I explained that Bernie and Fred do not get along so well and his brother is the kind of man who might cause embarrassing problems at the wedding. Ba said he had an uncle who would get drunk and start fights at family gatherings, so he understood, but we did not translate this to Bunny.

I told her we will hang the mobile in our living room area after we get back from New York, but I did not tell Bunny or my parents that I know she was at our wedding. I can reveal that to her later.

As we find the time, Fred and I are finishing the thank you cards to our friends and family and have completed packing for New York.

On Thursday morning, a large group of us took Me, Ba and Thao to the airport and made many wishes for a safe trip home and thanked them for coming and making a wonderful wedding surprise for me.

In return, they found it very enlightening to see my new home and meet my American parents and family members. This is their first time to America, and they promised it will not be their last.

I will miss them very much and made a special thank you to Fred from all of us to help my parents come to Riverton. He was humbled and said he was glad to do it. "After all, they're my parents too!"

Thomas Stimson

The City So Nice, They Named it Twice

Friday, August 18, 2000
Dear My Diary,

We left Riverton early this morning to get to New York before noon. The Dolly Madison Hotel had a car and driver waiting for us when we arrived. I asked Fred if he will be our driver for the whole week of our stay? Fred said no, just to and from the airport and maybe places close to the hotel, but mostly we will walk, take taxis or the subway.

Oh, I must tell you! The night before we left Riverton, Fred told me to make sure I bring my interstate passport. I am puzzled by the name, so I showed him my Vietnamese passport to see if the interstate passport was included. Fred looked carefully through the entire passport and got very upset.

"They forgot to include your interstate passport! You can't travel between states without one! I paid extra for it and everything!" Fred sighed and made a frowny face, "I guess we can't go to New York now."

I have never heard of such a thing as an interstate passport…and now we can't go to New York?! I was ready to cry as there are so many things I want to see and do.

Fred saw my crumbling face and quickly apologized for his poor attempt at a joke. He did not intend to make me upset and thought I knew there was no such thing as an interstate passport. Well, I do now! As punishment, I would not kiss Fred for two whole hours.

As we were checking in at the airport, the busy clerk asked for our destination. Fred, in a very good mood, said, "The city so nice, they named it twice!" The clerk looked at Fred blankly and repeated himself, "Your destination?"

"New York, New York. You know…the city so nice…" and he trailed off, having lost his audience of one. As we left the counter with our boarding passes, I hugged his arm and said, "I liked your New York joke. It's cute…like you."

Fred smiled, leaning over to peck my cheek he said, "Flattery will get you everywhere, my dear. Absolutely everywhere." I know he felt better, knowing that his joke had an appreciative audience.

The room at the Dolly Madison is not a room, it's a SUITE! Bobby and Robbie made sure we got a very fine room with a King bed, big bathroom with whirlpool and luxurious living room area. There is even a small kitchen, but Fred said most of our cooking will be done in the bedroom. I looked in the bedroom and saw no stove or microwave, then I understood his meaning and it made me blush!

A crystal vase of fresh flowers was placed on a table, along with a big fruit basket (I love fresh fruit!), bottles of sparkling juices and other treats. All from Bobby and Robbie and other friends. Different packages had personalized notes saying things like "Happy Honeymoon! Mom and Dad" and "What happens in New York, stays in New York! Auntie Ginger and family".

I did not tell Fred, but sisters have given me some very nice things to wear for our honeymoon trip…but not the kind I can wear on the street! I am shy to think about them, but they are beautiful. I tried them on at home and checked myself out in the mirror. I hope Fred likes them.

We unpacked a few things, then went out to explore the neighborhood. I wanted to go see some famous things right away, but Fred said it will be good to get familiar with this area first as we may

159

want to have breakfast or dinner before/after we go to the big things.

His explanation made sense and it is a very cute neighborhood with many little shops and food places to get meals or groceries. I think Fred does not plan to cook very much so we can see all that we can see.

We lunched at a café with outdoor tables to people-watch and the bill was almost $30 for not very much food. No wonder Tina warned us about this being a very expensive city!

I got worried and expressed to Fred that maybe we do not have enough money for all the things we want to do on this trip. In response, he took my chin between his thumb and forefinger and came close enough to kiss, "Kimmie, I have been living on a shoestring budget all my life. This is our honeymoon, and this is exactly the right time to spend some of what I have saved. YOU are worth spending money on." I feel better since he put it that way.

We kissed and Fred said in his work-truck voice, "Let's go spend some money!"

Central Park

Dear My Diary,

I had no idea that Central Park is right in the middle of very urban Manhattan. There is a zoo, big fields, and many paths to explore. People run and jog and I saw a big group doing Tai Chi on the grass. There were many kinds of people in the group, not just Asians.

I am still getting accustomed to seeing all the different races living in America. In Vietnam, to see someone not Asian is very unusual and they are always tourists or foreign workers, not citizens. Here, anybody can be a citizen. Maybe one day I will become a citizen of the United States too. I hope so.

There are performers everywhere in New York, and especially in Central Park. Musicians and singers, dancers, a man with a puppet and a group of actors putting on a show.

One magician had a small table and group of people watching him. He had three playing cards, all creased in the center to look like a small tent. One card is the Queen and the magician flipped the cards quickly around and people had to guess where the queen is. They paid money to do this. If someone finds the queen, they get more money back, but it did not happen often. The magician is very good. He asked us if we can find the queen. I wanted to try it, but Fred smiled and said thank you, but we will let someone else get lucky.

Later, Fred told me the man is not a magician, but a hustler and the card trick is a game called "Three Card Monty". The spectators are either gambling or are part of the card man's crew. Fred saw a TV show about how it works and if someone really picks the queen, the hustler can do quick things with his fingers to change the cards to a loser card just like a real magician. That is why Fred did not want to play. Very smart to know this!

We rented a paddle boat and went around the lake for a while. It's relaxing to be together like this and see many skyscrapers from the boat. It reminds me a little of the lake in Riverside Central Park, but Riverton has an island in their lake and Central Park does not.

After the paddleboat, we visited MOMA, the famous art museum. I tried to be interested in the art, but I do not know much about it, and I think Fred doesn't either. Some pieces looked interesting, but we left after a while when we both admitted to each other that it was boring. Sorry New York!

World Trade Center

Dear My Diary,

Today we visited the World Trade Center, two of the tallest buildings in the world and Tina works there! Asia International Bank, headquartered in Hong Kong, has their main US office here and Sister works with wealthy people and companies who want to invest in Asian businesses and banking opportunities.

Tina met us in the lobby, and we took a series of elevators to Floor 76 where she has an office with a view of the city. On her desk are two computers, several monitors, a laptop, blackberry phone and pictures of our family.

She introduced us to the director of the New York office…her big boss. He was friendly and asked how we liked the big apple so far?

I volunteered, "We have not had the big apple yet, but we did have big pretzels from a street vendor yesterday!"

Everyone laughed and Tina's boss said, "Your sister has a great sense of humor!" but I did not understand the joke. Later, Fred explained that "The Big Apple" is a nickname for New York City. I did not know this and feel foolish now, but no one made fun of me about it.

Now Tina's boss thinks I am the funny sister who makes clever jokes, so that is okay by me. At least, I do not look foolish to him, and it makes Tina look good too. I like that Tina simply introduces me as her sister and does not use Thanh's joke about being her "little" or "baby" sister to get a laugh. Tina is more mature than that.

Mom has visited New York many times since then and anytime someone asks her how she likes the Big Apple, she reaches for her joke, "I don't know. I have already had a big pretzel and a big chili dog but I have not tried the big apple yet!"

We had lunch at the company dining room on Floor 78. It's a buffet with no charge to employees and their guests. From the windows, you can see the East River, Brooklyn Bridge and much of the city. It made me a little dizzy to see everything from so far up.

Tina said they have a variety of popular foods from different parts of the world as you would find in the NY neighborhoods: Italian, Middle Eastern, Russian, Indian and others along with many Asian dishes. I tried some new and different things and most of it is very good.

After lunch, Tina had to go back to work. She works long hours every day and has all her meals at work to save money and be able to make as much commissions as possible. She gave us passes to the Observation Deck so we can see even more of the city from the very top floor.

"Fred, have you ever thought about moving to New York and working in a big building like this?" I asked, curious what he would say.

He looked puzzled and said, "No, why would I?"

"Well, don't you think it would be fun and exciting living and working in a big city like this?"

"I get enough excitement and fun being my own boss and getting out to do things when I want to. I don't need New York for that."

I said, "Tina makes a lot of money here," but Fred pointed out that she must work twelve hours or more each day and take all her meals here for free as it is hard to afford a place, even with roommates. "I'll take Riverton over New York any day," he concluded.

I have seen many pictures and movie scenes of the most famous statue in America, but I did not know the Statue of Liberty was so BIG! Many of us stood in line to go inside and walk up the narrow, winding staircase to the crown. We both had to keep our heads down to keep from bumping into parts of the statue's skeleton.

You must take a ferry boat to get there, and I got very emotional. So many people came to America by boat in the early days and their first impression of America was Lady Liberty, flaming torch in hand, welcoming everyone to their new country.

Now we fly in by airplane and can't have the same first impression as the immigrants of old. To see it up close helps me understand how it gave newcomers hope and the desire to be successful in America.

The first time we all went to the Statue of Liberty we were elementary school age and Mama and Dad told us the story about the statue and how it came to America from France to become the symbol of freedom recognized the world over. It really is impressively big. Almost every time we visited New York after that, one or the other of the folks would take us there, or at least view it from Manhattan for a little while and soak in its meaning. It might get boring to some to see the statue so often, but it gave Mama inspiration, and she always came away in a better mood and ready to take on a new project. I think most of us kids, and our kids, have had a similar "Liberty Moment" at some time or another.

Love Takes a Chance

August 22, 2000

Dear My Diary,

I am so disappointed…we could not go ice-skating! We spent much of today in Times Square exploring the many shops and interesting sights, including Rockefeller Center, but it is summer, and they only do ice-skating in the winter which makes sense now. I feel silly that Fred let me go on and on about wanting to ice-skate on the frozen rink while it is eighty-five degrees outside.

For years, we have watched the New Year's Celebrations from Times Square on television, so I know what it looks like in winter with tens of thousands of people packed together, but it so different in the summer, up close and in person. Lots of colorful characters and people in costumes are trying to get you to have a picture taken with them for tips or singing/playing instruments, selling things from tables or blankets on the ground…it is more like Saigon here than in Riverton!

And Rockefeller Center is not one building, but many buildings in a complex that includes TV studios, Radio City Music Hall and many shops and offices. Fred told me that we have tickets to watch a TV show being filmed as we sit in the audience.

We went back to the hotel, showered, and dressed up nice to go to the famous Russian Tea Room for dinner. SO expensive and the food was so different for both of us. It is one of New York's landmark restaurants and I am so glad we dressed up for it.

Everywhere I looked was lavish and eye-catching. The restaurant covers FOUR FLOORS! In Saigon, I have not been in a restaurant more than two floors and that is considered fancy. Lots of reds, golds and blues, huge mirrors and multi-level chandeliers, rich wood furniture. There was so much to take in.

They have a Pre-Theater menu of three courses: Appetizer, Entrée, and Dessert for a set price plus beverage. I had the caviar, pastry-wrapped salmon and chocolate mousse cake while Fred had the Borscht soup, Russian-style ravioli and vanilla cheesecake with fresh berries. We shared some of each other's dishes to get the full dining experience.

From the Russian Tea Room, we went to the Broadway show "Love Takes a Chance". I like to think the story is a little like me and Fred…in that we took a chance on a stranger to find happiness. The music came from a live orchestra and the production was dazzling. I sang along a little to the hit song "The Moment I Found You", but it has such a different sound and emotional impact to hear it live!

At the end of the show, we gave a standing ovation for such a wonderful performance. Then, the actors came out in small groups as we clapped and clapped and as more came to the stage, the larger their roles had been until the lead actors came out for the biggest applause of all.

We had backstage passes to meet the stars, get their autographs on our programs and make some small talk with them. I did not know what to say except "wonderful show", but Fred asked them if they will be "taking the show on the road" anytime soon?

Fred explained later that many shows travel to other cities and countries, performing for days or weeks so local people do not have to travel all the way to NYC or LA to see the show, the show comes to them!

Meeting Rock Rollins

August 24
Dear My Diary,

I got to be on TV yesterday…with a movie star! We went back to Rockefeller Center where they tape the popular late night talk show "Midnight Noise" even though it is early in the afternoon. Fred told me the host, Hugh Jarse, has been on TV for a long time but, since we do not have a working television, I do not know the show or the host.

There are a few hundred people in the audience, and we were sitting near the aisle and closer to the front. A crew member came out and thanked everyone for being there while explaining what time they will start, who will be tonight's guests and the studio rules. I recognized the name of Rock Rollins, but no one else. Then a comic came out to warm up the audience, but I didn't understand many of the jokes.

Pretty soon the host came out and thanked everyone for coming, announcing the guests again and with each name we clapped enthusiastically as instructed by the "applause" sign. Once he left the stage, the orchestra started playing the theme song, the announcer spoke his lines and then the host ran out on stage to bow and act like he just showed up.

Hugh spent a few minutes making jokes and some of them were about the American president and other people in government. The audience laughed but I did not understand the subject of the jokes. I glanced at Fred and he looked so-so amused.

Okay, now the good part: When Rock Rollins came out to visit the host, he was talking about a new movie he just made and that he learned a new skill – throwing knives.

The host questioned how many mistakes he made with the knives and his co-stars. Rock said, "Not many," and we laughed. Rock asked, "You want to see?"

Hugh said, "Sure!" so Rock asked the host to be the target and Hugh waved his hands, "Oh, no! I still have a show to finish!" Rock looked at us and called out, "How about a volunteer from the audience?"

Rock came down, approached our area and asked me to come up. I was surprised to be singled out but said "okay" and Rock escorted me to the stage. The crew brought out a target wall and some large knives on a table.

Hugh asked my name and I said "Kimmie." Then he asked, "Where are you from?"

I had to think about that…I was not sure whether to say 'Saigon' or 'Ho Chi Minh City' or 'Riverton' and I think I took too long to answer because the host prompted me with, "It's not a trick question," and the audience laughed, so I said "Riverton".

He asked me how I like New York so far and I said, "Very much."

"Are you nervous to have Rock throw knives at you?"

I repeated, with more emphasis, "Very much," and the audience laughed again.

Rock said, "Don't worry, I haven't hit anyone all week."

They brought me to the target and the host announced a commercial break. When the camera turned off, the show's director, Hugh and Rock explained that he will not really throw knives at me.

They showed how there are knife handles hidden inside the target that will pop out automatically through slits in the fabric. The people around me hid our actions from the audience and we talked very quietly.

The knives to be thrown will be tossed into a hole in the stage floor, away from the view of the cameras and audience. I feel better now. They just told me to smile and hold very still as though he were really throwing knives.

The host showed me tickets to several Broadway shows and asked me which one I want to see. There is one for a show Fred and I have talked about, a scary musical that sounds fun and so I picked this one. He said he will present it to me at the end of the act. Rock signed and personalized a photo of himself for me as a souvenir and a crew member held it until my part was finished.

When the show came back from break, the host and Rock made some more jokes about not hurting the tourist. It was very exciting as Rock fake-threw the knives and matching handles popped out around my legs, arms and next to my head. Then Rock asked me to put my arms over my head like a ballet dancer and the last knife popped in the center of the circle.

The audience applauded and Rock and I bowed to everyone. Hugh came over and announced that "for being such a good sport" he is giving me four tickets to see The Ghostly Ball and a crew member guided me back to Fred. Four tickets!

After the show was done filming, we went outside to call Tina. I told her to watch Midnight Noise tonight for a special surprise and she might want to record it, "And we have four tickets to The Ghostly Ball show tomorrow night. If you can, please come and bring a friend." She was surprised and will get off work early for this. She is on salary so can work what hours she wants, providing she makes her numbers.

I asked Fred why he thinks Rock picked me and he guessed it is because we were close to the front, and I am pretty. "If I were to pick someone from the audience, I would pick an attractive person near the front so it's easy to get to the stage." Make sense to me…and another sweet compliment!

Fred and I called some family members to watch or record the show tonight. We did not say why, but we would not call like this without good reason. We had dinner at an Irish restaurant that was very noisy with laughter and good cheer and was much less expensive than the Russian Tea Room.

I do not think New York has any American restaurants…everything is from somewhere else: Italian pizza, Indian tandoori chicken, Greek gyros, Russian caviar, German pretzels and Japanese sushi…the list goes on.

Well, ok, there ARE the fast-food chains with burgers, fried chicken, submarine sandwiches and so forth, but what I mean to say is that there are so many more options here than in Riverton.

After some more exploring and riding the subway trains up and down Manhattan, we went back to the hotel and had some sweets before going to bed and watching Midnight Noise.

NOW I know why I was picked…as the camera followed Rock into the audience, you can see Fred with his arm behind me and pointing his finger down to the top of my head, like saying "Pick her! Pick her!" Well, that mystery is solved!

It was so funny to see myself and think about how many millions of people will watch as I try to think of the answer to "Where are you from?" and Hugh Jarse saying, "It's not a trick question!" to make the audience laugh.

And I looked so serious and stiff when Rock threw the knives at me, with the drummer going

"Brrrrrr" each time before the knife is thrown, then the crash! of the cymbal when the knife "hit" the target. Finally, we took a bow and I bowed slightly to the host when gave me the tickets…my Asian side showing involuntarily.

After my part was over, Fred asked "What did you think to be on television like that?"

"I was a little nervous, but it was fun."

"So, who would you rather be with tonight? Me or Rock Rollins?"

"You, Fred, because you would not do a fake trick with me like Rock Rollins."

Fred winked and said, "Do you want to see a real trick?"

"What kind of trick?"

Then he went below the covers and…well, maybe that is enough trick talking for now…he he!

Frankie: You can still find clips of Mom's first television appearance on the Intercloud with a little searching.

For those who may not know, Rock Rollins was a top star from the 1990's into the 2010's pulling in $15-$20 million or more per picture for his action and comedy films.

Dear My Diary,

Fred told me not to tell anyone of the "rigged" trick and let people believe Rock was really throwing knives at me. I asked "Why shouldn't I tell them? Maybe they will think I could have gotten hurt!"

"Think about it, Kimmie. No one on the show told the audience it was a trick. You are in the United States just three months and already you are having knives thrown at you by a world-famous movie star on national television, and then being rewarded with tickets to a hot Broadway show!"

Fred looked deeply into my eyes with a look of pure pride on his face. "Do you know how cool that is, Kimmie? I mean, look at you…going from the quiet, shy Coconut Tree girl with no boyfriend to Cool Kimmie married to an American businessman and doing exciting, high-profile stuff in New York City."

I had not thought of it that way before. Fred continued, "Trust me. Leave yourself a little mystery on this one, Kimmie. You just joined the Cool Kids Club."

I do not know the Cool Kids Club, but I understand what Fred is doing for me. How did I get so lucky?

Very soon I started getting phone calls and text messages. Ohhhh! Everyone thought I was so brave to do have a dangerous stunt done to me. Soon after, someone uploaded the segment to VidLive and sent a link with a message to Ba and Me. My parents watched it over and over to see me on television through the computer. Fred said he bets that Thao will show the video to people at the office and then EVERYONE will know how cool I am!

Barry and The Ghostly Ball

Dear My Diary,

Yesterday Tina and her friend from work came to our hotel. We served chilled juice drinks and talked a little before leaving for the show. Barry is from England and speaks three Asian languages, but not Vietnamese. He knows a good place for sushi in Times Square near the theater we will be going to. It is a little hard to understand his accent, but it has a nice sound. I have always liked the British accent from TV and movies, but this is the first time I have heard it in real life, and it is so cool!

The restaurant was very colorful with much noise and activity which I am finding to be a common theme here. Barry and Tina drank Japanese rice wine served warm in small clay cups and I had some too. Barry spoke Japanese to the waitress, and I felt he was showing off for us, but he is a nice man. I asked him his last name and it sounded like "Pikah". I tried to pronounce it but not very well. Sister wrote it out to spell "Picker".

Fred looked over at the paper and said "Really?"

Barry responded, "Yeah, name I was born with. Brilliant ice breaker."

I did not understand until I put it together in my mind, "Barry Picker…Berry Picker". I had to hold my sides from laughing so much as Tina said, "She just got it!" and then they all laughed, but not at me. With me.

I shared with Barry and Tina about the Wood sisters, Hazel and Holly. They both liked my story. It felt good to share some fun thing in English and everyone liking it.

We told of our adventures so far in New York and Fred asked if it is worth going to the Coney Island amusement park? Barry said he went there the first month he was in NYC but the amusement parks there are mostly torn down or closed and there is not much to do. He recommended some areas of Brooklyn and said Staten Island was good for a day and told us about some places a short walk or bus ride from the Ferry terminal.

Fred told me the orange ferries we saw near the Statue of Liberty go to Staten Island and we can go tomorrow for a new adventure. Barry and Tina split the bill to pay for our dinner as a honeymoon present and for inviting them to the show.

I told sister Barry is a very nice man and she assured me that they only work together, and there is not "something more." I had not asked if there was "something more" so it was odd she felt a need to say so. Maybe others have asked her if Barry is a boyfriend.

It was another fun night, and we were just a few rows from the stage, considered to be among the most expensive seats, according to sister. This show is also a musical but with a much darker story than Love Takes a Chance. More drama and some intense and scary parts. I hung on to Fred's arm most of the time!

We took Tina and Barry to a nearby ice cream shop for dessert and discussing the show. After they left by subway back to their homes, Fred hired an old-fashioned horse carriage for a romantic ride. We cuddled under the blanket and warmed up with some nice kissing while listening to the blok, blok, blok of horses' hooves on the pavement until we reached the hotel.

Today we went to Staten Island and Barry was right…it is a nice relaxing place to go, not at all like Manhattan. We visited some public gardens, walked along a beach path called The Promenade and on to Fort Wadsworth which was used during George Washington's time. We had lunch in a cute cafe and visited the zoo, having fun looking and learning about the animals. Saigon has a zoo, but it is very different…run down with sad animals in iron cages and concrete floors. Here, they try to make the animal's house look like their real home in the wild.

Much of what we did today was free and there is the bonus of fresh sea air and trees. Yesterday morning and afternoon we went to the top of the Empire State Building, Greenwich Village, took a picture with the Wall Street bull, (it is very big!) and did a lot of walking around and visiting different places in mid and lower Manhattan.

I like riding the subway. You can hear them rushing and screeching below ground when walking over the metal grates on the sidewalk. Then you head downstairs, buy tokens and go through the gate to the trains.

The ride is bumpy and the cars shift constantly, like the way Fred showed me how he rode on the airplane by hanging on to a strap and bouncing around. He was joking about that, but it is as much like reliving a movie scene for me, much like seeing Saigon street-life was for Fred.

What I do not see so much from movies filmed in NYC are the many poor people sleeping on sidewalks, begging for money, or yelling nonsense to no one. I see it sometimes in Riverton, but not very much. Here, it is far more common and scares me sometimes.

When I told Fred, he said mostly they are harmless and besides, we are much bigger than they are, so if something happens, we can protect each other. Sometimes I forget that part about being tall and strong. I can protect myself or run fast if I have to. But no one bothers us, so I will try not to think about it and have fun while we are here.

Thomas Stimson

Fun in Brooklyn

Saturday August 26
Dear My Diary,

Tina met us at the Dolly Madison and we spent time chatting before leaving for our Brooklyn adventure. We have seen much of Manhattan and Staten Island and both are very different from each other. Brooklyn is mostly older neighborhoods that change their feel and style, depending on what kind of people are living there now and who had lived there in the past.

There are many pieces of public art, parks, interesting shops, and older homes. At one park, there was an outdoor party with Hispanic music and people selling different kinds of foods. We tried several things as we were hungry from walking around so much.

The people-watching was great until Fred tried to have me dance with him on the grass, but I was shy to do it with other people around. Fred encouraged me with, "This is New York life at its finest! No one cares how you dance!" so Tina got up and started dancing with Fred, then I joined and all three of us just got into the rhythm. People looked at us and nodded, some smoking strong-smelling cigarettes while others joined in the dancing. It was fun to be carefree and living in the moment.

We explored some clothing stores that carried things I have never seen in Riverton. More like costumes than clothes for the street, but to look at people in New York, I know many of them wear clothes like this too. These fashions would look strange and out of place in Riverton or Saigon, but I guess that is why New York is so well-known for being fun and hip while Riverton is…well…not.

When I realized that Tina and I are speaking nearly always in Vietnamese, I apologized to Fred for leaving him out of the conversations. We tried talking in English, but we also wanted to discuss personal things with each other. Fred shrugged his shoulders and said, "It's your language, go ahead!" He is easy-going like that. He probably does not want to hear a lot of girl-talk anyway.

Tina said she does not have a boyfriend or go on dates often. She is busy with work and is moving up well in the banking world, helping rich people with their investments. She said, "I will have time for men later," but she is thirty-five now and getting on the old side of having a baby, if she wants one.

I think maybe Tina will never marry, or if she does, will not have children. She has always been more independent and self-sufficient than the rest of us and not willing to compromise herself to follow cultural norms.

And I have no reason to criticize Tina about the way she lives as she is a good woman, hard-working and honest, like the rest of us. Thao is older, but she has Phung and I think they will come together soon. I see the way they look at each other, like "We should be as happy together as Fred and Kim".

We had dinner in a converted warehouse with an elevator out in the open near the end of the building. We watched the waiters roll carts of food from the open-air kitchen to an elevator, then up to one of the three dining levels where tables are spaced along the railing overlooking the main floor. No private booths here! The elevator and building appear to be most of a hundred years old, according to Fred's estimate.

The bartender's big moustache curled up at the ends and he spoke in a deep, rumbling voice, saying things like, "What'll ya have?" and "Straight up or on the rocks?" when Fred ordered a lemonade and cranberry drink. He is big and scary-looking, but sort of like a teddy bear, too. A big scary teddy bear.

Everything is fun to watch and the food is very good too. I had chicken covered with crushed nuts, baked nice and brown with creamy noodles and a salad. Fred's steak was topped with mushrooms and radish sauce and Tina had steamed fish stuffed with herbs and rice. We all shared some of our dishes with each other to try the new tastes.

Tomorrow, we leave for Riverton and I will miss New York and my big sister. We spoke of many things, but her most impactful statement was when she said that I look very happy in my new life, not like before.

"Not like before…" I did not realize I looked so unhappy with my life before Fred, but as I think about it, I should say that I KNEW I was not happy, but did not realize HOW unhappy until I met Fred, came to America and found a new kind of life.

I do not mean to say I am not happy with my parents or sisters…I have a wonderful family and love them very much. I even like our neighborhood because everyone knows me and sees me so much that my Cay Dua self was a kind of normal abnormality. But, away from familiar people and places, I am much stared at and made fun of or spoken rudely to.

In America, I am still taller than almost any woman, and most men, but not nearly so much. And people here are polite and do not feel a need to make clever or rude comments to me about my height. If only I could have this life in my own country, I think it would be most perfect for me.

I told sister that I am very happy with Fred and his friends and most of his family. "The work we do is not boring, always different, and I feel good to have the physical and mental exercise it all requires. And if I am bored or have nothing to do," I said with a wink to Tina, "I just look at Fred and I stop being bored."

Tina giggled at this as I know she thinks Fred is a good-looking man too. I recently learned the phrase "Eye Candy" and I think Fred fits this term very well. I translated it to sister and she agrees that it is a fitting term.

Fred asked what we are giggling about, sounding like teenagers. I said "Boys!" Fred smiled and shook his head, then we switched to English for his benefit and started making our good-byes.

Fred thanked sister for showing us around Brooklyn today and for everything we experienced together this week. She said it was nothing and was glad we came to see where she lives, works and has fun.

We never had a close relationship in the past due to our difference in ages. She moved to America when I was eleven or twelve years old and she did not return many times after that. Now, as adults, we have had some very good opportunities to converse over these last three months. With each visit and chat, I am finding myself growing closer to her as never before.

Later, when I explained to Fred these feelings I have for Tina, he said all my family have many good points and he likes Tina very much too. He has not had time to speak to sister as much as I have, but he can see and hear her attitude and tones of voice when she is not speaking English. I am glad Fred is understanding and does not appear annoyed or mad when we talk in our mother tongue. He is always sweet to me and my family.

Lois: Through the diary, it is interesting to watch Mama's relationships with her American sisters grow and develop as they had both been gone many years from Vietnam but for infrequent visits home. Each sister has a distinctively different personality, but despite their differences, they managed to become closer as time went on.

August 30, 2000
Dear My Diary,

We are just back from New York, and I can't think of anything else except the wedding, the honeymoon and all the things we did. But Fred? He is always two steps ahead for both of us.

Today we went to the Federal Building downtown with our officially signed marriage license, my passport, visa, and other necessary paperwork to sign up for my US Social Security Card. Once I get my Social, as he calls it, then we can apply for a green card.

I remember how Thanh and Vo got married in Vietnam, then she moved to Riverton and had a small legal wedding for the official US documentation. Vo was already a citizen, and she went through the same process as I am going through now. It took her five years to become naturalized so by being born in America, the twins were citizens before their mother!

Bernie's Big Case

Dear My Diary,

Today Bunny treated me to lunch at a Greek restaurant near her home. She couldn't wait to hear about our trip to New York, then to tell me about the big case Bernie is working on right now.

As I understand the type of law Fred's brother practices, people who have been hurt or wronged hire Bernie to file lawsuits and get money from those responsible. Bernie makes his money by taking a percentage of what the client gets. Fred calls Bernie an "ambulance chaser".

The current case is about a woman who, while opening a can of cat food, cut her thumb on the sharp edge of the lid. She did not go to the doctor until the thumb became so badly infected, she almost died, and it had to be removed.

She went to Bernie who decided to sue the cat food company, the can manufacturer, the cat food distributor, the store that sold the cat food, the doctor who amputated her thumb and the hospital where the surgery was performed. So many people to sue over one thumb!

Bunny said this is Bernie's usual way of doing business. She calls it the "shotgun approach" because the more people he sues, the more likely he will get some settlement money for the woman and the higher the chance he will get paid.

Bunny said this is a stupid case, Bernie won't win and he is wasting everyone's time because the woman could have easily gone to the free clinic or county hospital, gotten antibiotics and stitches and not have to suffer so much. She was careless to cut her thumb and careless to wait to go to the hospital. I think Bunny is right.

I learned more about Bunny during lunch, like her parents are divorced, she has no sisters and two much older half-brothers whom she is not close to and there was more, but it sounds complicated.

In her youth, she won local beauty contests that got her some scholarship money, but she spent more time partying than studying and failed out of college. So different from me…

She was hired as a secretary in Bernie's one-man law firm "based more on my skirt length than my skills", she said wryly, placing her fingertips half-way up her thigh to demonstrate. Bunny took the job because she thought Bernie ambitious, and he was in better shape back then…not fat and balding like he is now.

He was also loud and braggy, which Bunny thought was an expected attribute for a lawyer. Bernie told her he had quit one of the larger local law firms to start his own practice and "keep the profits for himself" but she now believes he did not quit but was fired for some reason, based on things she has heard from others.

This was around the time Frank and Maggie lost their home and business because they invested so much in Bio-Oil companies and lost everything when the bubble collapsed. Bernie told Bunny that his parents blame him for everything, but it was not his fault.

Nowadays, Bernie does most of the work himself and doesn't need a secretary so much. But when Bernie gets money from a job, he goes a little crazy and spends it very quickly and when business is slow, he complains about having no money. Bunny said no matter if business is busy or slow, she always has trouble getting the bills paid on time.

Bunny likes it better when Bernie is busy like he is now, and leaves her alone because when he is unhappy, Bernie is a jerk and blames others for his troubles.

I told Bunny about my family in the US and Vietnam and how we are close to each other in the heart if not always in distance. I explained that Fred is, in some ways, like my father in how he works hard at an honest living, every day is different, and the bills always get paid.

Bunny said I am very lucky to have such a good and close relationship with my family…not like hers who are scattered around and often at odds with each other.

Bunny confided to me that Barney is careless with his money as well as his mouth. Sometimes he does scary things and because Barney won't let her work other jobs, Bunny has been secretly saving money in case something bad happens to her husband. She calls it her "crash stash".

When Bernie has money and is feeling generous, he buys Bunny expensive gifts and clothes, which she then returns to the store for a cash refund or sells it and puts the money someplace secret. She also saves as much of her allowance and grocery money as she can by buying most of her things at discount retailers.

She said sometimes Fred gives her cleaning supplies, small appliances and other necessities from his business, so she spends less allowance money…he knows about the crash stash too.

Bunny said, "I feel like I can trust you and I don't have a real sister to confide in. Please don't say anything to Bernie, okay?" That's a promise I can easily keep!

As we left the restaurant, I thought about her Crash Stash and asked Bunny if I should protect myself from Fred with a crash stash of my own?

"Honey, Fred and Bernie may be brothers, but they are completely different people. I have never heard a bad word against Fred and if anyone has, it was because Fred was smart enough to say 'no' to them. Bernie doesn't have a nice word to say about anyone unless he wants something from them."

"But should I protect myself with some saved money?" I persisted.

"Kimmie, Fred will never let you down. I see the way he looks at you…believe me, he is in love!"

Then Bunny's smile turned wistful. "Can I tell you something? Sister to sister?" I said yes, of course. "Please don't take this the wrong way…but sometimes I wished I had gotten Fred instead of Bernie." Then her face got red, "I'm sorry. I shouldn't have said that. Now, you're going to hate me."

"It's okay," I told her. "I am not offended."

I did not tell Bunny that before I left Vietnam, my parents had given me my own "crash stash" money in case something went wrong with our marriage. I have not told Fred about these secret funds either and I hope I never need to use it!

Fierce 5

September 7
Dear My Diary,

Normally, Fred is such a nice, normal, average man of above-average stature…and then, like tonight, he surprises me with a completely different side of himself. Let me explain:

Fred often keeps Fierce 5 drinks in the refrigerator and takes a few with us if we are expected to be out for much of the day. He calls it an "energy drink", but it is too sweet for my taste. My preference is water, cold tea and fruit juices. Boring, but natural.

It's called Fierce 5 because, as it states on the cans, the drink contains "a blend of five special ingredients for a smooth, long-lasting energy high". It is a popular product for the younger crowd and Fred says he does not need it, nor would he buy it for himself, but he gets two free cases every month as an investor. Fred manages to hand out a few at auctions or when he meets with clients that he wants to do business with…kind of a marketing ploy while getting rid of excess product.

Fred had let me know we were going out to "a little business reception" and asked me to wear the red sleeveless Asian-style dress I have (the hem is mid-thigh and almost too short for my personal taste) along with heavier-than-normal make-up. When I asked him what kind of business reception it was, he either did not understand my question, or ignored it.

I have realized that Fred often does not understand either my grammar, accent, or both and will ignore the question or remark if I don't press him on it. I did not press him on it this time.

The reception was held in a downtown art gallery featuring out-sized pictures of women in highly stylized make-up, some with animalistic features. Very avant-garde.

But the art on the walls had nothing on the crowd of similarly styled, and very tall, women who attended the party…a forest of cay dua!

As we entered, the women looked me up and down, some very cool and distant as though sizing me up for a challenge while others smiled and said "hello".

They were of a range of ethnicities I have not yet experienced in Riverton: one was as pale as snow with a cloud of white hair and red eyes, another was the color of midnight and bald as an egg, along with more than a dozen others of every shade in-between. There were plenty of eye-popping outfits and heavy make-up as they confidently strutted about.

Not many men were present, but there was one who stood out from the rest. Short, stocky, and looking very arty in his colorfully framed eyeglasses and a beret cocked to one side, he was about sixty and clearly the center of attention.

In my three months here, I have rarely seen anyone so tall as myself, but these women are all about my height, give or take a few centimeters and were not the slender, anorexic kind of models I frequently see in fashion magazines, but muscular with well-defined legs, arms, busts and butts, not unlike my own.

Some stalked about, purring and making cat-like hisses, clawing the air in my direction with long painted nails, then smiled disarmingly to show it was just for play. It dawned on me that out of all these extraordinarily tall, beautiful women, I am the only Asian.

I smiled politely and spoke through my teeth to the stranger standing next to me, "Fred, what kind of party is this again?" I don't know what Fred was thinking to bring me here, but it felt like something out of a European art-house movie.

"You will see…" Fred answered softly in a sing-song voice, snagging an hor d'oeuvre for each of us from a passing waiter, "…you will see. Just go along with whatever is being said."

With those mysterious words, Fred took me to the group at the center of the studio to meet the gallery owner and "Zander". Zander is actually a woman, as I can see now by her ample chest, but dressed like Truman Capote.

Fred introduced me to Zander and explained to her that I came from Vietnam earlier this year. Zander, looking me up and down, asked, "You two are a couple? Fascinating!" She said the last word in a husky, drawn-out way. "What kind of work do we do?"

When I explained that I helped Fred with his business, she said, "I understand he does some very physical work," in a manner that was neither question nor comment. "That's why you are so fit," she concluded.

Zander asked me if I had done any modeling work before? I answered I have not and she nodded thoughtfully.

Fred took Zander's moment of reflection to explain how she is a very famous fashion photographer and will be working with Fierce 5 and a local advertising agency to create a marketing campaign that portrays the "fierceness" of Fierce 5. "These are samples of Zander's work," he said, spreading his hand out to the large portraits of animal-women.

That's when I understood why we are here.

Fred turned to Zander, "If you are looking for someone who is really fierce, you should have seen Kimmie with Rock Rollins!"

Zander's penciled eyebrows popped up as if she had just spotted a mouse. "Really! Rock Rollins?"

"Yes," Fred continued, "did you see him on Midnight Noise last month? Throwing knives at a tall woman?" Zander shook her head but some of the models near us came over to say "Yes! I saw that! Oh, that WAS you! I remember! Cool!"

"Do you know Rock Rollins?" Zander asked me directly. Her interest in me had been mediocre at best until Fred dropped a major name and now the room was beginning to buzz.

"Yes," I admitted, trying to sound confident, "Rock Rollins used me on national television." That brought a mixture of gasps and uncertain laughter.

Fred hurriedly followed up with, "Rock picked Kimmie out of the audience to be used as a human target for a knife-throwing stunt. Tell them what you got for doing it, Kim."

"Oh, yes! An autographed picture and tickets to The Ghostly Ball. He was very nice and funny with me, just like he is in the movies."

Zander pushed her lips together, squinted at me and said "Hmmmm!" She made an angry face and moved her hand in kitty-claw fashion, hissing like a cat as I had seen other models do, then had me do the same.

I thought it was silly but, with Fred's words in my ear, I did it anyway…several times with Zander repeating, "fierce!" and "fiercer!" and the other models around us were doing it too, as an encouragement.

Soon everyone was applauding my effort and Zander called several of the women to stand next to me, all of us doing the kitty-claw / hiss together. She kept rearranging different people in and out of the line-up, but always with me in the middle.

As Zander studied me some more. Fred asked, "What do you think? Is she the missing piece of the puzzle?"

"Hmm, she's not a pro…" Then to me, "Do you have any ink?"

I was surprised she would ask such a question, so I started digging in my purse.

"What are you looking for?" Fred asked.

"A pen. Zander is asking for some ink?"

"She means ink pictures on your skin, Sweetheart. Tattoos." Zander is smiling, but kindly. Fred answered for me, "No tats, no piercings and no sizable scars or birthmarks."

Zander smiled, "How refreshing in this day and age! Kim, do you like to dress up? Make yourself gorgeous?"

All this attention, along with Fred's word "gorgeous" got me shy and I involuntarily said, "Oh, no. I am not gorgeous."

Fred made a tiny head-shake of disapproval as Zander commanded, "Well, let me be the judge of that! Mitzi and Gaynor here are my make-up artists. Let them create a Fierce You that will make your Fred howl with delight. You would like that, wouldn't you?"

I glanced at Fred who gave me a nod and a wink. I smiled and said, "Yes, that does sound fun!" not really feeling like it will be fun. I have to trust Fred on this. I can always kill him later.

Zander led me to a corner where a mini-studio was set up to take a variety of pictures in my "before" state. Quickly and efficiently, Zander took head shots, half and whole body with relaxed and "fierce" poses.

From there, I went into the back where they had a full make up station. While the artists were making me up, I could hear Zander ordering the other models into various groupings as she had done with me, calling out, "Fiercer! Make the kings of the jungle fear you!" as a chorus of roars and hisses followed suit along with the clicks and flashes of the camera.

It did not take long for Mitzi and Gaynor to bring me back to Zander. My hair was brushed out and puffed up with hair spray, eyes more cat-like, lips fuller and cheek bones shadowed to look higher.

It's not as much make-up as I got on my wedding day, but the effect was much more startling when I saw myself in a mirror. When I joined the others, Fred's eyes were hungry with desire as Zander had me turn around and study my face from different angles.

She had me do the face and hand-motions again. "Fiercer!" she would say, clawing the air and I, returning the gestures in kind, hissed hotly as the other models called out encouragement and Zander took a new set of photos.

Finally, Zander said to me, "I know you're not a pro, but you do have certain qualities I am looking for." Then to Fred, "But no promises," as Fred nodded in understanding.

Fred explained later that the ad campaign will use five powerful-looking women of different ethnicities to sell F5 mostly to males in their teens and twenties. The agency has already selected a number of models to audition, some of whom were here tonight, but could not find an Asian to fit the team's physical requirements.

They were about to give up when Fred volunteered me at an investor's meeting. The ad agency, Fierce 5 board and Zander will make their final picks soon and then prepare the employment contracts and a shooting schedule.

I asked Fred what Zander meant by "no promises". Fred said it meant that they were not going to play favorites just because I am an investor. "If you get the job, it's because you are the right fit, not because of who I am."

We stuck around for a while to chat with some of the models and their partners as Zander interviewed and photographed others, making them hiss and kitty-claw the air. The women have stopped hissing and are acting normal now. I think they were trying out for their parts when we came in. We had some food and found the wine glasses were filled with Fierce 5, not alcohol. Makes sense now.

After we left the gallery, Fred asked, "So, what did you think about the evening?"

I had gone along with Fred at the gallery, walking into the oddest party I have ever been to and its unexpected twists and turns. I would much preferred this had been handled differently, for my sake, so I let Fred know my displeasure.

"About how you surprised me like that? Why didn't you tell me about this ahead of time? I could have been more prepared."

"I didn't think you would go, or even agree to check it out, if I had told you up front," Fred said, then adding, "I know how you are."

I turned on him, "Oh, you do, do you? And how am I? Am I so bad that you can't let me know I will be interviewed for a job I have never done before? A modeling job?!"

Fred looked uncomfortable at my pointed words and growing anger. Now that we are away from the gallery and the other women, another thought came to me. "Are we so poor that I have to get other work to pay the bills?" Fred was silent, stunned and, by his not answering, I suspected I was right. "Are we? Tell me!"

We had stopped next to the van. The dull, ugly, hail-dented work van we use to get around in. Fred's Proof of Poverty. He began, "First of all, we make enough to pay the bills. I did not bring you here tonight because we need extra money. I brought you here because you are beautiful, and they were looking for an Asian face to round out the Fierce 5 line-up. I thought you would make a good fit. That's all."

I was not convinced. "Why did you say you know how I am? What does that mean?"

"When I said, 'I know how you are', I only meant it as 'I know how shy you are about your looks. About not accepting what everyone else can see'. So, I brought you along to let Zander have a look and see for herself. And she is impressed." Fred dropped his head, "That's all I meant. And I'm sorry I didn't tell you what tonight was all about. I just figured if I told you, you would not have gone."

"You're right," I admitted. "I probably would not have wanted to go."

"If you're selected, the work will be easy," Fred continued, on a new line of selling me. "Photography and video posing a few times a year for the ad campaigns, maybe some appearances for the investors and press. The outfits won't be very revealing, and if you don't want to do it, you don't have to," Fred promised. "But it will be a way to make some extra money for yourself or family with very little effort. And hey! It might be fun!"

Grudgingly, I said, "I will think about it."

"Kimmie?"

"Yes?"

"Cool Kids Club!"

Lois: What surreal surroundings for Mama to be in! Dad was good about bringing someone into a situation without telling them ahead of time, and letting the news or event be a surprise. Like the F5 tryouts or secretly bringing family from Vietnam for the wedding.

Kimmie: Walking into that gallery and being amongst a group of tall, lithe, athletic women was very intimidating and strangely dream-like. Especially as many were heavily made up and hissing at each other like cats. Part of me wanted to leave as it was so weird and part of me was too fascinated by what was going on to consider leaving. I'm glad I stayed.

My New Idea

September 20
Dear My Diary,

Yesterday, my Conditional Green Card came in the mail…yay! I put the new card in my wallet next to my Social Security card, driving license and my heart (a picture of Fred).

I feel that I am becoming more of a citizen and less an immigrant in this country, except for my accent…that will never change. Sometimes Fred has a hard time understanding me or Thanh's speaking style, but he always blames it on his "bad ears" or some other nonsensical reason. I know this because he rarely has problems understanding other people. It's okay. I know I sound funny, and my pronunciation is not great…but I practice and try to do better.

On the second floor of the garage is an area with lumber and other building supplies. When I asked about it, Fred explained that it all came from a deal Fred made to buy the inventory of a local hardware company that was going out of business. Some things he sells to RPR at below-market prices, some he uses for projects around here like shelving, sorting tables and the greenhouses. What he could not use was sold off through Ubiddit, FreePost and the flea markets.

Fred owns some houses he bought very cheap over the years, fixing them up and either selling them for a quick profit or having RPR rent the property for long-term equity growth. He has not purchased any houses in a while because prices have shot up in recent years and it is hard to find a bargain anymore, so he does other kinds of buying and selling.

Looking at the lumber, I see one kind that gives me an idea for the resale stores. Fred likes to say that I am smart and clever, but I think he only says that to flirt with me or make me feel better about myself. However, I feel like one area of the resale stores could use some help and Fred has just the thing to make it work.

Frankie: Mom had seen how lots of smaller items at the resale stores were tossed together in boxes or on shelves and many would come back to the garage to be donated if they did not sell after a time.

Dad had many sheets of pegboard that he could not sell and were taking up space in the garage. Mom's idea was to offer up the pegboards with display hangers and different sizes of clear plastic bags to the resale stores, have them installed on a wall and fill the bags with related items (toys, sewing notions, paperback books, holiday decorations and the like) and charge a low flat price per bag.

Dad liked the idea and the next time they went into the stores, he would say "Kimmie has a great idea to help you increase sales…I'll let her tell you more about it." The first time he did that, it put her on the spot. Mom gamely made her pitch, but she was not happy about it.

After we left the first store, I asked Fred why he did that to me? Making me do the presentation without warning. In turn, he asked how I liked making the presentation?

I was nervous as English is not my main language, but when I saw the interest forming in the owner's eyes, I felt confident enough to keep going.

"That's why I had you do it, Kimmie." Fred explained. "It is your idea and it's best if you make the presentation. When you show someone that you believe in the idea, how easy it is to set it up and how it can increase sales and profit, it is hard for them to say "no". Besides, it won't cost them anything but some wall space."

He reminded me that they are buying most of our small goods for a dollar a pound, and if they can sell one pound of bagged products for two or five or ten dollars, then it is a good way to increase profits to the store and then to our pockets.

I had been wondering why Fred would not charge the store owners for the peg boards and hangers, even at a below-cost price. Now the answer came to me and I asked, "Are you a part-owner of the resale stores too?"

Fred made a quiet chuckle, then nodded. "You are getting the idea, Sweetheart. You are getting the idea."

Then, another light flashed in my head, "And this is how your mother got her job?"

"You are on fire, Kimmie! Popping like popcorn!"

Frankie: Another thing about Dad is how he would give credit to others, even if he had a hand in the idea or execution of the plan. It made the other person feel good and didn't cost him anything. We all benefitted from Dad's cheerleading of our efforts and if we failed at something, he would put a positive spin on the lesson learned and that we would do better next time.

So, now I have uncovered another layer of the onion I have married. No wonder he spends so much energy among a few resale shops, selling and buying back unwanted items to resell again at another. He has a vested interest in all of them!

Fred kissed me and said, "See? I said you are a very smart woman and you proved me right, yet again." I am happy now that Fred made me speak to the owners and proud that I did a good job selling my idea and figuring out Fred's connection to the resale stores.

But what I don't understand is why he does not tell me everything up front. I mean, how long was he going to wait until he told me about his role in the stores…or why he is so bitter about his brother…or how he got back the Starbuckle garage when his parents lost ownership of it…or if my sister repaid him for the limo, which I hesitate to ask him about?

As I think about all these things, and more, the biggest question that has crept into my mind is: What is Fred not telling me that, when I find out, will make me regret marrying him?

Special Delivery

October 2, 2000
Dear My Diary,

What a surprise today! A big truck came to the garage to deliver a shipping container of goods from Vietnam. At first, we were confused as we had not ordered anything, but the driver's paperwork showed it coming from Pham Lo International Trading Company and then we understood…sort of.

As the driver jockeyed the container into our fenced area between a junked truck and a recycling dumpster, I opened the envelope to find a key for the container and a letter from Ba saying all the contents are to be sold as we see fit. Total cost of the goods is about $50,000 USD and we are to keep half the profits once the initial investment is recovered.

I was not expecting this, and no one even hinted that a delivery was on its way. Fred was laughing at the whole scene, saying, "I guess Ba doesn't think we have enough to do!"

We unlocked the container and faced a wall of tightly packed boxes. That's my Ba's handiwork…no wasted space here!

We locked the gate and pulled out several boxes to see what we have: Carved stone horses frozen in mid-gallop, colorful wooden puzzle-lock jewelry boxes and old-style Asian jackets for small children with machine-embroidered embellishments. Fred held one up and commented, "Good luck selling this! T-shirts with cartoon characters would have been a better choice."

Other boxes have colorful ceramic dinner sets with designs like Koi fish, lotus flowers and butterflies. There are toys, kitchen gadgets, electronics…just a big mix of things. Some of them I recognize from the craft factories in Dalat, Hue and other provinces while some come from other countries.

I was appalled at what my family had done without checking with us first. "Fred, what are we going to do with all this? I am so sorry, but I did not know this was coming!"

Fred said he is not surprised. "I think we put the idea into their heads by showing them how to sell on Ubiddit. Then, when they came for the wedding and saw how much space we have here…yeah, we kind of invited this. But it would have been nice to be warned ahead of time."

After we pulled out about thirty boxes and inspected their contents, Fred and I started formulating a plan on how to sell it all. Fred reminded me that this is the perfect time as Christmas is coming and people are looking for interesting things to buy as gifts. "Honestly, Kim, this is more of a blessing than a curse because right now, except for the holiday decorations I have been stockpiling, I don't have a lot of worthwhile inventory…and all this stuff is brand new!"

Fred sucked his teeth, as he often does when he is thinking through a problem. "We can blow out most of the decorations at the flea market this weekend, wholesale some of this to our resale stores…we can do a last-minute sign-up with local Christmas bazaars and there's a big one at the coliseum the weekend before Thanksgiving. That will give us some good retail exposure as well…" and he rattled on, developing a plan straight out of his head.

Fred said we have enough things here and don't need to buy any lockers until after Christmas. For now, we will concentrate on the contents of the container.

Dear My Diary,

I called my parents to let them know we got their shipment box and what a surprise it gave us. Seems that Ba forgot to email us about the shipment and Me forgot to remind him…how are they running an international business if they can't remember to call their daughter about a single shipment? Honestly!

Ba followed up with an emailed spreadsheet of the container's inventory including prices in VN Dong. I will add a column next to the VN prices and recalculate to US Dollars so we have purchase prices we can use to determine selling prices and profit margins.

Tonight, we had Cam and Tam at our home while their parents had their date night at the casino. We showed them some of what we got from Vietnam to sell and let them figure out how to open the puzzle boxes. I let them help make dinner by opening peapods into a pan for boiling and they sang songs to me that they learned in school. It is so cute to hear them sing! I look at them and wonder how long before we will have our own children singing for us?

After dinner, I washed up while Fred sat with them on the couch, reading out loud from books. First, Tam would read part of a book, then Cam for a few minutes, then Fred did some reading. The girls cuddled up to their Uncle and looked at the book he was reading until they fell asleep. I took a picture of Fred with his arms around the sleeping beauties. Such a sweet scene!

Thomas Stimson

Happy Halloween!

October 31, 2000
Dear My Diary,

We had so much fun tonight! Last month Fred had a local costume designer create matching outfits for us to celebrate Halloween. The costumes are made of all black stretchy material with white bone shapes stitched all over. The leg and foot bones go down to our soft shoe covers while the arm and finger bones end in soft black gloves and even the skull is on the stretchy black cap. We left our faces without skull-shaped make-up as we were visiting children at the hospital and did not want to scare them.

Fred brought his popcorn wagon and small toys like cars, dolls, coloring books and crayons, travel games, funny hats and different things he has collected for them.

It is sad to see the sick children, but when they see us coming in, smiling and waving at them while in the company of nurses, their faces light up with surprise and happiness. Fred speaks well with them, encouraging the children to be nice to the doctors and not kick their legs or bite their fingers. This makes the children laugh and they promise not to bite or kick the doctors.

We served up bags of popcorn and let them pick a toy from the Halloween-decorated box while Fred tells two or three jokes and riddles. We spent a few moments making some pleasant chit-chat before saying good-bye and moving to the next room to do it again.

I don't feel like I have much to say as Fred is the funny one, but I smile and make small talk as I can with the children. Fred told many different jokes among the children. He told me later that if he tells the same jokes over and over, the children will try to share their jokes and then be disappointed that they all heard the same few jokes.

As a sample: What is a ghost's favorite fruit? Booberry! What did the skeleton ask the waiter? Can I have some more water? My glass is BONE DRY! How do you know vampires love baseball? They turn into bats every night! These are the kind of jokes Fred tells the children.

Fred says he does this to give something back to the community, as the children will miss more fun holiday events than adults who have seen many holidays in their lifetimes. Some of the children may not live to see the next holiday as they are so sick, but others will go home soon.

After our visit, we drove to Riverside Central Park to the city-sponsored party where lots of families come to make Halloween fun. We saw Thanh and the twins, so I ran up going BOOOO! The girls screamed with laughter at their auntie all covered in bones.

They are dressed as clowns and each has a different costume and makeup. So cute! We took pictures together. I picked them up and cradled one in each arm as they are so light. Perhaps I am getting stronger from working with Fred?

There was music and dancing and pretty lights on the water. Then I saw something I did not know we have on our costumes...the bones glow in the dark! Fred and I got into a darker area of the park and the bones shone brightly by themselves. Very nice!

Fred encouraged me to dance with him so we moved to the music, waving our arms, swinging our legs and doing funny moves. The twins came over and we all danced together. Other people are dressed as all different kinds of things like monsters, cartoon characters and cowboys.

It was so much fun and, as it got colder, we all hugged and went home. Now I can't sleep, so I am writing to relax and remember this special day.

The Taxman Cometh

November 2, 2000
Dear My Diary,

Sister Thanh is in some kind of new trouble now and she is panicking. She called me while we were busy with "Ba's Bonanza" (this is what Fred is jokingly calling the container box) by doing a "pop-up store" that we move from place to place around the metro area.

Soon after we got the container, Fred arranged with some of the larger retail and grocery stores in the area to set up one of his big moving trucks, tables, awnings, etc. in a corner of their parking lot that faces a busy street.

Fred had a large banner sign made saying "Christmas Gifts for Everyone!" and each day we set up in a different parking lot, send out notices on FreePost with our day's location and pictures of tables overflowing with products. Our rent is minimal, and we make back many times that amount. It also tends to drive more business to the store/shopping center we use as a selling location. Although we are still selling on Ubiddit, through the resale stores and at charity bazaars, the pop-up method eliminates selling fees, the hassles of shipping and it's all in cash.

That's what we were doing when Thanh called me. She got a letter from her bookkeeper that the US authorities want to look over her tax returns for the last five years. When I asked what is wrong with that, sister explained that she is paid largely in cash and has not reported most of her income so that she can pay little or no income tax and get a big refund every year.

Thanh said her bookkeeper is Vietnamese and is very helpful in finding ways for immigrant business owners to pay no taxes. The bookkeeper wants Thanh and Vo to come to her office after work so she can speak to them more about what is going on and find a way out of this problem.

I told sister that I will talk to Fred and see what he thinks. When I told Fred about the letter, he said that any bookkeeper who helps business owners report lower than actual incomes to the IRS to get a big refund is not an honest person. Fred does not want to get involved but advised that they find a good tax lawyer as soon as possible.

Fred added that he had a tax audit three years before and it was all very clean. "Bobby and Robbie take good care of me. I don't know what's going on with your sister, but it doesn't sound fun."

I called and left a message to sister about getting a good tax lawyer and please let me know what happens at the bookkeeper's meeting.

November 3, 2000
Dear My Diary,

Thanh called this evening crying so I could barely understand her. The story she told me is horrible and I am afraid for her and the children.

The bookkeeper gave Thanh a copy of a letter from the IRS saying they want to do an audit of their personal and business income taxes. She advised them that the audit will show that Thanh and Vo have made far more than reported and they will owe a great deal in unpaid taxes, fines, and interest. If that happens, and if they cannot pay it all, they will spend many years in prison for tax evasion, their home will be taken away and sold and the children will be put in foster homes to be starved by strangers.

When sister suggested getting a tax attorney to help, the bookkeeper warned them away from that idea, "She said the attorney will charge a high fee, then turn us over to the authorities for a big reward, so he gets paid twice. Miss Dung said the only way out of this is to give the IRS agent a cash gift of twenty-five thousand dollars to write up a good report and go away. What are we going to do?"

The bookkeeper also warned sister not to speak to others about this as it will make our family look very bad in the eyes of the community.

Thanh upset me to think that all these bad things can happen to my family. Thanh begged me not to tell Fred about this or he will think they are very bad people, too.

I said I wouldn't and asked how much she can pay on the bribe?

"Nothing! Or it might as well be nothing," she sobbed. "And she needs it in one week…one week! We owe more on the house than it's worth. Our credit cards are full, our suppliers won't accept anything but cash from us. I don't know what we are going to do…"

I didn't know what else to say and my stomach was in knots from everything sister told me. "I'll try to help you, Thanh. I don't know what I can do, but I don't want you to go to prison or the children to foster care…" Then, an idea struck. I blurted out, "Wait! Fred and I can take care of the children, so they don't go to foster care!" I said hopefully.

"Oh, and leave Vo and I to rot in prison? A fine sister you are!" she spat out and disconnected the call. I guess I should have phrased that better. Maybe I can give her the money, or Fred can help…but without knowing what it's for. What a mess!

Uncovering a Scam

November 4, 2000
Dear My Diary,

I could not sleep all night and all day my mind was on Thanh's situation. I must have looked as awful as I felt because Fred kept asking me what was wrong until I finally broke down and told him everything. He sighed and shook his head, saying, "That is the most bogus story I have heard in a long time."

"You do not believe Thanh is telling the truth?" I asked, hurt that he would think such a thing.

"Oh, I believe Thanh was told all these things, I just don't believe the bookkeeper's story," Fred clarified. "IRS agents are not known for taking bribes and the punishments don't sound realistic."

We have time to go see sister at Pretty Happy Nail Salon and Fred called the B&R office, asking to have one of their tax experts meet us at the shop. It is Saturday but Robbie was happy to call in one of his best people to help us.

Thanh was surprised to see us, and Fred spoke very sweetly to her, saying he wanted to help. He read through the IRS letter, shaking his head and rolling his eyes. Then Mahmood from B&R's office came in and introductions were made.

He read the letter, pointing out the spelling and grammatical mistakes that would never be made on an official letter.

In answer to Mahmood's questions, Vo said they have not given the bookkeeper any money and have not spoken to other VN business owners per Miss Dung's warnings.

Mahmood said his office has been getting calls about letters like this for the last two weeks from Asian business owners looking for tax advice and have the same letter and story. "If this were an audit, the IRS will not put business owners in jail except in the most extreme cases and they will not take away the children, but the house could be sold to pay back some of what is owed.

"However, the letter you have is not real." As proof, Mahmood took out three letters from his briefcase. Two of them are from the IRS to other Asian business owners, and both look identical to sister's letter.

The third letter looked very different because it is an official letter for a tax audit and review from the IRS. The other letters came from clients of Thanh and Vo's bookkeeper, My Dung.

Lois: I know how the bookkeeper's name looks to English speakers. The Vietnamese pronunciation is Mai-ee Yoong, but her American pronunciation fits better with her actions.

Fred explained that he has known Bobby and Robbie all his life and had had his bookkeeping done by them, and Robbie's father before that. "So, I know for a fact that whatever Mahmood tells you is the pure truth. You're being scammed by your own bookkeeper."

"Also," Mahmood added, "if this were a real audit, the bookkeeper would be in as much, if not more trouble, with the IRS for helping you file tax returns that she knows are not truthful."

Mahmood said the bookkeeper has created a scam to scare people into giving her money, then will likely leave the country to avoid jail.

The worry drained from Thanh and Vo's faces as Mahmood advised them not to call or talk to the bookkeeper anymore. If she calls for the money, say no and hang up.

"For now," Mahmood said, "we will report Ms. Dung to the police for attempting to defraud local business owners. You should expect follow-up calls from them for your side of the story."

Thanh hugged all of us and started crying again, but happy tears this time. "Thank you for not listening to me, Kim. Fred and Mahmood are good men."

Mahmood suggested that they call all the Vietnamese people they know to warn them of the scam and not to pay the bribe. Fred invited sister's family to the garage for a cook-out on Saturday after the shop closes. Thanh and Vo agreed to come and hugged us both again.

Fred told me in the truck that we will have a cookout, but also a serious talk with them about how they handle their business and taxes and get them out of so much trouble. "I know they might not listen, but maybe this big scare will change their way of thinking." Fred has also invited Mahmood to help, now that they know him and have gained some trust.

Dear My Diary,

Fred and I called all the stores where we installed the pegboards. The customers are happy to find small lots of things they want at bargain prices and sales are increasing to the point that two of the stores want more pegboards installed.

The store owners are thanking us for the idea and Fred always gives me the credit for it. And guess what? In the beginning, Fred had too many pegboards with no place to use them, and now they are all gone! It is a double-good thing for us and the stores!

Ears are Bitten

November 11th, 2000
Dear My Diary,

The cookout yesterday was a big success. It was colder than expected, so Fred and I set up a tent and warming lamps from the greenhouses so we could cook, but still stay warm and out of the wind.

Mahmood came with his wife Nezzie and their two sons who are close in age to the twins. She is an attractive Indian lady with a nice smile. The children ran about the rooftop and living quarters and the girls showed the boys the jumping bear. Grrr!

Auntie Giang also came with two of my cousins and three grandchildren. Auntie had heard about what happened to Thanh and others in the community, but she has always used B&R for her bookkeeping so never had any problems like this. I had asked her to come help with guiding sister and brother in Me and Ba's place.

We made grilled chicken and jumbo shrimp for the adults, hotdogs for the children and nothing with beef in deference to Mahmood's family.

We also served baked beans, corn on the cob, Auntie's family brought fresh spring rolls and Mahmood's wife brought an Indian dessert she made. Such a perfect combination for the cookout!

Then, a big surprise: Tina came to the cookout! Auntie had called her about Thanh, and she agreed to fly in from New York and use her banking expertise to help T&V with what is going on. She is such a good sister!

We agreed that after dinner, T&V would meet with Fred, Mahmood, Tina and Auntie in Fred's office while Nezzie, I and the others kept the children busy. Nezzie told us interesting things about India, and we shared things about Vietnam and how different it is from America.

Cam and Tam told us they started a Twins Club at school because of the books I got for them at the auction. There are a pair of boy look-alike twins, brother-sister twins and Cam and Tam who are not look-alike twins. They are all in different grades at the same school but play together sometimes at recess and make up pretend adventures like from their books. It is very cute to hear them talk about it and they are making new friends as well. I'm glad I bought the books for them!

After an hour or so, the meeting finished, and everyone came back to the tent. Vo tried looking tough but there was the soft sadness around his eyes and Thanh looked ashamed. Auntie and Tina held her shoulders and said encouraging things.

Fred gave me a nod and a wink to indicate that all is okay. From there, the party broke up as the reason for the get-together had been accomplished.

I told Thanh that I love her, and hoped Mahmood and Tina were a big help.

Thanh sighed, "We are lucky that Fred and Mahmood caught this before things went too far. We were so foolish to do what we did. Now we understand that we must make big changes." She added that Auntie bit her ears a lot, but with love, like a parent, and she and Vo let Mahmood and Tina give them expert advice.

After everyone went home, Fred and Tina told me more about the meeting as we cleaned up.

Mahmood said they were very lucky not to lose money to the scamming bookkeeper and advised them to get a reputable CPA to help them…not just with their bookkeeping and taxes, but to assist with financial planning for now and the future.

Auntie weighed in, reminding them there was too much gambling and drinking and spending money foolishly while the children are thin and hungry. They must be better parents and more responsible with their money.

Auntie told me in confidence later in the evening that sister has been selling her SNAP cards to customers for less than full value to help pay their bills. She knows because one time a customer came in and used a card with Thanh's name on it to buy snacks. No wonder the children are so underfed!

She recommended that sister meet with B&R's people to work up a money-management plan and offered to come to the meeting in place of Ba and Me, if they will permit.

Vo asked Fred how he keeps track of his business as they know much of it is done with cash. Fred showed them the notebooks he carries everywhere to record all our business transactions and how they work.

T&V said they have been talking since we came to the shop and have agreed to meet with one of B&R's CPA's for a top to bottom review of their business and personal finances. I feel good to hear this and hope it is not a false wanting but a true desire to make needed changes.

Tina said she will offer her language and financial background services to B&R and the Riverton police to help the criminal investigation of the bookkeeper, if needed. She can translate evidence and information written in Vietnamese and Chinese, assist in contacting Asian clients to ask questions and convince them to press charges. Mahmood will provide Tina's information and offer to help the Fraud Squad. Tina stayed with us tonight and will fly home tomorrow.

Dear My Diary,

I have two pieces of good news today:

This morning, as we were unloading the truck in Clarksville for another day of gift sales, I got a call from one of Zander's assistants letting me know that I got a call-back for the Fierce 5 advertising campaign, and do I want it? I said "yes", and she gave me a date, time and place in Riverton to meet, instructing me not to wear make-up as they will do that for me. I am expected to be there all morning.

I said okay, then asked Fred "What is a call-back? Did I get the job?"

"Not yet, my love," he said with a smile. "A call-back means they will narrow down who they want to use. They get some of the promising ones, like you, together with others, put on the make-up styles they intend to use, see how everyone acts and looks together to get the right mix. When they find the right combination, the final offers will be made."

That makes me feel good…at least I was not turned down after the first tryout.

And even better is that Thanh called to say the police arrested My Dung at the St Louis airport before she could fly back to Vietnam. An article in the Riverton Review said city police had sent out an all-points bulletin to airports and train stations as far away as Chicago and Denver.

Her suitcase was filled with bundles of cash hidden amongst the clothing. Some business owners paid her the bribe money, but many others did not due to the warning calls from Thanh, Vo, B&R's office and others. I'm sure she got much less money than expected.

Fred said it did not help that her name was so memorable. I asked what he meant by that, so Fred had to explain how the bookkeeper's name appears to English speakers. Ugh…I had no idea! I had not learned the word "dung" until today.

With Tina's encouragement, Thanh and Vo filed a police report against her for attempted fraud. We think many people will refuse to report the crime, fearing trouble from the police and the real IRS.

Fred heard that Mahmood and Tina have been asked to help the police figure out who all the victims are so they can return the money to the right people and build a case against the bookkeeper with as many charges as possible.

Thanh called Fred to say "thank you" many times to the point that he became embarrassed by the attention, and said, "You are my sister. I wanted to help you and Brother Vo." Fred spoke respectfully to her, but I know he does not agree with the way they have conducted their life. Maybe they will change now. I certainly hope so.

My First Thanksgiving

November 24, 2000
Dear My Diary,

Most of Ba's Bonanza is selling very well and our inventory is quickly evaporating. Every Monday morning, we bring new things to the resale shops and pick up what has been left at the university donation boxes. Every weekend we bring in a fresh variety of products to the flea markets (I work one and Fred works the other) so customers keep coming back to find new gift ideas.

I have become very good at selling to the public and, with Fred's help, developed my own style of showing and describing the products, answering questions, taking requests for items people want and getting their contact information, etc. It's hard work, but fun!

On Sunday nights we go through the completed Ubiddit sales, put out new auctions and prepare to ship out the paid goods. Mother Maggie is helping us by calling gift stores around the state and explaining what we are selling, emailing photos and descriptions and arranging for payment and delivery of box lots. In return, we drop off gift cards to her favorite grocery and drug stores as a thank-you.

We have long-since recovered the $50,000 price of goods and are making a healthy profit to be split with my parents' company. It has been a lot of work and time involved but Fred says it is also one of the best holiday sales seasons he has ever had. With sales slowing down, Fred is selling case lots to people and businesses on Ubiddit for a "Gotta Have It" price with overnight shipping to clear out the inventory more quickly.

Yesterday was Thanksgiving and we invited a lot of people over to celebrate. The living area is spacious with plenty of room for eating, drinking, and mingling. It looks so much better now than when I first moved in.

There are several vertical steel I-beams running from ground floor to roof that support the floor joists and two of them come up through the parlor area. They were exposed, unpainted and ugly, compared to the rest of the work Fred had put into the space to make a home for me.

At my suggestion, we took some of the lumber from the second floor and sheathed the beams completely, staining them in such a way as to better blend into the rest of the rustic environment. Working together, it didn't take long, and it feels so much homier.

We have decorated the beams with pictures and knick-knacks collected from locker sales and added Bunny's mobile to the twinkle-star ceiling, the birds nudged into flight by the drafts of our poorly sealed windows. That is a project for another day.

Fred got some more TV's (used, of course) and connected them all to the local cable system so we have the jumbo-screen in the living room along with one in each bedroom and another in the dining area to watch while we eat. Fred set the jumbo TV to the big parade in New York, followed by holiday shows for the rest of the day.

We had such a good crowd with Fred's parents, Auntie Giang and Mahmood and his family as they are newer to the area. Tina flew in last night and stayed at Thanh's so the five of them came over and we provided some board and card games for the children once they settled down.

Holly and Hazel came later in the day with Bobby and Robbie while Bunny and Barney spent Thanksgiving with her mother and stepfather's families. From the way she talks about their multitude of self-inflicted problems and feuds, I doubt that either of them had a good time. At any rate, we are not ready to have Barney over here, either.

Bunny sometimes stops by for a few minutes to visit while we work the pop-up store or a flea market. Barney has been working hard on a number of cases and she is lonely, so Bunny follows our ads on FreePost to know where we will be on any given day.

I don't mind her visits and neither does Fred. She holds back if we are busy with customers and when we do talk, the visits are short. She is polite and respectful in that way, which is appreciated, and maybe by visiting us, she recharges her social battery and feels a bit better. That's Fred's expression, not mine, but it sounds right. In my opinion, as long as Barney is not in the picture, she can visit whenever she likes.

This is the first time I have seen Fred serve wine and beer in our home. I noticed that Vo only drank fruit juice and Thanh confided, "Vo is trying to stop drinking alcohol, but please don't say anything or he will be embarrassed." I was pleased to hear this bit of news. It's not an easy thing to quit and I hope he succeeds. Still, I couldn't help but keep an eye on him, just to make sure.

Tina was acting oddly, but when I asked her, she would only say, "Everything is fine! I'm just so happy to see you and everyone!" Normally, she is relaxed and poised, but not today. There was an air of anticipation around her.

We played soft rock on the radio, everybody was having a nice time talking or helping us prepare dinner. The children were comparing Vietnamese and Hindi words and phrases and giggling when something sounded funny.

Luckily, we have two gas ovens and plenty of stove-top space to handle the large turkey, ham, steamed sweet potatoes in their jackets and homemade sauces (cranberry and apple) with everyone contributing other goodies to create a big buffet.

Fred has saved some tables from going to the resale stores and we cleaned them up, adding tablecloths to hide their flaws and a hodgepodge of chairs. We pushed them all together and Fred made a toast with many things to say about friends and family and first Thanksgivings with many more to come. Others around the table spoke up, giving their own reasons for giving thanks, as is the tradition.

Everything tasted so good and such interesting conversations were taking place: Frank explained to the children the story about the first thanksgiving between the Pilgrim people and native Americans, while Bobby told a story about Robbie having trouble with a biting, kicking donkey on their last vacation to the Grand Canyon and Maggie told a hilarious story about a customer who calls and emails, looking to buy antique toilets to grow things in them for her garden.

To help her, Maggie puts ads on FreePost requesting donations of old toilets to be brought to her shop. When the toilets come in, Maggie sells them to the woman who is happy to pay $100 to $200 each, depending on how interesting it looks…so many funny stories!

I couldn't help but notice Tina's furtive glances at Bobby until near the end of dinner. Then he nodded to her and sister stood up, tapping her wine glass saying, "I want to make an announcement everyone!" After we got quiet, Tina said "As today is a day for giving thanks, I want to share with you that I am thankful…very, very thankful that I will be…moving to Riverton to start a new job with Bobby and Robbie's firm!"

There were some quiet gasps as the news sunk in and Tina continued, "I gave notice to my employer on Monday and will work until Christmas, starting my new job at the beginning of the New Year!"

There was a flurry of applause, mixed with chairs being pushed back and bodies running around the table to hug Tina for her wonderful news and to Bobby and Robbie for hiring her. Such a surprise! Thanh kept saying, "She never said a word to me! All night and all day with me, and I never knew!"

Later in the evening, sister explained how it all came about. Mahmood had reported to his bosses how Tina assisted the police, helping interview the Asian victims, making some of them see the wisdom of pressing charges against My Dung which, in turn, led to her arrest.

And she did this voluntarily, refusing compensation when it was offered. Tina said, "I told them, I am doing this for my family. The bookkeeper's arrest is all the payment I need." So heroic!

Some of the victims have now become clients of B&R. From all of this, Mahmood suggested to Bobby and Robbie that Tina would make an excellent addition to the firm.

They made Tina an offer to work for them with her very own, unique job title, "Pacific Rim Client Manager", which means she will reach out to local Asian business owners (starting with the bookkeeping victims and growing from there) and help them become B&R clients.

She will start with a good, but not great, salary. From there, growth of the client base coupled with commissions from products and services will give her great earning potential. I pointed out that their starting pay is like a raise because the cost of living is so much less here than in New York.

Best of all, she will be near Thanh and me…Yay! There were many congratulations made to Tina, Bobby, Robbie and Mahmood for their hard work in helping to stop the bookkeeper's scam.

Most of the food is gone and we sent many people home with leftovers. Mahmood thanked us for inviting his family to our Thanksgiving dinner and all the interesting combinations of American and Asian foods and decorations.

Tina: I really loved New York as it had been my home all through college and the years I worked for the bank. However, the expenses and fast pace of the city were starting to wear on me.

Once Sister Kim came to Riverton, I began to consider a move. Then when Thanh got into trouble and I was able to help my sister and the authorities put that bookkeeper in prison, Bobby called and offered me a position. I didn't have to think long in accepting it! That was a great, great year for me.

Thomas Stimson

Tryouts Can be Trying

Tuesday, November 28th, 2000

Dear My Diary,

Fred took me to the Admiral Theater in downtown Riverton early this morning where Premier Promotions and Zander are doing the callbacks. Zander has several people working with her to get the models made-up, dressed and stage-ready for taking pictures.

Fred took a seat in the back rows with his laptop and cell phone, quietly making phone calls, catching up on emails and posting new things to Ubiddit while keeping an eye on our proceedings.

There are over a dozen other models, many with names I have not heard before like Alina, Shanondez, Ayla, Margritte, Gretel and others I can't remember. Some of the models were at the studio party and some I do not recognize.

They feel a little intimidating to be around because, for them, it is another paying gig and a possible stepping-stone to bigger and better roles. For me, it is an interesting outing.

I walked over to the very pale model with red eyes that I saw last time. I thought they were contact lenses, but when I asked her, she told me they are real, "Just like these," she added, cupping her breasts with her hands. I was taken aback and blurted out, "Mine too!" without thinking. Mentally I slapped my forehead for saying such a stupid thing.

She nodded, "I like that. All natural." She has a nice accent, but not American, I think.

I learned that Bettina is an albino, a woman with no coloring in her skin or hair, like a beautiful ghost. She has been in some movies and television shows and when I told her that we have a television but never really watch it, she said, "You're lucky." I don't know why she said that.

She has pointed teeth and when I asked about those, Bettina said they are fake, and we will all get pointed teeth. Then she hissed to show me how they look. Scary!

Each model is made up to highlight her unique features as I am made to look more Asian and exotic than in real life, including a wig. Getting made up is an interesting process: the assistants are quietly efficient and professional, making everyone feel welcome and comfortable. Some of the models smoke and chat, pointedly ignoring the No Smoking signs posted everywhere and there was plenty of food and drinks available until it was time for lipstick.

We were given costumes to wear…sleeveless vests and shorts, but not too short. I think they want to see toned muscles along with scary faces. The fake teeth are clipped on and feel strangely bulky in the mouth, but I don't say anything. I took a look in the mirror, and it makes quite an impression!

As each model is ready, we go to the photo staging area for solo head and body shots. I hold back a bit, watching how the others act and react so I can follow suit. They are my competition.

The solo shots start with a relaxed facial expression from different angles, then we pose, show our pointed teeth, and make kitty claws at the camera. Everything is digital so there is no waiting to print pictures. Zander supervises everything closely and tells us what to do, how to hold our head, hands and body.

If I squint past the stage lights, I can see Fred in the background. He gave me a wave and thumbs up. I gave him a little wave back. After everyone had taken their solos, Zander put us together in groups

197

of three, and later in fours and fives, posing together, looking fierce and hard at the camera and showing attitude. I think I kept messing up as Zander had to give me more directions than the others. She is patient, but firm in what she wants.

At first, I was nervous when working with Zander, but as the morning wore on, I became more relaxed. I don't know if I will get the job because I am the only Asian, but maybe, if I am not so good, they won't use me at all, Asian or not. I don't know.

I can feel tension on the set because others are competing for the job and very focused on doing their best. I don't care if I get the job or not, but I am trying my best, mimicking what others are doing and hoping I look confident. I want to help my family and I want to make Fred proud…it was he who suggested me to Fierce 5, after all.

By noon we are done. The makeup people showed me how to remove the heavy cosmetics with special creams and soon, I looked like Kimmie Starbuckle again in jeans and a blouse. They will be making their final picks in the next couple of weeks and making follow-up calls to those selected.

Fred asked me what I thought of today and I said it was kind of fun but kind of boring too, while waiting for the next thing to do.

"I hear that happens a lot in show business. Hurry up and wait," Fred commented, opening the van door for me.

Thinking about the times Zander had to give me extra direction, I asked Fred, "Will you be disappointed if I don't get the job?"

Fred looked surprised. "Noo! Sweetheart, you did great up there. Nervous, sure, but you are up against some heavy competition. If you don't get the job, it wasn't because you didn't try. I can never be disappointed with anyone who tries their best." Then he gave me a long, warm hug and kiss before settling me into the passenger seat and whisking me off to lunch.

Frankie: If there was one thing our parents drilled into us, it was to do our best. I think that individually and as a family, our successes have been largely due to preparation, assessing risk and doing our very best…it works, more often than not.

First Snow!

Thursday, November 30, 2020
Dear My Diary,

Today was the first day of snow! When we were out yesterday, Fred said "It feels like snow," but there was nothing coming down, so I asked him what it meant to feel like snow is coming. He had me pay attention to the air, the bite of cold tinged with moisture and increasing gusts of wind coming down from the North.

"That is one way to tell," Fred explained. "The other is to listen to the radio. The weather services have been calling for snow over the last three days," he said with a wink. It made me excited for the rest of the day and into the evening, checking every little while for snowflakes.

At about five, I got up to tinkle and peeked out the bedroom door. To my amazement, there were thousands of white confetti drifting diagonally past the big, multi-paned windows. Each flake glowed individually, like bits of cotton, as they fell toward the streetlamps and lightly touched down, creating a thickening carpet of white that masked the cracks and potholes of our street.

Watching the snow fall is like magic, mesmerizing the senses in the same way a waterfall's arcing path off a cliff can hypnotize me in the timespan of a single love song. Now I understand why people love to watch falling snow.

Fred came up softly from behind, slipping his arms around my waist and holding me close. He kissed my neck and asked, "How do you like it?"

I answered, "I love it…and the snow is pretty too." As I had hoped, he chuckled at my little joke, the kind of joke I have learned from him, and added, "What does this remind you of?"

Fred sighed, thought for a moment, then began reminiscing about riding on sleds pulled by bicycles, making snowmen with rocks for eyes and tree branches for arms, sliding on icy sidewalks in smooth-soled shoes and battling other kids in epic snowball fights.

I smiled to think of Fred and his friends having fun in the snow while there is a little girl in a tropical country who does not know what snow is except in picture-books and movies. Now she is here…and it is so beautiful!

I can feel Fred's desire growing and pressing against me as he speaks of his childhood…a childhood I wished I could have been a part of, or at least seen. Then we went back to bed, got under the thick covers, and made new memories of my first snowfall. Mmmm!

We were done by dawn and made a special breakfast of quiche, warm fruit compote made by Maggie and sweetened coffee. "I want to build a snowman," I said.

"Your wish is my command," Fred answered. "But not here."

We drove to Frank and Maggie's where they have a big front yard in a neighborhood with lots of families. It was so much fun!

Frank had gone to work as they get busier with bad weather, but Maggie was home as her store closed for the day along with the schools.

It was much like Fred had described: First we shoveled his parents' driveway, walkways, and sidewalks (Frank had cleared the porch and steps but little else), then rolled some of the piled snow into balls of different sizes. We stacked them together with a large base of five balls and building up from there to make a conical-shaped snowman taller than Fred.

Neighborhood children came to help, making suggestions and asking questions. Fred came prepared to add some weirdness to our snowman by inserting red, flashing LED lights as eyes (something from Ba's Bonanza) and embedding real dentures to make the mouth (something we find all too often in our storage lockers…ick!) and topping the whole creation with a wig and floppy hat.

We took pictures and had our own pictures taken with my first snowman, before going inside to have lunch and warm apple cider with Maggie. I will send copies of our photos to everyone so they can see the fun we are having here in the cold.

Fred had provided me with long underwear and waterproof gloves to stay warm and dry. Just the same, between working up a sweat and the snow sticking, then melting on my jeans, I still ended up wet, inside and out. That's okay…it was worth it!

After lunch, we walked around the neighborhood to see some of the early Christmas decorations people had put up, when we came across children and teens having a big snowball fight with snow forts and large homemade slingshots that could launch snowballs over the rooftops.

The children asked us to join so Fred went with one team and I with the other to make it fairer. All I can say is, I am so glad to be in such good physical shape because slogging through wet snow and ducking snowballs while slipping around on patches of ice takes a lot of exertion!

We finally retired from the game and visited with Maggie a bit more before heading home to a peach-scented hot shower for two…I love all the different body washes we have!

Kimmie: What a wonderful day that was, from beginning to end, especially after re-reading what I had written all those years ago. I don't think anyone who has never seen snow before, ever forgets their first snowfall.

As an adult, Fred had gotten used to snow, working and driving in it without giving a lot of thought to the matter. But seeing how it affected me and reliving some of his childhood memories through my admittedly childish wonder made the usual "oh, hell, it's snowing" into "Oh, WOW! It's SNOWING!" We often reminisced of this particular day with fondness. It was nice to re-live it again, if only on paper.

I am Chimera...Sssss!

Thursday December 7th, 2000

Dear My Diary,

I got a call this afternoon from Zander's assistant who offered me a contract as the character Chimera (I had to ask how to spell the name) for the Fierce 5 advertising campaign. The assistant said there will be a $500 modeling fee. I wasn't sure what she was trying to tell me, so I asked, "I have to pay a $500 modeling fee?"

She was quiet for a moment, probably thinking I was a simpleton, then clarifying with, "No. We pay YOU $500. Per hour. You get that for every day you come in for print or video work, plus transportation to and from the work location and a per diem."

I was a bit stunned. I did not know what to expect for pay, but certainly not this much. And PER HOUR. It had to be wrong. "Five hundred dollars per hour…is that correct?"

The woman sighed, "Yes, five hundred dollars per hour is what we are authorized to offer you, Ms. Starbuckle. If you feel that is not enough, your agent will have to contact Premier Promotions directly to negotiate."

I don't know if Fred knew about this rate of pay or not, but I am no fool and accepted the offer. Many people in my country don't make that much in six months and even here, that is a weeks' wages for many jobs. The assistant said she will send out the contracts and let me know when the first photo shoot is scheduled.

My heart was racing when I called Fred and told him that I accepted the offer to be a Fierce 5 model. "How much do you think they are going to pay me…per hour?" I asked, seeing if he knew.

"Twenty dollars," he ventured.

"Fred! I will be working with professional models and actresses and stuntwomen. Try again."

"Well, since you put it that way, twenty-two dollars."

Now I know he is playing with me, so I told him.

"Oh, that was going to be my next guess." Typical Fred joke!

He then admitted that he expected I would get about that much, to which I responded, "Why didn't you tell me, before?"

"Was it a good surprise?"

"Yes."

"Then that is why I didn't tell you. Now you got a good surprise. Do you still love me?"

"Of course. Oh! And is it okay to tell my family about the new job?"

He laughed and said, "Of course! It's not a secret. It's a real job for a real product. Why not tell them?"

Sisters will see the ads soon enough, but they might not recognize me as I will look so fierce and not like sweet little sister Kimmie.

I emailed my sisters, parents and Bunny. Bunny is like my American sister and makes me feel connected to Fred's family in a way that Bernie does not. Everyone said they are happy for me and to be careful not to get scammed. I did not tell them Fred is an investor in the company, but I did say he will be there when I am working, so it will be fine.

Later in the day, as my excitement settled down, the question came to me: What is a "chimera"?

Lois: Mama learned later that some of the other models were getting more money, but she never begrudged them since they were professionals with runway work, magazine covers, television and film roles to their credit. She felt lucky to be selected at all.

Merry Bucking Christmas

December 11
Dear My Diary,

Every second Sunday in December, Fred hosts a "Merry Bucking Christmas" party to celebrate with his business partners, go-to people, and a guest of their choice. Fred offered me the opportunity to invite someone from the Fierce 5 group since they are a part of our business ventures.

Bettina is spending time in Europe with her family, and I don't know the others well enough to invite them. Tina has much to do with her employer in New York before she moves here, so I am not sure who to invite. I don't know many people yet and this is for our, or really Fred's, business partners so I did not pick anyone to come over.

Fred has lots of Christmas decorations on the second floor, so we put up Christmas trees, one big and two small, with lights and fake snow and colorful toys and balls. We hung giant snowflakes from different parts of the ceiling among the twinkle lights and replaced burnt-out bulbs so it would not look so shabby.

Fred told of how he got the snowflakes and giant wreaths from a local department store that went out of business, along with a life-size electric Santa Claus that waves his hand and moves from side to side at the waist saying "Ho Ho Ho! Merrrry Christmasss!"

What a crowd! Most of the resale store owners/managers came, along with Auntie Giang, Robin and Rick Ryan of Flea City Market, Hazel and Holly Wood and Bobby and Robbie, of course! Others who came were bankers and lawyers that Fred does regular business with, the head of the Riverton Chamber of Commerce and the director of the school board.

We did not cook this time, thank goodness! Fred had the food and bar catered by a local German restaurant. The foods served were hearty, perfect for the cold weather, and the staff was dressed in traditional clothing with recorded German Christmas music playing in the background.

For this group, Fred said he makes sure to serve alcohol…otherwise not many people would show up. Fred did not need to tell me the other reason alcohol was served, because I know this from my own family's experience, is to loosen the tongues of those who can provide us with information, ideas and the possibilities of fresh business deals.

In that regard, I had had an idea for the resale stores that I shared with Fred last month and he thinks it will work well with our group. I got the idea from an American Christmas movie and, like the other idea I came up with, he wants me to present it to the store owners.

At one point, Fred was able to get the resellers together for what he called a "quick powwow" in his office and said, "Kim has a terrific idea that can benefit all of us, but I will let her explain it and you can decide for yourself."

After practicing with Fred, I had the confidence to explain how all the resale stores are connected businesses, yet do not compete directly with each other because no one store is near another and there are differences in the clients they cater to.

I said, "If you have customers looking for certain things, you can call, fax, or email the other stores with specific requests or lists of things your clients want. If someone has the item, it can be held while the customer arranges to pick it up or the store can have it delivered it at the customer's expense.

"An arrangement can be made amongst the stores to share in the profits of these sales or pay out a percentage as a finder's fee for working the sale together. Also, please let Buck or I know what customers are looking for and we may either know who has it or can try to find it for you. In this way, if everyone works together, we can all make more money and keep our customers happy and coming back."

Most of them seemed agreeable with the idea, but Chuck of Grandpa's Attic spoke up, "That all sounds very nice, but why should we share our business with others?" The "others" turned on him with unamused faces and Chuck added, "No offense intended, it's just that it's hard enough to make a profit some months."

I was ready for this question. "Does everyone remember the old movie of the department store Santa Claus? When a customer asked where a specific toy was in their store, the Santa said, 'We don't carry that toy, but the store across the street has them.'

"The store manager overheard the Santa sending a customer to their competitor and was about to fire the Santa when the same customer walks up and shakes the manager's hand, saying 'What a wonderful service you have, directing customers to other stores that have what you don't carry. I will come back to your store more often for the great customer service!'"

Everyone smiled and nodded at the memory of the old movie reference. Some spoke up in favor of my idea and told Chuck if he did not want to participate, he did not have to. Chuck grudgingly agreed to "try it out for a while" and everyone was happy to work more closely together.

Fred will let the group develop a plan they can agree on regarding how to compensate each other for these cross-store sales and we will make comprehensive lists of preferred contact information for everyone.

Fred gave me the smile I like best from him…the "You did a good job" smile.

Our parents were big entertainers. We always seemed to be having get-togethers of one kind or another with family, friends, business associates, etc. Sometimes we cooked the meals and sometimes they were catered and sometimes it was potluck. It got harder to get together as the folk's schedules became more diverse, but there was always good food and conversations and laughter. Dad and Mama kept with a good group and that rubbed off on us as we grew up so we tended to gravitate towards like-minded friends and colleagues.

Dear My Diary,

One thing I noticed at the Merry Bucking Christmas party was how the guests, Fred included, were trading envelopes with each other as they conversed but I was never within earshot of Fred when he was doing it.

For example, one of the attorneys was chatting with Holly Wood and I when he pulled a small envelope out of his pocket and handed it to her saying, "For the children. Merry Christmas."

Such a curious statement as I don't think Holly or Hazel have any children. Holly put the envelope in her purse and handed a different one back saying, "And Merry Christmas to you."

No one gave me an envelope, although many people spoke to me, made small talk, and wished me a merry Christmas.

I asked Fred about the envelopes, hoping it was not something illegal or something he would be upset about my asking.

"Oh, those?" he asked, mildly surprised. "We give each other donations to the charities we sponsor." We went to his desk and in a locked drawer was a stack of checks made out to Feed the Neighbors and Dissolving Debt.

Fred explained, "We not only get together to socialize and share information, but we also use the event to contribute our own money to a variety of charities. Everyone that was here are sponsors for, or have their own, non-profit groups as I do. I gave checks from The Orion Group to sponsors of veteran's affairs, the children's hospital, homeless outreach programs and many others. In return, I get checks to maintain and grow my Feed the Neighbors and Dissolving Debt programs. This little party probably generated a half-million dollars in combined donations. All the money benefits the community and," Fred added with a smile, "it's also tax deductible. That's helpful to us at this time of year."

The phrase that stuck in my head was, "This little party probably generated a half-million dollars…" There was between 40 and 50 people at the party, more than that, really, as some people popped in and out on their way to other parties. All those envelopes being traded and placed in purses and sport coat pockets, and I had no idea what was going on.

I wonder why Fred never told me about this before now…or why I had to ask?

My Fierce 5 Contract

Dear My Diary,

I got the official job contracts for Fierce 5 and Premier Promotions by delivery service this morning. Fred and I read it over carefully and he explained the different parts to me. Pages and pages of details but most of it sounds fair and standard for what is expected of me and the companies involved.

One important part allows me a choice on how I will get paid: in cash, shares of Fierce 5 stock, or a combination of the two. Fred and I went over the pros and cons of each option in detail, and I decided to go with the combination.

The way I see it, the worst that can happen is I will lose half the money (the value of the stock) if the company fails. If the company succeeds and grows, the stock price should grow with it.

Fred smiled, "Good choice. Half is guaranteed and half is speculation. I hope this works out well for you. Remember, I have some skin in the game myself."

I kissed Fred and said, "Win or lose, at least I am in good company."

I signed, initialed, and dated everything marked out for me and sent it back in the return envelope. This will be my newest venture into multiple streams of income.

Fred would not invest in this company if he was not very sure it would succeed. But I also know that there is no sure thing when it comes to investments…just like relationships!

Which reminded me of something I have hesitated to ask Fred for awhile, but I am curious of how things worked out. "By the way, did sister or brother pay you back the limo money?"

He stared at me for a long moment, trying to decide how to answer. I never told him that I knew about her credit card being declined for the wedding transportation or Fred covering the bill to avoid further embarrassment.

Finally, he said "I'm not worried about it, Sweetheart, and neither should you. I should have known to get limos for our wedding and I'm sorry that I didn't. It wasn't me being frugal…it was me being thoughtless." He kissed me and whispered in my ear, "I took care of it, so what's done is done."

"By the way," Fred added, with a wolfish grin, "Guess who's going to be sleeping with a model tonight?"

Thomas Stimson

My First Christmas in America

Monday, December 25, 2000
Dear My Diary,

Last year, my very first Christmas ever, was in warm and sunny Vietnam getting to know my American boyfriend/fiancé. This year I am in cold and sometimes snowy Riverton with my husband. Last year I was Kimmie Pham, aka Cay Dua, and now I am Kimmie Starbuckle, aka Chimera of the Fierce 5…Grrr!

I have learned many new phrases this year from Fred like AKA (also known as), ASAP (as soon as possible), FYI (for your information) and BS (bull stuffings).

There were presents under the Christmas tree this morning. "I wonder who put these beautiful presents here??" I asked the walls.

Fred came out of the bedroom in his long johns, his blue eyes widening, voice gasping like a little boy's, "It must have been Santa Claus! He's real! He's real!!" Fred jumped up and down, clapping his hands in delight as I laughed until my ribs hurt.

We hugged and kissed and Fred tasted cinnamon fresh with a new (old) brand of mouthwash we just opened. Then we settled under the tree to open our goodies.

Fred gave me two heavy knit dresses with matching tights to keep me warm, yet fashionable, a high-quality wok and utensils to make more of the Asian-style dishes that I like and some dangling earrings. Mostly practical gifts, I see. No car? That's okay. I did the same thing for Fred!

Some heavy flannel shirts I bought from the clearance rack at the Paul Bunyan shop, an appliance that can make both pancakes or waffles just by changing out the grilling plates for whichever you want (the last one, a floor model, and at a discount) and the last present is a specially formulated gel to make Fred's hair extra curly. I got two tubes from Thanh in exchange for some nice costume jewelry from our inventory.

We went to Frank and Maggie's for an early Christmas dinner and some of Fred's family were there, but not Barney and Bunny. Maybe they will come after we leave, I don't know.

The families appear to be working class and some are retired or on disability due to health problems. There are mostly pickup trucks and mini vans in front of the house and many people spent time in the back yard smoking.

One uncle went out frequently to smoke. Each time, he had to turn off the oxygen tank, take the tube out of his nose and then walk very carefully to a bench under the eaves before lighting up. Why is he smoking if his lungs need extra oxygen? No one said anything, but I found it painful to watch.

Fred and I brought sweet potato pie made from our own garden-grown yams. As I conversed with Fred's relatives, I got the impression that Frank and Maggie had been the most successful members of the family before Barney changed their fortunes.

Some of them asked me things like, "Does Fred still pick up trash for a living?" and "Is Riverton like where you grew up?" and "Did you fight for or against the Americans?" After asking my age, one auntie said, "When I was your age, I had my first grandchild! Why are you waiting to have kids?" I am only twenty-nine and just got married! Meanwhile, children were running about, yelling, interrupting conversations, or crying about something all the time.

These family members are not like Fred's parents or any of my family either. They have a different kind of living, thinking, and speaking style. I know some English curse words and they were in regular use, but not from Fred or his parents. I don't hear this language very much in my everyday life…except from Thanh.

As Fred spoke to his family and made polite conversation, his manner is not in the same fun, relaxed style that he has with me and others. Fred admitted later that his parents' siblings and their families can be "trying". I think he means, "Trying to get on our last nerves."

Fred said they are basically good, hard-working people, but now life is catching up too fast for many of them. Frank and Maggie look much healthier than most of the others. My American parents know about the work I will be doing with Fierce 5, but we did not speak with the others about it. I am not sure if they can understand or appreciate what it means to me.

Parents gave me a pair of warm dress-up gloves and a children's book about a boy growing up in rural Vietnam and the adventures he has with his family and their farm animals. Maybe they think I will enjoy the book as a connection to my homeland. I appreciate the gesture…it is sweet and something I can share with our future children.

From there, we went on to Auntie Giang's to spend time with her family and Thanh's. It is much more alive there and the children are well-behaved, sharing toys and asking permission to speak if adults are conversing.

I feel so much better to be among my family, especially as Sister Tina flew in from New York on Friday evening. We picked her up with the van as she brought everything she owns in several suitcases and large boxes. Tina is staying with Thanh but is hopping back and forth between their home and ours to visit and catch up.

Fred arranged with Father Frank to fix Tina up with a low-mileage, late-model sedan they got at a good price, and Hazel Wood is finding her a modest apartment.

Thanh and Vo have stopped going to the casino for Date Night, so we do not see the twins as much as before, which is good as we have been so busy the last couple of months. Also, Auntie confided to me that she convinced Thanh to stop taking SNAP payments since she was never eligible for it to begin with, and if the State figures it out, she will have to repay it all back and possibly face charges, especially for selling the cards to other people.

We gave the girls handheld gaming systems with an assortment of learning games along with a few fun ones. We are hoping the games will help them in their studies.

Vo looks healthier now and has lost some weight. I did not see him smoking at Auntie's and when I told Vo how good he looks, he made a self-conscious kind of thank you to me and said he is feeling better than before.

I said, "Well, it shows. Keep up the good work!" and patted him on the shoulder. He blushed and I get the idea he does not get complimented often. That is something Fred would have done, to recognize and encourage someone's positive behavior. My best friend's actions are rubbing off on me and I feel good in doing the same.

Tina and I got some alone time for a few minutes, and she asked, "How do you like married life and living in Riverton? Does it suit you?"

"Fred…he is the best. Always complimenting and telling me to be proud of who I am and how I look. He's a very optimistic man, and I think it's his attitude that brings him much good luck. Did you know he helped me get the job with Fierce 5?"

"No, I did not. How did he manage that?"

"I will tell you later when we have some time. But I do the first photo shoot next month. Then, if someone asks me if I am a model, I can truthfully say, "Why, yes I am! I am a Fierce 5 spokesmodel. Did you see my ad recently?"

Sister and I laughed as I struck a funny pose. "Of course, I miss Saigon because of our family, the warm weather, and the food. The going out in public, I don't miss. I like it much better here…and married life with Fred? Well, if you can find a man who treats you the way Fred treats me…then you will be a very lucky sister, indeed."

Tina squeezed my hand, "I can tell, Kimmie. Everyone can tell. And I could not be happier for you."

"What about you?" I asked, "How do you feel about leaving New York? Do you think you will like it here?"

"I've given it a lot of thought, believe me," Tina started. "I've spent my whole adult life in New York between college and work. There's no place like it and I loved my job, but it was all about helping rich people get richer. That was fine, until I came to help Thanh."

She shook her head. "The ignorance of finances, the trust placed in people they shouldn't and suspicion of those they should. I can make a difference in Riverton. I know I can, and I'm being given the freedom and tools to make it happen with Bobby and Robbie."

"Besides," Tina continued, meeting my eyes, "I missed out on your growing up…and even now you are changing and evolving before my eyes. I love the twins, and I want to be closer to my family…you, Thanh, auntie and all the rest."

I hugged Tina and told her how we are all glad she made this very difficult and important decision and we will do whatever we can to help her get acclimated. Then I changed the subject back to me.

"But there is one thing that bothers me about Fred," I began to admit, not sure if I should be confiding this to my sister, "but I feel like he does not tell me everything I should know."

"Like what? Do you think he has a girlfriend?"

"No! Not like that. At least, I don't think so. It's just that I keep learning things about his finances that he had not told me before. They are not bad things, but things he lets slip from time to time. I don't know if he does not like to brag about them, or because we are still so newly married that he is not comfortable to reveal them to me.

"Also, I still don't understand why he and his parents have such a terrible relationship with his brother and how he got the garage. That's another thing he won't talk about."

Tina put her finger on her chin and thought for a moment, "I remember a quote I read somewhere, I think it was Mark Twain, the popular American author. It goes something like this: 'Every man is a moon with a dark side he never shows to anyone.' Kimmie, if you want to learn more about what Fred is hiding, you will need to get behind that dark side and shine a light. Ask questions and see what answers he gives."

I stared at my sister, her wisdom shining its own light into my mind and heart. I hugged her and said, "I don't know how I will do that, but I will give it some thought and effort. Thank you."

Cousin Michael is home from college, looking very handsome and grown up. Grace, Auntie's middle child, has two small children with her husband who is an engineer at the local power company and Dorothy has a son almost seven years old and very smart in school. I learned that the common nickname for Dorothy is "Dot", and she goes by Dot Kahn at work. Guess where she is working? That's right…an internet company!

Grace's husband is Vietnamese, and Dorothy's is American, and all auntie's children are mixed Asian-American, so they have very much an international and interracial family. I don't think any country in the world has so much mixing of cultures as in America!

Fred has much more fun talking with my family than with his own, and I can share the Fierce 5 stories because they can appreciate how interesting it is. The family can't wait to see my first ads!

But Tina was the star of the day, I think, with lots of fresh stories to share about New York and everyone wanting to help her settle in. Luckily, Tina has been here enough times to know her way around the city without much trouble. She bought one of the new GPS systems before leaving NYC to help her get around Riverton and was showing everyone how it works. So cool!

We had a late dinner and everything is so wonderfully good! We brought another sweet potato pie for this party too, as we had so many yams. Easy to bake…healthy to eat!

Happy News from Family

December 27, 2000
Dear My Diary,

It finally happened…Thao and Phung are engaged! Thao called and gave us the details today. Phung invited Thao (with Ba and Me's permission) to Vung Tau, a popular seaside town not far from Ho Chi Minh City. They left the city by high-speed boat and arrived at the resort two hours later. Their hotel fronts the ocean with a private swimming area and many restaurants and night clubs nearby.

Phung rented a private boat to take them to one of the nearby islands and the crew set up a picnic lunch on the beach with a table, chairs, shade umbrellas and some fancy foods including a bottle of champagne.

A waiter poured the champagne so Phung and Thao could make a Christmas toast and Thao saw something in her glass. She carefully drank down the wine and at the bottom was a big diamond ring!

Then Phung got down on one knee and professed his love for Thao. Of course, she said "YES!"

Thao said she felt this was going to happen, especially as Phung has never invited her to a romantic place like this before. Moreover, it is Christmas time and I got engaged at the same time last year. Does that make me a trend-setter?

Thao has been very much in love with Phung for a long time and she knew he had strong feelings for her too. But since they work together and workplace romances are usually not a good thing, they were very careful about revealing their feelings to each other. Over time, they became much more comfortable, both personally and professionally, to the point where everything clicked for them. Ba and Me have a deep-seated trust, and love too, for Phung. Like the son they never had.

If I think the way my parents think, the combination of Phung's computer and operational skills and Thao's marketing and sales expertise, they make a powerful team to run the family business, especially when Ba and Me make the decision to retire.

I told Fred the good news when he came to the kitchen, so he took the phone and made his congratulations to them, wishing much happiness for the future. Later, I told Fred how Phung proposed. Fred smiled wryly, "Sounds more romantic than proposing in a Ferris Wheel."

"No!" I said, "It was very romantic in the Ferris Wheel, and different, and I was not expecting it." I took his hand in mine and looked into his eyes, so he knew I was serious, "I love that you proposed to me in a Ferris Wheel. It was a special moment on a special day and that makes you special to me."

I kissed Fred warmly on the lips to make sure he understood, and he kissed back just as passionately. Then Fred smiled and said, "If you say you prefer a Ferris Wheel proposal over lunch on a tropical beach, then I'll take your word for it."

Yes, it is very romantic to get engaged on a warm sandy beach with lunch and champagne, but Fred did not know about our beaches or how to make the proper arrangements.

I am very happy with the way Fred did it. It was clever and inventive of him to take the opportunity when it presented itself, much like in his business. I admit that maybe I am a tiny bit jealous of Thao for this, but I am still happy with my Fred!

New Year's Eve

Jan 1, 2001
Dear My Diary,

Last night, Fred and I went to the Rolling Acres Country Club for their New Year's Eve Fundraiser and Ball. Fred is not a member, but every year he is invited as a guest by one or another of his business associates.

He told me about it last month and said many important and distinguished people will be there so I should get "all dolled up" for the occasion and "hang the cost". What funny expressions! I asked Tina what the expressions meant. She explained, "Dress big and spend bigger."

After Thanksgiving, I took sister Thanh to Tree Top Gals where the clerks were very attentive and able to select some beautiful dresses for me. Since I do not have a reason to dress up very often, it was hard to decide which outfits to choose.

Luckily, Thanh has always had an eye for fashion and helped me select three outfits including shoes and purses for the party and any other special events we might attend in the future.

Many women were wearing outfits in Christmas red or white, but I chose a figure-hugging metallic-scaled dress that was full length down the back and left my legs exposed in the front almost to the knees. The dress scales were silver on top and blue underneath so any movement, like walking or dancing, caused the silver scales to shimmer blue and makes for a very eye-catching effect.

For this special occasion, I wore my diamond wedding ring and earrings and the coconut tree necklace. I saw a lot of women, as well as men, eyeing me as I passed and I could feel some of the old Cay Dua insecurity poking holes in my head. As soon as I felt the familiar pangs, I thought of Fred, straightened my back, and put on a confident smile to show them, "Yes, I *do* look good, don't I?"

I had met some of the guests at Fred's Merry Bucking Christmas Party, but there were hundreds of people in attendance so I could not meet everyone, even if I had tried. Fred spoke easily and confidently among the doctors, lawyers, bankers, business, and civic leaders that filled the hall.

I was proud in how he mixes with the distinguished gentlemen and their wives, dressed in tuxedos, designer dresses and jewels while introducing me in a gracious, respectful manner. The questions and comments directed to me were intelligent, thoughtful, kind, and not of the sort I had heard just the week before.

Dinner was a sit-down affair of salad, soup, a choice of roasted meats, starches and vegetables with several sauces, beverages and dessert served by an army of waitstaff. Meanwhile, the mayor and other notables greeted us from the head-table and shared stories of the different charities featured this year while encouraging us to "open your wallets as well as your hearts".

Bobby invited Sister Tina as his guest so he could introduce her around and get her acquainted with some of his firm's clients. She has already met with the staff, getting familiar with their products and services, putting together a plan of action, ordering business cards and organizing her new office.

While Tina had dinner with Bobby and his group, Fred and I ate with some couples, most of whom Fred has done one kind or another business with, and they spoke mostly of improvements being considered for the downtown waterfront, local politics, and home renovations they are doing.

I mostly smiled and nodded, not understanding much about any of the topics until they were talking about trips to other cities and Fred mentioned our honeymoon in New York.

That put a spark into Jessica who looked right at me and said, "You! That was you, wasn't it?" Turning to Fred, she asked, "That was her, wasn't it?" Then to the others, "That was her…I knew I had seen her before!"

Everyone looked as confused as I felt and her husband put his hand on Jessica's arm, "What are you talking about Jess? Did she do something to you?"

Did I? She had been eyeing me in an uncomfortable way from the time we sat down.

She jerked her arm away from Robert, "We just saw her a few nights ago…I can't believe you don't recognize her." And then to me, "You were on Midnight Noise with Rock Rollins. That was you, wasn't it?"

Now everyone was looking at me, waiting for my answer, including Fred who wore a smirky smile, so I answered, "Yes, that was me."

"I knew it!" she cried out, slamming her palm against the table, making the silverware jump. "Didn't anyone else see it? Rock was throwing knives at her and she couldn't remember where she lived."

"Please lower your voice, Honey, people are staring," Robert said nervously.

"That show was from a few months ago," someone else said. "You must have seen a rerun. I remember it because I recognized Fred in the audience pointing at Kim to be selected. That was August, I think."

Fred held up his hands in a gesture of surrender, "Guilty as charged."

"So, let me ask you something, Kim," Jessica was leaning forward, voice lowered and slightly slurred with alcohol, "Were those knives Rock threw at you real, or was it some bullshit Hollywood trick?"

Again, all eyes were on me, Fred's were narrowed. I had their attention, so I looked deep into Jessica's eyes and said, "They were real. Very real. And very sharp."

A collective gasp came from my audience, which included members of nearby tables. Linda said, "That's so brave. Why did you let him do it?"

"During the commercial break, Rock told me how he trained for months with weapons experts to get the technique just right…so I trusted him. And when the knives hit," I looked around the table during my story, making sure I had eye contact with every person, "it was with such force, the target vibrated deep into my body. Bvvvv! Bvvvv! Bvvvv! Just like that. Incredibly dangerous."

"Incredibly sexy…oops!" Jessica held a hand to her mouth as the others laughed.

"Yes, that too," I added with a wink. Fred shook his head, grinning like a naughty schoolboy.

The big draw of the party was a silent auction. A row of tables displayed a variety of quality items from signed art pieces and jewelry to golf clubs and high-end electronics that had been donated for the auction. If you want an item, you write your name and price your bid on the sheet of paper in front of it.

I saw people making bids far above the value of the item I would have guessed. When I pointed this out to Fred, he said that for charity, yes, people will often pay much more than retail price because all the proceeds are split between the children's hospital, Nelson Scholarship Fund and Homes for the Homeless. I put down some bids but did not win any of the items.

Sadly, I do not remember most of the names of the people I spoke with or what they do. Fred said not to worry about it as he has spent years getting to know many of these people, some of whom were neighbors, classmates, or customers of his family's garage.

Fred pointed out an elderly couple at the head table, Peter and Nellie Nelson, and told Tina and I the story of how they grew up in Riverton as childhood sweethearts.

Lois: Peter and Nellie married right after college and both became teachers, spending decades with the Riverton Municipal School District. Childless, they saw the unmet needs of poverty-stricken families and how it affected the ability of their children to learn. The Nelsons collected and donated money, clothing, food, school supplies and other necessities to help struggling students succeed in school.

The Nelsons lived frugally, living to the end of their lives in Nellie's inherited childhood home, even as both became district administrators and Peter rose to be Director of the State School Board.

Unspent money was regularly put into the stock market during its long climb from the booming post-war years onward, the Nelsons using much of their profits to help not only local children, but the community in general, donating generously to a variety of causes including the creation of the Nelson Scholarship Fund that has helped thousands of deserving students attend college and trade schools.

Now in their nineties, they have been retired for many years and are still active in the community, like tonight, to raise money and visit with old friends.

They look very sweet to me with cotton-white hair and holding hands while people came up to speak with them, smile and shake hands or give Nellie a kiss on the cheek. I should hope Fred and I live so long as them and be so happy!

As Fred went to refresh our drinks, a man came over to our table that I recognized as Shawn, a major beverage distributor and one of the Fierce 5 owners. He greeted me by name and gave his congratulations on my becoming one of their spokesmodels.

Pleased with the attention, I thanked him and said I looked forward to working with Zander on the upcoming photo shoot.

"When are you going to introduce me to your friend, Kim?" Shawn said, cocking his head towards Tina.

"I'm Tina," she said, reaching out her hand.

"My sister," I added. "She just moved to Riverton."

Shawn seemed surprised to learn this and remarked, "I assumed you were from a family of Amazons."

I know the English word "Amazon", so I corrected him, "Our family is from Vietnam, not South America."

He looked at me uncertainly, then burst out in laughter, "That's a good one, Kim!" then to Tina, "Is she always this funny?"

"Oh, yes," said Tina sweetly, "especially when she speaks Portuguese."

"TWO funny ladies!" Shawn said, pointing to each of us. "I like that!"

He leaned closer in, the whiskey on his breath making my nose wrinkle, "Welcome to our fair city Tina, and since you're new in town, I'd be happy to show you around. Help you get the lay of the land." Shawn pulled out a card and pen, scratching down a number on the back. "My personal cell, for when you want to get out of the house and see the sights."

Tina took the card and put it in her clutch without looking at it. "I'll keep that in mind."

"Amazons. Lay of the land…what a jerk!" she scoffed as Shawn walked away.

I was confused as to what just happened, except that he thought we were from the Amazon Rainforest and he asked Tina out to show her around, which I thought was a good thing, but clearly Tina thought differently. When I asked, she explained what was said, and what was meant.

Her English is so much better than mine. Now I wonder how often I am insulted without realizing it.

When Fred came back to the table, I told him how Shawn offered to take Tina on a tour of Riverton. Fred shook his head and warned sister, "Be careful, Shawn has a collection of ex-wives and children to support but is always looking for his next ex-to-be."

Tina made a face and said, "Even worse than I thought!"

I spoke to Tina off and on throughout the evening. She feels mentally prepared for her new job as the work is very similar to what she has been doing in New York. The big difference here is that she will be spending more time out of the office and meeting customers at their businesses.

Trinh: My clients in New York were wealthy, well-connected, and lived all over the world, doing business by email, fax, phone and video conferencing so they rarely had need to come to my office or vice versa.

In Riverton, my recruiting targets were Asian, mostly small business-owners who worked long days, so I had to meet with them on their terms, even if it meant nights or weekends. Moreover, these clients tended to not be financially sophisticated and were wary of products and services they did not understand.

My advantage was a combination of being culturally like them, along with a prestigious education, experience, and the ability to explain details, earn trust and overcome objections better than a non-Asian.

My role in helping the police interview My Dung's clients, translating documents and returning most of the recovered money added yet another layer of trust and respect among Riverton's tight-knit Asian community, making the potentially difficult job of recruiting clients, much easier.

The more Tina talked about her plans for next year, the more excited she became. On the spot, I told her, "I want to be your first client."

She gasped in surprise, "Oh, Kimmie! That is so sweet of you. I wish I could do that, but…" and a playful grin spread across her face, "You will have to get in line behind Thanh and Aunt Giang…they both asked me at Thanksgiving!"

We laughed and hugged as Fred came over for a dance, an amused yet puzzled smile on his lips as he asked, "Am I interrupting a private party, here?"

After explaining what just happened, he took us both onto the dance floor to celebrate against the backdrop of "Boogie Paradise" and "Bring it On".

During the announcements of the auction winners, I asked Fred if he had donated to the fund raiser. He said "Yes, of course, I do it every year." When I asked how much, he said "Ten".

"Ten dollars?" thinking it was not very much. "Is that all?"

Fred laughed and jokingly pinched my nose, "We couldn't get our coats checked for ten dollars, Sweetheart. I meant ten thousand." Oh! It surprised me that he can afford so much money. But the charities will help many people.

We danced more than we ever have before and celebrated the coming of 2001 with lots of confetti and balloons falling from the ceiling. We did not leave until after two…such a long night!

Kimmie: Our engagement and wedding parties were wonderful, but the annual New Year's Eve Benefit Ball took my breath away. The ballroom was enormous and dressed out in Roman style columns and décor. A live orchestra played and there were more jewels than I had ever seen before in one place…it was simply stunning. Kind of like Cinderella at the ball…but I came with my own prince!

For all the wealthy people there, most of them were down to earth, interesting to talk to and knowledgeable about Vietnam and many other topics. Fred was so handsome in his tuxedo and spent as much time with me as he did with others. I am glad Tina was there to keep me company when Fred went off to greet this person or that couple, but just as often he brought the other people to meet me and Tina for a few minutes.

When he told me he had donated $10,000, I thought certainly Fred was making fun with me. Five hundred or a thousand maybe, but not ten! He showed me the cancelled check later and the bank statement. That was the first time I was made aware as to how much money he might really have.

2001
Getting the New Year Started Right

Sunday, January 7th
Dear My Diary,

We got so much done in the last week…whew! Fred did the numbers from Ba's Bonanza and was impressed with the final figures. Over $200,000 in sales after costs, but before taxes, to be split evenly. Ba asked me to hold their portion for later use. I am not sure what "later use" means, but I have some ideas.

It was hard work, but we got rid of it all and collected a lot of donated items from the college boxes and dumpsters over the holiday break to re-sell. Luckily it was dry so no water damage from items left outside the boxes.

Now, people are calling us for their after-holiday "help me get rid of all this extra junk" pick-ups. Fred said it's like this every year after New Year's, during spring cleaning and after school lets out for the summer.

Tina found a cute apartment in downtown just a short walk from B&R's office AND she gets free parking in their building as one of her perks! Sister said it makes her comfortable to be in downtown, kind of like in New York with many shops nearby for food and sundry items.

We helped her get fixed up with some new/old furniture and kitchen items and she bought a new mattress and box spring set as you don't want to get those used (ick!!). She moved out of Thanh's place yesterday and the girls are already complaining they will miss her. Tina said she won't miss waking up to the family arguing and fussing at each other before they go to work.

Fred has been having some fun with me this week and it's getting annoying. He sees me and stops suddenly. Pointing, he says, "Is that you? That *is* you, isn't it? Are you sure you're you? I thought that was you…or is it me?" And so on, making fun of that Jessica woman.

When I asked Fred about her, he wasn't sure if she acted that way because of alcohol, pills, mental problems or a combination of things. "I don't know the couple all that well, but I have heard that she can be a handful." I can believe it by the way her husband showed concern and embarrassment.

Fred will stop soon enough as I have been ignoring his so-called comedy.

First Fierce 5 Photo Shoot

January 10
Dear My Diary,

Today was my official photo shoot for Fierce 5 and I have been told early on that I should stop saying "models". We are "The Talent".

First, we had a breakfast meeting with Premier Productions talent manager Crystal Bridges who made introductions all around and gave us the schedule for the day along with sketches of the kinds of poses and facial expressions they would require of us.

During our meeting, Zander and her assistants made their final adjustments to lighting, backgrounds and so forth. On a table nearby were dozens of cans of Fierce 5 in different flavors to be used as our props.

I already know Bettina who I learned is Dutch and her F5 name is Ice Queen. Jaguar is an African American from Georgia, Diabla is from Venezuela, Scirocco from Morocco (funny rhyme!) and my F5 name is Chimera.

I learned that a Chimera is a mythical fire-breathing creature made up from parts of different animals. The animal parts vary with which source is used but now I know why my character is Fierce!

Crystal took me aside and said I would be last in the taking of individual poses, with the understanding that I am new to the business and to watch the others carefully so I could mimic their actions. She was kind in her manner, and I understood she was doing this as a professional courtesy to me. I said I would do my best and thanked her for what she was doing.

After make-up, fangs and hair, we started with single full and half-body poses, moving on to close ups, then pairs and trios, most of the poses involving a stare-down with the camera, before bringing the full Fierce 5 team together.

We did groupings of five across; stacked up and down with a can in each hand next to our heads (ten cans total); in a circle facing inward, our right arms raising F5 drinks aloft to meet in the center, right legs bent slightly at the knee and our left legs thrust behind us in a kind of victory pose; and I can't remember what all else.

Thankfully, many of the shots did not require us to show our pointy teeth so we could put them in glasses of sterile water when they weren't needed. We were there all day as they tried many different set-ups, backgrounds and we went through four sets of costumes. They will have plenty of material to choose from for different kinds of ads.

The models are all friendly with me and each other. Some have worked together on other projects and all live in the US now. Throughout the day, they taught me tricks like how to look straight ahead, then snap my head to the side "with attitude", different ways of walking and standing and how to make certain facial expressions, then holding them for long periods of time as the photographer takes shots from different angles. It was fun to learn.

I had Diabla take pictures of me with my phone so I could send them to my sisters and parents and show them my Fierce Side. It's like Halloween, but I will get paid with cash and not candy.

We were there ten hours and even got paid for the time we ate lunch. They gave us pay envelopes at the end of the day and will tell us in plenty of time when our next job will be. Before we left, I opened the envelope and inside was a check for $2,500 and a Stock Certificate for 500 shares of Fierce 5.

Fred let me know that right now the share price is $8 but they give us shares at a discounted price of $5. That means I got $4,000 worth of stock for $2500 or a 60% bonus right away. I can sell it now and get the cash or keep it as is. I will keep it for now and see if it goes up. Yay!

Fred spent part of the afternoon cooking up a nice meal for us and we discussed my very interesting day. He said he is still chuckling about the story I told at our dinner table and how convincing it sounded that Rock had used real knives. "And I loved your sound effect. That was inspired! Bvvvv! Bvvvv! I could almost feel it myself!"

I reminded Fred how he told me not to tell anyone about the rigged target and let them think it was a real stunt. He remembered and added, "I guarantee you that story is getting around and your Cool Kids Club factor is going up with it."

"You think so?" I asked. "I don't think they will tell anyone."

"Are you kidding, Kimmie? People are going to spot you on the street, as striking as you are, and tell the person they are with, 'See that tall babe over there? I heard she was on Midnight Noise with Rock Rollins and he was throwing knives at her. Is she famous? I'm sure she is if she was on TV with The Rock.' That's what they're going to say about you. Cool Kids Club all the way for you!"

Fred is too sweet!

So far, I have had a good time learning to model and meeting such fun and interesting women from all over the world. I hope the ads work out for Fierce 5…looks like we are now BOTH invested in the company and its future.

I have seen Mama's stage name spelled "Chimera" in some of her earlier work but always thought it was a typo or misprint. Now we understand the details of how she got started…and it was all due to Dad's gentle persuasion. Mama had never considered being a model or actress due to her low self-esteem.

Between Dad's involvement with Fierce 5 and being on stage with Rock Rollins, it all kind of planted a seed in her that made her who she is now. When things weren't so good, Dad reminded her she could quit if she wanted, or do something else, or not do anything at all…but Mama was never one to quit. And neither are we.

Bernie's Big Case

January 17, 2001
Dear My Diary,

Bunny called to say hello and how she misses hanging out with me. Christmas was lousy for her and there has not been much to do between the cold weather and Bernie's preparations for the big lawsuit which started today.

The Riverton Review and local radio stations are giving a lot of coverage to Bernie's case due to the unusual injury and number of defendants being sued. Local opinion-makers say it is ridiculous, a waste of the court's time and many people are making fun of the case in general.

I gave Bunny a quick update about my Fierce 5 photo shoot and Tina getting settled into her new job. I promised we will try to get together soon but Fred and I have been SO busy lately.

Fred says the weather is worse than usual for January with sleet and freezing rain common this month. That does not stop us from going to the auctions when they haven't been cancelled due to weather. When we do go, there are very few who show up to bid.

Since they are also resellers like us, as a professional courtesy, we all quietly agree to take turns buying lockers. By doing this, we are not driving up the prices against each other and everybody gets something by the end of the day. Most of the lockers sell for ten dollars or less because of it. Not good for the storage company but good for us.

Fred and I have learned how to move fast and efficiently as a team to stay warm and get everything home. Then it's time to sort, list and sell!

Thomas Stimson

Bunny's Barney Update

Dear My Diary,

Bunny emailed me to say the court case is lasting much longer than expected. She thought it would last one week but has been dragging on for nearly a month. The defending lawyers are bringing up numerous legal arguments against paying and Barney is coming back with other legal arguments for his client to be paid.

Some of Barney's arguments, according to the news, are outlandish and the reporters are openly wondering why the judge does not cut Barney off when he goes on lengthy, rambling rants. When I ask Fred about it, he acts annoyed and says he does not care what Barney is up to. That's a lie because I have caught him sneaking looks at the TV and articles about the case…so he does care!

Bunny wishes Barney had taken the settlements offered early on so he can work on other cases and they could pay their bills.

The Six Million Dollar Man

Feb 12, 2001
Dear My Diary,

Fred's telephone rang while he was in the shower, so I answered it. A man was yelling, "Six-million-dollar man, GM! I am the six-million-dollar man! Ha ha ha ha ha! Take that, bitch!" and hung up. He sounded drunk and it was probably a wrong number, but his sudden announcement and hang-up rattled me.

Fred came out of the shower and asked who had called so I told him what the man had said.

"Sounds like Barney," he said, appearing unconcerned.

"Now, how do you know that?" I asked. "You didn't even hear his voice!"

"When Barney gets especially fired up, he calls me 'GM', which is one of his brotherly terms of endearment." With some encouragement from me, he admitted that GM stands for 'Garbage Man'.

"That is a terrible name!" I said, "But why did he say he is a six-million-dollar man?"

Fred shrugged, "Who knows…who cares?"

Dear My Diary,

Maggie called us to ask if we saw the news about Bernie? She would not say what it was and I did not tell her about the surprise phone call last night. I fetched the newspaper and on the front page was the story of how Bernie got a total of $6 million for his client and how the decision surprised everybody.

What happened is puzzling to us but here is what happened: After all the lawyers and witnesses were done, the jury made their decision that Bernie's client did not deserve any compensation. There was not enough fault found on those being sued and too much fault for the injured woman. No money was awarded, and Bernie lost the case. That should have been the end of it…but it wasn't.

The judge overruled the jury and very quickly awarded the woman $1.2 million from each of the five parties sued for a total of $6 million. That is what Bernie meant when he called. I still do not like that he called Fred a GM. Does that make me a GW?

I asked Fred if all the companies will have to pay the money and he explained that the sued parties will typically appeal the decision, making legal arguments about why they should not have to pay. Until a final decision is reached, the woman will not be paid.

"The appeals process can go to multiple courts, last for years and cost a great deal of money to continue. To save time and money, the losing parties can offer to settle the case for less than what the judge ordered and be done with it."

I had learned from Bunny that when Bernie wins a case or gets a settlement, his fee is 1/3 of the total collected. If his client gets all the money, Bernie will get $2M as his payday and he will be a millionaire.

When I informed Fred of this, he said "Well, good luck, Chuck!"

Excerpt from the Riverton Review February 13, 2001: In a surprise move, Judge William Davidson overruled a jury's dismissal of Bernard Bartlett's "Cat Food Can" lawsuit and returned with his own verdict of all parties being found equally at fault and awarding the plaintiff, Mrs. Lauren Leatherwood, a total of six million dollars to be divided among the five defendants. Attorneys for the defendants are expected to file appeals.

Valentine's Day!

Wednesday, February 14
Dear My Diary,

Fred and I got an invitation by email to celebrate Bernie's victory at the Rolling Acres Country Club. I do not want to go because Bernie is such a jerk, but Fred is willing because sometimes he can make good business contacts at the club.

"But why would he invite us after…you know…what happened?" I shuddered to remember when Barney had threatened me with Fred's arrest and my deportation if I would not sleep with him.

"Two words…no friends." Fred replied. "The little rooster likes to have an audience while he crows for his hen, or, in this case, his client. Oh, and to rub my nose in his success."

"What does that mean?"

"You know. 'I just scored a big win and you're still a junk dealer. Nyah, Nyah Nyah.' Kid stuff." Fred chuckled, "I'm a bigger man than to let something like that bother me. Besides, he doesn't know what I know."

Now I'm curious that he will tell me a secret he has been keeping from me. "What do you know that Barney doesn't know?"

Fred kissed me, "How lucky I am to have you in my life," he said, pinching my nose playfully. "Grrrr!"

That's when I got a call from Bunny asking if I am going to the gathering at the country club. When I said I didn't think so, she begged me with "pretty please?"

Apparently, Bernie is afraid of me now and we were invited as Bunny's guests, not Bernie's, because she wants me to keep her company while Bernie "makes an ass of himself."

The luncheon will be this Saturday and Bunny promised there will be lots of seafood to eat (she knows I love good seafood!) so we agreed to go, but I am not happy about it.

I have been looking at different kinds of cars as we go about our business…liking this one, not liking that one. Asking Fred, Frank and sisters about different car makers since many in the US are not found in Vietnam. I want my own car and not be forced to drive Fred's beat-up trucks all the time. I'm sure Fred is tired of my hints. Maybe I am not a good hinter. But then, maybe I am…

After visiting the OMV to change some car titles into both our names, we stopped in at a car dealership we pass frequently. "Why are we here?" I asked.

"We need a sedan for someone with long beautiful legs," he said.

"Oh, I see! Getting a car for yourself?" I teased, secretly happy for what he just said.

Fred asked the nearest salesperson for Charlie Thomas. Charlie is the Sales Manager and an old school friend of Fred's. This is my Valentine Day surprise…a car!

I already have an idea of what I want but tried several different makes and models to see the differences and get the right fit for my "long beautiful legs". I asked Fred if we are getting a new or used car? Fred asked Charlie to excuse us so we could speak privately.

Fred said, "Sweetheart, I know I'm frugal, almost to a fault. But when it comes to you, I want you to have your hearts' desire. You've worked so hard, and I am so very, very proud to have you in my life. That's why we are here today. I love you so much. Any car, any age, any price. You name it, and it's yours."

"Any price, Fred? Are you sure?" I teased, "I might have some secret desire that costs way more than any of these little toys." I stroked his cheek with my finger, gazing deeply into his sea-blue eyes, "Last chance to change your mind about what you just said. Mmm?"

He gazed back just as intensely, "I'll take my chances."

"Hmmm. Okay then, my brave lover boy, call your old school friend back over here."

I ended up with a beautiful demo model the dealership had been using, at a deeply discounted price with plenty of leg room for both of us. We took out a loan so I can start building my credit, another item for the "joint assets" file.

After a long, hot, sexy shower, we dressed up and Fred drove me in our new car to the casino for their Valentine's Day buffet. We had not eaten all day so we could "stuff ourselves silly" as Fred likes to say. Crab, lobster, steak and so much more. We toasted our love with sparkling cider and had our picture taken at a special booth in the lobby…no charge!

We even went into the casino and played some slot machines and then a quarter push machine. We had watched others do it, then give up after a short time so we got forty dollars in quarters and made a plan.

Part of the challenge is trying to knock over tall stacks of coins, one of them with a tightly rolled one-hundred-dollar bill poking out the top like a flagpole on a tall building.

Fred was so funny, making jokes and getting overly excited when quarters fell into our hands. We kept replaying the quarters that fell into the trough until the stacks collapsed and eventually the piles of quarters, along with the bill, fell out and filled several change cups. It took over two hours, but we won back several times our dinner bill. Much more fun than slot machines or card games!

Barney's Victory Party

Dear My Diary,

Such a party yesterday! It's the same country club we went for New Year's Eve and Bernie got a big table in the middle of the dining room. The restaurant is beautiful with a large chandelier, fresh flowers on the tables, cloth napkins and heavy silverware. I wore a long, knit dress with matching tights and some fur-topped boots to look nice and still stay warm.

As soon as we came in, I went straight to Bernie as he eyed me with suspicion until I extended my hand, as a kind of peace offering. We shook hands as I congratulated him on winning the case on behalf of my family and wishing him future success.

He was taken by surprise at my words and seemed to soften a bit. Bernie introduced me to his client and her family. Mrs. Leatherwood awkwardly offered me her left hand to shake and kept the thumbless right to her side.

Fred had helped me with properly expressing in English what I wanted to say to his brother, as an attempt to defuse any hostility he might still be carrying about my blacking his eye, which he fully deserved. As I made eye-contact with him, I couldn't help but notice that Bernie's nose looks a bit more lumpy and crooked than I remember.

The part about my family's good wishes…I have no idea if my sisters know or care about Bernie's case, but I wanted to show kindness when he expected different. Fred came in a moment later with a shopping bag and set it between the chairs he selected for us. As I arrived at my seat, Fred pulled the chair out and Bunny nudged her husband, whispering, "Why don't you ever do that for me?" as he pulled coldly away from her.

Bernie put on a real show for Mrs. Leatherwood, her mother and children. Besides Bunny, Fred and myself, there were Bernie's secretary (I did not know he had one…I thought he worked alone?) and an office assistant with their spouses. There were others we didn't know and whom Bernie did not introduce. Maggie and Frank were not there.

Bernie had champagne brought out and served to everyone, even me and Fred. Bernie knows Fred does not drink, so I think he did it more for show. Fred ordered ginger ale for both of us, which was fine by me.

As often happens, some people kept looking at me from the corner of their eyes but were too polite to stare. I instinctively straightened my back, smiled, and attempted some small talk.

As the appetizers came around, one man asked Fred what he does for a living and before Fred could answer, Bernie said, "He's a GM, aren't you Freddy?"

Fred replied to the man, "That's right, I'm a General Merchandiser." He answered so quickly and confidently that I could tell this was not the first time he used that line.

Bernie smirked while the man asked me the same question. I could tell he was just trying to be polite, so I answered that Fred and I work together as self-employed merchandisers. Fred looked pleased and patted my knee under the table.

Not wanting to lose the attention of his guests, Bernie spoke up, "Kim, didn't I hear you were a member of your countries' Olympic basketball team?" I don't know why he said this except to try to fluster or embarrass me.

I calmly said, "No. I tried to join but…I was too short!" and I pushed my hand down on my head to emphasize my height. People laughed and Bernie shook his head but did not pursue it further. Fred muttered "Good job!" to me in Vietnamese and Bunny winked at me as she laughed into her napkin.

It felt good to turn the tables on Bernie. Unluckily for him, this was not the first time I have had this type of question posed to me in the past, so I had a comeback ready.

Bernie talked a lot about his big win, how well he argued the case, and how the jury did not know anything, concluding that the judge was very smart to overturn the jury's decision. Then he turned to Mrs. Leatherwood and asked, "So, what are you going to do with your millions? Get some more cats?"

People groaned and I thought the poor woman was going to melt with embarrassment. Mrs. Leatherwood is a soft-spoken woman who was clearly not happy being the center of attention.

Her family did not speak much, looking uncomfortable in, what I assume, were their best clothes. I tried speaking to the children for a few minutes, but they just mumbled some polite answers and did not look interested in talking to me.

A middle-aged man in golfing clothes came to our table and spoke briefly to Fred, who then excused himself and went to the bar to speak with him in private. Bernie called out to the retreating golfer, "Did you hear about my big win?"

"Everybody in the room heard," he answered.

Bernie laughed, "Damn right!"

I told Bunny I had something to show her outside and as we put on our coats, Bernie frowned and said, "Where are you two going?"

"Back before you know it, Perry Mason," Bunny said, to the laughter of the others. Bernie beamed.

As we headed for the parking lot, I asked what a Perry Mason is. "He was a TV lawyer, never lost a case kind of guy. It was a compliment…sort of."

I showed Bunny my new car and she was very impressed. We got in and I showed how much room there is for my legs and some of the nice features. I didn't tell her it was Fred's present to me as I don't want her to feel bad or jealous, but I did want to tell her something that has been on my mind for many months.

"Bunny? I had you come out here to not only show you the car, but to personally thank you."

She cocked her head, "Thank me? For what?"

"For coming to my wedding."

Bunny kind of froze, not sure how to respond, like I was testing her. "You knew?"

"I learned about it afterwards."

"So, you're not mad that I came after you told me not to? I planned it so Bernie didn't know what I was doing and…"

"I know. That was a very sisterly thing to do," I said reassuringly, my hand on her arm. "Fred told me what you did and how careful you were. I appreciate that."

"Thanks, Kimmie," she said, dabbing her eye with a tissue. "It was a beautiful ceremony."

"And," I added, "your bird mobile is happy as the center of attention in the living room. It goes well with the twinkle lights."

Bunny giggled, "I'm glad. We better get back before the food comes out."

Fred had returned from the bar and the waiters were serving our table, beginning with our host. I asked how his meeting went and Fred said softly, "Will tell you later."

Then he retrieved the shopping bag from under the table and came around to Bernie as he was taking another gulp of champagne.

"As your brother, I wanted to say congratulations on winning your biggest case ever and," Fred shook the bag gently, "I have a gift appropriate for the six-million-dollar man."

Bernie looked surprised, then suspicious as Fred removed the gift-wrapped box from the bag and handed it to Bernie. We all watched as he opened his gift. Inside was a tall narrow box with a man-doll inside.

Bernie chuckled, "Will you look at that…a Steve Austin action figure! The Six Million Dollar Man!" The brothers shook hands and Bernie held the box up to show everyone, as we all applauded and cheered, even the people at the bar. I did not understand the cultural reference, but Bernie was so pleased, he behaved himself for the rest of the evening.

Dinner was steak and lobster, crab cocktail, saffron-seasoned rice, asparagus with sauce and other foods. I made small talk with the other guests who seemed very interested in Vietnam and my coming to America. I learned that most of the guests are potential clients whom Bernie is trying to court, and that Bunny is going back to work for her husband to help with the expected increase in cases.

After we came home, I asked Fred about the doll and its meaning. He told me that The Six Million Dollar Man was a popular TV show when they were children and when Bernie said, "I am the Six Million Dollar Man", Fred found the doll among some recently sorted auction finds.

Fred told me the doll is worth about $200 as a collector's item, "which is $200 more than I expect Barney will actually make on the case." Fred did it to make Bernie happy and make us look good to others at the table.

I asked what the other man wanted to speak to him about at the bar and Fred explained that he is an estate lawyer with an interesting business offer, but they must act on it soon. Fred will follow up with him tomorrow.

As we got into bed, I commented that Bernie must be very rich to afford this kind of party. Fred got a pained look on his face and told me something I did not expect.

"Barney is in the habit of having a lavish party like this to celebrate his wins and court new business, then charging it all to the client's bill as 'Incidental Fees'."

I asked what does that mean exactly?

"It means," Fred said with a sigh, "Barney charged Mrs. Leatherwood for her own party."

We never knew a lot about this side of Uncle Barney but over the years, stories got around in the family of some of the unethical and even criminal things he pulled off. More to come…

Sneak Peek

March 1, 2001
Dear My Diary,

I took part of the morning to get my hair done at Thanh's shop when I got a call from Fred making sure I was still there. "Don't leave! I've got something I want to show you…you are all going to freak."

I know this term, "to freak". I also know he went to the Fierce 5 office this morning, so I had an idea of what he was bringing…and I was right!

As he walked through the door, Thanh abandoned me in the middle of a rinse to run over and hug Fred. "There he is! My favorite brother-in-law!"

"I'm your only brother-in-law," Fred reminded her with a smile.

"And STILL my favorite!"

"Mine, too!" called out Vo as he came from the back room. "And I have three others!"

"Well, that's good to know," Fred laughed, then held up a large envelope. "Are you ready to see what's coming out in the next two months?" he said to the shop, while looking directly at me.

Thanh finished rinsing out the suds, then wrapped my head in a thick, heated towel as Fred waited patiently. The towel felt *so good!*

"Okay, I'm ready. Now freak me."

Fred went to the main counter and pulled out two ad mock-ups as we crowded around. My heart was beating faster as he spread them out to the "oohs" and "aahs" of everyone there.

It was one thing to do a whole day of getting made up, taking directions, posing, and waiting around between set-ups in a cold, empty theater wearing uncomfortable costumes. It was something else entirely to see the professionally shot and enhanced pictures of five women in stylized make-up, fangs bared, standing in a line with leather-booted legs slightly spread and locked straight, right hands on hips and left hands thrust out, gripping cans of Fierce 5.

The ad read, "Live Fierce. Be Fierce. Drink Fierce 5"

"Oh my God, Kimmie, look at you!" Thanh cried out, pointing at Diabla, "You look so different!"

"Because that's me," I said, pointing to the model at the end.

Thanh looked more closely through her reading glasses, "You look even more different here!"

"Fierce 5 Makes You Feel Alive!" had all of us in a half-body shot holding various flavors of product next to our faces as we presented fangy smiles in devilishly delightful ways. I remember that one being a fun shot to do…and it shows in our expressions.

"Do you still have the costumes?" Vo asked, his eyes shiny and focused on the models.

Thanh pinched his arm, saying in Vietnamese, "That's your sister! Don't be a pig."

Vo rubbed his arm, "I meant for you to wear, my love."

"Nice try. I would swim in clothes that size," Thanh reminded him as their workers stifled laughs.

Fred put his hand into the envelope in a teasing manner, "And this last one…this one will be used exclusively throughout Riverton and the entire state." He laid the photo directly in front of me.

It's a close-up of a Fierce 5 model, head tilted down, ready to take a sip of the Rockin' Raspberry in her hand. As if interrupted, her face is turned slightly towards the camera, eyes connecting with the viewer. A slight smile plays across her lips. She looks seductive. Inviting. The caption: "Find your Fierce. Drink Fierce 5."

In the lower left corner is a word in quotation marks: "Chimera"

It's me…I have my own ad!

"Ohh my God!" Thanh shrieked, "Ohh my God, that's you!"

I had no idea they would do this…and it looks so good! Thanh hugged me. Then Vo hugged me. Fred had his arms outstretched and I folded myself into him for an extra big hug.

"Are they really going to put that ad all over the state?" I asked Fred, afraid the news was too good to be true.

"The ads still have to go through a final approval process, and these were the top picks." Fred said with assurance. "And yes, Chimera will be seen locally in newspapers, convenience stores and supermarkets where Fierce 5 is sold. And just to let you know, each of your teammates have their own solo ad in the other major markets we currently sell in…I just didn't bring those." He smiled down at me, "I wanted you to see your ad first. So, what do you think?"

I wiped my tears on his shirt, trying to regain my composure, "They're wonderful, Fred. I can't believe how good they look."

"That's why they hired Zander…she's the best. And so are you," Fred reminded me, leaning down for a kiss, then whispering into my ear, "You, in that picture, are hotter than a firecracker. Let's go home."

"Hey, movie star!" Thanh called out, "We need to wet your hair down again or it's gonna stick out all over."

"Fred's going to need a cold shower," Vo joked in English.

"Speak for yourself, funny-man," Thanh shot back. "And you, Little Sister, don't forget about us when you go off to Hollywood."

"What? No! It's just a modeling job," I assured her, "I'm not going to Hollywood."

"Hmmm, those pictures tell me different."

Lang Starbuckle: Dad made high-quality color copies of all the mock-ups and kept them in a safe-deposit box for many years. The originals at the Fierce 5 offices have been lost, possibly destroyed after being digitally stored to the Cloud.

Word has gotten out about the copies and we have had significant offers made by wealthy collectors as they are among the rarest and most sought after Fierce 5 memorabilia known to exist. As of this writing, they are still not for sale.

Lois: Years after this incident, Aunt Thanh would boast how she was the first to recognize her baby sister as a star of the future and, based on that singular prediction, would later turn to fortune-telling as a side-job…and she did very well at it!

Fred the Chump

Dear My Diary,

Fred will be leaving soon with Dan McClurg, the attorney Fred met with at the country club, to finalize a business deal with some family members of a deceased client. They live in different parts of the US so there will be a lot of flying and driving involved.

This will be the first time we have spent nights apart since our wedding. When I mentioned this to his parents, Frank and Maggie offered to let me stay at their place if I want. I will think about it…but it might be nice to have some alone time with them and learn more about the family.

Today was our Dissolving Debt class at the library. I made a small speech about the differences between Vietnam and how we treat debt (don't have any or it is very expensive to get) versus the US where debt is very easy to get. Fred helped me write and edit what I wanted to say, and we practiced the presentation several times so I can look and feel confident.

I enjoy doing the class with Fred and felt even better when Vo and Thanh came to the class for a second time as a refresher course. They have made many changes to their lifestyle and are saving money towards opening another salon. Thanh often calls me and Tina for advice, which we are happy to give. This is what sisters are for!

During the class, I saw Bunny and Barney walk by the auditorium doors, then stop and look in. Barney stared at us, then the audience, like he was trying to understand what we were doing. Fred looked over and said, "Hello! Would you like to join our Dissolving Debt class?" Barney shook his head quickly and left as Bunny smiled and waved at me.

Tonight, we got a call from Barney who asked many questions about what we were doing at the library. Fred had the phone on speaker mode so we could both listen as Fred explained the class and how he teaches people to reduce debt and grow their savings. The conversation continued like this:

Barney asked, "How much do you charge?"

"Nothing. It's a public service."

"You don't charge ANYTHING?!"

"Like I said, it's a public service."

"Is that something court-ordered? Do you have to do this class as part of community service?"

"No. I do this to help people."

"Looks like you had 150 to 200 people there. At fifty bucks a pop, you could make a quick ten grand!"

Fred explained that these people would likely not want to pay, or be able to afford, a fee as they are already deep in debt and looking for ways to get out.

"Well, that's why you charge them! You have information they need, they're desperate and you have them by the balls! Charge them for the information and if it doesn't work, who cares? Fifty dollars isn't much and maybe it will help you get out of that garage!"

"Is there anything else Barney?"

"Are you going to charge them a fee?"

"No, Barney."

"Then you're a chump…and don't call me Barney!" and he hung up.
I asked, "What is a 'chump'?"
"It's another word for a fool."
"But you're not a fool for not charging them, are you?"
Fred smiled wickedly, "I'm only a fool for you, girl!"

Lois: In his lawyering days, they say Uncle Barney wouldn't do anything for anyone unless he got something out of it for himself. Not an altruistic bone in his body and he didn't believe in doing anything for the sake of being kind, helpful or generous. That attitude would eventually change, but not without hard lessons learned in the process.

Starbuckle Family Stories

March 15, 2001

Dear My Diary,

Such a sweet and sour night! I took Fred to the airport early this morning, flying out to Seattle with Dan McClurg. The plan is to visit five people in three different cities to sign some release papers and, if all goes well, Fred said we will be staying busy for a few weeks, but the project should be worth it in the end.

I don't know what that means, and he won't tell me any more than that so as not to jinx his luck. The important thing is that Fred will be back in time for our first birthday together…Yay! I hope he gets me a nice present from wherever he is going.

Now that he is gone, I had time to wrap Fred's present and put it away.

I took up Frank and Maggie's invitation to stay in their home for the two nights Fred is gone so I do not get lonely. Bunny joined us for dinner and Bernie is working on some new cases at the office. He has been busy since he won the case for Mrs. Leatherwood and Bunny is helping at the office handling inquiries from potential clients and preparing court documents.

We had baked fish, rice, salad and wine…healthy and tasty! The wine was sweet, fruity and not too strong. It went well with the stories parents told about Fred and Barney as children. I have not understood the reason why Barney became Bernie, but tonight I found out.

When Maggie was pregnant with her first son, they could not decide on a name for the baby. They tried many, but none felt right. During this time, Maggie's grandmother, Louise, had been ill and was getting worse. Maggie and her mother cared for Grandma constantly as she neared the end of her life.

Suddenly, Grandma's eyes flew open and she sat straight up in bed crying out "Barnabas! Are you there? Where's Barnabas? I need to see my dear Barney one last time! Oh! There you are!" With those words, she stretched her arms straight out, fell back in bed, and passed her last breath.

I got chicken skin all over when Maggie told her story…ooh! Maggie and her mother did not know who Barnabas was. Was he Grandma's first love? A secret husband? A married man she loved from afar?

The person was a mystery, but Maggie liked the name Barnabas and the nickname Barney, so she convinced Frank to name their child Barnabas in honor of her grandmothers' memory if it was a boy and Louise if it was a girl.

So, who was Barnabas? The answer came years later when an old photo album was found in Louise's' house. Inside, along with many other photos, was one of a little girl, about eight or nine years old, with her arm around a duck. The caption read, "Louise and Barnabas – 1910". Barney was named after a duck! I have not laughed so hard since I came to Riverton.

Barney did not think the story was as funny as the rest of the family and came to hate his name. Once he decided to open his own law firm, Barney applied to the courts and had his name changed to Bernard Bartlett because Bernard Bartlett sounded more professional than Barnabas Starbuckle.

Sang Starbuckle: I remember hearing about Barnabas the Duck when my sisters and I were filming a sitcom in LA and the episode that week involved a pet duck that got lost. It reminded Mom of this incident and she told the story during lunch to the group of kid actors and extras. That someone was named after a duck got a lot of laughs, but I never heard Mom tell the story again.

Parents also told me how they lost their home and business when Bernie broke their trust by taking and investing their money in the risky bio-oil stock craze that was popular a few years ago. Eventually, the bio-oil bubble collapsed, causing investors to lose most or all of their money.

Apparently, Fred did not take the bait and was smart enough to stay out of bio-oil. When his parents lost the family home to the bank, he gave one of his rental houses to them. Unfortunately, Fred did not have enough money to save the family business, so it had to close, and all the employees lost their jobs.

Eventually, Fred bought the building back from the bank, but by then Frank was too broken financially and emotionally to start over. Fred chose to keep the garage and make it his headquarters, proudly keeping the family name on the building.

Frank said, "Our wish is to give this house back to Fred when we pass on, as a 'thank you' for what he's done for us."

Fred had not told me this story before…I don't know if he meant it to be a secret or just didn't think it was important enough to share. Or maybe it is one of the hurts he carries around and does not want to burden me as I learn the ways of married life and living in Riverton.

Whatever Fred's reason for not telling me, their story made me understand some of the pain the family has gone through. I do not understand everything, but I hope to learn in due time.

To put a softer edge on the topic for my sake, Maggie said, "Barney meant well," but Frank showed a flash of anger saying, "No he didn't. One day he is going to go too far and get himself arrested!" Then he looked at Bunny and, lowering his temper a bit, added, "I'm sorry, but I hope I am wrong."

Bunny nodded, then everyone stopped talking, so I asked Bunny to help me with the dishes.

Now I understand why Frank goes quiet whenever Barney is around. In the beginning, I thought Frank didn't like me when he spoke so little during our visits, but he was very kind and sweet with me tonight. Now I understand his heart is broken because of Barney and I am glad they have a son like Fred. I am just as glad to have married the "good son".

Frank and Maggie had gone back to their room when Bunny, having had several glasses of wine, suddenly blurted out, "All I can say is, 'Thank God Fred married you!'"

"Thank you, but why do you say that?"

"We all thought he might be gay."

I asked, "What is gay?" and Bunny looked surprised.

"You know, like Robbie and Bobbie. Guys who like guys better than girls."

"Why did you think Fred likes men that way? He acts very normal with me."

Bunny said that no one she knew had ever seen Fred out with a girl or dating anyone. "I mean, he's so gorgeous, he could have any woman he wanted!"

I remember how Fred called me "gorgeous" the first time he saw me. Now Bunny is calling Fred gorgeous.

Then Bunny said, "I mean, even I tried to get him in the sack."

Bunny could have punched me in the stomach, and it would not have shocked me as much as her words. Fred has told me from the very beginning that he had never bedded a woman before me.

Bunny continued, "I probably shouldn't be telling you this, but since it happened before you guys got together, you will understand."

My English may not be great, but even I know that any story starting with 'I probably shouldn't be telling you this…' is a story that shouldn't be told. Yet, she continued…and I listened.

"One night Bernie and I had a fight, a real big fight, and I left the house to get away from him. We were both pretty drunk and high and I don't even remember what the fight was about now.

"Anyway, I was mad and lonesome and wanted to get back at Bernie for all his crap. After driving around for a while, I ended up at Fred's apartment. That was before he moved into the garage."

The more she talked, the more I didn't want to hear any more of the story…but I couldn't stop listening. I wanted to know just how bad it got…and see how truthful Fred has been with me.

Bunny told Fred about the fight, hoping he would feel sorry for her. He listened and assured her that everything would be all right in the morning.

"Then I told him how I was lonely. 'Lonely for a nice man. A real man. A man who can make me feel like a real woman.' I did my best cuddle-up and tried to kiss Fred, but he turned his face aside like I was an old aunt and held me away, like this!" Bunny demonstrated pushing straight out, elbows locked, hands gripping imaginary arms.

"I mean, look at this!" presenting her body like a model, "Lots of guys would jump on this if they had the chance. Believe me, I get offers!"

Now she is bragging about her body and 'getting offers' like a working woman of the streets. I felt sick to hear this kind of talk. It would have made me sick, even if she wasn't talking about my husband.

"Anyway, in the end, Fred did right by me."

Suddenly, my cell phone rang and I jumped.

"I'll bet that's Lover Boy wanting to know why his ears are burning!" Bunny sang out, as she left the room. I could hear her say goodnight to Frank and Maggie before shutting the front door. She might have been drunk, but I was the one dizzy from all her talking.

I snuggled into bed while Fred told me about his day. He is in Seattle and met with two people to sign release contracts, adding "So far, so good!"

But it was hard for me to concentrate on his happy mood when part of my brain was struggling to understand what the phrase "Fred did right by me" meant. Did Fred sleep with his sister-in-law?

He and Doug will leave for Saint Louis in the morning to meet with one person and then all the way to Baltimore and nearby Philadelphia for the last meetings before flying home.

We talked a bit about my having a nice dinner and chat with parents. I did not tell him about Bunny's awful story. We agreed that Fred would call me instead of me calling him because if I call, he might be driving or in a meeting with Doug's clients. It's so good to hear his voice and I miss him, especially in the evening. He said to say "hi" to parents and family.

After we hung up, I thought more about Bunny's confession. What did she mean? As soon as she said, "Fred did right by me," the phone rang and she left the house. No follow up, no explanation…nothing. I don't know what to make of it.

Fred's call was relaxing so I will try not to think about Bunny's story. Ugh!

Lang Starbuckle: Aunt Bunny was always very sweet with us and she was a kind soul, but some of the outfits she wore were not what one would call "age appropriate". She was often needy in that "look at me" kind of way. It helped sometimes when she was doing sales, but it was kind of hit or miss on how people reacted to her.

It was understandable that some people might suspect Dad was gay, if only because he could not find someone with similar interests as him and his frugal lifestyle. Both our parents were outliers in their respective societies, but once they found each other, that was it!

Bernice "Bunny" Bartlett-Starbuckle: Yeah, your dad was a real hunk in his day. A lot of us thought he was, well, you know…more of a man-lover if you know what I mean. No dating that we saw, no locker-room talk about women. But when he brought Kimmie home, and we saw how beautiful she was, well, that pretty much told us what side his bread was buttered on, if you get my drift. They were a real match made in heaven…not like my match with your uncle, God rest their souls.

Doing Right by Me

March 16, 2001

Dear My Diary,

Last night Maggie asked me if I wanted to invite my sisters and auntie for a barbeque this evening. I called and everyone will be here between five and six o'clock.

I am still thinking about Bunny's story from last night. I cannot believe Fred could be considered gay by anyone. He looks at me often with admiring, even hungry, eyes and we have so much passion for each other during our intimate times.

Fred is my first lover, and I like the way he keeps things fun as well as tender. I think we will both like the present I got for him…I just can't give it to him in front of anyone else.

I can understand now the how and why people love so deeply as a couple. But I am disturbed by how Bunny's story ended the way it did. I would understand and expect Fred, or any man, to have other lovers before marrying. But if he had lovers and then claimed to be a virgin at marriage…that would be an unforgiveable lie.

There is also the question of did he sleep with his sister-in-law? If he slept with Bunny, would he try to sleep with Tina…or Thanh? If Barney knew that his wife had slept with Fred, then no wonder he wanted to scare me into sleeping with him…it would be a kind of revenge!

I never lied about being a virgin and I never wanted to be with a man like that when I was single. What if he had had a sexual disease when we got married? That would be a disaster! And does he have children hidden from me? The more I think about all these things, the more it is driving me crazy.

Most of all, I need answers about what Bunny meant. I considered calling her and asking for specifics, but I don't think I could. I am sure I would not like the answer. It will be better to talk to Tina. Her English is far better than mine and she has more life experience. She will know what Bunny meant.

Dear My Diary,

I went home and posted several listings to Ubiddit before taking a nap that was more restless than restful. Fred called for a few minutes to let me know he had finished in St. Louis and just arrived in Baltimore. They will meet one person tonight and the last person tomorrow before flying home from Philadelphia. Half of me can't wait to see him and the other half feels icky about what he did, or didn't do, with Bunny.

I helped parents set up a large canopy in the back yard for the barbeque. It is sunny but cold and this will help keep out the cool breezes as we eat.

I am sorry that Fred is not here for the party, but it will be fun for my family to meet Frank and Maggie for a full evening. But it would not be a typical family get together without Vo finding a way to offend someone.

Thanh and her family came after Auntie Giang, and before Tina, with everyone being careful to speak only in English so as not to offend our hosts. Auntie brought a cake from a local Vietnamese bakery for dessert and the twins looked very cute in matching dresses.

Everyone left their shoes outside out of habit, but Frank and Maggie wore their shoes in the house like other Americans. As we were in and out of the backyard frequently, and there were no guest slippers provided, the family ended up putting their shoes back on, but it is mentally uncomfortable for us to do so.

Vo asked, "Where is Fred? I thought he would be here."

I said, "He is out of town on a business trip."

"Oh! Maybe Fred have out of town girlfriend!" he said, laughing. It is a typical joke of his but no one else laughed or paid attention to him. It stung me harder than it should have because I still don't have an answer to my question, but I said nothing.

Then, he said it again, like maybe no one heard his joke the first time. Auntie gave Vo a hard look, but he was oblivious.

When he said it a third time, Frank addressed Vo in a stern voice, "You have said that three times now. Do you know something about my son that I don't know?"

Vo, seeing Frank's steely-eyed gaze, looked nervous and he stammered, "No! It is just a joke."

Auntie hissed in VN, "Apologize to Kim's American Ba!"

"Please, do not be offend with my bad joke. Very sorry. Bad joke. Not again."

Frank said nothing but his jaw was very tight as he went back to the grill. Auntie took Vo's glass and sniffed its contents. Making a face, she poured the drink onto the grass and said, "No more!" Vo looked like a kicked dog and Thanh made a sour face at her husband.

Maggie tried changing the subject and asked Thanh about her nail salon. Thanh looked relieved and talked about their successful little business. Sister said, "Please come to my shop. I give Fred's mother very nice job on the house. You will like!"

Maggie looked at her hand and said, "I could use a fresh manicure." Thanh smiled and said to Frank, "You come too, please!" Frank looked at his nails and said with a smile, "Darn, and I just got mine done yesterday!" blowing on his nails as if to dry them. Everybody laughed and the mood settled down from there.

Frank cooked steaks for the adults and hamburgers for the girls. They call Frank and Maggie

"Uncle" and "Auntie" like we had instructed them, and my American parents smiled to be addressed this way.

Tina arrived and told us about her month so far and how she is staying busy with B&R Group. Auntie and Thanh gave her some new potential contact information. Tina can use all the help she can get to build her client base.

After dinner, parents surprised me with a birthday cake one day early and sang the birthday song to me. Of course, it will also be Fred's birthday but since he is out of town, this one is just for me! I called Fred and we sang the happy birthday song again into the phone so he can be happy too.

By 9 o'clock the girls were getting sleepy so we carried Cam and Tam to the car and my family made their goodbyes. I feel so good that both families are a good fit and can have a lovely time together. I will email Me and Ba with pictures and tell them about tonight, wishing they could be here for dinner and conversation with my American parents.

Once the others were gone, I walked Tina to her car and tried to phrase my personal concern in a roundabout way. "I was reading a story about a lonely woman who was trying to interest a man she liked into sexual relations with her. He physically showed his refusal of her offer, but then she said, 'In the end, he did right by me.'"

"Sounds kind of hot," replied Tina.

I was nervous to ask the next part, hoping my anxiety did not show too much. "The story was in English and the character did not specify whether the man bedded her or not as the story moved on to the next chapter. I know it's just a story, but I am puzzled with those words. Do you think he bedded the woman? Does the phrase 'he did right by me' mean he satisfied her sexually?"

"Yeah, sounds that way to me," Tina said. "She got what she wanted."

Did He, or Didn't He?

March 17, 2001
Dear My Diary,

Today is our birthday but I am not happy about what I have to do. My stomach is in knots and sometimes my hands shake. I have an idea how to start the conversation, but the end will be up to Fred's answers.

As I pulled into the parking garage, I put on fresh lipstick and practiced a casual smile while trying to smooth out the forced, unnatural grimace that is reflected in the rearview mirror. I look ugly.

I met Fred and Dan at the gate who said, "This must be the little lady who stole Fred's heart!"

I smiled at Dan's phrase 'little lady'. They wore tired smiles and said everything went smoothly. The deal is done. They shook hands and made plans to meet tomorrow.

As Dan walked away, we hugged and kissed but I didn't feel joy in doing so. Walking to the car, Fred chattered on about the trip and the hotels and the cities while my mind was preparing for the talk we would have.

Once the bag was in the trunk and we settled into my car, I began. "Fred, I have a question."

"I know what you're going to ask…your birthday present isn't here but it IS bigger than a microwave oven, I can tell you that," he said with a boyish grin.

This is going to be harder than I thought.

"Nice try, but that's not the question."

"You want to know where we are going to have our birthday lunch? I have a place picked out that you haven't been to yet, I don't think…"

"That's not the question, either." My patience, and willingness to move forward, were thinning, and it edged into my voice.

"Oh, okay. Sorry. What's your question?

I took a deep breath, "If an adult woman who has never had sex is called a virgin, what do you call an adult man who has never had sex?"

"Ummm," Fred looked puzzled. "Same word. A virgin."

"Wrong."

"Okay, I give up. What do you call an adult man who has never had sex?"

"A LIAR!"

The answer came out stronger than I intended and it shook Fred up. He pulled back a bit. Nervous? Frightened of me? Will he confess?

"I…I don't get it. I mean, sort of, because some guys, but…where is this coming from, anyway?"

"Were you really a virgin when we married?"

His mouth dropped open and color drained from his face. I would have expected it to redden in embarrassment. "Of course, I was! I told you I was! You are the only person I ever told and now…hey, are you calling me a liar?" There is a hint of challenge in his voice.

"Are you?"

"Kimmie, where the hell is this coming from? I leave for three days and come home on our birthdays, to be told that I lied to you about the most personal, most precious thing a man, or woman, can offer another…"

Fred stopped, then his face lit up. "All right, you want to know who my sex partner was before we were married? My lover since I was fourteen? Do you?"

I didn't say anything. His eyes were a little crazy. Fred raised his hand and I shut my eyes, steeling myself for what was coming…but nothing happened. I opened one eye.

Fred's right hand was still raised, palm out, fingers sideways and, pointing to it with his left hand, he introduced me to "Miss Right, the only one to give me sexual satisfaction from puberty until our wedding night." He curled Miss Right into a loose fist and moved it up and down in a way I had seen others do to simulate self-induced pleasure.

"Now that I have answered your question, I have one for you. Who, or what, gave you the idea that I wasn't a virgin?"

In a very small voice, I answered, "Bunny. She said you did right by her."

"I don't know what that means. Did she say I had sex with her?"

"Not exactly."

"What *exactly* did she say?"

So, I told Fred the whole story as she told it to me.

Fred nodded, clearly remembering the night. "Come to think of it, I *did* do right by her. Now you are going to do right by me."

"How?" I asked.

"You are going to call Bernice, tell her that when I had called, you missed hearing the end of her story. Do not tell her I am with you, even if she asks. All right? Just let her finish the story and then judge for yourself if I lied to you or not."

Fred got out of the car and I thought he was going to walk out on me, but he just retrieved a notebook from his bag and got back in the car. As I called Bunny, he began writing in the notebook.

When I got Bunny on the line, she was on her lunch break and not at the office. She sounded happy to hear from me. "Hey Sis! I'm getting a Big Beefy from Bob's Beefy Burgers. Have you had a Big Beefy yet? No? Oh, you gotta try them. They are sooo good!"

Fred was still scribbling in his notebook as I asked Bunny if she could finish her story from the other night.

"Oh God, I was so buzzed after dinner. I didn't finish the story? Oh, that's right, Lover Boy was calling his little Lover Girl," she giggled. "Is Lover Boy home yet?"

"Um, not yet." I felt weird having to lie to Bunny to get to the truth. "I had a few minutes and just wanted to hear what happened after you kissed Fred."

I saw Fred close the notebook, and then his eyes.

She laughed, "No, I *tried* to kiss him, but he wouldn't have any of that from me. He pushed me away and got mad…told me straight up that he wasn't fooling around with any married women, especially his own sister-in-law.

"Instead, he drove me home in my own car, made sure I got inside safely, then he walked all the way back to his apartment. That was like, I dunno, over two miles away.

"That's why I thought he might be queer. But now I know he was just being a gentleman. Yeah, he did right by me. Other guys would have taken advantage of a drunk chick, even a sister-in-law, but not Fred. You got yourself a good one, Sis."

"I think I see Fred coming now," I said, my voice cracking. I wanted to end the conversation and crawl into the nearest rathole.

Bunny giggled, "Make sure Fred treats you to a Big Beefy for your birthday!" as I disconnected the call.

Fred opened his eyes, then the notebook, wordlessly placing it on my lap.

I read his notes: *Bunny and Barney had a fight. She was drunk. Came to me for sympathy. Then for sex. I Refused. She got mad. Told her I wasn't that kind of man. Took her home. Walked back in the rain. Nothing happened between us.*

Teardrops fell on his words. The words of truth. The tears of shame.

Fred's long arms reached out and drew me to his shoulder as waves of sobbing racked my body. He stroked the back of my head in a soothing manner, whispering "It's okay, baby. Let it out. Let it all out."

And I did. I let it all out.

When the tears had run their course and I pulled away to catch my breath, Fred's shirt was dark with dampness and his eyes glistened with tears.

"Why are you crying?" I asked.

"I felt bad because you felt worse. I guess I caught the crying bug."

"I was so awful to accuse you of something bad. Are you going to divorce me?"

"What? Over a misunderstanding? No, of course not," he said, shaking his head. "I could never divorce the other half of my heart."

Those words touched me so deeply that we fell together across the console, kissing and making up with such passion that we practically jumped out of our skins when someone slapped the window behind Fred. A grinning, freckle-faced boy made kissy-faces at us as his exasperated mother hauled him away while glowering at us over her shoulder.

"Let's go home," Fred said, mirroring my thoughts exactly, "and celebrate."

Frankie: Mom had, and still has, an excellent memory, especially for things that were heard and spoken. This gift was a great asset in learning lines for TV and movie parts and it is fair to say that her diary versions of who said what and how are highly accurate.

Our Birthday Gift

March 17, 2001
Dear My Diary,

After we came back to the garage and had welcome-home/make-up pleasures, followed by an early dinner in Old Town, Fred wanted to show me what he got for our birthdays. I said "Of course!" and put out my hands for the present. Fred laughed and said it was bigger than that and in another part of town.

He drove us to Honeywood Heights, a part of Riverton we frequent for estate sales and buying collections. It is always a treat to see so many beautiful homes with large yards and expensive cars in the driveways. "Did you buy a house for us here?" I asked hopefully.

He smiled and said, "You could say that."

My heart lifted…first a car, and now a house!

We pulled up to a brick home with a large lawn and border garden in front. It looked picture-perfect! I asked "Is this the house? Is this our birthday present?"

Fred said with a big smile, "Not exactly, Sweetheart. Look over there."

I looked. Across the street is an enormous two-story house. The paint is mostly peeled off, parts of it appear to be sagging and the land around it is overgrown with high grass, trees, and weeds. A picture-perfect home…if it were a haunted house!

We got out of the car. Fred stared at the house and slowly looked up and down the street like he was thinking very hard. I looked too, but didn't know what he was looking for. I waited for the punchline to his joke. This has to be a joke. Please, let it be a joke.

Fred crossed the street and I followed. He walked around the house, scanning the structure and taking pictures with his digital camera while picking his way around the trash that littered the grounds.

I followed reluctantly, feeling sick that this is no longer a joke and wary of stepping on a broken bottle or falling into a hidden well. I have seen no other houses in the area that look like this wreck.

The two-story house is shaped like a fat "T" with the wider side facing the street and a slightly narrower addition hidden behind the main building. There are some smaller buildings on the property like sheds and what might have been a chicken roost. I can see no other houses on this piece of land. I don't like the house and I do *not* want to live here.

A man washing his car across the street was watching us. Here we are, in the midst of the wealthiest neighborhood in Riverton, and Fred is admiring a rundown old house and taking pictures. I think we look odd to him…I mean, more than in the usual way.

I asked Fred, "You want this house?"

"Oh, yes. That's why I went out of town with Dan. We had legal transfer papers signed by the family members who inherited the property from their deceased aunt."

I said nothing but thought to myself, 'The dead aunt's family got the better deal.'

"Are we are going to live here?" He can, but I won't.

He said, "Oh, no! This house is not for living in. It is for tearing down!"

"Why did you buy a house to tear down?"

"To make money."

Now I really don't understand, and I don't like how I feel. I think Fred got cheated somehow.

At the back door, Fred fished a key out of his pocket and a miner's flashlight that straps to his head. "Ready to go inside?" I said nothing. He unlocked the front door and walked in, saying in a happy voice "Honey! I'm hooo-oome!" laughing at his own cleverness.

I didn't. I don't think it is funny at all. Fred asked me to come in, but I refused.

"Okay, suit yourself!" and he left me standing there on the porch, spanning the width of the home, cluttered with old appliances and furniture. Looking up, I spotted a wasp nest the size of a ripe durian in the corner of the ceiling. Instinctively, I backed away. Great.

After a few minutes, I was curious about what Fred was doing. I peeked in and the house is full of stuff. I mean, it is FULL of stuff! To be cute, I yelled out, "Honey, I'm hooo-oome!"

Fred returned, ducking under the low doorsill between the kitchen and dining room, head lamp bobbing in the dusty air. "Welcome to le maison," he announced. "That means 'the house'."

"I know. And it's *la* maison. I know some French too."

The house is impressive with many rooms, high ceilings and old-fashioned architecture. Some rooms are so full of boxes and bags of who knows what, you can hardly get through the door. Some rooms have paths between piles of stuff and the whole place smells musty.

One room is a library with floor to ceiling shelves containing thousands of books, phonograph albums and art pieces. Many look to be antiques. As we dug through a mountain of books and magazines in one corner, we uncovered wooden legs but can't tell if it's a table or a piano. Fred laughed and shook his head, "No need to buy any storage lockers for a while…a *long* while."

We found a sofa in a rear parlor with blankets, pillows, tissues, and paperback novels scattered about. A dresser tucked into a nearby corner was topped with a hairbrush, jewelry boxes, photographs, medicine bottles and other personal effects.

Clearly, this is where the woman lived her last years, sleeping and living amongst boxes and bags, shuffling to and from the nearby kitchen which had less piled junk than the other rooms.

The entire house has two floors above-ground plus an attic. Junk littered every staircase. We found a door leading to the basement and went about halfway down the wooden stairs, treading carefully in case any of the steps were rotten. Fred's headlight shone on a jumble of random junk several feet deep. We could not see the floor, so we retreated.

Some of the storage boxes are so old, they had fallen apart, spilling their contents everywhere. Many items still had their original packaging and price tags.

Fred used his digital camera to take pictures of some of the rooms, the contents of boxes, some of the doors and windows and the wood trim around them along with the floor molding, or at least where we could see it. He took pictures of sinks and bathtubs, light switches and electric sockets, doorknobs, and vents.

I don't know why he took pictures of all these things, but I just watched and waited for him to talk while he was in his concentration zone.

Once he got his tongue back, Fred explained that he will have the utilities turned on after the property title is transferred to the Orion Group. Same goes with the recycling and garbage dumpsters that will be brought in for the trash and we (we?) will try to sell much of what is here to offset the cost of the property.

From the looks of things, a kitchen match would save us a lot of work…but I didn't tell him that.

Finally, we went outside. Fresh air! When we got to the sidewalk, Fred took a right and walked to the corner, turned right again and walked to the next corner without crossing the street. On our right there were no houses at all, just trees, weeds, bushes, piles of trash and empty land. On the left side were lots of pretty houses with manicured lawns and gardens and late-model cars parked in spotless driveways. Why didn't he buy one of these houses?

When we got back to the haunted house, Fred smiled with satisfaction and nodded as though someone had just commented on the beautiful weather.

"Why did you want to buy this house?" I asked, hoping he would not be annoyed by my asking the same question again.

"You can't see what I see, do you?"

"No."

He took me across the street and said, "Okay, we will walk, and you will count houses. Start with this one," as Fred pointed out the brick home in front of us.

I thought 'This is a silly game, but I will count the houses.' So, we walked to the corner and turned and walked to the next corner and turned. When we got back to the first house, I said "That was a total of thirty-six houses. Six on the short sides and twelve on the long."

"How many houses on the first block we walked around?"

I looked across the street. One house. Fred looked at me and raised an eyebrow. Then I understood. Then I "got it". But I am not sure I want to "get it" for my birthday. Looking at all the nice houses around us, I am disappointed with my birthday gift.

Lois: Mama has told us the story of the Honeywood Heights property many times. This was to be the biggest project they would work on together for a while. To think this is what Dad got them for their birthday! Well, it wasn't planned as a birthday gift, it just worked out that way.

Kimmie: The kids pointed out that in my entries of the time, I mentioned that I had gotten Fred a gift for his birthday but did not reveal what it was. My intent at the time, I think, was to write about his reaction once he got it. Instead, Fred offered the bigger surprise of a long-neglected home that someone had recently died in. The house was not intended to be anyone's birthday gift. Its' acquisition just happened to fall at the same time of year.

Fred brought home some souvenirs from each of the four cities he visited, and I gave him the birthday gift later in the week, after the shock of the house wore off.

The gift had been a book I found in one of the lockers we had purchased…a highly detailed picture-book entitled "Manual of Marital Bliss" that I covered with a sheer negligee before boxing it up. The book was highly educational for both of us.

Thomas Stimson

Barney's Bio-oil Debacle

March 21, 2001
Dear My Diary,

Fred has finally agreed to explain how Frank and Maggie lost their home and business and what happened to the relationship he had with his brother. It's clear that this is a very painful topic for the family, and I have been hearing bits and pieces so far, but I really want to understand it better, especially as it involves my best friend and his parents.

Hello Kimmie's Diary!

This is the first time I have written in any kind of diary, so I am flattered to be asked. It is important for you to understand what happened between my parents and Barney, and why there is bad blood that will probably never completely go away.

It is not a pretty story and one that may be hard for you to understand since you and your family get along so well with each other. That's one of the great things about being a part of the Pham family…the trust and respect you have in each other.

First, a little background: Soon after my brother got his license to practice law (fourth attempt at the bar exam was the charm), my parents, at Barney's badgering, gave him Power of Attorney (POA) to conduct business for them on their behalf. It was with the understanding that the POA would only be used if they were unable to manage their own affairs such as a severe disability, dementia, death, etc.

A few years ago, the price of oil was being driven up sharply by the major oil-producing nations and newsmakers were predicting ridiculously high fuel prices for a long time to come.

Some people got to modifying their cars to run on vegetable oil as it was very cheap compared to petroleum. Soon, former Big Oil employees and chemical engineers started creating their own fuels from cheap grains and used fryer grease along with selling instruction manuals on how to modify vehicles to run on these alternative fuels.

Before long, "Bio-Oil" was all over the news, and it became a growing trend. As the price of petroleum kept rising, many small start-ups were promoting their companies, auto repair shops were modifying cars and entrepreneurs were selling locally made fuels. It soon became a very hot sector for new investments. That's how the bio-oil industry got started.

Barney had all kinds of inside information about people who were planning, making, or selling bio-oil products and he wanted badly to get in on the action. Problem was, he had no money of his own to invest, so he asked our parents for seed money. His reasoning to them was to help Mom and Pops increase their savings and net worth to have an earlier and nicer retirement.

Predictably, they said no, no, no. "It's a gimmick. The price of petroleum will go down later. The companies are unproven. The prices of the new stocks are too costly."

My parents had plenty of reasons to say "No", but Barney had more reasons to say "Yes". He can be a real pain if he does not get his way.

My parents broke down and gave Barney several thousand dollars, figuring they could afford to lose that much. Barney, in his faultless logic, did not think this was enough. Without telling our parents, he used the Power of Attorney to take out loans, really big loans, against the equity of Pop's repair business and the family home. Since the buildings had been paid off decades ago, there was a lot of value to draw from…and did he draw!

Barney intentionally borrowed from out of state banks who did not know our family, so there was no reason for them to be suspicious of Barney's actions. No one contacted our parents to ask questions about the loans. Since Barney was an attorney in good standing, on paper anyway, the banks took his word and the required documents to happily give him open lines of credit.

Funny thing is, he never asked me to invest. That's okay, because the joke is on him. Barney never knew that I was investing in bio-oil companies, but carefully. I would buy into something on the rise, then set a trailing stop so that if the price pulled back a certain amount, it would automatically sell. So yes, I did make money and I never bought anything without the trailing stop.

He went on to purchase positions in a variety of bio-oil start-ups with promises of big profits and shiny futures. He also did a lot of the investing on margin, borrowing some of the broker's money to boost the number of shares he could buy. Along with increasing potential profits, it also added extra costs and a lot more risk.

As more and more people changed over to bio-oil products, gasoline sales dropped and, within a few months, the surplus generated pushed gas prices back down. A classic example of supply and demand working to balance everything out. You don't need a business degree to understand that.

Moreover, a lot of the bio-oil products were not very well made, causing problems to the cars and trucks using them. Pops' garage got a lot of cars coming in with gummed up engines, burnt valves and other major damage from poorly made fuels and reconfigured engines.

Gas prices go down, bio-oil products lose favor with the public and many of the new companies were poorly managed. As the bio-oil sector collapsed, so did the stock market in general.

Barney's investments sank with everyone else's, and he made the classic move of doing nothing, hoping the market would turn around.

And in classic fashion, they didn't. The brokerage firm who loaned some of their money to Barney on margin demanded their shortfalls be covered with more deposits into the account. Barney sold what he could at a great loss as the rest disappeared into a cloud of bankruptcy filings.

At first, my parents thought they had lost the few thousand dollars they had given Barney…until the banks started calling Mom and Pops for the payments on Barney's huge loans. He had made a few payments when things were going well and he still had his job with the law firm Dewey, Cheatham and Howe, but the debt-load was far more than Barney's income could cover and he wouldn't return our parents' frantic phone calls.

Once Mom and Pops contacted the banks involved, got copies of the signed loan contracts, including their Power of Attorney documents, Barney finally confessed to what he had done.

"But it was all to help you! I wanted to help you retire early and live the good life!"

I thought Pops was going to murder Barney…and who would have blamed him if he had succeeded?

My folks did not have a lot of money saved up. Their retirement plan was to eventually sell the family home and business and downsize to a smaller place. The money gained from both those sales would be their retirement fund and it would have been a lot of money. Would have been…

Mom and Pops had no way to repay the loans and Barney had squandered every dollar he invested.

I could not help my parents, as much as I would like to have done. It was far more money than I had at the time, so Mom and Pops talked to their lawyer about their options. Because of the way the POA was written, Barney could do what he did, and it was legal. Not right, but legal.

In the end, nothing happened to Barney, legally speaking. Once his employers learned what he had done, they sent Barney packing and no other law firm in town would touch him after that. That's when he decided to change his name from Barnabas Starbuckle to Bernard Bartlett and start his own law firm.

My parents were forced into bankruptcy. They lost the house. They lost the garage that had been in our family for over sixty years. About thirty people lost their jobs. My grandfather had started Starbuckle and Sons in the midst of the Great Depression and many of the employees had been there for decades. Some of them hunted Barney down and gave him a farewell ass-beating.

Barney also filed bankruptcy. He did not have a house, savings, or any assets to lose. He filed so he would not have to pay anyone back, not even our parents.

Mom and Pops had always been comfortable, but never wealthy. Not the kind of wealthy that could pay off over a million dollars in loans they never took out. When the bank took over the family home, I fixed the folks up with one of my rental houses and signed over the deed to them. It was the best I could do with what I had to work with.

I got Mom a job at one of the resale stores and Pops went to work for one of his former competitors as a shop manager.

One of the sidelines he had at the family garage was buying and reselling used autos and car parts to make extra income for the shop. I helped Pops get set up on Ubiddit and now he has quite a following with many clients seeking out specialty parts. It keeps Pops busy, and their savings are growing with it.

You had suggested one time that perhaps Barney was trying to help our parents financially but did a bad job of it. The truth is, he was not trying to help our parents. He was trying to help himself. No one takes out loans against someone else's home or business without their permission. That is just plain wrong, and doubly wrong when you're an attorney.

Barney knew it was wrong. That is why he did not ask our parent's permission and used out of state banks. I know Barney and the way he operates. His idea was to take the money, make a profit and then pay off the loans and keep the difference without telling anyone, but it backfired on him.

So, he stole from his own parents, lost the money, then filed bankruptcy and stole from the bank all the money he borrowed by not having to repay our parents, the brokerage firms, or the bank. In technical legal terms, Barney is a First-Class Turd.

I don't deal with Barney if I can help it. He does, however, have a wife he doesn't deserve. She is sweet to us and puts up with Barney's foolishness. The bio-oil event happened before they met, and I don't think she knows the full story. She isn't the kind of person who would get involved in something like that and I can tell she watches her step around Barney. She is a smart cookie.

I hope this makes clear some of my family's drama. Your family is one I wish mine were more like. Everyone helps each other, talks to each other, and respects each other. Fred

Dear My Diary,

I have read Fred's story twice and now understand what Barney did. I feel so bad for Frank and Maggie! The bits and pieces of information I have heard over the last year now make so much more sense. I hope Barney learned his lesson and will not do such a selfish thing again. I believe everybody should be forgiven and have a second chance to make things right.

Thinking back on it, I remember how Bunny had said Frank and Maggie invested and lost all their own money and blamed Bernie for it. She has also said that Bernie never takes the blame for anything. Since Bunny was not in the family at that time, I believe Fred's version of the story is more truthful than what Bernie might have told Bunny.

I told Fred that his parents told me he did not invest in the bio-oil companies, but he wrote in my diary that he did and made money on them while Barney lost it all.

"I don't tell my parents everything that I do," Fred admitted. "I have multiple streams of income where opportunities allow, and that era allowed for some good profit-taking to those who worked it smart. There is a saying in the investment world: 'Bulls make money. Bears make money. Pigs get slaughtered.' Barney was a pig, but it was my parents who got slaughtered."

His last words made me feel sick and now I want to hug Frank and Maggie so much. I want to give them something for their retirement losses. I don't know what Ba and Me would do if one of their daughters did such a terrible thing to them. I cannot imagine any of us doing a thing like this and I hope I never do.

Kimmie: Fred and Barney were never close growing up. Not only because Barney was several years older, but their personalities and interests were vastly different, which shows clearly in what happened during the bio-oil boom and bust. Fred was careful and self-disciplined while Barney was reckless and selfish. Barney left his parents ruined and Fred provided them with a home and incomes. Barney lost his job and Fred kept growing his.

It took Fred a long time to tell me what had happened, and yet, it wasn't the whole story.

The Gambotti Growler

Friday, April 14, 2001
Dear My Diary,

Bunny called today and is she furious! Without telling her, Barney purchased something called a Gambotti Growler.

I asked, "What is that?"

"You don't know what a Gambotti is? It's one of the most expensive cars you can buy!" Then she explained how Barney contacted a Gambotti dealer in Chicago, the closest city that has one, and traded their sedan for a Growler model at a price that stunned me.

"Where did he get so much money?" I was afraid that Barney got another falsified loan like he did with his parents.

"Bernie showed off his news story from the Review and based on that, the dealership gave him a six-year loan for $155,000 at 18% interest because his credit is so bad." Bunny sighed, "The payments are over $3,600 per month. That's more than our rent. Way more."

I didn't know what to say. They could have bought a decent-sized home in Riverton for that kind of money.

I asked, "Is it a big car, like the RV Fred has, with a kitchen and toilet?"

Bunny laughed bitterly, "I wish! Just two seats and barely room for anything else. How are we supposed to get groceries home in that thing?"

I was surprised to hear this. "It doesn't have a trunk?"

"Trunk? The engine fills the entire back half of the car! Bernie keeps bragging how it can go over two-fifty and I asked him 'Who are you running from that you need to go that fast?' He just laughed like I made a joke.

"I know business has picked up, but how the hell are we going to keep paying over three thousand every month? For a CAR! And don't get me started on the insurance! God, we are so screwed."

I can hear Bunny's voice building with emotion as she continued venting, "He keeps saying we will get paid by those companies, but that could take *years*! Maybe never! He knows that. I know that. Bernie says, 'It's only money' and 'I'm the hottest lawyer in town right now. Let's enjoy the ride!'" She said the last part in a voice that sounded so much like Barney's, I had to cut off a giggle so she would not think I was laughing at her.

The phone was quiet for a moment, and I said nothing. I have no idea what to say. Finally, Bunny sighed, "If he had to get an expensive car, why couldn't it be a really nice SUV?" Then she apologized for bothering me with her troubles.

I said, "It's okay. We are sisters, and sisters are good listeners."

"Thanks, Kimmie. I gotta go now." Bunny started crying as she hung up the phone. I feel sad for her.

At dinner, I told Fred about the Gambotti Growler and how upset it made Bunny. He just shook his head and made a call to Bobby, letting him know what Barney had done and to make sure none of our accounts have been affected.

I asked Fred if he thinks Barney stole from us. "I don't think he believes we have much money," Fred assured me, "but that doesn't mean he won't try to pull a fast one if he thought we did."

Thomas Stimson

My Awful Easter

Monday April 16th
Dear My Diary,

It is taking a long time to get the necessary permits for the Honeywood Heights property. It is such a big piece of land and so little has been done with it over the last one hundred and fifty years. The city wanted it inspected for hazardous waste, a family cemetery, and a list of other possible concerns on and under the land as well as a comprehensive title search.

Surveyors have been out multiple times while Fred, Holly, a civil engineering company and city officials have been planning, plotting and haggling over details of how the land will be divided into 36 roughly equal residential lots. This is Fred's first big property deal so he is doing whatever he can to get everything done right, and to the city's satisfaction, without costing a fortune.

One of the bigger difficulties is that there are several large, old apple and walnut trees on the property, most likely planted by the first-generation Robertsons. Fred spends a lot of time and energy figuring out what to do with them.

Removing the trees will be very time-consuming whether we do it ourselves or hire out the work. The roots run thick and deep, creating potential difficulties for home-building, excavating and landscaping. On the good side, the wood is valuable and can be sold to local furniture-makers and artisans.

Fred sees the trees as worth keeping, adding thousands of dollars to the value of the properties if they are healthy and in good locations. We will know more once the land is surveyed and divided. After all, you can't have a big tree in the middle of where a house will likely be sitting. Fred will have to remove two trees that are dead, or nearly so. The rest are healthy enough to keep if they don't interfere with property lines or home placement.

Yesterday, Fred's parents were kind enough to invite us to church for their Easter service. Fred learned soon after that Bunny and Bernie are coming too. My feelings toward Fred's brother are worse than before, now that I know how he cheated his parents. I'm sure Frank and Maggie have love for their other son and, as Christians, they try to forgive him to keep the family together.

Fred helped me pick out something appropriate to wear and when we arrived at the church, I felt my spirits uplifted. It was a sunny day, the grounds were freshly landscaped, many women wore hats or outfits with flowery patterns and children ran about in little suits and cute dresses with their baskets of treats.

We met up with Bernie who guided us to the parking lot to see his new "baby", the Gambotti Growler. Fred pointed out the personalized license plate "6 MIL MAN" and shook his head. The top of the car comes only to my waist. Bernie turned the key, and it really does "growl" like a big cat.

Red pinstripes form a growling tiger's face against an aerodynamic black hood and the expansive rear window gives an unobstructed view of the sleek, chromed engine. Subtle, it is not.

Other people came over and admired the car as Bernie handed out business cards and made his sales pitch to "call the six-million-dollar man". Some people were clearly not comfortable with his solicitations and after a few minutes of admiring the car, we went back inside to find Frank and Maggie.

251

Fred's parents go to church every Sunday and wanted me to see how Easter is celebrated. I met many of their friends, some of them saying "Oh! I have seen you at (some place or other), I did not know that was your daughter-in- law!"

As I do not know the songs or how to read music, I stood respectfully and listened. The church leader stood at a podium and welcomed everyone, asked for prayers to be given for this person or that and other announcements. Then he made a long speech that I could not follow, and neither could Bernie as he fell asleep and began to snore. Bunny poked him awake, winking and grinning at me as he grumbled, "I was listening with my eyes closed."

When the service finished, we went downstairs to a buffet lunch. Church members were slicing fresh roasted meats and dishing up different foods onto heavy ceramic plates. Everybody was cheerful, saying "Happy Easter" and "Praise be with you" and nice things like that.

We found a long table to share with some other couples, and as we started to eat, I asked Maggie, "What is Easter? What exactly are we celebrating?" Maybe this was the wrong time to ask, but I had been curious as to what it all means.

Maggie scolded Fred, "Haven't you told your wife about Easter?"

He looked abashed and defended himself with, "She never asked me!"

So, Maggie told me the story of how Jesus was turned over to the bad Romans who punished him for not believing in their god. They put nails into his body and hung him from the cross like I see in pictures and on people's necklaces. Once Jesus died, his followers put the body into a cave and rolled a big heavy rock in front to keep animals out. Three days later, some people came back to the cave and there is Jesus, outside the cave and alive again.

This story reminded me of something I have seen in movies, so I said, "Oh, like Halloween!"

Everybody around me suddenly got quiet, eyes grew wide, and mouths fell open as they understood how I understood the story.

"Oh my God! She thinks Jesus was a zombie!" Barney blurted out the words in a voice filled with glee and started laughing.

Others laughed too from behind their hands. Some people looked at me with sympathy and some in anger, perhaps because I insulted their god.

"She is a Buddhist! She does not know our Bible stories," said Maggie, as she attempted to stand up for me. Instead, it made me look and feel foolish and ignorant and very, *very* embarrassed.

I jumped up, almost knocking down an old man as I tried to get out from between chairs that were placed too close together and my legs got tangled.

I don't want to go to church anymore. I want to go home to Vietnam and never come back. Now I will be the big joke people will remember and talk about for a long time…the tall, awkward Asian woman who thinks Jesus is a Halloween monster.

Fred caught up with me and his parents were close behind as I stumbled towards the parking lot, hot tears stinging my eyes. With no car keys, I hit the roof over and over with my fist in frustration. My reflection in the car window shows that I am the one who looks like a zombie now, as make-up streamed down my face.

I am so ashamed. Ashamed of my ignorance. Ashamed that Barney could make fun of me without my giving him another black eye. People came outside to look while Fred and his parents stood quietly near me, waiting for my anger to settle down.

From another part of the parking lot, I can hear Bunny yelling at Barney, "Why do you have to act like that? I can't believe you!" and Barney saying, "It's not my fault Kim is so funny!" Then I beat the car some more. Ahhhhhh!

As my emotions subsided, I said through clenched teeth, "Fred. Home. Now."

He quickly unlocked the car, "Of course, Sweetheart."

Maggie came over and said "Kim, what happened inside was okay. No one thinks you meant to insult Jesus or the holiday. They know you are a foreigner, and this is a new experience for you."

I thanked her and apologized for being an embarrassment to them. Maggie took my arm and turned me towards her. She looked into my eyes and said, "Daughter, you can NEVER embarrass us. We love you too much." Then Maggie hugged me and patted my back. I got in the car, saying nothing, struggling to hold back the dam of emotions sweeping though me.

As we left, I heard Maggie say to Frank, "That is the LAST time I invite that boy anywhere!" I think she meant Barney. But then, maybe she meant Fred...for bringing his ignorant wife to church. With that thought, the dam burst and I cried all the way home.

Dear My Diary,

Maggie called to see how I am feeling. I said a little better but still very embarrassed. She said no one at the church is upset with me and if I want to come back with them, no one will laugh, and Barney will not be there either.

I thanked Maggie for her kind words and for checking up on me. "At the church, you said I could never embarrass you. Well, you can't embarrass me either as you are good parents to us. Thank you for inviting me to church and sharing your Easter holiday tradition."

I checked with everyone, and this is a story none of us had heard before. Likely because it was so embarrassing for Mama. Dad NEVER made fun of Mama regarding things she was sensitive about. That was one day she would rather soon forget.

When I brought it up to her recently, Mama hid her face in mock shame and said "I felt SO immigrant that day. I really wanted to go back to Vietnam and stop trying to fit in. Of course, I did not fit in so well in my homeland either, so I stayed. Your father and grandparents were very understanding and did not laugh at me or make fun of what happened. They are not that kind of people, and I have always…ALWAYS appreciated that.

Walnuts, Cherries and a Junked Car

Saturday, April 28th, 2001
Dear My Diary,

Fred and I visit the Honeywood Heights property almost every day to explore and plan what will be done with everything. Even though he does not legally own the land just yet, we have taken the initiative to collect and haul away all the loose trash we can comfortably retrieve, as some of the brush is quite dense.

Fred told me how families grew much of their own food and raised animals on their lots, but most of the barns and outbuildings have long-since crumbled back into the soil.

He has also arranged to have about one hundred workers come to clear the land of weeds and brush. I can't believe he is hiring so many men and women to clear the lot! It sounds very expensive.

Fred hired a firm to set up temporary fencing all around the block with a big gate at the driveway. An old car is blocking the access and it has turned into a rusty, dusty piece of junk that Frank says is not worth salvaging. Fred sold it to a scrapyard for $200.

That two-hundred dollars is our first bit of money from Fred's "investment". I don't see this turning out well, but in return for Fred's constant and cheerful encouragement for me to be more confident, I refuse to voice my doubts in the profitability of this deal. But I still think them.

Legally, we can't remove anything, including the car, from the property until the title is transferred to The Orion Group, so Fred is using his time to make lists of things to do and planning how to clear out the house. We sold off nearly all the inventory at the garage, mostly to the resale stores, in case we need the room, but Fred is hoping to sell directly from the property for quick cash and to save the time and money it would take to move it all to the garage, list it, and so forth.

Fred had already stopped all Ubiddit selling and thinks it will be many weeks before we start again. After listening to all this up-beat talk and studying the disaster awaiting us, I asked Fred how much he expects to make from the property after all the work is done. He just said, "Far more than I paid for it."

We have been wading through rooms full of boxes, bags and furniture bought over the course of decades. Some were bought new and are still in their original packaging and price tags. Others appeared to have been bought at yard sales, thrift stores and the like. Fred showed me how, in different rooms, you can see the ages of the things Miss Robertson bought and stored over the years. Some have mostly 1960's stuff, some from the 1970's or '80's.

I can't tell because these are American tastes, trends and fads that I did not grow up with. He gets very excited with some of it, sharing information like, "I got one of these for Christmas when I was ten and had so much fun with it!" or "My friend spent a whole week's allowance to get one of these and he broke it on the first day." Fred has so many nice memories bubbling up from our finds. I wished I could share his enthusiasm, but all I see is a tsunami of work ahead of us.

Every day Fred takes dozens of pictures with his digital camera of things that catch his eye. At home, we look up these items for their current values and record what we find. With two computer desks, we can research twice the number of items per hour. Then we box up the selected items that will make us the most money on Ubiddit while the rest either gets sold from the driveway, sent to the resale stores or in the dumpster if they are nastied up by mold or rodents.

I am learning a lot in the process and I must admit, his enthusiasm is catching!

The folks kept many of the pictures of the Honeywood Heights house before, during and after all the work was done. It was a packrat's dream with boxes stacked six feet high and full of everything described in Mama's entries and more.

Auntie told me recently that Cousin Michael will be out of college for the summer and is looking for work. The house is overwhelming in the amount of effort it will take to clear out, so I suggested that we hire Michael as a helper. I know Fred prefers to do as much as he can by himself, but for this project, I feel otherwise.

Michael is active in sports, is very fit and getting high marks in his business admin classes at Prairie State University. Fred admits that this is, by far, the biggest clean-out he has ever done. It will take several weeks to empty the house what with sorting, boxing, hauling, and selling what we can to reduce expenses. Having dependable and honest help for this project will be crucial, so Fred and I will talk to Auntie and Michael.

Lois: From details scattered over several weeks in Mama's diaries, here is a summary of the history of Riverton, Honeywood Heights and the property Dad bought.

As families moved west across the United States looking for new places to live, ten-acre tracts of land were sold by the territorial government to people wanting to settle in the new town of Riverton.

Each ten-acre plot was a rectangle with roads cut between them as they are now. The plots typically had a house, small farm or garden plot and sometimes a business like a store, blacksmith shop, furniture-maker and so forth. People typically had large families back then and, over time, families moved away or sold parts of their land to others who built more houses until the neighborhood became what it is today.

The land Dad bought was purchased by Albert and Claire Robertson over one hundred and fifty years ago and has been held by their descendants ever since. Albert was a wealthy merchant from Chicago who saw a chance to plant new roots in a promising location that offered little competition. A store and warehouse were quickly constructed along the river, a two-story home was built for his wife and children on a rise of land now known as Honeywood Heights, away from the crime and grime of Chicago. As the business grew, so did the Robertson family and their home gained a sizeable addition to accommodate them all.

Miss Gladys Robertson was born and raised in this house, a great-granddaughter of the merchant. By the time of her birth, the family's mercantile businesses in Chicago and Riverton had been sold off and

Glady's family lived off the proceeds while her father invested in a number of business ventures…many of them doomed to failure.

Over the decades, her siblings married, moved away and started their own families while Gladys remained single and became the head librarian and researcher of the Riverton City Library. She retired many years ago with a pension, social security and enough savings to provide for her basic necessities.

By the time of her death, all Glady's siblings had passed away, along with some of their children. All that is left of the original family are five first-generation nieces and nephews who were Miss Robertson's heirs in the will.

As Honeywood Heights evolved from pioneer settlers to suburban chic, the original homesteads were split and split again as smaller, older homes with large yards were torn down and larger homes were built onto smaller lots into the 1980's and 90's.

As property values increased, so did the taxes, but Miss Robertson's income could not cover the rising costs. She turned a deaf ear to generous offers from banks and developers as well as visits from city officials pressing her to resolve delinquent tax bills and improve the property, which was falling into disrepair.

In the end, the City of Riverton made exceptions and exemptions for Miss Robertson due to her age and status as a long-time city employee and descendant of Riverton settlers, allowing her to pay token amounts on what was owed until she sold the property or died.

At the time of her death, Miss Robertson owed over $250,000 in back taxes and various fines. For her heirs to get the property, the full amount would have to be paid within thirty days of her death or the family would have to forfeit their inheritance and the city would sell the property at auction to recoup what they could.

A few days after she died, Miss Robertson's attorney, Dan McClurg, spoke to Fred at the country club bar where Bernie was celebrating his court win to make him an offer. They had known each other a long time and after doing some research on the property and the financial state of the heirs, Fred offered to take the property off their hands for the cost of what was owed to the city.

None of the family, as individuals or as a group, had the money required to pay the back taxes. Mr. McClurg provided all the family members with legal descriptions of the property and photos of the broken-down house surrounded by overgrown, trash-littered yard. The family members may or may not have spoken to lawyers about the offer, but they clearly understood that they would either need to pay a huge amount of money for a seemingly worthless property in a far-away city, have it sold at auction or someone else could pay the taxes and take the property off their hands for the cost of a signature. Dad had to move swiftly on this before other people found out and attempted to gain ownership of this valuable property.

Dad and Dan took all the necessary legal documents to the five heirs in four states and they signed away their rights to the house and property to The Orion Group.

Kimmie: I couldn't believe Fred had so much cash to buy this property so easily. He made a joke at the time that it takes a lot of Ubiddit sales to save up that much money!

Once the property was in his company's name, Fred sold one-fourth of the property back to Dan McClurg for the same percentage of the outstanding tax lien. From there, they split the costs 75/25 for the clearing and surveying the land, insurance, taxes and other costs associated with the property while Fred would cover the removal of the house and everything in it. The splitting of the property was a kind of 'thank you' to Dan for helping him get this deal and would ensure that he got first look at other opportunities in the future.

May 15th, 2001
Dear My Diary,

The things Barney will do to get attention! I had just finished showering and the TV was on as background noise when I heard a familiar voice talking about the six-million-dollar man. The first thing I thought was, 'What is Barney doing in our home?' I put on a robe and peeked out the bathroom door…but no one was there. Barney's voice was coming from the TV!

Fred's brother sat behind a desk and the Steve Austin doll stood just to one side. Barney was saying, "You may have heard on the news how I got one of my clients six million dollars for their tragic injury. It was one of the largest personal injury awards in Riverton history. If you or a loved one have been accidentally killed, injured or wronged in some way, do the smart thing and come see me, Bernard Bartlett, for a free consultation. I got one client six million dollars…what can I get for you?" The camera zoomed in on the doll, and it said: "I am the six-million-dollar man!" in Barney's voice, but deeper, then the commercial was over.

I found Fred in the kitchen eating some fruit and I told him about the commercial. He said, "The action figure does not talk. Barney must have added that in for effect." I was not expecting this reaction.

"But Barney is on a TV commercial!"

Fred yawned, "That? Oh, yeah. Barney's done commercials before, but now that he's got the media's attention, not to mention an expensive car payment, he's going to milk this until the cow runs dry."

I asked, "Do you think Barney will ever get the six million dollars?"

Fred scoffed, "Oh, sure…right after he's elected president of the United States."

I have now watched Barney's commercial all the way through and found some parts a bit odd. It starts with Barney sitting behind a desk, hands clasped and the doll prominently displayed as he introduces himself and goes on with his pitch. This is what I heard from the bathroom the other night that made me think he was in our home.

But each time I hear the pitch, he says something that does not sound right to me, so I asked Fred, "When Barney says, 'If you or a loved one has been accidentally killed, injured…', it sounds like he is saying, 'If you have been killed, please call our law office'. Is that how it sounds to you?"

Fred agreed that the way the words are arranged, it sounds like he wants dead people to call or visit his office. "Like I said, bottom ten percent of his class. What do you expect?"

I feel funny that my English is not so good, and Barney is an American lawyer, but even I can tell his English does not sound right. No wonder Fred has so little respect for his brother.

Cousin Michael

May 30, 2001
Dear My Diary,

Fred finally got the property title and permits to tear down the old house. Last week, we had lunch with Michael and Auntie at the garage to discuss hiring my cousin for the summer. It's been settled that he will commit to sixty hours per week while we clear out the house and lot. We let him choose between working five twelve-hour days or six ten-hour days for $500 per week. When the property is done, he can assist in posting things to sell on Ubiddit and FreePost.

Mike was clearly unhappy with having to work so many hours and at a low wage, but he did not voice his displeasure. He is well-aware of the hours his mother puts into running her stores but perhaps he thought we would be easy on him.

Seeing his face this way, I explained that when Fred has a big project like this, he works around the clock and napping as he needs it. Fred continued my train of thought by saying "This job will be good for learning about the value of things, the best ways to sell and managing your time and resources. I like to call it 'Economics 101 in Real Life'."

Auntie told Michael, "Listen closely to what your cousins tell you. You can learn much that will be useful all through life. Don't worry, you will still have time to play this summer."

Then Fred laid out the ground rules: Come on time and keep busy. Not sure what to do? Ask. Find something that might be valuable? Let one of us know. Don't be tempted to take something without asking us first. Moreover, Fred made it clear that he will not tolerate laziness or foolishness.

Mike agreed to all the rules and Auntie assured us that Michael has always been a good worker in her stores and honest as well. Fred said, "I have no doubt Mike will be a big help this summer, but I still want to be clear on the expectations we have."

We took them to Honeywood Heights to see exactly what we are dealing with. As we slogged through the house and Fred pointed out various things, Auntie kept exclaiming in wonderment, "Troi oi! So many things!" "Troi oi! How did the woman live like this?"

When we showed them the area where Miss Robertson lived her last years, on a couch in the living room, with little trails to the kitchen and bathroom through all the clutter, Auntie gasped, "Troi oi! How sad…how terrible. Why didn't somebody help her?" For that, we have no answer. Troi oi, indeed!

Fred fixed Mike up with coveralls, a tool belt and rubber gloves. We showed him the crash carts and what they have and how to use some of the tools. Mike decided on the six ten-hour days so he will come at eight and work until six with flexibility allowed.

Today, by working out Fred's plan, we used a combination of trucks and a motorcycle to bring several vehicles and a dozen eight-foot tables to the property. Tomorrow, Fred will drive the big box truck and I will drive the dented work van to use for errands.

Fred has reminded me that the one hundred hired workers will arrive on Monday. It will be interesting to see so many people clearing the land. I asked, "What about food and drink for them?"

Fred assured me that that will all be taken care of by the work crew boss. "These workers know how to live off the land," Fred said with a wink. I don't know what he means by that, but I guess I will learn soon enough.

Fred is a nervous ball of energy and keeps making sure he has everything we need. He hates to stop a project for something he forgot. We will have cell phones, chargers, laptop computers and internet connection boxes with us. Electricity and water have been turned on at the house and everything is ready. As we like to say, "Let's go make some money!"

Our First Week in Honeywood Heights

Monday June 11, 2001
Dear My Diary,

Fred told me to take the day off to relax and recharge my batteries. That sounded good until I realized that I also need to do laundry and cook up more food for the week which *also* means grocery shopping. Since my day will not be as relaxing as Fred would imagine, I invited Thanh to help and chit-chat with me. The chores went faster with sister's help and now, with everything done, I can lay down and record my week.

We left home at 5am with our usual "Let's go make some money!" and a kiss. Fred backed the truck up to the kitchen steps and I pulled the ramp well onto the porch which we cleared last week for the crash carts, racks of tubs, wheeled garbage cans and folding tables.

Our first task was to fill the now-empty truck with most of the interior doors which are original to the house. Using cordless screwdrivers to make the work go faster, we removed and bagged the hinges, screws and strike plate for each one and taped them to the respective door before stacking them in the truck. There are dozens of doors in a variety of styles and conditions, and many needed to be wrestled out of overcrowded rooms. Fred has a wholesale buyer for them so, along with the quick cash, it will simplify moving things in and out of the different spaces.

When Michael arrived, we had him start emptying the kitchen drawers and cupboards down to the bare wood. Old food and broken or chipped items go in the trash and the rest into bins for further sorting. Fred reminded Michael to check all unsealed food containers, cans, cannisters, jars, mugs, glasses and bowls for money and other valuables that people often hide. "We don't want to be throwing out the family jewels she stashed in a can of cocoa."

The refrigerator was a horror show of spoiled food and I re-tasted my breakfast at the first whiff. We hauled it outside and Fred plugged it in to chill the interior so it won't smell so bad when it's time for Michael to clear it out. Once that is accomplished, Fred will decide whether to clean and sell it or send it to the recycler. I think my parents had one like this when they first got married, and it was old even back then!

A little testing proved the gas stove works well, is from the 1950's and can be sold for several hundred dollars after a good clean-up due to its vintage looks. We are using the newspaper stacks littering the house to wrap dishes and glassware before boxing them to sell at a later date.

After a break for lunch in the RV, Fred and I took prybars and carefully peeled molding from the doorways, placing them in the truck with the doors. Some pieces were weak or rotten and broke apart, but we were able to salvage most of it.

From Dad's sales records, the doors and fittings were sold for $50 apiece and were estimated to sell for $300 to $500 each once cleaned and refurbished. Michael admitted that he was not happy about the long hours and low wages but by the end of the summer, he had learned a great deal and got buffed up in the bargain. He was even able to use some of the experiences in his college coursework and *reports!*

There is a detailed account about how they broke down the jobs to make the work go faster, the kinds of things they found, the different ways they sold many of the items and so forth. Here are some of the more interesting entries:

The one hundred workers Fred told me about came on Monday…in two long trailers! Not busses or cars but horse trailers because they are goats! Fred kept it as a surprise for us.

William "Billy Goat" Hurd was hired by Fred to bring in the goats to clear the land of all the weeds, brush and brambles they can eat. They are so cute! We took a break to pet the goats and take some pictures. Once the goats got busy eating we went back in, but it was hard not to take a peek at them once in a while.

Fred called his mother about the three toilets in the house. Two are very old, from the 1920's or 30's with the tank high overhead and a pull-chain and one is more modern and ordinary. Maggie called a client who collects old toilets to create artistic planters. She came over and loved what we have. She was not interested in the newer toilet and offered us $1000 for the other two if she could take them now.

Fred explained the history of the house and the original pioneer family who lived and prospered in it for generations. He described the last surviving Robertson as being a much-beloved librarian who added to Riverton's education and culture. The woman said, "Yes, I remember her! She was always so kind and helpful."

Fred continued "And with the house being torn down in a matter of weeks, you can own not just a pair of antique pull-cord johnnys, but pieces of Riverton history that no one else can duplicate!" They settled on a price of double what she had offered.

Then Fred told her that the toilets are still connected to the water lines but once the work here is completed and the water is shut off, he will take them out and deliver both to her house at no extra charge. Fred did not mention that the toilets are still in use by us throughout the day.

Me and Ba will NOT believe this story! Fred took the payment in cash and wrote down all the artist's information so he can call her when they are ready to be delivered. Two thousand dollars for two old toilets…Americans still surprise me at what they will pay for things. And Fred told the story so well that I almost wanted to buy the toilets for myself! No, not really. But such a story!

Michael is a very hard worker and comes on time every morning. He likes to talk with me about school and with Fred about business but when he tried to talk to us about his favorite sports, Michael quickly found us lacking in knowledge and interest.

Meanwhile, Fred always keeps us feeling good by saying things like "Great work everyone!" and "Another room bites the dust!" while doing high fives to Mike and hugs and kisses with me.

This weekend, we set up all the eight-foot work tables in the driveway and filled them with a variety of things from the house in an orderly manner and advertised the sale on FreePost. Fred had considered sending the sellable goods to the resale stores but decided there is a better opportunity to make more cash and, more importantly, promote what we are about to do.

The neighbors are happy to hear that the land will be divided and sold to make new homes, calling the current state of the property an eyesore and breeding ground for mosquitos. Watching the goats at work has been attracting visitors as well who watch through the fence with their children.

Fred wants to build interest before we actually start the sales. He has already started getting offers from developers to buy the entire block as is, but he knows he can get much more by selling the lots individually.

After the visit of the "toilet woman", Fred removed the newer toilet, sealed up the bottom, filled it with soil and planted a flowering bush the goats had not yet eaten. He sold it on Saturday for $150. Fred really knows how to make money from junk!

Michael is also a very good seller as he is handsome with an easy charm, gaining the attention of more than a few ladies. With just three of us, and a lot of people showing up, buying and asking questions, I feel like we need more help. I will talk to Fred and see what we can do.

Today is Monday so it is just Fred and Mike working at the house while I come to rest and write to help me relax. There is still so much left to clear but progress is being made as well as cash. For now, I will be a cat and take a long nap.

Dear My Diary,

Thanh called to ask if we plan on going to the July 4th fireworks like we did last year? The girls want to go but I told sister that we are too busy to go this time. I invited the family over to see the goats and gave her the address.

I asked Fred about getting help for the weekend sales since the last one was so hectic. He agreed that three of us were too few. There was no chance to rest and so many visitors made it confusing between those wanting to bargain and those asking questions about the house and property.

Fred called the shops to find some trusted employees to work with us the whole day for $100 cash each. There will be two helpers each day and whatever is left over on Sunday afternoon, Fred will take to the resale stores where the helpers are employed. It is a fair deal and we will make sure there is plenty of food and drinks for everyone.

Vo brought Cam and Tam to see the goats and visit the house. Vo asked what we will do with the house and I told him, like everyone else, we will tear it down. He said, "Wait another year and it will fall down by itself!" He thinks Fred is crazy to waste time on such a project.

I haven't told my sisters or Bunny our full plan yet. I don't know why, but I think it's because I'm afraid Fred will fail in what he is trying to do. It just seems, I don't know, so big. So ambitious. I don't want Fred to lose face if he fails.

The girls had fun petting the goats until one knocked Cam down. "Goats do that sometimes," said Billy Hurd, "when you get in the way of their eating."

Cam was not hurt and she laughed, saying "Silly goat! Silly Billy goat!"

Vo said, "Goats crazy and you crazy too. So much junk in here!" and he took the girls home. When I told Fred what Vo said, Fred responded with, "Yeah, crazy like a fox!" I hope so!

The goats are gone now and the land is well-cleared of plants, but at one time Mr. Hurd let us know some of the goats found marijuana plants deep inside the property. Fred thinks neighborhood kids might have planted them as it was well-hidden from the street by trees and bushes. The goats were jumping and kicking and very playful before getting sleepy and falling down and Mr. Hurd pulled out the rest of the plants. The goats finally woke up and ate much more than before. Fred called it "having the munchies." Such a funny way to say "very hungry."

Shooting in Riverton Central Park

June 27, 2001
Dear My Diary

Today we had a print and video shoot for Fierce 5 at Riverton Central Park, so I went home early this morning and took a hot double-shower. It felt so good to scrub all the dirt, dust and stink from a week's worth of working on the house and sleeping in the RV. The camper always smells of mildew no matter how long we leave the door and windows open, but after a family of racoons trashed the kitchen while we were working, we took to locking the door and closing the windows.

I found the hair and wardrobe trailer near the lake and it's a hundred times nicer than the RV. I quickly got compliments on how buff I am looking with questions about how I was working out and who my trainer is. I didn't want to reveal my current workout routine so I just said, "Oh, do I look all right? Yes, Fred directs my workouts."

"Buff" is a new word for me and the admiring glances from the crew and my Fierce 5 sisters reinforce the meaning. It's funny, but in Vietnam I was ridiculed for being tall and muscular while in America, looking the same way, I am complimented and even paid to provide sex appeal for energy drinks.

Zander came in wearing knee-length man-shorts, a tropical shirt and red sports shoes asking "Is everyone ready to put the 'Fierce' into Fierce 5?" as she handed out fresh copies of the day's schedule.

We cheered happily and Jaguar went "Hoo! Hoo! Hoo! Yeah, let's do this!" and it made us all laugh. What a great way to start the morning!

We spent the day pretending to celebrate summer with cans of Fierce 5. There were male models posing with us to enhance the party atmosphere, like holding or toasting cans of F5 with big smiles or mouths opened in laughter. There was a lot of joking around and suggestions by cast and crew to get the right kind of facial and body expressions needed for the print ads.

One shot had model Aaron kneeling at my feet while holding up a can of F5 with both hands as though proposing marriage. His blue eyes gazed in seeming admiration as I reached for the drink, giving a fierce grin in return.

In the video shots, we get to say things like "Fierce 5 makes me feel alive!" and "Be Fierce! Live Fierce! Drink Fierce 5!" and "May the Fierce be with you!"

Many people came to watch the photo shoot, staying respectfully behind the barricades. We visited the fans and signed autographs between camera set ups. I watched how the other models made small-talk, posed for personal pictures and give some attention to each fan. I followed their example, using my experience selling things with Fred.

The interactions felt good, especially when chatting up the teens and young adults who looked self-conscious in our presence. I think we made a great impression. After all, it's these kinds of friendly interactions that will help sell drinks and keep our jobs longer.

We posed on the lakeshore with Riverton's skyline in the background and pretended to ride in a speedboat as large fans blew our hair back, holding up drinks and waving at the cameras.

Later in the afternoon, we were joined by some local sports stars who posed with us, toasting with

F5 drinks and making their own fierce faces with pointy teeth. Throughout the day, we went back to the trailer to refresh our make-up, hair and change costumes while grabbing a bite to eat and drink.

We were active all day and very warm, making us drink a lot. I filled an empty F5 can with water so I could drink, appearing to enjoy the product while avoiding the jitters from all the energy-inducing ingredients. Bettina has to stay well-covered except when we do the actual photography. Being albino, her skin tends to burn easily and she has to frequently apply sunblock and wear large-brimmed hats.

The pointy teeth are hard to wear all day and we have to keep them on with our costumes in the public areas. Once inside the dressing rooms, we can't wait to take the fangs off and drop them in glasses of antiseptic liquid. The fangs are custom-made and fit over our teeth with a clip which pushes our lips out a bit. But when we go "Grrr!" it is very impressive!

In all, it was a long day but I am not so tired…my work at the house has me accustomed to this kind of activity. We won't have to work again for a while as many different set-ups were done to create a variety of spots for store displays, billboards, magazines, websites and TV/movie theater ads. It was also *very* profitable for me!

And the best part of the day? Finding Fred home, freshly bathed with dinner prepared and ready to shower me with attention and body wash!

Hidden Treasures

July 6th, 2001
Dear My Diary,

Wednesday was July 4th, and we spent the day clearing out the home library. Fred sorts the books, like everything else, into Keep, Sell and Trash piles.

Miss Robertson, being a librarian, collected books and loved going to signings when authors came to town. We have found hundreds of autographed books so far, and they all go into the 'keep' pile. Fred thinks we can get decent money for them in Riverton, even if they don't show high prices on Ubiddit, because they were from her collection. We will see.

With each volume, Michael and I check the inside pages for autographs and quickly flip through the pages to see if any cash or valuable papers are hidden inside, then set them aside for sorting. So far, we haven't found very much in the way of valuables in the house other than some spare change and a few pieces of jewelry.

Suddenly Michael said "Bingo!" and held up a twenty-dollar bill from the book he was holding. It had George Washington's face on it and the number 20 in the top corners were crooked. It looked very odd.

Fred glanced at the bill, turned it over a couple of times, then pulled a $20 bill from his own pocket, saying "Mike, why don't you take the rest of the day off and go see the fireworks?"

Michael looked incredulous, then overjoyed and took the twenty dollars from Fred, asking "Are you sure?"

"Get out of here before I change my mind," Fred said with a smile. "You've worked hard enough, so go out and have some fun. We'll see you tomorrow."

"So, what did I find? Something special?"

"Looks like an older version of a twenty, or it may be a fake. I'll have it checked out to be sure."

It was 3pm when Mike left. Once his car was gone, Fred's face broke out in a big grin. "If there is one, there must be more!"

Fred placed the bill flat into a zip-lock bag and showed me some printing underneath Washington's picture: IN GOLD COIN.

"What does that mean?" I asked.

"It looks like a special kind of currency issued a long time ago. Let's find out how special."

On Ubiddit, we found Sold listings for US Gold Certificates from one to three *thousand* dollars…each! *Troi oi!* Fred began dancing with excitement and so did I.

After we settled down, I asked, "Do you really think there are more of these?"

Fred raised his eyebrows at that. "Look at this place, Kimmie. The house is over a hundred years old. The bill is dated 1906, and someone hid this money in an old book that no one was likely to read." He tapped my nose playfully and waved his arm around the room. "Still lots more to go through. So," Fred took a deep breath, "let's go make some money!"

We hugged, kissed for a few minutes to boost our luck, looked over our new treasure one more time and went back to work.

We had been sorting our way from the bottom of the shelves to the top and it was around the three-quarter high mark where Michael had found the first bill. Now we were finding its brothers and sisters and cousins amongst the volumes.

I soon discovered what distinguished which books had money in them…a small upside-down 'V' cut into the base of the spine. A little piece cut out, just a few millimeters in height. It would not have been seen or noticed on the books higher up as the edge of the shelf obscured the clue.

Gold certificates. Silver certificates. Regular bills. $10 and $20 and $50 and $100. "Bingo!" became our new shout-out word. Everything but the first bill went into a large envelope as Fred wanted to keep the note Michael found separate. We had a short, simple dinner in the RV and came back for more as the early evening shadows began to lengthen.

Fred was going back through some of the earlier books for anything we might have missed when, from a high shelf, I pulled down a book so unnaturally heavy that I nearly fell off the stepladder. Fred took the book from me and set it on a table as I climbed down.

The title on the spine read "The Practice of Pharmacology". The pages were stuck tightly together, and the cover was stiff, but once Fred pried the time-hardened leather away from the volume, there were no cheers of "Bingo!". We could barely breathe.

It was filled…filled with gold and silver coins! The book was real, but someone had heavily glued the pages along the outside edges and hollowed the interior to make a safe out of a boring looking book. None of the coins are newer than 1933.

"I'll bet a dollar she didn't know about this money," Fred said. "If she knew about it, she could have sold them and kept up on her taxes."

"Who do you think hid them?" I asked.

"Parents. Grandparents. Who knows? There's nothing in the book-safe or anywhere else we have looked that would give us an idea."

"This" said Fred, patting the large, black book, "goes in the 'Keep' pile!"

We heard the fireworks from Central Park and all over the neighborhood going off to celebrate America's independence. Inside, we quietly celebrated our financial independence…both our heads filled with the wonder of our good fortune, and I worry about how we will deal with it. After midnight, we only heard the crickets saying Chrrr! Chrrr! Chrrr! between the last pops and fizzles of the night's festivities.

It was very late when we finished opening all the books in the library, our new-found wealth loosely sorted and sealed within dozens of plastic bags. Then Fred got the idea to go through the old phonograph records in case bills were hiding in the covers, but no luck there. The sun had fully risen by the time we finished.

We were exhausted and Michael would be in soon. We left a note to have him box up the records and 'sell' books for the weekend, then we retired to the RV for breakfast and a nap.

In the afternoon, Fred put our new treasures into his safe deposit box at the bank after taking inventory pictures for our records. He used a different camera chip than for Ubiddit items and put that in the box as well. We said nothing to Michael about what we found and agreed to tell no one at all, not even our parents, until we had more information and a plan.

I showed this entry to Michael, who is retired now, and his face softened at the memory. "I remember finding this strange twenty-dollar bill and then Cousin Fred traded with me and let me go early. The next morning, I was tired from my night out with friends, but Kimmie and Fred were wiped out. They slept for hours while I did what I could in the house." Michael expressed surprise that they had found more valuables in the library and thought his gold certificate was a singular event. But more on this subject later...

I got a call from Ba this evening to let us know that everyone is fine, and would we take another container or two of things to sell for the Christmas holidays? Last year was very profitable for him and very busy for us! I asked Fred who just motioned with his hands at everything, as if to say "Are we not busy enough here?!"

Knowing the answer, I still had to ask Fred as a matter of courtesy to Ba who could hear everything. I explained briefly that we have a very big project in the works and can you ask us next year? Ba said he understood and wished us good luck with the project.

Fred appreciated my family's good wishes and added, "Last year was a lot but this year would be too much!" I agree. At least Ba did not try to surprise us again!

Barney the Chump

Dear My Diary,

I simply could not wait to write this down during my lunchtime as the news is too big! We have a boombox that runs throughout the day and every morning the announcers talk about the current news, weather and traffic while making jokes between songs and commercials.

This morning, the news was about how Judge William Davidson has been forced to retire. Not because of his age, but because authorities were concerned about some of the judges' more questionable rulings over the last few months.

After a review of his recent cases and a medical check-up, the judge was found to have a form of dementia that may have impacted some of his decisions. Now, all the cases he has ruled on in the last twelve months are being reversed and will have to be retried with a different judge.

Guess who is being affected? Bernie! His was the biggest and most publicized of the cases to be thrown out. After the news, the announcers made jokes about the "six-million-dollar man" attorney Bernard Bartlett and his talking doll commercials.

Fred heard the whole thing, smiling and shaking his head at the news. All he said was, "Who's the chump now?"

Dear My Diary,

It's hot and humid here in the summer, like in Ho Chi Minh City, so Fred often works without a shirt and it doesn't hurt my eyes when he does…but I cannot do the same! I work in shorts and T-shirts or tank tops and Fred makes lots of eyes at me too! No coveralls in this weather, ugh!

Yesterday, we found a new set of treasures in the house. Things that made us excited at first, then caused my heart to ache as I understood more. Let me explain.

We have completely cleared both main floors and the attic of the house, leaving the basement as our last obstacle before we start the tear-down. This area can be accessed down a short flight of steps from the outside, which would make emptying this large area into the dumpsters so much easier…except that the door is completely blocked with junk from the inside.

It took us two full days of hauling stuff up the stairs for further sorting and removal before we could get the door open. This was about the same time that we were able to reach the first of the floor-to-ceiling rows of shelves that cover most of the walls.

Hundreds of jars filled with preserved foods, thickly covered with dust, line the shelves. They are decades old and whatever fruits or vegetables were inside have mostly crumbled apart and settled to the bottom.

Mixed among the jars are tins of store-bought foods, many of which are rusty or swollen. Fred commented, "You could poison a whole city with what's in here."

But it wasn't the food that captured our attention, it was the packages. Boxes wrapped in brown paper and twine that had been mailed, sent back and never opened.

Looking more closely, we found that Miss Robertson had been sending gifts to her siblings' children in different parts of the country. They were returned by the post office with red-lettered stamps saying either "Address Unknown" or "Delivery Refused".

Fred opened one. It had a birthday card inside with a five-dollar bill and a Stork Baby doll that was popular a long time ago. Fred observed "Five dollars back then would be more like twenty dollars now. Pretty generous."

We opened more packages. Same thing. Birthday, Easter and Christmas presents with personalized cards, cash and toys or clothes. There were dozens of boxes. It was very quiet in the basement as the three of us tried to make sense of what must have happened.

"Why didn't she return the gifts back to the stores for a refund?" I asked out loud, "Or take the cash out of the cards and donate the toys and clothes?"

"I don't know," Fred admitted. "Looks like she just put them into the basement as-is. It must have hurt getting rejected like that, over and over again, by your own family. As for refunds, I think that back in those days, refund policies were not as generous as they are now."

"In Vietnam, most stores have a very strict return policy," I offered up.

"What return policy is that?" Michael asked.

"Returns not accepted." I said, making air quotes with my fingers. This is a gesture I recently learned, and my answer got both men laughing. "Not a joke," I emphasized. "It's true."

I asked Fred if we should try to return the packages to whom they were meant for, especially as he had recently visited with them.

"Oh, no!" he said. "I don't know what happened back then…maybe they moved and didn't leave her a forwarding address, or they chose not to be in contact with Gladys for any number of reasons. No matter. The heirs gave up the right to claim anything here. Anyway," Fred sighed, "it's ours now."

These vintage toys and clothes in their original boxes, unopened, unworn and never played with, will go on Ubiddit to the highest bidders. They will not be "ours" for very long.

We found sturdy wooden crates in the basement to transfer the hundreds of jars and cans to the dumpsters and prepare for our last weekend of selling from the driveway. Then we will take a few days break before tearing the house down.

As we cleared out each room, we also removed all the brass fixtures like light-switches and socket covers, heating vents and light fixtures. They have pretty designs and Mike is using strong solvents and polishes to clean them up as best he can. Fred will sell the covers for ten dollars each and the light fixtures for much more. I asked if we could keep some of the covers for the garage's living quarters.

"Why not?" he said. "We earned it." Except for some cleaning supplies, we haven't taken much else for ourselves.

I will feel so much better when we are done with this place. I am tired every day and sleeping in the RV is not comfortable at all. Even with all the work he does, Fred only sleeps three to four hours per night with sometimes a nap in the afternoon.

At least his energy level is not the annoying kind, like when someone can't stop moving or they talk all the time. We often go to bed together but when I wake up, he is already in the house clearing a room or doing Ubiddit research. I think Fred works slower in the late hours, but he still makes progress.

Bobby, Hazel and Holly have been out here several times for long talks with Fred about the property and how to prepare the lots for selling. Because Mike is here, I can't spend much time to hear the conversations. What I do hear is 'shop talk' that I don't understand so well, but Fred seems generally satisfied with the progress they are making on his behalf.

As problems arise, the problems get resolved with the expertise Bobby and RPR provide. Fred is equally happy with the progress we have made on the house and said we three make a good team.

I reminded him, "If you have good employees, it will work like this all the time."

"Ah," Fred replied, "the problem is *finding* good employees, and then keeping them!" He agrees that Mike is a very good worker and let me know that when everything is done, we will give him a bonus.

The old house feels enormous now that everything is out. The rooms echo as we talk, and I wonder what it must have been like to live here a hundred years ago. It has been an interesting experience and I have learned a lot about the Robertson family and Riverton history and how the city has grown and changed. Now this land, the last undeveloped block in Honeywood Heights, will see a new chapter form, catching up with its neighbors into the twenty-first century.

Nearing the End

July 24, 2001
Dear My Diary,

It feels *so* good to take a long, hot shower, crawl into a big, soft bed and curl up with a fresh, clean husband!

We've finished our last driveway sale, bringing in more tables and arranging the goods on top, underneath and within the open space of the giant 'U'. We also brought a truckload of lesser-value items from the garage that did not sell on the other weekends or were refused by the resale stores.

Even with four helpers from the resale shops to help, it was still hectic! Fred and I are always the cashiers and change-makers to keep things honest.

Hundreds of people came, bargained and bought from us like it was pre-holiday shopping at the Saigon marketplaces. We sold boxes and boxes of books and magazines, records, linens, tools and everything else worth putting out…even a few that weren't!

Along with cashier duties, we have been taking the names, emails and addresses of people who want to know when we will sell the lots. People give us business cards and text messages all the time. Neighbors, real estate brokers, contractors and others want to know when they can buy a plot and for how much. Fred hinted to me that he has a way to make maximum profits on this property and is developing the plan with B&R and RPR. It has been over two months now since we started work on the house and I am so glad the clean-out is done!

The surveyors are back taking final measurements, checking coordinates against plat maps and staking the lots. Fred does not want any one lot to be much smaller or larger than any other. It helps that the property is a fixed rectangle and not a strange shape.

Fred has been over the land twice with a strong metal detector he borrowed from a friend. He has been hoping for more gold coins and not old storage tanks that would have to be dug up. Mostly he finds beer cans, machine parts and the occasional corroded coin.

Now it's time for Michael to research the more valuable items that we have kept back from the driveway sales to either put on Ubiddit or list on FreePost. He has found that some of the older books from the library are worth hundreds of dollars.

We opened all the returned gifts and took out the cards and cash. The cards are signed 'Aunt Gladys' and dated, but she wrote no personalized message for the child but for what was already on the card. It looked very dry with no emotion or attempt to make a connection. The gifts are lined up on their own shelf to be researched and noted for the best way to sell.

Fred photographed samples of the wood floors from different parts of the house and shopped them around by emailed photos. A local decorator came in, made an offer and we are letting them remove the floors to be refinished and installed in wealthy people's homes. The boards are wide, smooth and richly grained. I would love to have them in the garage instead of the rough-hewn and splinter-filled wood flooring we have now. They are the reason why we can't go bare-foot or wear thin slippers in the non-carpeted areas.

Once they are gone, one of Fred's construction friends will be here to knock the house down with a bulldozer and a team of workers from Mulchables will help Fred sort out the wood from the metal and take all the wood away in big trucks. Then, the foundation will be broken down, the basement filled with dirt, the metals sold to a recycler and lastly, the land will be smoothed and leveled to look its very best for selling.

Fred likes to sing "Payday is coming! Payday is coming!" I asked him how much he expects the payday will be?

"I have some idea about it, of course, but I don't want to jinx it. But I can tell you this: I'm working on a plan that could help us get top dollar for the lots." And then Fred would not tell me what the plan is. Humph! He will have to tell me soon, but in the meantime, he is like a small boy with a bag of fireworks and a box of matches.

I think I would like to live in Honeywood Heights someday, especially if we have children. I don't want our children living in this big, drafty garage. There are no neighbors, grass or trees while Honeywood has nice homes, sidewalks, people jogging with baby strollers and washing their cars in driveways. Honeywood Heights looks like the America I saw in pictures and movies while growing up in Vietnam while the warehouse district looks like a photo from a Warsaw-Pact news story.

When I took a break from the dusty old, haunted house, I walked around a bit and looked at the beautiful homes and gardens. People waved and smiled at me. Sometimes we chit-chatted about the property or their flowers. It is not blocks and blocks of depressing gray concrete and graffitied doorways.

I understand why Fred lives there and he tried to make a nice home for me before I arrived. I truly appreciate his efforts, but it does not feel right to live behind a locked barbwire fence. Am I so bad to feel this way? Am I so spoiled?

I don't tell Fred my thoughts and I don't want him to think that I want so much when he is happy at the garage that has been in his family for many years. Time to try to sleep now.

Fred Sets a Date...and an Unusual Plan!

Dear My Diary,

Fred has set the date to sell the Honeywood Heights lots on Saturday, August 18th in a most unusual manner…he will do it as a live auction!

He and RPR will be advertising the sale heavily to the people who have expressed an interest in buying a lot, to the general public and the top realtors and residential developers in the region. The advertising should bring in many more potential buyers.

RPR is arranging with the city and police to block parts of all four streets so the auction crew and buyers can move freely from one lot to another. Bobbie and Robbie will be there with some of their employees along with Hazel and Holly's crew to handle the legal paperwork for each sale.

Fred was careful to purchase the property from the city under his company name The Orion Group LLC as well as presenting the company as the seller. Many businesspeople know Fred is Orion but most others do not, so it is a kind of screen for him to stay semi-anonymous, as the interest grows around the sale.

Some banks and credit unions will have booths for last-minute loan preapprovals and mortgage financing offers. Letters have gone out to all the homes surrounding the block, explaining what will be going on that day and apologizing ahead of time for the inconvenience of closed streets, and high foot traffic.

Fred selected the date because it is before Labor Day weekend, will still have warm weather and there is enough time to advertise and contact potential buyers.

Dan McClurg is taking a strip of nine lots along Grant Street and is not participating in the auction. His plan is to join forces with a local contractor to build houses to the specifications of the buyer, provide financing and so forth. He will have representatives from the construction firm and Midwest Best Credit Union to meet with potential clients on the day of the auction to take advantage of the expected crowd.

Fred and Robbie are finalizing an invoice for Dan to repay his share of the tax lien plus one fourth of the costs of the surveyors, goats, fencing, permits and other expenses paid out for the land, but not for the house. Fred took responsibility of those costs, and guess what Diary? Fred said his share of the tax lien has been recouped between the sales of everything from the house and the estimated value of the old money we found.

We have spent many hours researching the internet, library resources and local coin shops for items that match ours to learn more about them and get approximate values. Fred will not bring his treasures to the shops or use his "go-to guys". He does not want anyone to know of our big find yet and is "keeping everything on the down low" as Fred likes to say. We do not need the problems that come with news like this getting out.

Fred does not intend to sell any of it right away. The price of gold has started to rise after dropping for the last twenty years and Fred is hoping this will increase the desirability of the coins themselves and make for larger profits later.

Kimmie: I felt funny about keeping all the money we found, knowing that if Miss Robertson had been aware of it during her lifetime, she could have sold some of them to pay her taxes. Then her nieces and nephews could have inherited the property and made money from selling it like we are doing. I wanted to give the old money back to the family and told Fred the same. I will never forget what he told me:

"Sweetheart, do you realize how much money Miss Robertson spent on all the things she bought and stored in her house? Toys...who in the house were playing with them? No one. Clothes...for men, women and children and yet she lived alone. Enough home décor and linens for a hundred houses...that she purchased and put away only to gather dust. She could have paid her taxes with the money she spent buying tens of thousands of items she didn't need."

I knew Fred was right. She was a hoarder, a sickness that took over her life and home. It would have been different if the house was just a house filled the normal amount of furniture, clothes and decorations the family bought, used and accumulated over the decades. But it wasn't.

As far as Fred was concerned, the gold, silver and currency repaid us for all the extra work we put into clearing out the house.

First Wedding Anniversary

August 15, 2001
Dear My Diary,

Fred treated me to a four-day weekend in Saint Louis for our first wedding anniversary. I had not been to this city yet, but it's not such a far drive from Riverton. We left in my car on Friday afternoon, had a picnic dinner in a state park along the way and arrived at the hotel by early evening.

We did a lot of things in the few days we had. Some of them Fred was unable to do in the past, either because he was too young (jazz and blues music bars) or because he was there to buy at auctions and go straight home.

After watching a film about how it was built, we rode nearly to the top of the Gateway Arch in a funny little elevator. Once it stopped, we walked the rest of the way to look out the windows and gaze for many miles in all directions. The state of Illinois on one side, Saint Louis, Missouri on the other and the Mississippi River right below us.

I felt a little nervous being so high up, almost 200 meters, but the arch is steel and concrete and buried deep in the ground for stability. The arch represents how the citizens of the eastern United States used this area to gather and travel by wagons and horses to the California and Oregon Territories. Later that night, we came back to see the arch lit up with beautiful colored lights. I hope my pictures come out!

We spent a morning at the zoo and the afternoon at the famous Missouri Botanical Gardens. I love seeing and learning new things about plants and animals!

We went to a church (but not for Easter service!) called Cathedral Basilica. SO different from Frank and Maggie's modern-style church! We took the tour and as we visited the main hall, someone began playing the organ, filling the large, artistically designed building with rich music. It was such an emotional experience! We have a Notre Dame church in HCMC, but I have never been inside and do not know much about it even though it is in my home city.

The Tower Grove Park was once part of the St Louis World's Fair in 1904. There are still some leftover buildings or parts of buildings on the grounds from that time over a hundred years ago. It is much larger and fancier than Riverton's Central Park and we made a picnic under some big shady trees.

I asked Fred if he thought the Robertson family had come to St. Louis for the World's Fair. He said, "I would think so. It was a very big deal with all kinds of new inventions and entertainments. Since they were wealthy business owners, a trip like that would be the equivalent of taking the family to one of the big amusement parks in California or Florida."

That made me smile, thinking of families coming here by train or steamship to see strange and interesting new things among the large crowds. Certainly many of the inventions and products being introduced at the fair as new, revolutionary and high tech have become everyday items we now use and take for granted. The exciting fair is now long-gone and exists as a peaceful park. It was a fine way to spend a Sunday.

We ate St. Louis barbecue and went to music bars on two different nights for live jazz and blues that the city is so famous for. We danced, drank non-alcoholic cocktails and tried new kinds of foods.

Our hotel was not as fancy as we had in New York, but they had a free breakfast and a bed so soft, it was like sleeping on a cloud.

Fred made it a point to ask that we don't talk about work or the Honeywood Heights home, but to celebrate, have fun and relax from all we have done these last few months. Of course, we both thought about the work that has been done and what will be done soon, but we pushed our conversations towards "us" and our time in St. Louis.

Monday was our first wedding anniversary. We had dinner at the Broadway Oyster Bar and they served us a fancy ice cream dessert topped with sparklers that lit up the table. (Fred special-ordered it when he made the reservation). Everybody turned to look and applauded while the waiters sang us a short happy anniversary song. Later, the band read off a list of patrons having their birthdays and anniversaries, so we got another round of applause.

We leave St Louis on Tuesday noon for the long drive home. We had such a great time that I want to go back again someday.

Ba and Me called my cell phone to wish us anniversary happiness and to say that Thao and Phung will marry next March. Such a long engagement! Sisters and auntie and cousins and Fred's parents and Bunny all called to wish us a happy anniversary…but not Barney.

Michael will soon go back to school and we left him the keys to the garage so he can keep working the Ubiddit deals as part of his summer education. His anniversary gift to us is a nice card and two sweatshirts from Prairie State University. That should keep me warm in the winter!

Growing up, we went to St. Louis plenty of times for family vacations and work-related reasons. When we were older, one or two of us might accompany Mama on a commercial shoot or go with Dad for a Dissolving Debt seminar. We were more like little assistants, answering the phone, sending out messages, fetching something from the car or briefcase or taking notes. With everything we did, we were learning not only the family businesses, but by having one on one time with them, we could stay connected as parent/child and stay grounded no matter what and where our lives would take us.

Auction Day

Sunday August 19, 2001
Dear My Diary,

The Honeywood Heights auction is now officially over, and it was so much better than I, or more accurately, "we" expected.

Fred did a lot of pre-planning with Riverton Property Rentals and the B&R Group to generate as much interest as possible and make the sales process smooth and efficient. Let me explain:

After proposing and rejecting different ideas, they finally decided on using powdered limestone to mark off the property lines and post a large sign in front, with lot number and details.

They also rented a flat-bed semi to hold the support staff and their paperwork, a stage for Fred with a microphone and speakers and a special electronic sign. For each three lots sold, the truck would move forward to the center of the next three lots and so on. That way, everybody could see exactly what lot they are bidding on, the moving process will give Fred a short break and a chance for the clerks on the truck to process more information.

It took time and effort to get the necessary permits to have the police block parts of different streets and redirect traffic with some neighbors complaining 'Why can't they just put For Sale signs on the lots like everyone else?'

But everything got cleared through the city, lots of advertising went out, including faxes, emails, ads in FreePost and two eighth-page ads in the Review's Lifestyle section, Sunday editions.

Currently, there are no empty lots for sale in Honeywood Heights, so the auction has brought out lots of people to the neighborhood, both buyers and on-lookers, with everyone in a festive mood and hoping for a chance to build their dream home in the county's most desirable neighborhood.

Fred could have sold each property multiple times based on the number of people calling and emailing Fred and RPR with offers to pay in cash, raising their offers, trying make secret deals and so forth. Every one of them were told the same thing: attend the auction and place your bids...no exceptions.

A reporter and photographer from the Riverton Review showed up along with a camera crew from KAP-TV. I guess the auction has become an "event". They interviewed Bobby, Fred, the sign operator and some of the people milling about.

One thing I noticed right away is that only twenty-five lots are up for auction, not twenty-seven with nine others belonging to Dan McClure. I see that two of the lots have "NOT FOR SALE" signs in front. One lot is in the center of Falk Road and the other is around the corner on Marine Drive. Fred assured me that neither of them have been sold, but they are taken. He refuses to tell me more, even under the threat of the Tickle Monster. I am a curious cat now, but one thing about my husband, he will always tell me when the time is right.

I wore capri pants with comfortable flat shoes and a short sleeve blouse with a light jacket while Fred wore a colorful tropical shirt with parrots and a straw hat to make things fun for the audience. We held hands and met many people, some greeting him as Buck and others as Fred or Mr. Starbuckle.

The lots are clean, having been groomed by a road grader just days ago. The trees helped us as well, producing lots of ripe walnuts and cherries to add beauty to the property and interest to the lots they sit on. The two dead trees were taken down weeks ago, the stumps and large roots ripped from the ground, and everything hauled to Mulchables, since the wood was too poor for making furniture.

Many homeowners in the area have offered their driveways and front yards for parking at $10-$20 per car while other neighbors are selling food and drinks or having yard sales.

Registered prequalified buyers, or their representatives, were issued numbered paddles and some last-minute registrants are still lining RPR's tables for a chance at a property. I saw one person in line wearing a Coast Guard uniform with gold on his shoulders and cap.

Fred's properties cover both short sides, one long side and three lots on the other long side while Dan's nine lots are all in a row next to Fred's last three. The flat-bed truck is parked at the corner where Fred's lots start and Dan's end.

Dan's stretch of real estate was getting plenty of attention because the developer working with him had his own colorful banners flying and his sales reps were showing floor plans to prospective buyers, some of whom were gripping auction paddles. Looks like Dan's properties are some people's Plan B.

The hired truck was clean and shiny, festooned with balloons and the electronic sign made colorful moving pictures, scrolling information about the auction. Pop music blared from speakers, a pair of clowns handed out free bags of popcorn from Fred's popcorn wagon and police cars with flashing lights manned intersection barricades. The atmosphere was carnival-like with hundreds of people milling about, chatting and inspecting the block of land that, until recently, held a run-down house and a tangle of weeds and brush.

Yesterday, Fred and I came out and took pictures of the property…the "after" pictures to match up against the "before" pictures Fred took on our birthdays five months ago and the "during" pictures taken at one-week intervals after that. It has been five months almost to the day…but sometimes it feels like five years.

By afternoon, it won't be Fred's property anymore.

I found sister Tina who came to see the excitement. She said the auction has been the talk of the office and there are over one hundred and fifty people registered to bid, each one paying a one-hundred-dollar non-refundable fee for the privilege. That should take care of the truck and driver, sign rental and helpers.

Just then, Bobby and Robbie came over to wish us a late Happy Anniversary. I hugged them both, thanking them for all the work they have done for us. Robbie shook his finger at me playfully, "You might not be thanking us so much once you get our bill!"

Frank and Maggie showed up as well, marveling at the cleared land and big truck. I looked around but didn't see Barney or Bunny. I never told Bunny about the project when she called looking to hang out with me. I made the excuse that we were busy buying and selling stuff so had no time to meet, which is technically true. But the real truth is that we don't need Fred's brother learning about our business dealings if we can help it.

At 9:45 Fred and staff members from RPR and B&R got on the truck, adjusting the microphone and settling laptops onto desks to face the buyers as helpers blended into the crowd, ready to watch for bids and transfer needed items to and from the bidders.

At ten, Fred took the microphone and boomed out "Gooood Morning Riverton!". After the crowd responded, he introduced himself as the auctioneer and thanked everyone for coming. Then he warmed up the crowd, making some jokes and listing some of the more prominent residents of Honeywood Heights such as a bank president, the mayor, a couple of sports celebrities and a best-selling author.

"The land behind you is the last undeveloped parcel of the original 10-acre settlements that has grown to become the City of Riverton," Fred explained. "The original settler of this property, merchant Albert Robertson, purchased this land over one-hundred and fifty years ago, and proceeded to build a home for his wife Claire and their children, away from the crime and grime of Chicago…and who could blame him, even today? Am I right?"

The crowd gave a knowing laugh as Fred continued. "The last owner and resident of this property was Albert and Claire's great-granddaughter Gladys Robertson, a much beloved librarian of Riverton who was born in the original house and lived her entire life on this very land."

Fred had done the research and explained to me that having a true and meaningful story will help create more interest and higher bids for those wanting to own a piece of local history.

Next, he introduced the high-tech electronic sign, Glowmaster 2000, that would be assisting the auction along with its operator, thanking Signs of the Times for providing it. The operator waved to the crowd and set off electronic fireworks to show his appreciation at being invited and the crowd responded with applause.

The rules of the auction were explained: that all lots will start at $10,000. The winners will come forward, show ID and sign some preliminary paperwork pending final arrangements for the transfer of funds, title and the signing of all required documents.

"And I have gotten a lot of questions about this last item, so I am happy to report that there will be *no* auction fees or commissions added to the winning bid price." This caused much applause and cheering from the crowd. "However," Fred warned, "winners *will* be responsible for the sales tax and normal legal fees for titling, etc." This caused some good-natured booing which Fred waved off with a smile, "The governor always wants her share, am I right?"

The first lot up for sale stood behind the crowd. Fred explained Lot #1's dimensions, assigned address and asked for the first bid.

The crowd seemed hesitant, looking about to see who would go first. Fred had expected this and gave the audience a nudge. "Who takes the first swing for ten thousand? Ten, ten…" a paddle went up, Fred pointed "and ten starts the bidding for lot number one, do I have fifteen?" The sign lit with "$10,000" in a burst of color and animation with a smaller "$15,000" blinking in the upper corner.

And that's how it went. Fred talked and joked, encouraged and cajoled, and with each new bid, the sign updated, encouraging future homeowners to push their luck a bit more until Fred finally called out "SOLD" at $85,800. The Glowmaster 2000 flared "SOLD!" with electronic fireworks bursting around the word as had been planned. People applauded and Fred made a big show of shaking the new owner's hand as they reached the truck.

Fred had been practicing at Signs of the Times on ways he would be calling the auction and coordinating with the operator on what kinds of animations would be done throughout. Fred kept the pace of his calling much slower than normal since this was not a typical auction crowd and they were doing only twenty-five sales, not hundreds, which allowed the Glowmaster operator more time to keep up the images as needed

By the third lot, people were becoming attuned with how the auction was conducted. I saw couples discussing strategy as the bidding progressed and the final prices creeped higher. Applause was encouraged and Fred kept up his happy, joking, but very professional demeanor to keep the crowd engaged…and it worked!

The truck had to take a slow, wide turn onto Falk Road after the sixth lot sold and Lot 10, went for $110,000 to the Coast Guard Captain. Fred saluted him as he approached the truck to sign his paperwork.

At this point, people who had come to buy were getting nervous that they might not get a property. People became increasingly animated in waving their numbered paddles and shouting out their bid price over each other until the bidding slowed down and finally stopped.

As the truck stopped at its next station, Fred announced, "Ladies and gentlemen! Boy and girls! Before we start the bidding on lot number thirteen, please direct your gaze to the lot on your right." In unison, the crowd shifted their heads to the Not For Sale sign placed squarely in what should have been Lot 13.

"I am proud to announce, that Orion Group has generously donated this plot of land to the City of Riverton to be the home of its newest city playground!"

People clapped and cheered at the news, especially the neighboring residents. Their children and grandchildren will soon have a nice place to play close to home. I realized too, this will help push sale prices up as well, making *all* the local properties more valuable. Fred was so smart to do this.

So, if that is the reason for one not to sell…what about the other?

By the end of Falk, the price had crested to the $150,000 mark and sold to the owner of our favorite Asian supermarket, Hong Lo. His family is very rich, owning restaurants, a travel agency and other businesses.

On Marine Drive, just after Lot 19 is the other Not For Sale sign. I know this lot so very well. It held half of Mrs. Robertson's family home along with Lot 20. Fred did not say anything as the truck slowly rolled past the empty lot, but I could tell he was expecting to be called out on this…and he was.

"Hey, what about this one?" "Aren't you selling that?" "Is that going to be another playground?" "Why isn't this one being sold? I want to buy it!" and so forth.

"Like the sign says, that lot is not for sale. We still have six more to go so don't put your checkbooks away just yet." Fred said with a smile.

"But why isn't this one for sale? Shouldn't they all be for sale?"

Without losing his cool, Fred said, "That particular lot has been set aside by the owner and is not for sale."

"But I thought *you* were the owner. Aren't you the owner of Orion Group?"

"As advertised, there is a total of twenty-five lots for sale. That has not changed. And next up we have Lot 20 whose official address will be…" and Fred moved on, no longer responding to the whining man whose wife was feeding his ear with more things to say. Why couldn't she speak up for herself?

Now my curiosity is piquing about that lot. What plan does Fred have? A store? There are few stores in this neighborhood. Electrical sub-station? That would ruin home values. A community garden sponsored by his charity Feed the Neighbors? Possibly…but Fred puts those in low-income neighborhoods, not where people buy organic water collected from tropical rainforests at ten dollars per liter.

The last three properties sold in a frenzy of bidding that brought in prices of over $175,000 each and had some couples in tears for not getting one of their own.

Fred repeated his announcements about the nine new homes to be built further down the block, and there may still be availability for anyone who is interested.

Finally, Fred announced "For those still looking for a deal on real estate, we will be conducting another auction for pre-loved homes in the Riverton metropolitan area, with announcements going out soon to those on our mailing list. If you are not already on our mailing list, please contact Riverton Property Rentals at…" and he concluded by thanking everyone for attending. It was just after noon.

Some people hurried over to Dan's properties to see if any were left to buy, the police took down their barricades and cars started slowly moving in as others tried to leave. Fred and I helped collect the paddles and trash, thanking people for coming, congratulating the winners and shaking hands with many well-wishers.

Tina and I spoke with market owner Hong Lo who was smiling from ear to ear over his new purchase. "You know, we are getting more business from non-Asian customers. They see cooking shows on the internet and come to us for specialty products they can't find in their local supermarkets. Business is booming and living here will increase our status even more."

I agreed and said, "That is very smart thinking. Maybe we will be neighbors, one day. The schools here are among the best in the state." I said it without believing my own words. We will probably be living in the garage for a long time. He drove away with his wife and children in their new luxury car.

I kept track of each sale in a notebook and Fred grossed about $3.5 million dollars. I keep checking the numbers, but they are all right there. Three and a half million dollars in three hours. Unbelievable!

B&R will collect what Dan McClurg owes, pay the remaining bills and split the agreed-upon fees between RPR and themselves. We will know the final profit in about two weeks, but Fred already has his own figures at home to see how close he gets.

The only figures Bobby and Robbie don't have are the value of our Fourth of July Treasure. The Secret Stash. Fred has other names for it too. Fred swears he has not told them, or anyone else about it. Not even his parents.

He asked me one time if I told my parents or sisters and I shook my head, "Believe me, I am not telling anyone but my best friend…and he already knows about it!"

From the Riverton Review, Sunday August 26th Lifestyle Section: "Not since the Millennium Block Bash of New Year's Eve 1999 has Honeywood Heights seen such a gathering of excited citizens as Riverton Property Rentals (RPR) and CPA firm B&R Group LLC hosted an unprecedented auction of twenty-five home-ready lots for land-hungry bargain hunters. The land, bulldozed and leveled of everything but a scattering of majestic walnut and cherry trees, are ready for the architects' hand and landscaper's eye to transform the last undeveloped block in Honeywood Heights into a bevy of beautiful homes." So started the full page and half article with color pictures including Dad on the flatbed truck with microphone in hand and arm outstretched in the "Sooooooold!" pose. Other excerpts:

"Riverton Mayor George Gomez, a Honeywood resident himself, expressed sympathy for the recent passing of former landowner and long-time city librarian Gladys Robertson in February of this year. 'She was one of the last pioneer descendants living in the Heights and was a much beloved citizen to generations of booklovers. Sadly, due to age and infirmities, she had let the house and land fall into

disrepair. Now, with a fresh influx of families, we expect exciting new homes to be built and enjoyed by generations to come!'"

"Along with the twenty-five lots sold by RPR, and nine others being developed by local attorney Dan McClurg, one of the remaining lots has been donated to the city and granted approval to be Riverton's newest city park and playground."

Fred let Tina and I know that we will be going to the riverfront casino tonight. When I asked why, he said, "With everything that happened today, I feel lucky. Real lucky."

"How lucky do you feel, Brother?" asked Tina.

"So lucky, that I plan to bet one million dollars on a single hand of cards to see if I can double it. That's how lucky I feel." I stared at him in disbelief, and it made Fred laugh. "But I'm not stupid. We're going to celebrate with Bobby and Robbie, Holly and Hazel, Dan, Michael, and some other key people who helped us today. You're included, Tina."

"You're inviting me?" Sister asked, "But I didn't have a part in the property sale."

"Doesn't matter. You're family and our guest. Besides, it never hurts to have another sparkling personality or two at a table full of dull bean-counters."

That sounds more like Fred. Always making jokes and compliments. Of course, Tina agreed to come and headed home to rest and freshen up.

Fred asked me to drive us home as his shoulders and muscles are very stiff. He did not sleep well last night in anticipation of today's event and now it is over.

I looked down and saw Fred's hands shaking. It worried me and I said so.

"That's why I want you to drive. I think the adrenaline is starting to wear off and when it does, I get the jitters." Fred shook his head, "I can't believe we cleared so much in sales. Way more than I expected. Way more."

That makes two of us.

At home, I got the green medical oil while Fred peeled off his shirt. His muscles were rock hard, and it took a lot of kneading to soften them up. Fred rolled over and brought me to him. His muscles weren't the only things that were stiff! We made pleasures for a long time, then fell asleep in each other's arms.

Fred had reserved a private dining room at the casino decorated like an Old West bar. We feasted on seafood, chicken dishes and Prime Rib along with dozens of attractive side dishes and salads from the main dining room and had our own private bartender.

Bobby passed Fred two envelopes that he slipped into his jacket pocket. When Fred saw me eyeing the transaction curiously, he said it was "just some legal paperwork having to do with today's sale."

We had fun talking about the auction, what we observed and who we knew there, but not much actual business talk. I know Fred likes to save detailed discussions for the office. We made several rounds of toasts with champagne and sparkling juice to our successes with much to be thankful for as the summer ends and the holidays approach.

Fred gave Michael a thank you card from both of us for all his help this summer. Inside the card we included the $20 Gold Certificate Mike had found, sealed in a plastic bag. Fred told Michael that, as a Business Major, he should research the history and value of his gift and decide what to do with it. Mike was very happy to get the bill and said he would treasure the lessons from his summer with us.

Everyone had a good time telling stories and joking around. Bobby said Tina "is a breath of fresh air" and "has a good rapport with all kinds of people".

Robbie asked if I was happy that she moved to Riverton and I said, "Of course! Being in the same city as her sisters is really important to Tina. But now that she's been living here for a while, she says the best part of Riverton is hanging out with you two characters!"

Well, everyone around us laughed and laughed, including Tina, and I'm glad they did…I've been saving that line to use on Bobby and Robbie for a while now. So worth it! Fred smiled and winked at me in appreciation.

Robbie asked me, "What are you and Fred going to do next?"

"I don't know," I admitted. "We haven't discussed anything past Honeywood Heights. I guess we'll go back to buying lockers and estate collections."

They smiled at each other, and Bobby said, "Well, after all that hard work, you should take some time to relax!"

I agreed. "That sounds like a good idea."

The Biggest Gift

Sunday August 19, 2001

We slept in and had no plans for the day. While I was savoring the love-glow from last night, Fred spent time in the workshop and came back up while I was making lunch. He stood quietly with something behind his back until he got my attention.

"Kimmie, thank you so much for all the work you've put in over these last few months. I know it has been hard and unpleasant, working long hours in dirty conditions and eating crappy food. But you never complained, never slowed down, helped make the work go faster and Michael really benefitted from working with both of us. This was the biggest single job I have ever done and it would have taken far longer without you…and a lot less fun." He gave me a warm smile as I tried to peek behind him.

Fred brought out a book from behind his back. "This is for you."

I know this book. It is the fake book I found on the shelf filled with money. I shook it. "No more gold coins?" I asked.

"Spent them at the casino," Fred joked. "Look inside."

I opened the book. Inside were some envelopes, red, like for Lucky Money but larger and without the colorful pictures. The top one has my name.

"Open that one first."

Inside is a piece of paper. It is the legal title to a piece of land. 1336 Marine Drive. The address of the unsold lot. The land that half of Gladys Robertson's house had sat on. It has my name on it. And only my name.

"You earned it, Kimmie. Your own piece of real estate. You can do anything you want with it."

It is dated from two weeks ago and very official looking. I became emotional and Fred took me in his arms. I cannot speak. Such a dream I did not believe would happen. "Can we build a house there?"

"Of course, Sweetheart," he murmured. "That's what it's there for. I know you're not happy living in the garage. No neighbors. No trees. I saw you looking at other homes with that dreamy look on your face."

I smiled into his shirt…he *did* notice!

"When we have children, it will be better to live there than here. I know that as well as you, Sweetheart."

It's like he read my mind and my heart. I raised my face to his and we kissed deeply, tenderly. I whispered in his ear, "So, now you are a millionaire, yes?"

There was a pause. "What do you mean?" he whispered back.

"From yesterday. I kept track of the winning bids."

"Oh, you did, did you?"

"Yes, I did. You are a millionaire now, aren't you?"

I could feel his smile on my cheek as we whispered back and forth.

"Yes, I guess I am." We kissed some more until Fred pulled away. "Before you thank me all the way to the love-nest, you might want to check the book again."

There is another envelope. Inside are airline tickets to Miami, Florida. "What is in Miami?"

"Alligators, mosquitos…oh, and there will be a rental car waiting to take us to Key West. You will love it there. It's at the very, very bottom of Florida and the kind of sleepy tropical town where we can relax and play and make love like bunnies.

"We leave in one week and spend two weeks in Key West. After that, I will be setting up another round of auctions, but for now, we will just rest and relax.

I remembered what Bobby and Robbie said to me last night and repeated it to Fred.

"Oh, they already knew about this."

"You told them before you told me?" I asked, surprised.

"Actually, it was their idea. They offered their vacation home to us as a gift, Sweetheart. It's on the beach in one of the prettiest little towns in America."

I see now how my friends were having fun, giving me hints last night, and I was clueless.

There is one more envelope inside the safe-book. I opened it. I know this paper. It is our prenuptial agreement. I am puzzled by its inclusion. "Why is this here?"

"So I can do this…" Looking into my eyes, Fred took the paper from my hands and slowly, carefully, tore the document into smaller and smaller pieces and then threw them up in the air and it came down like snow. "No more pre-nup. No present nup. No post nup. No nups at all!"

I jumped up and down in happiness, then thought of something devious and narrowed my eyes at Fred.

"So, you trust me with your money now? Maybe I will want to divorce you next week and get half of everything?" I said this with, what I hoped, a playful, teasing look.

"No one is divorcing anyone because we love each other too much," he said with a confident grin.

We hugged and kissed some more. Then I saw the paper bits on some of the food and complained to him about it.

"Oh, Babe, it will make lunch taste that much better!"

Thursday August 23, 2001
Dear My Diary,

My mind is still swirling about what happened on Sunday. I am so touched by Fred tearing up the agreement and saying that everything belongs to both of us. It is an act of true love.

I could tell Fred never really wanted to make the pre-nup and was nervous about discussing it with my family. I know he feared a rejection from me, that I might be insulted by it. But I understood from the beginning that he felt the need to protect himself and his money. I had to protect myself too. He could have been a liar, out for my family's money.

I told Fred yesterday about the $10,000 Crash Stash and asked if he was upset with my parent's plan for me? He only smiled and said "Your parents were smart to offer you protection and a way out, if the marriage went bad." Fred was not mad at all. In fact, he seemed amused by it.

Then I went a step further and explained how I have saved most of the money he has given me as 'pay' along with my modeling money.

"I expected you would do that. Doesn't surprise me. Kudos."

He did not ask me how much I have or what I will do with all the money. I have an idea for some of it and will discuss it with him in Key West. I want to know what he thinks about it before I make a final decision.

The plan for tomorrow is to fly out early to Miami, then drive to Key West. I asked if we were driving because Key West does not have an airport?

"Oh, they have small planes that fly to the island, but it will be prettier to drive down."

We are packed and ready to go. Tina helped me find cute bathing suits and fun, warm-weather dresses at Tree-Top Gals after Fred told us to "go hog wild" and buy what I want. Such a funny phrase. Oh, and I looked up 'kudos' on the computer. It means "good job" or "congratulations". Now I know a new word.

Despite Fred's generosity and our newly-gained wealth, I am still careful to find good bargains. This is the time of year when bathing suits and summer dresses are half off. When I told Fred this, he grinned and said, "I like it when bathing suits and dresses are half off!" Then he winked at me. It took a moment to understand what he meant…Naughty boy!

Key West

Monday, August 27
Dear My Diary,

Key West is so beautiful! We flew to Miami and rented a convertible sports car for the drive down. Fred thought it would be more fun this way…and it was! We drove through over 40 islands and crossed 42 bridges on US highway 1, "the highway that goes to sea" as it is called by the trip-planner.

We stopped for lunch in Marathon and visited the Dolphin Research Center to learn more about these wonderful sea animals. They even let you swim with the dolphins, and we watched other people doing it, but it would take too much time and Fred wanted to move on. It was fun, just the same.

The area looks a little like the Vietnamese coastal provinces but has a strong Spanish influence. Fred said many people here are originally from Cuba, Haiti and other islands of the Caribbean and Atlantic seas. Moreover, many retirees from New York, Michigan and other northern states come to winter or retire permanently so there is a mix of people who live and work here, not like Riverton which is mostly white and Christian and few of other kinds of people like me.

Sometimes we stopped to take pictures and visit cute touristy towns. With all the stop-and-go's, it took about six hours to get to Key West, but we weren't tired with all the eye-catching scenery.

After we got to Bobby and Robbie's vacation home, Paco met us at the door. I recognized him from the first time I had dinner with Fred's best friends, a slight man with dark features and a pretty accent. He takes care of the home, cooks and helps with anything the guests need. Fred says he is also there to keep people from stealing and trashing the house, so he is like a security guard too.

Paco told us he would cook anything we like, but to give him some ideas or preferences so he can shop and prepare accordingly. "Key West is a very small town, so it is easy to bike or walk and see everything." Paco advised. "We have bicycles you can use, or I can drive you. I only say this if you want to turn in the rental car to save money."

Fred laughed, "You know me too well, Paco! What do you think, Sweetheart? Up for some walking?"

I like the idea of strolling hand in hand through this lovely town, or just hanging out at the house so that was an easy decision.

Paco had already prepared a light dinner for us with some chilled dishes that were perfect for cooling down after a long, hot drive. Spiced shrimp, ham slices marinated in pineapple sauce, a colorful tossed salad, cut fruits and coconut juice. So good! There is a fully stocked bar ("No surprise, there!" commented Fred) and Paco offered us any kind of drink we wanted.

Fred surprised me by ordering Pina Coladas for both of us. It's like dessert in a tall glass with rum in it. After a few sips, I asked teasingly, "Fred, why are you having this kind of drink? This is not like the man I know."

"After the summer we've had? I want this to be a fun vacation and fun vacations call for a fun drink. So, why not?"

"Yes, why not?" We toasted with a kiss and explored the house which is large and luxurious. Five bedrooms, *two* living rooms(!) that Fred thinks is for when they entertain, and one group might want to watch a sports game while others chat or play cards away from the noisy fans.

Fred peeked through a door and let out a whoop, "They still have the Monster!"

We walked into the four-car garage and lights came on automatically. At nearly twenty feet long, the glossy red car with four thick chrome exhaust pipes emerging from the side of the engine was nothing like I have ever seen. So long, that it had to be parked diagonally across two of the four bays, shared with a sedan and full-sized SUV. It was, indeed, a monster.

The tires were white from the hubcaps to the edge of the treads and there was a spare tire, with matching cover, on either side of the hood, just in front of the doors. Floorboards wide enough to stand on jutted out from the sides. The low-slung convertible roof is leather and polished chrome accents are everywhere.

"If you are ready, we can return your rental now and you will ride back in the Duesenberg, yes?" asked Paco, suddenly behind us. "I always love an excuse to drive the Dus."

"Don't twist my arm, Paco…it breaks easily under that kind of pressure," Fred joked. Then, turning to me, he added, "Pops spent two years restoring The Monster. It used to belong to one of Chicago's better-known bootleggers before he was put away."

"Put away, where?" I asked, not understanding the phrase.

"Prison, Sweetheart. He was a bootlegger, a gangster. Pops had to fill in a number of bullet holes you could put your finger through, with room to spare," Fred explained, circling two fingers loosely around another, for emphasis.

My eyes must have gotten big when he said this, because he put his hand up, palm out and said, "Really! Scout's honor."

Fred went on to explain how Bobby bought the car from Frank when he and Robbie took over the firm. It was a kind of present to himself, and they drove it on nice days for fun, before having it shipped to Key West.

Paco drove us all around town, pointing out things of interest. We waved at people who turned to stare and smile at our beautiful taxi. Paco stopped at the Southernmost Point buoy and Mallory Square so we could take pictures in front of the car.

Back at the house, we were too excited to relax so we wandered outside to see the swimming pool, tennis court and the bordering beach facing West. Robbie told us that Key West is famous for its beautiful sunsets, so this is the perfect place to be in the evenings.

There are many seabirds flying about, but no parrots as I hoped to see. We wore our gold Cay Dua necklaces for the trip and it feels like a new honeymoon. We walked the beach for a while and played games with crabs who got annoyed with us for blocking their way.

I asked Fred if we could take some home to eat and, as a reply, Fred picked up a scuttling crab and waved it at me while the confused animal pinched the air. "I am the crab of Key West present," said Fred in a menacingly crabby voice, "and if you take my life with boiling water and cocktail sauce, I will haunt your dreams for-ev-ah, ha! ha! ha! ha!"

Fred set the terrified creature down who made a beeline for the nearby rocks and quickly buried itself in the mud. "Actually, I don't know what we are allowed to do here with the animals, so let's leave the crabs alone for now. We can ask Paco about it later."

After watching our first Key West sunset wrapped in each other's arms, we went into town and wandered about, looking into store windows and listening to street musicians play for appreciative tourists like us. I am so glad Fred brought me here!

Dear My Diary,

We took a boat tour around the local islands (they are called "cays" here) and we both snorkeled for the first time. You wear flippers, a windowed mask and the snorkel is a tube for breathing. I have seen people do this lots of times in movies, but it feels weird to do it in real life.

The training was minimal and it's easy enough. You just swim on the surface and look down into the warm, clear water to see fish, coral and other things on the bottom, then take a deep breath and use the flippers to go down a few meters to explore. Lots of pretty fish, some small sharks, crabs and an octopus gliding across the sand like a magic carpet.

One woman diving with us must have been seasick or something because as she climbed out of the water, she turned her head and vomited into the sea. In seconds, there were dozens of fish churning up the water around her, gobbling the half-digested food. Ewww!

I almost fed the fish my own lunch with this unexpected show and then someone called out, "Hey! No feeding the wildlife!" which made us all laugh and the woman was even more embarrassed after being sick in public.

Best of all, Fred said my swimsuit is the best investment he ever saw…he always says such sweet things to me!

On a typical day, we have a light breakfast at the house and either lunch or dinner in town as we try out different restaurants, swim in the ocean, relax by the pool and explore the area by foot or bicycle.

We visited the home of the famous American author Ernest Hemingway who used to live and write in Key West. The house is now a tourist museum with many six-toed cats that were descended from his pets over the last sixty years or so. I will try to read some of Hemingway's stories so I can imagine him writing in this beautiful home.

During our relaxing times, I have been reading (finally!) the book Phung gave me as a going away present…the Vietnamese language copy of Blue-Collar Millionaire. It has been very interesting so far. It is a non-fiction book about people who have ordinary businesses and became very wealthy while keeping to their working-class roots. The authors do not tell their real names to keep the subjects anonymous, but uses titles like Mr. X or Miss M.

The book reminds me of my family and of Fred and his father. I don't think Frank was rich, but he had a successful business before Bernie drove his parents into bankruptcy.

Ba is very successful, and my family is wealthy, but you would not know it to see how we still live near the waterfront warehouses when we could be living in District 1 in a fancy high-rise apartment overlooking the city. We don't live there because Ba likes to be close to the business and the people who work for him. He is also very hands on, even as sister Thao and Phung handle most of the difficult parts. Thao will own the company when Ba and Me retire.

Fred and I discussed the idea of taking some of my savings to put towards Cam and Tam's college future. Fred agreed that this is a very generous idea and why don't I ask Tina for help in setting up a special education fund since that is a part of her job with B&R?

He said there may be ways to invest the money in tax free instruments for the girls. That is what Fred has heard but Tina and our friends at B&R will know the best strategies.

I have been wanting to do this for my nieces but frankly, I did not think to ask my sister's professional advice. I feel so ignorant sometimes, but Fred supports the ideas I have for my family.

When I told him this and thanked him for his kindness, he said, "Well, they are my nieces too!"

Fred's Secret Uncovered

Sunday September 2, 2001
Dear My Diary,

I can't believe Fred has been keeping this secret from me! Oooh!

After lunch, Fred and I were lying on lounge chairs, he was working on his tan, and I was reading Blue-Collar Millionaire under the edge of the patio umbrella. A small table with chilled scallops, lime juice and herbs sat between us.

In Chapter Eight, they discuss "Mr. M., one of the wealthiest men in Riverton…" and I thought 'Oh! I wonder if Fred knows this person? Maybe it is Bobby or Robbie? Or the old teacher couple, the Nelsons?'

I continued to read. "…this young entrepreneur works primarily in the recycling business, but with so much more in terms of unrelated revenue streams.". Fred always tells people he is in the recycling business. And he has rental houses. And partners in different businesses. And stocks.

The more I think about it, the more my skin prickles up. I looked at Fred but he was busy with his sunblock.

Further on, it explains how he "saved his family's former business building from the auction block and turned it into his home and business headquarters, complete with a roof top garden." I looked over at Fred. "Hmmm…"

Me: Fred? Did you know they talk about a millionaire from Riverton in this book?

Fred: Is that so?

Me: Yes. It is so. Can you guess who it is?

Fred: Is it Barney?

Me: No. You know it is not Barney.

Fred: Bobby, or Robbie?

Me: No, they do not "live in a former business building, complete with a rooftop garden."

Fred: No, I guess they don't. Would you like another scallop?"

Me: No, I don't want another scallop. I want to know if you knew you were in this book?

Fred, sighing: Yes, I knew I was in that book.

Me: Why didn't you tell me?

Fred: You never asked.

Me: I think Phung suspected you were in this book, and kept asking me to read the book, but would not tell me *why* he wanted me to read it.

Fred: Well, now you know what Phung knows. And if he only suspected what you now know, you can tell him he was right.

Me: Why didn't you tell me?

Fred: I did not think it was a big deal.

Me: FRED! You are one of the millionaires featured in this book! It is a bestseller and translated into many languages including Vietnamese! I did not know that you were a real millionaire before we sold the Honeywood Heights property!!

Fred said, "If you look on the office bookshelf, there is a copy of the book, signed by the authors as a 'thank you' for my contributions."

He went on to say that he had read it and was pleased to be anonymous, but of course, a lot of local people knew who it was right away.

"Does your brother know about it?" I asked. "It is a best-selling book after all."

"Barney only reads when it is necessary and, if he knew, he would have said something long before now."

I am still learning so much about my husband. I will keep reading the book as it is eye-opening in how there are so many wealthy people in America like Fred and not like the people who try to show off their wealth…or lack of it…with blatantly material things…like Gambotti Growlers.

Frankie: We still have Dad's autographed copy of Blue-Collar Millionaire, along with Mom's Vietnamese copy, among the books Dad and Mom have written or has been written about them.

Thomas Stimson

How Fred got the Garage Back

Wednesday, Sept 5th
Dear My Diary,

Now that I know Fred has been a millionaire for several years…not a few weeks like I thought…I have been wondering about the garage. I know Frank and Maggie lost their home and business because Barney took out loans against their value and could not repay them. But if they did, how did Fred get the garage back? Did he buy it back from the new owners? Did he sue for it? Finally, I just asked him.

Fred sighed, "Well, now is as good a time as any to tell that story."

I had Fred write about it in my diary as it is too much for me to understand and accurately convey.

Hello again Kimmie's Diary,

Since you understand how my parents lost their home and business due to my dear brother Barney's greed, here is, as they say, the rest of the story:

After my parents grudgingly filed for bankruptcy, the Starbuckle and Sons garage went up for auction by the bank. The date was set, legal notices were posted, and the bank sent out invitations to potential buyers.

Nothing had been removed from the property. The vehicles, tools, parts, office equipment, even the coffee maker, were still in the building and up for sale. Sixty years and a lifetime of hard work going to the highest bidder.

On the day of the auction, dozens of people showed up at the garage. The bankers and auctioneer looked pleased. This would be a good day for them. Large posters showed photos and legal descriptions of what was inside. Few people came forward to look at them. They opened the bay doors to show the interior, but no one could go inside. Mom and Pops started tearing up and friends put their arms over their shoulders. Bobbie and Robbie were there with their briefcases. Barney was not.

The auctioneer gave a rundown of the rules, the size of the building, all the good stuff inside and the usual sales pitch to get the crowd excited. He started the bidding at $100,000. Nothing. Crickets. The crowd was silent. The auctioneer did some more pitching about the value of the building, the stuff inside, great location near the freeways, etc. Still no bids.

He started again at $80,000. Still nothing. More pitching. Still nothing. The starting bid kept dropping, the bankers were looking nervous, scanning the crowd for clues. The auctioneer said "What's wrong with you people?" and "This is an auction, not a funeral."

Little did he know. He was from out of town. Any one of our local auctioneers would know the situation and keep his insults to himself.

Finally, the starting bid came down to $25,000. They said this was the lowest starting bid and if there was no sale, the bank would halt the auction and use alternate methods to dispose of the property. "Going once! Going twice!"

"Twenty-five thousand!" I shout.

The auctioneer looked surprised, as did the bank officials, mixed with relief. Now the auction could get under way.

"I have a bid for twenty-five, do I hear thirty?"

Again, crickets. Nothing from the crowd.

"This property is worth twenty times that. The winning bidder can make a quick profit on this place without batting an eye! I have twenty-five, do I hear thirty? Thirty? Thirty? Twenty-eight? Do I hear twenty-eight? Twenty-seven?" He breathed one last sigh. "Twenty-five thousand once? Twenty-five thousand twice? Sold! For twenty-five thousand dollars."

And the biggest cheer I ever heard went up from the crowd. That really threw the big-wigs for a loop. I went up to the desk with Bobbie and Robbie and got the property signed over to me for $25,000 cash plus taxes and fees. The bank lost buckets of money and believe me, I didn't lose a minute of sleep over that.

When I gave my ID to the clerk, the other bankers, curious, looked over her shoulder to see who I was. They looked at the license, then up at the building with our family name staring back down at them. They looked me in the eye, then wandered away without saying anything.

We had a quiet dinner that night in the old lunchroom. Me, the folks and Robbie and Bobbie. The next day I set to work clearing things out, selling stuff and renovating the garage to the way I wanted.

At this point, you are probably asking yourself, "Why didn't anyone else bid if dozens had come to the auction?"

And to that, I say, "Good friends."

I had sent word out to Pop's circle of friends, former employees and business associates of our plan. I could not make people *not* bid on the building, but I could ask, as a favor to Pops, to let me win it for the lowest possible bid.

Some of these friends could have bid against me, and a few could have outspent me, but they didn't. Pops and Grandpop were always stand-up citizens, honest, hardworking and trusted. Everyone knew what had happened, and felt bad for Pops, so they had come to show their respect and support of my family for what we had given theirs.

Bob and Rob said they heard our story making the rounds through the crowd accompanied by thinly-disguised threats to any non-Starbuckle attempting to make a bid. We got lucky, but I would have paid a lot more, if I had to, to get the garage back. I always felt blessed that I was able to keep it in the family.

Could I have sold it for a quick profit? Sure, I could. Could I have turned the building over to Pops and put the garage back in business? I could have done that too, but my father was too broken in spirit and funds to start over again.

The reason why I saved the garage is because it has been a part of our family for over 60 years. The stuff I was buying and selling was being stored in places all over town and I saw the garage as a way of centralizing my operations and providing me a place to live. Then I could turn those "storage homes" into cash-producing rentals and stop paying rent on storage lockers.

Thank you Kimmie for letting me tell this story. I hope it gives you a clearer understanding of why you are living in that big ugly building instead of a nice pretty house like other people live in.

Dad had considered re-selling the property and giving everything to Grandpa and Grandma to replace all the money they lost. After some consideration, he felt like he could be more profitable in keeping the garage and using it as he did, while giving his parents a small, comfortable home and making sure their bills got paid.

Plans for a New York Visit

Thursday September 6
Dear My Diary,

I got a call from Tina asking if I have any plans for the weekend of October 20th.

I said, "I don't think so, but you never know what Fred's going to do next. Why?"

"One of my former co-workers is getting married that weekend in New York and invited me and a guest. I thought you might like to go. She's from a wealthy Singaporean family…so, you know what that means!"

"It means shopping for extra-nice outfits with room for expanding waistlines!"

Tina giggled, "We'll make it a four-day weekend, two for the wedding and two for us to hang out, shop and take in a show. Are you up for it?"

"I'll check with Fred, but I would love to go. Especially with an expert in all things New York!"

That would be such a nice treat for us…I can't wait!

While Paco was out shopping for groceries, Fred and I went over the numbers from last month using the spreadsheet he created for this project. Including an estimated value of the old money we found and tax deduction for the donated land, Fred's total profit will be just over three and one-half million dollars.

Fred kept laughing and playing with the numbers a bit here and there. "I've never made a seven-figure profit off of a single project before," he said in wonderment.

And I have never dreamed of making so much money in my entire life!

It was during this time that interest rates were dropping, the traditional 20% down payment to mitigate foreclosure risk was history, aggressive, independent mortgage brokers were popping up everywhere, greedy homeowners were refinancing multiple times to milk their home of its growing equity. Adding to this feeding frenzy were lenders willing to turn a blind eye on getting proof of financial stability and creating thousands of "liar loans" that were bundled and sold to other investors at a discount. Increasing numbers of renters were turning into homeowners causing prices to skyrocket and amateur investors were flipping homes for quick profits.

Dad and his financially experienced friends saw the speeding train would soon crash and burn, taking a piece of the economy with it. It was why he chose not to carry the mortgage notes like Doug McClurg had and chose to keep the ball rolling by selling most of his fifteen rental properties, most of which were now vacant before the crash he was predicting would happen.

I said, "You have so much money now. If you sell those houses, what will you do with all the money?"

"If the opportunity is good, I'll buy more houses on the cheap again, along with shares of beaten-down blue-chip stocks. In fact," Fred said with a shake of his head, "I think it is so close, that I've put selling alerts on many of my investments. Better to take profits now than losses later."

Fred is also making a list of organizations to donate some of his money, in addition to the ones he already sponsors. Fred likes to make his donations within our state so he can make sure it gets to the people who need it.

Then he surprised me by asking for a list of organizations I want to give in the US or Vietnam. I have some ideas and will work on it right away. There are many poor people in my country, and I especially want to help children and the elderly. We have no social security, food stamps or any kind of state-sponsored welfare in my country, as there is in the US.

RPR, B&R and Fred are planning to sell his rental homes by doing another auction, like he announced last month at the Honeywood Heights event. He said the success and excitement of the last auction might be just the trick to boost selling prices even higher than they are worth right now.

When I asked if he will sell all the rental houses, Fred said, "There will be one that I am definitely going to keep," and he told me the address.

"You own Barney's house?!" I asked in surprise. "I thought he owned it."

"Well, Barney likes to say he owns the house, but he rents it from RPR. And here's the cherry on top: he doesn't know that I am the owner."

It's easy to see why Barney graduated from the bottom of his law school class.

So much talking has given me an appetite and Paco made us another wonderfully delicious dinner. He is a kind and quiet man and nearly invisible, giving us room for privacy. Fred will leave a $200 tip for everything he has done.

We watched the sunset from the beach and walked into town for dessert, fruit drinks and live music at one of the bars to celebrate. I feel very relaxed now and we have both turned dark from the Florida sun. Such a wonderful two weeks after a long summer of hard work!

A Special Conversation

Saturday September 8
Dear My Diary,

After a morning swim in the pool and lunch at Sloppy Joe's bar, we talked about building a house in Honeywood Heights. I have been thinking about this since before Fred gave me the land title, but kept my thoughts private until Fred brought it up.

"Do you have an idea about what kind of house you want, Sweetheart? A particular style that you like?" he asked, clearly interested in my answer.

But I must be honest and say I don't know. "There are many beautiful homes in the area, it is hard to pick just one or two styles that I might want. I like so many of them!"

Fred agreed. He has lived in the garage for the last few years and apartments before that. The houses he buys to re-sell or rent are mostly smaller two bedroom/one bath homes in working class neighborhoods built during the baby-boom years. The homes for his parents, brother and my sister are better than his typical rental homes, but nothing like what is in Honeywood Heights.

Fred asked me, "Do you know the most important part of a home?"

"The floors?" I joked.

He laughed, "Yes, that will keep you from falling into the basement, but something else?"

"Doors?"

"No."

"Walls?"

"Helpful, but no."

"Then what?"

"The love of the family inside the home."

"Fred, that is such a sweet thing to say!"

"You know, as a couple, we are a family. But it would be nicer if there were some little members too."

'Oh, my!' I thought. 'Fred is talking about children!'

"But we have been married only one year. Are you sure you want to make a baby with me?"

Fred took me in his arms and said, "You have been through a lot in the last year. Moving to America. Sister Thanh's family facing problems that you helped them get through. All the work you did for my business without complaint. Becoming a Fierce 5 model. And most challenging of all, putting up with my cooking!"

Looking deeply into my eyes, he continued, "You have been an absolute champ through all of it. A real trouper. I could not ask for a better wife and friend. And I firmly believe that our children could not ask for a better mother."

I took a deep breath, thinking 'I *have* been through a lot, haven't I!' I thought about how to respond.

"Fred, in my country I am the too tall girl. The freak. The one people stare at and make fun of. I had no reason to think I would ever marry, and if I did, I would be like a prize for that man, but not in a good way for me."

My heart swelled with emotion, "But you do not make fun *of* me. You make fun *with* me. That is so different. You make me feel special and smart, pretty and useful. You say the nice things that only my parents and sisters would tell me. Your parents accept me with love. Your friends and business partners treat me as an equal to them."

Fred and I held each other for a long time. He murmured "You *are* our equal. You *are* smart. You *are* pretty. You *are* respected. And you *are* very, very special to me and my family."

I said, "When I see you with the twins and other little cousins, the way you play with them and teach them fun things, I see you as a future father wanting to come out of his egg. Cam and Tam are getting healthier now that brother and sister have stopped gambling, smoking and drinking so much. They are making more time for their daughters and preparing better foods for them. Fred, you are the one that took the time to help them, and they love you for it. I love you for it. And I want very much to start a family with you. Do you want to start a family with me?"

"More than anything in the world, Kimmie. More than anything in the world."

And with that, I stopped taking the birth control pills…and spent the rest of the day in bed!

Monday September 10
Dear My Diary,

I hope we come back to Key West again. It is such a beautifully relaxing place with wonderful seafood and the warm ocean for swimming. I would love to bring my sisters here next year, maybe at Christmas time.

I never saw any parrots even though there are lots of signs and pictures of them everywhere. When I asked Paco, he said "Parrots are not native to Florida. The ones you might see used to be pets and there are small flocks around Florida but, alas, none in Key West." He shrugged, "Sorry to disappoint."

Tomorrow afternoon we will fly from Key West to Miami, then to Riverton where we expect to be greeted by sunshine and warm weather, but no palm trees or ocean breezes. Uck! In a couple of hours, we will take Paco out for a farewell dinner at a restaurant with live island music.

We just finished a three-way call with Bobby and Hazel, going over how they will sell most of Fred's rental homes, since so few are occupied and available homes for sale are scarce. RPR has already contacted the current tenants to see if they are interested in buying the home they are occupying and, if not, we will prepare the homes for the auction.

Since the Honeywood Heights auction was so successful, some real estate brokers who attended are now hiring professional auctioneers to recreate Fred's success.

Hazel Wood said some of her clients want Fred to auction their homes or vacant lots since he was in the newspaper and on TV. Fred will offer his services to RPR clients at a flat fee of $2500 per property to make some quick cash. His price will heavily undercut other auctioneers who will charge a percentage of the sale price.

The total number of empty rental houses is thirteen. I pointed to the calendar, "Thirteen could be a lucky number because next month, October 13th is on a Saturday, a perfect day for an auction!" Everyone reminded me that thirteen is an unlucky number, but in this case, it may become a very lucky number.

It was decided that one month is enough time to advertise and prep for the auction. All three cheered my idea and I got shy but Fred smiled and patted my back in approval. "Brains *and* beauty!" he said.

After our meeting, we called Bobby and Robbie back to give them many thanks for the use of their beautiful home, going on about what a relaxing romantic time we have had and how Paco was such a good host and cook.

"Stop gushing, you lovebirds!" Bobby said, with a smile in his voice, "We're glad someone's getting some use out of the place. Just get back here safely, have dinner with us on Saturday, tell us all about it and we'll call it even."

We did not tell them about our new plans…that they might be uncles soon! He he!

Now it is time to get ready for a night out with Paco.

Good Night, Dear My Diary!

America's Sad Day

September 11, 2001
Dear My Diary,

I am writing from the back seat of The Monster. I just finished my turn at driving and can't keep the images of falling towers and exploding planes out of my line of sight. Closing my eyes to rest makes it worse. I am worried about Trinh and want to get this down on paper while I can, even though I will never forget this day. No one will ever forget this day…

We are just north of Gainesville, having filled the car for the fourth time and taking time to eat, even though neither of us feel hungry. Such a terrible day for America and I am not sure where to start…so I will start with breakfast.

Paco had made the most wonderfully decadent breakfast: a crab omelet with onions, peppers and dill sauce, toasted baguette slices with creamed avocado and warm olive oil drizzled over and a fresh fruit compote with shaved coconut sprinkled on top. It was Paco's treat for us, and the perfect meal to end our long second-honeymoon time in Key West…until the phone rang.

Paco spoke briefly, "No Mr. Bobby. No. Yes, right away."

As Fred took the phone, Paco turned on the kitchen television. I could hear Bobby say, "I guess you haven't heard the news yet?"

On the TV, I recognized the towers of the World Trade Center. But instead of standing tall and majestic, their upper floors billowed smoke and there was talk of airplanes hitting them. But how? The skies were clear and blue. How could planes hit not one, but both towers on a clear day?

"No one is sure what's going on yet." Bobby started, "At first, we thought it was an accident but with both towers hit, it must have been planned."

We stared in disbelief as footage rolled of the second plane flying straight into the South Tower as cleanly as a playing card slides into the middle of a deck. Seconds later, flames erupted as though from a dragon. Newscasters were struggling to hold their emotions as they described the scene and what they knew so far.

I thought of Sister Trinh. We visited her at the World Trade Center's North Tower a year ago and, if not for Thanh, she would still be working there today. I shudder to think of losing my sister this way.

"Don't count on flying out of Key West, or anywhere else, today," Bobby said. "There may be more flying bombs out there yet."

Robbie got on the phone, "How are you two doing over there?" he asked.

"Well, we *were* fine, until now." Fred said bitterly, "I've never seen anything like this."

"I think this is our generation's Pearl Harbor," Robbie said. "Only, we don't know who the enemy is yet."

Paco pointed out things falling from one of the towers. It took a moment to realize it was people. People falling hundreds of feet to their deaths. I thought of Tina and hid my tears as I raced to the bedroom for my phone. No answer on either her cell or home phone.

I went back to the kitchen and spoke into the phone, interrupting Fred, "Did Tina come into work yet?"

"Oh, hi Kimmie. No, not yet. It's only eight-fifteen here," said Bobby. "Tina rolls in around nine unless she has a morning appointment." I had forgotten about the one-hour time difference. "I'll have her call you as soon as she's in," Bobby offered.

'But why didn't she answer her cell?' I wondered out loud.

I was deep in thought about sister when Fred got my attention, "Kim, Robbie says we can either stay here until things settle down or we can drive back. What's your idea?"

Thinking of sister and how much she loved New York and her friends there, and how I would feel if something like that happened to me, I had only one answer: "I want to go home."

A moment later, Fred said, "Bobby wants us to drive The Monster back."

But I could hear the couple bickering over the speaker, "Have you seen his trucks? The insurance company would…"

The television stated another plane had crashed into the Pentagon building and announcements were made that all air traffic was to be cancelled until further notice.

Fred said, "Look, if you want the Duesenberg, we'll be happy to drive it there and I'll keep the gas receipts. I don't call it 'The Monster' for nothing!"

Soon after, first one tower, then the other, collapsed in clouds of smoke and dust. Nobody spoke, but we all cried together. Paco went to the bar and poured a tumbler of liquor for himself, downing one, and then another. He turned to us, raising the bottle as an invitation to soothe our nerves, but we shook our heads. He nodded in understanding, then pulled a large picnic basket from the pantry and began to fill it with food for our trip north.

I kept calling Tina but now the lines for both phones were busy. How could both her phones be busy? I tried calling Thanh and Vo using their home and cell numbers, but all their lines were busy too.

Then it hit me…everyone was calling everywhere to check on family and discuss the crashes. Now it made sense. Tina must know what has happened by now because she likes watching the morning news shows as she gets ready for work. Poor sister!

Luckily, we had packed last night and there is plenty of trunk space in the car. After both of us practiced driving a bit on the unnaturally quiet streets, we left Key West in the Duesenberg for Riverton. Our plan is to drive straight through to Riverton, switching drivers every two hours, filling the tank, stretching our legs and downing cans of chilled Fierce 5 before hitting the road again. Fred estimates it will take about twenty-four hours, but I think it will be much less at the rate we are driving.

The car is very heavy and drives like a silken cloud, but if we drive much more than three hours, the tank will go dry, so we are keeping close track of the next towns and cities to keep from running out of fuel in the middle of nowhere.

The roads are emptier than we expected. I think everyone is home watching television and learning new things about the attacks. The radio in this car is original and does not work well so we keep it turned off. Neither of us feel much like talking, let alone listening to the news or music. Overhead, military jets and helicopters constantly patrol the skies.

I wish there was a way to recharge my phone in the car. My battery is dead from trying to call Tina so much and Fred wants his available in case of an emergency. I don't blame him. B&R said they would shut the office down today, and maybe tomorrow too so I don't know how Tina is faring with all this bad news.

It is getting too dark to write and my head is buzzing. It's going to be a long night..

Tina's Guilt Trip

September 14, 2001
Dear My Diary,

We left Key West at noon and arrived in Riverton at nine in the morning. As we approached the city limits, Fred used his phone and let his parents and Bobby know that we had made it safely back and our first stop was to see Tina.

She opened the door cautiously only after she saw us on the porch. Her face was red and puffy and her voice was as hoarse as a frog. I held Tina in my arms as she cried and cried. So many friends and co-workers are dead or missing and it is too early yet to know what happened to who. The phone lines in and out of New York are jammed most of the time.

Because it is an Asian-based bank, many of the employees work during the late-night/early morning hours when it is business hours in Japan, China, Korea and Vietnam so those workers had already left work to sleep during the day. But Tina and her staff worked through the day, typically from eight to five o'clock, and often later, selling financial products to local investors, managing brokerage accounts and the like.

Tina was most concerned about her former co-workers because the planes hit between 8:45 and 9 o'clock New York time, when her entire staff would be at work. We were both crying for her co-workers and all the other people lost or injured in the attacks and relief because it did not happen to Tina. She is safe with us.

Fred made tea and muffins from a mix to help out. It was kind of him, but we have no appetite and Tina is an emotional mess.

Fred called Bobby who understood right away why Tina will be more traumatized than most in Riverton. Bobby said several employees have family there and it is very hard to reach anyone as the phone systems are jammed with people calling family, friends, offering help to the city, etc. Bobby told Tina to take all the time she needs and come to work when she feels ready.

Fred is trying to be supportive, but it is hard for him because he does not know what to do and we are only speaking our mother tongue.

Trinh is a crushed woman. She has been keeping in touch with many friends in New York, some from college, some from the neighborhood and some who work in the WTC or nearby offices. She might not know for some days or weeks who is alive and who is gone. Many were not born in America and their families, living so far away, have even less ability to know what has happened to their son or daughter, brother or sister, niece or nephew in America.

Thanh came over later as they did not open the shops. I told Fred to go home and his being with us is appreciated, but Tina feels guilty about moving here and does not feel it is right that she is alive while so many of her peers have died. These thoughts and feelings are taking a toll on her heart and emotions.

I spent the next nights with her to be a calming influence. She has lived in America for many years and is significantly older so we do not have much in common. But she is my sister and she needs me and Thanh to get better.

I have also seen Thanh in a new light these last few days. Her normal talking style is either brief and direct to the point of being rude, or with flowers in her mouth as she does to customers or those from whom she wants something.

For now, she is gentle and kind and warm to Trinh, like she is sharing the pain. I think she is like this to her children when they are sick or hurt. It is not the style I am accustomed to seeing in her. Now that our older sister is hurting, I am impressed with Thanh's attitude and wished she would use it more often.

Ba called to see if we are all okay and if any terrorists are attacking Riverton. We assured him that the Army and Coast Guard bases are on high alert and many military planes are flying over us regularly.

When Trinh hears a jet plane or helicopter, she freezes with a panicked look because it reminds her of 1975's fall of Saigon. I am too young to remember it, but it is very real to my sisters. Especially how thousands fled the advancing communist forces to the waterfront where we lived to board boats and leave Vietnam in haste. My parents were very scared, unwilling to leave their homeland and unsure what the next day might bring…but it was not an unknown terror like it is now.

I may be the baby sister, but at night I sleep in the same bed with Trinh to give comfort. I wrap my long arms around her and hold her close. If she talks, I talk with her. If she is quiet, I stay quiet. I wonder if this is how a mother holds a child close when they are sick or frightened? I am glad I can do something to help Trinh.

Vo brought the twins to Trinh's apartment for a short time to cheer up their Auntie. They had made pictures and decorated them with flowers and cute animals and "I love you" and "Please do not be sad".

This made Trinh cry some more, but in happiness for their sweet thoughts and happy art. She held them very close for a long time before kissing them and telling them to be good. Cam and Tam promised to be good girls and blew us kisses on their way out.

Fred said all the local businesses, except for gun sellers, are very quiet this week so he comes to the house two or three times each day with food from our gardens and pantry to make something good to eat, but our appetites are off.

Trinh slept through last night and hardly woke up at all. Today she has more appetite but looks bedraggled. Having so many tears, worries and guilty feelings is like a cancer, and she has lost so much weight so fast.

I do not feel as close to New York as Trinh does, but I do understand how I would feel if this kind of unexpected attack happened in my home city to kill many thousands of people, some of them I know or close to me.

Good Night Dear My Diary

Lois: Although Aunt Trinh was not in New York at the time of the attacks, she suffered from survivor guilt for a long time afterwards that took a therapist to help her get through. It was simply a matter of circumstances that brought her to Riverton to start a new career and be near family that kept her from being yet another victim of the 9/11 attacks that we still memorialize today.

Dear My Diary,

Tina has been getting some emails and calls from her NYC friends with news of who is safe and who is missing, injured or confirmed dead. Most of the people she had worked with are in 'missing' status and presumed dead. Many of the bodies may never be found. Those who were not at work that day are transferring to other branches, returning to their homeland or leaving the company for other places. Staying in New York is too hard to bear. Most have promised to keep in touch.

Sister is making a list of everyone she knew and writing down little histories of each to remember them by, especially those who did not survive. She told me this is a kind of therapy for her, putting happy memories on paper to ease the pain.

She locates pictures of her friends among the still-unpacked possessions and includes them in the mini-biographies. She writes about their history together, how they met, where they came from, who they worked for and what they were like.

Tina intends to share the histories with those people's families if she can get their addresses. Maybe it will help them to know how their family member is remembered by a friend or co-worker and have another piece of their child or sibling to hold onto.

Tina's doctor has prescribed medications for anxiety and depression to help her get back to the office. "I need the money and, more importantly, being around people who won't feel sorry for me."

I will talk to Fred about getting together more often with sister for meals and fun activities that don't involve talking about nine-eleven…unless she needs to unburden herself. I will always be there for her when she needs it.

Good News! Barry Picker called sister…he is alive! Barry left the city just after Labor Day weekend to visit his family for two weeks. He is deeply saddened about everything and told Tina he will stay put and get a job in London. With so many bad things going on in America, he will not likely return for a while, if ever. He is relieved that Tina moved to Riverton when she did and got a job near her family as Barry is doing now.

Everyone is calling the attack "Nine Eleven", partly because that is the date it happened, 9th month and 11th day. Also, it occurred to me how nine eleven is the emergency phone number used everywhere in the United States and that the terrorist leaders intentionally planned the date as a cruel joke to America. I hate them.

I asked Fred if we are still doing the property auction on Oct 13th, and he said nothing has changed for that. "The country is starting to settle down and the stock market has opened back up again. Things will return to normal soon…at least mostly."

Sang: Mom and Dad told us that before 9/11, anyone could enter an airport terminal and go right up to the boarding gates, even if they didn't have a ticket. No long lines for security, no having to arrive two or three hours before the flight. None of us have ever been greeted coming off an airplane the way Mom was when she first arrived in the US, with family waiting right there with flowers, balloons and hugs and kisses. As Dad would say, "Nine-eleven killed the fun of flying for everyone." I'm sure the pun was unintended.

Dear My Diary,

I found Fred's copy of Blue-Collar Millionaire on his office bookshelf. I never noticed it before amongst the pricing guides and self-help books he likes to read. The title page is autographed by all the authors with personalized notes of thanks for his contributions to their study. It makes me proud of what my husband and best friend has accomplished for himself, and others, before he was even thirty-five years old.

Dad's copy of Blue-Collar Millionaire, signed by all four authors along with Mom's VN language copy are part of the Starbuckle archives at Riverton University.

Treasure Hunt

Dear My Diary,

While RPR and B&R prepare for the upcoming auction, Fred and I went to the locker auctions to get some clothes, furniture, household items and collectables for the resale stores. This will be our first time at the auctions since before the Honeywood Heights project, and what a sight that greeted us…my goodness!

There were far more than the usual group of bidders and many of them we had never seen before. In fact, very few of the regular buyers were there.

Fred found a cluster of our competitors drinking coffee and eyeing the better dressed and mostly younger crowd who had arrived, some openly counting large bundles of cash or talking loudly on cell phones.

Fred asked "Hey, what's with this crowd? Did word get out about a safe in one of these lockers?"

Bob the Bottle Guy asked, "Where have you two been hiding out? You've been missing a lousy summer and it's getting worse." The others nodded and made similar comments. "Everybody is here because of Treasure Hunt."

Apparently, Treasure Hunt is a hot new TV show where camera crews go from city to city and show professional buyers purchasing lockers at auction and then going through what they bought, often discovering "treasures" among the trash.

Francine, an older woman who sells regularly at the flea market, said many of the buyers on TH seem to find amazingly valuable things far more often than anyone she knows, and Francine has been doing this for decades. We explained that we do not watch much TV and don't have cable so never saw the show.

The seeming ease of finding valuable items as portrayed on Treasure Hunt has generated a lot of interest in buying storage lockers and bidding into the thousands of dollars. In retaliation, some of the regulars will push the bidding higher to have fun with the amateurs with no intent to win the locker. Sometimes they will talk among each other loud enough for others to hear, "I think I saw part of a car buried in there" and things like that.

Understandably, the regulars are upset by the high turnout of new bidders. By overpaying for the lockers, the regulars can't stock their resale stores, flea market booths or Ubiddit sites with affordable items, so many of them have dropped out of the auctions and finding other places to get their goods.

We took a chance and watched the auctions through the morning. The regulars were right. Things we would normally pay a few hundred dollars, people bid up to $2500 to $3000 or more. It was not worth it and bought nothing today.

Fred suggested that we will go through the neighborhoods on trash day like he used to do years ago when he was getting started to find sellable items, buy large lots of items from Ubiddit, shop charity shops throughout the metro area and tell the store owners to put ads on FreePost to encourage people to bring in unwanted items to donate or consign.

The Big Auction

October 12, 2001
Dear My Diary,

Tonight, Holly Wood called to update us on the number of pre-qualified bidders who have registered for the auction. Some signed up at the open house events but most had registered soon after the initial announcements were made. RPR had the registrants select which homes they were interested in, and she faxed the lists of names to Fred. Holly and Hazel think as many people are looking to buy a house for renting as they are to live in themselves.

Most houses have fifteen to thirty registered bidders, but some last-minute registrants are expected. We are not setting a limit because, as Fred likes to say, "The more the merrier!" The bidding will start at $50,000, and after that…? We will see!

October 14, 2001
Dear My Diary,

Fred did it again! He was so confident and funny and knows how to cajole people into placing higher bids…and make them feel good for doing it! I think more neighbors came to watch the proceedings than were there to bid.

As we pulled up to the first house, his sweaty palms gave away his nervousness. I knew this would happen, so at breakfast, as he fretted about last minute details, I took Fred into my arms and told him one of Ba's favorite sayings: Good Luck happens when Preparation meets Opportunity.

"My Love, you and everyone else have worked hard to prepare for another successful sale. The opportunity is like a tree full of perfectly ripe mangos. All you need to do today is reach out and pluck thirteen mangos. Very simple." I gave him a long, warm good-luck kiss that he eagerly returned. He may not remember the mangos, but I know he will remember the kiss!

The homes looked great, and the buyers cheered as we pulled up in a bus playing a catchy pop song over the speakers. Fred bounded out the door with a cordless mic in one hand and red clipboard in the other, calling out "Who's ready to spend some moneeeey?" and the crowd cheered louder than before.

Each stop was much the same routine: Fred thanks everyone for coming…what great weather to buy a home isn't it? Here are the rules…bidding opens at fifty thousand do I hear fifty? Final bid is reached…winner approached by RPR rep to finalize the sale…thank everyone for coming…hope to see you at the next auction (gives the address), and we get on the bus.

I went along to support Fred and provide an extra level of interest to the proceedings. I am becoming a familiar face to Riverton residents and sometimes people approach me for my autograph. Fred appreciates my company and the extra boost I provide with my presence.

Before the auction starts, Fred reminds the crowd that the winning price does not include the sales or property taxes but waives all the usual fees that a buyer would normally pay separately from the sale price.

This is not a normal practice in real estate, but the selling of homes by auction that are not in foreclosure is not a normal practice either. Fred offers to pay the fees to encourage higher bids and his announcement at each stop always gets some excited questions to clarify this or that point, even though the details were in the registration agreements that everyone signed. Fred answered all the questions in a friendly, informative tone so as not to alienate any of the bidders.

When it was all done, Fred grossed nearly $2,500,000 with many of the houses selling for over $200k, much more than comparable houses in terms of size and location. Fred said, "That's why we did the auction. It doesn't give people a chance to negotiate for less because they feed on each other's energy to drive the price *up*. I love it!"

The combined total of what Fred originally paid for all the properties was less than $400k so after legal fees, taxes and commissions to RPR and B&R ("Gotta spread the love around!") he will clear a profit close to two million dollars, not including the rent he has collected, or the payment of property taxes and management fees paid out over the years. "Still, it is a pretty penny," as Fred likes to say.

I lunched with Bunny today for the first time since Bernie's cat food case was dismissed. She said his business has dropped to nearly nothing now that Bernie's name is a big joke in the local law circles.

He has been pushing to negotiate any kind of settlement with the companies he sued but they just ignore him, and the local judges throw out his motions for this or that legal action so the six-million-dollar man is not even a six-dollar man anymore.

Bernie is now sending bills to Mrs. Leatherwood for his work, even though he advertises "You don't pay unless I win!". Of course, Bernie claims to have won the case and it was not his fault that the case was overturned. Mrs. Leatherwood has no money to pay anything and Bunny said "That dog is barking up an invisible tree." I almost choked on my salad, laughing so hard at the picture in my mind.

"But do you know what I don't understand? With the price of homes skyrocketing and every landlord in the state raising rents, ours has stayed the same the whole time we've been there."

I remember Fred saying that Bernie pretended their home was his, so I feigned surprise, "Oh, I thought you owned your house!"

She scoffed, "Bernie tells people that, but we rent. His income is too upsy-downsy for a mortgage. Of course, that didn't stop him from getting a sports car that we can't afford. No, we rent. And it hasn't gone up a dime since we moved in. I know people whose rent has doubled in the last three years, and they can't believe my luck."

"Hmm," I pretended to consider the matter, knowing full well that Fred could have sold the house out from under them with all the others, but he didn't…and I couldn't tell Bunny either. "We have a saying in Vietnam: 'When being offered an animal as a gift, do not ask the status of its health.'"

Bunny started to say something else, then her face lit up, "Oh, I get it! Like, don't look a gift horse in the mouth!"

I don't know that American saying, but I said, "Yes! Like that. I mean, maybe they forgot to raise the price of the rent or the owner does not need the money or…"

"Fat chance of any of those things," Bunny said dismissively. "But I sure as hell won't bring up the subject with the landlords either. I may be blonde, but I'm not dumb."

I don't know what being blonde has to do with being stupid or incapable of speech, but when Bunny asked what we were up to these days, I just said, "Oh, you know, the usual." I don't have the heart to tell Bunny about our trips to St. Louis and Key West while they are struggling to make money and Bernie won't let his wife work an outside job.

Since she doesn't seem to know about the auctions we have done, I guess Frank and Maggie have not told her either. As Fred likes to say, "The less said around Barney, the better."

Frankie: The auctioning of properties became a short-lived trend in the Riverton area. Many professional auctioneers and real estate brokers jumped on the bandwagon when they saw what Dad was doing, how quickly the properties could be sold and at higher prices than using traditional methods.

But auctions only work well when the housing market is red hot with low supply and high demand. And, like the bio-oil boom, the direction of the real-estate market would soon change.

Michael's Gold Certificate

Saturday, November 3
Dear My Diary,

We invited Tina, Auntie and Michael over for dinner tonight and he had an interesting story about taking his gold certificate to a coin shop in the town where he attends college. The owner said the bill is a fake because George Washington was on a twenty-dollar bill. He offered Mike ten dollars because he wanted it as a novelty item. Mike refused and the shop owner offered a little more and a little more and, finally, offered him two hundred for it, final offer and won't offer it again. Michael *still* refused to sell.

Fred asked, "Why did you turn down two hundred dollars and how did you know the bill was not a fake?"

"We found it hidden in an old book in that house. Who would hide a fake bill in a book? Besides, Uncle Fred, you seemed to know there was value in the bill or you would not have given it to me."

"Smart kid," Fred said, "using your noodle like that."

Mike had refused the store owner's offer because he had done his homework ahead of time and checked it out on Ubiddit against similar ones that had already sold, just like the researching he had done for us over the summer.

Mike opened a Ubiddit account and sold it for over four thousand dollars. Fred and I congratulated him on doing his homework "and not falling for one of the oldest tricks in the book" as Fred would say.

"That dealer knew very well what it was worth and would have had it resold to a collector before the day was out for a big profit if you had believed the guy."

Tina told us about her meetings with Hong Lo, the owner of our favorite Asian market. Tina is getting him interested in buying some financial products and maybe even to switch over to B&R for his tax returns next year. He has a bookkeeper, but finds that person is making mistakes and possibly causing him to pay more in taxes than he should.

I don't know anything about American tax rules, but they must be complicated. Tina said, "If that goes well, we will offer to go back over the previous years' taxes and possibly get more money refunded. And if THAT goes well, it could lead to valuable referrals from Mr. Lo."

"I'll put in a good word for you and the firm," Auntie said. "We've helped each other out a few times, so Hong knows I won't lead him down a blind alley."

Later, when we were alone, Tina asked if we are thinking about having a baby? I told her that I feel the time is right for us. Fred has been a wonderful husband…kind, funny, giving me confidence and proving that he is not a phony like his brother. He will be a great Ba to our children.

No one but Fred knows that I have stopped taking birth control pills and we do not want to give our families too much hope in case we can't conceive. We don't have a reason to think that we can't make a baby, but I also know there is no guarantee. Fred has not told anyone either, so it is our secret until it happens…or not.

November 6, 2001
Dear My Diary,

I had a Fierce 5 modeling appointment today with the full crew for more print and video ads. So far, F5 distribution has been limited to the Midwest and some of the Southern states, but Fred says we are going to "kick it into high gear" now. He always has such colorful expressions!

After we had our hair and make-up done and updated costumes put on, we met at the stage and there was a group of people I have only seen a very few times: The owners and top executives of Fierce 5, including Fred. They were smiling and shaking hands with us, awkwardly high-fiving and such. It felt like good news was in the air.

Zander began the meeting, directing her words to the crew and looking very mysterious. Believe me, 'mysterious' is not a normal look for her. Zander's announcement went something like, "Congratulations, everyone! Our Fierce 5 campaigns so far have generated a lot of fresh, or should I say 'fierce' interest, sales, and fans to the brand. We are getting into more stores and requests from larger grocery chains to carry Fierce 5 in other markets." We clapped and cheered at the news, as did the execs.

"Based on the company's research of sales figures, one of the biggest drivers of sales has been you five," Zander waved an open palm in our direction, "the faces of Fierce 5. The characters who embody toughness, energy and animalistic sex appeal to our target audience."

This time, the execs began the applause and cheers, smiling broadly at us and giving thumbs-up gestures. I put my hands over my heart and bowed slightly, embarrassed at the attention, but pleased, nonetheless.

Jaguar pumped her fist in the air, going Hoo! Hoo! Hoo! as she does when excited and Bettina said, "We could not have done it without Zander's genius behind the camera," We cheered for Zander who took a rare turn at shyness as the attention was now put on her.

Regaining her composure, Zander went on. "In order to ride this wave, and the success it is bringing to the company, we will be quickly expanding our exposure across the country. Some of the ads we did earlier, along with ones we are doing today, will be launched into other regions of the United States with beverage distributors signed up to deliver F5 to select national and regional store chains." More applause from everyone. Such a secret Fred has kept from me! He stood among the owners grinning widely and giving me a big wink, which I returned.

"In order to boost Fierce 5 to the next level, to make this the number one energy drink in the country, to make Fierce 5 known to one and all…our promoters have signed up one of the hottest, toughest, and might I add, *fiercest* action stars to help promote Fierce 5. Aaaand rumor has it, he even knows one of our own Fierce 5 tigresses!"

Zander wiggled her eyebrows, then swept her hand back and raised her voice, "Please help me welcome the newest member of our Fierce 5 team…international action star, Rock Rollins!!"

My heart leaped into my throat as Rock strolled out from backstage, putting his arms up and shouting, "Fierce 5 makes me feel ALIVE!" and we went from cheering to a shrill screaming. He came over to our group saying "Be Fierce! Live Fierce! Drink Fierce 5!" and we surrounded him like teens meeting a pop star.

Rock was dressed in a costume similar to our own, but more masculine, with thick black lines painted under his eyes and over the top of his signature shaved head to emphasize his fierceness. He was ready to model with us!

Rock turned to me, "Kimmie! So good to see you again!!" Needless to say, with the heavy make-up, wig and fangs, I don't look anything like the newlywed who couldn't remember where she was from in front of a national television audience. Fred must have told him.

Thinking quickly, I said "Thank you! So good to see you again, especially now that you are not throwing knives at me!"

Rock said, "You were great on the show! I still have people asking me about that appearance." I could see Fred watching everything with a very pleased-with-himself smile.

Rock was then introduced to the other team members and the owners came around to make some speeches about what we will do and how important it is to make ads that show the passion of F5.

Then Rock made his own announcement, speaking directly to us: "Heads up, everyone! How would you like to help me kick some ass in my next film?" As we whooped and cheered, Rock continued, "I've got a great scene made just for the Fierce Five crew and I would be honored if you said 'yes' to doing it." We laughed and nodded and said 'yes' in a handful of languages and went a little crazy. Troi oi!

The details have not been worked out yet, but we are expected to do a scene involving fighting and stunts with Rock against some bad guys. Some of my co-workers have TV and movie experience, so they know more about this kind of work than I do. We also need to get a SAG card, if we don't already have one, to work on the film. I don't know anything about union cards, but company management will get us what we need.

After so much fun news, it was hard to look fierce for the cameras, so Zander gave us time to settle down as they finished setting up cameras and lights and Rock made small talk with us. Fred came over and asked me what I thought of everything?

"How did Rock know me after such a long time and with all the makeup?"

Fred's eyebrows went up in mock surprise, "Gosh, I don't know!"

As always, when we are working, Fred sits in the back of the theater to research new investment ideas and offers from people all over the Midwest. But unlike most times, I saw a woman I do not know sitting near him and they were speaking to each other off and on. She does not look like a model and Fred does not hide the fact that he is talking with her in a casual-conversation sort of way.

During a break, I went to see Fred and Rock followed me because…the mystery woman is Rock's wife! Introductions were made and her name is Kathy Rollins. She and Richard (Rock's real name) are childhood sweethearts and I can see the love-glances they give each other.

Rock got his nickname from the many body building competitions he won. His friendly personality caught the attention of Hollywood, and everything went up from there.

Fred told me later that his own muscles are home grown, not beefed up by specialized exercises and performance drugs. I told my best friend, "Do not worry, Fred, I like your big muscles better!"

When Rock and his wife were leaving, he gave us all energetic handshakes and high fives while telling us how much he enjoyed "working with such pros". He let us take some personal pictures with him and was very upbeat about everything.

I have read articles how he is always nice to fans and the people he works with. Clearly, it is true. And I feel good for his wife too, as they grew up knowing each other and have stayed together all these years, despite all the temptations that can make and break a couple in this business.

Thinking about it, I guess Kathy is also Rock's rock. I see this in my relationship with Fred…supporting each other's successes.

At the end of the day, we were given one more piece of news: that because we are working with a guest celebrity and our ads will be nationwide with so many more people seeing them, we will get more pay…MUCH more pay! I am keeping my special arrangement of half cash and half F5 stock. It is so much more, that it's hard to believe. I wonder what we will be paid for our scene in the movie? I will have to wait and find out.

A Surprise from my Family

Thursday November 15
Dear My Diary,

I met with Tina to discuss how to invest and grow what I have built up over the last year. I may be entitled to half of Fred's assets, but for myself, I have over $50,000 in my personal account plus F5 stocks and a clear title to the land in Honeywood Heights. I have never had so much money of my own before!

We met at Sister's apartment where we can speak freely, and I brought some homemade Pho and herbs from our garden to get the afternoon started.

As we ate, I told Tina how much I have in savings and the desire to create multiple streams of income. She understood this term and wants to help. She gave me a list of investment types from the very safest to the more aggressive kinds, with notes about how each works and the possible risks involved.

Tina explained, "With the money you have right now, you can get into some domestic and international index funds, real estate and petroleum trusts, things that will pay dividends and help you with growth, but fifty thousand won't give you much in terms of multiple income streams. Besides," she added, "you do not have fifty thousand to invest."

Her last sentenced surprised me. "Of course, I do! Why would I say it if I did not?" Did she think I was lying or mistaken? I don't think she meant to insult me because that is not her way. "Please sister, explain what you mean by that."

A knowing smile crept across her face as she began, "When family came to the wedding, do you remember Ba saying he had some family business to discuss? Then you interrupted him to give back the get-out-of-town money?"

"I remember it very clearly. Is he upset about this? I know I should not have interrupted him like that but how does this make me not have money to invest?"

"I did not say you do not have money to invest. But what I am about to tell you does involve our family and your financial future. Have patience and let me explain."

I made the 'zip my lip' gesture I learned from Fred and let Tina continue.

"By giving back the money, you threw Ba off the little speech he was about to make, but he was so pleased with your gesture that parents decided to hold off telling you what needs to be told now."

I thought, "Uh-oh! Here comes the bad news!"

Tina took my large hands into her tiny ones, look directly into my eyes and said, "I am speaking for all the family when I say this: Kim, you have worked very hard for many years and taken so little of your wages in return. We could see you did not desire material things as Ba and Me kept you in food, clothing, and pocket cash. Even so, sometimes you returned the extra money to help buy food or holiday items.

"Now you have a new life in America, and it is time to take all the salary you have earned from the family business. On behalf of Ba and Me, I present you with this."

Silently, I accepted the envelope, nervous to see what they had given me. The red card was decorated with bees gathered about a shiny golden honeycomb, a symbol of teamwork and diligence. Inside, Me's beautiful handwriting thanked me for all the hard work and effort I had put towards our family and business and how proud they are of my new life in America.

And there was a check.

I felt my heart stop in my chest. "This is US dollars?"

"Yes, Little Sister."

"This is not possible!"

"It is possible, Kim."

"But how can this be?"

"It is your earnings that you did not take, and we re-invested it back into the business. Your salary grew with our successes. You worked hard for it and made a good face for our family. It is yours to keep now."

The check is over $750,000! Most of our employees make about $150 per month.

Tina continued, "We prefer if you do not tell Fred about this money. You have the prenuptial agreement and need to keep this separate from Fred's money."

"I never told you or the family, but Fred cancelled our pre-nup after the Honeywood Heights sale."

"Oh! Well, are you comfortable with that? Fred dissolving the agreement?"

"Tina, this check in my hand is only a fraction of what Fred has. Yes, I am comfortable with it."

"That's wonderful, Kimmie. By the way, the check is only for show. The money is already in a money market account we set up for you."

I stared at the check again, astonished at the amount.

"Ba said it was difficult to come up with a fair figure for you. Vietnam has had such a high rate of inflation, but the company made good profits and, as you know, we now have offices all over Asia. We can thank Thao and Phung for helping us with some modern financial tools, so this figure is better than if we had given you a salary in VN Dong for all those years. Your money has gone up and the family is now releasing the money you earned back to you with our most heartful blessings."

I think I was quiet too long as Tina asked, "Are you ill? Do you need some water?"

I took a big breath and said, "I'm sorry, it's just so much to take in. I was not expecting this very wonderful gift."

"Kimmie, it is not a gift," said my sister gently. "You earned the money."

"Yes, of course. But it is still a surprise."

She nodded and smiled, laying her hand on mine, "*Now* you have money to invest!"

I kept thinking, 'I must remember to breathe.'

All this new information was too much for my head right now, so I thanked sister for her help and, before I left, we called Ba and Me and I gave them my most heartfelt thanks for the money. I promised to use it wisely and donate some to those who have less than myself. I could not keep the emotion out of my voice and my parents, I could tell, got caught up in the moment as well.

Today I came to Tina's with $50,000 and walked out with over $800,000 plus stocks and land. Now I am personally a millionaire! It is like a dream. A really, really good dream!

For a time, we believe the Phams were one of the wealthiest families in Ho Chi Minh City, and one of the least showy. They prided themselves on being, much like the book Dad was featured in, their own version of Blue-Collar Millionaires. Our grandparents remained humble to the end of their days as well as frugal in their spending and savvy in their business dealings.

Since then, many families have eclipsed the Phams in terms of wealth, building upon large privatized factories churning out electronics, pharmaceuticals, clothing and brand name cosmetics. No matter, the family business still thrives profitably in what they have always done, goods for the common household: foodstuffs, clothing, cosmetics, housewares, decorative items and tools.

Kimmie: Every time someone wanted to "talk to me" in a private setting, I always felt like when one is being called to the principal's office: nervous, scared, that "what did I do this time?" feeling. I had never expected anything like this from my family, but they had thought of it, and carefully. I think once they saw how Fred was with me and our family, that I was happy and he was so supportive of my personal growth, they decided it was the right time to present me with what they felt was a fair compensation for my time working in the family business.

When I read my old diary of that meeting with Tina so many years ago, the feelings of surprise, shock and humility returned to me almost as strongly as they did the first time. I felt, and still feel, truly blessed for the kind of parents I had and how fairly they treated everyone.

Dear My Diary,

I have been thinking a lot about the money from my family and, although I understand why they would prefer I not bring it up with Fred, I feel I can't keep this from my husband and best friend. He has been so good and honest to me, encouraging the personal and professional confidence I lacked in my homeland.

And in all the time we have been together, he never asked me about my personal money unless I brought it up first. I decided to broach the news in a round-about way to test his answers and make it fun.

At dinner I asked him, "Were you disappointed that I did not bring a lot of money into our marriage?"

Fred looked surprised at my question and said, "What do you mean?"

"You can see my parents have a big business and offices in other countries, yes?"

"Yes, of course."

"And I worked for them for many years?"

"Yes."

"But did you expect me to bring much money into the marriage?"

"I did not expect that you would or would not bring any money into the marriage. It never crossed my mind. I had enough to take care of you and that's all that mattered to me." Concern clouded his expression. "What is this all about, anyway? Are you in some kind of financial trouble, Kim?"

This was not going as I expected. I intended to tease this out some more, but his annoyance was starting to show because he called me "Kim" instead of "Kimmie". It was time to be more direct.

So, I told Fred everything from how I did not formally take my wages as others would have done, felt no desire to shop or have fancy things for myself and never asked my parents for anything. They would simply slip me pocket money from time to time or bought my necessities like clothing as needed.

When I came to America, I felt bad for not having my own money to bring or expensive jewelry or anything especially nice, forcing my new husband to have to pay for everything.

Fred patted my hand and said, "Oh, Sweetheart, I was so thrilled to have such a beautiful, good-natured woman by my side that I was happy to give you what you wanted…and you've never asked for much to begin with."

He was so sweet that I kissed him and continued my story about the meeting with my parents to return the $10,000 escape money. "It turns out, that my parents had their own surprise for me but were so taken aback by the fact that you had been so generous to give me part of your business profits, they held off on giving me the money I had earned working for them." Finally, I told Fred about my meeting with Tina, the amount I got and the conclusion of my story.

I asked Fred, "What do you think?"

"About your parents not giving you what you earned all the years you lived with them, or that they gave you the money now, plus interest and accrued profits or however it is?"

"Yes, both."

Fred looked at me a long minute and asked, "What do *you* think about it? How do *you* feel?"

"I always assumed the work I did paid for my food, clothes, and bed. When my parents gave me so much, of course, it surprised and humbled me."

"Do you think what you got is fair?"

That was a good question. "I worked full time about twelve years so the check averages out to over sixty thousand annually compared to less than two thousand for the average worker."

"You didn't answer my question," Fred gently reminded me. "Do you think what you got is fair?"

"Even if, as a manager, I should make two or three times more than the average worker, I really made thirty times more." Then I worried what Fred was thinking as he is much better at business dealings than I am. "Fred, do *you* think it is fair?"

A slow smile spread across his face. "Your parents always impressed me as honest and fair people. I like them very much. No, that's not true. I *love* them very much. They understood your attitude about money, and you did not question about not getting a regular paycheck. They reinvested your wages back into the company, making it grow, and then returned it to you when they thought the time was right. The investment has grown far larger than anything you or I, could have done on our own. Kimmie, you did very, very well."

Then he stood up and give me a big hug and kiss. "You know, they could have given you nothing and you probably would never have given it a thought. Just the fact you tried to repay them showed your parents your honesty and conscience to give it back after you earned your own."

"What should I do with the money?" I asked.

Fred sighed, "Right now? Nothing. Lots of things are going on and it's hard to tell which way the wind will blow next. A lot of my money is in cash now because I think things are going to go sour soon and if it does, I want to be ready to take advantage of it."

"Is it a bad time to build a house in Honeywood Heights?"

"I don't think it is a good time but don't worry, you will have your dream home before long."

Saturday, November 17
Dear My Diary,

I went to Thanh's grand opening of her second nail salon, just in time for the holiday dress-up season. Now that she and Vo no longer go to the casino, they have been able to save up the needed cash to hire more experienced workers and find a good location with the help of the Wood sisters. It is well-decorated with all new chairs and equipment.

I told sister that I stopped taking the birth control pills more than three months ago and nothing has happened yet even though we make pleasures often. She said it can take some months for the pills to wear off and not everyone gets pregnant right away. Some people try for months or years and still can't conceive.

"You both are young and very healthy. I think you should see a doctor if you are not with child by, hmm, Valentine's. Hey! That would be nice…a Valentine baby! A Christmas baby is even better. Don't worry, Little Sister, with Fred I predict twins, like us!"

Sister is right, I should give it more time. I know it is common for couples not to ever get pregnant, but I hope that is not us. I will wait, but still worry a little.

I let one of the employees give me a mani/pedi and facial. She was very chatty and funny, talking about her new puppy and how much her two children love the animal. The services are complimentary from my sister, but I still left a generous tip for Qui and wished her good luck with her new job at Happy Pretty Salon II.

When I got home, Fred said I looked like a million dollars. I threw my hands up in surprise and said, "My face is all green?!" Fred laughed and laughed at my joke. I like to make him laugh!

Trang: Mom could pull off the funniest lines out of nowhere. She could make us all laugh at the most unexpected comments and reactions to ordinary things people would say. Sometimes she would tell one of us to "turn off the lights in the chicken", knowing full well she knew she was exchanging kitchen for chicken. It wasn't until later in life that I realized how many of her little word jokes originated from when she and Dad were in their first years of marriage, and she would mix up words or parts of words together in error. When she got a laugh from it, she would mentally file it away and use it later to make others laugh too.

Thanksgiving

Friday, November 23
Dear My Diary,

Yesterday we had a big Thanksgiving dinner at home, like last year and all our families came except for Barney and Bunny, whom we did not invite. Robbie, Bobby and Robbie's parents flew to Hawaii to visit Bobby's parents who retired to the islands. Fred said that part of Bobby's parents' retirement income is the monthly payments he gets from his son.

My Fierce 5 friends Bettina and Consuela share an apartment in Chicago, so they drove down at my invitation. With her natural red eyes, Bettina can look very cold and fierce for the characters she plays, but she is actually quite warm and friendly and has a pretty accent, being from The Netherlands. As unusually attractive as Bettina is, Consuela gets her fair share of admiring looks from the men as well.

Bettina asked what designer we hired to make the unusual decorations like the mannequin hands for coat holders and twinkle lights on the ceiling? When I told her it was our sister-in-law, she said it was very avant garde and she likes it.

Tam was listening in and asked Bettina if she wanted to see our pet? Everyone jumped when they heard the GRRROOOWER! from the kitchen as Bettina nearly fell off her high heels when the bear jumped out. She laughed more than Tam and was a good sport about it. She told Tam, "Mein Gott! You got me good!"

Cam and Tam are getting tall now. They are ten and a half years old and becoming less like little girls as they develop their sense of style regarding clothes and hair. They like getting manicures at the shop when business is slow. They are also eating better because when I have been to Thanh's home, I see a bowl of fresh fruit on the counter and the refrigerator is full of healthy-looking foods.

Vo's manner is much nicer than before, but I had heard that he had difficulties while undergoing doctor-controlled withdrawals from tobacco and alcohol. He has lost some of the puffiness in his face and shows more energy in his movements.

Thanh also mentioned that with the extra income from the second shop, they will start a college fund for the twins and I congratulated her on the decision. Fred will be happy to hear about how my sister's family is turning their lives around.

Frank and Maggie looked relaxed and held hands sometimes which I find very sweet. It's nice to see that spark of romance in older couples. Fred has told me that no matter what happens, we will make sure his parents are comfortable in their old age. After what had happened to them, I agree it is the least we can do.

We know they are saving up their extra earnings and Frank loaned, or maybe gave, Bunny a used car he bought cheap and fixed up for her to drive after Barney traded their sedan for the Growler. Moreover, they have asked Tina to take charge of their retirement investments. It's not hard to see why they trust my sister over their elder son.

Riverton is a far cry from NYC, but Tina has really settled in, making many new friends and building her clientele. There are numerous small towns surrounding the city and she has created a brochure and business letter printed in English, Vietnamese and Chinese that she mails out to Asian business owners in small batches of fifty or so at a time. After one week, she follows up with a phone call to make sure they got the letter and did they have questions or want a free financial consultation?

Tina targets one town at a time with each new target town close to the others she has worked. That way, if she gets some appointments, they will all be in the same area rather than going North in the morning and West in the afternoon to make her presentations. She is very clever and organized that way. Fred calls it "working smarter, not harder".

Mahmood, Nezzie and the boys came also, bringing Indian spiced potatoes for their side dish. It smelled heavenly and tasted better! Mahmood told me how Tina shared with him the way she collects customers, so he does the same now with his South Asian clientele. They advertise to the same areas at the same time to be more efficient.

As he is the tax expert with B&R Group, he solicits for tax work but will send clients to Tina for other kinds of products and she refers her clients to Mahmood for tax services. Each uses the other as interpreters as needed, and they share commissions for the referral work. This is a nice way of helping their clients and earning more commissions for each other.

Auntie let us know that Michael will graduate this May from Prairie and though he does not have a job lined up yet, he is starting to look around. My cousin would like to stay near his family, but is open to taking a job in St Louis or one of the other cities within a four-hour drive from here as a second option. Grace and Dot also visited us with their families after having dinner with their in-laws.

I called Bunny from our office to wish her a Happy Thanksgiving, but it is not a happy holiday for her. She is alone and does not know where her husband is. "Barney was real upbeat for a while, talking about how our fortunes were about to change and he had something in the works. When I asked, he wouldn't say what was going on. Then last week, his whole personality changed. Barney got all paranoid and bitchy with me, stayed away for long stretches and still won't tell me what is going on."

I was quiet while Bunny spoke, not knowing how to respond. My man is so predictable, the opposite of what sister was describing. Fred will tell me what's going on if I ask, and even when I don't.

She continued, "I can't figure if he is having a mental meltdown, got hooked on dope again or is on the wrong side of some bad dudes looking to hurt him. And honestly? I don't want to know."

I invited Bunny to dinner, but she said she had better not, in case Barney comes home. "If I'm not home, he's gonna be pissed."

I think she should be more upset that Barney is not home with his wife on Thanksgiving. But I left those words unspoken. "Is there anything I can do, Bunny?" I asked, not knowing what Fred would say to my offering, "Do you need some food or rent money or something?"

Her voice went soft, "Oh, Kimmie. That's sweet of you to offer, but I'm okay. Well, not okay, but I can manage for now."

Bunny thanked me for calling and I hung up, feeling bad for her and a little guilty that I had so much to be thankful for.

Our families have been asking about a time frame for a new house so I explained how we are waiting for a better time to build and do not even know what style we want yet. When I mentioned this to Hazel, she offered to show us some homes in the wealthier neighborhoods to get ideas for interiors and exteriors.

At dinner, when we made our thanks, Fred and I had already agreed to not mention the property sales, even though it was our biggest success story. I gave thanks for Tina coming to Riverton and having all the sisters in America living in the same city. Fred gave thanks for having so many good friends, both new and old, to share our good times as well as inheriting such a large and wonderful family.

Maggie made everyone laugh when she said, "I want to see more family at the next Thanksgiving feast!" while pointing at Fred and I. Everyone understood she meant grandbabies! I could not help but blush at that.

Everyone had a good time and we let Consuela and Bettina stay overnight in the guest room as it is a long drive back to Chicago.

I went grocery shopping today and asked Bunny to keep me company. She did, but I had ulterior motives in mind. We took two shopping carts and filled them both. One cart for me and the other for Bunny. When she realized what I was doing, she begged me not to do this.

"Please let me," I said, putting my arm around her shoulders "I want very much to help my American sister and you would do the same for me if I were in trouble, wouldn't you?" Bunny's normally rosy cheeks are getting pale and thin. Moreover, I saw a big bruise on her arm when she reached up for some cans of soup. Was Barney hitting his wife?

She looked ashamed and said "Yes, I would."

"Then it's settled. My treat." I also brought leftovers from Thanksgiving dinner since we had so much that we cannot eat it all. It will be a feast for Bunny and Barney.

Now Bunny has food enough for weeks to come and I feel better for her. For Barney, I do not.

Thomas Stimson

Merry Bucking Christmas

December 10, 2001
Dear My Diary,

Last night was a very special Merry Bucking Christmas party I don't think any of us will ever forget.

It began snowing in the early afternoon, but lightly, so it added some Christmas flavor to the party. Tina came over to help us decorate on Friday and Saturday and it made me wonder if we will have another Christmas party here next year. When I asked what he thought, Fred said he will keep the building as our main workplace, but we might do the party at a local restaurant or civic hall.

This year, we catered the meal from a Scandinavian restaurant in Old Town. The cuisine comes from the very northern countries of Europe and the waitresses wore traditional costumes of long white dresses with a red sash and a crown of woven tree boughs with candles in them. Not real candles, like in the old days, but electric ones to be safe. Still very pretty!

We learned to say "Skal!" when we toasted each other and got some lessons about the different dishes from the owner who is from Sweden. Learning about the food makes it taste that much better!

There were about thirty of us finishing dessert and a thick drink called Advocaat, having a good time when Robbie stood up and tapped a wine glass with his knife. The glass broke and shards dropped into his plate. Someone called out "Skal!" and we all laughed. When Robbie got his breath back, he said, "I have an announcement, everyone!"

As we settled down, Holly retrieved a flat rectangular gift box from behind our couch and came back as Robbie was speaking. "As you know, 2001 has been a great year for the real estate business and business in general, despite the recent efforts of some misguided souls, and some of us have had a better year than others! Would our gracious hosts join me, please?" I do not know what is going on and I can tell Fred does not either.

"I put the word out to find something that would be an appropriate gift for our Merry Bucking Christmas host and hostess. They have really done a number on their numbers, and we found something that is one in a million, or should I say, one in ten million!" Everybody is curious now and speaking softly to each other.

Robbie handed us the gift. Fred took it and I opened it as Holly started a CD of an old song that I hear on the radio sometimes. The gift is a black frame with matching background and a gold record covering the top two-thirds of the space.

It is a music award and Fred read the words on the plaque to the group: "Presented to Carlyn George to commemorate the sale of over 500,000 copies of the country single record 'Ten Million Reasons Why'." Then I realized the song on the CD is that very same song!

Robbie asked me "Kimmie, do you like this song?"

I said, "Yes, I think so."

"Fred, how do you feel about this song?"

Fred answered, "I like the song, but I think you are going to tell us why we should like it a whole lot better."

327

"This gold record is a way of recognizing that, as of last month, Fred and Kim have officially become Deca-Millionaires! That's ten million reasons to celebrate!!" Everyone stood up and applauded us for at least a full minute. Robbie gave us big hugs and soon everybody was hugging us and making many congratulations. I know we are not the only Deca-Millionaires in the group, but we are the newest. A very special kind of Cool Kids Club.

Robbie explained how the gold record had been sold to a collector some years ago by the estate of Carlyn George and recently, the collector put it up for sale on Ubiddit, which is how our friends got it for us.

Bobby told the group that my pegboard idea, and encouraging everyone to share information to help customers find what they are looking for, has increased sales of all the stores by an average of twenty percent.

I feel proud and humbled to be hearing this from Robbie and getting looks of respect and nods of approval from our friends and business partners. Fred draped his arm around my shoulders and said in my ear, "We couldn't have done it without you, Sweetheart."

After we went to bed, we were too excited to sleep. I asked, "Fred, do we really have ten million dollars?"

Fred wrapped me up in his thick muscular arms and cradled me like a child. "No sweetheart. Not at all." After a long pause, he said, "More like twelve million."

Lois: The gold record was a prized possession in our home, for a time hanging prominently in the living room, and later relegated to our parents' bedroom. When people asked about the gold record, Mama and Dad would just say it was something they had collected over the years and they liked it. It wasn't until we were adults and starting to make our own way in the world that they told us the story of "Ten Million Reasons Why" and how they came to have this bit of musical history. Years later, our three sisters, as a group, joined the "Big Ten" club long before they graduated high school.

Thomas Stimson

Barney Strikes Again

December 25, 2001
Dear My Diary,

I went a week past my regular moon time and over four months since I stopped taking the birth control pills. Fred suggested I take a home-test to see if we are pregnant. I have not heard this term before, but I like it. *We* are pregnant…not *I* am pregnant. A team effort. My spirits are buoyed.

With a nervous knot in my stomach, I got started, but while I was making water on the stick, the home phone rang and Fred picked it up. I could hear him in the next room.

"Fred here. Yes? Yes, I am his brother. No. No I hadn't. No. Who is this again? Are you sure about your information?" I wonder who he is talking to. It does not sound good.

The test is finished. I have the answer.

Fred is sitting on the edge of the bed, still talking, "Hold on, I have another call coming in. Mom? Hi, what's going on? I have a reporter on the other line trying to tell me about it right now. What happened? That's what the reporter was trying to say. Well, of course he did! Didn't we expect it?"

'No,' I thought, 'not now. Please, not now.'

"What? There's more? What more? What about Pops? Oh my God! Oh, no! Where is he? He's there now? You're there too? I'm coming straight over." and Fred dropped the phone. It clattered on the ancient wood floor. A woman's voice was saying "Hello? Mr. Starbuckle? Are you still there?"

I gently picked up the receiver, disconnected the call and placed it back on the cradle.

Fred was staring at nothing. The test stick was in my hand, the results waiting to be shared. My heart sank at the next words.

"Barney's been arrested. FBI. When Pops heard the news, he collapsed. Mom called 911. He's at the hospital. They think it's a stroke. I have to go. I have to go to Pops."

I helped Fred to his feet. He is not steady. I think he will have a stroke too.

I embraced my husband and said in his ear, "I will drive. Pops needs us."

Fighting back tears, I looked one more time at the stick and threw it in the trash.

Now it is midnight of Christmas Eve going on Christmas Day. Ten days since Barney was arrested by federal agents. Ten days since the stroke. Ten days Ba Frank has been in a coma after the operation on his brain. I will sit with him until eight.

We have been sitting with Ba Frank in shifts, day and night, so he will see a familiar face when he wakes up…if he wakes up. Many people have volunteered to sit with Frank: Tina and Thanh and Vo, Robbie and Bobby, Auntie Ginger and Grace, members of Maggie's family and people from their church. And, of course, Fred and I.

The doctors say that if Frank does wake up, the damage to his brain will probably never fully recover. We sit and pray and talk to Frank, hoping he can hear us.

Frank is the only one I have told about the baby growing inside me. I want so much to tell Fred that he will be a Ba.

A Father.

A Daddy.

I want so much to tell Maggie and Me and Ba and everyone, but this is such a bad time. I do not have the courage to add to the drama, even if it is good news.

Not that anyone would be upset about me, I mean 'us', getting pregnant. We planned for this. More like 'another big thing to worry about Kimmie and the baby' kind of upset. Taking the focus away from Frank's near-fatal condition with my happy news.

When Fred asked me the next day about the pregnancy test, I shook my head and changed the topic. I did not lie, but I could not tell him either. Fred never asked me again. His head is very full right now.

This is the first time my head is clear enough, and the news is complete enough, to write about what has happened.

On the morning Barney was arrested, and the news began coming out, my sisters and local family started calling and texting me, asking what happened. Was Fred arrested too? Did I know this thing his brother was doing?

I quickly understood that I must call Me and Ba and tell them what has happened before other family members contact them with what they have read or heard, combined with assumptions and gossip, and cause them needless worry.

I asked Fred if I could tell my parents. My poor Fred has other things on his mind, and I do not want to burden him, but asked out of respect to his family. He said "Of course, they need to know. Please give them our love from me and the folks."

I reached Thao first as she was at work already. It was early morning in Ho Chi Minh City, but she was very bright and chatty about her wedding plans and how much Phung is helping.

My insides were dying and she is talking about the wedding. Finally, I said, "I am sorry to interrupt, but I called to say that Ba Frank is in the hospital with a brain problem. It may be a stroke and he might die."

"Oh Kimmie, I am so sorry to hear! Ba! Kimmie is calling! Bad news about Fred's Ba!"

Ba came on the phone and I explained it again, adding "I must tell you something before you hear it from someone else. A very bad thing happened, but Fred and I are not a part of it. Ba Frank did not have a brain problem without reason. His other son did something bad and was arrested by the FBI. The shock of the bad news caused Ba Frank's brain to break."

Ba asked, "What did the brother do?"

"Nothing is very clear right now except that it had something to do with the brother trying to sell his expensive Italian sportscar while pretending it had been stolen. If the FBI did the arresting, it is a very serious crime."

I assured Ba that I knew nothing before this, and do not believe Fred knew anything either. "He has not spoken very much to his brother in a long time. Especially not enough to make a criminal plan."

I warned Ba that he is sure to get communications from other family members with news that may or may not be accurate. Even so, please do not worry about me and Fred but to make prayers for Frank. He is very sick right now and needs all the prayers we can give him.

"I am very sorry to hear of these things and promise not to make others aware of our family problems. I only ask that you keep strong and drink Fierce 5."

It took a few seconds for his words to make sense to me, then I had the first good laugh in days. Ba made a joke to help me break the nervous energy. "I will drink a Fierce 5 in your honor Ba. You are the one who taught me to be strong." I gave our love to everyone, and we hung up. Then my laughter melted into tears. Such a shame!

Poor Fred has been so busy "putting out fires" as he calls all the urgent things he must attend to. Like dealing with reporters, all of us being questioned by the FBI and lawyers for the insurance company, dealing with doctors and tests and family and friends calling and asking if there is anything they can do. I help where I can, but everyone wants to deal with Fred or Maggie. In this way I am kind of invisible and lonely too…just like when I was single.

Most Asian homes have an altar to honor the ancestors, but I had not made one in my American home. Everything here is so new, and all my close family are still alive, so even with Lunar New Year and other holidays, I did not have an altar to honor the old families.

I made an altar from a cabinet we have in storage and put it in the corner of the living room. Then I set candles, bowls of fresh fruit, flowers, small glasses of water and a vase filled with sand to hold the incense sticks and made many prayers for Ba Frank, Maggie, Fred and our families to be strong during these difficult times.

Lastly, I made a prayer for the baby in me to be healthy and strong and not feel my worries but to be a happy child always.

Last night, for my Christmas gift, Fred gave me a model of the Honeywood Heights house we tore down. It is made with wood and window glass from the house along with walnut and cherry wood from the property. Fred had taken many pictures and found color photos of the house in Miss Robertson's home, then gave them to a local artist who made the model from the pictures.

It is so pretty with eye-catching colors and a porch that is not sagging. The model is so thoughtful and reminds us of what we did together and what we will have in the future with our own property.

I am ashamed that I did not get Fred anything this year. The last ten days have been so busy, so confusing and so sad, that I forgot to get anything and, when I finally did remember, there were other things to take care of. It is a very Un-Merry Christmas, no thanks to Barney.

I will stretch my legs, get some coffee and explain, as best I can, what has happened over the last ten days.

Barney's Tangled Web

Dear My Diary,

With much-needed coffee in my blood and mind as clear as it can be, here is what happened as I understand it from the newspapers, TV, police, Fred, Bunny and others:

After the ridiculous cat food lawsuit was thrown out, a man offered Barney the real estate deal of a lifetime. With the price of land skyrocketing, and Barney going broke as his law practice dried up, he was desperate for a big score.

But the big score required a cash purchase...a very large cash purchase. With no cash and even less ability to secure a loan for this great deal, he went looking for partners. He found two: An elderly couple and a young man, and he sold them on the promise of five acres of prime undeveloped land on the Riverton waterfront.

Barney bargained with the seller to take six million in cash from the other parties and Barney would be included on the contracts as one of the purchasing partners. While the other partners split the full cash price between themselves, Barney, with no cash out of pocket, would be listed as having one-third ownership so when they re-sell the property, Barney would get a share of the profits. This detail would not be disclosed on the contracts, and I am not sure that the partners understood this part of the arrangement.

Barney did not tell his partners, Bunny or anyone else about this. He did hint at having some "lucrative real estate investments" planned, but little more than that.

Meanwhile, the seller never showed Barney this "prime real estate" he was buying. Apparently, he just kept describing it as five acres of undeveloped land with a water view in every direction, a perfect location in downtown Riverton, etc. but never giving an address or showing it to see if the land was any good or not or if zoning laws would permit building on the site. And Barney, foolish Barney, took the seller's word for everything and did not demand a due diligence investigation of the property.

Barney helped his partners withdraw their cash from the bank and loaded into suitcases, delivered it to the seller and signed all the documents. The paperwork was rushed through, the property description given in technical terms with no maps or diagrams and questions asked by the partners were answered in vague, glowing terms.

Only after the papers were signed and the cash handed over, did the seller give the location so they could admire their new property...in the form of geographic coordinates.

Barney took his partners in Bunny's car and, with a GPS device, went looking for their new investment. Each search kept bringing them to Riverton Central Park, frustrating the group as they were miles away from the Riverton waterfront district. Barney took everybody home, then visited the City Planning Department for some help. It turned out that the given coordinates were accurate.

Are you ready, My Diary, to know the location of Barney's big investment?

The property, five acres of undeveloped land with a 360-degree view of the water is Duck Island, in the middle of Riverton Central Park! Of course, the island belongs to the city, so no one can buy it.

By now, the seller's phones were turned off and the office abandoned. The seller was gone. The cash was gone. And who were his business partners? Who had the money to invest but not the capacity to question the deal?

Barney's business partners were the sweet, old Nelsons, now in their nineties, who we met last New Year's Eve, and a young blind man named Nicky Vamkros who won one of the big lotteries last year. The sweet Nelsons who had helped so many students, and a blind man with new money. I felt sick when this was reported in the Review.

This all happened around Thanksgiving, and I remembered Bunny saying Barney got kind of crazy at Thanksgiving and went from being very happy and hopeful to upset and staying away from home for long periods.

Fred said that if it was only this, Barney might not have been arrested, but could have been sued by the investors and probably been stripped of his license to practice law. But no, Barney had to make things worse.

At first, Barney felt like he had to show the investors something, but not the island. Much of Riverton's waterfront is lined with docks, warehouses, shipyards and similar industries, areas not suitable for luxury hotels or high-rise offices. The nicer waterfront areas are completely built-up with no empty land that Barney could point out as being theirs, even as a ruse. As a last resort, Barney took the easy way out and just stopped taking the investors phone calls.

Now Barney was angry at being duped and wanted compensation for all the work that had, so far, netted him nothing but mounting losses.

He read in a news magazine about how people in other countries will pay very high prices for luxury cars from America, even several times their cost, due to their country's high import taxes. To feed this black-market demand, many luxury cars are stolen or bought through fraudulent means by professional criminals and sold overseas, hidden in shipping containers.

Barney came up with a plan to ship his car overseas to a buyer, then claim the Growler was stolen. The insurance would pay off the car, Barney would get a lot of extra money from the overseas buyer and not have to spend anything out of pocket but for fees to the middleman. It would all be a win-win proposition.

But Barney did not have the knowledge or resources to find an overseas buyer or work out the logistics of such a deal, so he contacted some low-level criminals who were also prior clients. One said he knew a guy who knew a guy that maybe could help him.

Soon, Barney was introduced to the "big boss" Stecchino. Stecchino was fifty-something with a barrel-chest, slicked-back hair graying at the temples and a vaguely European accent.

Barney told Stecchino his idea and the crime boss made a show of how his people can ship the car to Eastern Europe with other goods packed around it. Stecchino would also arrange things to make it appear that the Growler was stolen so the insurance company would be forced to pay.

The buyer he had in mind would pay up to $500,000 for the Gambotti Growler, but there would be some risks and possible bribes involved from shipping inspectors, informants or unforeseen circumstances. If they were caught, there would be prison and other punishments. Barney said that he had read that this kind of crime is common and was willing to take the risk as it was a low risk/high reward venture.

Barney had several meetings with Stecchino and, each time, the crime boss or one of his people reminded Barney of the risk of getting caught, saying things like, "I sure wouldn't want to share a prison cell with you."

Barney was actively involved with Stecchino in the planning and execution of the entire project, even giving his own ideas about how certain parts should work.

Twice, Barney pushed to negotiate more money for himself and on the second attempt, Stecchino reminded Barney that it was he who had the connections to the buyer and the insurance company to sell this very expensive car, and if he didn't like it, Barney could find someone else to do his bidding, so Barney backed down.

At the arranged date, Barney brought the car to the shipping docks late at night. Stecchino asked him one more time if he was sure he wanted to do this? "You keep asking me the same question over and over and I keep giving you the same answer over and over. Yes, I want to do this. Now where is my money?"

Stecchino spread out his hands, smiling and said in a soothing voice, "Hey, I have to ask. People change their minds all the time. I'm just making sure."

"Well hurry the hell up. I don't want to be out here any longer than I have to."

The crime boss scowled at Barney's rudeness. "Yes, I can see you are ready for the big payoff. Sergei!"

Another man brought a briefcase and laid it on top of a fuel barrel. Stecchino said, "Open it. You've earned it."

Barney hesitated, then pressed the buttons to release the latches. The camera recording the transaction zoomed in on the single, white, legal-sized envelope taped to the floor of the case with the words "YOU ARE UNDER ARREST" in thick block-print letters and Barney's voice rising in anger as he said "What the fu…"

A face suddenly filled the screen, a beefy hand pushing Barney's head roughly into the briefcase as the sound of multiple guns being cocked were recorded for posterity.

The camera zoomed back out and Stecchino's European accent has changed to a familiar Mid-West twang as he announced, "I am FBI Agent Robert Hollis and you are under arrest for…" listing Barney's crimes and reading his rights while they cinched handcuffs on his wrists.

I know all the details because Fred and I have seen and heard the tapes. It plays like a movie, but it is all too real. All the meetings and phone calls had been carefully recorded with cameras and microphones on the agents and hidden within the meeting places. Barney was stung big time.

Bernice: Boom! Boom! Boom! Four o'clock in the morning and the FBI are banging on my door. Barney's not home, spotlights are shining in the windows and men outside yelling to open up because they got search warrants. Right away I knew it was about Barney. I cussed him out in my head that whole night. Mostly I remember that and badges, warrants and questions…lots of questions.

I told the Feds I would tell them whatever I could, but I didn't know much of anything. If I had known more ahead of time, I probably would have called them myself and I said as much. They wouldn't tell me exactly what had happened, but they did say Barney was in FBI custody. When I said "it figures", that opened up a whole new can of worms and a whole lot of new questions like I knew more than I was letting on.

I kept saying that I just meant Barney was stupid enough to do something wrong and get caught, but the only thing I knew was he planning on some kind of land deal. When they asked me what I knew of Barney wanting to sell his car, I said I didn't know anything about that, just that he had some kind of real estate deal lined up but where it was or who he was dealing with, I had no idea.

I figured out later that they didn't know about the land deal in the same way as I didn't know he was trying to sell his hot-shot car. It seems we both gave each other information the other didn't know about.

The Feds came in, took all our computers, all the paperwork and files Barney had at home and my cell phone for any text messages or calls I might have made. I gave them Barney's office keys and combo to his safe, not that there was anything of value in it.

Lots of questions about the Growler, our finances, if we had any firearms, who his business associates were…it went on and on, let me tell you. I didn't get arrested as they had nothing on me, but Bernie? I told the Feds they could keep his ass as long as they wanted.

Excerpt from the Riverton Review December 16, 2001: Local attorney Bernard Bartlett was arrested last night in a sting operation carried out by local FBI agents. He has been charged with attempted insurance fraud and intent to transport stolen goods out of the US among other crimes. The arrest took place without incident last night at the Governor Bremer Tunn dockyards. Few details are known at this time and contact with Mr. Bartlett's family have been met with "no comment".

Mr. Bartlett, a Riverton native formerly known as Barnabus Starbuckle, became the most well-known recipient of one of now-retired judge William Davidson's questionable rulings in which Bartlett's client received a $6 million dollar award for losing her thumb to a poorly opened can of cat food. Bartlett then used his new-found celebrity to promote his services as "The Six Million Dollar Man" using an action figure prop from the popular television series in locally aired commercials. After Judge Davidson was determined to be mentally unfit, all of his rulings for the previous twelve months were vacated and Mr. Bartlett's business has reportedly suffered in the aftermath.

When Frank heard the news of his son's arrest, he collapsed from the stroke. Frank and Maggie have limited health insurance that cannot begin to cover the costs of what Frank is facing.

Luckily, due to all the money and time Fred has donated to the children's ward, the hospital's director flew out a neurological specialist from Chicago to operate on Frank at no cost to our family.

When news of the arrest became public, the Nelsons and Nicky Vamkros called their lawyers and the police to find out about the land they invested in through Barney, causing a fresh frenzy among the news services and local police.

That led other people who know the Starbuckles, especially former employees, to share with the news outlets about what they knew of Barney cheating his parents out of their home and business. This particularly painful and private affair got into the news and "our world has turned upside down and inside-out", as Maggie has said many times now, usually during fits of sobbing.

This is a huge embarrassment for our family. None of us knew Barney was involved in all these dealings, and now old family hurts have become public knowledge that we can't control.

It is almost four o'clock and I am tired of writing now, with so much more that needs to be said. The orderly has brought me some food, so I will rest and eat.

Lois: All of this unfolding over a period of ten days and Mama was hiding the fact that she was pregnant so as not to upset the family any more than it was. That had to be so tough on her!

Thomas Stimson

Fred and I Go to Jail

Dear My Diary,

I am back and feel better now that I have eaten. The room is quiet but for the soft wheezing of Frank's respirator and gentle, rhythmic beeps of the heart monitor. As I write, I say the words aloud so my American father hears a familiar voice, even if it is in Vietnamese.

It is best that I speak in Vietnamese because if I spoke in English, and Frank could understand me, he would surely die of shame. I touched Frank's cool, dry arm and said in English, "Time to wake up, Pops. We love you and want you with us for a long time." Ba Frank does not awaken, so I will continue.

Barney has become famous from coast to coast. "Bernard Bartlett Busted!" "The Six Million Dollar Man Strikes Again! Local Lawyer Charged with Insurance Fraud" "Duck Island is Site of Waterfront Real Estate Scam" and many others. The news is especially juicy as the victims are a blind man and a sweet, elderly couple. Barney is in jail and bail is denied as he is a flight risk.

Right away, the police and FBI are arguing over who has jurisdiction over the land scam but clearly the insurance/auto theft scam belongs to the FBI. Both agencies are asking many questions, taking statements of what we know, what we do not know and so forth. Lots of family and friends are calling to see how we are and what a terrible thing Barney did. It is all very hectic.

When the doctors asked Fred if they know of any reason for the stroke, Fred replied "You know the lawyer who just got arrested? That's Franks son."

I heard this and asked Fred later why he did not say that Barney was his brother? His answer chilled me. "He is no longer my brother. He did pretty bad stuff last time but this time he practically killed Pops."

After his arrest, Barney called Bunny and said, "You've got to help me! I need money! Ask your family for help!" Bunny told Barney to jump in the lake he bought.

Barney had the nerve to ask his mother for money for a defense attorney. I was standing by her side when Maggie said "How dare you call me for money! Your father and I paid for your entire law degree…then you repaid us by throwing everything we own down a rathole and destroyed the family business in the bargain."

As Barney tried to say that that had not been his fault, Maggie raised her voice over his, "And even if I *did* have any money, I would not give you one damn cent! The only thing I want to hear from you is how you intend to repay us…but those are words I never expect to hear from your mouth. Not ever. You made this bed all by yourself and now you will have to live with the fleas that come with it." Mother Maggie's shoulders sagged as she hung up the phone and I went to hold her. She did not tell her son that Pops is in the hospital.

On top of everything else, I went to jail for the first time.

Barney has run out of people to ask for help, so he is calling his least favorite GM to get a defense lawyer. At first Fred refused and refused. After much soul-searching, I broached my idea carefully to Fred. "Why don't you go and talk with Barney and see what he wants to say? Getting that off his chest might help and you will show Barney your good face by doing this much, even if you do not help." Fred eyed me warily as I continued, "Maybe give him a suggestion about how to help himself or you can find a lawyer for him if you want to help. Barney is your brother. Maybe he did not know it was wrong?"

But even as the words left my lips, I knew how stupid that sounded. Barney knew *everything* he did was wrong.

He cheated an elderly couple. He cheated a blind man. He cheated his parents. Most of all, he cheated himself. Barney is in a world of cheat.

Fred was not happy with my suggestion but reluctantly agreed to speak to his brother. I felt better that my husband would make the effort.

He made some calls from his office and arranged with a detective to meet Barney in a private room. Fred asked me to come along as support. I did not know what I could do as support but I was happy to help Fred help his brother. Maybe after Barney comes out of jail, he will be a good man as he can never be a lawyer any more.

We got to the jail and went through the metal detectors before being searched by police officers, a man for Fred and a woman for me. We were led to an office where we emptied our pockets, the contents recorded and put into a lock box.

The police had me wait in the hall and Fred went into a meeting. When they came out, I was surprised…no…shocked, to see Fred's wrists handcuffed behind him! I was on my feet in an instant, "Fred, have you been arrested?"

The officers told me to come along and Fred explained that he asked to be shackled as he does not feel he can keep his control when he meets his brother. "This is to protect Barney from a well-deserved ass-beating"

I was skeptical of his story…maybe he is trying to protect me from knowing his part in Barney's crime? I followed in silence, hoping all goes well.

Outside a guarded door, the police gave us final instructions. There is a two-way mirror and we will be watched and recorded. We are limited to thirty minutes for the visit and if we are done early, to just say "We are ready to leave," and we will be escorted out. We said we understood everything. My hands trembled a bit.

In the room is a thick metal table and three equally heavy chairs. Everything is gray but for the big mirror on one wall.

Barney is already seated. His hands are in front of him, elbows bent. I can see his arms cannot fully extend due to the connected chain around his waist. The officer said curtly, "Your thirty minutes start now," and locked the door securely behind him.

Fred just said, "Okay, I'm here. Talk."

Barney: What's with the bracelets? Did you kill somebody?

Fred: Pop had a stroke after the news about you came out. He nearly died and is in a coma right now. The cuffs are to keep me from wrapping my hands around your scrawny throat for all you've done to our family. If Pop dies, I can't make any guarantees that I won't. Even if you're still behind bars.

Barney looked surprised at Fred's words, then asked, "What is she doing here?"

Fred: Kim is your savior. She wanted me to come to see if we could help you. Otherwise, I would have just left you to rot. You should thank her.

Barney made a face and said, "Whatever. Look, I need help in getting a good lawyer to help me out of this mess."

Fred: Why are you asking me? I am not a lawyer. Call one of your lawyer buddies to take your case.

Barney: I don't have anybody who will help me, and I don't have enough money to afford one.

Fred: And I do?

Barney: You've got a business, if you want to call it that. But mostly, you got the garage property so just take out a loan to help me out. I'll repay you later.

Fred: The way you repaid Mom and Pop? Don't get me started.

Barney: But this is really important, and I know I can beat this rap. Come on, be a sport. Help out your big brother.

Fred: Barney, you are the rich one. At least that's what you tell everyone. You've been bragging for years that you have the degree, the prestigious job, you live in a nice house, drive an expensive car and make lots of money.

I don't have a college education, a regular job or an expensive car. To you, I am just the GM, the garbage man. The guy who buys and sells other people's trash. The embarrassment who lives in a garage, drives old trucks and wears second-hand clothes. Why don't you take out a loan on the equity of *your* house to hire a lawyer, instead of mine?

Barney: I would, but it's complicated. I am having cash flow issues.

Fred: It's not complicated. Your house is a rental. You pay $1200 a month for the house plus utilities.

Barney (looking surprised): How do you know?

Fred: I know the owner. So, you don't have any lawyer friends who will help you out?

Barney: I don't have any lawyer friends and the firms I have called won't talk to me.

Fred: Big surprise. Why don't you use the defense attorney appointed by the court? That's free.

Barney: Public defenders are a joke! They are either fresh out of law school or losers that can't get hired by a decent firm.

Fred: Sounds familiar.

Barney, (getting annoyed): Look, are you going to help me or not?

Fred: Okay, Counselor, what's your defense going to be? The FBI has you on video and audio tape trying to sell your car to commit insurance fraud. They say the cash you gave that scammer has been traced to Miami and no one is sure if you intentionally or accidentally cheated your investors. If it was accidental, that won't be so bad against you.

Barney: That's why I need a good defense attorney, to help me get clear of the charges! Just like that sports star that was found innocent of killing his wife and her boyfriend. He's still walking around free!

Fred: The jury didn't find him innocent, they just couldn't find him guilty. Whole different thing and you know it.

Barney: Either way, he's still free.

Fred: Look, here is my best advice. Tell the truth. Just tell the truth. Tell the police, the FBI, all of them…tell them everything you know from start to finish and be damned sorry about it.

Barney: Oh, yeah, and go to prison for years and years. Not if I can help it!

Fred: You know as well as I do, the more you make the courts, the judge and the jury work to convict you, especially with the sympathy factor of the Nelsons and the blind guy, the more likely you will spend a very long time in prison. If you tell the truth, help the police sort everything out, beg for mercy and offer to repay your debts, the better it will be for you.

Barney leaned forward and said in a quiet voice: Easy for you to say. You are such a boy scout. I didn't mean to scam those people. Or our folks. It just happened. But I'm not going down without a fight, either.

The office door opened and a policeman put his head through the door. Barney yelled, "That's not thirty minutes! Get out!"

The officer gave Barney a hard look, then said in a kindly voice, "I was told to let you know that your father just passed away. Sorry to have to tell you." And he left, the lock clicking heavily.

My stomach dropped into my shoes. I started to cry. I could not help it. Poor Frank!

"AAAHHHHHH! AAAHHHHHH!" Fred jumped up, the heavy steel chair clattering behind him. He rolled his shoulders, the muscles growing and straining at the handcuffs as a shirt button flew off.

Fred screamed, "You killed Pops! You killed Pops! Now I'm going to kill YOU!" His thick neck muscles strained as he pulled and twisted his body into painful contortions.

POP!

Fred's wrists were free!

I screamed. Barney screamed. Fred screamed and jumped ALL THE WAY OVER THE TABLE knocking Barney backward.

"Tell the truth, damn you! Tell the truth! TELL THE TRUTH!!" and as he shook Barney like a rat in a terrier's mouth, I ran around the table and tried pulling Fred off, but it was impossible. I've never seen him like this before. Where were the police? This was crazy!

Barney screamed in a high-pitched voice, eyes bulging in terror while trying to hold his hands up to his face and Fred screaming at his brother, spittle flying from his lips.

Barney saw Death, I am sure of it.

Finally, several officers rushed in, pulling Fred off Barney while two others gripped my arms and we were rushed back to an office around the corner while other officers stayed with Barney.

My heart and mind were racing. Frank is dead. Fred broke steel handcuffs and tried to kill Barney. Is Fred going to be arrested? Am I? What will my family say about this? I can't bear to think about it!

As soon as the door closed, everyone's attitude changed…they started laughing! Laughing and laughing!! Different voices said, "Did you get all that on camera?" "Three different angles!" "Did you see Barney's face? That was classic!" "Priceless!"

Fred said, "Man, that felt good!" Turning to me, he asked "You okay Kimmie?"

I could not believe what they were saying. Like it was a big joke!

"What the hell was that?" I asked. "What is going on? Why is everybody laughing? Is Frank dead or not?"

Fred made the first of many apologies to me before explaining how they wanted to trick Barney into making a confession. For starters, the handcuffs were not real and are often used by magicians.

Fred showed me how easy it is to snap the connecting chain on and off. His struggle to break the shackles was all acting, as was the news of Frank's death. The police were watching through the mirror the whole time. When Barney refused to "tell the truth", that was the signal to send in an officer to give the "bad news" about Frank's death and give Fred a reason to attack Barney.

Fred said he did not hit Barney with his fist as he could have easily done, just shook him up and screamed at him. "Put the fear of God into him," was the expression Fred used.

When I asked, "Why didn't you tell me this before we went in?" Fred said he wanted my reaction to be genuine when they announced Frank's death and everything after that. Fred showed me how to do it and I played with the cuffs for a few minutes. Even a child could "break" them.

I hit Fred hard in the chest one time to show him I am mad at being made a fool and scaring me so much. Then I hugged him as I knew he was trying to do the right thing for everyone, even Barney.

Maybe I can laugh about this later, but I only felt better after I called Maggie and she assured me that Frank is still very much alive. I did not tell her about the jail. I will let Fred tell her if he wants to share this with her.

I asked Mama how she got such a detailed account of the conversation. She said Dad had been wired with a mike for the police and they let her have a transcript of the conversation that took place.

The fake handcuffs have been around the house for years and years and all of us kids have played with them. Dad showed us how to pretend struggle and "break" the cuffs for dramatic effect...but he never told us the story of how they were first used.

Apparently, Dad and maybe Mama, has told the story to others because over the years, at least 3 TV shows or movies have contained a jailhouse scene very much like Mama described. The earliest one starring, guess who? Yes, Rock Rollins!

Fred's trick worked! The headline of the Riverton Review's front page announced "Attorney Bartlett Gives Full Statement. Duped into Buying Riverton Park's Duck Island." The 'unnamed source' for the story stated that Barney gave full statements about the property scam, admitting that he intended to make a profit without investing his own money, but did not know that the property was not for sale, or even sellable. As for the Gambotti Growler, Barney was trying to recover some of the stolen money for his investors after the property sale fell apart.

Now Barney is helping the FBI to try to identify the scammer who goes by the name of Charles Parker and while Charles Parker is a common name, it was also the name of a New York criminal who frequently and fraudulently sold the Brooklyn Bridge in New York City to immigrants and tourists a very long time ago. The scammer was using the name of another famous scammer!

Over the years, the Riverton Review and other media outlets, have reminded people of the time Duck Island was "sold" to a local attorney. It had its own anniversary for a couple of decades and has dwindled in interest to becoming a minor piece of trivia, used by tour guides and local authors.

This morning, the scammer George Parker, not his real name, was arrested in Miami. It did not take long because someone at the Nelson's bank was very clever. Here is what happened:

When the Nelsons went to get cash from the bank and said it was to buy investment property, the bank managers knew this was not a normal request from the Nelsons, so to protect the elderly couple, and themselves, they recorded all the serial numbers through a high-speed computer scanner before handing it over to the Nelsons and Barney with the couple calmly assuring the bank managers that everything was in order.

When the bank learned about the scam and Barney's arrest, they gave the list of serial numbers to the FBI. The FBI soon found the cash being spent at luxury auto dealers, a boat seller, high-end electronics and jewelry stores. Security cameras in all these places were reviewed and quickly helped to identify, find, and bring about his arrest.

Fred and I were visiting with Maggie and Frank at the hospital when an orderly delivered the morning newspaper. As Maggie began to read the front page, she screamed suddenly! Not like Fred at the jailhouse kind of scream but like she saw a mouse kind of scream. She was staring at a picture on the front page saying, "This can't be!" and "Oh my Lord, this is all my fault!" She dropped the paper and went to vomit in the toilet.

I picked up the Riverton Review. The arrest photo and real name of the scammer was on the front page. The man looks very much like Barney, but much older and with less hair. He has the same mean look in his eyes and the set of his mouth.

The name of the scammer is Brad Luzerk who has a long history of criminal arrests and time in prison for fraud, drugs and other crimes.

Maggie came back and her face was flushed. She pressed tissues to her wet eyes saying, "I never thought I would ever see that man again."

When we asked how she knows this man, Maggie said, "That's Barney's father. Barney got scammed by his own father!"

We both turned to Frank who is still in a coma with tubes and wires all over his body, then at the picture in the newspaper. The man in the picture looked more like Barney, than Frank does. From there, Maggie proceeded to tell us a story that neither she nor Frank had ever told anyone.

Frank and Maggie were childhood sweethearts through much of their teens. He went to work at the family garage while Maggie went to college in Chicago. In her sophomore year, she made the mistake of admitting to a classmate, Brad, that she was a virgin and he started pressuring her to sleep with him. He had dark skin, black hair and was quite handsome back then along with having an outsized ego and plans about making it big.

One night, he took advantage of Maggie after some drinks, and she became pregnant. Brad refused to admit that he was the father or help in any way with the baby and proceeded to trash her character by spreading rumors of how Maggie was a loose woman. This was 1962 and pregnant students were not allowed to continue school so Maggie had to drop out in shame.

Maggie returned to Riverton and, once she and Frank got back together, she told him what happened. Frank had always loved Maggie, so he asked, and she agreed, to say that Frank is the baby's father. Soon after, they got married with Frank's name going on Barney's birth certificate.

As he grew up, Barney turned out physically and emotionally very like his birth father and Fred turned out more like Frank and Maggie. We are the first ones to know that Barney is Fred's half-brother. Not even Fred's grandparents knew.

"Well, that explains a lot," Fred commented after Maggie had told her story. I, too, always felt there were too many differences between Fred and Barney.

When we were told the story of how Uncle Barney got arrested, Mama said Grandpa Frank used to call Barney "that little bastard" sometimes. Mama knew "bastard" was a bad word but did not know the meaning until it came up in a script and she asked Dad the specific meaning.

Dad said once he learned about Barney's real father, it dawned on him WHY his father called Barney that name. He could see it being said in the manner of a general curse word and out of anger or frustration, but once the truth was revealed, the word took on more meaning than he had imagined.

Fred showed me the Editorial Page, a part of the paper I never read, and the chief editor wrote an opinion piece headlined "Attention Mr. Bartlett! I Have a Bridge in New York…" The story goes on to point out Barney's ignorance of basic law and doing research before buying property for himself or others. He called it "due diligence" which is doing the homework and background checks so everything is right and correct. The editor's letter made Barney into a cautionary tale.

Along with the fictional Riverton property, Luzerk had offered up to other potential investors a "luxury high rise tower overlooking Puget Sound and the Cascade Mountains with a 5-star restaurant on the top floor" (Seattle Space Needle), an "island retreat in San Francisco's Bay Area whose existing buildings can be transformed into a luxury resort" (Alcatraz Island – a famous prison) and "Luxurious 15-bedroom residence in the heart of Washington DC includes deluxe office spaces, secure entrances, large dining room and formal garden. Perfect bed and breakfast opportunity! (The White House)

Of course, none of these places can be for sale. The idea was to convince the buyer with lots of talk, phony documents and some story why they cannot visit the place in person but urged to pay and sign contracts to beat out the "other investors" who wanted in on the deal.

Of all the scams, Brad only found one buyer…Barney. The other buyers were too smart, asked too many questions and made too many demands to be taken advantage of. Barney did not push hard to get the location as Brad "did not want the word to get out and have buyers fighting each other for this great opportunity" and he wanted only cash "to avoid all the delays in getting loans processed and holding times for checks to clear."

New details are coming out almost every day about Barney, our family, the scam victims, the way high-end cars are stolen and sold overseas, etc. Everyone from our local paper to the national networks and popular magazines are covering this story. It is so strange to be in the middle of all this.

I have been writing all night, but I feel better now…and worse. The sun is coming up and Frank's physicians will be here soon to check on him. My joints are stiff from sitting so long. Time to go home and get some sleep.

2002
Kimmie's Rising Star

January 3rd
Dear My Diary,

I got an email from Thao regarding a date change of their wedding plans to June. The original date for March is too close to the Lunar New Year and business will be too hectic to allow for proper planning.

She said they had already changed the date some weeks ago but did not want to bother me while so much was going on with Fred's family. Moreover, it will be better for the children to attend after school is out for the summer. The wedding will be Saturday, June 22nd and Thao asked if we can come at that time? She has already gotten yesses from the other sisters, but this is the first time I am hearing about this, so I have to ask Fred. We have not been back since we married so I responded with a tentative 'yes', but I need to make sure and let her know as soon as we can.

I asked Fred what will happen to Barney's Growler? Will Bunny get it? Fred said the car is being held as evidence. Luckily for Bunny, her name is not on the car loan or she would be in deep financial trouble as well. On the good side, the FBI has cleared her of any wrongdoing since they found no evidence of her involvement.

The Growler was eventually sold at government auction and the proceeds used to pay the costs of the investigation by federal agents, court fees, impound fees and so forth (those get paid first, before the victims). Same goes for the cars, boat, jewelry and other items purchase by Luzerk as well as the remaining cash that was recovered.

Even with the purchased items being new or very nearly new, the auctions only recover a portion of their original purchase price. Luckily, most of the cash had not been spent yet so after it was all done and accounted for, Barney and Brad ended up owing the victims about $1.5M, split evenly between them.

The bank that held the lien on the Gambotti Growler tried to go after Bunny for the balance of the loan, but since our state is not a community property state and she was not on the contract, she had no obligation to the loan. That was not the case for the tens of thousands in credit card debt she held jointly with Barney along with the back rent on his office space that sat unused.

Mama quietly loaned Bunny the money to pay off the cards and the Wood sisters were able to sub-lease the office for a premium. In this way, Bunny did not have to file bankruptcy, was able to rebuild her credit and not drain her Crash Stash or savings any more than necessary. Bunny did repay Mama over the course of several years and, to our knowledge, never had any more financial problems.

Ba Frank Wakes Up

Dear My Diary,

Ba Frank is awake! Maggie and Aunt Dorothy were in the room when Frank opened one eye and rolled it around like he was trying to see.

He is very weak but can move some fingers and look around with his good eye. Only half of his body is working, but Fred said this is common for stroke victims. We got the call this afternoon while cooking dinner and I am so relieved it was not the other kind of phone call we could have gotten.

We turned off the stove and rushed to the hospital to see Pops. We were asked to stay only a short time as he is so weak. He will need time for his mind and body to recover.

We spoke to him quietly with big smiles and told Pops how happy we are to see him awake. We promised to come back tomorrow and see him again. He cannot talk with the oxygen hose in his throat, but one side of his mouth made a lopsided kind of smile, so I know he is happy that we came.

Maggie said when she first saw Frank's eye open and moving, it made her own heart almost stop as she thought she was dreaming. Then her sister Dorothy said "Lord Jesus, I do believe Frank is back to us!" and they buzzed the doctor right away. The doctors say the worst is over and once his vitals are stabilized, they will work on making Ba Frank stronger so he can go home in a few weeks. Everyone is optimistic. Fred called his father "a tough old bird". I like that phrase! It reminds me of some of the chickens we have had to eat when we were children.

We've agreed to only speak of positive things around him and not bring up family problems, especially Barney. I emailed my family and let them know the good news. Everyone loves Ba Frank…even if he is "a tough old bird"!

I told Fred about Thao and Phung's updated wedding plan for June 22nd. He smacked his forehead with his palm and said he forgot all about them getting married and said he thinks we can go.

With so much going on, it's been hard to plan for even the next day, but with Ba Frank awake now, it should not be a problem. Fred will arrange for nurses to help Maggie care for Frank once he is home. Then Fred said, "Yeah, tell the family to expect us for the wedding…what the hell! We could use a break from all this craziness."

Thomas Stimson

Helping Bunny

Saturday, January 26th
Dear My Diary,

Bunny invited me to lunch at her home, saying she missed my company. I've missed her as well and we spent time catching up on Frank's recovery efforts. Bunny is filing for divorce, something I had heard rumors of among the family, so it is not a surprise to me. I think she should have done that a long time ago, but didn't say as much.

When Bunny asked if Fred would be upset about her doing this while Barney is in prison, I said "Of course, not! Neither of us would blame you for doing such a thing. If Fred ever did something so terrible, I would file for divorce, get on the next plane to Vietnam and go back to work with my family."

Bunny said she felt better hearing that from me. I can see she looks happier and more relaxed than I have seen her in a long time. Barney calls her sometimes, but she checks the Caller ID and lets the calls go to voicemail. Who could blame her?

Bunny confessed, "Even when I'm divorced, I still want us to be sisters. Is that okay with you?"

I said, "That is happy to my ears."

She laughed and hugged me. "God, I love the way you talk!" I don't know why she said that.

As we ate lunch, Bunny said when she applied for work at some of the local law offices, they treat her like poison. I asked her why, and she said it's because of Barney. No one liked him and maybe they think she helped him do what he did, even if she didn't. Bunny is having a hard time finding work and does not want to dig deeper into her Crash Stash.

Bernice: I had Kimmie over for lunch one day and asked her how she liked working with Fred doing the auctions and reselling stuff. She made it sound fun and different and not boring like office work, so I had her look over Barney's stuff and the jewelry I got from him. She had all this professional testing equipment and really knew how to use it.

Kimmie said most of the stuff was costume jewelry. Even my engagement ring! His ROLEX watch was actually a RQLEX but you had to look hard to see the tail in the "O". Just a big bunch of crap.

Kimmie said his designer clothes and suits, even if they were genuine, were going to be a hard sell as Barney was only five foot five so too small for most men to wear. I ended up giving Kimmie all the jewelry in a coffee can so she could price them out and decide on the best way to sell them. For all the bad news, Kimmie made it sound like I could get money for it all, if not nearly as much as I was hoping for...even the engagement and wedding rings.

She offered to take me to one of the flea markets where she sold stuff sometimes and I could come along. I needed money more than I needed stuff and wanted to rid myself of Barney as much as I could. Kimmie gave me some hope that day and selling at the flea market sounded fun. Hanging out with her was always an upper for me, so I thought, "What the hell, I might even learn something useful!"

I saw a picture of Bunny and Barney in front of the Eiffel Tower and asked, "You went to Paris?"
Bunny kind of laughed, "Yeah, you could say that."
"Was it beautiful?"
"No."
"Was it romantic?"
"Not at all."
"Was the food wonderful?"
"Not especially."
I was puzzled. "Everything I hear about Paris is very beautiful, romantic and they have wonderful food."
"Sure, if you go to Paris, France."
"This is not Paris, France?"
"It's Paris, Texas. Big difference."

Lang: We talked to Aunt Bunny about this story none of us had heard. Uncle Barney had told Bunny they would be going to Paris and would not need a passport. She bought a bunch of new clothes on credit and told everyone where she was going. They flew to Dallas and Bunny knew something was wrong when they left the airport and rented a car instead of changing flights. Two hours later they were in Paris, Texas for a poker tournament Barney had been invited to. There IS an Eiffel Tower there…all of 65 feet high. One of the many disappointments in her marriage.

I told Fred about helping Bunny sell off her husband's things and he wished me good luck with it. I asked Fred if he wanted anything from Barney's and he said "I can't think of anything I want from Barney except all the time and headaches I have wasted on him. That, I would like to get back!"

I don't know what I would do if Fred was caught doing bad things and sent to jail for a long time. But then, Barney and Fred are so different from each other and now we know why. Different fathers with very different personalities made Barney one way and Fred another.

We all knew Barney would mess up one day and Bunny knew it most of all. At least she has her Crash Stash. Now, if she can just find a job where nobody cares who her husband was…

Applying for Permanent Residency

February 20, 2002

Dear My Diary,

Do you know if you put today's date in the same order as we do in Asia, it is the same number frontward and backward? I think 20/02/2002 is a lucky number for me!

Today Fred and I filled out and sent off the paperwork for my Unconditional Permanent Resident card. If approved, my new status will be good for ten years. I've been worried that Barney's arrest might hurt my chances, but the immigration lawyer Fred is using assured us that Barney's problems will not be our problem.

We've collected bank statements, tax returns, truck titles and other things with both our names legally attached to prove to the US government that we have a real marriage and not a fake one. The lawyer reviewed everything, made a couple of small corrections and we sent it off registered mail. I am nervous about being accepted but Fred assured me over and over that I am the perfect person to become a permanent resident, and later, a citizen.

I feel bad for not having told Fred about the baby, yet. I want to, I really do, but between the drama surrounding Frank and Barney's problems and Fred constantly stressed and stretched in different directions with all of it, I don't feel any time is the right time to bring it up without adding more stress to my husband.

What's worse, I have already waited too long since the test and we have not made pleasures since Barney's arrest. I can't lie and pretend that I didn't know I was pregnant until now. I need to be brave and just tell him, even if he gets mad that I did not tell him sooner.

February 28, 2002
Dear My Diary,

A funny thing happened today. Bunny, Tina and I were having lunch in the University District at a small café we like. Two young teen boys at another other table kept looking at us and talking to each other excitedly while pointing at a magazine. Finally, Bunny had enough and called to them, "You got a problem over there?" The boys came over and said, "Are you the Fierce 5 girl?" while pointing at a picture of me in a skateboarding magazine. There I was in a solo shot, holding a can of Brutal Berry and making a fierce, pointy-toothed grimace.

"Yes, that is me." The boys grinned and asked for an autograph.

I did not know this word and Tina helped out in Vietnamese "They want your signature as a souvenir." I got out a pen and signed the ad. The boys studied it and their faces fell. "Who is Kimmie Starbuckle?"

Attempting to save me some embarrassment, Bunny said "Oh, that's her alias." Then to me, "Sign your real name, 'Chimera'" and winked.

Oh, I see. They want my character's name. I signed it again and the boys thanked me before running off with their prize.

"Awww! Your first fans!" Bunny gushed. Now I know that if someone wants me to sign an F5 souvenir, to sign as Chimera.

Tina advised me "If this happens again, you should ask the fan's name and use it in the autograph like 'To Mike, Make it a Fierce 5 day! Chimera' or something like that and if you have time, make a bit of small talk like what is their favorite flavor and thank them for being a fan."

What a great idea! I will practice signing my autograph and keep some extra pens with me.

How sweet…Mama's first autograph request! It would not be her last by a long shot…she is still giving out autographs, even at the nursing home. Luckily, she still has her wits about her and will tell her favorite entertainment stories if so inclined.

Thomas Stimson

A Son's Quest

March 1, 2002
Dear My Diary,

I got the script for Rock Rollins new movie "A Son's Quest", but they only sent me the section with Fierce 5 in it. I'm glad because I want the rest to be a surprise. I read it over and our parts are action-packed with only a few lines. The studio helped us get our union card and F5 paid for the one-year membership. If I want to do more acting in the future, I will have to pay my own way unless it is done with Fierce 5 again.

Fred called the scene a "throw-away" as it is not important to the story except as product placement and Fierce 5 is paying the costs of filming the scene since Rock is our celebrity spokesman. If the movie is a success, our brand will be seen by millions of people who will want to buy and drink Fierce 5 and go fully nationwide, and maybe even international!

Another part of the contract is for our scene to be filmed in Riverton using local talent and merchants. The same scene can be done very easily in Hollywood as it is an indoor shoot, but this also means I do not get to travel to Hollywood…uck! I complained about this to Fred but he just laughed and said he will take me to Hollywood "soon enough." Maybe that means our next vacation? I don't know how he means that.

Fred and I read my parts and those of the others. While we were reading, I got a call from Angie, the stunt coordinator, and she will travel to Riverton to teach me and the others our parts. She asked me how fit I am? I said my clothes fit fine.

She said, "No, I mean are you strong, flexible and exercise regularly?"

I said, "Yes, my husband keeps me active and I am quite strong, I think."

She is arriving next week and gave me the address of Golden Boy Gym where we will be training. Fred said he knows that gym and we went there to look at it. I have never been to a gym except in school for physical fitness class.

It was very bright inside and heavy with the smell of sweaty men. The manager verified that some of the training rooms have been reserved by the studio. I am excited to be part of making a movie after watching so many over the years.

Later that night I got a call from Zander. I thanked her for getting the movie scene for us and look forward to this new experience. She said Consuela and Bettina will be training with me at Golden Boy for our parts with Malia and Jasmin joining us before the final rehearsals. They are currently on location with the fantasy TV show "Swords of Algiers" doing stunt work and fight scenes. As Malia likes to say, "It pays the rent, but not much else!"

Dear My Diary,

Business at Flea City was busier after Christmas than before. People have less money to spend so they use the flea market for bargain-hunting. This was a good weekend for the stuff Bunny had to sell as people are getting their tax refunds and have more money to spend.

Bernice: Kimmie really knew how to dress things up for selling. Before we went to Flea City, she had me clean up everything we were going to sell like washing and ironing clothes, putting jewelry into detergent baths and polishing them with soft toothbrushes so they would sparkle better and stuff like that. Her van had clothing racks on wheels, display cases from department stores for bracelets, necklaces and earrings and all kinds of professional-looking stuff. She said Fred had bought all this from stores that were going out of business for practically nothing, but it made what we were selling look way nicer than just all jumbled in a shoebox.

Kimmie also advertised my sale with pictures online and she showed me the ads. It looked so good, it made ME want to come to Flea City and buy my own stuff! I wasn't happy with the prices she wanted to charge, especially knowing what we paid for them, but it also makes sense that people want to buy things for as cheap as possible while sellers want as much as possible. I had to think more like a buyer and less like the person selling her own stuff. Kimmie said volume and presentation is the key. And it sure was!

Actually, it was pretty fun. Kimmie would talk to browsers and show them this and explain about that. We sold that fake Rolex for nearly $200 and we even showed them the "Q"! They understood it was fake and it worked fine and they only bargained a little. I listened to Kimmie and started copying what she was doing and pretty soon the cash was rolling in. I could tell some people were only coming over to check out her bod, but they often ended up buying stuff.

Fred brought us a hot lunch even though we had packed sandwiches and fruit. He took over for a while so each of us could take a breather and I got to checking out what other people were selling. It was an eye-opener to see what and how different stalls sold their stuff. Some were like us with good displays and some were just boxes of random stuff, real junk and people were pawing through them looking for who knows what.

That was the time I started understanding what Fred and Kimmie really do with themselves. Seeing how different it was from what I imagined and from how bad Barney made it sound. I forgot exactly how much I made that weekend but I think it was over a thousand and I still had a lot of stuff to sell. That weekend was a real turning point for me…and for my future.

Bunny made a few hundred dollars and has more things to bring next weekend. She was not happy to sell so many things so cheap but I had to remind Bunny that she might be able to get more money for some things but it would take much longer to find the right buyer and people are comparing our prices with that of GnG or other discount stores.

The important thing is selling in volume. What she and Barney owned was not so special or different from many other people's things, so the prices are expected to be lower. I told her that after next weekend, if she still has things to sell, we can try posting on Ubiddit and FreePost for a month or so.

I told her it is much better to get things for free or almost free, and then sell them. She asked me how do we get free things to sell? I promised to show her this week and she will see how we make some of our money.

Bernice: Oh, and that stupid Six Million Dollar Man doll that Fred gave Barney? Around the time we were doing the flea market, Kimmie ended up selling it on Ubiddit for over FIVE HUNDRED DOLLARS!

I couldn't believe it! What she did was so clever, let me tell you. In the description, she included a link to a VidLive site where someone was running Barney's commercial. She made it clear that the doll we were selling was that very same doll and included links from the Riverton Review that talked about his bust and that he had had that commercial running up until the time he was arrested. Several local people bid the hell out of that thing until it sold. Better me than him to make money off that damn doll!

Trashy Treasures

Dear My Diary,

Bunny has been after me to see and learn how we do our re-selling business, so early this morning I picked her up for work. I had told Bunny to dress warm in things she doesn't mind getting dirty, but when she came out of her house, she was dressed way too nice. I reminded her that we are not going shopping but to dress like she was going to do serious gardening. She came back out in what she called her "grubbies" and boot-shoes. Much better!

I brought the tall, two-seat work van with room for large items like furniture and lawnmowers. We drove to the General Quarters military housing neighborhood as today is their trash pick-up day. I told Bunny that we will pull over as we see things piled up next to the garbage cans to try to find some sellable goodies.

We drove for about four hours up and down the streets and alleys of three different neighborhoods, pulling over, inspecting boxes, bags and loose items, and collected boxes of perfectly good books, clothes, toys and two lawn mowers.

The working mower we can sell for $40 or $50 after we clean it up nice. If we can get the other one to work, great. If not, it will be good for scrap metal money. We also got framed pictures, small appliances and an older video game system with a box full of game cartridges.

I told Bunny that I will be training and filming a scene for the new Rock Rollins movie so I won't be able to do very much reselling work for a while. Now that she has some new skills for pricing and selling at the flea market, she can go out on her own to find free things to sell and make her money last longer until she gets a job.

After we got home, I estimated that we can sell the load in the van for $200 or so. She said "Really? That's like making $50 an hour!"

"Not quite. We still have to spend time cleaning, testing and pricing the items before trying to sell at the flea market, on Ubiddit and other venues. But yes, we made money with not much more in costs than gas, time and selling fees."

Bunny thought it was a lot of fun and good exercise. I agree. And it was nice having someone with me today. It's always easier, faster and more fun with someone else to work with, especially since Fred is so busy with his parents right now.

Stunt Training

March 17, 2002
Dear My Diary,

Today was a very busy and happy day for me as it is my 31st birthday and Fred's 34th. I had told him last night not to make a heavy breakfast as I will be training hard. He scored points with me by making a thick fruit, vegetable and yogurt smoothie for both of us. So healthy!

Then he gave me my present, saying it is a good luck charm…and what a charm! It is an action figure of Rock Rollins dressed in shorts, no shirt and boxing gloves. The gloves are held close to his chest and one glove has something sparkly attached.

I removed the figure from its box and 'Rock' was holding a pretty necklace with a sparkly star in the center. "For the newest star in Hollywood!" Fred announced before giving me a kiss.

"I will never be a star, but I will give you a twinkle from my eye!" I responded.

I gave Fred an "Outdoor Sportsman" watch to use for our dress-up times. I found the watch in one of our auction lockers and hid it away, then got it inspected, replaced the battery and cleaned it well at one of our go-to Jewelry stores. No charge for a good customer like us!

When I showed the watch to Bunny and explained how I got it, she told me that if Barney had gotten a used watch as a present, he would feel very insulted. Then again, knowing Fred, she believed HE would be insulted if I bought it new and at full price!

She is right, of course. She said, "It's so funny how different two brothers can be from each other." And I cannot tell her how really very different they are.

We met with Angie Smith and two assistants this morning at Golden Boy Gym. She is the stunt trainer for our movie and is all business. When she took off her street clothes to the shorts and sleeveless shirt beneath, taut muscles were prominently outlined on her slender frame and I knew she was serious about training us.

She asked if any of us have health or medical problems she needs to know about. We all told her "No" and I feel guilty for not admitting my pregnancy. The scene will be shot in about a month so I think it is not so important and I don't want to miss this chance.

We started with stretching exercises, then trying out different moves to see how high we can kick, how fast we can move this way and that and how much we can lift. When she asked me how much I can lift, I admitted that I have never lifted weights like they have at the gym, but often move heavy boxes, bags, furniture and etc. as part of my regular job. Once we used some of the equipment, it was determined that I can lift between 130 to 160 pounds without difficulty. Angie was impressed at my strength for someone who does not train in a gym.

My part involves kicking, rolling and throwing of people. Some of the stunts will use wires that other people will control to make the action look bigger. Later, they will erase the wires so it looks like I am throwing a big man across the room.

The whole scene will last about three minutes, but there will be a lot of moving parts using a variety of camera angles. Angie said sometimes it can take all day to do part of a scene if multiple takes are required for angle and lighting purposes.

We had lunch with some of the other trainers and men who will be fighters in the scene. I have seen a couple of the men around town and, as we made introductions, I learned that most of them are from the local area, picking up work as they can in movie, theater and TV productions and going as far as Chicago and St Louis to get the work they want while staying near home.

I know Bettina and Consuela live together in Chicago so they are centrally located for lots of big modeling and acting jobs in North America. They often work together on projects too, so I guess that is why they were picked for Fierce 5.

I have looked up everyone on VidLive and MovieMadness websites to see their work. I am the only one who does not have any prior experience. I feel very junior to them, but when I told Fred, he said, "We all have to start someplace!" and "Look at it this way, you went from being teased as a Coconut Tree to being a respected member of Fierce Five…which do you prefer?" Of course, I like my F5 job and Zander and everyone treats me as their equal. Fred knows how to keep my balance when I am feeling unsure or down about myself.

Some of the stunt training was filmed and photographed for promotional purposes and to add to the Special Features section of the home video editions. Mama usually wore T-shirts and gym shorts for ease of movement during the training sessions and she was very fit in those days. Great muscle tone and little body fat. While reviewing these old films, Frankie said "I hate to say this about my own mother, but she was really hot!" I think we all felt that way.

Today, I learned to kick, punch and fall in such a way as to roll back up on my feet in a smooth motion. Consuela and Bettina know how to do this already and their rolls are powerfully graceful, especially when they tried out different flourishes to the starts and endings. Angie said I did well for a first-time effort.

We will keep practicing and next week we move to a warehouse studio for another week of training with the rest of the actors and stuntmen. We will be there for two weeks, I think. This is where they will connect wires to us for jumping and throwing.

I am nervous about this stage, but find it fun too. By the end of the day, I feel good-tired. Fred and I went out for a quiet dinner, talking about what each of us had been doing today. Times like this make me feel closer to Fred. After so much going on with our families, this is the kind of activity to free our minds. I had never thought that I would have a day like this on my birthday!

Dear My Diary,

Bunny wants to help us with re-selling stuff. She thinks it is fun to collect things and try to re-sell them. As I am training for the movie, and we make preparations to go to Vietnam, it would be good to have a helper. Bunny is honest, fun and when we sell at the flea market, she is a very good seller, making compliments and suggestions to people who are "just looking" and helping us make a few extra sales.

Fred has everything with his parents more or less under control, so he is back to collecting, delivering, shipping and etc. We both agree that having Bunny helping out will be beneficial to all of us. Fred brought her to the gym during our lunch hour to discuss the idea and during that time, I had her meet my co-workers.

Bunny was bubbling to meet everyone, especially the stuntmen. Her eyes were non-stop scanners! It's cute to see her this way…cute, but kind of sad. She is happy that we want her to help us and we can use the help of someone we can trust. Fred took her around today to all the stores for the pick-up and delivery of goods.

Now, as we near the end of our practice session, Angie brought in some props we will use in the scene and practice certain moves. One of the props is the top half of a man with one arm holding a knife. The body is on a stand and can be turned back and forth by using a handle.

One of my parts is to be threatened by a man with a knife. I distract him by looking past his shoulder, causing him to turn towards the imaginary danger and his knife arm turns with him. At that moment, I scissor-cross my arms and SNAP goes the knife-wielding arm!

We practiced until I have all the parts down good and can make a fast snap. Angie says the stuntman will be wearing a fake arm so I will not break, or even hurt, his real arm. Stunt trick!

Angie brought out a cushioned piece of furniture with no back or arms, like a foot rest you'd find in front of a chair, but larger and higher. Angie said this item will represent a man's bent-over back and when I see two men coming to jump on him, I will take some steps, roll across his back and kick the bad guys into tables. Today there are no men to attack so I practiced rolling smoothly, timing the kicks and trying not to fall off the man's back as I did the first few times.

Angie showed me what she wants and I imitated her. Soon, it is feeling more natural and I can put some power to my kicks. Then two assistants wearing chest protectors come at me as the bad guys and let themselves be kicked over and over. I practice timing the roll and kicks so there is a pattern of rhythm, smooth movements, power and grace. During the shoot, the "bad guys" will be on wires and will fly backwards much farther than I can really kick them. This is so fun!

Next week will be pre-production training and setting up the stage for the bar fight scene. Angie will leave for another project and her assistants will take over. By that time, the rest of the F5 team will be there and we know what to do. Now it is time to make it smooth and powerful as though we have been doing this kind of fighting for many years.

March 23, 2002
Dear My Diary,

We invited Angie to our home for dinner as it is her last night in Riverton. She told Fred that I am a 'natural' when it comes to learning the action sequences and Fred responded with, "She's a natural all right!" and winked at me. I don't know if Fred meant to be naughty or not. Sometimes I can't tell.

Angie is flying out to Northern California to work on more stunt training and, at the end of dinner, she told me that the back I will be rolling over is Rock Rollins…he picked me for that stunt!

After Angie left, we had such intimate pleasures as we have not had for a long time. Before our love time, Fred gave me more attention than usual as we cleared and washed the dishes. He apologized for spending so much time with his parents and dealing with Barney, whose sentencing will be in May.

Ba Frank is recovering, but very slowly. I visit as often as I can after training and when he sees me, Frank's eyes sparkle with happiness. I hold his hand and tell him about my day and what is happening with the family or tell stories of my time in Vietnam. I do this to take his mind away from all the bad things going on. My mother taught us how you help the sick, sad and lonely people…talking about nice things, interesting things, happy things and soon their troubles will go away, even just for a short time.

March 30, 2002
Dear My Diary,

I am relaxing in bed now. The makeshift studio was not ready for the crew in time, so training is running longer while construction and wiring is being completed. Rock and the main cast members are filming in the redwood forests of California, so the production time is not wasted. They will be arriving over the weekend.

Two of my F5 sisters will have green screen stunts, but my parts do not require flipping in the air or complex techniques. Malia and Scirroco are here now so we can practice everything as a team.

We trained all week with the weekend off for some "fun and sun". It is sunny here, but cold…brrr! All week we have been inside a barely heated studio from early until late and when there was a break in practice, we got final fittings for our costumes. Some of the people go drinking after work but Fred and I are not so interested, and I want to be at my best for the movie.

It will take four days to film the bar scene, then the rest will be finished up in editing and post-production. I like learning new Hollywood words like 'post-production' 'gaffer' and 'foley artist'. Foley artists make the sound effects like smashing chairs and hitting fists. Smashing chairs is so much fun! The chairs and tables are made to break apart and no one gets hurt but it looks very exciting.

During the break times, I like to talk to Baby through my thoughts. I never speak out loud to Baby except in the shower or when I am alone and only in my language. Fred understands a little, but we do not practice anymore. I have not told Fred about Baby yet, and I am ashamed for not doing so but I will tell him right after we finish filming. I am afraid if I tell him now, he will pull me out of the film to protect me. I am not worried as there are a lot of safety protocols in place. I will be fine.

At the same time, I can't hide the baby much longer. Fred might remember that I took the pregnancy test the morning Barney was arrested. Between that awful day in December until last week, we did not make love pleasures as Fred was not in the mood with so much going on. What to do?

I am learning a lot about the entertainment business from the cast and crew. Rock Rollins is so funny and sweet, but when we practice our fighting moves, he puts on what he calls his "game face". By doing so during practice, his character's expression will be natural during the fight scenes. We all practice this too, but sometimes our faces are so distorted as we go through our moves or yell "Yahhh!" that we can't help but to stop and laugh at ourselves and each other. Luckily, it is getting more natural now and I am more than ready to do this scene.

With everything else going on, we are doing interviews and photo sessions with local and national news and entertainment shows in a special media trailer outside the studio. It's fun to pose and talk about the movie and Fierce 5 along with our personal stories.

When Zander told me I needed to have some prepared remarks and biographical information for the media, I had Fred help me, so I do not sound too immigrant. Zander sent me a list of typical questions and my F5 sisters filled me in with other things they have been asked…including some very ridiculous ones.

Learning about my coworkers' lives growing up, I see that I was not the only one who had problems fitting in with their schools and making friends. Bettina's father was transferred to Japan for two years and brought his family. Bettina said she felt even more out of place among the Japanese students than in Europe because where she is from, blonde and nearly white hair is common. In Japan, people stared at her a lot and spoke to her very little. They wanted to touch her white hair and called her Ghost Girl instead of her given name.

Malia would buy beer for her friends when she was 14 as she looked and acted much older. They also called her Queen Kong (Fred explained the joke to me later. I can see why it was not funny to her.)

Consuela and Jasmin became models at a young age and have traveled all over the world but their formal education was off and on and neither graduated from high school because of it.

Rock has invited all the cast and crew to his hotel suite Saturday after work for dinner and drinks. I can't wait to go!

Clam Bake

Sunday March 31, 2002
Dear My Diary,

I had so much fun this weekend! After the final dress rehearsal and fittings for our costumes we all went to the Central Park Hotel where Rock had rented the rooftop garden for his party. A large tent had been erected with tables and chairs around a big box of sand that was protected by security ropes. The tent smelled of burning wood and smoke crept out of the sand like steam on a Saigon street after an evening monsoon rain.

Most of the crew came to the party and there was much talking and laughing and eating locally-made cheeses, sausages and specialty breads.

Rock and Kathy are so much fun. Rock asked me how I like movie making so far? I told him that I like it fine but it is hard work. Then he asked me how warm it is right now in Vietnam? I said it runs in the 90's or so, during the day.

"And it's a mild thirty-eight here in Riverton…can't beat it!" Rock said with a grin.

He officially introduced me to the movie's director Dodge Harrison. Dodge was a Hollywood action star when I was a girl but turned his talents to directing and producing the same kinds of movies and TV shows he was best known for. He makes it a point to have a cameo appearance in all his films, as a treat for the fans. He is very friendly and said he was looking forward to working with Fierce 5 this week. I could not help but notice that Dodge was drinking "Cherry Charger" Fierce 5. Cool!

Rock asked me if I want to stay in acting. "With your looks and a good action skillset, you can get work easily in movies and television shows."

I said "I don't know. I never thought about this before, being an actor." Of course, I've had my fantasies of film stardom. But that's all they have ever been. Fantasies. And I've never told anyone, not even Fred. Why should I? With my looks, I've never felt it could happen.

Rock said "Give it some thought. I can hook you up with my agent and you can see how busy she keeps me!"

I thanked Rock for his kind words and offer and promised I will think about it. I turned to Fred who lifted his eyebrows and nodded, not saying a word. He is always encouraging me to be brave and try new things like the Fierce 5 modeling. After filming is over, we can talk about it.

Almost everybody was drinking beer and wine with their food, but I stayed with the Arnold Palmer drink of iced tea and lemonade. I find it very refreshing. Fred had his usual ginger ale.

The clam bake preparation and feast is very interesting. I will explain: When we arrived, all I saw was a big box of several square meters with rope around it and many people gathered around talking about a 'clam bake'. I looked but it is just sand and some sea grass poking out. I asked Fred "What is this?"

"They call this a clam bake."

"So where are the clams?"

"They are under the sand, just like at the beach."

Soon some of the caterers came over and began removing the sand, while doing this, one of them explained how early this morning they put together this fire-proof box, then layered several inches of sand and large flat rocks to act as a floor. A wood fire was built and allowed to burn down to a thick mass of charcoal, like when we roast a pig at home.

From there, a thick cover of wet seaweed is laid over the coals, and then the foods to be cooked, then another layer of seaweed woven into a fishing net for ease of removal and a last layer of sand. The hot coals, rocks and wet seaweed, act as a giant steamer.

Once the seaweed net was pulled off, steam rose in a cloud of wonderful smells and such a sight to see! There were lots of 'oohs' and 'aahs' from all corners of the tent at the feast of clams, mussels, lobsters, crabs, unhusked ears of corn, sausages and potatoes were uncovered.

Tables had been set with heavy-duty paper plates and utensils as the caterers surrounded the pit with long tongs, filling large platters high with seafood, meats and vegetables that were then set one platter to a table of eight

Rock had ordered hundreds of pounds of fresh seafood from New England for our party. It must have been so expensive! But then, he is also a very generous man.

The actors and crew have so many stories to tell that I have a hard time believing them all. The kinds of tricks people play on each other, on-set accidents (mostly funny ones) or romances that come from working so closely together. Now I have lots of new and fun stories to tell sisters and cousins when I see them again…too many for telling now.

Some people brought musical instruments and were soon playing while others sang along to popular songs and some songs I have not heard before…there were so many talented people at the party. One woman played her guitar in a kind of fast rhythm and another man joined in with a harmonica, matching his style with her playing as we all clapped to the music and she sang.

I found out later that she had some hit songs in the 1970's and 80's and still plays often at music festivals. In fact, she makes her home here in the Riverton area and came with a person in the crew. I did not recognize her name but Fred knows who she is. I am afraid I do not know very many of the popular Western entertainers but for a few of the bigger stars.

We left when too many people were getting drunk and, as we started to drive home, Fred took the car one time slowly around Riverton Central Park as a romantic ending for our day. I looked at the island in the lake and thought about Barney. I know I will never look at Duck Island the same way again.

I am exhausted but very happy. We smell like smoke and seafood and have made many new friends in the last two weeks. We took a shower together, made pleasures and slept deep into Sunday morning. At breakfast, I felt some little tickles in my tummy. I turned around but Fred was not close enough to tickle me. When it happened again, I thought 'Troi oi! I think the baby is kicking.'

Without thinking, I blurted out "Fred!" and when he turned to me, I caught myself and said "Can you bring me the plates?"

I almost told Fred the baby is kicking and he does not know I am pregnant. What am I waiting for? I know. For the movie to finish and then tell him. But I can't wait forever. I see my tummy beginning to swell, but not a lot. Fred did not even notice last night…he had his mind on other things!

Mama has pictures from the party taken with Dad, Rock and Kathy Rollins, Dodge Harrison, all the F5 team and lots of other cast and crew. Some of the pictures were taken by the folks and others were

taken by studio photographers to be distributed as promo photos in the US and abroad, especially in the countries where the Fierce 5 team members came from.

Dear My Diary,

I accidentally made a change to our fight scene that the director likes, and he thinks it adds 'a little something extra'. Let me explain:

In the original scene, Rock and the bad guys are building towards a fight and the F5 team sees he will need help, so we each stand and say a line. The camera moves from one to another of us as we stand, step forward and say our line. When the last one speaks, we charge forward as a group and the fight scene goes from there.

When the first take is done, the director looked at the playback with other staff and he was pointing at something. Dodge called me over from the group and showed me what they had just filmed. Then I saw what mistake I had made…I was nervous and said my line in Vietnamese! No one seemed to notice, or they simply stayed in character as the other F5 women said their lines as written. Needless to say, I was embarrassed and apologized for the mistake.

The director ran the film back again and looked thoughtful. Then he called the rest of the team over and asked what languages they spoke? We have Dutch and German for Bettina, Spanish for Consuela, Moroccan Arabic for Jasmin and English, or as Malia likes to say, "Georgian".

The Director asked us to do the scene again, but this time deliver our lines in our own language. He had Malia do the last line and make her Southern accent stronger. I don't know how the audience will know what we are saying if we deliver the lines in our own language, but no one questioned the director, and he did not tell us his plan. We did the scene a few times until Dodge was happy.

The Accident

April 5, 2002
Dear my Diary,

I am afraid I hurt our baby. I was so stupid to do this! If Fred never forgives me, I will certainly understand.

It was our final day of filming and Fred watched part of the time before leaving to help his parents with something. Everything was going smoothly, but during one part, I made a mistake and turned right instead of left. My right turn put me in the path of another person's stunt, and I got kicked in the stomach. Ooof!

I fell and was struggling to breathe. Dodge yelled "Cut! Cut!" and people rushed to aid me. Donnie, the man who kicked me, was apologetic, saying "Sorry! Sorry! Are you okay?"

Crew members helped me up and the EMT rushed over at the same time. As I started to breathe again, I could only think of one thing to say: "Oh my baby! Did I hurt you Baby? Please be okay Baby."

Someone asked me in Vietnamese "Are you speaking to your baby? Are you with child?"

I started to answer in Vietnamese until I looked up and saw not an Asian man speaking to me, but an older black man in an EMT uniform. "What did you say?" I asked in English.

The EMT answered in English "Are you pregnant? It sounded like you were talking to your baby." This made me very shy and did not answer right away. The man asked me again in Viet if I am pregnant?

I admitted that I am. "But you are American. How do you know my language?"

He had been a medic during the war and often helped care for women and children in the villages. In the US, with the growing Vietnamese population, especially in Southern California, he still has opportunities to use his wartime skills. He told me his name is James and is employed by the studio.

Now I am caught with the truth. I said yes, I am maybe three or four months pregnant. James asked who my OB/GYN is and I admitted to not having one yet.

James checked me over and asked questions. He said that I have very firm abdomen muscles and that is likely protecting the baby from any real harm, but I should go to the hospital for a more thorough check-up.

Dodge and his assistant came over to make sure I am all right. They said my part is done now and thanked me for my efforts in the film. They will let Zander know if they need anything more from the Fierce 5 team and wished me a speedy recovery. The studio will pay for whatever is needed.

The EMT drove me to the hospital and Malia came with me for company. One of the film crew also joined us to help with the insurance paperwork. My tummy does not hurt so much but I had to make a very hard phone call to Fred.

I called while waiting to be seen for the ultra-sound. When he answered, I tried to be light-hearted with my words saying, "I have good news and more good news."

He said "Great! Are you done filming?"

"Yes. And more good news: I have a baby inside me."

"Whoo Hoo!" he cheered.

"But I also have some bad news," and Fred got quiet. I explained about accidentally getting kicked in the stomach and I am at the hospital to learn if the baby is all right or not. Without hesitation, Fred said he was leaving for the hospital that minute.

Fred found me before the scan was started and Malia left for the cafeteria to give us privacy. He asked me what happened, so I told him again, in more detail. He asked, "When did you learn you were pregnant? Was it today?"

I deflected Fred's question by saying "They will give me a scan and see what to do next. I am feeling better and do not think I am badly hurt."

Fred held my hand in his lap and was quiet.

The ultrasound did not show any damage to the baby, but they also said it is hard to tell when the fetus is so small.

Bruises are now showing just under my breasts, well-above where the baby sits and the doctor said it is a good sign. No broken or cracked ribs either. The doctor told me much the same as James, that my toned muscles helped protect the baby, but we will not know fully until after the baby is born and maybe even later than that.

The doctor advised me to keep an eye out for any blood spotting, and if there is, to have it checked out right away. Same goes for cramping or other pains in the lower belly area.

Malia gave me a hug and said she will fly home tomorrow. I feel better that the baby may not be hurt…but then, it still might be. Now I will have to confess when I knew about the baby to Fred. Maybe he will be very mad at me…but he is also one that forgives easily. Still, I feel sick in my heart for having done this.

Good Night Dear My Diary, Wish me luck…

We have heard this story many times from Mama. As we got older, she used this story as an example of being honest with your partner (or parents, or teachers, etc) regarding important events or changes. Even if by holding back the information it means you will get something you want, the risk of continuing the path could spell danger for yourself or others. At least we know why Frankie turned out the way he did…

Kimmie: Originally, I held back news of the pregnancy because it fell right into the firestorm that was Barneys' arrest and Franks' stroke and I did not want to burden the family with more things to deal with. Once that settled down, I kept the news hidden because I saw the movie role as a way to jumpstart my entertainment career, even if I was not sure I really wanted such a thing. I did not want to let the F5 team down and wanted Fred and my family to be proud of me. Even now I feel bad for having waited so long and especially for endangering the life of our first child. As I expected, Fred was kind enough to forgive me, but I never held back important information again. It just wasn't worth it.

Thomas Stimson

The Announcement

April 7, 2002

Dear My Diary,

Fred and I had a long talk today about the baby and why I had not said anything before now. I apologized many times to Fred about holding back this important news, but he just held me close, saying that it was okay and I am forgiven.

Fred blamed the combination of Barney's arrest and all the personal, legal and media-related chaos that went with it. On top of everything else, Fred is busy planning stock short-selling strategies with Bobby, Robbie and other local investors as they expect the markets to go through, what they are calling, a major correction. When I asked what 'a major correction' means, Fred said with a straight face "A major correction is a polite way of saying that the market will take a big, and very painful, dump on investors."

With no time for Fred to do the resale work that we depend on, I had to take it over while still working my Fierce 5 obligations. Fred feels terrible to have let things go like this and making me hesitant to tell him.

I said, "Fred, I wanted to tell you and my family so many times, but I knew if I told someone else first, then you might hear about it before I could tell you and then I would lose face with my very best friend. It would not be fair to you not to know first. I am so ashamed not to tell you until now."

Fred asked, "You really didn't tell anybody?"

I sighed and said, "Well, I admit that I did tell Ba Frank during his coma, and I told him in Vietnamese, as insurance."

Fred smiled at that and said, "Well, he always knew how to keep a secret."

We agreed that I should see an ob/gyn doctor at the hospital and make extra double-sure that our baby is okay and then schedule out prenatal examinations.

I told him that I am feeling much better but still bruised and tender above the tummy. I showed Fred the bruise and he touched it lightly, then a little more. Then he started talking to my tummy. "Hello? Hello? Daddy to Baby. Daddy to Baby. Do you read me, Baby?"

It was very cute and sweet. Soon we were kissing and …well…I will just say now that Fred has forgiven me and demonstrated his love and tenderness for me and our new family.

Frankie: This is the first time Mom mentions the short selling of stocks. In the early part of 2002, what Dad and his friends expected to happen, happened…the beginning of the 2002-2003 bear market.

Dear My Diary,

We have been flooded with good wishes since we shared our news about the baby with our families and friends. Needless to say, we said nothing about how long I knew, just that we are expecting and the due date is mid-August. This also coincides with our wedding anniversary so it makes the baby an extra-special gift!

But before we let everyone know, Fred made an appointment with Dr. Amy Sedaris at Riverton Memorial who saw me after normal business hours. She is typically very booked up, but took time for me because of our good name with the hospital and my recent accident. Fred was there, of course, as my support and to make sure we both understood everything about the pregnancy.

Dr. Sedaris is very kind and asked many questions in a straightforward and professional manner, very unlike the often rude and condescending style of the doctors back home. She listened carefully with her stethoscope and had the sonogram team give me a thorough examination of my insides. We asked her not to tell us the gender of the baby so as to keep it a surprise. "Doing it the old-fashioned way," was how Fred stated our wish.

Luckily, they did not find anything wrong, but if there is damage, it might not be clear until weeks or months after the birth like the possibility of mental or behavioral problems as the child gets older.

After I told her how the accident happened, the doctor asked me if I have plans to make any more action scenes in the next few months. Fred blurted out, "I hope not!"

Dr. Sedaris gave us a list of important foods to eat and drink and what to watch for that might indicate a problem. We already eat a very healthy diet of fruits and vegetables, lean meats and other good things but I will definitely step-up my consumption of dairy products.

The doctor also seems familiar with my culture because she asked if I am taking, or planning to take, any herbs or Asian medical treatments? I said that I have known women who took herbs during pregnancy, but I had not considered it.

Dr. Sedaris warned me against taking them as they may contain toxins that can react badly with any medicines the doctors want to give me. I promised to only take medicines that she prescribes or I can find easily at the local drugstores.

After the appointment, we had dinner with Fred's parents. Frank is looking much better now and has gained some weight, but he still cannot eat or speak very well. We pay for nurses to come in and help with his bathing, feeding and other chores.

At the table, Frank has a clear plastic bag on a stand that hangs over his head and a tube leading into his arm. He said something I could not understand, but Maggie translated that his "Dinner" is in the bag. Then Frank said "Yum!" with his crooked smile and rubbed his tummy with his good hand. It made me laugh and feel sad at the same time.

Maggie is very excited to be a grandma and Frank shook his good arm and leg to say he is very happy too. I came over and hugged him as best I could and kissed his cheek saying that I am very happy to make a grandchild for them.

We went on to Thanh and Vo's house to make our announcement in person. Tina was there visiting and when I told them about the baby, the sisters made happy screams. That caused the girls to come from their room and jump up and down when they learned they will have a new cousin. We stayed for dessert and a blended fruit drink to toast the new baby.

While we were with sisters, I called Me and Ba and told them the good news.

"*Finally* you will be a mother!" Me said. Ba told Fred he will be a very good father and wishes one day to hold his grandchild to show everyone. He also told me that I will be a very good mother and for both of us to come to Vietnam very soon!

At times like this, I miss my extended family as we have not been back to Vietnam since I left to marry Fred. I told Ba and Me that we will be there very soon and gave them the date we will arrive. I did not tell them about my accident…just the happy parts about how all went well with filming and having a clam bake on the hotel roof with Rock Rollins and Dodge Harrison.

Lois: It was around this time that Mama saw the future difficulties of continuing the reselling business. Dad and his friends were deep into researching and short-selling stocks as the market headed into freefall, intending to purchase multi-unit housing complexes once the prices had bottomed out. This would allow for a larger return on the property investments while they paid for themselves through rental incomes. At the same time, Dad was considering selling his share of the resale stores back to the owners, if they were able and willing, but had not yet discussed it with anyone but Mama.

Grandpa Starbuckle was slowly recovering from his stroke and still needed constant care while Grandma needed his support both financially and emotionally. On the bright side, Dad increased his attentions with Mama after the pregnancy had been outed. Conversely, she would have to ease up on the strenuous physical work involved in collecting and delivering goods to the resale stores, especially in her last trimester. Aunt Bunny was starting to get involved with the business at this time but had no real experience in the different areas of its operation.

With her lot in Honeywood Heights still sitting empty, Mama wanted to start designing and building a home. She still had no clear idea of what she wanted, Dad had no preferences and the complexity of the project daunted her.

Moreover, she still had to prepare for her sister's wedding in Vietnam and the Fierce 5 marketing team was planning more work for the spokesmodels in anticipation of A Son's Quest to boost sales even further. So much was going on!

Dear My Diary,

I am feeling better in some ways: Ba Frank is home now and slowly getting better, the movie scene is done, and Bunny is learning our business with enthusiasm, if not with the speed as I had hoped for. I prefer the enthusiasm, plus she is very honest, which is important to us.

As we prepare to go to Vietnam for Thanh and Phung's wedding, I am disappointed that we have done nothing with the Honeywood Heights land. I have lived in the garage now for almost two years and I really want to raise our child in a proper house.

The homes of our families are not like the homes in Honeywood Heights. Theirs are the common two- and three-bedroom homes found in most areas of the city and, I am sure, in much of America. But if we choose to live in HH, I know we will need a house to be of a similar size and style to fit in with our neighbors.

I would be happy with a house like my other family members, but Fred gave me this piece of land as a gift and an investment, so I do not want to sell it and act like it is not important to me. Also, it will be good for our children to socialize with other wealthy families and develop friendships among Riverton's influential citizens. Fred told me the schools in HH are among the best in the state due to the extra fund-raising and attention cultivated by wealthy parents…another attractive feature as well.

Holly Wood was sympathetic regarding my confusion about designing and building a new house from the ground up. She said there is no way to plan a proper house without having some ideas and preferences, so we took time today to visit a few of the homes for sale in HH. I made sure to bring a digital camera and notebook for referencing, and I am glad I did.

I have never seen the insides of such fancy houses before! Many homes are up for sale now as the economy is shedding jobs and reducing incomes. For some families, the value of their recently purchased homes has gone down so much that they are simply giving the houses back to the bank.

We drove to my block and saw several homes partially built, but most of the lots are still untouched. We only saw three houses being worked on today.

We visited a total of ten houses and while some looked very similar in terms of size and layouts, others are very different. Holly and I took pictures and made notes of things that I do and do not like or want. Fred wants me to be happy with my choices and claims that he doesn't care how it looks.

Fred often says, "Whatever you want will be all right with me." It must be nice to be so laid-back and casual. This attitude does not help me narrow down ideas and I doubt he will help much with the planning as I get to know better what I want.

Luckily, Holly is patient. I'm sure she works with many people like me and, best of all, she does not push her ideas or selling points like a salesperson. She treats me more like a friend who knows a great deal and wants to share.

Some homes have long staircases that curve up along the wall or centered to the front door like you see in mansions or fancy hotels in the movies. Some homes have a separate, smaller house in back that goes by different names like the mother-in-law apartment, guest bungalow or pool house. Personally, I like the idea of a library / playroom for our children. I don't know how many children we are going to have, but I am wishing for two or three.

Some homes have swimming pools, which surprised me as I had not heard that people have swimming pools in Riverton. Holly warned me about having a pool, saying "They are more trouble than they are worth" as they can only be used a few months out of the year, are lots of work to maintain summer and winter and other issues. After Holly gave me the price range for installing a basic pool, I quickly decided "No pool for us!" My decision was finalized when Fred told me that several times a year young children drown in privately owned pools throughout the state. That sealed my decision!

Not only does every master bedroom have its own bathroom, like ours, but they also have a Jacuzzi tub. It looks interesting but I can't see myself using one. When I asked Fred his opinion about having one, he said the tubs are good for the home's resale value but mostly people do not use them very much. Apparently, like with swimming pools, the tubs require lots of maintenance, cleaning and people mostly do not have time to use them.

I do want a good-sized backyard with fruit and shade trees along with a garden for herbs and cooking greens. The problem with that is how short the growing season is and how the cold will kill most of the plants I want. I like the green houses at the garage as they protect the plants, but they also take up a lot of room. I need to give more thought on this.

Anyway, I got lots of ideas and Holly has plenty of contacts for builders and architects who design these kinds of homes. When I get a clearer idea of what I want, then we can interview different firms for the project. I thanked Holly for her time and she said "Anytime you want to look at more properties, just give us a call!"

In the midst of all of this, Mama came up with the idea of offering her cousin Michael a job, or maybe even a partnership, in the reselling business once he graduated. Dad did not think it would work since Michael was such a good student that he would most likely be able to pick and choose from a variety of job offers that would certainly come his way. But, since he was family and had worked out well the summer before, Mama took the tact of one of her newer lessons in America, "If you don't ask, you won't get."

A New Business Partner

April 10, 2002
Dear My Diary,

I called Auntie Ginger and arranged to meet for lunch at her favorite restaurant. She looked so happy to see me, asked about the baby and told me how my skin had the rich glow of an expectant mother. We have not told anyone, not even our families, about my accident as we do not want to cause unnecessary worry, so I just told her how I feel and that we cannot wait to meet our new child.

After our first course of dim sum, I asked Auntie about Michael and how he is doing in school.

"Very good!" she said, happy to speak about her only son. "Very good grades and during this last year, he has earned more academic scholarship money than before. It has helped to pay for most of his school expenses." She took a bite of a crab puff and added, "Of course, I could pay for it all, but if other people want to reward my son with gifts, who am I to refuse?"

I asked if Michael has had any job offers yet and she said "Oh, yes!" but not with as much enthusiasm. "He has had several very good offers from banks and other firms, but now the offers are being cancelled or reduced in terms of pay."

"But why, Auntie?" I asked. "Did Michael do something wrong? Was it Fred's family problems getting back to the employers?"

She shook her head, "Of course not, my Niece, it is the economy. Financial institutions are laying off workers and managers from top to bottom and have frozen any new hiring. Michael has done nothing wrong. It was the greedy banks doing something wrong and it is affecting everything now."

Of course! How stupid of me not to consider this as the reason. Fred has said as much several times, but I did not connect it to Michael's job search in the business and finance industry. I said to Auntie, "I might know someone looking for a business partner...a smart, honest, hardworking person who has some experience in the field he would be working in."

Auntie's eyes brightened as she leaned forward and simply asked "Who?"

"Me! And Fred, of course." Now her face slowly spread into a big pearly smile. Auntie has a beautiful smile, and I am glad to have put this on her face.

After I explained what we are considering, she said "Oh, Michael likes you and Fred very much. He has great respect for you and...and...oh!" Emotion overcame her and Auntie sipped some tea.

Then she got on her phone, "Michael! Where are you? What are you doing? Are you hungry? Good, you are always hungry! Come down to the Golden Waterfall right now. Yes, right now. I am fine and you will be fine too if you come here. Yes. I have a very pretty woman here wanting to talk to you." Auntie winked at me as she continued, "Fifteen minutes? Ok, make hurry!" and she flipped her phone shut. "I give him twelve minutes," she predicted smugly.

"Your cousin is on Spring Break time and is home now before starting his last term." Auntie ordered the waiter to bring another chair and place-setting.

Ten minutes later, Michael made a beeline to our table, looking out of breath as he rushed over. After greeting us, he saw the table set for three and not four. "Where is the pretty woman you said wanted to speak with me?"

Auntie made a show of pointing to me, "Your cousin, of course! Do you see any other pretty women at the table?"

Michael grinned, "Only you, Me."

She took his face and kissed his cheek. "That kind of talk will get you a very nice wife one day!"

As the waiter brought more food, I told Michael of the problems we are facing and how much we admire his earlier work with us. The offer is that Michael would be an employee to start and, if everyone is happy with his progress, the job could turn into a partnership. The specifics would be worked into a contract if he was interested.

Michael admitted that he is disappointed at the job offers that had been withdrawn before he could accept. Worse yet, many of his fellow classmates who had accepted offers, have had them cancelled due to layoffs and cutbacks. Some banks are even filing bankruptcy or asking the government for assistance. This is a very tough time for new graduates.

I told him how the resale business is getting better as more people offer to sell things to our stores for food and rent money while others are buying from us to save money on things they need. "Fred says that when the economy is down, people use us to get necessities and when the good times come back, people use us to get fun things. Either way, we tend to stay busy no matter what. It's just a matter of finding and selling the right kinds of goods at the right time at the right prices."

I felt it necessary to add that Bunny is helping us right now but is not part of the partnership idea we have for him. She is learning the business fast, is energetic and has a knack for sales pitches. Michael does not know Bunny very well but has agreed to work with her.

Now that Michael understands our situation better, and is showing an interest in working with us, I called Fred and told him the, tentatively, good news. I asked Michael if he has plans for the afternoon and he said "If the plans involve talking about this more, I will give you all the time we need!"

Fred heard this over the phone and said "Good man!". By the end of the day, we had a verbal agreement about the next steps going forward towards the possibility, but not a promise, that cousin will take over a portion of the business for his own.

In the meantime, one of Fred's lawyers will draw up a formal agreement to prevent any misunderstandings and present it to Michael and Auntie for their approval. As an adult, Michael does not need his mother to go over the agreement, but as we are all family, I feel obligated to share the contract with her, let them take it to their lawyer if they wish, so no one feels like Michael is getting cheated.

Michael will spend the rest of spring break getting more familiar with what is going on, so that when he graduates, he can step in right away. His first big responsibility, sort of like a test, I guess, will be to take care of business while we are in Vietnam.

We had dinner together at home and had a very nice chat about many different things. After cousin left, Fred and I talked some more about it. The situation feels good, and Auntie is pleased, I know. Her youngest child will have a job and some of the stress of running the day-to-day affairs of the resale business will be in good hands.

Michael: I was surprised to get the phone call from my mom to meet with Cousin Kimmie about a job. Solid offers for graduates were far fewer than in previous years and I didn't have anything secured yet. I was worried, even though I knew Mom would provide me with a place to live until I got work, but I really wanted to have something ready to go by graduation.

I really liked working with Kimmie and Fred the summer before and I knew the work would be varied and loosely structured, which was appealing to me. Once I understood that they were moving away from the resale business and getting into other ventures, it was apparent that I could eventually take over most of the business as my own. Again, a very appealing idea, and not something I could have done in a large firm.

Kim mentioned that Bernice was assisting them with their online auctions and selling at Flea City as a way of earning money after what happened to Fred's brother and that she may want to continue in this way as a helper. I had met Bernice a couple of times but did not know her well. I wasn't sure if this was a good idea, but I knew Fred and Kim would not have her working with them if she was not up to their standards, so I accepted Bernice as part of the deal.

Thanh and I Have a Fight

April 21, 2002
Dear My Diary,

With all the bad things going on with Fred's family, a bad thing is also happening in the US but, according to Fred, will be good for us. Fred had explained how short-selling works to me more than once before I was able to grasp the full concept. He even showed me his accounts and the exact sequence of how he trades. It is the opposite of how he has been investing before, while still making a profit. Sell and buy back vs buy and sell.

Lois: Mama went into great detail in this section about the upcoming recession and how Dad and his business partners and friends planned to short sell a number of companies related to the housing, real estate, building and banking industries.

Fred explained how he borrows the shares from his broker for a fee, sells them and buys them back at a lower price when they drop a lot, then returning the shares to the broker.

I asked Fred if this is legal? "It sounds like you are betting the company will fail so that we can make a profit."

"Oh, it is perfectly legal, but some people find it morally wrong to make money on other people's misfortunes. Besides, Sweetheart, I would never do anything illegal and my chances of failing at this is low." Fred and his friends, including Bobby and Robbie, have lists of companies they plan to short.

"Is there *any* risk to this?" I asked.

"Only if the price of the stock goes up, and quickly. Then buying it back will cost more than I sold if for and I would lose money. But the companies we are short-selling are connected to the real estate market, and as they go down, our profits go up. Plus, I have alerts set when a company's price gets too close to the amount I am willing to lose, so I won't lose too much. See? I'm covered in both directions."

Mama got more nervous after this exchange with Thanh soon after:

I was chatting with sister on the phone and explaining what Fred is doing and she does not believe me. She said "You cannot sell something that belongs to someone else, and then buy it back for less and return it! Who would let Fred do such a thing? I have never heard of such a ridiculous plan! If he is, it must be illegal as it makes no sense."

I said, "Fred would never do anything illegal."

"Well, his brother did illegal things. Maybe cheating runs in the family and you are too stupid to see this. Everybody is losing money in the stock market now and making money from stocks that go down is a fairy tale...idiot!"

I am shocked that Thanh would not believe me and, moreover, think Fred would do something illegal, especially after he helped her out of some financial jams. I did not know how to respond to her insults so I said I had to go and hung up.

I thought and thought about it, then I called Tina who verified everything Fred told me and that even our very successful CPA friends are short selling to enrich themselves. "Like with any investment, there is risk in what they are doing," explained sister. "But it is a controlled risk. I learned about it at Columbia and saw it in action while working in New York. Set your mind at ease, Little Sister. They know what they are doing and I am doing it also."

I believe in Fred and I believe in Tina and I am not going to bother Fred about this again...he has enough troubles on his mind than to have me pestering him over my sister's ignorant rants.

Kimmie: Thanh could drive me pretty crazy with some of the things she heard from others or opinionated on without researching or asking those who had expertise. I can't tell you how many times she thought something or another was illegal, bad for the body, etc. based on gossip from customers and employees, but would not dare spend a dollar or a few minutes to learn the truth from an attorney, doctor, CPA, etc. Over the years, I had to learn to ignore the poisonous seeds she liked to sow in other people's ears.

Dear My Diary,

I decided to make another big decision in my life. It is something I have been thinking about for a while and now feel it is the right time.

My long hair takes so much time to dry and style, then I have to tie it up when I work, and now with Fierce 5 and the wigs we must wear, it is one big bunch of hair on top of another and it makes my head very hot.

Two of my Fierce 5 sisters, Bettina and Jasmin, wear what they call a Pixie Cut style and is very much like the cute boy-style, I wore in Vietnam. Malia also keeps her hair very short in the naturally tight curls of her race.

Despite my sister's previous insults, I went to the Happy Pretty salon and Thanh cut my hair very nicely and we kept to pleasant topics of conversation. It was like nothing had happened before, and I was glad.

Then, one of the customers asked me if I am a model. Thanh's face lit up to hear this question asked of me and I said "Yes, I am. For Fierce 5 energy drinks. Thank you for asking!"

Then she asked, "Why do you come here, instead of one of the high-end salons downtown?"

I saw sister's face tighten but before she could say something back, I jumped in with "Because Thanh is one of the best stylists in town. My employers like her work, the prices are reasonable and I wouldn't go anywhere else."

The look of pride on Thanh's face was priceless. Despite our differences, we are still sisters and we look out for each other.

May 1, 2002
Dear My Diary,

Bunny asked me if she could come to the auction I was attending and help with things, "Just for fun." I reminded Bunny that the work will be kind of dirty and physical like before, but she can come along if she likes. "Before we go to the auction, I want you to help me with some of the boxes we got from other auctions, and then you can see what we do with our treasures once we get them home."

Bunny changed into her grubbies and came over. On the second floor we have a big pile of boxes and bags to be gone through. I hefted a box onto one of the sorting tables, slipped a cutting ring onto my middle finger and Zip! Zip! Zip! right through the taped edges.

Bunny showed amazement at the ring which has a hooked blade. I explained how Frank had made several of them for Fred to make opening boxes faster and easier without moving and losing box cutters all the time. "That's wicked!" she exclaimed.

I put on three more rings and made kitty claw motions, saying "Fierce Five makes you feel alive! Hissss!"

Bernice: I remember when Kimmie brought me to their big storage area for the first time and showed me these wicked looking rings with hooks on them. She ripped open taped boxes like they were butter, and it was the first time she saw what was inside. I couldn't believe how quickly she could go through a box and recite what different things could be sold for and a few items she set aside for more research. She saved a lot of the boxes to reuse for shipping and sorted different kinds of things onto different storage shelves. They had a really organized system.

Kim showed me how they look things up on Ubiddit for pricing and how a lot of the stuff they were selling are being kept out of landfills, filling a need in society for recycling and saving money. She sounded just like Fred when she pitched me like that. Anyway, I had an idea I wanted to share with her and since the computer was already on, it was a good time to do it.

Bunny asked me if I ever looked at VidLive.com? I said I like to watch Vietnamese entertainers on it and have watched myself with Rock on Midnight Noise.

Bunny logged onto VidLive and found what she wanted to show me. There was a child who introduced a new toy she had bought. The young girl, about six or seven years old, showed the front and back of the box to the camera and read out loud what it said. Then she removed the toy from its packaging, showed how to play with it while telling us what she did and did not like about it and, at the end, gave it a grade based on five different faces, from a frown to a bright smile.

Bunny asked me what I thought of the video? I said, "I don't know. It's cute, but what is the point?" I wanted to get to work on opening boxes and showing Bunny how we operate, and she is showing me a video of a child describing a toy.

Bunny pointed out the number of subscribers to the child's VidLive channel (more than one-hundred thousand) and how many had watched that particular video (over twenty thousand views and it has been up less than a week). "This is all she does, Kimmie! She buys toys or companies send her toys, she makes a video review and people, especially children, all over the world watch it. She has so many subscribers and video views, that she makes money from VidLive and sponsors and gets even more free toys out of the deal."

I could tell she was impressed with this discovery, but I wasn't so sure. "Are you saying we should buy and review toys too?" She laughed and said, "That was just to show you how easy it is to get a channel started...so easy, a kid can do it. Well, the parents help too, of course."

Bunny typed something else into the computer and came up with a different video. This one was a middle-aged couple who buys pallet-sized boxes of returned products from GnG and other big retailers at auction, sight unseen. They called their channel "Treasure or Trash?" They filmed themselves pulling out and showing us, the audience, all the different things contained in this roughly one cubic meter box. Garden tools, linens, toys, hardware, kitchenware, underwear and more. Some things were in perfect condition, some had damaged boxes but the product was fine and a few of the items were chipped, scratched or had other defects.

They made lively and funny chatter while describing how much they expected to get for each item from their local flea market, Ubiddit store and monthly yard sale. At the end of the video, they used a giant paper pad and marker, outlining how much they paid for the box and shipping and how much profit they expected to make.

They encouraged viewers to email them if they wanted any of this stuff and would work out a payment and shipping arrangement through their website. The couple estimated a $400 profit from it all, which I thought was a fair estimate.

By now, I understood what Bunny was trying to show and offer me. I asked, "You want to make videos of us buying lockers and then show whatever we find inside?" She said "Bingo!"

I asked Bunny if she had heard about the TV show Treasure Hunt. She had not, so I explained how the show worked. She asked me how the buyers on the show sold their finds? "I think some of them have resale stores like we do or sell at flea markets and on Ubiddit."

Bunny said, "If we do this, we can direct the watchers to your Ubiddit site the way the pallet guy does. You could get all kinds of new business from that!"

"That sounds good, but who will handle the camera and who will do the showing and telling in front of the camera?"

"You will be in front of the camera because you are the expert and know what to say about everything."

I put my hands up, "Oh no! My English is not so good, and no one wants to see me on VidLive."

Bunny argued back, "You are going to be in a movie with Rock Rollins! You have been on late night TV, and you do interviews for Fierce 5! You make presentations with Fred for Dissolving Debt! How can you not want to go on the video?" I finally admitted that she had made some good points and agreed to be the face of our video.

Bunny has a good camera with tripod and has been practicing with it. "We can do the video together and it will be fun!"

"I don't know if this will be a good idea or a bad idea, but you make sound like a fun idea!"

"We don't even have to use our real names!" she said. "You can use Chimera. Maybe call it Chimera's Treasure Chest."

I asked, "What about my accent? Maybe people will not understand me."

"Do you have lines in the movie?"

"A few."

"Well, if they let you talk in the movie, then you can talk on our video! Besides, I understand almost everything you say. You sound great!"

I will set up a staging area for the unboxings with plenty of lighting and room to move around while Bunny sets up a VidLive account and teaches herself how to edit the videos we make. I asked how she will learn to edit and she said "Easy! There are videos on VidLive that can teach you almost anything!" But of course!

In the afternoon, Fred and I went to our pre-natal appointment with Dr. Sedaris and everything looks as it should. I am lucky never to have had morning sickness, always eat healthy foods and I take the pre-natal vitamins every day. The baby's heartbeat is normal, and they did another scan to make sure the baby is not damaged. The doctor said everything looks perfect including the head. It is the head I am most worried about, and I feel better after Dr. Sedaris reassured us.

It has been such a long day! Bunny has my mind busy with thoughts about making videos and the more I think about it, the more I think we can make it work. Bunny is a bubbly kind of person and fun to listen to. I don't know if I can be like her, but I can try, for the sake of the videos.

I don't know how to tell Fred about our idea, but I think he will like it. Also, he likes Bunny and if there is a way to help her and we benefit from it, so much the better. Besides, he is fast asleep and snoring next to me. Not a good time to tell him. He he!

Dear My Diary,

At Bunny's suggestion, I entered Kimmie Starbuckle into Knowitall. I didn't find very much: our wedding announcement, some news items talking mostly about Fred and bits that connected my name to Chimera.

Then I typed in Chimera and mostly got information about the mythological creature. Finally, I typed in Chimera Fierce Five and boom! Pictures and ads and some of the interviews I have done on TV or for newspapers and magazines. I was so surprised! I never thought of looking myself up before.

I read the comments about me or the other Fierce Five members. Some of them were very dirty, uck! But mostly were complimentary about our good looks or they can't wait to see us in the new movie or which of us is this or that person's favorite.

That gave me an idea. I opened a new Ubiddit account call "Chimera's Treasure Hunt" and emailed Bunny the link. I was very pleased until she called me and said that maybe it's not a good idea to call it "Chimera's Treasure Hunt" because it sounds too much like the TV show.

Being married to a lawyer, she understood that I might be sued for using part of the show's name and by doing so, we are trying to take advantage of their name for our own profit.

I asked, "What can we call it to make it different enough?"

"How about 'Chimera the Treasure Hunter' or 'Hunting Treasure with Chimera'? That's different enough and the word 'hunting' fits your tough-ass character."

I liked her thinking, so I changed our site name to 'Hunting Treasures with Chimera' and 'Chimera' for my official Ubiddit name.

Bunny has been practicing filming, editing and uploading sample videos to VidLive. She also wrote an introductory script for me to say at the beginning of the video and asked if we can go to an auction soon and try out our new idea? I gave her the next two dates when local auctions are taking place and we settled on next Wednesday.

I also let Bunny know about our bringing Michael into the business after graduation but did not tell her of the possible partnership we offered him. I just said that we will be gone to Vietnam for a long trip, and since he knows much of what we do already, Michael will be a big help.

When I suggested that she and Michael can work together to help us as my due date gets closer, her eyes lit up, "Oh, he's dishy!"

I'm not sure I like the sound of that, but I think between the two of them and our contacts, they will stay busy enough to pay for themselves with something left over for us.

At dinner I told Fred about our idea to make videos of the auctions, opening the lockers to describe what we find, then inviting viewers to bid on some of the treasures we are selling.

Fred thinks it is a nice idea and sounds like fun. "She can be very creative and some of her ideas might help everyone out. I will help her financially and, best of all, it will help keep her mind off Barney."

I told Fred what Bunny said about Michael and asked what "dishy" means?

Fred gave a short laugh and said, "It means, Michael had better be careful of Bunny's charms!"

May 14, 2002
Dear My Diary,

I had Bunny watch some episodes of Treasure Hunt to better understand what to expect when we go to her first live auction, then I wrote some sample things to say during the videos and Bunny cleaned up my grammar before I practiced in front of the camera. I dressed nicer for the auctions today so I can look good for the video.

We did not bid on the first two lockers as I wanted something for Bunny that we can sell easily and maybe the VidLive watchers can make a connection. We still filmed the lockers and made some comments about why we were not interested so we could lead up to the good stuff.

The first locker contained many rolls of leather and a large heavy-duty sewing machine to turn the raw material into purses, jackets and so forth. The machine would have been hard to sell and even harder to load onto the truck.

The second was smelly and moldy and no one bid on it…Ugh!

The third locker only had a few bags and boxes and I felt like no one would bid on it. I whispered to Bunny "This one".

Bunny started the camera and described what she saw in there. The auctioneer started the bids at $20, and when no one bid, she dropped it to $10, then $5 and I called out "One dollar!"

No one upped our bid and Bunny looked like an excited puppy to learn that we won a locker for a dollar.

Our second win was a small locker stacked high with boxes, suitcases, and some furniture. We paid $150 after some spirited bidding against a couple of regulars. I think two small lockers is enough to get started.

We went to each locker and filmed the opening of our "treasure chest" before opening it and reviewing what we found inside. Bunny and I already decided to treat each auction and locker as its own, individual show.

After the introduction, I explained to the audience why I bought an almost empty locker while others did not bid. I said "Some people will think it is not worth their time and energy for maybe a lot of junk, but even a few things sold will be worth the dollar invested. Sometimes good things come in little packages. Let's see if that is true today!"

Then I put on my cutting rings, showing off my kitty claw moves and hissing at the camera. I explained the purpose of the rings and took off all but one to open boxes.

There were many empty DVD and game boxes, some children's clothing and toys in good condition. Under some of the bags I found most of the missing DVD's and games on the ground. Some are scratched but most look to be in good, but not excellent, condition along with a DVD player and the game system with cords and controllers.

As I worked, I explained how much I think I can get for the different items and which ones would be sold at a flea market or on Ubiddit under my seller's name Chimera.

For the second locker, Bunny started with a close-up of me standing in front of the stack and as I spoke, she pulled back until she had me at full body with the top door edge inches from my head and the stack going up even higher. "Are they full? Are they empty? Do we have treasure or do we have trash? Come on, everybody, let's find out!"

Bunny set the camera on a tripod and I introduced "my sister in treasure hunting". She said "Hi!" while grinning and waving into the camera. Because there were so many boxes, we both took turns taking them down and pulling out a few things at a time. After a bit, I commented to the camera, "Honestly, it looks like a whole apartment's worth of stuff was moved in here."

As we lowered the wall of boxes, we uncovered a dining set, TVs, a queen bed, couch and loveseat, appliances and wall art. "Since we are not finding any toys or child-size items, I am guessing this belonged to a young couple," I observed, for the education of the audience.

Bunny asked, "Why do you think a couple would have left this all behind?"

"That's a great question, Bunny," I said. "With my experience doing these kinds of unboxings, my best guess is that one or both lost their jobs, moved back in with family and didn't have room to bring most of their stuff. They stored it and, sadly, they stopped paying on their rent and now it's up to us to find new homes for all these great items. You can see how clean and well-packed everything is. They took good care of their belongings, so all this will be very easy to sell."

"That's awesome, Chimera!" Bunny said. "Now how are we going to sell all this great stuff?"

"We have two ways for our VidLive friends to get in on some good bargains. First..."

That's when I gave directions to my Ubiddit page and what kinds of items we would expect to sell that way, "And for those of you living in or near Riverton, you will find us selling at Flea City near the old train station. Check FreePost for the exact days we will be there, then stop by our booth to browse, buy or get an autograph."

Before we left the facility, we made a general introduction that went like this: "Hi! And welcome to Hunting Treasures with Chimera! I am Chimera from Fierce 5," (holding up a can of F5, then taking a pretend sip) "and in my spare time, I like hunting treasures for fun and profit. Come with me and see how I do it! Later, you will have a chance to bid on the treasures I find thru my Ubiddit site. As a bonus, every auction winner will get a personally autographed picture," (I held up a sample picture) "as an extra thank you for your support. Let's see what we can find!" (I motion with my hand towards a group of lockers). We will use this intro for each video to keep things simple.

After we got back to the garage, Bunny and I sorted out the items to sell on Ubiddit and finished up both videos by going over each item to sell individually or in bulk lots, announcing the starting bid and wishing everyone good luck.

Two lockers and two videos, one timed at less than thirty minutes and the other ran just over an hour, because of all the stuff crammed into it. Bunny said we should not go on so long as people will change the channel if it is too long or boring. She will edit the longer one down as she thinks is best and we can check it together.

I have had something on my mind and at the end of the day, I took the chance to ask Bunny if she is going to Barney's sentencing? Her up-to-now happy face turned hard and she asked, "Are you or Fred?"

I said I am not and am pretty sure no one we know is going. "I'm sorry to ask such a painful question, but if you are going, I can go with you for moral support...if you wish."

Bunny's face softened and she gave me a hug, thanking me for the offer and adding, "If Barney is going to prison, he doesn't need me there applauding the judge."

I didn't know if she was trying to be funny, but I almost laughed once I understood her meaning.

At dinner, I asked Fred if he or his parents are going to attend court on Thursday. Fred shook his head and said, "We agreed that by not going to court, by not being there for the sentencing, we will send a message that we do not approve or support Barney and his actions." He sighed, "And we don't want to deal with the press, either. We've all had enough of that for a long time to come."

When I told Fred what Bunny said about applauding the judge, he just said, "Not bitter, is she?"

Thomas Stimson

Barney's Sentencing

May 16, 2002
Dear My Diary,

Barney was sentenced to eight years in the state prison for attempted insurance fraud. No one in the family attended the sentencing…not even Bunny. Even so, the day was a somber one for us as Fred and I caught up on our own projects, each lost in our respective thoughts.

Fred said that Barney got a lighter sentence and was only charged with one crime because he confessed and cooperated with the police and FBI, did not commit a violent crime and they were able to catch Brad Luzerk with his help and recover much of the money. If he had fought the charges, it would have gone a lot worse against him.

The courts also decided that Barney was, in part, a victim of the scammer. That is, they understood that he was not directly trying to sell the island to his clients, but was still very much at fault for not doing his due diligence as an attorney to make sure the land deal was legitimate and in his clients' best interest.

But because Barney had Luzerk make the contract out for $6M that included Barney as a partner without disclosing to his partners that he was not putting any cash or property into the deal, the court determined his actions were misleading and fraudulent and for that, as well as the insurance fraud conviction, his law license is permanently revoked. Fred said the chances of his brother being able to practice law anywhere in the country after this "are less than zero".

Barney will also be required to repay the victims half of the money that was not recovered, plus fines and legal fees. Brad Luzerk is expected to be given the same requirement at his sentencing.

The victims still have the right to sue Barney in civil court for even more damages if they wish to do so, which means Barney may have to go to court again.

I don't know if Brad knows that Barney is his son. Neither the names Starbuckle or Bartlett would mean anything to Brad and Maggie's maiden name was McGillicuddy when she was in college.

I asked Fred what will happen to Barney when he gets out of prison? Like, what kind of work could he do and where would he live?

Fred said, "I don't know and I don't care…that's a long way down the road from now. Barney made the mess so he will need to deal with it himself."

From the Riverton Review, May 17, 2002: Local attorney Bernard Bartlett, formerly Barnabus Starbuckle, was sentenced to eight years in prison for attempted insurance fraud. Bartlett had pleaded guilty and waived his right to a hearing after attempting to sell an exotic car to federal agents with the stated intent to report it stolen afterwards and collect the insurance fees along with profits of the sale of the car to unspecified foreign buyers.

Federal law enforcement officers conducted a sting operation after a tip from an anonymous source and uncovered not only the intended insurance fraud but also Bartlett's involvement in a land sale scheme involving prominent Riverton couple Peter and Nellie Nelson and recent lottery winner Nicholas Vamkros. The fraud, which Bartlett claimed to be an unwitting victim, involved the purchase of Duck Island in Riverton Central Park as a site for a business development.

Criminal charges in that case have been dropped in exchange for information leading to the arrest of mastermind Brad Luzerk and an agreement to repay the victims plus fines and court costs. In addition, Bernard Bartlett has had his license to practice law permanently revoked. Members of Bartlett's family have been noticeably absent from all court proceedings and have refused comment to the press.

Prior to sentencing, Bartlett, 39, read a statement in court expressing remorse and taking responsibility for his actions with personalized apologies to the Nelsons and Mr. Vamkros. Only Mr. Vamkros was in court along with legal representatives for the Nelsons who made no public comment on the sentencing.

Mr. Vamkros said he forgave Mr. Bartlett and does not intend to pursue civil damages as he feels that the losses he has suffered will never be repaid, even with a court ordered judgment. Mr. Vamkros summarized his feelings: "I don't trust lawyers anymore."

Dear My Diary,

We had a get-together meeting today with Bunny and Michael. Michael wore khakis and a polo shirt and Bunny wore a light cotton dress with a floral pattern and high-heeled sandals. It's hard not to smile too broadly as Bunny looks dressed more for a date than to meet a new coworker. After all, she is almost twice Michael's age.

When I try to look at Michael through the eyes of another woman, I can see what a good-looking young man he is. I don't know if he would be considered "eye candy", but he is attractive, confident and smart as well as a gentleman. Add to that, Bunny is a lonely woman who had been in a loveless marriage for a long time, but I don't think she is interested in getting a new man right away. I think Michael falls into a good middle ground for Bunny...easy on her eyes but understanding that he will not want to be pursued by this older woman.

Fred ran the meeting, bringing Michael up to speed on the current events of the business. We showed him clips of the videos Bunny has been making and he is impressed with what she has done so far. Maybe they can keep doing the videos without me, or use me sometimes when I am available. They are also encouraged to find new ways to buy and sell that we have not tried yet.

Bunny brought some books from the library about collectables and antiques with the goal of learning more about some of the older and more interesting things that we find and what can bring in the most money. When Michael agreed that the books are a good idea and that he will also do extra research, Bunny look pleased that her idea is being taken seriously. So very unlike the last man she was dealing with.

The meeting went well and we shared more information about our expectations. We reminded Bunny and Michael that they will need to work out their differences and how to divvy up the duties that are to be done together or separately, as skills, effort, and time demand.

Bunny has accepted to work full time for a salary and a percentage of the weekly profits. She can stay in her house rent free and if all goes well, we can consider a contracted partnership. For Michael, we made the same business arrangement to start after graduation, and he can live at the garage rent free once we move out. Bunny and Michael exchanged phone numbers and emails, and they will take care of our resale business while we are in Vietnam…that will be their first test.

Fred and I made our own private plans for how the partnership will work. We will determine a buy-in fee for each that can be taken out of their share of profits until we are paid in full and we believe an even three-way profit split is fair since we are providing them free rent and they will continue to use the garage for working as is done now.

We feel good to have them both join us, and Auntie will be pleased as well. Her youngest child will have a job and Bunny can help build her income with hard work and clever ideas in a new job she thinks is fun.

Letter from Prison

May 22
Dear My Diary,

I picked up the mail yesterday and Fred got a letter from the State Prison. The hand-written address is unevenly spaced and a bit crooked like that of a young child. I think this is the first time I have seen Barney's actual handwriting.

I gave the letter to Fred who took one look at it and just threw it in the trash like it was junk mail. I was stunned at his callous action but did not say anything, wondering why he is not the tiniest bit curious or concerned about its contents. As close as Fred and I are to each other, I know better than to ask why he did this. Simply put, Fred is sick of everything concerning his brother.

After we went to bed, I told Fred the baby is kicking me too much so I will drink some warm milk to settle the child. Once Fred began snoring, I pulled the letter out of the trash. Fred may not be interested, but I am. The writing is hard to read, but here is what it says:

May 18th, 2002
Dear Fred,

I don't know if you heard but I was sentenced to serve eight years in the state pen. Afterward, I will have to repay a shitload of money, more than I can ever possibly earn, even if I can get my law license back, which I won't. I was never a very good lawyer to start with, which is how I got into this mess in the first place.

I am not asking for sympathy. Nobody came to my hearings and I get the reason loud and clear.

I am not asking for forgiveness. That went out the window when the folks lost their house and business on account of me.

And I am not asking for any kind of help, because I know you won't give it to me anyway. I think the only smart thing I did was to tell the truth like you said. Confess and act damned sorry for what I did.

And I am that…sorry for what I did. Really. Not just because I got caught, but because I hurt people who did not deserve to get hurt. The Nelsons and Mr. Vamkros were nice people who really believed what I had to offer, because I believed it myself. I was just too greedy and lazy to look deeper into what was being offered and seeing it for the scam that it was.

Bernice divorced me double-quick and I don't blame her. She did not deserve what she got either. I don't know what she is doing for money or a job, but she is smart and scrappy enough to make it on her own.

I know she likes your wife and thinks a lot of her. Maybe they can stay friends, but even if they don't, could you keep an eye out for Bernice and make sure she is okay?

I hear the Luzerk guy may spend the rest of his life behind bars because he's old and has a long rap sheet. I might be here the rest of my life too if I don't survive this sentence.

This is a tougher place than the city jail and a lot of guys here have been in and out of prison since they were juveys. I am already being messed with and tested to see how tough I am. And I'm not tough.

Not at all. I thought I was, but I'm not.

I don't expect a reply and if I never hear from you again, I understand. I really am sorry for everything and hope you and Kim have a long and happy marriage. By the way, congratulations on your impending parenthood. May your children be better citizens than I ever was.

B. B.

I read the letter over and over again, his words burning into my brain. Quietly, I took the trash out to the dumpster but am keeping the letter hidden in one of my VN novels as Fred never looks at them.

If he changes his mind and looks for the letter, it is gone with the trash. I don't know if Barney is really as sorry as he says, but he made prison sound like he is a mouse in the middle of a bunch of hungry cats.

I will not say anything to anybody but will see if someone else gets a letter from Barney. If he wrote to Fred, he will certainly write to his parents and maybe Bunny.

Now I am wide-awake, knowing something that Fred does not know and does not want to know.

Troi oi!

May 29
Dear My Diary,

Bunny posted the videos to VidLive three days ago and the next day we posted the auctions to Ubiddit with a stack of autographed Chimera photos ready to go into each package. Cam and Tam called me today with excitement in their voices. It seems the twins make regular internet searches for their auntie and 'other famous celebrities' and today they found my videos and recognized Bunny as my helper. They think it is "so cool".

I thanked the girls and gave Bunny credit for the idea of making the videos. The girls begged me to come to the flea market and see how it looks. I said "If it is okay with your mother, we can all go together. But it will have to be for the whole day as I can't drop everything and take you home if you get bored."

"We won't get bored!" they said together, then giggled.

Bunny told me that she got a letter from Barney saying he was sorry for hurting her and everyone else and that she did not deserve someone like him. What she told me sounded very much like the letter I read, but of course I did not tell her this. "He told me that I was smart and would do better on my own without him than I ever did with him," she said, adding bitterly "Yeah, no shit, Sherlock."

She went on, "Funny, he never told me before that I was smart. He liked to tell me I was nothing without him, but I always knew better. Now that we're divorced, he's singing a different tune. Go figure, right? He didn't tell me that he loved me or anything. Not that I care, but yeah, I feel good about what you and me are doing and I want to learn more about the business. One day I want to be my own boss, you know?"

I told her she is a good student of what we do and I have every reason to believe she will find much success. She squeezed my hand and said "Thanks, Kimmie. That means a lot to me." And I felt good to tell her. Especially as I really believe it too.

Dear My Diary,

I have visited with two of the biggest custom-home contractors in the state...the ones who have their fingerprints all over Honeywood Heights, Admiral's Row and other upscale neighborhoods. They require so many details of what I have in mind for my new home, meaning, I have to know what I want. The problem is that I have never paid much attention to the style of houses anywhere before and American homes are so much different from Vietnamese homes. Back home, the houses are tall and thin because the land underneath is very expensive so there is not much room for a variety of styles.

Here, houses can be spread out on one level or two, with or without basement. Rooms can be open or partitioned from each other. These are the kinds of questions I am expected to know: Do I want the exterior to be wood, stone, stucco, brick or a combination? Colonial, Craftsman, Cape Cod, Split-level, Ranch, Manor or Farm Style? What kind of cabinets, windows, frames, blinds, counter tops, floors, faucets, lighting, colors, textures? The type of this, style of that, color schemes of everything.

I am still dizzy from all the questions. I have already looked at many houses with the Wood sisters and they are all very nice, but soon different features are all mixed up in my mind. They show me samples, pictures, layouts. They explain the differences between styles and how they can make combinations, variations and other kinds of tions. How do people make all these decisions?

The architects explained how most people who want a custom-built home spend hundreds of hours poring through specialty magazines, books and catalogs, touring other homes, visiting furniture stores, specialty shops and, I suspect, fortune-tellers and self-styled experts, before putting together lists of ideas for the architect.

When I talk to Fred about his own ideas of what he would like in a home, he is of zero help. He is happy with the garage, or an apartment or maybe just a floor with a mattress. He said, "I don't care what our home looks like, as long as you are happy."

I will not be happy if I have to spend hundreds of hours researching every detail and costs of the details and the time it takes to order and build or install those things. I think it will take me years to build a home and hope it looks good when it is finally finished.

A good architect can create pictures of my ideas and how it might look when finished, but a picture can't really give a true representation. It's like the difference between seeing and ordering a dress from a catalog and going to the store, picking out the dress and trying it on. At the store, you can see and feel the dress and determine right there "Does it fit right? Is the fabric comfortable and hang right? Is the color pleasing or the pattern too busy?"

When I talked more to Holly about my difficulties in choosing details, she said some people take years to create a "dream home" or I can pick one of the contractor's ready-made designs as a starting point, then adding, subtracting or modifying features as desired.

I don't know what I want or how to put it all together. Now I wish Fred had not given me the property.

May 31, 2002
Dear My Diary,

Troi oi! I can't believe how active the bidding has gotten on our Chimera Ubiddit site! Bunny is hopping up and down with excitement, saying it is because I am a celebrity and people can brag to their friends about how they got this or that from Chimera and have an autographed picture to prove it.

Bunny asked if we can sell the furniture on Ubiddit too instead of at the flea market? I told her that it is expensive and impractical to ship the couch, bed or dining table so we would be better off to sell them through FreePost.

I told Bunny how this kind of bidding is not the norm from what Fred and I see on our own site so she should not expect these kinds of high bids all the time. The auctions end in two days and most items are bid up several times their normal going prices.

Bunny kept saying "Hot damn! Hot damn!" at all the high bids for what are very ordinary things. We are packing everything today in anticipation of the auction's close. I also announced on FreePost that Chimera will be at Flea City this weekend selling a variety of merchandise and signing autographs.

Cam and Tam will join us as they are now eleven years old and can be good helpers. When it's slow, they can explore the flea market, but only together. It will be more fun than staying at the salons all day, as they often do now.

June 3, 2002
Dear My Diary,

I could not believe how busy we were this weekend. Cam and Tam came with us on Saturday to help with the set up and we brought folding camp chairs for the slow times, but by Saturday afternoon we sold out of almost everything that we were not selling on Ubiddit.

After an urgent call, Fred showed up with more things from storage to sell to keep the momentum going. I let Bunny know that the proceeds from our personal inventory will not be split with her, but I will give her some money anyway, like as wages, for her help and she said "I'm cool with that". I like that line.

Many young men and women came to our booth wanting to get an autographed picture, take a photo with me and buy something from our tables. Sometimes I would see a mother or father nearby pretending to look at things while their child met a "celebrity".

Some people were disappointed that I was not in full costume and make-up but I made sure to have short conversations and ask questions of the fans so they felt liked and appreciated and could walk away happy. I may not feel like a celebrity, but I am beginning to see the power it can have, and it makes me feel good about myself.

The twins helped with selling and keeping the tables in order. They giggled sometimes at the cute boys who came around and shared their observations with each other in Vietnamese so they would not be understood. It amused, and sometimes disturbed me, to hear them talking that way because they are only eleven! Hanging around the shops with women who gossip all day, their mother included, does not help. Still, I will keep what I hear to myself...it's safer that way.

I made sure to tell the fans about the Fierce 5 team having a part in the new Rock Rollins movie. Bunny filmed some of the fans meeting with me or buying our wares and giving a thumbs up to the camera. Bunny wants to add this footage to our VidLive channel to encourage our sales and show my popularity with the fans. Bunny always asks permission first before she starts filming and nobody said "No" to her request all day and we tell them to check our site often for new videos.

Bunny has a real talent for selling and chatting up the customers, saying things like "That's a great CD, I have it in my collection!" or "You totally rock that shirt!" holding it up to the person's chest. Bunny has always been an outgoing person and it is very good for sales. Many of the younger customers buy this or that from her suggestions and seem happy with their purchases. She is, how to say, charmingly pushy. I can see this partnership idea being a good thing for us.

I gave the twins five dollars each for helping us and they went off together to explore the market. They came back later with caramel-corn, cute hair clips and many stories of what they saw, meeting up with a school friend and so on.

Later in the day Robin Ryan, the owner, came over and remarked how popular I am. People she had not seen before came in asking for the Chimera booth. At first, she was not sure who they meant, but when they showed her my picture from a magazine, even with the heavy makeup, she recognized me and gave them our booth number. She did not know that I am a Fierce 5 model but she does know that I am the only tall Asian woman in the flea market.

On Sunday, Fred and I kept the Chimera meet-and-greet opportunity alive by bringing in things from storage that we think will be good selling to my fans and I brought many more pictures too!

Bunny came along as I told her that she is good for business and I like her selling-style. She said, "I like to be around people and didn't get chances like this with Barney. It's like a new kind of freedom and I get a real buzz doing it.

Fred asked, "Are you sure it is not the Fierce 5 talking?"

She giggled, "Well, maybe some of that too!"

In the end, we split all the sales with Bunny as Fred said she worked very hard to make a good day of selling, and I agree.

Cousins Cam and Tam both had fond memories of going to the flea market and helping Mama and Aunt Bunny during the time they were selling there. Tam is still a big fan of yard sales and flea markets for vintage clothes, jewelry and reading material.

Tam: Aunt Kimmie's life was so different from our parents, always doing cool things and buying and selling interesting stuff. Not like spending all day in a salon gossiping about the customers and each other. All you had to do was ask a seller "What's this?" and "How does it work?" or "Why would someone want that?" and they would often be able to tell you the history, the mechanics, the reasons people would want to buy it and then offer it to us for a discount. I've learned a lot from going to flea markets, garage sales and auctions about all kinds of things. I've learned so much that my garage and attic are full to bursting with things I had to have.

June 4th, 2002
Dear My Diary,

The auctions closed Sunday night and my estimate of what we might get was very low. We made triple or more with many watchers and bidders on most of the items. My arm will be sore from autographing so many pictures, he he!

Bunny said we got several tens of thousands of views on each video. I guess a lot of people are doing searches of my character name and when they find a new thing, like the videos, people want to see it and tell other friends and fans.

We made over $1700 in sales from $151 cost of goods. I taught Bunny how to do the spreadsheet for Ubiddit and she asked me when we can do this again, as it was so much fun. If this is the kind of money we are making because people want to buy used things from a celebrity, it will be a very profitable business!

Humble to a fault, Mama never liked to call herself a celebrity, even with all the work and appearances she has done over the years and all the goodwill she has generated from it.

Appointment for Green Card Interview

Dear My Diary,

Today we got an appointment notice for my Permanent Resident interview. Lucky for us, the date is just after we get back from Thao's wedding. I am nervous about it, but Fred says the interview "will be a piece of cake". I sure hope so…the Barney issue still weighs on my mind.

Michael's Graduation

June 6, 2002

Dear My Diary,

Yesterday we celebrated Michaels' graduation from Prairie State University, about an hour's drive from Riverton. It has a well-respected business degree program like Riverton University's, but Auntie wanted Michael to live far enough away to force some independence on him, instead of taking it easy by living at home. "To help Michael grow up and solve his own problems like getting up in time for classes!" Auntie joked with us. "Close enough to visit but far enough away to live his own life."

A few thousand students graduated with a main ceremony at the football stadium and then smaller ceremonies for the individual colleges. Michael looked so handsome in his cap and gown! My own graduating class had less than one hundred students. So different!

We sat with Auntie, cousins, and their children, catching up on family news, about our newest family member and the visit we will making to Vietnam for Thao's wedding.

We don't know what their plans are regarding children. Thao is kind of old, maybe, to get pregnant but Auntie and cousins said that with good health and balanced nutrition she should be able to have a few more good baby years. We will see. I will ask her about this when we get together.

After it was all over and many photos taken and congratulations made to our newest graduate, we packed some things from Michael's dorm into our van and drove it all back to Auntie's house.

I could not believe how much time we spent in traffic! Fred explained how the university is the main employer of this otherwise small town. Whenever the school year starts or finishes or has a long break, thousands of students and their parents arrive and depart by the local highways which are not big enough to handle these short-term migrations.

When we got to Auntie's, we dropped everything off and met up at the Golden Waterfall for a private celebration with many gifts. We gave Michael a high-quality PDA to help with his new job, appointments, keeping track of mileage and many other features.

We didn't tell Mike, but we found this one still sealed in the box at Riverton University during Winter Break...right there in the donation box! It sells for $200 new, but we kept it aside for Michael's graduation present. Which makes me think...do the parents of the person who donated the PDA wonder if their child is still using it, or why they don't see it around? I imagine it was a gift or purchased for the start of school, and the student never even opened the box...such a shame for them and a score for us.

We invited Bunny to the dinner so she can meet with Michael and his mother again before they start working together on Monday. Bunny was in a great mood after making $400 at the flea market today. She emptied her garage, loaded up her car with tools and holiday decorations and sold what was left to another wholesaler before packing up in the early afternoon.

Thomas Stimson

Heartbeats and Hiccups

Dear My Diary,

This week Michael and Bunny are working together for the first time. We visited all the resale stores, met with the owners or general managers, and explained how we are letting them take over the bulk of the resale business while we go on holiday and spend time with our new baby.

They have all met Michael and Bunny in the past and understand we are going through some changes, but I assured them that the quality of the goods and level of service will not decline.

Bunny took detailed notes about the stores, the computer system, times certain things need to be done, etc. while Michael can remember lots of details with minimal note-taking. Aunt Ginger has this same skill, so I think it runs in the family.

Bunny and I have filmed a number of videos in the last few weeks to prepare for VidLive viewings and Ubiddit auctions, but not for the flea markets as I will not be there as regularly as before.

In the time since Barney went to prison, I've seen such a change in Bunny as I would not have expected. She's lost weight, got a new hairstyle, courtesy of Thanh who gave Bunny one on the house as a kind of celebratory gift. She calls it "short and sassy" and I had to look up the word to understand it. The dictionary says "lively, bold, and full of spirit". Yes, that certainly suits Bunny and her hair these days and it looks good on her.

It's been a lot of work packing four suitcases and carry-ons for the trip. Fred helps of course, but men are simple when they pack. A few shirts, a few long and short pants, underwear, socks and they're "all done!" in less than fifteen minutes and one suitcase. I reminded him to pack some nice clothes for the wedding, dinners out and the like and then I need to check his things for holes, stretched out necklines and nothing too tight or baggy.

For myself, I have to coordinate my outfits with shoes to match, purchase gifts for everyone and leave room in Fred's second suitcase to bring gifts back for the baby.

Fred has made the short-selling process automatic and easier to manage so he has more time to pay attention to me and help with planning.

I will tell you a cute story, My Diary: Sometimes as we lay in bed, Fred or I will lay hands on my belly and we feel this "bump, bump, bump" under the skin. It is very rhythmic. Sometimes we feel it and sometimes not. We ooh and aah over the baby's heartbeat and make love talk to our child who will soon be here with us.

It is all very sweet…until we went to the New Parent's class at the community center. There, we learned that the baby's heartbeat cannot be felt through the many layers of skin and fluids. What we are actually feeling is the baby's hiccups. HICCUPS! How does a baby have hiccups when it's surrounded by water? Anyway, that is what the teacher told us, and we have to believe it, but now it is not as romantic as before.

Dear My Diary,

I finally found the answer to my big headache about how to have a house built in Honeywood Heights: I won't.

After filling my head with so much information and ideas and variations of those ideas about how to build and decorate a house, something I had read somewhere began to tickle my brain. Tickle, tickle, tickle. What was it? I went back to The Blue Collar Millionaire and found what my memory is trying to tell me.

Chapter four explained how most self-made millionaires do not try to build a house from the ground up but look for existing homes in the neighborhoods they like and purchase one in very good condition, perhaps needing minimal repairs and touch-ups. But what they won't do is waste a lot of time and money designing a home, chasing after the contractors to complete the work, haggling over building code regulations and facing mounting costs that come with the unwanted surprises contractors have a knack for discovering.

I feel so much better now...but I also feel that I wasted so much time trying to understand everything about designing and building a house. I don't want to impress people, just be comfortable and in a good neighborhood where our children can be happy and safe.

June 10, 2002
Dear My Diary,

We have been so busy since arriving in Vietnam. Journalists have been calling my cell phone and parent's house from different newspapers, magazines and TV/radio stations. They want to interview me about what I do in America as a model and actress and how do I feel about returning home? Questions like "When will Fierce 5 be sold in Vietnam?" and "What is Rock Rollins really like?"

My question to them is, "How do you know about me?" and they say "Our sources tell us…" "We heard from others that…." "We saw the news from Hollywood…" and similarly vague answers. I generally do the interview right over the phone, often in front of amused and impressed family members. I have done enough of these in America, so I have easy answers to the questions they most often ask.

At breakfast this morning, one of the celebrity magazines had me featured on the cover, using a picture cropped from a Fierce 5 ad along with an article about me further in. I do not think I spoke to this magazine, but the article quoted two of our neighbors saying what good friends they are with me, how nice and pretty I am, and they always knew I would have great success in America. These neighbors have never been friends and often made fun of me. Suddenly they are my best friends?

I showed Fred the magazine and explained what it said about me, kind of complaining about it and about all the phone calls and requests for interviews.

"Have you ever been on the cover of a magazine?" Fred asked.

It was not a question I expected of him and thought for a moment. "No, not even with the group."

"Then I think this is your first magazine cover," Fred pointed out. "That's a big deal…a really big deal for anyone. You should be proud, and I will even frame this for you. As for the rest of it, the remarks are harmless and makes for good copy. At least they are saying nice things about you and nothing bad."

"But I wonder how the press knew about me and my life in America and that I would be here now?" I did not expect an answer, but I got one anyway.

"I told the press." Thao had said little this morning until now. I am shocked at her words. "I am sorry if this upset you, Little Sister."

I said, "I am not so upset as puzzled as to how the local press knew about my side-work in America and why would they want to write about me? Why did you tell them? I am a nobody."

Fred stayed quiet as the conversation unfolded in English for his benefit. Thao explained, "I have watched my sweet-natured little sister be disrespected and made fun of for too many years. Now that you have become a kind of celebrity in America, as small as it may be to you, I wanted to share the news of your good fortune in such a way that the neighbors and our employees will treat you differently…with the happiness and enthusiasm and respect as you did not get before. You are not a nobody, Kimmie. You have always been a somebody."

Fred wrapped his arm around my shoulder in a half-hug, "Like I am always telling you, Sweetheart. You're just too modest to accept it."

Sister continued, "I shared the news clippings and VidLive sites you sent to us so the press would have someone new to talk about…a new rising star in American entertainment from Vietnam. They are hungry for nice, new things to write about, so why not you? When they call the office asking after you, I paint a flattering picture about what you are doing, how proud we are and the good luck you have could not happen to a nicer person. I hope you are not upset with me."

By now, tears have formed at the corners of my eyes and I don't know what to say. I am surprised and pleased that Thao made such an effort to help me make a better face to everyone. And I feel stupid and ungrateful for complaining about it in the first place.

Fred said, "Thao, that is one of the nicest things I ever heard of someone doing. Believe me, Kimmie has earned everything she got. She works hard and everyone really, really likes her."

Thao smiled and said, "Can the press quote you on that?"

Fred laughed, "As much as they want!" Then he turned to me, "How can anyone be upset with her sister after an explanation like that?"

I agree, it was a very sweet thing for Thao to do and I will not complain anymore about this. I also understand that the good press I get today will help me tomorrow. I said to Thao, "There is one thing missing from all of this."

"What is it?"

"It was Fred that got me started with Fierce 5 and encouraged me to accept this type of work. After that, it blossomed like a pond of lotus. He is the reason for my success."

Fred spoke up, "I just planted the seed. Your hard work and dedication made the blossoming possible."

I hugged Thao and said "You are one of my many blessings and I am proud you are my big sister."

"The whole family is very proud of you too…and they know that Fred is your biggest fan."

"Hear, hear!" said Fred enthusiastically.

I am so lucky to have a sister like Thao!

Dear My Diary,

This is Cam and Tam's first time in Vietnam, and it is SO different for them. Ho Chi Minh City is very active and noisy with motorbikes and cyclos everywhere and every meter of the streets are packed with stores, homes and people selling goods and services from the sidewalks. Not like Riverton where things are more spread out and slower paced.

Thanh has been gone a long time and is too nervous to drive anything having less than four wheels, so Thao gave both girls a ride on her motorbike through the city, one in front and one behind like a sandwich. They could not stop laughing and talking about how scary and fun it was. We said traffic is like this all the time and sometimes worse! Later we will give them a ride in a cyclo as they are very popular with the tourists.

We took them to our neighborhood market to buy food for today's meals and is not at all like GnG or SuperFoods. Here, you need to bargain and chat with the sellers. The girls did not like it when their mother chose a big fish for dinner from a barrel. The seller whisked the catfish out of its temporary home, clubbed it while the animal thrashed about and expertly gutted it before wrapping it in newspaper and smilingly presented it to Cam.

The girls' faces were filled with disgust and they refused to touch the package. We told them that this is the way of many other countries too…and we know the fish is perfectly fresh for cooking. We did not take Fred as the prices will magically go up when they see a foreigner in the family. Sorry Fred!

Cam Nguyen: The time we had in Vietnam was so surreal for us. We heard all about it growing up, how great it is, how good the food is and so on. But until you can actually see it, smell it and hear it, you can't appreciate how really different it is from anywhere in the US.

I imagine when Mom came to Riverton, how slow-paced and dull it was in her new country, compared to HCMC. Same goes with knowing how fresh many of the foods are when the growers are not there to tell you or seeing how healthy the animal is before you pick it out and take it home or have the seller prepare it in front of you. I STILL remember the fish seller conking a fish in the head with a wooden club. It was sudden and quite jarring when you are not expecting it.

One of the children in the neighborhood asked Tam if she had some American money he could see. She handed him a dollar and he ran off so quick we could not catch him…that was the last time we let someone pull that trick on us!

The girls do not read or write well in Vietnamese but they understand everything and speak with a very nice accent. Everyone is praising Thanh on how well they speak and related stories of first-generation Vietnamese children living in the West who refuse to learn the language.

Fred does not get praised. We have not practiced very much and he can just say a few simple words and phrases. I have a hard enough time with the expressions, slang and cultural references that go "whoosh!" over my head.

Tam and Cam have a good time speaking to the neighborhood children, cousins and other family and their behavior earns nice comments from everyone. Thanh could not be prouder of her daughters and, I think because of that, her own behavior is less sharp here than at home. I am so glad for that!

Vo has also been on his best behavior about drinking alcohol. When I see him being offered beer or wine, he always turns it down, though I see some desire for it in his eyes.

This is Vo's first time back since he met our family and became engaged with Thanh, about fifteen years ago, I think. His family lives in the Central Provinces but I don't think they will go to visit this time. Vo and Thanh have never taken a vacation together because they are so busy running the salon, now two salons! But I am glad the whole family has come to visit Me and Ba and the girls can see where their Me and aunties grew up.

Some of the people ask me if American women are as tall as me? I tell them that they are mostly taller than our women here, about halfway between VN women and my size.

As I pay more attention, I see many younger generation VN men and women are taller than their parents. Better nutrition is the biggest reason, I think, compared to the time during and after the war.

Dear My Diary,

Before we came, I asked Fred if I can make some donations to help my countrypeople? He said "Of course, Sweetheart! That's one of the good things about money, you can help yourself and you can help others as well. I feel good that Fred is frugal but not cheap. A cheap man will not help others with his money, but a frugal man will spend wisely to help those in need.

I took Fred to the temple near our home and explained to him how my family, and others in the area, have made contributions to grow the temple and raise money for food, clothes, medicine and other needs for the poor and sick of our district. I have told him about this before, but now I give him fresh words so he can see and understand for himself exactly what I have been telling him.

Once we entered the temple, we burned joss sticks and made prayers. I do not know what Fred has prayed for but I made thanks for the many blessings I have in my new life with Fred, the health of my growing baby, protection for my family, Fred's family and all our close friends.

Then we met with the high-ranking monk and leader of the temple. He knows my family very well and I told him something of my life in America and what a kind and loving husband Fred is. Fred heard his name and smiled and nodded and the monk smiled and nodded back. I asked him if there is any program or special needs that we can contribute towards?

He said "There are so many more orphans now than years before. After 1975 the old money became worthless, many government employees and officials were arrested as spies and sent to re-education camps and everyone else who could not escape the country were thrown into poverty. Many children were abandoned and left without anyone to care for them.

"As our country rebuilt and became economically stronger, there became many fewer orphans as parents had money to feed the children they had. But now, because of growing drug addictions and the loose morals of young women and men, there has been an increase of abandoned children whose mothers are either in jail or seek the pleasures of the needle over that of their offspring. Many grandparents cannot, or will not, raise the children of unmarried addicted daughters. It is a both a burden and a shame to have such a dilemma, so that is where we have our greatest need."

I translated all this to Fred as we walked three streets over from the temple to a large building that I remember used to be a high school. Thao and Trinh went here before they closed down and opened a larger, more modern school.

We all went in and the monk gave us a tour. Different classrooms are used for the sleeping quarters of different aged children, so infants are in one area, toddlers in another and etc. The rooms are painted in bright colors with pictures of animal, trees and pretty things.

It is also very loud and very hot. The walls are of concrete causing noise to be amplified rather than absorbed. There is no air conditioning and many windows are broken with no money to replace them. The more we looked, the more Fred wrote things in a notebook. We stopped and spoke to the children and caretakers. The older children have school here, but few books. Many other children cannot learn well because of being born with addictions from their mothers or infected with STD's at birth and other problems that complicate caring for them.

Most people do not want to adopt diseased, addicted or mentally ill children, the preference and the highest fees go for healthy and attractive children. There is very little government money to help orphans and when people make big donations to the temple, they often request the money to be used for a new statue or gold decorations or silk carpets to make the temple pretty, things they can point to and say, "I bought that for the temple!" but, as the monk said, "You can't eat a statue and you can't cure illness with a silk carpet. The orphanage is our most pressing need but gets the smallest amount of donations."

We thanked the monk leader for his time and praised him for the work they are doing. I said, "We have made many notes and will meet with you again with what we can offer."

He said "You look to be a happy couple with peace in your hearts. Your children will be much blessed."

I relayed this to Fred and he smiled, bowed to the monk and said "Cam on nhieu lam".

This was the beginning of a very long and fruitful relationship with the local temple and their orphanage. At the time they visited, there were about two-hundred children being served and many others in the neighborhood were cared for during the day for the parents who wanted to work but had no dependable childcare so there were many children in and out of the facility at any given time.

Cousin Ca

Dear My Diary,

One of Me's sisters, Auntie Duc, came to visit with her daughter Ca. I do not know Ca very well but I remember her as having a sweet nature and she never teased me about my height. Auntie spent much time telling us how good Ca is with children and the elderly and how she wants to go to nursing school, but it is so sad she can't attend for lack of funds.

Auntie asked me if we have a maid or nanny to help care for the baby? I told her we do not have servants as is not common in American families but she countered that many rich people and entertainers have cooks, nannies and drivers.

When I said "We are not rich, nor are we entertainers," she said "Oh, I know better! Your mother told me and showed me the videos that you work with Rock Rollins, do modeling and starred in a movie. A busy woman like you needs a competent and trustworthy nanny for the baby and who better than a member of your own family?"

I told her one baby is not such a burden and I thanked her for thinking of me in this way.

I have not heard cousin talk about wanting to be a nurse, but I did watch her play with the younger children, telling them a nice story and gently broke up a fight between a boy and a girl, making one apologize to the other and giving a hug afterward. All this was done with a kindness that one rarely sees in adults. And despite Auntie's boasts of Ca's fluency in English, I quickly discovered that she is limited to a few simple words and phrases.

When we were alone, I asked Fred if we need a nanny so we can help Ca get into an American nursing school. He said that we don't need anyone, especially as we are still at the garage and have not made progress with building a home in Honeywood Heights.

I began carefully, "I don't know how to say this so as not to hurt your feelings, but I am not in love with the idea about living there anymore." Fred's eyebrow lifted in surprise as I pushed on, "I know it is getting very cheap to build a home now, but every time I think about all the details and decisions we need to make, then buying all new furniture, decorations and appliances, it gives me a big headache."

I put both hands to my head to emphasize the point and Fred chuckled sympathetically. "I don't want to raise children in the garage, but Honeywood Heights is too much in the other direction." I put my hands on his broad shoulders, "I love that you gave me the land and a chance to build a dream home in a dream neighborhood, but I would prefer something more...in the middle. Please don't be mad at me." I batted my eyes like a movie vamp, hoping to get his sympathy and a laugh. It worked.

"How can I be mad at my little Kimmie when she opens up to me?" Fred took me in his arms and kissed me long and tenderly. "I want you to find the perfect home for us anywhere you like, my love. Whatever you pick will be perfect for me too."

I am so glad Fred is giving me his blessing to follow my heart. Speaking of which, Fred is purposely moving away from buying and selling household goods and towards bigger investment projects using his newly minted profits. He has a good head for business and lots of experienced friends to guide and support him.

Now that the worry about building a home is no longer an issue, I pushed about how I will care for our child, if I take over the resale side of our company. Even with Michael and Bunny working with me, I can't bring the baby everywhere, what with having to stop frequently for a feed and a change and working in the cold, heat, rain and snow.

I am not confident that I can do so many things and take care of a little baby at the same time. And what about the benefit dinners and special events where no children are allowed? Do I, or we, stop going to them? Hire a babysitter that we don't know like Thanh did with Cam and Tam when I first came to Riverton?

Troi oi! I am beginning to have doubts of my abilities to bring a new child into our busy lives. Fred looked uncomfortable and said he did not know I felt this way, apologizing for not asking even once if I needed help.

Maggie has so much to do now with Ba Frank, the twins are getting older, but not old enough to handle a small baby, and Aunt Ginger's children have their own families keeping them busy so we do not have much in the way of family support as we continue to grow our business life.

Fred sucked his teeth as he often does when he is deep in thought. Then he said, "Okay, let's consider your cousin. I want to meet Ca and Duc to learn more about them with my own eyes."

I did not think Fred would agree to this, even a little, and I am not sure it is a good idea, but it is a good idea to learn more before we make any serious decisions.

Dear My Diary,

After several discussions with Fred, my parents and sisters, we have some ideas of how to help the orphanage using our company's contacts with the reputable firms we are associated with.

First, Trinh and Thanh will cover the costs of replacing all the windows with tinted, shatter-resistant plastic material to cut down UV rays and keep out the dust, rain, birds and insects that constantly come in through the broken panes.

Second, Ba and Me will pay for cushioned pads to be attached to the walls. They can be made with different colors and patterns for decorative purposes, but more importantly, the panels will absorb much of the sound that currently bounce off the walls and make the rooms loud and echoey.

Third, and this will be the most expensive part, to install solar panels on the roof, providing cheap and reliable electricity to power an energy-efficient AC system. Electric power is very expensive here and the grid is often not reliable in a city as large as ours. The two systems working together will keep costs down and the children cooler. Fred and I are funding this portion.

To help with costs, our family knows many companies throughout Asia and will send out specs and take bids to get the best prices for all the projects, especially as it is for a charitable cause.

Lastly, our family will provide regular deliveries of food and clean water to help feed the children. All of us will contribute an equal amount to cover the next twelve months as Me and Ba recruit other business owners to contribute with similar donations of food, clothes, toys, books and medical care.

We know that if we just give the temple money, we will have no control over how it is used. But if we give the help directly…by our company making sure the solar panels, wall pads and windows get installed properly and healthy food delivered, we can control how efficiently the funds will be used. It will cost a lot, but Fred agrees this is a great way to help my people and our plan will keep the children healthier, happier and conserve resources. It feels so good to help my community…especially the children.

The Twins Book

Dear My Diary,

I saw Cam reading a book about twins and I asked if she is enjoying it. She said, "It is interesting, but sad too." The book talks about identical twins, and even a set of triplets, who were adopted individually by other families through an agency. The families who adopted were not told about the other twin.

The adoption agency then did follow-up interviews with the families to see how the children were doing. But what they were really doing is studying how different and how alike the twins were to each other, never revealing to the families that their child had a twin. It was all done in secret.

Later, some of the twins discovered each other and, over time, uncovered details of what the agency had done, causing much controversy about the study and the cruelty of separating siblings, or at least the adoptive parents should have been told up front and be allowed to decide whether to keep one or both.

Cam offered to give me the book when she is done and it does sound very interesting. Even though our nieces are fraternal twins, they are very close to each other and often one will finish the other's sentences. Thanh said that when they were very small, they even had a kind of secret language that only they understood but the girls have not used it for some years now. It was cute at the time, but maybe there was something more to it? I thanked Cam for offering me the book.

Dear My Diary

Through one of Bobby's clients who works for the INS, we learned that we can bring Ca over on a work visa and it will not take very long to process if we use the Premium Service. It costs more but is very fast and Ca could be in Riverton before the baby is born. If we decide to get the visa, we will give the reason of needing someone from Vietnam for cultural and language needs and that is why we can't hire an American nanny.

I spoke to Me and Ba about Ca and contacted Auntie Giang too and they all told me the same thing: Ca is nice, sweet and a bit simple but will probably be a good caregiver to our children. However, her mother is not nice and can be tricky about getting things that she wants. "Be careful in dealing with Duc," is what we heard from everyone.

We had lunch with Auntie Duc and Cousin Ca at their home as a kind of interview, without saying it directly. They prepared a very nice meal of pho, crispy vegetable egg rolls and a salad that Fred raved about. Duc puffed up and said that Ca made everything as cousin smiled and bowed her head shyly.

I asked Ca if she knows how to make any Western foods, but she shook her head. I told her that I did not know how to make Western foods until I came to America.

The house is very clean, tidy and well-cared for. Uncle works long hours as a taxi driver so he is not at home. Auntie said he taught Ca how to drive during late night hours when traffic is light and there is less chance of an accident. When I told Fred this, he laughed and said that is a very smart way to learn here.

Ca stated how she has been taking English classes for two years now, but when I encouraged her to say some of her best English to us, she became painfully shy and mumbled out "My name is Ca. I want go to America." When I asked why her English is so limited, she admitted that learning a new language is hard for her and classmates who started with her are now many levels ahead.

Fred told her nursing school in America will not be in the Vietnamese language so if she wants to go to college, her English needs to be very, very good. Much of our time visiting is spent speaking VN and translating to Fred as Auntie does not speak English and Ca, as we found, as good as none.

Duc and Ca run a childcare business from their home for the neighborhood families. They showed us toys, sleeping mats, child-sized tables and chairs, cleaning supplies and the foods they prepare for the children.

I must admit they have it set up very well. Duc complained that getting paid is haphazard at best. The mothers work for low wages and it is hard to pay all their expenses if they must help other family members or husbands take their money away for drinking and gambling.

I have heard that some daycare businesses just take the parents money and do not feed the children more than crackers and water to make more profit, but Duc and Ca are showing a good effort. There are books for stories and teaching children to read and toys and games and dolls to play with.

Ca also earns extra money or food by helping families of the elderly by giving baths, cooking or babysitting while someone goes to the market or doctor. Sometimes she gets paid and sometimes not. It is as much charity work by helping long time neighbors and friends.

Cousin is the opposite of her mother who did most of the talking. Auntie asked us if we will take Ca to America with us as a nanny, how much will we pay and so forth. Fred said we have not decided whether to have a nanny and we must discuss it further. Auntie looked disappointed and Ca did not appear interested either way. When I asked cousin what she thinks about working for us in America, she shrugged and said it sounded nice.

As we were making our thank-yous for the lunch and visit, Auntie whispered something in Ca's ear. Cousin gave Fred a hug and tried reaching up to kiss his cheek, but Fred would not bend down and she was too short to reach his face. I understood what Auntie wanted: Please the husband for a 'yes' decision, but Fred will not play this game.

In the evening, we had a long talk about if we want Ca as a nanny or not. It's sort of a 50/50 split, so we made a list.

Reasons for Yes:

Ca showed that she can take care of children and old people, so maybe she can help Maggie with Frank as needed.

Ca has a gentle nature and does not have the sharp tongue of her mother or will be demanding as far as we can see.

She is family and it is good for family to help each other in the same way as how my American cousins help watch each other's children when they have appointments, want a break, etc.

She can cook, drive, do laundry and other daily routines.

She can be of help when our schedules are busy like having appointments or meetings, making deliveries, photo shoots and the like. I may still keep the Fierce 5 job so Ca can come with me and keep the baby company and fed while I am working.

Reasons for No:

Her English is too limited after two years of school, so she will not have the ability to run complex errands, answer questions or follow directions without help until she can learn English better.

Her mother is pushing for Ca to go to America with us. I understand it will be a way for her parents to get US dollars while still working. She sees Cac as going to nursing school but Fred and I agree that Ca has much to learn before she can go to college. And how long will she be with us before attending college? Will we still need a nanny when Ca is gone?

Then there is the cost of a nanny such as wages, food, clothes, health insurance and more. At the same time, having a nanny will free us up to do more and other kinds of work and investment opportunities, offsetting the extra costs. Of course, we will still be parenting our child, but an extra person will help so much making this "no" reason balanced with a benefit.

I told Fred about my feelings that Auntie will try to control or influence Ca against us, even from across the world. Fred said, "Oh, I have no doubt about that. I've dealt with plenty of people like your aunt before, so I'm not worried about it affecting us very much."

I am so glad to hear this from Fred.

Frankie: Nowadays we call what they did a 'Cost Benefit Analysis', but back then I don't think either of them knew the term. To make important decisions, Mom and Dad often laid out Pros and Cons, Yes and No type lists and weighed one kind of thing against another. In this respect, Aunt Ca was no different than a house, a car or a decision on where to go for vacation. Mom and Dad nearly always made good choices using this method. Nearly.

Dear My Diary,

Today we took the entire family to the orphanage to meet with the head monk and several temple officials. This is especially important for Cam and Tam as they do not understand just how desperately poor some children's lives are. Because there are no orphanages in America, they have nothing to compare such a place with.

Officials welcomed us at the gate as uniformed children greeted us with bundles of flowers, giving words of welcome to their home and thanking us for our goodness. In return, we handed over brightly wrapped boxes, asking them to share the contents with the other children.

Once the children returned to their quarters, we were given another tour, more for the rest of the family's benefit than for Fred and I. As we passed one large class room, children were tearing into the boxes full of toys we had given them, a mixed assortment of books, puzzles, jump ropes, dolls, small cars, etc. that came from our warehouse inventory. The children waved at us in excitement as adults passed out the gifts.

When it came time to talk business with the temple officials, Thanh asked her daughters to mix with the other children, using their best manners. The lead teacher took over, introducing the twins to the other children and we left them alone, knowing they will be fine.

We met in an empty classroom to explain our offer of assistance for the orphanage. Ba did most of the talking as he can speak like a flower to make his points heard and appreciated. The monks are pleased with our generosity, but concerned that there is not enough room on the roof for solar panels and fearful that local thieves will try to steal them, even during the daytime.

We inspected the rooftop, observing the numerous pipes, vents and litter strewn about. The men agreed that some of the panels can be set higher up to avoid rerouting the utilities and increasing the ability of catching more rays. Theft can be discouraged with a razor wire fence surrounding the roof and reinforced brackets with lock-nuts to secure the panels.

Ba and his people will hire reputable companies to purchase and install everything we promised along with wholesale distributors to deliver high quality, nutritious foods for the children so they will grow strong and happy.

The monks said that because we are paying for the foods, they can use some of the saved money to hire better teachers for the children. Better education means that when it is time for the children to leave the orphanage, they will have good basic life skills to get decent-paying jobs and make their own future. Overall, it was a good meeting so we returned to the classroom to get the twins.

The girls had a good time playing games with the other children who begged us to let Cam and Tam stay longer, but we must go home. On the way back, the girls talked with amusement about the silly questions they were asked, like if they ride horses every day, eat ice cream for dinner and do they have their own car to drive around everywhere?

The girls explained what they typically eat for meals, that they have never ridden horses before and they are much too young to drive anything but a bicycle.

Thanh said, "They ask the silly questions because they hear things from other people and see things on TV and imagine what a luxurious life you have because you live in a rich country. They think we are all rich because they are so very poor with no family who can take care of them. Maybe they will never have a life like you have, but they all dream to be like you." This sobered the girls a bit.

I added to my sister's explanation, "Maybe, by being there and playing with them, they will have some hope and create a desire to work hard to have nice clothes like you wear and live in a house with a car to drive and money to buy good food and travel to nice places. For now, they only have what is given to them by others, much of it second-hand. That is why we gave gifts to them, to make their today life better for tomorrow. Do you understand?" The girls nodded.

"Thank your parents every day that they did not hand you over to strangers. That every day you get good food and toys and clothes and a home where you only have to share the bathroom with your sister and not fifty other children." The girls giggled at this last part, but now they understand how their lives could be far worse.

Thanh told me later that the girls are now being extra nice and sweet with their parents and thanking them many times for their good life and not making them orphans. Thanh said "If more ungrateful children in America could see what we have here, they would have their eyes opened and stop being such spoiled brats."

"Yes," I agreed. "But we still have so many children like the orphans here, but living in foster homes. Orphans are less obvious in America, but their living conditions vary a lot and can be, from what I have heard and read, just as bad, if not worse sometimes, from what we have here."

Dear My Diary,

I have a cute story to share: As we took a walk around the neighborhood with Tam and Cam, pointing out people and places of significance to us, the girls kept hearing the neighbors, especially the children, call their auntie by her old nickname.

"What do you think it means?" I asked the girls.

Cam said, "Because you have a head as hard as a coconut?"

Laughing, I said "No, but Uncle Fred might disagree. What else?"

"Your skin is brown and rough like a coconut tree trunk?" said Tam, trying to outdo her sister.

I stared at my bare arm in pretended shock. "My skin is NOT like the cay dua trunk!"

"Your hair is green and thick and sticks out all over like the leaves on the tree?" Tina said, with both girls breaking out into gales of laughter, along with my sisters.

"Now you are just being too silly! It's because I am so tall and strong looking." I said, throwing back my head and preening.

"A cay dua is strong, but not strong looking," observed Cam. "It is very slender!"

"Ah! But I have never been slender, like you. And especially now that I no longer have a flat tummy."

"Because you're having a baby!" both girls said, giggling.

At home, Me asked me if I've had the ultrasound to see if we are having a boy or girl and I asked her to guess. She felt my growing belly and, after a minute, told me it will be a boy.

"How can you tell?" I asked.

"We have four daughters and two granddaughters...we are due for a boy!" It made me laugh and my laughing caused Me to laugh, causing Ba to come in and ask what is so funny, so I told him and he said "It's true!" But to be fair, my parents also assured me that if we have a girl, it will be a happy occasion as well. "No pressure," as Fred likes to say.

They asked me if we have names picked out and I said yes. If it is a boy, his name will be Frank, like his American grandfather and for a girl, it will be Lois, to honor her Vietnamese grandfather. My parents are not familiar with the name "Lois" and neither was I, but as we were looking for names, Fred had made the suggestion of Lois or Louise for a name that is close to my father's. I like Lois better as the sound of Lo-is is closer to Lo than Lu-weez. My parents are very touched by our considerations to family names. Either child will have the middle name "Pham" to show their mother's roots, as well.

Dam Sen Park

Dear My Diary,

Yesterday we took the family to Dam Sen Park where Fred proposed to me and it is a very nice place to take the girls. We don't have an amusement park like this in Riverton, so that makes it extra-nice for them.

I told the story of how Fred asked me, in Vietnamese, to marry him while stopped at the very top of the Ferris Wheel. The man who ran the machine that special day was not there and poor Fred is embarrassed because, when asked to repeat the proposal, he could not remember any of the phrases except "Anh yu Em". Everyone smiled and said "Those are the most important words to know!" I never get tired of hearing Fred say "I love you" in any language.

They had a live band featuring young teens doing the playing and singing, so we took a break to watch and listen. While the girls hopped about to the pop music, I accepted Fred's invitation to a dance, but not too energetically as I am so big with child. He took my hands and we moved about, spinning me slowly, then taking me into his muscled arms. I could do that all day if I had the chance. Me took pictures of us and we will print them out at home. The girls came over and danced with us too. Even Me and Ba took a turn, like in the old days.

When Fred, Vo and Ba were getting lunch for us, I took Phung aside and let him know that he was right about Fred and the Blue Collar Millionaire book...but how did he know?

Phung said he read BCM a short time before meeting Fred and when he learned Fred was from Riverton, it sparked something in his mind. The more he learned about Fred, the more things he matched up to the book, so he suspected the BCM from Riverton might actually *be* Fred. It was an educated guess and he was absolutely right.

Phung Nguyen: When I first read Blue Collar Millionaire, I could relate to it as how the Phams lived and worked as working-class people who happened to be wealthy business owners. That's why I liked the book and, in the process, I learned things from it that I could use in my own life.

Once I learned that Kim was dating by email with an American, I was happy for her but little more than that, until I started hearing stories about Fred, that he was from Riverton and had a recycling business. I went back to the book and found the section on the Riverton millionaire and thought "Nah, couldn't be."

But after having long talks with Fred and Ba Lo, it became more evident that maybe he was the same man from the book. He never told us he lived in the garage...we would not learn that until after Kim moved to the US...otherwise I would have pegged him for sure. I had just enough reason to keep suspecting that I was right, so I gave Kim a copy of the book as a going away gift. But I did not think it would take her so long to get around to reading it!

As we are in a fun and relaxed atmosphere, we also discussed the interview I am to have soon for the unconditional Permanent Residence card. It will be good for ten years and three years after it starts, I can apply for citizenship.

Me asked me if I want to become a US citizen and I said, "Of course! My husband is American, two of my sisters are American, my child will be American, my adopted home is America. I would be proud if I were to be accepted as a citizen." As Me patted my hand, I added, "But I will always be Vietnamese in my heart. You know that."

Ba said, "No matter where one goes in the world, your past is always a root you cannot break."

And Phung said, "You can take the girl out of the country, but you can't take the country out of the girl!" which made us all laugh at his clever wit.

Thanh said the interview is very easy and she did not speak English half so well as me but it worked out fine. Trinh's employer in New York helped her file the residency and citizenship paperwork as one of her perks and now she votes and has the coveted blue passport. Everyone told me I will get it done, no problem...especially as I have a little citizen coming soon!

Dam Sen is so romantic. At one point, we were all holding hands: Thao and Phung, Fred and I, Thanh and Vo and my parents...even Trinh held hands with the twins. One of the park photographers got a candid picture of all of us and Ba bought copies enough for everyone. So sweet for so many couples to be in love and relaxing together before the big wedding.

Fred and Basketball

Dear My Diary,

Today, some cousins asked Fred if he would play basketball with them. Fred tried to politely turn down their invitation as he does not know how to play any games well, but the cousins and their friends begged and begged, "Do not be shy with us," and "All Americans know how to play basketball!" Fred reluctantly agreed and I went with them to help translate.

There was an argument as to whose team Fred should be on so they decided to play two rounds for twenty minutes each with Fred and another top player changing sides for the second half.

I do not know anything about basketball but it was easy to see that Fred had no idea of what to do. They complained when he took too many steps without bouncing the ball so I had to explain this to Fred. Other times, players on the other team grabbed the ball away from Fred and made points for their team. And when Fred threw the ball to the loop, mostly he missed the whole thing while other players put it in the loop much more often.

Many times his teammates yelled "Donkey! Donkey!" at him in English. At first Fred responded with "Hee Haw! Hee Haw" at them but cousins got upset and told me to tell Fred to Donkey the ball. I did not understand the word either. In exasperation they showed us to have Fred jump up high and push the ball directly into the loop. This move is hard for the other players as they are so short, but with Fred being tall, it is an easy move, they explained. Sadly, Fred proved them wrong.

After twenty minutes, the other team was leading by many points and they no longer wanted Fred on their team. Fred's team argued, "You promised to take him! Give us your best player as we agreed!"

Fred went to the other team and when he tried to donkey the ball, he injured his wrist on the metal loop and had to retire from the game and go to the local doctor. His wrist is not broken but he is in a splint and a sling.

Fred was the butt of many complaints and jokes with the family about how can such a tall American not know how to play basketball? "I told them from the very beginning that I don't know how to play, so it's not my fault that I didn't meet their expectations."

Fred wasn't like other kids who played sports outside of school or watched it on TV. Fred was busy making money, his favorite sport.

How We Met

Dear My Diary,

Cam and Tam and their young cousins think it is very romantic to get married. The house is full of family and the monsoon rains are drenching the streets so we are catching up and sharing stories. The girls asked Thao about her romance and she explained how she and Phung fell in love by working together at the office and finding their common interests. They had to hide their liking of each other, especially around parents and a sister, but soon love took over.

I said "We knew long before you told us!" and she laughed, admitting it was hard to hide their feelings for each other and from family.

The girls thought the workplace romance, especially surrounded by family and trying to keep it a secret, was kind of exciting. Then they asked me.

Mostly when someone asks how Fred and I met, we just say that we were introduced by a family member and later Fred came to Vietnam to meet me in person and propose marriage. All this is true, but we rarely divulge much more than that. I do not think I have told Dear My Diary this story, so I will tell you what I told the children. Since Auntie was there too, she filled in some parts from her side. Here is the story:

"Even as a young girl, I was much taller than others of my age and was teased terribly for it. As a teen, I understood that no man would want to marry a woman taller than he unless he is very rich and she is very beautiful or famous like a model or singer. This kind of marriage will make him feel very manly for having a tall, beautiful and talented woman. Of course, she feels very rich when he gives her money, jewels and other nice things.

"Also, I have a college degree and most men in our area do not. Men often do not want a woman who is smarter and more educated than he as it makes him look less masculine and a smarter woman is more difficult to fool with his lies, if that is his habit.

"I had never had a boyfriend and gave up on the idea of finding a tall, educated Vietnamese man with clean habits or even a shorter, less educated man who would marry me for my nice nature and not care about our differences."

Auntie joined the story now: "My brother Lo told me how he wanted to find a nice man for Kimmie. He said many people were making fun of her and she felt very bad about herself. Her confidence is very low and she does not like to go out for entertainments. He said, 'Many tall men live in America, Sister. Maybe you know someone who might like Kimmie? She is a very nice young woman, quiet, smart and works hard for her parents.' (I did not know this before…that my father asked his sister to find a man for me.) I told my brother that I don't know any tall Vietnamese, but some of my customers are tall like Kimmie. Then I thought of my business partner. Fred is not married, is much taller than most men and very clean habits as I never see him smoke or drink. Sometimes I would tell Fred, 'We got a good deal on this kind of beer, you can have it cheap!' and Fred would say, 'You know I don't drink! A waste of time and money.'

"The next time he came for fuel, I asked Fred, 'You have a girlfriend? You have a wife? You have any children you not tell me about?' He said no, no and no. Too busy with work and what he likes to do for fun, other girls don't want to do. When he said that, I asked Fred if he has a boyfriend. You know, in America it's common, so I have to ask. If he does, I would stop the questions.

"Fred asked 'What's going on? You've never asked me questions like this before, and no, I am not gay.'

"I said 'I know a nice girl for you' and I explained about Kimmie. When I showed him pictures, he smiled and I was encouraged. He said 'Well, I don't know.' and I said 'She speaks English, and works hard in the family business. They buy and sell things like you. She will understand you better than any silly American girls.' Fred said, "I admit, she is pretty, but if she is so good and her family has a big business, why doesn't she have a boyfriend in her country? Is something wrong with her?'

"Then I explained about our cultural differences regarding women like Kimmie and once Fred understood everything, he said 'Okay, I will write to her.' I know that maybe he only says this to humor me, but I think part of him really wanted a nice girl. As we are business partners, he knows I never lie to him."

So much of what Auntie has just said is new to me! Even Fred never told me about this conversation. Huh! I decided to continue the story and have it out with Fred later: "One night during dinner, my parents said that Auntie knows a nice man in America who wants to make friends with a nice Vietnamese woman. He is a white American, works with Auntie and she knows him well enough to recommend him to me. They showed me a picture of Fred in front of a work truck with jeans and blue T-shirt, big muscles on his arms and chest (I puffed up my chest and arms in imitation to make the girls giggle) and a very warm, relaxed, kind-looking smile.

"And I thought 'Oh no! An American?!' (I made a sour face and stuck out my tongue) I have heard this kind of thing all the time and I wonder in my head 'If he is so nice and good looking, why can he not find a girlfriend, even an Asian girlfriend, in his own city? Maybe something is wrong with him?' I tell you here and now, I would rather live alone all my life than with a man who acts like a dog to women.

"Please understand, I did not say any of this directly to my parents…that is disrespectful…but to be polite I said, 'Oh, I am not interested in having a boyfriend right now. This man is far away. I will not be interesting to him and he will go away eventually. I do not wish to waste his time.'

"Me said, 'Please talk to him a few times and see what happens. Just be a pen pal for now and try to learn about him. Yes, perhaps nothing will happen, but if you do not put a hook in the water, you cannot catch a fish.'

"I was not so interested in catching a fish but, to please my parents and Auntie, I agreed to give my email address to this American and see what happens."

This was the time Fred wandered over to say "What's happening ladies?" in his happy, smiling way.

The girls giggled and Tam said "You are a fish! And Auntie Kim caught you!"

With a look of surprise he said, "I've been called a lot of things, but never a fish!" as he made swimming motions and puckered his mouth.

After explaining the expression to Fred, I apologized about having to switch languages so all the girls will understand the story. He gallantly bowed and swept his hand toward me saying "Carry on M'lady!"

I continued the story: "Fred sent me a short email as a test to check that he had my address exactly right, and if so, please let him know. He said his friend Giang Greene gave him my email address and that if I am looking for a pen pal, he would welcome an answer from me.

"I wrote back saying 'Yes, I want to practice my English with an American. If you have time and want to help me, it is okay to write back.'"

"Did you really want to practice your English with him?" a young cousin asked.

"Oh, no, it was just a way to see if he would write back. Good girls do not want to be so forward as to say 'I am looking for a boyfriend!' and anyway, I was not. I was just being polite to please my family.

"We started writing maybe two times a week with little things like 'Hello! How are you? What have you been doing? Oh, that sounds interesting!' Early in our friendship we learned that we have the same birth month and day, but different year. I sent him a card I found in an expat store for his birthday with my first handwritten message and a picture of me to here," as I made a cutting motion just above my breasts "so he does not see that I am a very tall woman.

"And on *my* birthday, I got a very nice card with a heart-pictured postage stamp and his hand-written wish for my birthday to be happy and lots of fun and he wished to be here to share it with me. In his new picture, he was wearing winter clothes and pretending to throw a snowball at the camera. It looked very cold there…brr!

"Soon, we were emailing four or five times a week with things like 'What did you have for lunch?' 'I had a busy weekend selling electronics,' and things like that. After a while the emails were sounding much the same from one to another and a little boring. I liked talking to Fred as a friend but the sparkle of earlier conversations was fading. Then I got an unusual letter…"

"I will fill in this part," said Auntie who explained that over time, Fred was feeling comfortable writing with me and wanted to show his increased interest, but was nervous that I might turn him down. "He also understood how your correspondence was sounding more and more the same.

"One day, he came to me and asked if I knew of Kim's interest in him? I said 'I do not know but why don't you just ask her? Americans are very good at being direct, so just let Kim know of your strong desire to have her as your special girlfriend and does she feel the same way towards you?' The clouds on Fred's face broke away and he said, 'That's a good idea!' That's when I realized how little experience Fred had with courting a woman."

The girls turned back to me for more of the story. "So, Fred wrote a letter and sent it by Express International Mail, which is quite expensive, stating in a very serious manner about the strong feelings in his heart for me and do I have the same kind of feelings for him and do I desire to make a more serious relationship with him?

"His words took me by surprise me as we had not met yet and I had not thought in this way about Fred. I read his letter several times, to absorb his thoughts and feelings toward me. Then I thought about what he wanted and considered how I felt about him, deep down."

The girls were quiet, absorbed in the story unfolding before them. "I found that I was looking forward to his emails every day as they often arrived in the morning as he is sending them out before he goes to bed. If he misses a day, my family knows as my mood is not so cheerful.

Fred seems nice and sometimes has interesting stories to share. Meanwhile, I have no one outside the family who takes an interest in me. I felt that if Fred had another girlfriend, he would not write to me anymore, or not as much as he does, so I thought 'Well, okay…why not? I think I have serious feelings for him too.

"I responded with an email explaining that I got his letter and was strongly affected by his words. I said 'You are a very nice man and I am honored that you wish to make a stronger relationship with me and be my special boyfriend. In turn, I want to be your special girlfriend and grow our relationship."

By now, some of the girls are wiping away tears of emotion so I emphasized to their young hearts, "Remember, one should have friendship as a base for lasting love. I felt much better once my words were sent out and I had said what was in my heart.

"Right away, Fred's writing became much happier and more personal to me. He told me more about his family and friends and the city he had spent his whole life in. He confessed that when he is alone, he speaks to me, tells me things, shares memories and holds hands with me, even though I am not there. Like an invisible girlfriend that only he can see and hear and touch." The girl's faces went dreamy as I spoke this last part.

"A most special moment came when Fred asked to visit with me in Vietnam. Actually, at first, he asked if I could come to Riverton. How I could stay with Auntie and we can be together during the day. I had to explain that Vietnam is a communist country and it is very hard for citizens to get a tourist visa. Fred did not know about this, and most Americans I have found do not know this either, so he offered to come here.

"With his serious offer of a visit, I became very nervous because I never told Fred how tall I am and I honestly did not know how tall he is either. When Fred had asked me how tall I am, I would say, 'Tall enough so my skin fits my bones.' I thought that was cute and vague and Fred responded back with, 'Me too!'

"Moreover, as we live near the river in our working-class neighborhood, I was afraid he would be disappointed or disgusted that our homes do not look like what we see on American TV shows. You know, big and beautiful with lots of grass and trees and sidewalks and nothing like here where it is crowded, noisy and dusty. I asked Auntie about the idea of Fred visiting."

Auntie answered "I told Kimmie, 'Fred is not picky about where you live or how you look. He only cares that you are nice and the same person in real life as in your letters!'"

I said to the girls, "Auntie was right. If Fred wanted me forever, he needed to understand exactly who Kimmie Pham is and how she lives. I also wanted to meet Fred. To look into his eyes and heart and know that he really is the same nice man that has been writing to me.

I had already told Fred about my parents and sisters and you and you!" as I pointed to the twins who said "We know! Fred came to our house with Auntie Giang and said he is coming to ask you to marry him! He was very nice and brought us dolls and told funny jokes to us!"

So, today I also learned that Fred came here with the plan to get engaged with me and he told Thanh and Vo and Auntie first! So many things I am now hearing for the first time.

"I was careful to tell Fred that he can come and be our guest, but he would have to agree to stay at a hotel because I am a nice girl from a good, respectable family."

One cousin asked, "Were you nervous to meet him?"

I admitted that I did not sleep the whole night before his arrival and I had kept my true height a secret all this time. "I should not have done it, but I was scared that he would run away once he saw me. And did he run away?"

The children laughed and said "NO! He is sitting right over there!" They pointed at Fred and he waved back to us.

"He only ran TO me, not AWAY from me. He did not make me feel like a cay dua because he is even more cay dua than I am."

It has taken a long time to write this and I am emotionally drained. Looking back on all the nice things about our courtship, I regret my silliness about not simply telling, and showing, Fred my most obvious trait…all because I feared his rejection. I have read that most of the things people fear and worry about never materialize…just like this.

Now I am hungry and baby wants some Bun Bao or whatever I can find in the kitchen.

From Dad's email sent July 5th, 1999: I went to the park yesterday and thought about holding hands with you along the lake. In my mind, you are right beside me, smiling at some silly joke or kicking off your shoes to walk barefoot in the soft grass.

I watch the children along the shore digging in the sand and feeding ducks…maybe a couple of them are ours (children, not ducks). The Independence Day activities are everywhere: you have a butterfly painted on your cheek and a spider on mine. We dance to live music, eat fried chicken, barbequed ribs, buttered corn and coleslaw for dinner and once the sun is down, fireworks fill the night sky…just for us.

I can't wait for you to be here and make each other's dreams come true.

From Mama's email sent July 7th, 1999: How sweet you are to walk with me in the park and holding hands during the holiday time. I do not see people with painting pictures on their face but I like the butterfly for me. For you, maybe a horse or dog, not a spider! I do not know the coleslaw food but I am sure it is very tasty if you like it.

For me, I think of you with my family at dinner I make by myself. I am not such a good cook, but I help my mother often and she is very good! Do you know to eat with chopsticks? I do not know to eat with fork and knife but I will learn. It will be fun for each other to learn this new kind of eating.

At my dinner with you, we will have many kinds of foods and speak of many interesting things. After dinner, we walk along the streets in my neighborhood. The children play football and the adults sit outside to visit with each other. The many cooking smells from the homes make us hungry all over again and we buy a cold coconut with 2 straws and drink the sweet juice together. Do you like my dream to come true?

Negotiation

Dear My Diary,

After much consideration, Fred and I decided to bring Cousin Ca to America as our nanny and agreed on an offer. Fred would do the important talking points and I would both translate, and fill in details as needed. When we arrived at cousin's home, there were four small children playing on a mat and two babies in open dresser drawers asleep.

Fred asked if Ca is still interested in coming to the US? Of course, they said 'yes'. Fred explained how Ca will live in our home and we will provide a private room, food, clothes, health insurance, phone and other necessities. In return, Ca will help take care of the baby, do errands, housework and other jobs as needed. Moreover, she will accompany us if we need to travel for work.

Auntie's eyes sparkled as I laid out everything. Then I asked what kind of pay they were thinking of?

"Five Thousand dollars!" Auntie Duc announced, "And one month vacation with pay to come home and visit her poor parents. You pay the airplane."

"Five thousand a year?"

Duc looked sourly at me. "Five thousand American dollars a *month!*" she said, holding up five fingers pressing her palm out in emphasis.

Fred understood this clearly enough as he muttered "Like hell!" With a shake of his head, Fred took my arm and said "Let's go!" in Vietnamese to let Auntie know he was serious.

Duc said "No, no! Do not go! Sit! Sit!" while I shrugged off my husband's arm, saying "Let me do this."

With deference to my elder, I explained that $5000 per month is not possible and Ca will be living with us while we pay all her basic expenses. "It is very expensive to live in America and most people there do not make $5000 per month but still have to pay for housing, food and so forth."

Duc said "You are very rich and can afford the high wages a good nanny like your cousin is worth."

When I insisted that we are not rich at all, she said "I heard you went to New York for an after-wedding holiday!"

I admitted, "This is true, but the flights and hotel were a wedding gift from Fred's best friends, and most of what we did in New York was low-cost or free. We actually spent very little on our honeymoon."

Duc countered, "Fred is an important businessman, I am sure. What does he do?"

I glanced at Fred and decided to tell her the truth. "Fred is a reseller Auntie. We spend most of our days traveling the city, seeking out things we can get for free or low cost and reselling them to others at bargain prices. Things like clothes, furniture, tools, toys, scrap metal and such."

Duc look at me with a sneer, "Like the poor people who collect scraps from the street? I don't believe it!"

"Maybe one or two steps above them, and we use a truck, but it is true." I pressed on, waving an arm towards my husband, "Almost everything Fred is wearing right now was not new when he got them. Same for me."

"Humph! What about you being a magazine model and knowing Rock Rollins?" Auntie wagged a finger at me as Ca played quietly with some children, ignoring the unfolding drama. "I've seen the pictures! That is very big money!"

"Yes, Auntie, I have modeled a few times and get a flat fee each time. And the part I have in Rock's movie is small and may not be seen by many audiences. I was paid for it, but not a great deal.

"I may do more, but it is not certain. My main job is mostly to help my husband with his business. It is very physical work and we do not want to have our child in cold, rainy or hot weather and in dirty areas like warehouses. That will be Ca's job to take care of the baby when we are working."

"But your home must be very big?"

I thought about the garage and said, "Well, yes. It is very big." I showed her a picture of Fred and I in front of the garage.

Duc squinted at the building and asked, "What is this place?"

"That is our home, Auntie. It used to be a car repair business, but now we work and live there and the cost is very low because it is in an industrial area of the city."

Her face began to fall. "You have a car?"

I pointed to the trucks and van in the background. "That is most of our vehicles and I have a plain sedan I drive for myself. As you can see, we have no expensive cars, no fancy house, no designer clothes." I put my hand on one of her bony shoulders. "I am very honest with you. You can ask my parents or sisters or Auntie Giang. They have all seen where I live and what I do. My parents have a much bigger business than Fred."

I did not lie to Auntie, but I came prepared to paint an incomplete picture of our life in order to make a stronger bargain. As Fred stood quietly to one side, nodding occasionally as though he understood our conversation, I pointed out that Ca's English is very limited for someone who has been attending classes. She will need to learn and understand much about Riverton, where and how to shop, making of American foods, the use of appliances that her family does not have like an oven and washing machine.

I offered $500 per month cash and all her expenses paid by us including English lessons and we will try to help her get into nursing school, although I did not tell Auntie that Fred and I have serious doubts that will ever happen.

I also would not promise that Ca can come home for a full month every year. "All things considered, Auntie, this is a very good offer. For all the things Cousin is not paying for, it is really close to what you were asking. However, if our offer does not suit you, then we will understand."

Duc was not happy with so little cash which, we knew, she would have her daughter wire home each month, but not before pushing for some of the wages to be paid up front. After a firm refusal, she finally agreed. At no point did Auntie consult with her daughter, so I asked Ca what she thought and she said, "It's okay." I could see she did not want to be involved as her mother is the boss of their home. I found it strange, as this will be her new life and not her mother's. I find it unsettling that Ca does not act pleased or excited to go to America.

As a finish to our negotiation, I followed Fred's rule to be direct and advised the two women that if Ca cannot or will not be a good nanny and housekeeper, is lazy or makes trouble, we will send her back to Vietnam and we will find another helper.

Ca nodded and Duc said she will work hard for us. I gave Ca a cookbook I found about how to make many kinds of Western dishes with instructions in English and VN.

I got the information we needed about Ca and her family to fill out the worker's visa paperwork. As we were leaving, Duc pulled me into the kitchen and asked me, away from Fred's ears, for $1000 per month instead of five-hundred "to help your poor hard-working aunt and uncle". She said "Fred will not miss the money."

"But I will, Auntie. This is my choice, my money and not Fred's. Please do not ask again or I will stop the paperwork like this!" and I snapped my fingers, startling her. Duc apologized, promising not to ask again.

I explained to my family at dinner what happened during the meeting, including the finger snap which I learned from Bunny. She often says something dramatic, then snaps her fingers to emphasize "like that!"

Everyone agreed that I made a good argument without resorting to lies. Ba called me "Silver Tongue" and Fred said he understood parts of my explanations here and there, winning my case "like a really good lawyer".

I felt very good about today and Fred is very proud of me. I hope this all works out to everyone's benefit.

Dear My Diary,

As I approached a room where the children were talking, I heard this from the different cousins: "Your aunt is really pretty." "She's really smart too! My parents say she is doing very good work since she moved to the little city near Chicago."

Hearing this, I thought it was so nice that they talk about me in this way…and then I heard more: "What's wrong with your other aunt? Why is she so big?" "She's going to have a baby!" "I know that, but she is too tall! She almost touches the ceiling she is so tall." "My mother says her mother was watching a movie about a twenty-meter-tall monster woman attacking a city and it made her like that!" "That's not true. My parents say her mother dreamed to be married to a dragon and it caused her baby to be so really big!" "Maybe her baby will be 3 meters tall!"

I felt terrible and tears came to my eyes. I know they are children and I have heard these stories and much worse while growing up, but old hurts never really go away when brought back to life.

Then Tam spoke up, indignance in her tone. "That's mean! Aunt Kimmie can't help being so tall. And being tall has made her a famous model in America!"

The other children start laughing at her and Cam added, "It's true! She just made a movie with Rock Rollins and he is a BIG movie star!"

"Oh, she did?" the others taunted. "Can you prove it?"

I took a big breath and forced a smile like I have not heard their discussion. Entering the room, Cam said, "Auntie! Cousins don't believe us about your modeling and acting!" The other children looked at me curiously to see my reaction.

"Who does not believe I can be a model?" Called out on their comments, they looked away, rolled their shoulders and mumbled "I don't know."

With a smile to disarm their shame, I asked, "Would you like to see pictures?" and their eyes came back to me. "Come. I will show you."

Taking the digital camera from my purse, the children gathered in a semi-circle behind me as I lowered myself to the floor and brought up my favorite files. "Here I am with the Fierce 5 models. Guess which one I am?" They laughed at the big hair styles and pointy teeth and heavy makeup but could pick me out easily. I showed them other modeling pictures Fred has taken of me for our personal records. Then I make the kitty-claw pose and said in English "Fierce Five makes you feel ALIVE!" and I hissed to show my teeth and the children laughed and giggled some more.

"Did you know that I got to make a movie with Rock Rollins? I got to fight bad men with my Fierce 5 friends." I showed pictures Fred took during rehearsals including shots of me and Rock with his wife. "Do you believe Tam and Cam now?"

"Yes."

"Do you think you need to apologize to them?"

"Sorry for not believing you."

"That's better," I said. "Now I want to show you one more picture." In a moment, we were all standing in front of the picture of Ong Noi. "You see how he is very tall compared to everyone else? Even so, all his children were normal sized and all his grandchildren were normal sized but one great-grandchild was not normal size. Do you know who that one great-grandchild is?"

In unison, the children said "You."

I proceeded to explain how any family member with his blood in their veins can pass on the gene to be very tall to their future generations. "It is from genes found in every cell of our bodies that make us who and what we are, not what movie our mother watched or the dream she had. That is old-fashioned and ignorant thinking."

Now they understood I had heard their words and became uneasy with me.

I asked them "Do you feel bad when someone makes fun of you?"

"Yes."

"I grew up with people making fun of my height, thinking they were being cute or funny, but in America I get much more respect. Not just because I am tall, but more because Uncle Fred and others see how smart, honest and hard-working I am. My height got me a modeling job, but my good attitude and clean habits help me keep my jobs and grow the ways I can make friends and earn money. I am not ashamed anymore about my height, just as you should not be ashamed of who you are or what you do or how you look. Remember, if you are strong on the inside, you will get respect from the outside."

I gave each child a hug to show I am not mad at them, then asked Tam and Cam to come with me. When we were in my room, away from the other children, I thanked them for standing up for me and telling the others about my good features. "This is a good way to act with others and will help you with friendships for many years to come."

The girls said they love me and their Uncle Fred and do not like it when people talk bad about us. I gave them each a kiss and we returned downstairs for dinner.

I see a new respect in the eyes of the other children now, and I am certain they will tell their parents some of what happened today. Perhaps it will help their parents understand too.

Needless to say, as we were growing up, Mama and Dad drummed into us the importance of good work and living habits and treating others fairly and with kindness, no matter their station in life. They had many good things come their way and, when something didn't turn out well, they did not blame anyone but took the event as a life lesson and moved on. As Dad would say, "You need to turn those lemons into lemonade, then life will be much sweeter!"

Cam: I still think back sometimes on the day Aunt Kimmie came in and caught those children talking trash about her. She turned the situation around without getting angry and when it was all over, the kids had a whole new way of understanding what she was about. Aunt Kimmie had also heard us defend her and she really appreciated that. I felt a little more grown up that day, having done a mature thing and being praised for it. It was a lesson I have used, and shared, throughout my life.

Thomas Stimson

Baby Shower

Such a surprise awaited me today as Me and Thao rented a private party room at a nearby restaurant for my baby shower. It was Thao's wedding time, but my family wanted to celebrate our new child too. I am so touched…really, *we* are both touched. Fred did not go as he would be bored with a lot of chattering women, all in Vietnamese, but he expressed his appreciation with hugs and plenty of "Cam on nhieu lam's" to my mother and sisters.

All my sisters, Cam and Tam and many relatives, workers and neighbors who have known us a long time were invited. Most were surprised to hear that we are choosing to wait until birth to learn the gender while most women find out as soon as they can.

Thao bought a fright wig and had me wear it with my F5 fangs…Grrr! Everyone laughed and laughed as we showed Fierce 5 magazine ads that had been scanned and projected onto a big screen. Throughout the shower, many of our guests shared words of friendship and support regarding my new life in America. Their attitudes toward me have changed and softened…perhaps even wistful of my upward climb while most are caught up in the same day to day struggles as they have suffered for many years.

I got so many clothes, toys and other things for the baby: a breast pump and nursing bras, books on baby care, blankets, a mobile with gentle lights and music to hang over the crib and the list goes on. We may have to use our company's shipping account to get it all home.

We had so much good food and drink, especially wines from the upland provinces, that some of the women took to telling naughty jokes and stories. That's when it was decided to break up the party and give thanks to our guests…the twins do not need to hear these kinds of stories and I am not a fan of such humor, either. I did not tell anyone that Fred and I have been collecting many sizes and styles of baby clothes and toys from our reselling inventory over the last few months as we did not know about the baby shower to come.

Fred and I filled out, scanned and emailed the paperwork for Cousin Ca to Bobby who will then print and add the required business and financial documents required so cousin can come over as an employee of The Orion Group. Fred said, "I just hope this works out like we want." But his face told me that he believes otherwise.

The Wedding

June 23, 2002
Dear My Diary,

The wedding was so lovely! It was a small formal ceremony for family and close friends at the big temple near our home. Hundreds of fragrant flowers surrounded the altar and guests as special incense was burned and the elderly head monk, who has been the temple leader since before my birth and has watched all of us grow up, performed the ceremony. This is the first time in many years that all four sisters are together in Vietnam, and now with two children and one on the way.

Phung's parents, brother and two sisters with their spouses and children are here, wearing the finest suits and ao dais as can be found in Ho Chi Minh City. His Ba and Me have worked with us many years, as a distribution manager and accounts receivables clerk respectively, along with several other of their family members.

All three of us, along with Phung's sisters, made a line next to Thao. Phung's brother stood directly next to him followed by three of his closest friends and Fred. Fred and I agreed to stand at the ends to help make the tableau a bit more aesthetically balanced. Fred said it best: "It will look more even in an odd sort of way."

Thao had been nervous about asking us to do this, feeling that we might take offense or feel disrespected to be put at the ends instead of ahead of her new in-laws. I told Thao, "It does not matter if I stand next to you or at the end of the line or across the world, I am always your little sister and will always love you…that goes for your American brother as well," and I gave her a hug. I do not want to stand out so much as I already do, and Fred does not care either way. He is happy to be with my family wherever we are.

I had to have a new ao dai made to fit my growing tummy. I hear it is sometimes called a "baby bump" but our baby is not a "bump" anymore! And speaking of 'bumps', I was a little shocked when I saw Cam and Tam dressed up…they wore ao dais like the rest of us, but their chests were poking out. I had not noticed this development on them and asked Thanh about it.

She said the girls wanted to look more grown up, so Thanh allowed them to wear sports bras with socks as filler as well as more than a hint of make-up and lipstick. They look like such young ladies now!

The reception was held at the Rex Hotel…the most famous hotel in all of Ho Chi Minh City. I know most of the five-hundred plus guests as they are family, co-workers and business partners. My family calls everyone we do business with a "partner", not "associate" or "client" or "customer", as we all try to make money together equally and fairly.

Lois: The Rex Hotel, for those who don't know, dates back to the 1920's French Colonial era of Vietnam's history. The hotel went through a big remodel after Reunification in 1975 and was a real showplace in the 1990's and 2000's. As much as it was a landmark for the city, The Rex was torn down a number of years ago when it could not compete with many modern high-rise hotels that now dominate

District 1.

Tam "Tammy" Greenberg: Are you going to publish this? Oh, my God! I remember the wedding and a lot about that trip to Vietnam. We were about eleven years old and after growing up in Riverton, HCMC was so exotic. There was a restaurant with jungle snakes you could pick out and they would cook. People were making all kinds of businesses on the sidewalks like cutting hair, selling anything you could think of, even a guy doing dental work! Motorbikes and cyclos and taxis zipping by everywhere all the time.

We really got to spend a lot of time with Aunt Kim and Tina. Even though we lived in the same town, they worked a lot, so this down time really allowed us to talk and learn about each other. Aunt Kim told us one time that the book we gave her about orphan twins being separated to different families gave her inspiration later to do what she did. It just goes to show that even kids can influence the decisions of adults in a big way.

I looked back recently at pictures of Thao and Phung's wedding and yes, there we were with our first make-up and pretend boobs. It looks pretty weird as I look at the photos now. We were so small, especially for our age, but it was a big deal for us to look more grown-up in front of the adults and our cousins. I remember sneaking some champagne from unattended glasses and dancing my first dances with a cute boy in a bow tie and shiny shoes. Good times!

Many of the guests can speak some English and wanted to practice on Fred while others wanted to have their picture taken with their "new American friend", maybe to show off to others as a kind of trophy.

I also had many conversations with guests about my marriage, life in the US, the baby and working with Rock Rollins and Fierce 5. F5 does not have a distributor or license to sell in Vietnam yet, but Fred and I shipped over fifty cases for the wedding and another fifty for promotional giveaways.

The idea is to promote Fierce 5 with me being Vietnam's most visible spokesperson and, in part, I think Ba was hoping this would cut down on the bar bill for the wedding. Frugal Ba! Of course, Fred is pushing for Pham Lo International Trading Company to be the main distributor for Southeast Asia. Who better?

With so many people, the family hired a large photo team for the wedding and reception. For the reception, Thao changed into a beautiful white wedding dress, a European design that opened from the bottom so her legs were showcased just above the knees as the rest of the dress draped to just above the floor in the back. Phung wore a 1920's era tuxedo, complete with tails, spats on his shoes and a top hat like from the old movie musicals. The only thing missing was a monocle and cane…So handsome!

Something we noticed throughout Mama's diaries is how often she refers to movies and television as to how something, or someone, looked or did something "just like from a movie". How little she knew then how her life would evolve in that very direction!

June 25
Dear My Diary,

It was heart-warming to see my parents and family and the sights, sounds and smells of my old neighborhood. I feel like I could stay in Vietnam forever to enjoy the music, foods and sounds of my own language everywhere. However, returning to Riverton, I feel much better with the cooler climate as the heat and humidity were a bit tough to handle when we traveled out of doors. It can get fairly sticky here too, but not consistently every day.

We stayed in the same hotel Fred had used while he was courting me so Thanh and her family could stay with our parents and give them the gift of time with their granddaughters. Soon Me and Ba will have grandchild number three and number one for Frank and Maggie. I guess it is a good thing Barney and Bunny have no children or they would only see their daddy on Visitor Day, as Fred explained it to me in the same manner he would describe a bad smell.

Barney has been in federal prison for a month now and I can't help but think that he would not be there if he had children and more responsibilities to make him good. Then again, he had Bunny and a law practice but he still got into trouble. I guess Barney was born bad.

Bunny and Michael have been working very hard and Bunny seems happy with her new job. Michael is not unhappy, I think, but he does not show emotions easily, so it is hard to tell sometimes.

After Fred checked to make sure the stores are well stocked and money has been regularly deposited into our accounts, Fred paid them for the time we were gone. He has gone to B&R's to catch up on things while I drove to neighborhoods I like, looking at the homes listed for sale.

We've made the decision not to move to Honeywood Heights…so what to do with the empty lot? We don't know, but will let it sit as the real estate prices begin to recover. Meanwhile, I drove around the block twice to see that a few homes are being built on the lots we sold, and it looks like McClurg has stopped construction for the time being.

Fred has heard that some of the people he sold homes to have pulled out of their contracts and McClurg may be forced to file for bankruptcy. If so, I wonder if Fred will buy the lots? I think it would be a messy deal with several homes only partially built. I mean, how do you finish them? Use the same plans and contractor or tear down and start over?

Buck's Park is still in the planning stages and they want to open by next Spring, but that may be a problem too. With property values down and abandoned houses scattered across the city, there is a severe shortage of property taxes being paid and budgets are cut to the bone.

I drove to different neighborhoods that appeal to me and took down the addresses of homes I like the looks of, helping myself to a flyer and taking some pictures. Ultimately, none of them really suit me.

Our late-afternoon OB GYN checkup went well. The baby is active, my weight is good and I know my diet has been excellent after three weeks in Vietnam. Junior, that is what we call our son/daughter for now, is due August 7th and I pray very hard for a healthy child!

Fred says he wants a little girl who looks like her beautiful mother (So sweet!) and I told Fred that I want a handsome little boy that looks like his Ba. We will see in a very few weeks.

Thomas Stimson

Bunny and the Pop Boxes

Dear My Diary,

Bunny came to the garage today as excited as a puppy! She brought in a rectangular plastic thing, red and kind of thin. She asked us if we knew what it was? When we answered that we did not, she held both sides, made a quick jerking motion and it popped open into a complete six-sided box!

Imprinted on the plastic is the word "Pop-Box" because it pops open easily, folds shut and can be stacked on top of each other. Bunny showed us how strong and well-made they are so we opened and closed them many times with no problem.

Bunny bought them from a man selling from the back of a trailer at a local strip mall. She bought three, one of each size, and chatted up the man who travels from town to town throughout the region selling Pop-Boxes and other things he can get at discounted prices.

Fred asked "What will you do with them?" And Bunny replied, "I'm glad you asked!"

She looked up Pop-Boxes on the internet and found the importer and distributor in Chicago, calling and negotiating a bulk price deal, but she has to provide proof of a business license before she can take delivery.

Bunny wants to use our license for the Orion Group to get the discount. Fred, never one to allow others to take advantage of him, suggested the she invest twenty dollars of her own money, fill out some forms, and get a business license of her own from the city. She was surprised that it could be done so easily.

The minimum order is one thousand units and the seller was charging triple the purchase price she got from the Chicago office. Bunny feels like she can sell them at the flea markets and other places around the metro area.

"I even made a song for them! It goes like this:

"You can pop it, you can lock it, you can fill it up and stock it! It's the Pop! Pop! Pop! Box!

"You can pack it, you can stack it, if you drop it, you can't crack it! It's the Pop! Pop! Pop! Box!

"Ohh, let's all pop the box!" (she snaps the box open) "Let's all Pop the Box!" (snaps another one open) and she waved her hand toward the other boxes as an unspoken invitation to try it ourselves while still singing "Let's all Pop the Box…let's go!"

"You can shake it, you can take it, to the closet or the lake, It's the Pop! Pop! Pop! Box!"

We were laughing so hard as Bunny sang and danced with such attitude, I could really see people buying from her just for the entertainment value of it all. Bunny admitted that the song needs some work, along with her dance moves, but she wanted something that will get attention and make people want to buy.

Fred said "The pitch is the biggest part of selling and I think your pitch is terrific."

Bunny wants to save on shipping costs by picking them up directly from the warehouse, but she does not have a truck and one thousand or more pop-boxes will take a lot of room. Moreover, she wants this to be her own money-making project by using her own funds and selling skills.

I helped Bunny with calculating costs for fuel, time figures about shipping here and mileage depreciation. Fred is not comfortable to have Bunny drive one of our trucks and it will take a full day to drive round trip, plus loading and unloading cases of pop-boxes.

For storing the inventory, Bunny has already sold the bed and furniture from the guestroom as she never has overnight visitors.

Lois: Mama ended up going with Bunny to Chicago to get the Pop-Boxes. Bunny paid rent and fuel for the truck, fed Mama and paid a flat fee for helping. Mama would have done all that for nothing but Dad did not want Bunny to think this was going to be a free-all-the-time kind of thing, especially as she was buying the boxes for her own profit.

Mama said they had a great road trip and Bunny ended up selling many tens of thousands of Pop-Boxes over the next few years. She even recorded her little song and dance for VidLive along with her contact information for people to buy them from her online. If you can still find the video, it is HYSTERICAL!

Lang: Aunt Bunny found an old Pop Box commercial she made with Mama in it. It is so cute! Mama stands on the left while a much shorter man stands on the right, holding her hand and looking adoringly up at her. He gives her the "wait a minute" sign and brings back three pop boxes, a large, a medium and a small and stacks them up in front of her. He climbs to the top to present her with a ring box. At this point Mama's expression goes from puzzled to delighted, clasps her hands and nods enthusiastically, then takes him by the shoulders and leans in for a kiss while the scene changes to the words "Pop Boxes. For just about any job you have."

Dear My Diary,

Fred and I got an email from the Fierce 5 management team last week, upset that I am using my character's name on VidLive and Ubiddit for my own monetary gain, even though I am also promoting their drinks in the videos. Management says they own the rights to the character, including the name, and if for any reason, I am no longer working for F5, they retain the option to use a different person as Chimera. It is a trademark infringement issue.

Fred read my F5 contract again and we talked about it with one of Fred's lawyers. The lawyer's explanation was that the company wants to keep close control over all parts of marketing their products and my way of helping is not authorized.

It makes sense to me so I will stop. I called Bunny and explained why we have to remove videos with Chimera's name off VidLive. She was disappointed to hear this and said she would do it.

A few minutes later, Bunny called back and asked "Maybe you can change the spelling of your name a little and not promote the drinks?" Then she spelled out some variations like "Kimera", "Kymera" and "Chymera". Suddenly I saw something I never saw before: Kimera is almost like my own name! I said I would think about it and hung up.

I looked over the spellings and played with it in my head. I ran the details by Fred about a "stage name" as he concentrated and sucked his teeth. He likes the idea and suggested that Kymera is different enough and has a nice look in print. As often happens, Fred had read my mind.

I asked Fred what he would do if I legally changed my name to Kymera? He said, "Then I would have two lovers, Kimmie *and* Kymera and you would be loved twice as much!" as he took me into his arms for a warm kiss.

He is so sweet, but I will not change my name. I said that to tease him and fish for a compliment. I like Kimmie…but I also like the idea of Kymera as a stage name if I pursue acting, maybe with no last name. I have to think about how that might work.

I like my married name, but when I look at other Western names, I think Starbuckle has a funny sound. I also know that many entertainers change their names to be more pleasing to the eyes and ears of their audiences. I looked on the search engine Knowitall and cannot find any Kymera person or companies listed. Hmmm!

And this is when Mama came up with the name she has used professionally ever since. My parents did check with F5 management who grudgingly allowed that Mama's new variation was different enough that she could use it as her own name, as long as she did not promote Fierce 5 with that name without their express permission.

I visited with Thanh and she is upset about something that happened while they were gone. The trusted employee who was to manage their salons was caught cheating the business as soon as Vo and Thanh were barely out of the country.

Right away, the other employees heard the manager tell customers, "Oh, the credit card machine is broken. Please pay with cash!" Inconvenienced customers had to go to an ATM machine for the required cash. While the manager was on break, one of the employees tested the machine by charging a penny and it worked fine.

When the manager returned, the employees, as a group, accused the manager of cheating Vo and Thanh. The manager told everyone that they were all fired and she would hire a new crew before the end of the day. The workers demanded she empty all the collected cash on the table and leave or the police would be called. One very large worker stood in front of the door and another started calling 911. The manager got angry but she put all the cash from her pockets and purse onto the table and said many terrible things before she left.

The workers elected a new manager to run the business until sister and brother returned home. They contacted the other shop and told them what happened so that when she did try to go in, those workers locked the door and pretended to call the police so she would go away.

I told Thanh how lucky she is to have good employees watching out for her. They could have lost several thousands of dollars too easily. I think the employees have seen how much the owners have changed and wanted to protect them.

Moreover, they are now using their profits to invest in nicer things for the shop and increasing the pay of long-time workers who have been loyal to them. When I told Thanh these thoughts, she asked, "You really think so?"

"I am very certain of this. Otherwise, they would not care and let you lose all the cash and then claim ignorance of what happened. Good treatment equals respect and loyalty."

Sister was very lucky this time. Maybe next time they will not all go on vacation together and one will stay back to watch the business.

Cam Nguyen: I remember that happening after we got back. After talking with Aunt Kimmie about it, Ba and Me decided to take all the employees out for an Appreciation Dinner to thank them for their hard work and honesty to them. They hardly had any more problems after that. But then, we never went on full family vacations anymore until after they retired. Usually, it was Me who took us out of town so Ba could keep a close eye on things.

Thanh told me how the girls have become extra nice and sweet with their parents, telling them 'thank you' many times for their nice life and not making them orphans. Thanh said visiting the orphanage is something many children in America need to see as it has made a lasting impression on Cam and Tam and they will not forget for a long time.

July 5, 2002
Dear My Diary,

Ca's work visa has been approved! I called their home and spoke to Auntie Duc to let her know the good news. Then she asked, "What about me?"

"What do you mean, Auntie?"

"Did you get a work visa for your auntie and uncle?"

Confused, I replied, "We only got one work visa for Ca so she can help take care of the baby."

"I am disappointed with you, Kimmie. If you really love us, you would have ordered two more visas so uncle can drive you around and I would cook for you on the days you do not take us all out to eat."

My anger began to rise at her raw nerviness. "That was not our plan and never was. You and I never discussed this and I only applied for Ca. Even if we had thought about it, we do not have the living space for all of you nor the amount of work needed to keep you busy. It is only me and Fred and a soon to come baby. Fred does not need a driver who does not know Riverton and does not understand English and we do very well at making our own meals."

"Do not be disrespectful to your elders, just because you are a famous model."

"I am not a famous model and if you demand I get two more work visas, then I will cancel cousin's visa and you can all live together in Vietnam as you do now."

As I was about to hang up on Auntie for wasting my time, she laughed and said she was just making a joke and didn't I find it funny?

"I do not understand or appreciate this kind of humor. I am pregnant, tired, working for our living and then you ask for more than we had already discussed and agreed. I know you are my auntie but I do not have the time or energy for playing guilt games." I bit her ears especially hard.

Auntie apologized for upsetting me and I told her we need Ca to get a VN passport as soon as possible. Auntie assured me that they had applied for the passport the day after we took copies of Ca's documents and it should be ready to deliver anytime.

I asked, "Are you sure? You did this before we got the visa approval?"

"Oh, yes. I believed you would get it done so we made the preparations."

When I told Fred about the call, he was annoyed with how auntie was acting. He did not say much about it so maybe I should not have told him the story and just say that cousin will have her documents ready.

We did not do the July 4th picnic on the roof this year or see the fireworks. It is very hot and humid here and, with the baby, it is making me more tired than normal. We've been running the AC all day and much of the night to keep cool so I can do things to get ready for little Frank or Lois.

Michael and Bunny sometimes come up for lunch to cool off and discuss what they are doing or share a funny story with me. I like this kind of family time with them…sort of like what we do with my own family.

Dear My Diary,

I have been looking over the baby shower gifts from my family and friends…so many pretty clothes and toys. Before we left, I had already picked out many things from our inventory for the baby, and now we have so much more. I am trying to decide whether to put the old clothes back into inventory or to keep them and sell the new clothes with tags still on for the money.

I have mixed feelings about both ideas so I asked Fred what he thinks we should do?

"Well, do you like the new clothes?"

"Of course! They are very nice, but the baby will grow out of them quickly. We can make more money from the gifted clothes as they are brand new and cost us nothing."

Fred asked, "Do you know what is one of the greatest things you can do for the people who gave you the gifts?"

"Send them a thank you card?"

Fred shook his head, "Well, yes…that. But even better is to take a picture of the baby wearing the gifted clothes and send it to the giver." Fred smiled and continued, "Show them how cute the baby looks with the clothes, how happy the child is playing with the new toy or snuggled up in the pretty blanket. To me, that is a gift worth one-hundred times that of re-selling the new clothes for cash."

It's funny, but when I thought of re-selling the new clothes, I was thinking that this is what Fred would expect us to do, so his actual answer surprised me. He is more thoughtful than I expected…and I am so bad to think of selling the gifts!

The Interview

July 16, 2002
Dear My Diary,

The interview is done and I was so happy that I started crying before we got out of the federal building. Partly, it is the hormones, I know, but still, I am filled with happiness and a feeling of security to have become a permanent resident.

We drove to the state capital for the INS interview with a briefcase full of paperwork that has been ready since before we left for the wedding. But even after we got home, I kept checking and made Fred recheck everything just to make "absolutely double sure" as Fred likes to say. He also says "Measure twice, cut once," which kind of means the same thing.

After going through the metal detectors and bag searches, we were taken to separate offices and asked a series of questions. It did not take long, maybe fifteen minutes with a very nice INS officer. We went over my personal identification, then she checked our joint bank statements, car title and other legal documents with both our names, asked if I had been out of the US for an extended period of time (just to Vietnam for three weeks with Fred) and I showed photos of Fred and me with my family in and out of Vietnam. I know they want to be sure we have a genuine and not fake marriage so I can be a real US resident.

As I said, she was very nice and was careful to speak English slowly with me, in case I did not understand her so well, but it was fine. I have been here two years now with Fred and I must speak, hear, read and write English almost all the time and with people who are sometimes difficult to understand.

She asked me if I am employed in the US and I explained that my husband is self-employed and I work with him and also do some work with Fierce 5. She asked "What is that?"

I spotted a magazine on her desk and recognized it. "Give me that magazine and I will show you."

Yes! There it was on page 67, a full page F5 ad with all of us. I pointed and said, "See, that's me!" She laughed and said, "If you say so!" and the interview finished soon after that. I mean, how else would I have known that a Fierce 5 ad would be in that magazine?

I have a growing collection of F5 print ads as was recommended by the other models, along with clips, scripts and other items from whatever jobs I do to create a portfolio for future job assignments. I don't know if I will continue this in the future, but it is fun to collect these things for myself.

Fred was already finished and we met with an official in the lobby to sign the final paperwork for my card and take my fingerprints. It was almost noon and baby was very hungry so Fred took us to a VN restaurant he read about on the internet. My best friend knows that at times like this, I like my comfort foods and we took our time savoring the flavors of my homeland.

Fred held my hand many times under and on top of the table…so romantic! Afterward, we toured the beautiful capitol building and I learned more about how they make the laws and where they meet to debate and vote. It gives me such pride to be a part of our state and country.

I get tired more easily now, so Fred drove and I napped off and on in the back seat. I felt better by the time we got home.

Bunny came in to work soon after we got home. She asked about the interview and I told her everything that happened. She liked my story about showing the official my picture in her magazine. With so much make-up and big hair, I think she was amused that she could not see my real face. I don't care. I got the card and it will be in the mail soon. That's the most important thing.

Bunny handed me a package wrapped in pretty paper…a present! "It's a combination Congratulations and Baby Shower gift."

Bunny gave Baby some very cute onesies in green, yellow and purple in three sizes to grow into and with different patterns, along with two boxes of newborn diapers, wipes and some other items we will use a lot of. She is so sweet!

Fred admired the clothes and thanked Bunny as well. In return, Bunny thanked us for giving her a chance to work with us and Michael. She called Michael "a swell kid" and "a real gentleman". I think that means that he does not try to sleep with her like some men.

After a refreshing shower, I sent out emails to the family about our good news. I feel so much better now!

Trang: Mom had whole rooms set aside for not only her own memorabilia, but that of Dad and the rest of us. All but Frankie since he didn't get into the entertainment business. Most of it was kept in a general chronological order with magazines, videos, you-name-it in different areas for each person. All of Dad's books and his stuff in one corner, Lois's books and magazine articles in another, etc.

It got harder to catalog everything once the electronic stuff came out, or rather poured out. There were so many e-zines, graphic novels, niche publications, news articles and online interviews that popped in and out of circulation within days, or even hours featuring one or more of us. And from all over the world!

Just the same, there was a LOT of memorabilia. It has been really fun to go back through some of it with our kids and grandkids, especially the older items. We get a lot of "Yeah, that was me when I was your age!" "Yes, Aunt Lois really did write all those books. That's why you need to do better in school." and "Grandma did look like an old-fashioned rock star, didn't she?"

The Boston

July 21, 2002
Dear My Diary,

What a mess of a day…and it was up to Fred to be the hero of this latest misadventure. Let me explain:

Today is Ca's coming to America day. With my parents help, we purchased the necessary plane tickets and gifted $200 USD to fly to Riverton by way of Seoul and San Francisco. Thao and a company driver went to Duc's home and took the family to the airport to make their goodbyes. Thao gave Ca detailed verbal and written instructions along with the tickets, visa and passport. As are the rules of the airport, only those with tickets can come inside.

In Riverton, we joined Auntie Giang, Bunny, Frank and Maggie and others to greet Ca as she came out of the security zone. The plane from San Francisco was on time and we waited and waited until I had to sit down as Baby is getting so heavy inside me. Riverton is not a large airport and once the bulk of the people had come through, we waited a bit longer for the stragglers but no Ca came through the gates.

Disappointed, we checked with the ticket agent to learn that Ca had successfully flown from Seoul to San Francisco but did not board the flight to Riverton. We became concerned and worried that she is hurt or sick or kidnapped. Fred made the unhelpful suggestion that cousin left the airport and maybe ran off so as not to come to Riverton. I pinched his arm for saying such a mean thing.

Hours later, my cell phone rang. It was Ca saying she is in the boston. I asked Fred, "What is the boston?"

"The boston what?"

"Yes, the boston. What is the boston?"

"Who is on the phone?"

"It is Ca. She can not find us. She says she is in the boston."

"Boston? Massachusetts?" I have not seen Fred this surprised in a long time. "That's on the East Coast! North of New York. How the hell did she end up in Boston?"

Ca explained that she was at the San Francisco airport at the exact gate they told her to be and was written on Thao's instructions. At some point, everyone around her stood up and went away to another part of the airport, leaving her alone. She did not know what to do, so she stayed put.

Soon, other people came and gathered and waited until they were called forward to present their tickets. By now it was almost two hours past departure time. The agent took her ticket and Ca went to her assigned seat but someone else was sitting in her seat so she sat somewhere else and soon the plane took off. Now she is in Boston with no money and does not know how to get to Riverton.

"Where is your money?" I asked. "Did Thao not give you $200?"

Ca said when she went into HCMC airport, there is an exit tax. Of course, we know this. It is $20 USD and has been for a long time. "When I asked how much it is, the cashier asked me 'How much US money do you have?' and I said two-hundred and she said 'That is exactly the amount of the exit tax.' I said I thought it was twenty dollars and she said 'It went up yesterday to two hundred' and she put out her hand, so I gave her the money.

To keep it simple and short, I told Fred that Ca lost the cash and got on the wrong flight. Fred asked for Ca to get an airport employee on the phone and, after some time and multi-translations, it was determined that in SF, the flight was moved to a different gate and that is where the passengers went.

Ca did not understand the announcements and did not question why everyone had left the gate. A Boston-bound flight arrived at Ca's gate and during boarding, the check-in person was chatting with someone and did not notice her ticket was for the wrong flight and city. The flight was not full so Ca was able to get an unclaimed seat.

Fred, after much back and forth with an airline manager who agreed that it was, in part, their fault that Ca got on the wrong flight. Ca's suitcases are not in Boston but luckily, she has a carryon with clothes and toiletries.

The airline offered to put Ca up in a hotel tonight and make sure she gets on the next flight to Riverton tomorrow morning, all for no charge.

Fred said "That's very kind of you, but I want her to stay at the airport tonight so she doesn't get lost again."

The airline made up for the hotel by giving Ca a debit card to buy food and other purchases as she has no money and is hungry. Fred is very good at negotiating and getting things done without making others mad at him. I am very grateful to Fred and very ashamed of my family member to get into so much trouble.

We know now that cousin's suitcases are in the Lost and Found at Riverton Airport after Fred called there. Ca will be here tomorrow afternoon. Fred grumbled that Ca is "simple" and I tried to explain that she has never flown before and did not know what to do.

But I have to agree, Ca is not willing to ask questions if something does not sound or look right. I hope the airport cashier enjoys her $180 profit from Ca…Grrr!

Ca is with us now after spending a sleepless night at Logan International. She said the seats were hard and no place to lay down except the floor. Her mother had warned about gun-carrying robbers in America, so Ca just sat and looked at fashion magazines and ate food from the Asia Express fast-food stand with some of the debit card money. In the car, she showed me an F5 ad in one of the magazines and pointed to my picture with pride.

As Fred drove us home, Ca looked about everywhere and asked "Where are the motorbikes?"

Ca Driving

Dear My Diary,

Now I have another problem: I have just learned that Ca does not know how to drive.

This morning, I wanted to see how well Ca can drive and it is very easy on American streets, not at all like Ho Chi Minh City. I thought, "How hard can it be? Cars are much the same…same side steering wheel, same placement of gas and brake, not like Japan.

The car was outside in our heavily fenced lot when Ca sat in the driver's seat and looked around like everything is very new to her. She started the car, put it in neutral and gave it gas, then more gas, not understanding why the engine got louder but the car would not move. Then she dropped it into Drive with her foot still on the gas. The car lurched forward, then stalled because she had not taken the emergency brake off. Without the brake, we would have gone straight into the concrete-embedded fencepole.

"What are you doing?" I cried out, partly in anger and mostly in fear of hurting my baby once again. Thank heavens I have the habit of clicking the seatbelt right away. "I thought you knew how to drive?"

Ca admitted that on her second night of lessons, she was driving on the street and her father said, "turn right" and she did…straight into the sidewalk, hitting two parked motorbikes and damaging the front wheel and fender of the taxi. Her father had to pay for the repairs of all the vehicles out of the family savings as he had no insurance. She was meant to turn at the intersection ahead.

When Fred heard the story, he did not think it was funny. He said, "It shows again how simple she is and how much her family has lied to us."

Luckily, she CAN cook. Fred took us to our favorite stores where we picked out many quality ingredients and some cooking tools I did not have. Ca also brought the cookbook I gave her and she will learn Western dishes as she gets used to everything.

Dear My Diary,

There is a new song on the radio that reminds me of the first time Fred and I met in person. After I heard it a few times, and paid more attention to the announcer, I learned the singers are H2Ho…the couple who sang at our wedding! The song goes like this:

Stranger from a strange land
Could you be the one?
To chase away the darkness
And reveal to me the sun?

Stranger from a strange land
I feel so close to you
Perhaps we knew each other
In a past lifetime or two

Of all the things that we can share
Holidays, food and fun
It's our hearts that set us apart
And make our love as one

Now I'm a stranger in your land
Adopted as my home
Show me all its wonders
And never leave me alone

When I told Thanh about the song, she said she has heard the same song in Vietnamese on the international music channel. She recorded it for me and it is even more beautiful in our own language. Fred has now listened to both versions and he likes both very much.

July 25, 2002
Dear My Diary,

This morning, Ca and I were grocery shopping when someone behind me said, "Hi! Are you Chimera?" I turned around and there stood two girls in their early teens, possibly sisters.

I smiled, knowing fans when I see them. "Yes, I am."

Returning my smile nervously, they asked for my autograph on their cans of Fierce 5. I keep pens and markers in my purse for just this kind of occasion and am happy to oblige. We chatted for a minute or two, making polite conversation.

They kept glancing at my very large tummy, then quickly bringing their eyes back to my face. The older one asked me if I had been a model in Vietnam before coming to America?

"No, this is my first time being a model anywhere, and I like doing it. And thank you for being fans of mine and Fierce 5." I offered my hand and we shook before they ran off, excited with their new prizes.

I explained to Ca what had just happened, even though she did not ask me why the girls stopped us. She nodded and said, "That's nice."

Speaking of fans, Fred is not one of Ca yet. He does not speak much about her, but I know he thinks she is simple, and he has said so before. She almost always wears a small smile like she is thinking of something pretty or sweet but does not share what is on her mind. I realize now that this has always been her nature, even when I had met her at family functions in the past.

I looked it up in my dictionary and the words that describe her best is "pleasant" and "agreeable". She does not complain if she does not like something and rarely states her opinions or desires. If I ask, "Do you want to do this or that?" She will say "It is up to you," or "Whatever you want," or words to that effect.

Sometimes I have to teach her one thing several times to get it right, but once she learns, she does it very well. She may not be so bright, but I would not call her "simple" either. That word is not accurate for Ca. And not fair. Or nice.

I feel like Ca will be a good companion for me. This is another word I find that fits Ca well. I would not go so far as to say "friend", but maybe she will be later on. For now, I can speak with her in our common language, and she nods or comments about what I say.

I know I need to speak more to her in English and her with me. Our shopping helps with this as I use English to give names, prices and what to look for on the labels.

Meeting the girls has put me in a good mood. I feel pleasant and agreeable too!

Dear My Diary,

I found the house! I found the house I want to raise our children in and my heart is racing with joy. Ca and I were visiting the neighborhoods I like and I saw a For Sale sign on a two-story house. I have seen this house before, but not with a For Sale sign. There were no cars in the driveway and the blinds were up so I could see inside. It is completely empty and ready for occupancy.

It is so perfect, located in an older, middle-class kind of neighborhood with lots of big shade-trees up and down the street. The house sits on a much larger lot than its neighbors with an enormous backyard containing an overgrown vegetable garden, fruit trees and a combination garage/workshop in one corner. The yard is protected by a cyclone fence that stretches from the edge of the house to the property-line and all the way around with a double-wide gate for auto access to the garage. There is even a swing-set left behind by the owners!

A big bonus for our new family is that the back yard abuts the playground of an elementary school with the building about a hundred meters away.

The house next door is also for sale on a normal-sized lot and a smaller, ranch-style home trimmed with flowers out front. It didn't take long to make a decision and call RPR. Hazel said she will help me today as Holly is contracting with a bank to maintain some foreclosed properties before they are auctioned off. I know the Wood sisters have been getting more work like this in recent months.

I apologized for wasting her sister's time in Honeywood Heights but now I have a strong interest in a different part of town. I gave Hazel the address and she said to give her an hour. Then I called Tina and told her what I found. "Since you are helping me with investments, I want your opinion on my plan. It is a slow day so she was able to come right over.

Cousin and I walked around the houses and then I sat on one of the swings to rest and reflect. I could see us making a life here, with children playing on the swing set, climbing the fruit trees like little monkeys and scrambling over the fence to go to school.

My reverie was interrupted by a man who entered the back yard and said "Hello!" He is around my parents age and had a gentle demeanor. "Are you looking to buy this house?"

"I don't know yet," I said cautiously. "I am just looking for now."

He said, "I've lived next door for over thirty years and just wanted to be sure no one was trying to break in."

He was not threatening or accusing us, so I said lightly, "The only thing I have ever stolen is my husband's heart."

He chuckled and said, "The world could use more of that, couldn't it?" When I stood up from the swing, he looked more closely and asked, "Have I seen you somewhere before?"

"I don't think so, but maybe you have seen me in town or at the grocery store. I don't think there are so many tall women like me in Riverton."

"That is true," he said, tapping the side of his nose in concentration. I introduced Ca and myself with first names only and the man's name is Al. We all shook hands and he said he hoped I will find what I am looking for. Pointing at my tummy, he asked, "You have any other children?"

"No, this is my first."

"For what it's worth, this is a good neighborhood for children young and old," he said, before trudging back to his home. I would be very happy to have him as our neighbor, and I am sure Fred would too.

Tina showed up as the man was leaving and, looking around, said "It's not Honeywood Heights, but it's certainly a better neighborhood than where you are now!"

I showed sister both houses and shared my idea with her. Her eyes got big and asked, "Have you told Fred?"

"I just found both these houses for sale and am making my own decisions. If they are in as good a shape as I think they are and have you help me strike a good bargain, I'm going to buy them with my own money and tell Fred later."

She whistled appreciatively and said in English, "That's bold!"

When Hazel arrived, she said "I thought the address sounded familiar!"

We went into both houses and inspected them thoroughly, especially the larger one. I could feel special things within its walls that I never experienced in the many other homes I have visited. So much so, that I became very emotional, and not in the hormonal way. I want very much to buy them both.

Before she left the office, Hazel had done some quick research and found both sets of owners are, as they say, "motivated sellers", meaning they are months behind on their mortgages and the banks holding their titles are willing to bargain to keep them from going to auction.

The prices of the homes here are a fraction of the cheapest Honeywood Heights mini-mansions. Hazel said the schools in this neighborhood are not as good as HH schools but they have very good teachers and lots of the graduates go on to college.

The homes appear to be in good shape, but we will still have a professional inspection done. Fred will take care of any repairs or upgrades that need to be done, assuming the homes are not rotting away from the inside out or, God forbid, declared as hazardous waste sites.

Hazel will get one of her inspectors on it right away and let me know. I asked her to please say nothing to Fred about this and winked at her. She pulled her fingers across her mouth like a zipper and said "My lips are sealed!" Ca copied Hazel's motion and smiled.

Hazel will run the numbers and let us know what she thinks we can get away with as an asking price for the houses. "There are no offers on either house right now as there is far more supply than demand." That means this is a good time for us. Yay!

At dinner I told Fred to move some of my short sale profits to my personal savings account. When he asked why, I said, "I have plenty of extra money now and do not want to invest it all. I just want to have some cash put away for a rainy day." I so like that expression!

Fred shrugged and said he will take care of it over the computer. He has no idea how rainy it will be soon!

Dear My Diary,

Hazel's assistant called me to say they have submitted the offers on both houses and it will be up to the lienholders to accept or reject our proposals. If accepted, we can close within ten days if I pay with cash. If rejected, then I will make a new offer and try again.

The inspections show that both houses are in good, but not excellent, condition, which is better than I expected, considering they are well over fifty years old. The list of things that need to be fixed are small and easy enough to do. There is no need to get the old owners involved as they are most certainly without money.

Fred is getting used to Ca. He does not speak to her much but I see that he tries to be polite and considerate, using simple English, pantomime and physical expressions to get his meaning across. Fred does not act with Ca as he does with other people and I am sure it is because things started with her in a difficult way because of Aunt Duc's transparently manipulative manner. It will take time for Fred to warm up as she is also living with us, but not as a visitor and maybe that is what is making him uncomfortable too.

Ca is getting used to our home now as she learns to use the microwave, oven and washer/dryer, none of which she has used before in Vietnam. When it comes to my cousin, patience is a required virtue.

We found an ESL class for her at the community college to improve her English. It's one of those classes people can join or drop out anytime. We think her English will improve more quickly with no one but me around her who speaks Vietnamese, and I am using as little VN as is practical with her. We will see.

August 16, 2002
Dear My Diary,

It has been a busy week so let me catch up and write like it is August 13th, our wedding anniversary:

First of all, the second-best news I have is that the official closing on both houses will be late next week, but Hazel and Holly are letting me take the properties now as I have paid with certified checks from my account. Now I have the keys for just long enough to do what I want.

Before giving Fred his present, I arranged with a caterer for an early dinner at Frank and Maggie's home. Dinner was a mix of Vietnamese and American foods and Ca made the jasmine tea using our best service. There was very little work on our part so we could spend more time relaxing and enjoying the delicious meal.

Frank is getting around pretty good with an electric wheelchair and Fred purchased a specially equipped van with an electric lift. We do not have vehicles like this in Vietnam and Ca is clearly impressed with how easy it is for Frank to be more mobile. Frank and Maggie like Ca and she is kind to them in her quiet way.

We had a nice chat through dinner, but I am nervous of what will happen later. I think Baby understands this and has increased the tempo of its kicks, making me even more uncomfortable, but I try not to show it.

Maggie is excited about being a grandma soon and Frank gives me his funny smile and winks with the half of his body that still works. Everyone is in a good mood, so I said, "I want to take everyone out for a drive, if that is okay, but we will need to use your van."

It is a warm evening and they agreed, as long as we are not out too late. I promised parents it will not take long.

Fred offered to drive and I said "No, this is my treat." Ca got to see how Frank is loaded into the van, then sat next to him and held his hand in hers. So sweet!

I did not drive directly to our destination but in a roundabout manner, through other pretty neighborhoods as the Starbuckles reminisced about how this neighborhood has changed and how pretty that home is and so on. Then I stopped the van and gave everyone a sleep mask to put over their eyes. "I want to show you a surprise, but you have to close your eyes until we get there." They were puzzled but agreed to play along as I made encouraging comments like "No peeking!" and "Almost there!"

When I stopped the van, I told them to keep their eyes covered as I led Fred out of the passenger door and Ca led Maggie, then she turned Frank's chair toward the open van door.

"Take off your masks!" and Ca helped Frank with his. "SURPRISE!"

My husband and his parents stared at the big house. Maggie was the first to respond. "This is our old house. What are we doing here?"

I said "This is the surprise. I bought the house for our anniversary present!"

Fred turned to me, his mouth agape. "You didn't!"

"Yes, I did! Look. The sign says SOLD! It says Sold because I bought it. See? I even have the key!"

Maggie had her hands over her mouth, chanting "Oh my Lord! Oh my Lord!" as Fred looked at me uncertainly. "And why did you buy this house?"

Now I am not sure if I did a good thing or a bad thing. I thought everyone would be very happy right away but I cannot read their reactions at this moment.

I turned to my American parents. "I bought the house because I think this is the perfect place for us to raise our children…in the house where their Daddy grew up and went to school. I know you lost the house before, but now it is back in the family. I hope you like it!" and I wiggled the key at them.

Now, in my best TV announcer voice I said, "But wait, there's more! As a special anniversary bonus, you get an extra house free!" and I pulled out the other key and pointed to the house next door. "And I got this one for the two of you so you can be right next door to us. We can help you more easily and our children can see their grandma and grandpa whenever they want!"

"You bought TWO houses?" exclaimed Maggie and Fred at the same time.

"Yes, really, I did. And I wanted parents to have the big house but since Frank can't climb stairs anymore, I got the one-story house next door. Even better, it already has a wheelchair ramp, wider doors, a roll-in shower and other handicap designs in place."

Frank had tears streaming from his good eye so I went over, hugged him and asked if he likes the present. He shook his head, "Not like. Love. Love you. So good." His voice is croaky like a frog but with much more heart.

Suddenly, Fred wordlessly hefted me up in his arms and gave me a passionate kiss, his salty tears flavoring the moment. He set me down and Maggie took a turn at hugging and kissing me. By now, I was crying and everyone was emotional but for Ca who accepted the scene with quiet detachment.

Maggie stuffed a sodden tissue into her bra and said "You are the sweetest, most thoughtful, most generous child! I can't believe you did this and we can't begin to tell you how much this means to us! Frank! Let me get you out of that van!"

Fred looked a little embarrassed. "After all this, I feel a little silly giving you your anniversary gift." And he gave me a small box. Inside is an expensive designer key chain.

"It's not a silly gift, Fred. It is very practical for our new house keys…and since it's a Tiffany key chain, it looks like we are even!"

We went into the small house first and Frank is able to get in and out of every room with his wheelchair. Maggie said, "The McDougals used to live here and Fred had SUCH a crush on their daughter, you wouldn't believe!"

Fred sounded like a little boy when he said, "Mom! I was only in the sixth grade!"

Then we visited the big house and I can't imagine what was in their minds as they went through their old home and all its memories. Fred told me that when he was a young teen, there was a tornado on a Sunday morning that destroyed the elementary school on the other side of the fence. The building there now is not the same building Fred attended. No one was hurt as it was empty and very early in the morning.

As we were coming out, the nice old man from next door, Al, came over and said "Well, as I live and breathe! Frank! Maggie! Visiting the old neighborhood?"

Maggie said, "As a matter of fact, we are moving back here, just to keep an eye on you!" and they both laughed as old friends do. Maggie put her arm around my shoulder and said "Al, I want to introduce you to my daughter-in-law, Kim. She is helping us get moved back here."

Al's eyes lit with recognition, "Now I know where I saw you…at church! On Easter! Oh, yes, you were quite popular that day."

Maggie looked a little embarrassed and said "Well, she didn't know any better and…"

"Oh, I know that! After I thought about what she said, I couldn't help but see how she thought Jesus was a zombie. After all, when you don't know the bible and its stories like we do, some of the miracles can sound a little crazy. People are going to match up what they hear or read with something that they can connect with. It's human nature." Then to me, he asked "So, are you going to be my new neighbor?"

I said, "Yes, with Fred." and Fred came over to shake hands as Al asked "Are you still growing?"

"More out than up these days!"

After Al returned home, I reminded Frank and Maggie how much I love them. I feel so much a part of the Starbuckle family that when I saw the houses for sale, I knew I had to get them right away. Maggie thanked me so many times and said that I am the daughter she always wanted. It was just at that moment when I felt warm water trickle down my legs.

I was embarrassed, thinking I had accidentally wet myself, but Maggie said "I declare, I do believe your water just broke!"

I was not sure what Maggie meant, but Ca saw it too and said "I think the sac has opened and it is time for the baby to come out." She is much more familiar with these things than I am.

Fred took off his T-shirt and helped me clean my legs while Maggie got Frank back into the van. Fred drove his parents home, then drove us straight to the hospital in our car with the baby bag.

Next the first best thing happened: After nine hours of labor, Franklin Pham Starbuckle arrived at 1:35 am on August 14th, the day after our two-year anniversary. He is a very healthy-looking boy at seven pounds, five ounces and twenty inches long.

After Frankie was cleaned up, I got to hold him first. It is so beautiful and wonderful to see our new son, so tiny in my long arms. After all my worries of our baby being damaged from the kick, he looks so perfect and the doctor said all his functions appear normal.

Even through his surgical mask, I can see Fred smiling like a child at Christmas. Frankie, I think this is how I will call him, stared and stared at me like "Who are you? Are you the same one who's been talking to me while I grew in your tummy?"

Fred and Ca got to hold him for a few minutes each before Frankie fell asleep after working so hard to come out and visit. The hospital provided a crib next to my bed so we can watch him, nurse him and do everything right there. The doctors and nurses are so kind and thoughtful, making sure we have everything we need and answering all our questions.

At about five o'clock, Fred took Ca home, then emailed all our family and close friends before coming back and sleeping in the big chair near my bed.

I stayed in the hospital for two days to rest, get used to nursing, learning to change tiny diapers and make sure our little son is in perfect health. I also had many visitors, but Fred made sure their stays were short: Frank and Maggie, sisters, nieces, Bunny, Aunt Ginger and the Woods. Everyone brought some gift along with their good wishes and fawned over the baby who mostly slept through the visits.

On the morning of the third day, we left the hospital as a family of three, securing Frankie into the car seat for his first ride. On the way home, Fred talked and talked about the houses, saying it is the best thing that has happened to his parents in a long time. "I love you so very, very much and I don't want you to ever change."

We cannot move into the houses until the closing process is officially completed. but Holly says not to worry as it is a "done deal". I like that expression!

Fred will direct the workers from RPR in the cleaning and repainting of the big house inside and out, removing the carpets to install laminate flooring and other upgrades. The house was not in bad shape, but still looked very much the way it was when Fred grew up, which was fine for back then. Fred understands enough about home-styles to know we need more outlets, more counterspace in the kitchen and easier to clean walls and floors everywhere with lighter colors.

RPR has some real experts on their staff to make renovations faster, cheaper and with less negotiating than with an outside contractor. Fred thinks everything will be done in about a month or so after closing is completed.

Very little work will need to be done for his parents' home as it was clearly remodeled before it went up for sale. Once the recession took hold, the last owner could not afford to pay both the mortgage and their apartment rent anymore and that is how they lost the house.

Frankie's eyes are blue and not shaped like mine. At first, I thought a newborn's eyes are sometimes blue, then changes later but the doctor said his eyes are really blue like Fred's and his parents. Frankie will sleep in a crib next to my side of the bed and I have a rocking chair with big cushions for nursing.

Speaking of which, my breasts have swollen so much that the nursing bras I bought are way too small now. Thanh will help me get some new ones in a few days as I can't trust Fred with that job…he gets red-faced just walking through the lingerie section of any store.

I am worried about my tummy still being puffed out like I have another child to deliver, but the doctor and Thanh say it will shrink back down soon. I sure hope so, if I am going to continue modeling. Sister showed me her stretch marks from the twins as she was very, very big before their birth.

That is all for now, My Diary. A new baby, and soon a new home.

Dear My Diary,

So many good wishes are coming in from everywhere! Beginning, of course, with my family in Vietnam and Fred's family throughout the state. I do not know many of Fred's family very well, but it seems Maggie has been sending out Frankie's photos to everyone she knows.

Thanh and her family came to visit and the girls are so excited about their new cousin. They have other cousins from Vo's side of the family, but they are in Vietnam so we only got to meet a few of them during this last trip. As for Frankie, the twins can see him much more often. We took pictures and videos of the girls holding Frankie and talking with him as he stared and stared at them in puzzled wonder.

My Fierce 5 sisters all sent congratulations, good wishes and gift cards, as did Zander. She has asked if I will stay with Fierce 5 now that I have a child? I said, "Oh, yes! I love being part of Fierce 5. It is like having four more sisters!" I could hear Zander smile over the phone when she responded, "Well, we love having you as part of the team, too!"

August 25, 2002
Dear My Diary,

This morning was so crazy and Fred is furious at Ca. He was up late last night reviewing investment opportunities and was sleeping in as Ca and I ate warmed sardines for breakfast and discussed what we plan to do today. Then I nursed Frankie while Ca made eggs and ham for Fred.

Soon, I heard Fred yell "What the hell are you doing? Get off of me!" Poor Frankie was still latched on as I rushed to the kitchen and saw Ca run out of our bedroom and into hers, slamming the door behind her.

Fred came out in his underwear, very red-faced. "What the hell is wrong with her?" he asked. "I want her out of here and I want her out NOW!"

I followed Fred to the bathroom as he took in gulps of water and spit it back into the sink. I said nothing, knowing he will tell me soon enough.

"I was sleeping and dreamed that a fish swam into my mouth. It was so weird, that I opened my eyes." Fred shuddered and made a bitter face as he continued, "And there she was, kissing me with tongue and touching my tool with her hand. Nasty, yech! That's when I yelled and pushed her away. I don't know what kind of man she thinks I am, but I am NOT that kind of man. Jeez!"

Fred began brushing his teeth with an intensity I had not witnessed before, attempting to clear the fish taste out of his mouth. Frankie, upset at the breakfast-time drama, let out as much of a wail as an infant can muster as I tried to understand why cousin did such a thing. It's not like Fred has been flirting with her…or the other way around that I can see.

Fred cleaned the bedroom floor of the spilled eggs and rinsed the slab of ham as I made a new breakfast, and we left Ca alone. Fred was too mad to eat, so I packed his breakfast as a lunch and he headed out to B&R's offices.

With Fred gone, I knocked on cousin's door. She let me in, head hung in shame and eyes red from crying. Avoiding eye contact with me, I got the story. It was as I suspected: Ca said her mother wants more money from us and instructed Ca to do some sexy thing with Fred so he will give her more money. And if he refused to pay, then Ca would threaten to tell me about their sexy fun times.

Ca admitted that she did not want to do this and has never made sexy time with anyone before, but her mother put on pressure and told her what to do.

In the back of my mind, I thought, 'Well, for starters, you do not kiss a man right after you have eaten fish for breakfast,' but instead, I said "Fred is not a man who has sexual pleasures outside of marriage. Fred is very true to me and only wants me. He is loyal to me and I am loyal to him. That is why he yelled and got very upset when you did this bad thing."

Ca said her mother told her all men do the sexy thing away from their wife and even her father has many girlfriends.

"Yes, it is true that many men do this, but many other men do not. What you did is very wrong, even if your mother told you to do it. Now you will have to leave our home and go back to Saigon in shame."

This made Ca cry and say she did not want to do the sexy thing and will never do it again. "I want to stay with you and will never touch Fred again."

"What about your mother?" I asked. "She pressured you to do the bad thing and even instructed you to threaten us? For what? More money? That kind of trouble is not worth it to us." I took her slender shoulder in my hand and looked directly into her eyes. "If we give you more money now, then mother will soon ask for more and the demands will continue going up like a ladder without end. We can't have that…and we won't have that. You must leave."

"I will divorce Me and Ba and never speak to them again or send them money."

"You cannot divorce your parents," I pointed out. "You should have a good relationship with them. But the good thing is that you are living far from their hands and you can stop listening to their poison talk and demands. And you should send them some money as children should do, but save some of what you make and grow a nest egg to be more independent."

I told Ca how Fred, my Fierce 5 friends and others helped me understand that it is okay to say "No" to bad requests and stand up for what is right. "It's very simple, Cousin. If you are told do something bad, and you know it is bad, then do not do it."

After a long, heart-to-heart talk, we agreed that she will stay with us. But should anything like this happen again, we really will send her back to Saigon and she will lose much face among the family and neighbors as the girl who went to America and then was kicked out.

"What about Fred?" Ca asked.

"I will take care of Fred," I assured her, though I was not so sure of his reaction to my decision. "But now, let us not say any more about it."

Dear My Diary,

Bunny used the intercom to call up and see if she can visit her nephew. "Of course!" I said and once in our living quarters, she washed her hands and face at the kitchen sink before taking Frankie from his crib.

Bunny is so gentle with him and makes the sweetest talk. I guess she is still an aunt, even though the divorce is final, and I still think of Bunny as a sister, so yes, she is Frankie's aunt and he does not know the difference. He looks and studies his aunt so much, as he does with the rest of us...always studying whoever is holding him or is nearby.

His hair is beginning to curl and is a bit light. I wonder if that will be part of his permanent self, like his father. It is hard to tell as babies often change over time, like how hairy babies lose all their hair soon after birth or fair-haired babies can turn dark or the other way around. It is as interesting to watch him change and develop day by day as whatever he finds fascinating about all of us.

I told Bunny about the day my water broke right after showing the house Fred and Barney grew up in and the house next door for our parents as a gift.

Bunny looked puzzled, "You bought the house they lost after investing in all those Bio-oil companies?"

I said, "The house they lost when Barney invested money he borrowed against their equity to buy bio-oil stocks." Then we went back and forth about what we know, since that all happened before either of us met our husbands.

Bunny shook her head. "I can't believe that I fell for that stupid story from Barney. I never thought his story made much sense, knowing Frank and Maggie. And that Power of Attorney was like giving him a license to steal."

I explained that after Fred bought back the garage, his father did not have the money or heart to start the business over, "So that is why Fred took over the building and here we are!" I spread my arms out in an encompassing gesture.

Ca said "Here we are!" and spread her arms out in imitation, then smiled. Bunny repeated the action and then we all kept saying "Here we are!" and spreading our arms like game-show models as we laughed harder and harder at our own silliness. Frankie got bored and let me know it is time to eat...Whaaa!

Needless to say, Fred was not happy that I did not send Ca back home. In my sweetest and gentlest manner, I told him of our discussion and he grudgingly agreed to let Ca stay as long as she avoids listening to her mother's bad ideas and is respectful to all of us.

At dinner, after everyone was served, Ca sat and, while staring down into her bowl, said "I make sorry, Fred."

I said, "Speak to Fred's face, not your food."

She sat up, looked directly at Fred and said in a small, sad voice "I make sorry, Fred. Please, I make sorry."

Fred's face fell, then he firmed up again and said quietly, "Ca, I accept your sorry. Do not do that again. Okay?" She said "Okay" and that was the end of that.

I don't think any of us have heard that story before…and I would not expect our parents to tell it around either. How embarrassing! It worked out well though. Ca has remained a part of our family all these years. Quiet, dependable and good-natured Aunt Ca. She never went to nursing school but helped all us kids, and some of our own, through all kinds of childhood diseases and boo-boos.

Kimmie: That was the maddest I think I have ever seen Fred that did not have something to do with Barney. We had been warned time and again about Aunt Duc and she lived up to her expectations as a trouble maker. Luckily for us, Ca does not have a mean bone in her body and has been a constant and faithful companion and helper to this very day. We never discussed that incident ever again, and now it's being published for all the world to see. Troi oi!

September 3, 2002
Dear My Diary,

Today, I was at the Vietnamese store getting groceries with Frankie and Ca when a woman stopped us and asked me about the baby and my husband. Tonight, I shared the story with Fred and the woman's questions, asking if my husband is white because of how Frankie looks. Of course, I told her 'yes'.

But Fred disagreed with my answer. "That was very nosy of her to ask that," he said. "That is none of her business. Do you know what you should tell someone if they ask you that again?" I asked "What?"

"Tell them your husband is Asian, but your BOYFRIEND is white!"

I laughed to think of the look on the woman's face if I had said this to her…I know Fred is not serious, but I could never say such a thing, not even to a rude person. I told Ca what Fred had said and she laughed and laughed!

I wish we had a dollar for every time we've heard that story from Dad…and it always got a laugh. Frankie looks so Caucasian, he used to call himself "Whasian".

At the store, there are stacks of free Asian language newspapers, and I found an ad for a local church that offers free ESL classes. The church is not far from our new home, so I spoke to Fred about it and he agreed it would be a good thing for Ca.

If it is well-run and helpful to cousin, we can make a donation to the church. I am now speaking to Ca mostly in English with some help on words and phrases in VN. To help further, sometimes we watch TV so Ca can hear English from different kinds of people as I explain some of what they saying, like the news or children shows which are easier to understand.

Sept 14, 2002
Dear My Diary,

Today is Frankie's one month birthday and we had a little party for him. We invited my sisters, Auntie Giang and her family, Frank and Maggie and Bunny to celebrate. Maggie asked me why we are having a one-month birthday?

I explained that birth and the first month afterward is the most common time for babies and mothers to die from infections, illness or any number of other complications related to childbirth. After the first month, the biggest dangers have passed so we make a celebration for the continued good health of both. We served tea and cakes and Frankie got some new clothes and toys, red eggs for good luck, Lucky Money and so much attention from everyone.

He is staying awake longer now and is more active. The doctor says he is growing normally and everything looks great, which pleases me to no end. After what happened during filming, the more Frankie grows, the better I feel.

Ca is becoming more helpful to me now, anticipating our needs and what is to be done, as she did for the party today. I heard Auntie ask Ca how she is getting along in her new life and Ca said she likes us very much…that we are nice to her, and she loves caring for the baby and helping us.

Auntie looked pleased and I felt good too. I can see Fred is becoming more relaxed around Ca now, especially after what happened with them last month. I think they are at the point of "forgive and forget" now.

Everyone is asking Fred if he is changing diapers and yes, he is a good Daddy this way, except when Frankie makes a sudden pee-pee fountain on Daddy, then Fred shrieks like a little girl…it is too funny! I shared the story in my language so as not to embarrass Fred in front of his parents, but he understands when I am telling the story.

The party lasted just two hours, but we had such fun and Cam and Tam love looking at their new cousin, talking to him and Frankie makes nice faces back at them. He *loves* the attention! He fell into a deep sleep after the party which made me a bit jealous…I really wanted a nap as well!

MFAP.

Dear My Diary,

Fred took me to a very interesting meeting tonight. He did not tell me where we were going or what it was about but said Bobby and Robbie would be there with some good information to share.

This is the first time we are leaving Frankie alone with Cousin Ca so I am a bit nervous, but I would not go if we did not trust her and I left two bottles of expressed milk for feedings.

We went to one of the smaller downtown hotels and entered a meeting room with many men in attendance and a few women. The stage had a long table, chairs and a dais with microphone with a couple of hundred chairs in neat rows facing it.

Over the table is a flag with the letters 'MFAP' in the center with the words "Marriage For" above and "All People" below the main letters. At the left edge of the stage is an American Flag, State Flag and a rainbow flag. Many of the people attending appear to know each other well, are dressed stylishly and it feels like a cocktail party with beer, wine and soft drinks for sale at a bar in the back corner.

Fred got ginger ales for both of us and we met up with Bobby and Robbie who asked after the baby. "Frankie is fine and can't wait to meet his uncles," I said, pointing at them. They smiled at being called 'uncles'.

Bobby thanked us for coming and expressed the hope that I enjoy the meeting tonight. "You might find this interesting, Kim. Just keep an open mind," he said, putting his hands on either side of his head and making a blossoming motion. So funny!

Robbie is looking thinner than I remember, so I asked him "Are you losing weight?" Robbie and Bobby's eyes made contact for a tiny second, then Robbie smiled and said yes, he has lost a few pounds recently. I congratulated him, but his smile was not of one who is happy to be losing weight. Maybe he is working too hard or has deeper worries on his mind.

"I am losing my baby fat by getting up four times a night to feed," I said, trying to lighten the mood.

Bobby said, "If I got up four times a night to feed, I'd be as big as a truck!"

Fred and I recognized some of the attendees through our business, charity committees and one or two from auctions. Soon we were asked to take a seat and I asked Fred what kind of meeting this is? He said "You will see."

I looked around and some of the men were holding hands or draping their arm over the back of their neighbor's chair like Fred does with me sometimes. Then I remembered the meaning of the rainbow flag and I began to wonder why Fred brought me to a meeting for gay people? I did see a few man-woman couples, but not many.

The man in charge welcomed everybody and they introduced the members of the MFAP committee, explaining their goal of making people aware of their current rights as citizens and to get more rights passed including marriage for all people.

When I first came in, I thought the banner meant for all couples like me and Fred...now I understand it is to gain the right of marriage for ALL people who want to marry including gay people. I wonder why they want to be married with a license like me and Fred? And it was from this meeting that I learned more.

They introduced "Riverton's own dynamic duo of financial wizardry" as Bobby and Robbie stepped up to the microphone. After welcoming everyone, they explained how there are many rights and privileges that legally married couples have that non-married couples do not have and how it is not fair that the laws accept one kind of marriage but not others.

Many of the unfair treatments regard taxes, wills, social security, health insurance, life insurance, giving legal authorization to another for a variety of reasons. The general feeling of the group is that any two people of consenting age should be able to marry and have all the legal rights afforded them without question. As it stands now, gay couples can not marry or have the full legal rights that others have, even if they have been together for many years.

Bobby and Robbie, along with other speakers, shared stories and information, some were very sad like the story of a long-time gay couple where the one who owned the home died and the dead partner's family came and took everything from the house they had shared for many years, kicking the grieving partner out and calling him "a roommate" with no rights to the house or its contents. The widow-man sued for the house and contents but the family won because there was no will and the widow was not considered family in the eyes of the law, so he had no rights to protect him.

There was much nodding and agreement with the audience and I feel that many of them have had similar experiences. Bobby and Robbie face the same legal problems as those they spoke of, especially as they get older and have much shared wealth between them as a couple. Luckily, both their families accept them as a couple and I don't think they would do something ugly against their son's partner. But not all families are as accepting as them. It is clear now why they want to make gay marriage a legal reality in American society.

The meeting finished with requests to write letters to the President, Governor, Senators and Congressmen for more equal marriage rights and finding more effective ways to bring attention to these issues.

After the meeting, many people lined up to give checks and cash donations to help the committee promote their goals and agendas to the press, lawmakers and the general public. Fred already had a check in his pocket that he handed over for ten thousand dollars.

We talked with others as the meeting broke up. Robbie took my arm and asked me what I thought of the meeting. I explained how very different this is for me and that gay couples are not legal in my country.

Robbie said, "It is not legal to be gay in many parts of the United States, but times need to change. Love should not be confined by the boundaries of laws. But without laws to protect everyone, there will still be discrimination and unfair treatment." He went on to explain how Massachusetts and California are very close to becoming the first states to legalize gay marriage and, if that happens, "the rest should soon fall like dominoes."

Fred told me at home that the money he and others gave will help educate people like they did tonight, help pay for lobbyists to push politicians to change the laws and so on. I feel very sorry now for gay people as they have so few rights. The way I know our friends and how much they love and respect each other, as well as others we are acquainted with, some of whom I did not know are gay until the meeting, it makes sense to me to have more freedoms for them.

Moving Day For Parents

September 30, 2002

Fred will not let me do much work on the new homes…my job is to be a good Me to Frankie, teach Ca things that she needs to know and make decisions for the new house like placement of furniture, who will be where and so on.

For example, Fred and the RPR workers are making the kitchen bigger by extending it three meters into the yard. The original kitchen was very small so we are adding a work island and pantry with plenty of new counterspace, shelving and storage.

As much as Fred loves what we have at the garage that he got free over the years, I insisted on splurging for new appliances and furniture. I mean, what's all this new money for, if not to make our living space more comfortable and attractive?

We are leaving the old stuff at the garage for Michael to use except for the super-king mattress that fits us so well. Everything we need is coming from one of the larger locally-owned furniture stores who are giving us a 10% discount on the full bill if we use their store credit card. Since we will pay off the card right away, we won't pay their high interest rate. We spent a lot, but we will save a lot more…plus, the owner has offered me a job as their spokesmodel for television and print ads!

Frankie: Mom did Arnold's Furniture television and print ads for over twenty years and it was a steady paycheck for her, year after year. As her star rose and she got more roles in films and television, the owners accommodated her schedule for three or four days a year to tape commercials.

Kimmie: In the earlier years, I simply posed, pointed and gestured. Later on, as my accent became clearer, they gave me lines to speak, with a commensurate bump in pay. Whenever a new store was opening, I usually attended, helping to cut the ribbon, hobnob with the customers and Chamber of Commerce members and sign autographs.

Between Arnold's, Anh Hai the Sandwich Guy, Fierce 5 and Riverton Auto Mall, I had a tidy sum coming in all year round for some of the easiest work I have ever done. Strangers smiled and waved to me on the streets, asked me for autographs, asked me for advice on breaking into show business and more. So different from my earlier times…

Our home is bigger than average for the neighborhood, but not as large as the Honeywood Heights mini-mansions. We have four bedrooms, two and a half baths, and two spare rooms, one for the library/office and the other was a playroom that, once the boys were older, Maggie had turned into a sewing and hobby room. Now it will be a playroom again.

The lot is double-size from that of our neighbors and on one end of the backyard is a small barn where Frank and his brothers used to work on old cars and re-sell them when they were teenagers.

How strange that I only just learned that this was also the house Frank grew up in. If someone had told me this bit of family history before, then I did not catch it. Anyway, once Frank took over the garage business, he had no time for hobby cars and Fred used the barn to store his treasures for re-selling. There is so much family history in this home and running into a fourth generation of Starbuckles!

Frank and Maggie have already moved into their new home and they are *so* happy. Fred said "If they had tails, they would wag them right off!" I translated this to Ca and she laughed and laughed at Fred's comment. She thinks Fred is very funny…and I agree!

Frank and Maggie had so much to move into their new home…decades of memories and belongings plus all their furniture and appliances. This house is a bit bigger than the one Fred got them and with many nice features for Frank and his motorized wheelchair. Moving was a lot of work, but worth every hug and kiss of appreciation.

Now they want us to help them sell what they can't or won't use anymore and add that money to their retirement accounts while making more room. We will get Bunny and Michael involved with this project as we are getting ourselves settled in. Now why couldn't they think of selling all that stuff *before* they moved? Oh, well.

I have a lot more clothes now than what I brought from Vietnam, but it's not as much as what Thanh has, as she often likes to point out to me. We only needed a few large boxes and totes to pack our personals, along with the TV, VCR, and not much else. Fred and I will use one of the work trucks to bring everything over in one load once the furniture is delivered and set up to make the move easier.

Ca has found a series of cooking videos on VidLive. They are cleverly presented as they do not speak, but just show how to make the dish with only basic English instructions printed on the screen. Ca will watch one video several times, making careful notes of the instructions in VN using her dictionaries to translate, then make the dish for us.

Fred is happy with the new meals as they are very healthy, tasty and cover a variety of ethnic styles. We praised Ca for her efforts, which is the opposite of how we saw Duc treat her. Fred is growing softer towards Ca, speaking kindly to her when just weeks ago he was cold and indifferent after the kissing incident. Actually, Ca is not lazy at all and, if you have patience with her, is not as mentally slow as she first comes across.

I have started leaving Frankie with Ca and either going to Golden Boy Gym for workouts or running in different neighborhoods to trim down and rebuild muscle tone so I can keep doing F5 jobs and other modeling or acting gigs as they come to me, like for Arnolds Furniture stores.

Ca's English is steadily improving to the point where I allow her to answer my calls with the most basic responses when I am busy nursing or otherwise have my hands full. When someone asks for me, Ca is instructed to say "Who is calling please?" then, "One minute please!" or "She is not available now." Today, I got a call from a woman I do not know and Ca did the right steps until I took over the phone.

The woman said "I called because I heard you might be looking for representation." I did not know what this last word meant, so I asked who she is.

"I'm so sorry, I thought you were expecting my call. My name is Takeela Rockett and I represent Rock Rollins as his agent. Rock gave me your number and was insistent on my calling you."

Oh, I remember now! Rock had said something about this at the clam bake. I wasn't quite clear of all the things she said, but I understood enough to keep the conversation going.

"Yes, I might be interested in doing this, but I don't know yet if I want an agent. Can you please explain to me how this works?"

Takeela said I must first provide a resume and any copies of pictures, videos, sound recordings, etc. of work I have done. If what I have is acceptable, we will have a meeting and discus what I am looking for, my abilities, interests and so forth along with reading parts of sample scripts that will be sent to me ahead of our meeting.

If the agency feels like they can get me work, which is not a guarantee, the agency fee is a percentage of what Takeela can negotiate for the job to be done. I have read how agents push for the highest prices along with merchandising and residual clauses for entertainers and athletes. That will be Takeela's job, but only if she believes I will get the work and pay to make it worth her time.

She asked me questions regarding my entertainment history and I went over my contract with Fierce 5 and Zander and I have an actor's union card. Takeela said that because I have so little experience in this kind of work, normally she would not take me on, but because Rock had recommended me, we will do the interview and audition steps to judge my talent potential.

If her agency is willing to take a chance on me, it will not be on an exclusive basis, meaning I can work with Zander on F5 projects and other jobs I can get on my own while Takeela shops me around. In other words, it will be a kind of open-door agreement that I can find my own work to build my experience and resume while they also find jobs for me. Later, if my desirability increases greatly, we can set up an exclusive contract and they will push much harder to find lucrative roles for me.

I think that sounds fair and I said as much, so I will speak to Fred about it and get back to her. I got her contact information and thanked Takeela for calling. She understands this is a new thing for me, like modeling and acting work and said she was interested in one-on-one meeting.

She works with Rock Rollins, so she must be VERY good at what she does.

We are finally moved in…Yay! The new furniture and appliances were delivered last week and set up in the most attractive way we could arrange them.

Frankie's room is next to ours and is painted in soft yellows and blues with my nursing rocker in one corner. The pastels are much happier colors for a little child than old brick and wood. Fred added cartoon character decals on the walls that can be removed easily when he is too old for them.

Frankie is not sleeping all the way through the night yet but is waking fewer times than before, so more sleep for Mommy and Daddy! We have decided to use these American terms for Frankie, but in speaking with Ca I still fall back to using Me and Ba. She understands the English parental nicknames but old cultural habits are hard to break.

Dear My Diary,

I found some time to speak with Fred about my discussion with Takeela Rockett and I openly wondered if I should continue to do acting and modeling. My thoughtful and considerate Fred asked me what *I* think and desire.

"So far it has been fun. I've made new friends and I feel it is a good way to keep busy."

"I don't keep you busy enough?" he replied, waggling his eyebrows at me.

"Oh yes, you and Frankie keep me plenty busy! But really, one of the reasons I brought Ca is that I might want to continue with this kind of career. I feel like I want to, but I will not do it if my husband does not want me to."

Fred smiled kindly at me, with a bit of hurt around the corners of his eyes. His attitude has always been to let me make my own decisions and not be ordered about by my husband, so my comment of submission hurts him a bit.

"Kimmie, acting is not like a nine to five job. With entertainment, some work might be for a day or a week and sometimes can last for years, like with a television series. You can pick and choose the jobs you are selected for depending on the part, the schedule and how it affects the family."

Fred took my hands into his. "I think it's great if you want to keep on with this. I have watched you change so much since I met you, and all for the better."

I am touched by his words. We kissed and hugged and made plans to call Rock. I want to understand better how things work for him, if he thinks we need Takeela at this point in my new career and, most importantly, if it will help me or hurt me to make a career of acting.

Fred is so supportive, and Ca is becoming a good helper. I almost forgot! She has her driving license now! So cool! She and I practiced a lot and she passed the final exam on the first try...Fred is *very* impressed with this. Honestly? Me too. I am so proud of my cousin. She just needed positive encouragement to blossom, same as me.

Dear My Diary,

Rock called to let me know he just finished filming "A Son's Quest" and will soon go to Texas for another film. Jokingly, I asked if he needs an Asian co-star? He laughed and said "Maybe in the next movie." The new one will be a cowboy movie with almost all men in the cast.

Fred, Rock and I did a three-way call about Takeela and what Rock thinks about me moving towards acting? I said, "I don't want you to say things to be nice. Please be honest and straight with me. I need to know your true opinion."

Rock explained how there are many kinds of actors. Some play a wide range of characters and types of stories, while others are more specialized to suit their specific looks, voices or style. Some stick to television shows, commercials or theater and others work wherever they can.

Rock said I have a unique and distinctive look that plays well to the camera and I performed my scenes very well. He said he could see me in action stories but that I should try other kinds of roles, like comedy. "You have a great sense of humor, and I think if you take some acting classes, and take them seriously, it can help you find characters and personas within you that can translate into parts."

He also said that with so many kinds of ways people watch and listen to entertainment now, that I have a good shot at getting parts "where they need a particular character to stand out in one form or another" was how Rock phrased it.

Rock recommended Takeela after having some not-so-good agents in the past. "Her fees are a little higher than most, but she is worth it!"

Fred asked "So you get what you pay for, and then some?"

Rock said "That's right. She will work hard to get you gigs, but she does not take on just anybody. You will have to prove yourself and be willing to take on some low-budget projects as you find your style. She will kick you off the roster over drug or alcohol habits, showing up late, not learning your lines or being difficult to work with. And that's why I recommended you, Kimmie. Clean habits, hard-working, you do what you are told and have a great attitude. Besides, Takeela owes me a favor. You have to have a strong resume to even be considered a client, but she has agreed to take you if you want her."

My heart nearly burst with happiness knowing that Rock thinks so highly of me.

"That sounds about right," Fred said. "She is not afraid of hard work and has been leaning towards doing more work in front of the cameras. We appreciate your kind words, Rock. You are a smart man, despite what Dodge says about you!"

"You wanted my honest opinion and I gave it to you. Now, do me a favor and don't tell Takeela that I said you have a spot with her. The best thing you can do now is accept her interview offer and do serious preparation for the script readings so that Takeela can do a proper assessment and give you directions on how to prep for future jobs, okay?

"Good luck with whatever you decide, and maybe we can work together in the future!" We said our goodbyes and hung up. Fred looked at me with a big, goofy grin. "Do I need to ask?"

I said, "Let's go make some money...Roll 'em!"

October 25, 2002
Dear My Diary,

Ca is now Trinh's newest client, helping her set up a savings and retirement account. Ca is only twenty-five, but she understands the importance to have a secure place to grow her earnings and not put it all in a hidden shoebox like many of our people do.

I asked if she still wants to send money to her parents, but she shook her head. "My parents have plenty of money and I know some of it is not honestly made. They do not need my money and I want to stay with you and Anh Fred because you are very nice to me."

Ca has been helping Maggie with Frank when I want some one-on-one time with Frankie. The first time Ca helped them, she came home with $40 and wanted to give it to me, saying Maggie gave it to her for helping out. At first Ca refused to accept the money, but Maggie was firm and pushed it into Ca's pocket, saying "You earned it. Please keep it."

I said "That's a good thing, Cousin! It is okay for you to keep the money. You help, you earn, you keep and save or do what you like."

"My parents always kept the extra money I made before."

"We are not your parents and the money you get for extra work is your own, I promise."

She hugged and thanked me before putting her new earnings away.

The other day, Maggie invited me and Frankie over for coffee and cookies to meet some our neighbors. While we visited, Ca attended the ESL class she now takes three hours per day, three days per week. The class is free and she likes the teachers and fellow students.

One of the stories I learned is how Fred used to knock on neighbor's doors and leave flyers offering "Spring Cleaning" and "Junk Removal" services. He would get paid to help clean homes and remove unwanted stuff. Anything that was worth re-selling was set aside, researched and put away for safekeeping. It was how Fred made his first money.

He started with his bicycle and built his own trailer to haul things home, and later moving up to an old pickup truck while in high school.

He used the small barn on the property to store his things and re-sell them at flea markets or to people who specialized in whatever he had to offer. By learning from these specialists, he was able to better judge the value of what he was buying and get better prices for them. Maggie even showed us a picture of the bicycle and trailer…he was so young then! Maybe 13 or so, but very tall for his age…of course!

It makes me wonder how Frankie will grow? Will he be tall like us? Frank is just over 6 feet tall and Maggie not much less. Yes, I think Frankie will be a tall one like us.

When I talked to Fred about the pictures I saw of the bicycle and trailer, he smiled. "Yeah, those were the days! I learned so much about so many things from that job. My folks gave me some guidance and even Bobby's father, once he learned what I was doing, offered to school me on saving and investing. Actually, I have been a client of Bobby's firm since I was about 15. It was just natural that I stayed with them when Bobby and Robbie took over. Well, look where we are today, huh?"

Another way Dad made easy money from cast-offs was to find free or very cheap car wheels that were left on sidewalks or advertised in the papers. People would often dress up their cars by changing out the factory rims for racing-style wheels. Dad could then turn the free wheels into a quick $50 or $75 at a flea market or to one of the local tire stores for $30 if he could not get rid of them after a few weeks.

November 1, 2002
Dear My Diary,

Takeela is flying into St. Louis next month and catching a shuttle here to have dinner and pick my brain. She asked me to think about, and write down, my talents, interests and things I might like to do in entertainment. This will be my interview and she will send some script samples to practice as though I were auditioning for a part.

I have a pretty good idea what to tell her and will have Fred help me with phrasing my thoughts. He will also contact the university theater department to see if one of the instructors can be hired to help with the script readings.

Yesterday was Halloween, so we went to the hospital in the afternoon to visit the sick children and Ca stayed home with Frankie. I feel very different about these visits now because it makes me think of what could happen if Frankie gets sick or injured and has to be treated in the hospital for a long time.

When I told Fred of my fears, he held me in his arms and gave me a long hug and a tender kiss, telling me that we cannot tell what the future holds for our children or ourselves. The best we can do is keep ourselves healthy and happy and help others who are not in the same condition. If something bad does happen to one of us, then we will deal with it the best we can. I don't know if I feel any better, but I know he is right. Life comes with no guarantees.

We dressed as the characters Raggedy Ann and Andy with bright red yarn wigs and big red spots on our faces and freckles and funny clothes. We had a woman at the costume shop help us with the make-up and how to act. It was so nice and fun to do it and the children were happy to see us...until we got home.

Waaahh! Frankie was terrified of us because we do not look like Daddy and Mommy. He cried and cried, even when we tried to say sweet things to him in English and Vietnamese. It was only after we washed off the makeup and changed into our regular clothes that he finally recognized us and was happy again. Poor boy!

Lois: So that's why Frankie is so scared of clowns! Now we know why.

Frankie: You take that back! I have never been scared of clowns!

Lois: If you say so, Frankie. Anyway, years ago I was reading in a child-rearing book that one of the stages small children go through in development is the inability to recognize a parent if their faces are hidden. Thus, the reason the peek-a-boo game is so popular with a certain age group. Hide the face behind your hands and the child thinks you are gone. Remove your hands and there you are...peek-a-boo! When Mama and Dad come in with full make-up and colorful clothes, the child won't recognize his own parents. There are color photos of Mama and Dad doing their Halloween bit in the Riverton Review dated November 1, 2002. They looked really good!

We had dinner early and around six pm we had children coming to the door for Trick or Treating.

We never had this at the garage as no one lives around there, but many dozens of children visited until about nine. It was so much fun to see the different costumes and many parents made sure the children said "Thank you!"

Fred wore his Raggedy Andy costume and make-up for the children and I did his make-up the best I could, but not so good as the costume store lady. It was fun to see the giant Andy lean way over to offer candy from a big bowl and say hello to the children. Some were brave enough to shake his big hand when he offered it to them.

Ca and I stood nearby to watch and take pictures as it is our first time seeing this part of Halloween and Frankie slept through most of it. Some parents asked to take a picture of "Andy" with their children, which he is always happy to do.

It was a very nice evening and we have only a few candies left. We do not have anything like this in Vietnam and Ca found it very amusing. One day we will be taking Frankie out for trick-or-treating too.

Lang: Mom and Dad loved taking advantage of their height to exaggerate the costumes they wore during Halloween or the occasional costume parties for charity. They have been dressed as Ninjas (black for Dad and white for Mom), cowboy/cowgirl with lassos (and we were dressed as little cows…can you believe it?), space aliens, a sultan with his veiled wife (charity event where it was warm as Mom's costume was kind of thin), scarecrows and all kinds of other things. We kids and Aunt Ca were usually dressed in similar fashion.

It was fun until we got older and asked our parents to stop dressing up with us so we could all do the kinds of costumes we wanted and let one or another of them tag along like most parents did. I think they kind of missed dressing up for Halloween, but even after we stopped trick-or-treating, Dad or Mom or both would dress up to greet the kids at the door. We were always one of the most popular stops in the neighborhood…especially as we gave out full size candy bars instead of the tiny bite-size ones more and more people took to handing out.

Dear My Diary,

This week, Michael, Bunny and I did a lot of auctions and videos for the holiday selling season. They get along very well and have become friends as much as co-workers. Bunny has invested in a much better camera with tripod and editing programs as well as amassing a collection of reference books and guides on antiques and collectables to help them sort the good stuff from the commonplace.

They have been doing their own videos off and on but they really want to do a bunch of Kymera videos to make them more interesting and popular to view. Now, all three of us team-up either at auctions or as a show-and-tell with a variety of unusual things we have found before sending them off for sale.

For the show-and-tells, we work inside and the items are spread out over a large table. We pick one up and describe it, focusing on condition and details along with close-ups of recently completed Ubiddit sales listings. Finally, we inform the audience when and what venue we will be selling the item. Each of us take a turn showing and describing the different items to keep it from being too boring.

In September, we got another shipping container full of things from Ba and Me to sell. Michael has been successful in finding distributors for many of the products and is figuring out which items will do well on Ubiddit and at flea markets, so we can concentrate on increasing profit margins along with our brand.

Michael and Bunny have split up to work the two largest resale markets, Flea City and the Farmer's Market, which are in different parts of town. They hire dependable and friendly workers from our resale shops to assist each of them, creating more exposure, more sales and more profits than if they worked together at only one venue.

We did a video of the craft goods we got from Vietnam and I am the narrator, wearing an ao dai to catch the viewer's attention as I describe the many artistic items, how they are made and what part of Vietnam they come from using a map and some pictures for details. The hope is that when people see the videos, they will click on our Ubiddit links to buy what they like as gifts or for themselves.

I like doing the indoor videos as we can keep Frankie nearby with Ca. As Michael uses his education to make our business more efficient, Bunny uses her people skills and bubbly personality to garner more sales from the "just looking" crowd. She has lost weight, with rosier cheeks and energy in her manner. I can also see, by the way she acts with Michael, that she really likes him and respects his ideas. Fred says they have good chemistry for the work involved and it shows in the profits we are making. Good job!

Dear My Diary,

Fred does not know any acting teachers or related classes in Riverton, so I thought a bit, then had an idea and emailed Zander. I almost never have a reason to contact her directly as her assistants contact us for the F5 assignments.

Instead of an assistant, Zander personally sent me a very nice return message to say she is glad that I am interested in acting lessons and gave me some names with contact information and little summaries of what they specialize in.

I am not sure who to contact first, with so many names and impressive credentials. Fred said Riverton University has a good arts program including acting and dance but I don't know if I want to learn dancing. I mean, how many men besides Fred can I dance with and look normal?

Fred explained that people often take dance to be more graceful in actions like walking, running, jumping and fighting so it looks more fluid and effortless.

I had never thought of things like this and asked Fred how he knew so much about dance. That's when I learned something new about my husband: Fred took dance lessons when he was a boy! At first, he did not want to go, telling his parents that only girly-boys took dance lessons. The teachers were a husband/wife team and the man explained it to Fred in much the same way he told me…only he phrased it in the language of sports.

Of course, Fred did not care about sports, but there were plenty of boys at the school of the athletic variety including some teens. *They* wanted to learn dance to make their muscles stronger and improve the way they run, kick and throw balls as well as jumping with more grace and power. Even some of his high school's best athletes had taken years of lessons from this couple and a few ended up married to girls they had taken dance classes with!

This couple was smart enough to know how to market the same products to boys as well as to girls, appealing to different interests. Fred had never told me this story before. Now it is giving me daydreams of Fred in tights…ooh!

Sang: We don't know how long Dad took dance lessons in his youth, but Mom got connected with the Arts Department at Riverton University and made arrangements to attend classes and workshops across a range of skill sets, work schedules permitting. To do all this, Mom used a mix of attending scheduled classes and hiring private tutors to help her with upcoming projects and learn new skills to make herself more marketable.

These classes, and the support she got from students and teachers alike, were a huge help in boosting her self-confidence and her abilities to project emotions and attitudes, improve her English skills, adding physicality to her performances from the broad to nuanced and yes, she even learned to dance! She has had major dance scenes in three of her films and looks so graceful on the screen! I love watching some of her older work.

Many of her teachers became our teachers as we learned about acting, dancing, singing, makeup and all the rest. Because of Mom, Fierce 5 and later, Triple Treat, Riverton became a magnet for entertainment production companies for low-cost locations, accommodating permit processes, high quality facilities and lots of eager local talent. A little piece of Hollywood in the Midwest!

Thanksgiving

Saturday November 30

The first Thanksgiving in our new home was very special for all of us. Fred, Maggie and Frank shared stories of past Thanksgiving dinners as we ate around the new dining table that seats ten. Ca, Maggie, Bunny and I prepared much of the food on Wednesday while Frank listened to music from his youth on the multi-disc CD player stereo system Fred bought for the home. Thursday was mostly for roasting the turkey, warming the ham and decorating the table with Maggie's wedding china and silver set.

The dining area is not so big as the garage, but Fred had added space by removing the wall between the kitchen and dining room during the renovation. Besides his parents, we had Tina and Thanh's family over for dinner. Fred also had a ramp built onto the front porch for his father's wheelchair and the twins love running up and down the gentle slope.

A few days ago, I explained Thanksgiving to Ca and how it is the tradition at dinner to say what you are thankful for and did she want to speak at dinner to the family? She was brave enough to say 'yes', so we practiced what she wanted to say in English and did this several times to reinforce the phrases.

When it was time, Fred started with how thankful he is for his father to join us in another Thanksgiving alongside his namesake grandson.

Maggie said she got her wish from last year to see a new family member at the table, "Correction…*two* new family members," she said, indicating Ca sitting across from her. "Ditto," added Frank in his croaky voice, patting his wife's hand.

I gave thanks for our healthy son, for Ca's help and an all-around good year and Bunny thanked us, "my brother and sister", for her new job. Cam and Tam gave thanks to their parents for being good to them and taking them to see where we grew up. Thanh and Vo gave thanks for a good year in general, with Thanh adding, "Also, having a closer relation to my sisters in America. It is most important thing I have now, along with my good husband and appreciative daughters."

Ca was the last to speak. I could see she was nervous but she said what we practiced: "I give thanks to Cousin Kim and Fred bring me to America. Aunt Maggie and Uncle Frank very nice parents. I give thank to everyone," as she waved her hand around to indicate all of us. I put my hand on Ca's knee and whispered "You say very nice!" and she smiled shyly at the compliment.

Nobody said anything about Barney during the thanking time or later. It is like he disappeared from the family. I am sure many of us thought about him today…his first Thanksgiving in prison. I wonder if he is thankful for anything on this day?

Everyone brought some special dishes to share along with the basic dinner menu we prepared. Maggie taught Ca, Bunny and I how to make apple and mixed-berry pies on Wednesday and that was fun. It was good to see that Bunny is still friendly with Maggie and Frank and they talked off and on through the day.

Late in the afternoon, other people came over with good wishes and more food and drinks to share. Auntie came over with Michael, her daughters and their families, spoiling Frankie with attention along with the Woods sisters. We gave everybody a tour of the "Starbuckle Homestead", as Fred calls it, and they enjoyed the story of its history directly from Fred and Maggie.

Tina let me know there is a rumor going around that Bobby is sick and may not be working much longer at the office. I asked Fred if he knows anything about this and he said yes, it is true. Bobby and Robbie are keeping it quiet for now but it is getting harder as Bobby has lost so much weight and the treatments are not working well.

Tina asked Fred if he thinks the company will close? Fred said he could not speak for his friends, but the company has grown over time with many good people working there and having built strong relationships with their customers. Fred said "I would not worry about B&R closing. It's a strong operation and Robbie is a good planner."

I remember Bobby looked thinner at the MFAP meeting and now I know why. Perhaps that is why they did not come to visit as they often do on the holidays.

In comparison, Vo and Thanh look healthier than I have seen them in a long time. They have promoted some employees to assistant managers so they can spend more time with their daughters. They are doing more family activities like walking around the lake and cycling through different neighborhoods. The girls look bright and cheery too.

I shared my observations with Thanh and she is pleased that I noticed such things. I told her "Of course! You are my sister so I notice these things and you all look better than before."

Thanh explained how they invested in ceiling-mounted exhaust fans to pull the heavy chemical fumes out. Employees are feeling better and more customers are visiting now. Sister added that Vo has not had a drink in many months and his health is so much improved that he spends more time in bed, giving me a big wink.

Then she asked me when we will make a new sibling for Frankie? I laughed and said "Frankie is only three months old…I am not planning for another baby so soon!"

Thanh made a little shrug and said "You are not getting younger!"

"Do you know anyone who is?" I retorted.

She stared at me, then broke out into laughter. "No. No, I don't know anyone who is getting younger. Not without Botox anyway!" Then Thanh told me that she has been saying "You are not getting younger," for many years and I am the first person to say the obvious thing back to her. "I don't remember you being so clever and funny in your growing up years, but it makes me happy to see you like this now."

Ca came over and I said to Thanh and Aunt Giang how much help Ca has been and we are glad she came to us. Ca smiled and hugged my waist as Thanh gave her a warm smile even though I know she was against Ca's coming because of her mother's meddlesome ways. "We are happy you are making a good face for our family Ca. Come by my shop whenever you want."

Ca nodded and thanked her as Auntie asked after her parents. Ca's smile faded and she shrugged as I explained how Ca's parents tried making problems for us through their daughter but Ca is refusing to do what they want. Cousin nodded in agreement.

Auntie gave Ca a hug and told her that if she wants to talk about anything, just call and Auntie will always make time to listen. Then Fred came over and spoke slowly and nicely to Ca about how much he appreciates her help with our family. She understood and it affected her to hear kind words from Fred after our prior problems. Ca can feel the acceptance of everyone on this day of giving thanks and I could not be happier!

Kimmie: I remember that Thanksgiving well. Our first party in our new home and with a new baby! Moreover, I spent much of the time thinking about Barney in prison during the holidays. I did not think anyone would write to him or send him some kind of gift except maybe his mother. I was sure Bunny would not as she often talked like she was glad to be rid of him.

I wanted very much to send a greeting card with some money and maybe a picture of Frankie. That way, he would know someone was thinking about him and he could buy whatever it is the men buy in prison. I wanted to do it as a gesture of kindness as it is a part of my culture.

But I also had to consider what might happen if Fred or his family found out I did this. I knew Fred would not do something terrible to me, but I think he would be very unhappy with my action. Like being friendly with the enemy or betraying the family. Plus, Fred did not know that I had read Barney's letter that he had thrown away and I still had the prison's address.

After balancing that with how the previous year's holidays had been ruined by Barney, I gave up the idea to send him anything. I never learned if anyone had sent Barney letters or gifts during his time in prison, but in hindsight, learning what I did later, I wished I had.

Dear My Diary,

Takeela came to our home for dinner with Ca doing the cooking, me helping and Fred entertaining Frankie. She is much better than I am and the dinner turn out beautifully. Our son turned on his charm with Takeela and she was quite taken by him. I think it helped set a positive mood for what was to come later. Fred and I have had several talks about what I might want to do if I wish to pursue acting.

"It has been fun so far and if I get parts, that would be wonderful. I will make every effort to prepare for the role and do what is asked of me except nude or sex scenes…I won't do those. If I can't get parts, then it is not the end of the world," I explained to Takeela. "In Vietnam, I tried to hide myself from ridicule of being so tall and unattractive. But since I came to America, I am treated well and told I am very pretty. Companies want to put me in their advertisements, people strangers ask for my autograph and even Rock Rollins is encouraging me to move forward in the industry."

"I don't know who told you that you are not attractive, because you are, and you have the kind of look I believe I can sell. You will lose out on a few parts if you refuse to do nudity or sex scenes, but it's not a deal-killer in my book. Lots of actors won't do them, and I won't offer you a part that calls for it either. It's a perfectly legitimate request."

Takeela's words put me more at ease with what kind of agent I am dealing with. Fred sat with us and took notes, but let me handle the interview. His body language was relaxed, so I pushed on.

"I cannot sing or do any real dance steps so that is out, but when I put on a wig or costume or heavy makeup, I feel more like a character and want to act differently than my everyday self, so maybe that is what I can do. In giving this a lot of thought and discussion with my husband, I would like to be considered for roles in comedy, action or maybe drama. I think those areas would be a good fit for me, but I will also follow your advice, since you are the expert in these matters."

Fred had me add that last part to show Takeela that I will not be a difficult or demanding person to work with. I am not in a position to be egotistical or make frivolous requests.

After dinner, we retired to the study and did some script-reading and role-playing so she could see how I present myself in a variety of planned and unplanned situations. Over the last three weeks, I have spent about sixty hours with three different tutors…two from R.U. and the other from the Triptych Players Community Theater along with many more hours of practice on my own and with Fred. Projection and enunciation, body language and cues, pacing and improvisation among other skills. It was fun and a bit grueling…I wanted to prove my worth not only to Takeela, but to myself as well.

Fred helped here and there as a third character to play off the dialogue. It was a new kind of experience for me, but Takeela said this is a very common way for directors, producers and casting agents to get an idea of an actor's fit for a role. I was nervous but confident with the time spent in training. Takeela kept the interview moving at a good pace as we jumped from one exercise to another to explore my range, strengths and weaknesses.

She will work up a resume for me including a head-shot and a variety of photos showcasing my stature. This will be a *very* short resume so I included some copies of interviews I have done with the American and Asian press. Takeela said that studios are looking more for ethnic and minority types for bigger roles in films, TV and stage-work to make shows more diverse and realistic of what is found in real life. This means I have a better chance to get work than how it was in the past.

I will probably not be picked for typical first jobs like an extra or a walk-on where they want people to look ordinary and blend in to the background unless it is a particularly specialized crowd scene like a fantasy setting. Takeela will push to get bigger, more specialized roles for me and asked if I am available to go to overseas for filming? I pretended to think a minute, "Um, yes!"

"I might be able to find more roles in Hong-Kong made films than American or European. Asian films do a lot of martial arts and old-style fantasy stories so you have a good chance to be picked due to your height."

Takeela became more serious, saying "I will do my best to get work for you, and I have some ideas, but if you want to become a successful actress, and especially to take advantage of your appearance, you should shop around to find or make your own projects or you could end up being typecast for the same kinds of parts over and over."

Fred asked what she meant and Takeela gave an example: In the early days of television, there was an actor getting regular work in small parts, but not getting much notice. He learned to scuba dive and became very good at this sport. He came up with an idea and, working with diving experts and professional writers, created the television show "Sea Spy". In every episode, the hero solved a crime or mystery or found something lost at sea by using his diving skills along with fighting criminals, sharks and other dangerous things underwater. The show made him famous and soon he was getting much bigger parts in other TV shows and movies. And because he had created and developed the story and character, he got more money for being the executive producer, co-writer and sometimes director of later episodes.

I asked, half-jokingly "So, I should learn to scuba dive?"

Takeela smiled and said that if I think about things that have happened in my life or read a book, article or a news story that I find interesting and relatable to me, especially something where I can use my specialized look and style of acting, then perhaps I can work up a story idea for developing.

"The right role can help you get better jobs and more interesting parts," she explained. "For example, you might create a role for yourself as a sports player or coach for an inspiring story. Or…" she said with a shrug and small smile, "…a very tall, very lonely woman who finds love in some unusual way."

Lois: The interview was a success and Mama signed a contract with Takeela Rockett to represent her. Other Fierce 5 models had representation, but none half as prestigious as Rockett to the Stars Talent Agency.

Thomas Stimson

Christmas 2002 – Merry Bucking Christmas!

Dear My Diary,

This year we had the Merry Bucking Christmas at our home as a potluck dinner with the theme "You CAN go Home Again!"

This year, Michael and Bunny were invited as they are our newest partners. We brought extra tables and chairs from the garage and placed them in several rooms so people can mingle, eat, drink and visit around the house.

Ca and Frankie stayed for the first part of the party so everyone could meet the new family members, then they went next door to Grandma and Grandpa's for the night. Maggie spoils him so bad…he he! I went over once during the evening for feeding and a little play time before he went to sleep. We are so lucky they live next door now!

Many of our guests had not been to the house when the Starbuckles lived there before. Fred shared with them some of the home's history except for the bad parts, even though many of them are familiar with what happened. It is a small city after all, and the events were much talked about at the time, but there was no reason to re-open old wounds tonight.

Auntie was not feeling well and did not come. Neither did Bobby and Robbie. They asked us to say "Hi!" to everyone but they were "under the weather." Fred explained the expression as it puzzled me. Such a strange term! I am still learning much about American slang and idioms.

The last time we went to Vietnam, I got a book called American Idioms. At first, I thought it said "American Idiots" but the second word was misspelled, but after Fred explained what idioms are, it was a fun book to learn from. It is written in Vietnamese and English with cartoon pictures for the different idioms. Trinh came to represent Bobby and Robbie and share some things they wanted to say to all of us.

I helped introduce Bunny and Michael to the partners who are not in the resale business so everyone knows who they are and what a good job they are doing. I like our parties because everyone gets to dress up nicer than we usually see them. The Woods sisters always dress fashionably well as part of their job, but many others we deal with dress more casually during their working hours.

Dan McClurg came with his new wife who was cordial but did not speak much as I don't think she knows many of us. Dan finally sold the last of his lots in the Fall, about a year after we sold all of ours. Fred said he barely broke even after all the expenses he had to incur including property taxes, foreclosing on properties the new buyers could not pay on, contractors going out of business and abandoning their work and so forth. That investment cost Dan time, money and a wife.

Bunny came to me and said "I have something to show you!" She took me to another room and showed me a library book…The Blue-Collar Millionaire. She explained what the book was about while I nodded and murmured words of interest. "Now, look at this!" she said in a conspiratorial tone, showing me the part about the Riverton recycling millionaire living in a garage. "Did you know about this?" she asked.

I said, "I have something to show you too!" We went to our office and took down two copies of BCM. I show her Fred's copy signed by the authors, and my own Vietnamese-language copy. I explained how I got my copy and discovered Fred's inclusion in the book over a year after we got married.

Bunny was disappointed that she could not surprise me with this bit of new news and said, "I was thinking I would like to be an auctioneer. It would be part of what I am doing now with you guys, but funner. Do you think Fred could teach me?"

I explained "Fred does not do auctions much anymore, but you can ask him and see what he says." She smiled at the idea.

Bunny said she is trying to educate herself and find new ways to make our business easier to operate and more profitable. I congratulated her on the efforts she and Michael are making while realizing how Fred is doing the very same thing by having partners do the work while we share the profits!

Everyone had a good time. Tina made a short speech on behalf of Bobby and Robbie, thanking everyone for their hard work and patience during the recession as we work our way out of it. I know some of the business owners have had a tough time of it, especially those with large loans on their homes and businesses. Others, like us, came through with even more profits and fewer problems than many families.

Bernice: I remember during that time I was going through a lot of books about how to be a business owner and what kinds of jobs you could do. I really liked what I was doing with Fred's business but felt like I could do more, if I had enough know-how and experience in the reselling of stuff. I went to dozens of auctions, estate sales, yard sales, flea markets, you name it. I asked questions, got pricing details, talked to the workers, saw how they set stuff up, advertised, maintained security, priced items, collected money and found out what they did with what was left over.

I took lots and lots of notes, pictures, wrote down what I liked and what I didn't like about each place and how they were doing things and how I might do them better. Fred taught me the auctioneers' song and I watched videos over and over of different auctioneers, trying to imitate what they were doing. I had never felt so alive and sure of myself in my life.

Michael and Fred worked with me on some of my suggestions and we started taking on jobs like buying an entire estate for cash then reselling the stuff as quick as we could. Michael said they did that one summer from a big old house that got torn down later and that job took weeks and weeks.

We created Pop-Up Shops in the parking lots of abandoned businesses that faced busy streets and then set up signs to direct traffic to us. The Pop-Up Shop was a big truck full of stuff along with tables, canopies, racks for clothes and things that hang. Really, it was a rolling garage sale that we could take from place to place every day, at least when the weather was good.

I never was very good in school, but I sure learned a lot during those years.

Dear My Diary,

At first, I thought I ate some food that did not agree with me at the Christmas party. I was nauseous and vomiting, but Fred was fine and it went on for three days, but not all the time. Ca suggested what it might be and, thinking back on the last few weeks, I have been so busy with everything that I don't think I have had my moon time. Sure enough, the pregnancy test confirmed what Ca thought…we are having another baby! Frankie is only 4 months old and now he will have a sibling. I don't know if I am happy or not about this. Fred and I had not even talked about when to have the next baby. Well, now we know!

This time, I told Fred before anyone else. I don't want anything to happen like last time. But last time I did not have morning sickness, but now I am, so I wonder if this is a bad thing? I emailed Dr. Sedaris who said the sickness can happen with some pregnancies but not others with the same woman. Every pregnancy can be different. Ca said much the same thing from her experiences with the neighborhood women. She had lived in the same house all her life so she has seen many things with many of the same families over the years.

Fred was not mad and I did not think he would be. He is more amused than anything else about the baby. He laughed and said "What can we do? Can't send it back to the store! No refunds, no exchanges!" Then Fred let me know that he loves me very, very much and is happy with another child. He finished with a shrug and said, "Well! The more the merrier!" He is so good to me.

I did the math and the baby was conceived on Halloween. When I told Fred, he said "Wow! That's scary." He is so bad with his jokes! But I remember that we had a wonderful love time that night after such a busy day and how good I felt afterwards. Maybe that is why the baby is coming…the result of special-time lovemaking.

Now I wonder how this will work when "A Son's Quest" comes out in June or July, around my expected due-date. If Fierce 5 wants us to do promotions for the movie, and they most certainly will, they might have to get another Chimera. We will see. It is not as important as the baby, but it would still be nice to do some events for my first movie part.

Christmas 2002

Dear My Diary,

This is Frankie and Ca's first Christmas. Everyone is excited about the new baby and some have too-personal questions about why we got pregnant so soon. I simply tell them that we planned it this way for Frankie to have a playmate close in age. We do not tell anyone that the baby was an "accident", as some people here have rudely phrased it. We wanted another baby and it makes more sense to do it now than in one or two years.

Besides, when someone says their child is an "accident", it does not sound nice to our ears, and gives a bad face to the parents and child alike. Fred is a good Daddy to Frankie and he is happy about having another child, especially in his old home with many nice memories. Frankie is too small to understand the colorful decorations and Christmas music on the radio, but we sing the songs to him and show him the pretty tree and make sweet talking with him.

He is sleeping almost all the way through the night now and I get up three or four times to check on him. Oftentimes, Ca is doing the same. We like to hold Frank up so his feet are on the floor and make him pretend to walk. "Step! Step! Step! Step!" and Frank moves his feet and pushes with his chubby little legs and we make some bouncy movements to encourage exercise. It is so much fun and he laughs and smiles so pretty!

Frankie got a lot of things for Christmas from our families, as did Ca. We asked to get nothing for ourselves but, of course, we did get some things and we gave much as well. Frankie has many toys he is too young to play with right now, but will grow into them before much time passes. Books, clothes, simple puzzles and things with flashing lights and music. We had our first snowfall of the season on Christmas Eve.

I took Ca out in her warmest clothes and we caught snowflakes on our tongues and made patterns in the grass with our boots and swept the sidewalks and paths for both our houses while Fred stood in the window to show Frankie what we were doing. Cousin had so much fun, calling the snow "magic". I agree. I never get tired of the snow…except the cold part!

And, like magic, the snow was washed away by Christmas Day rains, saddening Ca. I assured her that we will get snow at least several more times before winter is over. We spent the day inside, cooking comfort foods and relaxing with Tina.

Now that the stock market has been running flat over the last few weeks, Fred has decided the worst is over and is happily using our profits to buy up shares of strong companies that have been beaten down for another round of profit-taking. He is also spending more time at the garage with Michael and Bunny while they come up with new angles for the business based on everyone's ideas and research.

Fred is teaching Bunny the auctioneer sing-song and they will start moving into the Estate Sales business as a couple of the smaller outfits doing this have gone out of business and two of our resale shops are looking to close as well.

One owner is having increased health problems and his location is getting too run down and crime-ridden to attract good customers. The other store's owner is ready to retire to "anywhere warmer than here!" I laughed when Fred imitated Old Joe saying "Too damn cold for my blood these days!" Of course, he has been saying this for years, but it is going to happen now and Fred will do auctions of both stores' inventories and the Woods will help sell the properties and split the proceeds.

Thanh and Vo's business has done well through the economic troubles for two reasons: Even though many women slowed down the amount of beauty treatments they are getting, many of the salons competing with Happy Pretty Salon have gone out of business. They have bought out two locations with their own money and I helped with a third as a half-partner located inside a GNG superstore.

Sister explained that when the money is good, salon owners tend to buy lots of luxury goods, take expensive vacations, buy property in Vietnam and lease high end cars. But when business is slow, they have no savings to get through the hard times, so they either have to sell the business at a discount or just walk away from it all. I helped Thanh only because it is such a great location and they spent much of their savings buying the other salons. Even better, the workers from Thanh's current salons do not have enough work, so they get spread out to the new locations and work is increased for everyone.

When the economy goes back up, the salons will be more profitable and they may expand even further. In fact, Tina helped Thanh make Happy Pretty Nail Salon an LLC with a well-planned profit-sharing program for the employees and other benefits. It keeps the good workers from going elsewhere and attracts higher quality help…luckily my sister is very picky now about who she hires and does research on them before they can work for her. Drug tests, police records, verification of their work license history and a test on Thanh's own hands with specific styles on each finger to see how they perform.

I am very impressed when she told me all of this, and so was Fred. He thinks, with the way they are going, my sister and her family will be millionaires one day too! When I shared that with Thanh, she was very pleased and touched by his encouraging words. She said that much has changed in their lives since Fred became a brother…and all for the good.

Frankie (With help from Aunt Tina): Aunt Thanh and Uncle Vo approached Aunt Tina about ways to grow their business. They had given up going to the casino and Vo was now more than one year clean and sober, so cash was building up and they wanted to open more shops but were afraid of employees taking advantage of them. On the good side, many of their employees had proven loyalty stopping the manager who tried to cheat Vo and Thanh when they were on vacation, so they wanted to keep that loyalty strong and consistent.

Aunt Tina suggested a plan to provide a benefits package such as health insurance, a retirement and/or profit-sharing plan and paid vacation/sick leave. The idea being that if the employees had a personal stake in the business, they would do what it took to increase traffic, sales and profitability so they could get more in return and everyone would benefit.

A plan was eventually put in place that all workers who had been one year or longer with Happy Pretty Nail Salons would get a health plan and a share of the profits proportional to the amount of money each worker brought to that store in a given quarter and that money would be paid quarterly. If the store had no profits in that quarter, there would be no profit sharing.

People who had more skills typically earned higher individual sales so would get a larger share of the profits. (This did not include tips which are harder to track) This practice induced lesser skilled workers to learn new techniques, get advanced licenses and earn more money leading to larger bonuses and, over time, they could become managers or assistant managers of a shop.

Under this new benefit plan, more services could be offered, sales increased dramatically, the cost of inventory decreased due to volume discounts and Mom's resale business provided her sister with discounted jewelry and accessories that could be sold along with the personal care products, driving up profits even further. Best of all, top-notch employees from other shops wanted to work for Thanh and Vo, even if they had to wait a full year for the benefits to kick in.

Soon, they were opening or taking over an average of three shops per year all over the metro area and into other counties. For the shops they acquired, Thanh and Vo would also start off the older employees they had personally vetted (one-year plus at the shop) with benefits right away. By the time Cam and Tam finished high school, there were close to twenty shops in their portfolio and a long waiting list of people wanting to work for Happy Pretty Nail Salons.

To help her sister, Mom would attend Grand Openings as a "local celebrity" to cut the ribbon, taking pictures with customers and fans, handing out Preferred Customer Cards to everyone and generating local buzz in general. Needless to say, we all got our nails and hair done at HP gratis and learned early on to tip well and be extra polite to everyone. Oh, and yes, they did become millionaires…several times over. Thanh and Vo left healthy trust funds to Cam and Tam and their grandchildren when they died a few years ago.

2003
A Birth Too Soon

January 16th
Dear My Diary,

We had unexpected visitors today who gave us a scare. Let me explain: Auntie Giang was visiting us along with Maggie and Frank while Fred was out on business all day. Auntie so enjoys playing with Frankie and he loves her too. Even Ca was having a good time though the conversation was mostly in English for the benefit of parents.

I had just finished telling everyone about how Takeela got me a small part in a movie filming in Chicago next month when there was a knock at the door. Two serious-looking women were at the door, one Asian and the other an African American who stood slightly ahead of the other and seemed to be in charge.

She asked me if this is the home of Ca Nguyen? I said yes and she introduced herself as Dorothy Johnson while presenting her badge and identification card as a member of the INS. She politely asked to speak with Ca, so I called Cousin over in English, to be respectful of the officer. The other woman was introduced as a licensed Vietnamese interpreter, Tuan Nguyen. I explained to them that I prefer to speak in English but Ca will need the interpreter.

Ms. Johnson explained that they received a complaint that Ca is being forced to live with us without pay or freedom of communication. She made it sound like we kidnapped Ca or made her our slave.

I was a little confused by what they were saying, and I explained that Ca is my cousin and we legally sponsored her to help care for our child while we work. Auntie and Maggie heard us from the door and came over to see what was going on. The officer wanted to question Ca with the interpreter.

Auntie came forward, introduced herself and how she is related to Ca and me. She was very polite and used her very best English, but I could hear the steel within her words.

Ms. Johnson explained again the reason for the visit and wanted to see Ca's papers. We invited the women out of the cold to show our good faces and I retrieved Ca's papers, leaving Cousin with Auntie so there was no suspicion of bad intent if both of us left the room. After all, we have nothing to hide.

Maggie came with me, asking "Is everything all right? What's going on?" I said "They are asking

483

about Ca because of some complaint, but more than that, I don't know."

The officer looked over Ca's passport, visa and other paperwork to make sure they are in order, then asked again to speak with Ca privately.

"May I sit in on the questioning?" Auntie asked. She is very knowledgeable not only in both languages, but in many areas of law and immigration issues. When the officer said "no", Auntie said, "Then we can't let you speak to her until a Vietnamese-speaking lawyer comes to represent Ca, as is her right to do so."

After a moment to consider, Ms. Johnson agreed, saying Auntie could take notes and listen, but not speak without permission. I think so she will not warn Ca or feed her answers. Auntie agreed to the terms and I let them use the home office for privacy.

I became worried about Fred coming home because if he thinks Ca is making more problems, he will almost be sure to send her home. After fifteen minutes, everyone came out of the office and went to see where Ca sleeps. Cousin showed off her nicely decorated room with twin bed, desk, ESL study books and the like. She showed them drawers full of clothes she bought and was given and her bank statements with regular deposits and balances as the INS officer took photos and made notes during the visit.

Lastly, Ca made a point of unlocking her cell phone and showing the officer the many calls from her mother that were not answered or returned. Ca explained to Ms. Johnson that her parents want her to do bad things to our family and she does not want to do bad things. She loves us and wants to stay in Riverton to be a United State citizen. Ca then stepped over to me and hugged my waist to emphasize her feelings of belonging.

This satisfied Ms. Johnson who explained to me that because Ca had cut off communications with her parents, they had filed a complaint with the American Consulate claiming that we had kidnapped Ca, were starving her and other terrible things. Complaints like this are taken seriously and that was the reason for their visit.

Now she was satisfied and will report what she had found along with the pictures and copies of our documents. Ms. Johnson apologized for interrupting our day and we all shook hands. Auntie thanked them for the good work they are doing to protect our country and they went on to their next assignment.

Although the visit ended well, it left Ca frightened that they might come back for her. We hugged her and gave assurances that we will not let her go back to Vietnam if she does not want to go.

Aunt Giang told Ca that she should make a phone call to her parents. Ca's eyes got big and she shook her head in fear. Auntie smiled gently and said, "You should call and thank them for having the authorities come to visit. You can tell them how nice they spoke to you and your cousin, how much they liked your living quarters and found everything to be in perfect order." Auntie winked as Ca's face relaxed. "Thank them for their kindness in thinking about your welfare, and then you can finish the call however you choose. It is your choice how you want to deal with your family, but at least let them know what happened and how you will act with them from now on."

Frankie had fallen asleep but the happy, chatty mood for us was spoiled. Although the visit turned out well, I asked everyone not to bring this up with Fred as I do not want to upset him about Ca's parents, and anyway, the event is over now. They all agreed and we parted company. Auntie reminded Ca to call her parents today and not later than tomorrow to avoid more problems with the authorities.

Fred had a good day and was in a happy mood, letting me know how his day went. He knew we would have company today and asked how everyone is and did I give his love to Auntie and so on? He brought our moods back up and it was easy to set the uninvited visitors to the back of my mind.

Small wonder we never heard this story before. They never wanted Dad to know about Ca's government visitors! Mama always said, if you want to keep a secret, don't tell any person and if you want your secret known, tell the wrong person.

When I spoke to Ca about this, she said she was very scared to be sent back to her parents by Dad or the government. Mama said Dad may or may not have tried to send Ca to Vietnam if he knew, but by that time she had established herself nicely into the household and Dad may have been persuaded to let her stay. Mama said it was easy for her not to tell Dad as there was no reason to bother him with it, the authorities were happy and nothing ever came of it. "No need to stir the pot too much," was how Mama put it.

Feb 13, 2003
Dear My Diary

I just got back from Chicago where I shot a party scene for a movie. It is my first acting job not with Fierce 5 or as Chimera. It stars one of the newer comic actors, Idi Ott, and is called "Lost in L.A.". It's about a bumbling, low-class man from another country trying to make a success in Los Angeles.

In my scene, the star and his friend sneak into a fancy party to pick up girls. I am standing alone with a glass of wine wearing a short skirt and high heels. After admiring my figure from afar, he walks up and says "I love a woman whose legs go all the way up to her ass." I look down, give him a sour look and say "I hate a man whose ass goes all the way up to his face." Then I turn away, flip my hair across his face and walk off with my nose in the air. The star says to his friend "See? Hot women love talking to me!" as his friend rolls his eyes.

I worked two days to film the party scene and made $2000 because I have a line. They filmed my part a few times to get different angles and reactions from the star. I had to be careful to say my line exactly the same way each time while Idi said his part in different ways and they will use his best line in the movie. The rest of the time during filming, I was mingling with other guests as an extra.

Ca wanted to come to Chicago with me, but I explained that my work time is short and my part is small so the studio will not pay for Ca and Frankie to fly out with me. Takeela said they were looking for a tall, leggy woman to deliver the line and the casting director liked my looks. I don't know if I will be credited or not, but it was good experience, it will be added to my resume and that's what counts right now.

I bought cousin a pretty scarf from one of the fancy shops near my hotel. I also got autographs from the two main stars in my script on the same page as my scene along with a musical toy for Frankie. Fred said not to bring anything back for him, except for me…so sweet!

Fred's 35th Birthday

March 17, 2003
Dear My Diary,

Such a lovely birthday! Today is Fred's 35th and my 32nd. All these years Fred has been driving old trucks, vans and sometimes sedans. Some of them look like, well, rolling garbage bins. We have so much money and he looks so poor in some ways. I keep telling Fred that he needs a nice car to create a better image of himself. He likes to say that he doesn't care so much about his image…but I do.

The car does not have to be fancy, or even new because he does not believe in buying new cars, but at least something newer that is not splotched with rust and does not make people stare in wonder that it is still running under its own power. He bought me a car two years ago, so now I want to return the favor. I told him my plan while having breakfast after our morning pleasures.

Fred made a face to me about the subject, but he admitted that he has been thinking about it for a while. He does not like shopping for things unless it is to resell, but he also knows he needs a better car for everyday use. One that does not break down as much as the van is doing now with one door stuck shut, an engine that is getting louder over time and a rattle somewhere in the front whose source cannot be found. I told Fred that the van needs a party…a retirement party.

We went to see Charlie Thomas, along with Ca, Frankie and a second car seat to make sure both will fit in the car with three adults. Fred has no idea what brand or model he wants as he does not pay much attention to what other people drive. His lack of knowledge about cars made the shopping much longer.

At the end of the day, he got a big, American-brand SUV with three rows of fold-down seats so he can put lots of things in the back. It is four years old with very low miles and looks brand new. I wrote the check because it is a birthday present for my favorite husband…he he!

Fred also made a deal with the owner to buy up all the old inventory they can't sell anymore. Charlie had told Fred that an efficiency expert was hired to come look at everything to see what they can do to make more money and reduce costs.

One thing the expert found was so many thousands of car parts in their inventory going back to the 1970's and even earlier! Things that had not sold for decades were taking up space and the money paid for them has long been wasted. The owner has six different dealerships up and down the street and all of them have too much old inventory.

Fred told me that he can scoop up the parts for next-to-nothing and try to sell them at flea markets and on Ubiddit with Michael and Bunny's help. Lots of people with project cars have a hard time finding original parts they need like filters, lights, gaskets, engine parts, body parts and etc.

Fred thinks it will be fun to go through it all and resell them on both the wholesale and retail markets. "It might take a long time, but we can make a bundle," Fred said optimistically. Only Fred can walk into a car dealership to buy a car and walk out with parts for hundreds of others. The profits will easily pay back the money we spent on this car and many more besides.

After finishing the paperwork, we were all so hungry! We went out for an early buffet dinner at the casino with Frank and Maggie, and after we dropped parents at their home, Fred took me to Tree

Top Gals for some new dress-up and maternity clothes. I need to have nice outfits for what I hope are many special events this year. Frankie loved the attention from the saleswomen and Fred and Ca got to admire the beautiful clothes I tried on.

Ca does not know this yet, but tomorrow I will let Fred be a Daddy Daycare and I will take her out for her own new clothes shopping. Ca has been so good with Frankie and very devoted to us. She and Fred get along well and his parents love her very much as Ca always helps them as she can. She deserves some new clothes. After that, I will take her to Happy Pretty Salon for mani/pedies. Kind of a Girls Day Out, like the movie title.

It took a couple of months, but eventually the Clauson Auto Group sorted out and assembled over 50,000 new old-stock auto parts, many of them considered "vintage" by dint of their age. Each time one of the stores finished a top-to-bottom inventory, Michael or Bunny and a crew would come in, pick everything up and bring it back to the garage to be sorted and listed on Ubiddit, car collectors' websites and sold at flea markets and local racetracks as a pop-up shop.

Not only were there all manner of car and truck parts, but also manuals, promotional items, die-cast models, hats and shirts…all kinds of stuff. Some of the parts had gone rotten over the years like cork gaskets and some of the rubber, plastic and liquid products. On the other hand, others turned out to be hard to find and highly collectable, fetching good prices from buyers all over the world, so it all balanced out.

Dad paid $10,000, or about twenty cents apiece for everything and cleared over $2 million in the course of two years, most of it going to Michael and Bunny through their partnership with Dad. As Dad would say "Winner, winner, chicken dinner!"

Dissolving Debt – The Book

March 24, 2003
Dear My Diary,

Last Thursday we went to the OB GYN appointment and sonogram and guess what? Frankie is getting a little sister! Yay!! Doctor Sedaris says everything looks good, my blood tests are fine and although I am not showing a bump yet, I will be soon. By the weekend, we had received many good wishes for the child we will call "Lois" in honor of her Ong Nguoi.

Fred had a meeting today at Riverton University with the Dean of Economics and asked me to join him. I brought Frankie and Ca with us as it is a warm and pretty day and they can walk around the campus.

The nickname of the school is "R.U." and their marketing motto is "R U Ready". Fred explained how it is both a phrase and a question to say "R U Ready?" like "Are you ready to go to college? Are you ready to change your life?" as well as how, once you graduate, you will be Riverton University ready for a good job and exciting career. I think it is rather clever.

In attendance were economic professors, one representative from the President's office and the head editor of the RU Press office. All were holding copies of our Dissolving Debt workbook.

The Dean, a distinguished looking man named Dr. Webber, saw our presentation of Dissolving Debt at the library and asked Fred if he would consider taking his lessons and turning them into a book? After the recent economic crash with so many people losing their savings, homes and jobs, Dr. Webber said the public needs to learn the lessons of getting out, and staying out, of high levels of debt and learning to make smarter financial choices. He likes how Fred makes his points easy to understand while using common-sense ways of explaining how and why it is important to increase income and reduce spending to get out of debt and build wealth.

Dean Webber had Fred explain the Dissolving Debt class to the others at the meeting. Someone asked if we have a video recording of our presentations and Fred admitted we do not as we never thought to film our classes, but we did do an impromptu part of one of our lessons, so everyone could get an idea.

The Dean said that if we put our lessons into book form, along with a separate workbook, RU has a publishing office that can edit, design, format, print and sell the books with some of the profits going to the University and some going to us. The publishing office is one of their side businesses as part of their own multiple streams of income. If the book sells well, it will look good for RU and we can do other projects together.

Dean Webber offered to have us do a presentation of Dissolving Debt on campus that will be videotaped and used to sell the idea of publishing our lesson book to the Board of Regents. If approved, the book will get a budget and we will have a contract. And even if the answer is "no", we will be paid for doing the presentation. Either way, the school will pay for the filming and editing of the class.

Fred looked a little embarrassed and admitted that he did not graduate from college and is not sure he can be a good writer for the university. The Dean pointed out how many successful people did not attend or graduate from college but have been influential in their own rights.

Another member of the group explained how many of their students graduate with huge debts that hurt their ability to accumulate assets. With Fred's permission, the book could also be used as part of a class on Physical Responsibility, helping students reduce their loans more quickly and save money from their earnings to buy homes and help their families without the burden of so much debt.

Fred explained that all of what he teaches are things that frugal people have been doing for hundreds of years and the Dean Webber broke in to say "And look how many people today do not know or learn or practice these lessons! You have a great way of presenting knowledge and this will translate well to the written page. In fact, I foresee your lessons being turned into DVD's, audiobooks and even a regular class that can be taken for college credit."

I could see Fred was unsure about the offer and, although I said very little, I was thinking in my head "SAY YES! SAY YES! WE CAN DO THIS! SAY YES!" and hoped Fred could hear me.

When Dean Webber asked if we will consider their offer, Fred turned to me and I gave a nod with my head and a kick to his foot under the table to make my answer clear to him. Fred agreed to work on the book and asked what kind of time frame did they have in mind?

Knowing Fred is a busy man, they gave us ninety days for a rough draft and during that time, we can do the presentation at one of their lecture halls. Fred's eyebrow went up and he sucked in his lower lip and I could see that he thinks this is too short a time for the project.

I spoke up and said, "We are a team. We will make sure you get the first draft in ninety days along with a Dissolving Debt presentation to be filmed in front of a live studio audience." The last part caused a chuckle among the professors but I don't know why. I hear it all the time on TV.

Fred raised his eyebrow at me, but did not suck in his lower lip. We shook hands all around and were escorted to the front door of the Economics Building. It was a beautiful day and the campus looks like a city park with mature trees, big lawns and impressive buildings lining sidewalks filled with students going to classes and talking in small groups. I want Fred to make a bigger mark on the world and I want Frankie and Lois to attend Riverton University with the Starbuckle name to have a meaningful relationship with the college.

Fred said, "Well, looks like we have a new project!"

"Yes, we do," I responded. "R U Ready?"

Fred smiled at my little joke, then asked me more seriously about my idea on how to get the rough draft done in three months.

"The workbook is on the computer. I have been helping you with classes for over two years now and I understand all the concepts and know all the stories you tell to make your lessons clear. I will simply blend our class lessons and the workbook information together, but I will need you to review and correct my spelling and grammar and add whatever things I might have missed or that you want included to make it more complete." I sighed, "Thank goodness Ca is here to help me. This is the kind of thing I thought might happen where I would need full time help with the baby. You know Fred, it's funny, but of all things I thought we might need Ca for, writing a book was not one of them!"

April 15, 2003
Dear My Diary,

I've been so busy with writing the DD book that I haven't had time, or even thought about, writing in my diary. I find it interesting that sometimes it is very easy to write entries for the diary and sometimes I have trouble thinking of what to say. But with the Dissolving Debt book, it is almost like repeating back a favorite story.

I'm surprised that Fred did not think to write this book before, but then, he was always busy buying and selling. Writing a book takes a lot of time with no guarantees of success. By doing this for the university, the book is guaranteed to get exposure, if not income.

Now that Michael and Bunny have taken over our old time-consuming job, it gives Fred and I more time to spend with each other and develop bigger money-making projects. They now have two full-time helpers and several others from the resale stores that they can call on for bigger projects. The garages' living room space now has desks, computers and big white boards with dates, duties and projects for everyone. It has become quite an operation!

As I write this book, the words flow easily for me. I do not have to think of what to say when I hear Fred in my head telling the "It's Only" story and how investing money makes babies that makes more babies and so on. I think the rough draft is nearly done and it has taken just under a month to write. My goal is to have it finished when we do our presentation at the university.

As I finish one part or another, I send Fred emails for his review. Isn't that funny? I have to send my husband emails like he is in another state or country when he is often in the house or in town doing things. In this way, I can keep writing while he reads what I have done and make needed corrections which I plug back into the document.

I do not know why the university wants the book done so quickly, except that we think they want to "ride the wave", as Fred puts it, of the terrible economic disaster and put our self-help book out while the events are still fresh.

I still can't believe how well we did financially when many others did so badly. Many of our friends and family did very well, or at least did better than most, especially if they followed Fred's advice on how to protect themselves.

The resale stores are doing big business right now: So many people are coming in with treasures and ordinary things to sell and consign because they need money for food and bills. Behind them come the poor people to buy the ordinary things because they cannot afford new and people with money get treasures at bargain prices.

Meanwhile, people are filling FreePost with ads of things to sell and give away as they are being evicted from their homes or moving to smaller lodgings. Michael and Bunny spend their days calling and emailing those people to ask questions and haggle for things they can resell quickly or drive to the addresses for Free Things if it looks like it is worth their time. Oftentimes, "Free" means "Can't afford to take it to the dump." If the free stuff is large and metal, like heat pumps, air conditioners, car parts and exercise equipment, it can be worth picking up for the scrap metal value, if nothing else.

They have also taken up Fred's very first business of hauling away people's junk for a price, putting up signs all over town along with FreePost and at the flea markets. And Bunny is filming a lot of what they are doing, then posting them onto VidLive. Now she is starting to make money from the videos due to having so many subscribed watchers. So many streams of income!

Frankie is hungry and is letting me know now.

Lois: And Frankie still lets us know when he is hungry! But seriously…As the readers of Dad's books know, the "It's Only" chapter is one of the more popular point-making stories he told. "It's only a lottery ticket." "It's only five dollars." And so on. Each "Its only…" is expanded into what the money spent regularly on a small, frivolous item could turn into over a long period of time by investing in index funds including the "babies" created by interest and dividends that, if reinvested, compound over time.

May 1st, 2003
Dear My Diary,

The rough draft is done now. It took thirty-eight days to complete and I think it sounds pretty good. When Fred makes corrections, they are not big ones mostly. Oh, and it is not Physical Responsibility but Fiscal Responsibility. Fred taught me the word 'fiscal' as I have not heard it before. Or maybe I have but did not pay attention to it. Anyway, it makes more sense now to teach Fiscal Responsibility in Economics and the auto correct feature did not catch the error. My English is still not as strong as I want it…but I am learning!

Writing the book felt good and Fred is surprised at how much I got done. I am too! The words and ideas flow like the Mekong River when I am in a good frame of mind.

The date is set: next Saturday at 10am we will have the Dissolving Debt presentation at the main economics lecture hall. Yesterday we met with the AV crew with a copy of our computer presentations to be shown on big screens. We learned how to use the wireless microphones and electric pointers and there will be a director to keep our visual aids in the correct order. Two camera operators will record us as we teach the class, getting audience reactions and so forth.

The presentation will be over four hours long…longer than normal, but Fred and I have broken down the sections that we will each present into roughly twenty-minute segments that allow ten-minute breaks each hour for the audience.

We filmed several practice segments for the crew to get used to our pacing, how we move about and so forth to make the filming go more smoothly. Ca and Frankie were there, coming and going outside, napping and staying out of the way. Each of us took time to play with him when we were not needed by the AV crew. We were there almost six hours but are satisfied with how it will be filmed.

The hall is so big! It can hold over a thousand people for classes and special speakers like us. We have never used microphones before as our audiences have always been just a few dozen people, and maybe a hundred at the most.

The director said they expect most of the seats will be filled and some of the audience members will be high-ranking members of the University. The staff told us to just act natural and do what we normally do. Parts of yesterday's filming may be mixed with our live presentation on Saturday for possible future productions and showings.

Fred has been working with an attorney that specializes in intellectual property contracts. She will work with R.U. over the details of the book and its variations along with promotions and who pays for what from that.

I told Fred last night that I will wear one of my F5 costumes so the audience will pay more attention to my words. Fred said, "Do that, and they will be paying more attention to your legs than to your words." Of course, I will not wear the costume, but it is funny to think about.

Oh! One last thing: We got emails that post-production is completed and "A Son's Quest" will premier in Hollywood and New York. Finally! I get to go to Hollywood! The Fierce 5 team are required to come to both events, riding together in a fancy limo and fully costumed to walk the red carpet.

Fred was not invited to the premier, as he is not an actor or big investor of the film. Our part is small, but Fred says our being there in costume will bring 'color' and 'buzz' to draw in more ticket sales and, of course, buy more Fierce 5.

May 12, 2003
Dear My Diary,

Saturday's Dissolving Debt presentation was standing room only, and by far the largest we have ever done. Every seat was filled with adults ranging in age from late teens into their sixties. Dozens more lined the back and side walls, many with notebooks or recording devices. Either there was a lot of advertising done by the college or many people need our information. Fred thinks probably both. Graduation is at the end of the month and I think many students and their parents are already worrying about how to repay the loans they took out to pay for it all.

Ca and Frankie took Grandpa and Grandma to the zoo to get out of the house and Frankie would not miss his parents so much than if they had stayed home all day.

Bunny came out of curiosity since she and Barney had seen us that one time at the library. She said "I wanted to see what you are teaching and maybe learn something to make my life better."

I told Bunny that her friendship makes my life better, then she made the "Awwww!" face and gave me a big hug. She is such a sweet woman and I am glad she is 100% not like Barney…or maybe 90%.

Tina was there with some clients who, even though they make a lot of money, live in beautiful homes and drive finer cars than we do, are deep in debt and their net worth is in the negative. Tina has not told them that we are her family, just that it might help them to come, listen and learn. She is well aware that some will listen and learn and some will not.

Luckily for us, the school revamped, printed and bound our workbooks for this event. They look and feel so different from the homemade ones we made at Copy Counter. With so many people, we ran out and the event manager quickly had another three-hundred run-off in time for the first break using their high-speed copiers and binding machines. Dr. Webber was a huge help for us, providing security, a large sign-in desk where student helpers collected names and personal information and so much more to help us look and sound our best.

Dr. Webber introduced us, giving everyone a little history about Fred and the class he has been teaching for over six years now, how many hundreds of families have been helped by the Dissolving Debt program and that Riverton University is proud to be offering the DD book for sale to the public in the near future with some of the proceeds going toward the School of Economics and Finance.

I did not wear my Fierce 5 outfit, but we both wore better clothes than we normally wear…new khaki trousers and light blue polo shirt for Fred and a mid-length khaki skirt with dark blue top for me. My baby bump is showing clearly now and I feel good about being on my feet all day but there is a stool nearby we can use as needed when the other is presenting.

We have been practicing every day to make it as clean and smooth as possible. I imagine it is like practicing for a play before going live in front of a paying audience with no cuts or do-overs. Make a mistake and pretend it didn't happen. Keep the momentum going…a good exercise for what I hope to do in the future.

Looking over the audience, I can tell who the members of the Board of Regents are as they sit clustered together in the front rows. Older men and women with perfect haircuts and expensive casual clothes. They do not look like they need Dissolving Debt but, as Fred would say, "You never know!"

There was a little trouble with the AV system, but it got worked out before we started. We were both a little nervous I think, in a different room from the library setting we are used to and *so* many more people. I was afraid I might freeze or forget what I have to say, but once we started speaking, everything fell right into place.

One camera was stationary and followed us as we moved around, speaking and gesturing. The other was used to take close-ups, audience reactions and so forth. Once I started, I let my knowledge of the topics flow from my heart until my part was done and Fred took over.

During the breaks, people came up to ask questions and a few asked if I was one of the Fierce 5 girls and could they get my autograph? I found that surprising and sweet, so of course, I obliged them.

The Q&A lasted nearly an hour after the presentation finished and, due to the large crowd and noise, assistants took microphones into the audience so everyone could hear and learn.

Afterwards, by pre-arrangement, Tina brought her guests to us for a personal meet and greet. This was to impress on these high-dollar clients that she knows us personally and has a strong relationship with these authors of important information.

Per our earlier meeting with Sister, Fred offered the clients an opportunity of personalized one-on-one debt coaching. They looked pleased to hear his offer and said if they choose to get it, they will make arrangements through Tina.

She called us later that night and thanked us for doing this as it raises her status in the eyes of the clients to know they can get a personalized consultation from an expert. Of course, Fred has never met with others privately for paid consulting, but it can be another one of our future income streams. I think it is a wonderful idea!

We were escorted into a nearby meeting room where, in front of members of the Board of Regents, we presented five printed copies and a computer disk of the DD rough draft to Dr. Webber in half the agreed upon time.

They were very impressed and we chatted and answered questions with the highly educated group, who could not have been nicer, for another half hour or so. They liked our presentation and can see our collaboration will be a positive experience for everyone concerned.

Fred did not sleep most of the night as he was wound up from the big presentation and gave me many compliments about how well I did. Once he calmed down a bit, he proceeded to show me how much appreciation he has for me. Needless to say, it was a very special day *and* night!

Yesterday was my very first Mother's Day! Frankie and Fred gave me a necklace and pendant that opens with Frankie's little picture inside…so sweet! Fred and Ca made lunch for me and his parents while we told them all about the big DD seminar and the making of the book. We hope the school will like our draft and not make too many changes.

Ca is calling Fred's parents "Mama Maggie" and "Papa Frank" and they love it! She comes over and helps them as she can when I do not need her. She is always quiet and sweet and likes to hum Vietnamese folk songs and sing children's songs to Frankie.

I had forgotten some of the songs she sings, it has been so long since I heard them last. Now I find myself humming or singing with her and Fred likes to hear this very much, especially when the house is quiet. Ca has a sweet singing voice and Fred says that my singing pleases his ears but I think he is only sweet-talking me. And even if he is, who am I to complain?

Birth of Lois

May 19, 2003

Dear My Diary,

On Thursday night I was having tummy pains and I thought it was gas. I tried to remember the right word for this part of my body and told Fred how I am having pain. He gave me a strange look and told me I do not have testicles. I put my hand low on my belly and he said "Oh, that's intestines. Testicles are on a man…farther down," and he pointed to the right place. I laughed at my mistake, but got another sharp pain.

I said, "It feels like labor pains, but it cannot be. It's much too early." I am only six and a half months along. Fred thinks it is maybe my appendix or gas. I hope it is only gas.

Fred did not want to take any chances, so he drove me to the emergency room. I did not have a baby bag ready yet as it is too soon, but Ca quickly prepared one for me and stayed home with Frankie.

When the doctor checked me over, she quickly determined that my body is indeed going through labor. A team of medical personnel was rounded up while the doctor worked on ways to slow down or stop the contractions so the baby can stay inside longer and grow more. After more than half a day of trying different methods, an ultrasound showed the baby's way out is blocked. The doctor explained how they will have to cut open my tummy to get the baby out. It is a common, but serious procedure and the doctors do not see a better way to deliver our premature baby.

At 3:07pm on May 16, Lois Pham Starbuckle was born and put right away into an incubator. She is so tiny! The doctors say she appears to be normal for a baby of her very young age, but will need to stay in the hospital for several weeks until she gets stronger and is able to breathe and feed normally.

We were warned that complications may arise, even with the best of care, and there is a chance that the baby might not survive for any number of reasons. Despite the warnings, the doctors are optimistic that she will be going home with us in a few weeks. No promises, but they are doing everything they can.

Fred has already contacted our families asking them not to come to the hospital until we know more details. The last thing Fred wants is causing unnecessary worry and confusion…I am doing plenty of that on my own. Fred is very attentive, comforting and tries to lighten the mood, but I am so worried about our daughter that it does not help much…but I do appreciate him trying.

I was awake during the entire operation, but my hands and body were shaking involuntarily from whatever pain drug they gave me. Once they put Lois in the incubator and made all the necessary adjustments, they rolled her over to us.

I started crying. She is so small and pale, blood vessels webbed all through her translucent skin. I feel terrible that maybe I did something wrong to make her come out so early. She is only two pounds, nine ounces and 15 inches long. She is too small and weak to breast feed and they have her connected to machines and tubes to help her breathe, feed and take medicines as well as monitor so many functions.

The doctors found a lot of scar tissue and fibers inside my womb and the baby was running out of room to grow. The fibers are also blocking the birth canal so she could not come out to say "Hi!" by herself.

The worst part is that they recommend we do not try to get pregnant again or the pregnancy may be worse for me and the baby.

Was it caused by the kick last year? Did I do something wrong in the way I eat or work or something? Fred asked the doctors for me but they said it is not uncommon for this kind of female problem and was not caused by the kick or something I ate. It is just something that happens for different reasons like from a certain kind of illness or changes in body chemistry. They are not sure what it is for me.

Lois: The cause of the scar tissue and growths was Uterine Fibroids, which became so dense inside our mother, that she was unable to have a normal delivery. The doctors removed what they could during the C-section, but it left Mama's insides so scarred, the doctors determined that an embryo would either not stick to the walls or would have problems developing normally.

There are many possible causes of fibroids but trauma (like getting kicked) is not considered one of them. However, I know Mama believes deep down that the kick during Frankie's pregnancy caused her later issues. Based on the doctor's recommendation, Dad had himself sterilized to prevent future pregnancies.

I am sad to know that I can't make babies any more. I had hoped for maybe one more, but we have two now. That will have to be our family. The doctors say Lois' chance to live and grow healthy is very strong, but there could still be complications in the hospital or later in life, just so we are aware.

I asked Fred how much it will cost for Lois to stay in the incubator over the next few weeks? Fred shook his head and said "Money is the last thing you or I need to worry about. Let's worry about our daughter and how Frankie is going to react when he finds out he has a little sister taking away his Mommy and Daddy time." This made me smile, but does not make my worries less.

Lois: There were a lot of detailed entries during this time about me so I will summarize: I was born two months early and came home six weeks later on June 30th. No huge complications developed, but during my hospital stay I had a couple of infections, anemia and Respiratory Distress Syndrome early on and all are fairly common conditions in preemies. Luckily too, there were no long-term effects like developmental delays or lung issues.

Mama was in the hospital about a week recovering from the C-section and spending hours and hours watching over me, hooked up to machines and tubes, through the big nursery windows. Dad spent a lot of time at the hospital comforting Mama as well as monitoring their visitors and dealing with hospital staff. There are pictures of me all along the path to wellness and a really sweet one of Frankie pointing at me while being held up by Mama.

Another picture we love has Mama in the middle staring into the nursery window with Dad on the left with his arm around her shoulders and their heads are resting against each other and Ca is on the right with her arm around Mama's waist and her head rests against Mama's arm. Their backs are to the camera so you can't see me or much more than a couple of nurses heads and some medical equipment beyond the glass. I had the photo re-done in black and white for a lonely, haunting look, which is how the scene feels to me.

Mama and Dad were finally able to hold me in my third week. She still tears up when she talks about how she felt to finally hold her tiny daughter and our eyes connecting for the first time.

Thomas Stimson

Fred's First Father's Day

June 16, 2003
Dear My Diary,

Today is Fred's first Father's Day. I gave Frankie a card to give to Daddy but he likes the colored envelope and wants to keep it. He put it in his mouth and I had to take it away which made him cry. So spoiled! We spent time at the hospital, as we do every day, to see Lois and how she is doing. I am still worried about her but so far, her only health issues are minor and she is growing. The doctors and nurses are happy with her progress, so that's good too. Lois is one month old today and I feel that the worst is behind her.

I make prayers every day at the altar to keep her healthy and to grow big and strong and smart. I did not have the traditional one-month party as I did with Frankie because Lois is not home yet and I think it is too sad to have a baby party without the baby.

To appease my guilt, I made my own private party with tiny girl clothes and a small bear, a cupcake and a candle. Fred walked into the bedroom and asked what I am doing. I was embarrassed but I told him as he is my best friend. He took me into his arms and rocked me and told me that he knows how I feel…Father's Day without his little munchkin. I do not know what a "munchkin" is, but it is a cute name.

Fred assured me that Lois will be home as soon as the doctors think she is ready, then he picked up a little dress and made it dance with his fingers. It was cute how he did it, so we went to Frankie and showed him the dancing dress. He laughed and waved his arms about before finding something else of interest.

We took Maggie and Frank out for lunch and spoke of many things coming up for the rest of the year. Frank's talking is getting better and he has therapy several times a week to make his unparalyzed side stronger and his speech clearer. It is still difficult for him but he is always trying to do better. I like his spirit!

Last week we got news that Buck's Park will start construction at the beginning of July and should take about three weeks to complete. The Riverton Parks Department ordered the playground equipment in May and it has just arrived. It will be a very small park, just swings, a slide, jungle gym plus benches and two or three picnic tables.

One nice feature that will stand out is an exercise trail around the outside edge of the park where kids can walk a balance beam, swing on a rope over a small hole, jump through tires, do chin ups and other healthy activities with instructions at each stop of the trail. I think the neighbors are excited to have the park in the middle of their neighborhood even though many have swimming pools and trampolines in their backyards, which I think is much more fun. Fred had helped design the park and he has already gotten the tax break for his donation to the city.

As for the rest of the block, a few houses are fully built including Hong Lo's stunning mini-mansion with several luxury cars gleaming in the driveway. I heard he had brought over dozens of artisans from Asia to do the decorative trim and landscaping inside and out.

Then there is my area, full of grass and weeds. We mow it as often as we can to keep from getting fined by the city for an untended lot.

Some of the people who bought lots from us have already abandoned them and given the land back to the banks. With no house on the property, it was easier on their conscience to give it back. Of course, they still lose what they have put into it so far, and it hurts their credit, but the bank will lose a lot more, especially if they can't find a buyer quickly. Fred was smart not to take on the financing of the lots and let the banks accept the risk.

July 27th
Dear My Diary,

The Dissolving Debt draft was returned with a long list of required and suggested edits. Some parts need clarifying, other areas are too long and need to be trimmed or too short and need to be expanded. There are lots of marks and notations in different colors to indicate the changes to be made. It reminds me of a poorly written school report handed back by an unhappy teacher.

They are also requesting "side bars" to be added. Fred explained how side bars are the boxes of text sometimes found in educational books used to highlight a particular topic such as tips and tricks or an anecdote to emphasize a point, breaking up long pages of text and making it more attractive to read.

In a separate file, they sent samples of approved fonts and layout designs for us to consider. We will worry about that later. Fred complimented me on the good first effort I made in writing the draft. With so many things to change, I don't feel the same way but I know he is sincere so I thanked him with a warm kiss.

The problem now is that with Lois home and needing a higher level of care than Frankie did at her age, Frankie learning to walk and getting into more mischief and my parents coming soon for a visit, I have no real time to concentrate on editing the book. When we discussed my concerns, Fred understood and will rearrange his schedule to do the editing himself and I will help when I can. "Two heads are better than one!" he said.

Looking at all this new work we are taking on, I thought of another way to get the book out and make less work for us. I asked, "Do you think we can get more money from a big publishing company than from the university? A place that will do their own editing and design?"

Fred said "I don't know as I've never written or published a book before, but I have heard that it is very hard for a first book to be published by an unknown author or non-celebrity. Remember, R.U. made the offer to us because of our free presentations and they heard good word of mouth about us and how we help others. That's a big compliment to us."

He went on to explain that if we go to another publisher, they may pay us more, but most of the profits will go to the publishing house. With Riverton University, some of the profits will go to making the school, and the students, better.

Put that way, I agree we are making the right decision. I told Fred that it reminds me of the term "charity starts at home" where you help your family and community first like the way we do things for our hospital, community gardens, library and such.

My family does the same, having built a recreation center in our neighborhood and doing things to help our local temples, clinics and the orphanage. By helping our community from the outside, it makes us stronger on the inside.

Frank: Our parents gave generously to charities, with most of the money and goods going to either our hometown/state or Mama's home district in Ho Chi Minh City. Over the years, Dad was offered large sums of money to switch the Dissolving Debt series to competing, for-profit, publishing houses with stock incentives, generous royalties, etc. He could have made much more money but always refused and Riverton University has benefitted from his largess for decades.

Dissolving Debt and its spin-offs have been, by far, the largest selling publication for Riverton University Press. The school is now considered to be one of the top regional universities in the country in several fields, particularly the Economics and Drama departments, for obvious reasons. Because of that, competition for out of state and international student spots is fierce! Or, as Mom liked to say: Grrrr!

July 3, 2003

We are so grateful to finally have Lois home with us! I feel more complete now that she is almost the same size as Frankie was when he was born. Frankie is trying to walk now, but with no success yet. He can pull himself up and walk along the couch or the crib or with us to hold his chubby little hands, but he has to hold on or he will fall down.

He is very curious about his tiny baby sister and likes to watch her sleep. He babbles at her when she is awake, talking whatever baby things are in his head. Does Lois understand him? She might, but I certainly don't. At least he does not appear jealous of her and I let him nurse after Lois is done.

Frankie and Lois are physically so different from each other: Frankie has Daddy's blonde, curly hair and round, blue eyes but a flatter nose than Fred's family and Lois has brown eyes with the eye-fold. I do not think people will believe they are full-blooded brother and sister from the same parents, but I don't care…we will know!

Frank and Maggie come to visit often. Frank has so many medical needs and the bills come in constantly. The hospital did some free services for them at the beginning, but that soon stopped. They are too young to get Social Security retirement benefits or Medicare, but Frank gets SSI and Maggie is given money by the state as Frank's caretaker, which helps pay for their basic needs. I like that there is government money to help people like them. Vietnam is too poor to have social services so the disabled depend on their families, religious groups and begging to survive.

Bunny came to visit yesterday. She did not want to hold Lois as she was still in her work clothes, but cooed and said sweet things to Lois who stared and stared at her auntie. Bunny visits often to cheer me up with funny stories about work and Michael and what they are doing while she plays with Frankie, who adores her.

I asked Fred if he still considers Bunny as a sister-in-law and the children's aunt, even though she is divorced from Barney? Fred made his "considering" face and responded with "I have no problem with Bunny. Yeah, even divorced she is more of an aunt to the kids than almost anyone else in the family. Why?"

I said "I was just thinking about how great she is and wonder how Americans treat people who are divorced from their blood-family members."

"Well, she thinks the world of you, and you both get along really well. I like her and the folks love her. No need to change the way things are now, is there?" I agree, no need to change things.

Ba and Me called last month to ask if I want them to visit. I said "Yes, oh please come!" They will be here in one week and stay for three more. They want to meet their new granddaughter and look for a place to buy in Riverton.

I am so happy to hear this nice news! We have one spare bedroom for guests and Ca has started cleaning it and shopping for good things to eat.

When I told Maggie and Frank that my parents will look for a place to live, they said that our next-door neighbor Al is talking about moving to a retirement home near Central Park. He has been widowed many years and is getting tired of cooking, cleaning and yardwork. He is much older than Fred's parents, close to eighty, and is having a hard time walking as well as hearing and seeing. Maggie said that if we talk to Al and make an offer on the house, this might push him, in a good way, to move to the retirement home and my parents could stay next door to us!

It's a smaller home and will be just the right size for Me and Ba. I think it is a wonderful idea and I told Maggie so, giving her a hug and a kiss. She will arrange for all of us to have lunch with Al so he can meet my parents and we can bring up the subject about the house then.

Ba and Me Come to Visit

July 13, 2003
Dear My Diary,

We are so happy to have Ba and Me back in Riverton. Frankie began crying when two strange old people made a fuss over him, saying "Hello!" in two languages and trying to hug him, but soon he was showing off and acting too cute.

Our dining room was crowded that evening with the entire family gathered and Fred trying to stay unobtrusively nearby as he cannot follow the conversations. We talked much about Lois' birth and how scared we are for her survival including the potential for long term effects, even years from now. My parents reminded me that in Buddhist theory, we learn to accept what happens to us and make the best use of our lives as we can. With that said, I will try to keep a positive outlook for the future, no matter what.

Me and Ba want to buy a home either in our neighborhood, or in Thanh's and asked about the cost of a modest home, the taxes we pay and so forth. I explained how the US economy is still depressed and many homes are sitting empty so now is a great time to buy, but I did not tell them about Al's house yet. We want to keep that as a surprise if he chooses to sell.

Yesterday, I took parents around our neighborhood, a few blocks in each direction and then around Thanh's neighborhood too. Fred drove while Ca stayed home with the babies. We stopped at houses posted with For Sale and Foreclosure signs, looking around, discussing the pros and cons of what we could see. They found two or three homes they liked but were not "in love" with them due to distance from my home or other flaws they found.

Today we had lunch in my home and invited Maggie, Frank and Al to join us. Ba's English has gotten better, as Phung has been helping him by speaking more frequently in English to reinforce vocabulary and grammar. Me has been practicing also but is still too shy to speak to foreigners.

The meal was a blend of VN and American foods and everyone had a nice time chatting. Al asked if I have any brothers or sisters and I said, "I have three older sisters and I am the baby of the family," as is my little joke to say.

"Are your sisters as tall as you?"

"Oh, no! They are all a little taller than my parents, but not much."

Fred added, "Kimmie's so tall because she was special ordered by me from Heaven."

Al's eyes widened with surprise, then crinkled as a smile spread across his face. "I do believe the Good Lord listened to your prayers, son. And did he deliver!"

I translated what was said to my parents and they smiled and nodded approvingly.

During lunch, Ba told our guests how they are looking for a home in Riverton to live part time and be near their children and grandchildren. Al asked some questions to clarify what my father was saying, then said "Well, I have lived next door for over forty years, and it's been a fine home for me and my family. But it's getting to be too much work now, at my age, to keep it up." I translated for my parents, and I saw the subtle signs of interest in their manner.

"I've had my eye on a retirement home downtown where some of my friends are living. It's a nice place and I won't have to cook or clean." I kept translating and they kept smiling and nodding. "I haven't put it up for sale yet, but I would be much obliged if you wanted to come over and take a look-see," Al said, jerking his thumb in the general direction of his home.

Ba said in English, "I see the house next door. Very nice." He looked at Me and she nodded, as did I. "Yes, very much. I…we, would like to see."

The home is very tidy and is constructed in the same style and size as Maggie's house. The walls are covered with pictures of Al's wife and children spanning over fifty years. All his family live far from Riverton and Al's wife, Karen, who died a few years ago, now sits in an urn on the fireplace mantel beneath their fiftieth wedding anniversary portrait.

Al showed us all the rooms and we went into the basement as Al does not do steep steps anymore. Like many basements, it is full of old, dusty, unused things and it was hard to get around and check for cracks, mold, and pests.

After looking at everything inside and out, we told Al that parents will consider his offer to sell but we do not want to talk price just yet.

"Fine! That's fine! I'm in no rush. No rush at all. You think about it as long as you need." With that, we said our goodbyes and headed back to our respective homes.

July 16, 2003
Dear My Diary,

Last night, all my family came over for barbeque and catching up on family news, with the biggest topic being Al's house. Yesterday morning Fred, Ba and Me went next door and Fred carefully inspected the condition of the house while asking Al lots of questions.

First of all, the furnace is very old and will need to be replaced with a fuel-efficient model. The back porch is rotting away, but luckily the framework of the house shows little sign of decay or termites and the roof is fairly new. The backyard has gone a bit wild, but overall "The place could be a lot worse," said Fred. Except for the furnace, most of what needs to be done can be handled by Fred or the RPR crew like the porch, new curtains, fresh paint, carpets, etc.

Ba had taken pictures of each room and was showing them around to the family. The style is old-fashioned, but cozy. Vo suggested knocking down the wall between the kitchen and living room to make it roomier, as is the current style and Thanh said they should remodel the bathroom with shiny fixtures and take out the half-tiled walls.

Auntie, the voice of reason, pointed out how the house has its own special charms and only needs a minimum amount of updating. Ba and Me are happy with the style and do not want fancy upgrades, just what is needed like the porch and furnace and brightening up the interior with new paint, flooring and airing out the mustiness.

Parents really like the house so, as a group, we discussed the possible range to offer. Fred said Al's intention is to use the money from the sale to help pay the rent of the retirement home he likes, as his SSA and pension will not cover everything.

When Fred told us how much Al will pay for rent, we could not believe our ears. Thanh said, "That's like a mortgage payment for a big, fancy house!" Auntie Giang said she has heard similar figures for the nicer retirement homes because the rent covers all the meals, utilities, housekeeping, outings and activities.

Thanh said, "Maybe so, but for that kind of money, I want a cute house boy included!" I have not seen Me laugh so hard in a long time when she heard that. Even the twins came over to see what was so funny, but of course we did not say. Eventually, with Fred's help, we came up with a plan.

This morning, as arranged, the four of us went over to Al's to discuss the purchase of his long-time home. Al was warm and welcoming with coffee and bakery treats on the kitchen counter to set a friendly mood for our discussion.

Al is old and kind, has known Fred's family for decades and attends church with Frank and Maggie. My father is a skilled negotiator in business deals, pushing for the very best price and conditions he can get, but today he knows this is not that kind of negotiation. I think he sees a future self in Al and how he would feel to be widowed with no children nearby to help.

As for Al, he sees a new generation of Starbuckles growing up next door with loving grandparents coming from halfway around the world to share their lives, something Al does not have in his life.

After making pleasant chit-chat about this fine home in such a nice neighborhood, so well-taken care of with this and that needing to be replaced or repaired, Ba let Al make the first offer.

Al did not state his price right away but made his own little speech. He spoke about how much love has been in his home and he sees the love in our family and believes that Lo and Le will keep those good feelings going for many years into the future. At that point, Al made his offer.

Ba did not make a reaction.

Fred asked, "Are you sure, Al?"

Al said, "I've been checking around. I know what the house is worth, even taking into account the work that needs to be done. But most importantly, I want to make sure this house is going into the right hands…your hands." Al reached out and grasped Ba and Me's hands. "God bless you both."

They shook hands on it and Al agreed to have RPR draw up the paperwork. We did not dare counter Al's offer as the agreed upon price is about twenty percent lower than the low end of what we were expecting.

Ba and Me will have Tina draw a cashier's check to pay for the house in full. Fred told me later, in private, that once he knows Al is contracted for an apartment, he will go to the retirement home and pay the first six months of rent in advance to help make up for the amount he should have taken. We won't tell Al of course…it will be a surprise.

Before we left, Al sighed and said, "The apartment is pretty small and I have so much to get rid of. I don't know where to begin with it all. Any suggestions?"

I said, "I have one."

I told Bunny and Michael that I might have a job for them, filling them in on Al and his home and would they be interested in doing an estate sale for him?

Bunny jumped up and down, clapping her hands with excitement and Michael looked happy with the idea too, but he is not as exuberant as his partner. I know Bunny has been doing a lot of research on estate sales and has visited several in the area to get ideas of how they operate.

I told them of what I saw all around the house that could be sold, and since Al has a good relationship with Fred's family, it should be a simple matter of making introductions and going from there.

"If you do a good job with this sale, it can lead to more business from Al's church friends and people in the neighborhood," I said. "Just keep plenty of business cards on hand and make it a fun sale. You can't go wrong."

Dear My Diary,

I arranged a meeting with Al, Michael and Bunny, explaining to our neighbor that both are trusted family members who have taken over most of Fred's reselling business and that they will do a good job for him.

When Al met them, he cocked his head in recognition and said to Bunny "Aren't you the one whose husband went to prison? Barney's wife?"

She made a funny "sorry" face and raised her hand. "Guilty your honor!"

I told Al that Bernice had nothing to do with what Barney did and we would not have her if she were not honest and hardworking. Al nodded and said "Well, we can't always help what other family members do. Lord knows I've been there. If Fred and his family trust you, then I trust you too." Everyone relaxed and Bunny gave Al a thank-you hug.

Michael and Bunny shared in presenting the sales pitch they created starting with moving Al's furniture and belongings that he is keeping to the Bedford Arms Retirement Center. With Al moved out, they and their team will spend two weeks to sort, price, set up and advertise the sale.

As this is their first time doing an estate sale, they wanted to take the extra time to make sure everything is done right. The sale will take place on a Friday at the full tagged prices, Saturday everything is discounted 30%, and Sunday is the blowout at 60% off.

Whatever is left, Al can decide to donate to charity or let us buy it from him to resell elsewhere. The fee will be 25% of the gross sales which we know is lower than most companies charge, but since this is their first time out and Al is a close family friend, it will be a favor to all involved.

I wish them luck and hope Al gets a healthy check from it all.

Bernice: That estate sale was the first and WORST one we ever did. First, Al Paulson was the sweetest man and so easy to work with. We generated a contract with him and had it reviewed by Fred's lawyer for fine-tuning. We got insurance, permits, you name it and thank God we had all the paperwork with us at the estate sale, otherwise, who knows?

We did lots of advertising, Maggie had announcements done at her church, flyers all over several neighborhoods, Freepost ads and everything. Friday? Beautiful! Strong sales day. Saturday is always the best, right? Discounted items, everyone off from work, pretty day…until a bunch of people stormed in, moving fast and yelling, "Ok, everyone out! This is an illegal sale! Stolen items! Everyone out!"

Customers are dropping things, running out the door. Lots of shouting and confusion. I go to the guy who came in first and asked what the hell is going on? He pushed me aside and said "Where's my coin collection? Did you sell it already?" Another woman gets in my face, "What about my antique dolls? What did you do with them?" I said they got the wrong house or something. All this stuff belongs to Al Paulsen and they said "Yeah? Well, we're his kids! Where is he? We want to see him NOW and get our stuff back!" I saw some of the family hauling boxes out to their trucks in a fat hurry and I yelled "You bring that back here!"

I called the number Al gave me, then the phone next to me starts ringing. I pick it up and can hear what's going on in the house through the phone. He gave me his house phone number! Screw it! Then I called 911 but Michael was already calling them and trying to keep any more stuff from leaving the house.

One of our guys was a bouncer on the weekends but he was able to do only so much. The family was getting all in my face and that of our helpers, trying to get the money from the registers and saying it was theirs.

I called Bedford Arms, but Al was on some tour of retired ships on the river and that's when we learned that he doesn't own a cell phone. Kimmie was out of town, I think, and Fred was with his parents somewhere so we were in deep crap until the cops showed up.

Al's kids ran out and started shouting at the cops like they were victims and wanted us to be arrested for selling things that belonged to them. The police did a good job getting everyone's side of the story, looking over our paperwork and saying we had permission to do the sale because everything was in order.

Turns out someone from the neighborhood contacted one of Al's kids to say he was moving out and selling all his stuff. His kids were worried about all the old toys and junk they had left in the house 30 or 40 years ago and wanted to get it back. The police reached Bedford Arms, who radioed the tour bus, who brought Al and his new friends to the house. Then poor Al had to deal with the police, prove he was the homeowner and had given us permission to hold the sale.

Meanwhile, all these old people were staring out the bus windows and taking pictures while the estate sale customers were trying to figure out if we were still in business or not. While the cops were sorting things out, one of the family members spent time making lewd hand gestures at the bus. Al was such a nice guy and ended up with kids like that. The old Barney would have fit right in with that crowd.

The "kids" were in their 50's and 60's, yelling at Al and demanding their stuff. He looked shaken but stood his ground saying they left all that stuff at his home forever ago and if they had wanted it so bad, they should have come got it before. I remember him saying, "No phone calls! No cards! No visits! Now you want your stuff? Go to Hell!" One of the men tried to grab at Al but the police blocked him and made them put all the stuff back and had me and Michael make sure nothing in their trucks belonged to Al.

In the end, I'm pretty sure they got away with some jewelry we couldn't account for later. We decided to stay open a lot later that day to make up for the lost selling time and many of the neighbors who had been watching everything came over and bought a lot of stuff too.

As the police and Al's ratty kids were leaving, I had the bus leave and told Al I would take him back to the Bedford Arms when he was ready. I took him out to the back porch and had him sit in a chair with some coffee and cookies we had been serving. Then he started to cry. And cry. My nerves were so rattled and he was so pitiful, that I started to cry too. We shared some tissues and after a while he stopped crying. He said very softly "Thank you." I kissed the top of his head, patted his hand and went back inside.

About a half hour later I went to check on Al and from behind, it looked like he had fallen asleep because his head was leaned over. I touched his shoulder but he didn't wake. When I came around, I saw his eyes were open. I tried to feel for a pulse but couldn't find it. Al wasn't sleeping.

I went back in the house trying to decide whether to call an ambulance or 911 or what. I never had to deal with something like this before and I didn't want to say anything in front of the customers. That's when Fred, Maggie and Frank came in saying "Heard you had some excitement today!"

I said, "And it's not over."

Frankie: The coroner determined that Al Paulsen had died of heart failure. My father said he had died of a broken heart. But the Paulsen family wasn't done yet. Short version: Al's last will and testament left his money and estate to his church, some charities and several individuals and families, but nothing to his children and grandchildren from whom he was estranged for many years.

The Paulsen families filed a number of lawsuits against the estate, Orion Group, Bernice and Michael. They also filed challenges to the will, causing a probate to be opened. In the end, the Paulsen family did not get anything and most of Mr. Paulsen's money went to attorney's fees to fight the lawsuits against the estate so very little money went to the beneficiaries.

Luckily, our grandparents were spared any inconvenience of all this drama as RPR represented them as the legal buyers of the home. Besides, they had already returned to Vietnam and would not be back until Spring.

Kimmie: Hundreds of mourners from all over the area came to pay their respects at Al Paulson's funeral. Members of his church and the social clubs he had belonged to, neighbors, fellow veterans and charities he had worked with crowded the church and cemetery services.

The only noticeable absences were his children and their families. I never learned what had happened to cause their estrangement but I hoped and prayed our children do not abandon us over some hurt feelings or a disagreement. I can't imagine Al or his wife, who I never met but heard much about, could have done anything so terrible that could not have been easily forgiven and forgotten. As it is, my prayers were answered.

Friday July 31, 2003
Dear My Diary,

Buck's Park is now open! Yesterday was the official dedication and ribbon-cutting and nearly all my family came except for both cousin's husbands who were working. Frank and Maggie were there with some of their relatives and it was such a proud day for us all. We brought Frankie but had Lois stay home with Ca as she is still so small and susceptible to illness.

Dozens of neighborhood residents and city officials came to watch and celebrate with us. Fred thinks about three hundred or so were there which I think was a pretty good turnout for ten o'clock on a weekday morning. I was happy to see lots of mothers and children there, ready to try out the new playground.

The mayor and head of the parks and recreation department made speeches praising Fred and his family for all the civic work they have performed over the years including the generous donation of land for the benefit of the local children and their families.

Maggie took pictures and videos of Fred and I as we stepped up to the podium, shook hands with the mayor and Fred made a short, well-rehearsed speech. He spoke of how the future is in the hands of our children and, in a world that is becoming more complicated and troubled, children more than ever need clean and green places to play, use their imagination and let kids be kids as nature intended.

I also made a small speech from my own perspective, about growing up in Ho Chi Minh City where we do not have playgrounds like this for children, with such fun activities to do. I said, "For fun, we mostly ran foot races, played hop scotch or chased the neighborhood cats."

That brought laughter, as I had hoped, even from Ba! I continued, "I am very proud to be a part of this beautiful city in my adopted country and we want everyone to have fun in their new park." When the applause began, I said "Oh!" and held up a finger like I just remembered something. "And whatever you do to have fun, please do not chase the neighborhood cats! Thank you."

After we cut the ribbon and officially opened the park, Fred and I and some volunteers handed out little stuffed deer with a collar-tag marked "Bucks Park, July 30, 2003" as a keepsake for everyone.

Fred told me later, "Kimmie, if you really want to be an actress, I think comedy will be a good fit for you! That was funny stuff about the cats. People are going to remember your bit, and share it with others more than whatever the mayor or I said."

He said this in a kind and loving way, so I know he supports me as I support him. And his words about my words gave me more food for thought.

Dear My Diary,

The mail came today and there is a thick envelope from the hospital. I opened it up and stared in disbelief. It is a bill. Pages and pages and the total due is more than I paid for both houses. I remember, before we married, how Fred told us that he does not have health insurance because he is so healthy…but this is just too much! Plus, he paid for most of Frank's hospital and other healthcare bills. Luckily, Frankie was an easy birth and has been a healthy little boy, but what if he gets sick? Or any of us?

When Fred came home, I gave him the envelope and apologized for opening it. He shrugged and said "No big deal. It's your mail too." I told him what I saw and how much the bill is. He was quite nonchalant about it, saying, "Yeah, well, things happen sometimes. That's why we have plenty of health insurance to cover all this."

I said, "We have health insurance? When did you get it?"

"We've had it all the time since you got here. I always hand over the insurance card when we check in." He looked at me oddly, "I got it because you said it was important that we have it, so I got it like you asked. I thought you knew."

Funny, when he was giving them the insurance card, I thought he was using a different credit card from his usual. He explained that Frankie's birth hardly cost anything and Lois's bill will be just a few thousand dollars as there is a limit on how much co-insurance we pay in a year's time.

I pointed out some figures and asked "Why does it say we owe over $300,000?"

Fred showed me the words "This is not a bill." It is a summary before the insurance pays its part. Fred promised me that we will only pay a tiny fraction of the amount for Lois' birth. Now I feel better, but I wish he had explained this to me a long time ago. So much worry for nothing!

Dear My Diary,

Over the last few weeks, Fred and I have had many discussions about my continuing with Fierce 5…should I quit? Should I work? If I do, do I bring the babies or no? Fred can make his own schedule for teaching Dissolving Debt seminars but my F5 schedule for the movie premier is Labor Day Weekend with many scheduled events before and after.

Our decision is for Fred to stay home with Frankie and I will travel with Ca and Lois, paying their way out of our own pockets. It won't cost much more than transportation and some food since we will stay in the same hotel room. I let the F5 office and Zander know I will be there. If I did not go, they would have difficulty in replacing me and I feel ready to move forward with my career.

Ca has been so much help during these difficult times and I am so glad to have her with us. She is quiet, makes no complaints and is wonderful with the children when I need space to work and workout. As we travel, I will nurse Lois when I can and pump milk the for times I can't. I use the "kangaroo pouch" to keep Lois close to me much of the time. It was recommended by the doctors to increase our bonding and Ca will do the same when I have to work. It will be good for the baby to get used to both of us, I think.

Oh! And the word 'kangaroo', reminds me that Frankie has a new exercise seat that he loves, and it's so much fun to watch him. It's a padded harness that hangs from the door jamb on a spring-loaded cord. Frankie stands in the doorway and can bounce up and down or just stand there and watch what we are doing, but mostly he like to bounce.

Fred likes to say "Boing! Boing! Boing!" as Frankie bounces and the boy just laughs and laughs, so it makes us laugh too. Now we can do chores while Frankie stays out of the way, gets his exercise and has a lot of fun.

As for exercising, I am working out more to get in shape for the premiers. I go to the F5 office for costume fittings and the updated schedules of where we will go, the different cities, hotels, TV and radio studios and press conferences we will be attending. Looks like some very full days ahead!

I will not be the only one to bring extra people with me as Malia's fiancé will be coming as well as Bettina's mother and young son who is eight. It will be their first trip to America. We are flying on chartered jets hired by the studio, so no extra charge for our guests and it will save us from going through security lines and hauling our own luggage.

Even better, we will be able to rehearse for the upcoming interviews and finalize last minute itinerary changes without strangers overhearing us. I understand there will be twenty-five to thirty of us with plenty of catered food and drinks. It sounds like a flying party…so Hollywood!

I feel like Lois is feeding much more than Frankie did at her age and my breasts have swollen even larger to keep up with her needs. Fred thinks maybe her body is trying to catch up from all the time she was so tiny.

When Lois was born, Frankie was still nursing at night and eating solid foods during the day. While Lois was in the hospital, I worked with his pediatrician to get Frankie free of his favorite "bottle". It worked out well so when Lois was able to latch, I was ready and Frankie only rarely complained about wanting to nurse. Now she has an almost constant demand to be fed when she is not sleeping. The pediatrician said to let Lois feed as much as she wants and she will slow down in her good time. I just hope the plane has a private area, like sleeping quarters, where I can nurse.

The Fierce 5 promotions team has many things for us to do in New York, Chicago, Riverton and Los Angeles in preparation for the movie premiers. The company has produced a "Collector's Edition" of Fierce 5 cans to promote 'A Son's Quest' and there are six different designs, each with a different F5 girl on it in a "fierce" pose and, of course, our celebrity spokesman Rock Rollins. They look so cool! Fred already got several cases of Chimera for us to give away as gifts.

August 16, 2003
Dear My Diary,

I just heard about Al's death today. I don't know if I should tell my parents about it because they will think it is bad luck, even if the cause was natural and not by violence. But Bunny did say his children were angry, yelling and threatening, so maybe that kind of indirect violence was part of the cause. If I tell Ba and Me, they might think Al's ghost will hang around to haunt them and they will want to sell the house and move elsewhere. The easiest thing will be to not tell them unless they ask me specifically.

Fred and his parents will go to Al's funeral and Bunny said she wants to go, but is afraid his children and grandchildren will be there and give her a hard time. She calls what they did "an invasion' and she is still very upset about the whole thing. I would be too, if it happened to me.

We are in Los Angeles doing promos for Fierce 5 and the movie. Ca is getting more comfortable about exploring the area around our hotel and asking the concierge where to take Lois for walks, get some exercise and see nice things around the neighborhood, without going so far that she might get lost.

We have a routine now: After I get back, I take a shower, we have dinner, I have Mommy time with Lois, call Fred and Frankie and then we take a taxi to tour the local area so Ca and I can see nice things about the city we are in. That is *if* I do not have to go to dinner with executives, media people, marketing people, etc. which happens often. If I come back late, we take in a small meal or some fresh fruit, I feed and play with Lois and prepare for the next day.

The first times I called home, Frankie was being himself in the background but when Fred held the phone to him and I said "Hello! Hello Frankie!", he burst out crying because he suddenly realized I am away from him and not at home. Now he is used to it and babbles happily at me.

I call Fred when I can during the day to catch up and let him know my day, then I call Ca so she knows what to expect and do for the rest of the day. For meals, I let her order room service or go to a restaurant…whatever she wants. She takes such good care of Lois and I let her know my appreciation often.

But I am starting to see one new thing about Lois: She is starting to get hair. Since her birth she has been "as bald as an egg" as Fred will say, and I know this is not abnormal for preemies, but what is abnormal to me is how the hair is coming in very light…a little darker than blond but more orange, or at least it looks orange at certain angles.

It looks strange with her Asian features. I think it will turn darker as she gets older. Ca agrees that it might, but she also said that black-haired people usually have black hair from the very beginning. We will have to wait and see.

We went home for two days between Chicago and LA to celebrate Frankie's first birthday. He was so happy with a chocolate cake and funny hat to wear and many new toys and clothes and Lucky Money from the family. We took many pictures, and he is walking now! I feel bad missing his first steps while I have been travelling. Fred took some videos of it and he is so cute to watch. And I had to leave again so soon! Ugh.

Fred is taking good care of Frankie and his mother helps out here and there so Fred has time to work on the DD book edits. Fred often takes breaks from the editing to go down a long list of selected colleges, universities, bookstores and libraries provided by RU, contact and find places willing to host DD seminars.

It is hard work to keep track of all the people he contacts, who give him other people to contact, how to apply for space and time, etc. Most of the dates he has scheduled so far are for next year with a few for late this year. I expect to be done with the promo tour by mid-October or so, and then I can stay home with the babies and help with seminars.

I make time every day to run, in whatever city we are staying, to lose weight and tone muscles. I never know when one of the entertainment people we meet will remember me for a job and how good I will look for the part!

Most mornings I run with my F5 sisters and I learn a lot from them about all kinds of things, but mostly I concentrate on learning about the business side of what we do to increase my chances for success. Other times I use the hotel's gym machines if the weather is not good or I want to concentrate on toning other areas of my body.

When I run in our Riverton neighborhoods, many people smile and wave. Sometimes children call out, "Hi Chimera!" and I wave back…so different from what children used to call me. I find running helps me clear my mind to think and plan for the next days and weeks. I did not run in Vietnam, but in America it is a common and normal activity. Mostly, when people are running in my country, it is because they are running from the police or are late for work.

We filmed a segment on the popular daytime talk show "Chick Chat" last week. The show has three women hosts: a news reporter, an actress and an author of books and blogs about women's topics. We were all dressed in stylish street clothes and, to introduce the audience to Fierce 5, they did a side-by-side picture of each of us in our full character costume and makeup.

When I learned we were going to be on Chick Chat, I watched it for a few days as homework and found that they do not make fun of their guests like some shows do, so I felt better about being on the program.

They showed a clip of the bar scene and everyone politely applauded and the hosts asked us about the challenges of being so tall. I talked about how difficult it was to find a husband in my country and they put up a picture of me and Fred on our wedding day in our ao dais. The hosts went "Oooh! He's cute! Does he have a brother?" and I thought about newly-divorced Barney in prison, so I said, "Yes, but he is taken!" "Awww!" and they laughed good-naturedly.

We discussed the difficulty of finding shoes and clothes to fit and I brought up Tree Top Gals stores as a quick plug for them. They asked us if there were any mean-spirited nicknames that we wanted to share from our childhoods? Bettina, because she is so pale, was called Yeti or Giant Snow Girl. I shared my names of Head in Clouds and Coconut Tree. This is the first time I have told this to strangers, but I am more comfortable with myself now and thought it would add color to the interview.

Jasmin was called Date Palm and Consuela was Amazon. I did not understand that nickname until I asked Fred its meaning. He said the Amazons were a mythical tribe of warrior women in ancient Greece and not from South America like many people think.

When they ask Malia the question, she did not give a word name. Instead, she pushed out her jaw, hunched her back and scratched her underarms making "Ooo! Ooo!" sounds. Even I understood the meaning. No one dared laugh as they had with the other names we gave. On my videotaped copy of the show, Malia's part of that segment had been edited out. I think it was considered too…what?

Controversial? Maybe. But Sad, I think, is the best word. Too Sad.

But there is one more thing about the Chick Chat show that was the most interesting to me. When we went into the Green Room to wait for our segment, there were two black men who looked very much alike. One was with an older white couple and they spoke English with an accent like Barry's, but different. The other black man spoke in a different language and a blonde woman with him was translating back and forth between them.

I did not think much about it until the end of our interview, then the camera did a closeup of the host Jillian who said, "Up next, Somalian twins separated at birth and living on different continents, were recently reunited and are here today to tell us their heartwarming story. You don't want to miss this!" and they cut to a commercial.

I thought, 'Oh! I want to see this!' but we were led away as the twins, with the translator and older couple, waited in the wings to be introduced. We went to another office to meet the producers and have a light lunch until the show was almost over. Afterward, we went to the lobby to sign autographs, answer questions and take pictures with the audience members.

After reading the book from Cam and Tam, and finding other articles about separated twins, I find this topic most interesting to my heart and now, I was just feet away from a live example and I could not watch their story as they talked about it. Ugh!

I went to the restroom and called Maggie as she had promised to tape the show which is on a two-hour delay to our local station. I asked her to please tape the entire show, even after our part is done. She said that was no problem as they have all three TV's in the house taping the show and promised to tape the full hour. Maggie is so good about taping any of my commercials and appearances as she can, which is not many.

After we came home from our tour and rested up, we invited family members to come over for lunch, watch the interview and tell all about our travel adventures. But in private, I watched the interview about the twins. They were born in Somalia, a country in Africa, and because of the war there, their parents and family were killed or sent to camps. The boys had been rescued, cared for by an international agency and, while still very young, adopted out. One went to an Australian family (that is the funny English accent I heard) and the other to a German family.

They found each other recently because the Australian twin was trying to become an actor and was filming short videos on VidLive to promote himself. Meanwhile, friends of the German twin said, "There is someone who looks just like you on VidLive. Is that you? I did not know you speak English." He does not, and after much researching, he found the videos and felt he was looking in the mirror.

With help from friends, he sent an email to the actor and asked some questions. They found they were both born in the same country, but did not know who their parents were or anything about their past.

After much back and forth, doctors from both countries worked to get DNA samples to see if they were related, or just look much alike…and they are real identical twins! Part of the confusion was their records show different birthdays because the people at the orphanage or the local government did not know the history of the baby boys so they made up dates that they thought were close to actual.

Anyway, it was extremely interesting to me and I talked about it so much that Fred asked me if I thought I might have a secret twin somewhere?

I said, "If there is another two-meter-tall Asian woman in the world, I would probably know it by now!" Besides, my parents would never give any of us away, even in the poorest of times. I don't know why I find this so interesting, but it is. I feel bad for the separated twins who sense something is missing in their life, and then, when they find someone out there who is just like them, it makes them feel more complete.

At the end of the interview, the show arranged for each brother to fly with his parents to the other one's home for a two-week visit, so two visits of two weeks each, paid for by the show. It is a wonderful story and the happy ending made me cry.

Trang Starbuckle: During this time, the F5 team promoted the movie and the product with local morning talk shows all over the US. Most of them were done as live feeds from a major studio in New York, LA or Chicago and they would do quick five-to-seven-minute interviews for one or another of the many dozens of network affiliates all over the country. One after another, bang, bang, bang. Many of the same questions over and over with fresh ones tossed in randomly.

Fierce 5 management had given guidelines on the kinds of answers the team members could/should give…kind of a dos and don'ts list, if you will. By the time we were doing them as kid actors, Mom was an old pro at them and helped us develop stock answers and reactions we could say in our sleep.

Special Guests

Thursday, August 21
Dear My Diary,

I showed Fred the new orange hairs growing on Lois and asked him if he thinks they will turn darker over time or stay light. He said "How am I supposed to know?" Big help, Fred! Then I showed Frank and Maggie and she said, "We do have some red-heads on my side of the family, Kimmie. You met a couple of them before!" I really don't remember who has what hair color except one older woman who has blue hair and a couple of the teens sporting green and purple hair with nose rings and chains around their necks, but I don't remember any red heads.

When I told Fred about what his mother had told me, Fred said, "Oh, yeah! Now that Mom brought it up, we do have two or three redheads in the family!" It looks like Lois will be the first red head on my side of the family.

Lois: I was, and am, the only redhead on the Vietnamese side of the family, only most people don't know it as I have been dying my hair black since college. Too many unwanted stares and questions about whether my red hair was "real" or not. Apparently, if you look Asian, you can't have red hair without having dyed it…so I dye it black to make it look like it's not dyed red. Only my husband knows for sure! It would have been easier if Frankie had inherited the carrot-top genes instead of me.

Fred let me and Michael know we will prepare two rooms at the garage for next Tuesday. I reminded him that next Wednesday is the Riverton Premier of "A Son's Quest" and then I fly straight to New York and LA for the main premiers so I won't have time to entertain guests.

Fred said he knows all this perfectly well but that it will be important for this particular guest to stay at the garage and not in our house.

I asked, "So, who is so important that we have to put him up during premier week and why the garage?"

"Oh, someone who does not want to be bothered by thousands of fans at the Central Park Hotel," he said, giving me a big smile and waggling his eyebrows.

"Are you kidding? Rock will be staying with us?"

"Yes indeed. Rock and Kathy will be our guests. The promotions team heard about our little hideaway in the industrial district and asked if we can keep the Rollins there for a couple of nights. I said we would be happy to…unless you don't want them to?"

"No, that's fine. I think it will be fun. Oh! Can I tell my sisters? Maybe they will want to meet him?"

Fred shook his head. "You know how secrets are. Once somebody knows…"

"…everybody knows."

Thomas Stimson

A Son's Quest Premier

August 28, 2003
Dear My Diary,

The Premier yesterday was so glamourous. Many limousines were lined up at the Central Park Hotel where most of the studio people were staying. I went there to get in costume while Rock sneaked in through the back entrance. Kathy will spend the evening with a good book in the suite that F5 has rented for the Rollins. I understand that she does not attend the premiers as they are very boring for her. She will join us in the hospitality suite for an after-premier party.

When Rock and Kathy arrived at the garage on Tuesday morning, they found it "refreshingly different" and quiet compared to the hotel with lots of security and fans trying to meet with him at all hours. We gave them the five-dollar tour while Michael and Bunny are out working.

We did not tell Bunny about our special visitors, but Mike knows and will stay at his mother's for two nights to give them privacy. Rock and Kathy took one guest room and Fred and I the other. I will shuttle between the garage and home as I don't want to disturb our guests with crying babies and Fred can drive them around and cook meals.

Ca brought Frankie and Lois over for a while and she was quite shy to meet our guests, but used her best English to greet them. Her English is getting better and clearer to understand. Frankie made his little boy show-offs to Rock and Kathy until it was time to go home.

The largest and oldest movie theater in Riverton, The Palace, was fixed up special for the premier with a real red carpet and velvet ropes to hold back the fans. The first Premier is in Riverton as Fierce Five is one of the larger investors, and Rock is our celebrity spokesman, so we got to be first to show his new movie. Over the next few days, we will attend premiers in New York, Los Angeles, Chicago and Houston. F5 will not be attending the overseas premiers as we are not known there (yet!) and to save costs.

Many people walked the red carpet before us: the Director, producers, lesser stars of the film and local celebrities. We were in the last limo. Handlers assisted us out of the car and once we were lined up on either side of the car door, Rock got out of the limo and waved to the cheering fans. We lined up three on one side of Rock and two on the other, linking arms and strutting down the red carpet. People went crazy, snapping pictures, fans waving autograph books and putting their hands out to High Five and shake.

Once inside the theater, the mayor formally greeted Rock Rollins and gave him the key to the city. Rock made a short speech on how much he likes visiting Riverton, what a big honor it is and etc. We each got a Swag Bag, as did all the attending guests, then we went inside to see the movie, sitting a few rows away from Rock who was surrounded by the mayor and members of the F5 management.

It was so exciting to see all of us in the movie, and how it looks after all the editing and the addition of special effects, music and all the trimmings.

Our scene starts when Rock's group, who is travelling through our country, and the guide Abja with his helpers, come in to a bar arguing with each other. The place is dark and smoky with small groups of men at the bar and we are at a table drinking cans of F5.

Abja is demanding much money to take Rock's group through the Valley of No Return and that he is the only one who knows the way and, more importantly, its dangers.

Rock states how they don't have that kind of money and it is very important to get across quickly to save his father. Scirocco calls out, "Where are you going, stranger?"

"To the coastal town of Graa. But we must get through the Valley of No Return and this guide is asking for a princely sum!"

Ice Queen says, "Abja calls it the Valley of No Return so he may pick your pockets clean, but the journey to Graa involves little difficulty."

I say, "And you look well equipped to handle such a journey!"

Abja is annoyed. "Do not listen to these foolish women for they wish to see you dead by the thousand traps that await you." (then to us) "Tend to your own business and let me get on with mine."

We get up and surround Abja and his men.

(Jaguar) "No. We are tired of you and your men making a bad name of our homeland and robbing those who fear what you tell them."

(Diabla) "Go back under your rock and let these strangers travel in peace." Then to Rock, "You face no dangers here but from Abja."

Abja turns angry, stating "I have warned you to stay out of my business. Now it is time to teach you a lesson!" The bad men pull out different weapons and threaten us silently with them.

Each of us crush an F5 can in different ways to show how tough we are. One on the forehead, another twisting between her palms, another between forearm and bicep. I place a can between my thighs and push them together.

There is a closeup of Rock's face as one eyebrow goes up in surprise and it made the audience laugh.

As a group, we took a step forward and each of us speaks our line in our own language with subtitles beneath:

Ice Queen (Dutch): This has gone on long enough.

Diabla (Spanish): Thieves and tricksters do not belong here.

Chimera (Vietnamese): Safe passage should be had by all.

Scirocco (Moroccan): These wretched dogs must be put in their place.

Jaguar (English): Time to kick some butt, y'all!

When the last line is spoken in English and subtitled exactly in English, it makes the audience laugh, which was the intent of the director. It worked!

This leads into a fight scene between us and Abja's men with Rock and his men helping out. At one point, I am faced with a large dagger, so I call over the man's shoulder "Scirocco, no!" and the man turns to face the new danger…but no one is there! With his attention diverted, I use both my arms in a scissor-like action to snap his elbow and drop the knife. As he screams, I pick up the knife and throw it at another bad guy, the blade sticking through his coat-sleeve and into the bar.

At another point, two men are coming at Rock from behind while he is on one knee, choking a bad guy. I see what is coming and, making a short run, I roll across Rocks back and kick them both backwards, flying across the room and crashing onto tables that break apart. Other things that happen in our big scene:

Ice Queen blows frigid air on a man about to conk her with a chair and freezes him, then takes the chair away and uses it creatively to fend off Abja and others.

Jaguar is chased by a bad guy, runs up the bar and completely flips behind him. The man slams into the bar, turns and is head butted by Jaguar who then hisses at his collapsing body.

Scirocco grabs one man by the shirt and crotch, turns him sideways and uses him as a battering ram against three oncoming attackers knocking them down.

All these stunts and more happen very quickly and without bloodletting or killing. Abja and his crew run out the door, yelping like kicked dogs. This last bit also made the audience laugh.

Once the fight is over and we are thanked for our help, Rock and his group go up to the bar and say to the bartender "We will have what they are having," pointing to our table. Closeup on our group and the assorted F5 drinks in front of us. The bartender brings F5's to rock and his men who begin drinking.

The whole movie was very good and everyone gave a standing ovation as the credits began. A spotlight was shone on Rock, Dodge Harrison and others in their group who all waved and bowed. Then they put the spotlight on us and we waved and bowed too. We had a very nice time and signed autographs until it was time to go. We were loaded back into the limos to attend a small party in Rock's suite until Fred came to bring us all back to the garage.

This morning, we were having coffee and breakfast when Bunny came upstairs. She had seen my car and wanted to talk about last night. At first, she was happy to see us awake and having breakfast until Rock turned around to see our visitor. Bunny made an "Oh!" face and her words froze in her mouth.

I introduced Bunny as my sister to Rock and Kathy. Rock said "Good looks sure run in the family!" I know he says things like that all the time to be nice and friendly and, of course, we don't look anything like sisters, but Bunny blushed and said "Thank you!"

I invited her to breakfast as Michael was eating with us, so Bunny helped herself to a cup of coffee and sat with Frankie to play with him and tried not to look at Rock too much. It is one of the rare times I have seen Bunny speechless.

Kathy looked perfectly as ease as I am sure this is a very common thing for them. Before they left for the airport, we all took pictures with Rock and Kathy and they thanked us for our hospitality and such a quiet place to sleep. I will make some prints for Bunny of her with Rock.

Rock and Kathy know I am new to the entertainment business and want me to be successful so they laid out some good rules that I never want to forget:

1) Your agent can be your best friend or your worst enemy. Treat them as your best friend and they will not become your worst enemy.

2) Always remember what city you are in, who you are working with and they are always the best, no matter what. The best fans, great director to work with, awesome co-stars, beautiful city and so forth. No one wants to hear that their city was awful, or worse, you call their city by the wrong name.

3) Learn to pack light and live out of a carry-on. Keep a "Go-to" bag handy at all times with everything you need. You do not want to waste time at the baggage carousel or lose your luggage. Time is money and schedules are often tight.

4) Be polite to fans, the press and your support people, even if they are being jerks. They are

your bread and butter. (I like this term!) Too many stars have fallen by being rude and even violent towards others due to the stress of their jobs and celebrityhood. I hope I never get this way!

5) Learn to cat-nap, especially on planes, long car rides and on the set when there is down time. It is a valuable way to keep fresh.

6) Make some personal time for myself and family, otherwise the business can eat you up and burn you out. This is part of the reason there are so many divorces and drug/alcohol problems with people in the entertainment business. And the reason why Rock and Kathy have been together for so long…good private time away from working.

These are good things to remember and I do not want to endanger myself or my family if I get more work in TV and movies. I know I can stop at any time if I don't like the work anymore or it becomes a problem because of the support I have from my best friend Fred.

Even more-so as he is changing his career from the recycling business to the Dissolving Debt book and seminars. Fred was with me to hear all these great rules so we will see how that goes too! We both need to follow these rules and Rock is living proof of how well it works. He is not considered "The Nicest Guy in Hollywood" for nothing!

Lois: Mama and the team went to several premiers around the US and Canada along with some of the co-stars and she went to the premiers in Hanoi, and HCMC without the F5 team in the "local girl makes a splash in Hollywood" kind of way. These were sponsored by the Department of Cinematography and the Vietnamese Cinema Association which would lead to some work for her later in local TV and movie productions. While in Vietnam, she also did video interviews with some of the Asian news networks and entertainment shows.

It was a busy time for her and Fierce 5 did a "fierce" business along with it. Admittedly, it was a bit silly to have people sipping canned drinks in a movie where the most sophisticated form of transportation was horse and wagons, but it was a good popcorn kind of film and is still fun to watch.

Ca came along with Frankie and me and we stayed a few days with our grandparents. By now, Aunt Thao was pregnant with Vui. It must have been quite the homecoming! Mama offered, but Ca refused, to visit with her parents. Dad stayed in the states preparing seminar dates for Dissolving Debt and hiring assistants and a co-presenter for the upcoming lecture tour.

September 11, 2003
Dear My Diary,

The price of gold keeps going up and the value of the gold coins we found at Gladys Robertson's property are going up with it. Fred has been researching the coins and wants to sell some of them.

I have never felt good about keeping found money, even if they were unknowingly included in the price of the property. I feel it is bad luck to keep it. I shared my thoughts with Fred but, of course, he thinks it is a silly Asian superstition.

But Fred knows it bothers me more than most things and I have argued with him not to sell the coins, even anonymously. He finally asked me "What do you want to do with the moneys if not to sell them and keep the profit? Keep it hidden in the bank vault, doing nothing?"

My first idea is that it should go back to Miss Robertson's family members, but Fred pointed out that he bought the property and everything on it from them fair and square and no one knew about the gold coins or certificates. "If I give them the money we found, it might open a can of worms with questions being asked about how much we made versus what we paid them. That could lead to lawsuits and a big mess for us, so I would rather not get them involved. Do you have any other suggestions?"

My second idea is that since Miss Robertson was a long-time library worker and book lover, is it possible to donate the coins and certificates in her name to be sold at auction to raise money for the library?

Fred put his tongue on his front teeth and sucked. Then he nodded and said, "I think you've got something there." He will meet with Dan McClurg to put together a gift from the estate of Gladys Robertson and have Dan present it to the library board at a public meeting. Fred will make sure our names are not tied to the gift but only the three of us will know. This makes me feel better.

I asked Fred if he is unhappy that we will not get the profits he had hoped for? Fred looked kindly at me as he said, "If this is so important to you, then it is the right thing to do." Fred already got more than he expected from the land sale and this will be a good way to give something back to Riverton's citizens in return for Miss Robertson's love of love of books and education. We also will get a thrill out of making a secret donation like this and Gladys will publicly get the credit.

I called Tina today as it is the two-year anniversary of the terrible 9/11 attacks. I talked to her a bit as I felt that she would be depressed like she was last year. She said, "I feel a bit down, but I try to keep my mind off of it, which is not easy when it is all over the news."

She has been talking to a therapist off and on about something called "survivor guilt". Even though Tina was in Riverton when the attacks happened, she feels badly for her friends and co-workers who died or are still missing and that she survived only because she had moved away.

I told Tina that she is making up for what could have happened by being a good sister, auntie, daughter, financial adviser and citizen of her adopted country, as I am trying to do in my own way.

"I love you and will give you every support I can, anytime you need me."

Tina was quiet a moment and then said, "You have changed so much since you've come to Riverton. I barely recognize my baby sister as the one I knew in Saigon…and I mean that in the very best way!" It was a good talk and we both felt better when we hung up.

September 15, 2003
Dear My Diary,

Hilaire has opened five new Tree Top Gals stores in the Midwest since I moved here. Now that the Fierce 5 team are gaining popularity from the movie, Hilaire has arranged to hire us for a special-edition catalog and appearance tour, modeling outfits in each city's shopping malls to promote her stores.

Three months ago, she asked me how to reach our manager, so I shared Zander's contact information. Now, with the new movie out, more stores stocking our drinks and advertising has increased, Fierce 5 is a "hot commodity" as Fred likes to say.

We will do six fashion shows over an eight-day period with fifteen other models, some of whom are also locally-known actors, models and athletes. All kinds of winter and holiday outfits will be presented throughout the show…Casual, working, fun, sporty, dressy and sexy time.

Thank goodness we will not have to wear our heavy F5 makeup at the shows but when they introduce us, they will put large pictures of our character on the video screen so people will know who is who.

Additionally, we are the featured celebrity models for the Tree Top Gals Christmas Catalog. The front cover will have our team in full Fierce 5 makeup, hair and costumes with our character names underneath. The expanding centerfold will have us in the same order, but natural-looking with our real or stage names underneath. I will use "Kimmie" as my name for the catalog.

I hope this will help Hilaire with her in-store and online sales. She even has her own website!

The catalog Mom mentioned above has become a popular collector's item and we have several copies. Those that are autographed by all five members can go for a few thousand dollars in very good condition. It's surprising how many Fierce 5 memorabilia collectors there are, along with a smaller, but very dedicated group of our mother's fans. The actual catalog is tastefully done and nicely showcases the original F5 models.

Fred has finished the second draft of Dissolving Debt and sent it back to RU Publishing for another review. He has pushed hard to finish it, but I have not been of much help, I am afraid. He told me not to worry about it as I have been so busy with the babies and the movie premier and soon to be going back on the road for the fashion shows.

As Fred is not a man who needs a lot of sleep, he has time at night to work without disruptions. He said the RU team can clean up the minor details and edits and send it back to us in the way they want it to look. I am glad this part is done now.

Dear My Diary,

We visited Dan McClurg's office with the coins and certificates today. Dan did not know what we were bringing as Fred was intentionally vague about our reason for coming in. Each item has its own clear bag or envelope with a descriptive label that includes a value range. Fred also provided a complete spreadsheet with the same information as a backup inventory summary.

When Fred opened the box and pulled everything out, Dan's mouth fell open. He asked, "Where did you get all this?" and Fred replied, "From the Robertson property."

As Dan looked everything over, Fred explained our idea that this will be a donation from the Gladys Robertson estate to the Riverton Regional Library Services. The Library Board can decide whether part or all of the gift will be kept, sold or auctioned off and any money raised is to be used to fund book purchases, special programs and improved accessibility of information.

Dan said, "Everybody thinks Gladys was broke when she died. How do we explain the coins?"

Fred described how the coins were found "among her things" after she died, "…and you believe that she would have wanted them to go to the library that she loved so much." Fred made it very clear that we are not to be named as knowing anything about this.

Dan promised to take care of it. As an attorney, he has to keep things confidential for his clients and even though we are not Dan's client exactly, he understands our desire to stay anonymous.

September 23, 2003
Dear My Diary,

Today's Riverton Review has a feature article including color pictures of our gift to the library…I mean, the gift from Gladys Robertson's estate. What a welcome surprise it was to the board of directors and the many people attending the monthly meeting two days ago.

There is a picture of Dan McClurg presenting a special book he had made for the coins and certificates, a group picture of the board with the opened book, a portrait of Miss Robertson and some close-up pictures of the coins and bills.

The article said they did not have a detailed estimate yet, but one of the people at the meeting is an experienced coin collector and she said its value is well over $100,000 just from looking at them and reviewing the summary sheet. Dan had put this together rather quickly and it looks very good from the pictures I saw.

Fred said the newspaper usually has one reporter at the meeting to take notes and write a short report that gets buried somewhere in the next edition, but Dan made sure to let the Features editor know that there would be a surprise special presentation and it would be a good idea to have a photographer there. The Board Chairman said they intend to have the collection professionally appraised and then make some decisions as to what they will do with this gift.

Dear My Diary,

We have received an invitation from the Riverton Library to attend a costume party and Halloween-themed fundraising dinner featuring the auctioning of authentic gold coins and gold and silver certificates donated from the estate of Gladys Robertson. One of the more popular and entertaining local auctioneers will handle the sale, not Fred. Wouldn't that have been a weird coincidence if they had asked Fred to help with auctioning off the estate we had donated anonymously?

Fred asked if I want to go? I asked, "Will we buy something?"

He said "I would very much like to buy one piece as a memento of this entire adventure that we have shared, and help the library too."

"Didn't you keep anything back from the collection for yourself?"

He frowned. "No, Sweetheart. You said it would be, like, bad luck to do that. So, I handed over the entire set."

"I just meant it would be wrong to sell it all and keep the money for ourselves. Found money like that should not be treated lightly, especially when it was probably unknown to Miss Robertson and she could have used it to pay her taxes."

Fred sighed, "But it would have been okay to keep some of it if we weren't going to sell it, is that what you are saying?"

"Yes, I think that would have been fine."

He shrugged, "Well, what's done is done. I wished I had known what you just said, but I was just trying to respect your wishes."

I gave Fred a kiss and said, "What you did was the best thing. I believe Miss Robertson's soul will rest easier if the money is used for the good of the community."

Fred pinched my nose playfully and said, "Well, my soul will rest easier once we figure out what we will wear to the costume party."

Dear My Diary,

The movie I filmed in Chicago, "Lost in L.A." came out three weeks ago. Tina went to see it and said the movie was just okay, and she spotted me a couple of times in the party scenes but my scene with the star was not in it. That surprises me as we filmed several takes.

I called Takeela about it and she said it is a common event. That very often scenes are not used for various reasons like time constraints, pacing, did not fit the mood right and so forth. Takeela said it has happened to many actors, including future stars.

"Am I a future star?"

She laughed politely and said "You might be. Never can tell!"

She is nice, but I do not take her flattery too seriously. I am sure she says this kind of thing to everyone as part of her work as an agent. I am not so interested in seeing the movie at the theater and will wait for it to come out on DVD.

Thomas Stimson

Halloween Time

Nov 1, 2003
Dear My Diary,

Last night was unbelievable! Fred and I wore wedding ao dais as costumes, which stood out from the usual scary and naughty outfits adults here like to wear. I should be honest and admit that Fred's ao dai still fits great, but after having two children, constant breast-feeding for over a year and working out to build muscle mass, there is no way I could wear mine at all. I had a new one made by Thuy using a similar pattern to Freds, but in red while his is a brilliant blue. I accented my look with multiple bracelets, rings and the best jewelry I own, many pieces of which came from our storage lockers including a lady's Rolex.

We thought we would save money by re-using our outfits but that was not to be. On the bright side, I will have an ao dai I can wear on special occasions in the near future.

Vo brought over a black wig and helped Fred achieve an Asian appearance using golden tan foundation and expertly applied eye makeup. Fred said I look like his beautiful bride all over again…so sweet! And he is very handsome too! Maggie and Frank helped Ca babysit Lois and Frankie who went looking for Daddy when he saw a strange man with Mommy!

The cream of Riverton society attended in an array of impressive costumes. Fred said some of them traveled as far as St Louis, Minneapolis and Chicago to find the most exclusive designers and selections. It was funny how many of those same people admired our matching outfits and asked where we got them.

Guests crowded around the selection of monies on display in fancy frames with etched descriptive labels and a window on the back to admire and study the obverse side. Some were combined into sets, such as five of the same coin from different years or the same year, but in different denominations.

The security personnel guarding the display tables were dressed like warriors of Aladdin's time. To build interest for the upcoming auction, owners of local coin shops were dressed as wealthy merchants to show and explain the features, details and history of what the guests will be bidding on. These are the same experts who helped the library assess and provide the display cases for our found treasures.

I saw one coin I have had an interest in for a long time. I nudged Fred, "I want that one!"

Fred gave me a smile. "You want this one? To bid on?" and I nodded. I did not give Fred a reason but I have had a special feeling for this gold coin since the first time I saw it. Fred simply said "Then I will get it for you," and he wrote down the item number in his notebook.

The mayor, head of the library board, Dan McClurg and others made small speeches about Gladys Robertson, who she was to the community and how her beloved collection had been donated to the institution of which she had spent her entire working life.

The speakers painted a kindly picture of the founding family and their wealth, how it was passed down to their last surviving offspring, who now wished to see her family's name live on for generations to come through this most generous donation. They skipped the part about how she had lived in poverty during the last part of her life, surrounded by tons of near-worthless junk and owed the city many years' worth of back taxes. But that would not have helped the library raise very much money, would it?

It concluded with some vague plans that hinted at great things for the library system to be paid for by the proceeds raised by tonight's auction. The room was absolutely buzzing once the speeches were over.

As he promised, Fred bid and bid until he won the coin I wanted for a princely $2,100. And, like the other winners, we stood up and waved to the applauding crowd.

After the auction, we danced and chatted with different people that we know and some who were new to us, but have seen at other functions.

We also met with the Nelsons who were polite and pleasant with us. I don't know if they remember us from past meetings or if they know that Fred is Barney's brother. Either way, I was nervous with them at first, but they were sweet and we spent a few minutes making small talk.

After the party, we figured out about how much money was raised for the library. Fred has a spreadsheet of all the pieces, their details and a general value of each one and I saw him writing down all the winning bids in the auction program we were given. He determined that most of the items went for far more than their market value, but since this was for charity, what was paid for the coins and dinner is tax deductible and that's what most of this was about…tax deductions and getting something unique along with plenty of networking.

I asked Fred if he is sorry that I made him donate all the monies to the library and lose the chance of getting cash for them?

He took me in his arms, smiling tenderly until his eyes crinkled at the edges and said, "No, I am not sorry, and I will tell you why. First, if we had sold everything on Ubiddit and donated it to the library, we would not have gotten anywhere close to the amount they ended up receiving tonight." He kissed the center of my forehead and continued. "Second, a lot of people have become more aware of Miss Robertson's quiet service to the community and what a treasure she has been to generations of local readers." He kissed the spot between my eyebrows. "Third, the coins, and their history to Riverton, will be much more appreciated and treasured by those who won them at auction than strangers in faraway places who were just looking to fill blank spaces in their collections." He kissed the tip of my nose. I liked where this was heading. "So, to answer your question, you had a far better idea, and created a much better effect, than anything I had in my mind to do with what we found." Fred's warm lips met mine and we spent a long time appreciating each other's commitment to community service.

After a mutually invigorating shower together and, as we readied for bed, Fred took the time to look over our new treasure as I sat next to him. The gold coin had been expertly cleaned prior to framing and shone like a sunrise on the Mekong Delta. It was mesmerizing in its beauty.

The profile of an American Indian with a feather headdress stared, unsmiling and solemn, to our left. The man looks older, very strong and serious and he appears to be a leader or veteran warrior. The word "LIBERTY" is crested over the top, with thirteen stars framing the portrait, six on one side and seven on the other and the date at the bottom.

On the back is an eagle standing on a log with some leaves sprouting from it. The coin was worth two and one half dollars when it was minted, as stated on the back, along with the words "In God We Trust" "E Pluribus Unum" and "United States of America".

"You wanted this coin specifically and no other," Fred said, and asked "Why this coin?"

"Because I like the year of it. No other money in the auction had this year."

"Really?" Fred looked surprised. "Is that the only reason? The year 1911?"

"Yes. Actually, there is another reason," I admitted. "The year 1911 is the same year as my Ong Noi's birthday. The Ong Noi who made me tall and beautiful for you."

Fred smiled broadly. "Ah, yes! My favorite Ong Noi!"

The only pictures I have seen of Ong Noi shows him looking very strong and serious like this chief, this warrior, this man of great dignity and respect. This coin is the only one with his birth year and when I saw it, I felt a tug at my heart…a new connection with my great grandfather.

Before I came to America, I fervently wished I did not have this man in my family. His genes made me an object of wonder and ridicule. But now, even though I have not physically changed, good things are coming to me and I have respect from others as never before.

"Yes Fred, he is my favorite Ong Noi too."

The Big Vote

Tuesday November 4, 2003
Dear My Diary,

Today is the day our state is voting on gay marriage. Fred said he will vote "For" because he has an open mind about love and believes it is only fair that all adults should have the freedom to marry whom they wish.

I asked him to vote for me too, but of course he laughed and said he wished he could vote a second time on my behalf. "One to a customer!" he said.

Of course, I know Fred cannot vote for me and I cannot vote as I am not yet a citizen. But if I were, I would vote "For" also. I want our friends Bobby and Robbie and all their friends to have the same rights Fred and I have. As an immigrant and married just three years, I have more rights in the realm of marriage than Bobby and Robbie who have loved each other many more years than I have.

November 5, 2003
Dear My Diary,

Last night was a sad night. Fred and I went to the hotel where MFAP meets and there was a big party in progress as the votes were being counted. There was plenty of food and drink and big-screen TV's on the stage and in the corners of the room with different stations being broadcast.

High up in the ceiling was a net with many balloons to be dropped like at a New Year's party and everyone was in a good mood as the votes were being tallied. The ballroom had been open since noon, but we arrived about five pm after an early dinner and playtime with the children. The vote was kind of close, more "Against" than "For", but with many votes yet to be counted so it could have gone either way.

As we have been to some of the MFAP meetings and rallies to support Bobby and Robbie, I have made many gay friends. They are a fun bunch who like to tease me about being a Fierce 5 girl, my friendship with Rock, my height and how cute Fred is.

I asked Robbie, if the law passes, will he propose to Bobby? He grinned at his partner who was chatting excitedly nearby with some friends, "Oh, he said 'yes' a long time ago!" Then Robbie said, "Do you mean, would we get married? Oh, absolutely! Sign us up tomorrow, I say."

"I hope we are invited to the wedding," I fished, already knowing the answer.

"You and Fred and five hundred of our closest friends!"

Tina arrived to support her bosses and make some business contacts. Both are a good thing to do, but I have been thinking about my sister, after meeting so many of these gay men and women. Tina never seems to date, that I have seen anyway, or the men she goes out with are "just friends" or "men I work with". She is 36 years old and only in these last few months have I been thinking about her not having a man. Is my sister gay? And if she is, is she afraid to tell me or our family?

Then I thought about how many people believed Fred was gay because he did not date and never had a real girlfriend. It made me laugh as he is *very* good with me.

I asked Fred if he thinks Tina is gay or not? I admit, I threw that question at him quite suddenly, without any lead-in. He responded in such a typical American way: "Why don't you ask her?"

I said, "I cannot ask such a thing of my older sister! It is disrespectful." Fred shrugged his shoulders and said, "Well, I'm not going to ask her. It's none of my business."

I know he's right…it is none of our business. And even if she is gay, Tina is still my sister and I should not care about something not my business. Fred's bluntness has a strange way of grounding my attitudes, sometimes.

As the evening wore on, news reporters put people on camera, asking "Do you think the gay marriage law should be passed?" People who said 'Yes' got cheers from our party and people who said 'No' got booed. A few times people in our party were shown on TV explaining how important this kind of civil right is to make society more equal and we cheered and high-fived the person who was on TV.

But soon, the happy party turned quiet, and then sad, as the votes for 'No' grew until there was no chance for the 'Yes' vote to win any more. The balloons did not drop, some people were crying and others were quietly cursing as the banquet personnel came in to clean up.

We hugged our friends and told each other "It will happen one day, but now is too soon" and things like that.

I asked Tina what she thought of tonight's election and she admitted that she did not expect it to pass this time, but was happy to see the number of Yes votes got over 30%. "It could have been much worse," she said. "It shows that many people who voted have some belief that this is the right thing to do. But many more must think and feel the same way for this to pass into law."

Fred said it was a good try. There are several lawsuits pending to try and force the courts to recognize gay marriage as a constitutional right, but it could take many years to be heard and the courts may not agree with the arguments.

It is all so very complicated.

Friday, November 14, 2003
Dear My Diary,

We had a small party today at RU. The first copies of Dissolving Debt are done and the book looks SO beautiful. It has been done in what they call a Trade Paperback with a glossy cover, thick paper, attractive fonts that catch the eye and make you want to read it. They even used my cover design idea and it looks perfect because it tells the title in a picture as well as words.

Fred was as emotional as I was. And Fred did such a fine thing without telling me…he has *both* our names as the authors. I said, "Fred, this is your program, your words and stories and your passion. You should have just your name on it."

"Sweetheart, we are a team. This was a team effort and you should get equal credit."

Ok, I will not refuse my husband, but it really is very sweet of him. On the page where they have copyright date and publisher, is my name again: "Cover Design by Kim Pham Starbuckle".

The cover design of the book "Dissolving Debt: How to Decrease Debts and Increase Personal Wealth" is one of its lasting trademarks and has never had a major revision in the forty-plus years it has been in continuous print. A fist grips a bundle of bills with labels like "Auto" "Mortgage" "Credit Card" and "Education" sticking out from the top. From the bottom of scrunched bills is a rain of small bits falling onto a growing pile of cash. As DD grew in popularity in the US, Dad, and later Frankie, created specialized editions for other countries and made slight changes to the cover such as a growing pile of Euros, Pounds, Yen and the like.

The book has some additional features that we like such as perforated worksheets that can be easily removed or left in the book as the reader prefers, a CD-ROM with worksheets and calculators so people can do their DD work on a home or work computer to easily create and adjust the amounts of spending, saving and investing based on the individual's circumstances. The university team did that part for us since we have no idea how to program such things.

The University Book Store created a big display for us and we took pictures together with Dr. Webber and others who helped make this dream come true. RU will also put our book on their website and will promote it under their 'New This Month!' heading.

The university has a marketing department but it is very small, or, as Fred describes it, "understaffed". It will be up to us to start promoting the book locally. That should be easy as so many people have taken the DD course with us and will most certainly want to buy the book for themselves or others.

We will also interview with regional newspapers, magazines and local talk shows and expand from there. What we really need is to make a website for Dissolving Debt and we should have done this sooner. There's always something that needs to have been done yesterday!

I agreed with Fred, but we have been so busy with moving into our new home, the babies and two sets of parents. Even more importantly, neither of us know anything about making a website.

Fred called around to some of his friends and business partners and we got the names of half a dozen individuals and companies that can do the work, with varying degrees of expertise. It is still a fairly new technology that is quickly changing all the time. His friends advised us on what kinds of questions to ask and have a strong idea of what we want the website to do.

As the recession has turned around, Fred is starting to re-invest some of our profits back into S&P 500 and NASDAQ index funds. This will be far less work than researching individual companies and gives us more time to enjoy our new home, children and book selling!

Website Developer

Dear My Diary,

After researching and interviewing several companies, we have selected Berger King and Associates to develop our website. One of their clients is Riverton University and this is a big plus for us. Another plus for me that is Berger's wife is also Vietnamese. Phuong King married her soldier love, like Auntie Giang and came to America in 1967. Her English has almost no accent. I asked her how she came to speak so clearly and she said, "A lot of practice!"

Phuong and her grown children are the "Associates" of the company, so it is very much a family business with a few non-family employees. All the children have been to college for computer programming, graphic design and similar specialties so they all can share their skills in the growing business.

They can easily connect our book ordering page to the RU publishing department to handle everything regarding sales, returns, discounts, etc., so that will be less work for us. The website will also allow us to update our calendar of events for DD classes and book signings, make a Blog and lets viewers ask questions that everyone can see as well as our personalized answers.

Fred and I had to be educated on how a Blog is like a computer diary that we can write to let everyone know our thoughts or advice on different matters. For example, at the beginning of the year we know people are looking to get a big tax refund, which in our DD class, we frown upon. In our Blog, we can remind the readers that for every $1200 of tax refund they receive, it means they are overpaying the government $100 per month that they can be using to pay down their debts or use for investing. Things like that.

Phuong is very nice and said she will help me with tips on how to make my English sound less immigrant and the sounding out of certain words to be clearer. I know my grammar is not so good sometimes, or I make mistakes like saying "I need to clean the chicken floor." Or "Who left the light open in the bedroom?"

"Sounding immigrant" was a regular worry for Mama. She thought people would not take her seriously if her accent was so strong. She had also heard a story, a true one in fact, of a foreign-born actor who, in his first starring role, was humiliated when he went to the premier and all the words coming out of his mouth were in perfect English…he had been dubbed by another actor! Later, despite his strong accent, he became world-famous and his distinctive European accent was frequently impersonated by other entertainers. Over time, his first movie was re-released with his own voice as it should have been.

Mama was afraid that if she tried to make a serious attempt at acting, either she would be turned down or would be dubbed as this actor had been and be thought of as ignorant or backward by those in charge. Mama has been many things, but never ignorant or backward. The fact is, her voice has a smooth, musical quality to it and when she laughs, it is almost like the tinkling of a bell, as Dad liked to put it.

Phuong King gave Mama some tips, tricks and vocal exercises that, over time, she constantly put to use until her "American accent" became a near-permanent part of her being. It has helped her a lot with everyday situations and Mama could speak near-perfect English for interviews and acting roles. Honestly, none of us knew her as having a heavy accent unless we look at old Fierce 5 commercials or wedding videos and the like. As an interesting result of her vocal exercises, Vietnamese people say Mama speaks her native language "with an American accent." Talk about a switcheroo!

How did she do it? Some of the tips were pretty simple. Mama pushed Dad, Grandma, Aunt Bunny, Michael and the twins to correct her grammar or phrasing anytime she was "off". She would ask questions like "When is the time you use "Say" "Says" and "Said" and push for answers that she could understand and use.

She would listen to recordings of voices on one tape player, then say the sentence or phrase several times into another recorder and listen to see how close they sounded to each other. She worked hard on certain sounds she had difficulty mastering and Dad would try doing different things to help her re-create the sound he could do easily but she could not. When Mama wants to master a skill, she is tireless to get it right. For many years now, one of the biggest compliments to Mama's ears are "Were you born here?"

Dear My Diary,

I got a call from Takeela asking me if I want a part on "Swords of Algiers", the same television show Jasmin and Malia are in. My F5 sisters talked me up to the producers who now want to hire me for one episode as a "guest star". Takeela said a guest star role can lead to more episodes or parts on other shows later.

Filming takes place the second week of December, just before they break for the holidays. It's a five-day shoot on location in New Mexico and I asked Fred if I should take the job. I did not have to ask, but I did it out of respect for my husband. Of course, he said yes!

I will bring Ca and the babies with me as the filming is mostly on sets, but some of the outdoor scenes are done in the desert mountains nearby. Malia said it is much better to film this time of year than in the summer when it is very hot.

They are overnighting me the script and a trainer will come to Riverton the week before filming to prep me for the scenes I will do. Thank goodness I am not pregnant this time!

Frankie: This was Mom's second acting job outside of Fierce Five. It was the Season 3 Episode 15 of Swords of Algiers, in case you want to look it up. She had a fair amount of dialogue to memorize along with one major and two minor fight scenes. Dad helped with the script reading and, not only that, he managed to get a Dissolving Debt seminar booked for Albuquerque that same week so they could all fly down and back together in business class as was their practice.

They also booked a suite for the first time, instead of two separate rooms, so the whole family could stay together. It was arranged that the budgeted allowance the studio normally paid for "the talent" would go towards the cost of the suite, with Dad paying the difference.

Arrangements like these became a standard practice with our family as we grew because having multiple rooms would have been impractical and more costly. Mom did not get a regular spot on "Swords of Algiers", but it was added to her resume and helped her get future gigs as well as helping cement Mom's friendships with Malia and Jasmin.

November 24, 2003
Dear My Diary,

We have a new niece today! Nguyen Nghy Vui was born November 24th and is a very healthy little girl. Frankie is still the only boy grandchild, but Vui is now the closest one to my parents. I am sure they will spoil her to no end!

Ba has worked out a system for Thao to work from home through a special phone line. The warehouse phone operator will transfer calls directly to Thao's home business line and it is like she is at work! Even better, the computer system and fax lines are connected to Thao so that she can do everything from the privacy of their home while giving her more Mommy time. She won't have to work from the warehouse like our mother had to do.

Thao said the pregnancy went smoothly with no serious issues. They will try for another one before long as Sister is getting on the old side to make many more babies. Thao's doctor said she is healthy enough for one or maybe two more pregnancies, if she does not wait too long. She already knows what happened to me with Lois, of course, but we are different people.

Saturday November 29, 2003
Dear My Diary,

This is my first time going to a restaurant for Thanksgiving dinner. Between two small children, frequent air travel and the smaller house, Fred does not feel comfortable to keep hosting the big family dinner at the garage with Michael living there. We took parents, Bunny, Tina and her friend to Big Bob's Country Buffet for dinner. It's not as nice as the casino buffet and lacks good seafood, but it is American-style comfort food that pleases Fred's family.

The women wear old-fashioned long dresses and aprons and the men have on white shirts, vests and bow ties along with dark trousers. It is a fun and friendly place with many kinds of food. Frankie is wearing a cute little dress-up suit and Ca looked extra-nice in a slacks and sweater outfit. We all dressed up for the holiday to make it fun and I saw many other families doing the same. It was a long wait, but very much worth it.

Tina had already arrived with her friend…guess who?? Barry! Such a wonderful surprise, especially when he said, "Kimmie! Fred! Good to see you, mates!" How English is that? Bunny had driven Frank and Maggie's van and showed up a few minutes before we got seated…good timing for them!

Big Bob is the owner and he is really big! Almost as tall as Fred and twice as wide. He greets guests at their tables, making sure we got two high chairs and extra room for Frank's scooter.

Frank is feeding himself pretty well now with his one good arm. The love I see Maggie give him as she helps her husband always inspires me to be the same to Fred if he ever gets in a bad way like this.

I have asked Fred if he will help me if I become very sick or injured, and he says "Of course! You're my best girl! And you would do the same for me, so turn abouts fair play." He is so sweet to say! But now I wonder: if I am his best girl, who is his second-best girl? Hmm!

We learned that Barry and Tina have been keeping in touch since he left for London two years ago. This year, he kept making contacts with banks in the US, looking for a position in or near Riverton. That has not been an easy task with the economy, and especially the banks, having major problems for some time.

He finally found a job with one of the bigger regional credit unions doing risk analysis for domestic and international business loans. It sounds like a very important job and the best part is that their headquarters is in Riverton, just three blocks from B&R Group. Barry arrived on Monday to settle in before starting his new job and Tina had fun keeping Barry a secret from me until today. Such a surprise!

Barry has a beard now that is popular with the younger men…it looks like he has not shaved in about five days, but his features are strong so the beard adds a level of ruggedness to his naturally good looks.

Fred asked Barry how he keeps the beard looking the same way, day after day, without completely shaving it off or letting it get bushy? Barry said the secret is in the attachment to his electric razor that leaves a centimeter or so of length. I find that I can understand his accent better now since I have had much more practice in listening to, and speaking with, many people like my F5 teammates from all over the world.

I caught Bunny taking peeks at Barry when he and Tina were not looking at her. I agree that Barry is very good looking but she had better behave herself. I worry about Bunny being lonely and picking on the wrong lover boy…especially someone else's lover boy.

I explained to Frank, Maggie and Bunny how we met Barry in New York, that he worked with Tina at the World Trade Center and how he left in the Spring for a new job in London before the attacks.

It was good to catch up with everybody. Bunny is working seven days a week…five with Michael and two for herself. They have now done five estate sales since the first disastrous one and are smoothing out their operational style, gaining experience and becoming more profitable. I feel good for what Bunny is doing with her life…not a lazy person at all!

By the time we finished dinner, the children had fallen asleep and we all had a wonderful visit together. On Friday we called or visited with the other family members, as did Tina with Barry, introducing him to everyone.

I noticed that Tina does not say "boyfriend" or "fiancé" but "my friend". I think he is her boyfriend, but Tina has always been more private than her sisters. Otherwise, why would Barry look so hard for work in Riverton, of all the places in the world he could work? The answer is very simple.

Barry will begin looking for an apartment but is staying at a residence-style hotel for now. It sounds like he will not be living with Tina…that is Tina's way, I know, as it would be mine if Fred were not my husband yet.

I peppered Fred with many questions and ideas as I am a curious cat about their relationship. He said, "A while ago, you asked me if Tina was gay. Now I think the answer is clear. She looks happy in Barry's company, so let her and him get settled into their new relationship, okay?"

I asked "What new relationship? They have known each other for five years or more."

"Ok then, the next step of their relationship. Time has increased their desire to be together. He has worked hard to get a job near her. He's here now. Let nature take its course with them." Then Fred took me into his strong arms, caressing me with his sky-blue eyes and large, gentle hands. "Now, let's see what kind of course nature takes with us tonight." He has such a wonderful way of giving thanks!

Merry Bucking Christmas 2003

Dear My Diary,

This year, we rented a meeting room at the Commonwealth Hotel for our MBC party. The number of guests has grown with the inclusion of Zander, some of the F5 investors and three of my F5 sisters came to the party while Bettina is spending time with her family in the Netherlands.

Because I am now a partner in their salon expansion, Thanh and Vo came as our guests while the girls stay with Ca and the babies. We introduced them around to meet some of our other partners and possibly make some business contacts of their own. I am so proud to have both my sisters at the Merry Bucking Christmas party as business partners within our group.

Tina and Barry were there, along with Mahmood and Nezzie, the Woods Sisters, Bobby and Robbie, Dr. and Mrs. Webber, Auntie Ginger, Michael, Bunny and about twenty others. The hotel catered the dinner and there was a cash bar.

Dr. Webber announced that Dissolving Debt has sold over 1,000 copies since last month's release and we got some applause for that. It has kept Fred busy, booking seminars and signings, coming up with ideas for the blog that is not up yet…The Kings are still working on creating the website for us.

Everybody got a copy of Dissolving Debt who does not have one yet. Believe me, no one in this group needs our book, but we did it more as a celebration of the publishing and promotional efforts we have put into it. And, let's face it, we all know people who could use some help managing their debts.

RU is helping Fred connect with other schools around the country to put on one or more seminars while using the difficulties of paying off student loans and accumulated credit card debt as selling points to make their pitch. Ultimately, the seminars benefit everyone: RU and Fred split profits from the sales of books, the other school gets a speaker who can benefit the students and their parents, while promoting and selling Dissolving Debt in their store.

Fred has been putting much of our proceeds from short selling stocks and his property sales back into commercial real estate, working with Holly and Hazel to create partnerships with other local investors to buy up apartment complexes and commercial office buildings rather than individual homes.

In this way, the risks and associated costs are spread among several people and over multiple properties. Of course, the Woods will be managing the properties, signing tenants, collecting rents, maintenance and etc. The values have dropped so much that everything is selling at "bargain basement prices," as Fred would say. Once the economy gets stronger, many of the vacant offices and storefronts will find paying tenants and bring in good income.

Fierce 5 is now selling in some of the larger cities of Canada and finalizing licensing deals in Mexico, Brazil and Venezuela while putting out feelers in different parts of Europe and Asia including Australia. The business plan calls for concentrating on major metropolitan areas of wealthier countries where the citizens have plenty of disposable income and follow popular trends.

Zander told us that each country or region will have their own version of the Fierce 5 team. Some will have all women, like ours, but some may have mixed men and women. In this way, they can promote heavily in their own languages and style with local talent.

And one or more of us are expected to visit the areas where F5 will be sold. In part to help promote the brand and perhaps our presence will give some ideas and encouragement to make the local F5 team more successful.

Of course, the best help we can give is to have an F5 member who speaks the local language(s) well enough to make the visit, but that will not always be possible. For example, Bettina knows four or five languages but Malia knows only English and I know only English and Vietnamese with only a few dozen words and phrases of some other Asian languages.

We showed our scene from "A Son's Quest" for everyone at the party and it received enthusiastic applause. Zander thanked everyone for their support and belief in the product and, as a result, our sales are growing rapidly since the film was ranked number one at the box office for three weeks in a row.

I am not surprised as I read the Riverton Review daily and watching how my shares of F5 stock are growing in price. I keep receiving more shares with every paycheck and residual: half cash, half stock.

Fred and I share notes about our investments and he has been very happy with Buzzy Brew as the company has been expanding through the recession. People have lost their homes, their jobs, their spouses and their luxury cars, but they still run out to get their Buzzy Brew fix!

The company even authorized and conducted a stock split recently…three shares for each one we own. I asked Fred if that means we get triple the money? Of course, the answer is "no", but that would have been nice. It actually means that the stock price is reduced by two-thirds and we gain two shares for every one we own, so the value is equaled out.

The good news is that as soon as they did the split, the share price rose several dollars as it is now more affordable and is attracting buyers looking for a bargain.

Bobby looked tired but happy to see us. He wore a hat indoors which is not his custom, but was very stylish with his suit. Robbie did his annual roundup of what is going on with everyone, and announced that B&R will begin expanding into other cities around the state over the next three years with certain current employees taking on larger roles as branch managers and such.

I wonder what this will mean for Tina? I am sure it will be good news for her as she really likes her job and is helping grow the business with new clients being added every month. I asked Tina if she has been asked to move to another city, but she is not willing to give details. She did tell me that the company is, in her words, "facing challenges both good and bad" and that her job is secure.

I am not sure what she means about good and bad challenges, but I will have to trust her. Clearly, Tina has to be careful about saying too much outside the office, so I will respect that and try to get information from Fred. He's more fun to prod.

Auntie now has five stores and the business has become a cash cow, with plenty of profits coming in. She asked me at the party if Fred had told me what he and she had discussed? He had not, so Auntie said that she had met with Fred during the summer and offered to buy him out for his share of her business so Auntie could be the full and sole owner.

Fred had told Auntie "You can keep the cash and my share of the business. I have already been repaid." When she asked Fred what he meant, he said "You gave me Kimmie. That's all the repayment I need."

It took a minute for the words to sink in and Auntie took delight in watching my face change as I came to understand her meaning. She grinned and said, "THAT is a man in love, dear niece, a man very much in love." I hugged Auntie and said to her, "I could never, in a hundred lifetimes, thank you enough for introducing us. I am also very, very much in love."

Tuesday December 28, 2003
Dear My Diary,

Such a fun Christmas for us! It has now been four years since we were engaged and I can't believe all that has happened between then and now.

We went to Cam and Tam's school for their Christmas play. Frankie liked it and tried to sing along with some of the songs he knows from the radio, mostly "Jingle Bells" and the Falalala song. On another night, we visited a church where they had live animals and people doing the Jesus in the Barn scene.

They had camels, donkeys, goats, sheep and other animals you could pet. The kings were dressed in colorful robes while Jesus' parents were as peasants. Fred had to explain the story to me again as I know what it looks like, but I don't remember the details so good, then I shared the story with Ca to help her understand as we did not grow up with these stories.

But we did enjoy petting the animals, especially the sheep! We do not have sheep in Vietnam as it is so hot and humid in the South. I know about wool fabric, but real wool hair is so thick and soft, not scratchy like army blankets. It feels quite wonderful.

We said the different animal names to Frankie and tried to get him to say the words. He likes to talk, but mostly it is baby talk and a mix of English and Vietnamese sounds. He does not yet know the difference, so what he does say can be one, or the other, or mixed together. Sometimes I have to translate Frankie's words to Fred's parents, like when he says "toi doi" to them, it means he is hungry. It will take time for Frankie to sort out which words and phrases to use with which people.

It was not too cold that night, but we still dressed the children warmly and brought Cam and Tam and Thanh as we knew it would be a new experience for them too. The girls saw some of their friends at the church and made excited conversations with each other.

It was nice to watch them socialize with their peers. They have just turned thirteen and are shooting up tall and slender, but not skinny like the hungry kittens as I saw them when I first came to Riverton. They have perfect American accents and a very pleasant VN accent when they speak to us. They are good students, good girls and they love their little cousins too!

The church had singing groups and gave tours for new visitors as well as a place to warm up and use the restrooms. Plus, it was free! We did make a $20 donation in their box to help with the costs. I let Frankie put a quarter in the box too, so he can understand how to make a donation.

This will be a very important lesson to learn for later. I can't believe he is sixteen months old now and walking very good, but he still needs the stroller for longer periods. I think Lois will be walking about the time my parents arrive in the Spring.

We took Frankie and Lois to see Santa Claus at the mall for pictures. Frankie was very excited and happy about it all until he got on Santa's lap, and then he cried and cried, but Lois was just fine. It was not a good picture!

This is the first year Frankie can recognize Christmas things and when we came downstairs on Saturday, he was so excited to see the pretty presents under the lighted tree. He jumped up and down with happiness and tried to tear open the presents. We have to stop him and say, "Some presents are for you, some for Auntie Ca and some are for Mommy and Daddy and Lois. We will give you your presents if you say 'please'."

"Plee! Plee! Plee!" It was so funny and cute. This is how he will learn good manners.

Many guests came and went over the weekend with a big dinner here for the family. Barry brought Christmas Crackers for everyone to serve at dinner. I had not heard of Christmas Crackers before, but they are popular in the UK, Australia and other British-influenced countries. A Christmas Cracker is a tube surrounded by colored paper. One person holds one end, someone else the other, then you pull together and it makes a Snap! or Crack! sound. Inside are small candies, a toy and things like that. We did the crackers after dinner and before dessert and they are so much fun!

Ba and Me and everyone in Vietnam are in good health and did a very good business for Noel season time. Very soon it will be Tet and once that is over, parents will get ready to come to their new American home…yay!

Fred or I check on the house two or three times a week to make sure the furnace is running at a low temperature and everything is in order along with paying the utilities. We will have cable TV and things like that connected just before they arrive.

Al had left much of the furniture and appliances with the house when he sold it…stove, fridge, living room set, etc. Some of it is kind of old looking and not so attractive so I replaced them with new appliances as a secret Christmas/Tet gift.

I will let my parents get some new furniture after they are here to suit their own taste as it is still a few months away. Al's children are still making problems about not inheriting his money and his having sold their abandoned belongings, but they live too far away to bother us and his lawyer is working out the details.

Friday we will attend the New Year's Eve party and I have a new dress from Tree Top Gals. My tummy is very flat now from so much running and exercise which is great because the new dress clings closely to my contours. It is mostly red with spangles and white fringes around the bodice.

When I tried it on for Fred, his face lit up with desire. While the gown is long and covers everything, it still manages to show off plenty. I have to say, I feel very good in it…and I will wear red heels and ruby earrings to match.

Fred will wear a tuxedo with red accents to complement my outfit. And speaking of accents, I have been working on my American accent and trying to remember to do it regularly, even at home. Fred says I am getting better and Maggie says she finds my diction clearer than before. This makes me happy and encourages me to keep practicing.

If you told me four years ago that I would be wearing a dress that hugs my curves along with high heels to a party, I would have told you that you are talking about a different woman, and not me.

But now? My confidence level has never been better. The other attendees know and respect me and will treat me as an equal. Ok, maybe not as an *equal* equal, as I was not born here or look or sound like most of them, nor am I the wife of a doctor or lawyer or engineer, but I will stand out…and look fabulous doing it!

Frankie: There are pictures of Mom and Dad from that night in the Riverton Review Society section and more formal pictures taken at the party by a professional photographer. They looked REALLY sharp! Mom was just about as tall as Dad in her heels as her hair was kind of puffed up. She was keeping her hairstyle short back then, but a little gel or hairspray really made a difference!

Lois: Before she married, Mama's body was more developed, that is to say, had more curviness, than her sisters and female relatives...likely as part of the genetic anomaly that caused her extra height. After having two children, her hips and chest became more enhanced, but not overly so. By staying fit with her work with Dad, and later, with regular focused exercises, she was able to maintain a very attractive body well into her sixties. It was heartwarming to read the above section where she was finally able to embrace and appreciate the body she was so ashamed of just a few short years before.

2004
A Wedding of Two Grooms

January 5th
Dear My Diary,

Ca and I took Frankie and Lois to their pediatrician for a check-up and everything shows that they are growing well and they are within the normal ranges of children their age, especially when taking Lois' premature birth into account. The doctor said that means she will likely start walking, talking and so forth a bit later than average, but that is to be expected from a preemie.

Lois is almost nine months old now and has never had any serious problems from her early arrival. We are happy to hear that and very thankful. The doctor let Frankie hear his own heart with the stethoscope and he made big eyes to hear it. "Ohh!"

As we were leaving through the lobby, we saw Bobby and Robbie coming in. Bobby was in a wheelchair and looked too thin! I hesitated to say hello, but Robbie saw us, smiled, and came over. They admired the children and commented how much Frankie looks like his father and Lois looks like me, but for the red hair and we made a bit of small-talk.

Despite trying to maintain a casual air, clearly my face gave away the discomfort of seeing Bobby in a wheelchair, looking frail. He wore a hat, but there was no hair that I could see on his scalp and his eyebrows were completely missing, making his face even more barren of life.

Robbie asked "Fred never told you, did he? About Bobby?" I admitted that he did not.

Bobby spoke up, "Fred probably did not want to worry you, what with the baby and all. I have cancer and it's not looking too good right now."

"We are going up for another chemo treatment right now," added Robbie. "A cure worse than the disease."

I told them how sorry I am to hear this and wished I had known earlier. I gave them both a hug and Ca hugged them too. This news is breaking my heart. They and Fred are all of the same age and for Bobby to be with cancer…I feel terrible for both of them. Here they are, making plans to expand their business as one of them is dying. They are very brave to do this, but sad as well.

When I got home, Fred had already collected the mail. I was about to ask him when he knew about Bobby's illness when I saw an envelope separated from the rest of the pile…a very fancy envelope with our names on it. Inside was an invitation.

Mr. Robert Farris and Mr. Robert Beuhler request the pleasure of your company for a celebration of Life, Love and Eternal Commitment. Save the Date for Saturday, February 14th, 2004 at the All Faith Community Church in Downtown Riverton. 2pm service, 3pm to 7pm reception. Recommended attire: "Don we now our gay apparel"

I asked Fred, "What does this mean? Is it a wedding?"

"That's right. Not a legal wedding that will be recognized by the state, but a celebration of their union, their long-time partnership and commitment to each other for now and forever." Fred smiled softly to himself, then added, "All of these beautiful things, with an open bar and a kickin' DJ thrown in."

"What does this last part mean, about the recommended attire?"

Fred gave a short laugh and shook his head, explaining how the words come from a Christmas carol and means, in the old style of English, 'Now we put on our fine clothes' but, in this case, it is a play on words to mean "wear what makes you feel fabulous" then he threw his hands up and said "Whoo!" in a funny manner. I understand now that 'gay' has more than one meaning.

Frankie imitated his Daddy, putting his hands up "Whoo! Whoo!" and fell down on his bottom, laughing. Soon, we were all flipping our hands up and saying Whoo! Whoo! Even Ca joined in, having no idea what we were talking about.

Imagine…getting married and having a party in the midst of their own personal tragedy. I have heard Fred use the idiom "When life hands you lemons, make lemonade." I can appreciate the saying under these circumstances.

Bobby and Robbie's Wedding

February 15, 2004
Dear My Diary,

Yesterday was the most unusual wedding I have been to. Bobby, Robbie and Fred have all known each other since they started Kindergarten. It is hard to know exactly how long B&R have been a committed couple but Fred guesses it was during their mid-teens.

Now they are thirty-five and getting married to show their love to the world. The sad part is that Robbie will soon be a widower if doctors can not cure Bobby. Fred calls it "bittersweet" and although I am not familiar with this word, the meaning is clear enough.

The wedding venue is a church downtown that accepts people of all faiths, even those that other churches will not accept. I know people like to dress up for weddings and many people did dress in nice suits and pretty dresses, but some of the suits had women in them and some of the dresses had men in them.

We did not take the babies as we do not want fussy children to interrupt this most special ceremony. Maggie, Frank, Tina and Barry joined us, but Thanh and Vo did not want to go and Auntie Giang is visiting in Ho Chi Minh City so we will share their good wishes to the happy couple.

Fred and I met with many people, and he introduced me to some of Robbie and Bobby's family members. I have met some of them before, but Fred has not seen others for many years as they live out of the area.

Holly Wood gave me a hug and asked about our family and are the houses working out for us? I said "Everyone is wonderful and the houses stay full of love all the time."

She made an Ohhh! face and said "That doesn't surprise me a bit! Fred brought the babies by the other week and they are just so precious. Was that your sister with Fred? Ca…is that her name?"

"She is my cousin and is helping us with the children."

"Well, you and Fred are two very lucky people. I gave up on men a long time ago…too much trouble!" She laughed at her own words and then saw someone else to say Hi! to.

Organ music played softly in the background as we mingled and chatted, then the volume suddenly increased and people treated this as a signal to return to their seats. Soon, the houselights dimmed and colored lights began to twinkle from the flower arrangements lining each row and at the front, creating a very pretty effect.

Several men and women walked slowly to the front of the church and split off one left, one right, one left, one right until there were four on each side. A wedding march played as Bobby rolled down the aisle in a very dressed-up electric scooter with his mother and father flanking him, followed by Robbie and his parents. Each parent gave their son a kiss, then another to his partner before removing themselves to a seat in the front row. Both grooms were dressed in black suits with matching top hats.

Fred turned on a tape recorder to hold this memory of his best friends for posterity…and this is how I got the exact words to write down for myself.

The woman who performed the ceremony welcomed everyone to join in the Celebration of Life and Love as God has intended for all people to enjoy. She introduced Bobby and Robbie as her friends and parishioners of many years. She went on about what fine, upstanding members of the church and business community they have been, good friends to each other and selfless in their work with many charities and causes.

"This being Valentine's Day, a day to celebrate those we love and care deeply for, is an appropriate occasion to show the world that the heart knows no boundaries in terms of color, race, gender or age."

I heard people saying "Amen, Amen" and I thought of my own situation, finding love with Fred, even we are of different races, color and the societies we grew up in.

She finished her part and said at this point, "Bobby and Robbie have some things to say to each other and share with their guests." Bobby got up from his wheelchair with some difficulty and stood by himself as Robbie stepped forward and took his hands. As they did so, a big movie screen lowered from the ceiling and a school picture of a very young Bobby came on.

Bobby: "Robert Phillip Farris. When I was five years old and getting ready for my first day of Kindergarten, I was apprehensive about what school would be like. Would the other kids like me? Is the teacher nice? Should I bring my teddy to comfort me? I asked my mother these questions and she told me 'Bobby, you are a nice, smart boy. The neighborhood children already like you, your teacher is very nice and you won't need your teddy because you will make at least one new friend on your first day.' And she was right. I did make one new friend on that first day of school." (Other pictures of Bobby from that age have been forming and dissolving from the screen. Now Robbie's kindergarten school picture came up)

Robbie: "Robert James Buehler. When I was five years old and getting ready for my first day of school, I was a little terror to my parents (people laughing) because I was perfectly happy staying home and watching soap operas with my mother and Maw Maw and learning all about the real world from television. Who needs school when you have "Days of our Lives?" (more laughter) Mother said, 'Just try it for one week and if you don't like it, you can stay home for ever and ever'. I didn't know it at the time, but that was her first big lie to me…thanks Mom!" His mother called back "You're welcome!" and we all laughed. "It didn't matter anyway. I only needed a day to decide if I wanted to stay in school. I knew from the first day, and the first friend I made, that school was the place for me." (applause) More pictures have come and gone from the screen as before.

Robbie: "And do you remember the name of our kindergarten teacher?"

Bobby: "How could I ever forget?"

Both: "Mrs. Gaye!" (even more laughter and Fred is nodding at me saying "True! True!")

Robbie: "Can you believe it? And if you don't…Mrs. Gaye? Can you stand up please?" and a woman in the 2nd row, in her 60's I think, stood up and waved shyly to the crowd. A full class picture came on the screen with about 18 children and a young Mrs. Gaye to much applause. I saw Fred as he was the only one with curly blond hair…so cute! Bobby sat down at this point as he is too weak to stand for long.

One of the women at the front stepped forward and Robbie handed her the microphone. Bobby's sister told a funny story about how, as children, Bobby and Robbie did not play cowboys and Indians or cops and robbers or war like the other kids…they played IRS agent and tax cheat with the tax cheat going off to prison. Each of the other seven friends and family members took turns telling stories about one or both of them and sometimes Bobby or Robbie would comment on the anecdote or share a story in between.

The stories were told in chronological order, progressing through their lives as children, teens, college students and so forth. The stories were accompanied by photographs from either that particular story, or from around that time, to show their growth into adulthood, then on to more recent events like buying the building they are in now with a grand opening party. Fred was in three of the pictures, two as a boy and one at our wedding with me and Bobby and Robbie.

One story that touched me was what led to their first kiss. It was in Bobby's room with the door locked and shades down, dancing to a slow romantic song ("Love in the Afternoon" which they played a bit of).

They attended the same college but could not get a dorm room together for the first year, so they hung out at Robbie's room while his dorm-mate lived mostly off-campus with an older woman. Bobby: "Lucky for her!" Robbie: "Lucky for us!"

They were fortunate that their parents, and most of their family, accepted their relationship and how Robbie's father took them both under his wing to learn his business. There was a picture of Mr. Farris, Bobby and Robbie under a banner saying "Junior Partners". Mr. Farris in the center, arms crossed in front of him and shaking both their hands together in a sign of true partnership. They looked to be about twenty-five years old in the picture.

The lights came up, the screen rolled back into the ceiling and Bobby stood up again as the priest came back to finish the ceremony as a traditional wedding. The men exchanged rings and vows and it was a very emotional time for me and many others within earshot.

At the announcement of, "You may now kiss the groom!" Bobby and Robbie started a kiss on the lips as the lights went out, the church plunged into darkness and their suits and top hats lit up with hearts beating, fireworks exploding and cupids on each top hat shooting arrows at each other.

As the grooms parted and slowly turned around, it was very much like the animated sign from our Honeywood Heights auction, but on their clothing. The applause and cheers were deafening as the suits and hats went through butterflies flitting, hearts beating, flowers blooming and other designs that I can't remember them all. I am sure none of us had seen anything like it before and, as Fred told me later, "That was a real showstopper!"

The lights came up again and "Love in the Afternoon" crooned from the speakers. Bobby and Robbie were holding each other and singing, and *everybody* took up the song together. I do not know this song so well but the lyrics were on the screen, like in Karaoke. I looked around and so many people were kissing. Fred did not waste any time in pulling me close and then we were kissing too…

The wedding and reception were so much fun. I could see Bobby was tired from the day, but he kept wanting to stay and flash his suit. Fred said the suits cost almost $5000 each as they are very high tech and contain many thousands of tiny LED lights woven into the fabric.

I told Bobby and Robbie that I hope to be a citizen in time to vote for letting gay people have a real legal marriage, but in my heart, I have always seen them as a happily married couple. They were so pleased that they gave me big hugs and a kiss on the cheek. Even Fred kissed them on the cheeks in a show of love and friendship I have never seen him do before!

Some of the women at the wedding were as tall as me, especially in big heels and platform soles…but I could see most of these tall women were really men with heavy make-up, big wigs and well-muscled legs.

Many of the guests know I am with Fierce 5 and they kept introducing me to their friends and asked me many questions while I gave autographs…I felt very popular last night! I also saw Tina chatting with many of the guests and introducing Barry to her client friends. They look very happy together, which made me feel happy too.

Fred and his parents knew many of the people at the party like old classmates, Mrs. Gaye and some other teachers, former neighbors, business partners and people I have never heard Fred talk about. Of course, he knows so many people after growing up here all of his life and this is not such a big city. Fred and I even had some champagne…two glasses each! It surprised me to see him drinking, but the wine is not strong and it is a very special occasion.

The reception lasted about four hours and Fred heard that many of the guests went on to the La Cage au Folles nightclub to keep celebrating. We left about six and it was already dark, cold and raining but we didn't care. We took Frank and Maggie home and they shared stories in the car about many of the people at the wedding party.

Ca was telling bedtime stories to Frankie and Lois with Vietnamese picture books she found at the library. The children were so happy to see us and we made lots of cuddling time with them. Time and Life are too short and I want our children to know how much they are loved. This wedding taught me that.

Fred let me know that what I said to Bobby and Robbie was very heartfelt and sweet and they very much appreciated the kind words. I told Fred "I am sad that Bobby won't see the gay marriage law passed and it could be many years before it is. Do you know how long Bobby will be with us?"

Fred shook his head and said "Months. Maybe weeks. The treatments are not helping and he finally stopped them as there was no point to keep going on." We were quiet a moment, getting undressed. Then Fred said, "One other thing…this was not something said out loud or in so many words, but along with being a wedding, it was also a way for Bobby to say good-bye to a great many people who mean so much to him."

I nodded in acknowledgment. I had felt that too, with the way people were speaking to Bobby, hugging, kissing him and stroking his face with a sad expression in their eyes, trying to cover it with smiles and cheerful banter.

"I'm sorry if you didn't pick up on that. I know it's kind of a sad note to end the night, but…"

"But what?" I asked.

"But we still have each other and we are not going anywhere for a long, long time…are we?"

"Maybe you are not…" I teased "But if I find a 6 foot 10 inch man who is single, you had better be careful I don't fall in love with him!"

He grinned and said "Then I will get my legs stretched longer to be seven feet and get you back…ha ha!"

Not to worry My Love, you will always have me.

Anh Hai the Sandwich Guy

March 17, 2004
Dear My Diary,

Happy Birthday to us! Today is my 33rd birthday and 36 for Fred. It was three years ago today that Fred bought the Honeywood Heights property. I remember thinking that the old house was the worst present in the world, but Fred made it a very good present after much hard work by both of us.

Today, Tina had me come to her office to give me a present. Well, really it is two presents: the first one is a beautiful necklace, large and wide, designed to fit easily on my chest. It is a Phoenix bird created with semi-precious stones. Tina explained how the Phoenix rises from the ashes to start a new life, in the same way as I started my new life in America from the ashes of my life in Vietnam. I had never thought of my life in Vietnam was in ashes, but I can see her point. I do love my new life in America with Fred and consider this a most thoughtful gift with great meaning behind it.

The second present is that Tina has interviewed a client who is looking for an investment partner in his food business. He is having some success, but can only do it part of the year because where he is now gets too cold in the winter to operate. He wants to make this a full-time business in his own store and has most of the money he needs but wants to get a serious partner to put up the rest.

I asked if I will have to work in the business and Tina said "No, he is seeking a silent partner to provide money and help him find a good location. He has some family and friends that know how to work the business with him."

"How much do you know about this person and his business?"

"I have interviewed the client, visited the business, gone over the last three years of tax returns and cross-checked them against his bank statements. It looks like he reports everything he makes and does not report excessive expenses as many people do to avoid paying income tax. He is honest, a hard worker and will be a good investment."

"What is his name?"

"Trung Nguyen, and his business name is Anh Hai the Sandwich Guy."

My heart jumped, "I know him! I have had his sandwiches in the park!"

"That's right. He works most of the time in Central Park with some other food vendors. They all have special permits from the city to work there, but in the winter, business is dead so he closes for the season. That's why he wants to get into a more permanent spot."

I really like his Banh Mi sandwiches and when I have seen him at the park, there is usually a line of people. Tina went on to explain how much investment needed will depend on the final location and how much it will cost to fixup and decorate the property. Trung has most of the equipment he needs now and has some cash saved for deposits, renovation costs and advertising.

But even with all of those expenses covered, he will still need a cushion of cash to cover operating costs during the first year or longer at the new location as it always takes time to build a base of regular customers. That is where the partner comes in, to help the business stay solvent and to assist with finding a permanent location at a reasonable price and with professional equipment to cut labor costs. He will re-open his shop in Central Park in early April as the weather is warm enough and really wants to be able to move into a new shop by Fall. If so, he will still keep the park location and have other people run it as a secondary income.

I asked Tina if she has spoken with anyone else about Trung's business and she said "No, you were the first one I thought of. He has probably asked others before coming to me, but I thought you might like this one, since it is one of our own people."

I told Sister that I will give it some thought. I really would like to help one of my countrymen and Trung always looks cheerful and good natured when I am ordering food. This helps me with part of my decision but there are more parts to consider and discuss with my not-so-silent partner Fred.

Fred is in Omaha, Nebraska this week for DD seminars, so we cannot celebrate our birthdays ON our birthday. Instead, we will have it during the weekend when he is home, and I can discuss the sandwich shop idea with him then.

I have not written for a long time now, as it has been so busy for us. Fred has developed a routine on how he handles the Dissolving Debt seminars: He rents a large hotel meeting room or seminar hall at a local college/university, flies or drives in on Monday and prepares the room, spends three days doing two to three seminars each day and selling books, then returns home on Friday.

He works in collaboration with RU's marketing department to make the arrangements, signing agreements, advertising the event on local television and radio stations, shipping the materials, etc. RU also arranges to have three local area helpers, typically hotel or university employees, for running AV and the registration/sales desks.

Since I am so busy with children, parents and modeling/acting work, I can't help with the presentations, so RU found a professional co-speaker for Fred who quickly learned and understands how to present it. Her name is Crystal Dahl, a very educated and professional woman with an MBA and is sometimes an adjunct teacher in the Economics Department.

If Fred had to do all the speaking for three hours at a time, three times a day for three days, plus managing the local details, he would be completely exhausted by the time he comes home, so that is why RU hired a co-speaker. Crystal and Fred often fly out and back together with the flights and hotels paid by RU and sometimes by the hosting university.

We have had lunch with Crystal so I could meet her and give my own perspective on Dissolving Debt. I think Fred's other concern would be jealousy on my part for him traveling and working with another woman. I trust Fred, and besides, she is closer to our parents in age than to me and is also married, so I have no concerns about them working together. Moreover, Crystal has been teaching Fred some tricks and tips on better styles of public speaking and Fred says it has helped him a lot.

After a few seminars, Fred had me filmed and added my segment to the program to give both of them a break while including my personal views and experiences of debt use in Southeast Asia.

My filmed part is eight minutes long and is cut in with stock film clips of people making business with large amounts of cash, families riding on a single motorbike and such as that. Fred said that when I come on the screen, it makes him feel a little less lonely, even if I am only speaking about money…so sweet!

Every evening, Fred calls so we can catch up on the day. Frankie likes to say "Hi Daddy!" and Lois can hear his voice. She is not speaking yet, but I can see she knows Daddy is on the phone. It helps with my loneliness too!

Ba and Me will be here next month for the summer. The flights are booked and they have sent a container of furniture, foods, personal items and many more things for Michael and Bunny to sell. I do not have to worry about taking them shopping as much as I thought.

Dear My Diary,

I spoke to Fred about Trung and how Tina has reviewed his financial status and everything appears to be in order. I do not know fully how much cash or other help he will need and that information will be determined more closely by Tina and Trung once some locations are found and narrowed down, and that will determine what ownership percentage I will have, if I choose to join him.

Fred said it sounds good so far, but in the end, this will be my own decision so he will let me do it my own way. "But I will give you one piece of advice: Look at everything carefully. Use all your senses: eyes, ears, smell, taste, touch and common. If everything looks right, sounds right, tastes right and makes sense, then you can move to the next step."

I asked "Why will you not help me with more detailed information?"

He replied, "You are a smart cookie and I believe you will make the right decision if you use your senses, then your head. It will be a good learning exercise for you." Hmm!

From here, Mama went into deep detail about how she staked out Trung's business at the park from a picnic table on a nearby hill. She bought his sandwiches, did research on food costs, studied the freshness of his ingredients, the number of customers he served daily, what he did during the slow times...you name it. His menu at the park was limited to eight kinds of sandwiches and canned soft drinks, but he really wanted to expand his menu and grow more locations.

After looking at the Riverton Mall food court (too expensive), Flea City (only open weekends) and some questionable strip mall locations, Mama was able to get Trung a spot in the Riverton Hospital food court.

After helping him secure the hospital location and figuring out a way to keep the Central Park stand running for eight months out of the year, Mama became a 25% not-quite-silent business partner with Trung. I will let Trung tell the rest of the story...

Trung Nguyen aka Anh Hai The Sandwich Guy: I was a young guy at the time, with lots of ambition but not a lot of money. Most of my family had come to Riverton in 1975 after the fall of Saigon and I was born here soon after. I called my shop "Anh Hai the Sandwich Guy because I am the oldest brother and, in Vietnamese culture, my family title is Anh Hai. Also, it sounds way catchier than Trung Nguyen the Sandwich Guy.

I had seen Kim now and then at the park and she or her husband bought food from me sometimes, or hired my family for catering jobs. She was hard to miss...tall, beautiful and athletic...I remember seeing her filming a Fierce Five commercial one summer day and, even though they had catered food on the set, she brought her Fierce Five friends and crew members over to try the banh mi and that drove a LOT of business to me that day. Like I said, she was hard to miss.

I met Kim formally through Tina Pham as a possible business partner. I had no idea until much later that they were sisters. I mean, one is tiny and the other really tall. Anyway, after considering several locations, Kim got me a spot in the Riverton Regional Hospital food court. The rent was reasonable and lots of doctors, staff and patients ate either at the food court or had foods ordered up, sometimes in bulk, for meetings and other events.

With Kim and Tina's help, we created a business plan to present to the Director of Food Services with menus, cost analysis, previous business experience (I had 4 years selling at the park and doing catering on the side) and proof we had enough funds to stay solvent for the long term...and that's where Kim came in.

It was surprisingly busy when we started. We were new, with an appealing menu of things many people were not familiar with, but not so strange as they could not understand what we were selling. Over twenty kinds of banh mi sandwiches, bubble teas, spring rolls, bun bao, soft ginger tofu and Vietnamese coffee. And, of course, we also served Fierce Five. Can't forget that!

We developed an advertising campaign that is still in use to this day, with me front and center mugging for the camera in a variety of costumes and situations. I am short with a kind of funny looking face that I can exaggerate to great comic effect. Kim often posed with me and did other advertising for the shop...especially after she developed a sizable fan base. She was a big draw for us...especially at grand openings! Sometimes she would get behind the counter and ring up customers with a stack of 8x10 signed glossies ready to hand out to customers who were thrilled to have "Kymera" take their order. But I'm getting ahead of myself...

The hospital food court was a newer concept in the early 2000's and the Riverton Regional was part of a large medical corporation. It did not take many years to move into member medical facilities in other states. By that time, we had enough cash flow to open stands in malls and shopping centers at the same time, and in the same cities, where we had contracted hospital space. In this way, the medical staff and patients who knew our name and products from one place, were able to connect with us where they shopped, and it grew organically from there.

Eventually we went the franchise route, doing television and radio commercials, product placements in TV shows and movies (thanks to Kim) and it was a great ride. Now Anh Hai's is America's 8th largest sandwich shop chain and I still mug for the cameras occasionally along with my kids and grandkids.

Kim was a wonderful business partner and a good friend, generous with her time, talent and business acumen. One of my favorite stories about her was a day soon after we opened our first mall location. Not many people were familiar with our sandwiches and lots of people were passing us by after looking at the menu and deciding against trying anything. Kim, Fred and their family were lunching nearby with their banh mi's and bun baos and watching all this going on. I was embarrassed to have my business partner see this.

When they finished, Kim walked up to our counter, gave me a big wink, then turned around to face the food court and said very loudly, "Attention Everyone! Anh Hai the Sandwich Guy is giving away one free sandwich to each of the next 20 people who visit him, right here!" and she points at me with this gesture, like arcing her finger down at my head. I took the cue and put on a big smile, waving to everyone with one hand and making motions for the staff to get ready for a rush with the other.

You should have seen the people surging up to the counter! Kim kept it up, saying things like "One free sandwich of your choice per person! Don't forget to buy a drink and a snack to take with you! This is a limited offer to the first 20 people, right here! If you like us, tell your friends! If you don't like us, tell US how we can be better!"

And Kim went on, talking to the customers, making suggestions, encouraging additional sales, you name it. The looks from the other vendors as customers fled their lines for a free sandwich was priceless! I could see Fred laughing and shaking his head at everything.

Well, word got out all over the mall and business did not slow down for hours. Long after the free sandwiches were handed out, people were coming up to buy things and I think some were hoping there would be another "free sandwich" offer.

Kim settled with me later and that was not the only time she did something like this. You never knew when Kim would pop by one of the stores in whatever city she was in and start giving away sample cups of bubble tea or soft ginger tofu, meeting and greeting fans and making everyone feel special.

Frankie: We ate at Anh Hai's a lot when we were kids and teens. It was only much later that I learned it was because Mom would charge our meals to her personal account and take the expenses as tax deductions at the end of the year. Did I ever get sick of the food? Never! Too much good stuff and great memories to go with them.

Anh Hai the Sandwich Guy stayed as a private corporation until Trung and Mom sold it to Big Eats! Inc. a few years ago. Trung retired as a very, very rich man!

Dear My Diary,

As the economy is making a turn-around and our family is growing, Fred purchased two properties in Honeywood Heights at a deep discount from where they were valued three years ago. The smaller one will be a rental and the other will be used for our family if we have a big get-together. The bigger house still has most of the original furniture and décor left by the owners who abandoned the property and moved back to their homeland. Fred bought the property directly from the bank with cash.

The property Fred gave me is still sitting empty and he said we can sell the land in two or three years when the values go back up as before. I certainly hope so! I feel guilty for not attempting to build on it, but we agree that it will be too much work and trouble dealing with contractors when we can get a big, beautifully furnished home with two kitchens (one for parties and a smaller one for everyday use) and many bedrooms and bathrooms for far less money and time.

There are some repairs needed to be done in both homes, but Fred will have RPR start renting the smaller home soon. I intend to keep our Starbuckle home a long time so our children can go to school next door and have their grandparents on either side of us. But I am glad Fred got the two other houses as they will grow our net worth into the future.

May 5, 2004
Dear My Diary,

Behind the main library, between the parking lot and the rear entrance, there is a fountain with a series of low walls segmented around the perimeter. It is a pleasant spot for people to sit and read or enjoy the weather, where children can play and walk on the walls and jump between the gaps or splash in the bubbling waters of the fountain.

Walking in from the parking area with my parents and Ca, I saw something I had not seen before, so I pushed the stroller over to get a closer look. It is a bronze statue of a woman sitting on the wall with an open book in her hands. Surrounding her were various storybook characters engrossed in the tale she was telling. They sat in front on the grass, to her sides on the wall and one peering wide-eyed over her shoulder. To one side, there is a plaque that says: In Loving Memory of Gladys Robertson, Beloved Riverton Librarian. Dedicated 2004

I explained to my family who the woman is. They know all about our Honeywood Heights story and are familiar with her name. I then filled them in about the found monies and how we donated it all to the library…they did not know this part of the story and were impressed that Fred agreed to donate such a valuable treasure to the benefit of the library.

I put Frankie on the woman's lap to take a picture as he tried to look inside the book. It is such a cute picture! Then my emotions rose to the surface as I thought about Miss Robertson. I think the library spent part of the money raised to make the statues and honor her like this. I feel so much better to do what we did, rather than to keep the money and spend it on ourselves.

Mother's Day 2004

Sunday, May 9th

Today is a very special Mother's Day for me as I am celebrating with BOTH my children. Fred gave me a bracelet with both of their birthstones. The bracelet is white gold with two different green stones. The Emerald is for Lois (May) and something called Peridot for Frankie's August birth month. I have not heard of Peridot, which is more of a lime green than the deeper green of the Emerald.

Fred reminded me that the color green is traditional for Saint Patrick Day, our own birthdays, so I guess all of us have the color green for a special day in our lives, even though our March birthstone is Aquamarine and is a bluish color.

Colleges are now having their graduation ceremonies from this month and into June so DD is taking a break until after mid-June when campuses are less busy but can still draw people in and hall rentals will cost less. Over 50,000 books have sold so far and Fred is signing up more clients to pay for his time as a personal debt-reduction consultant. He does most of this work by phone, fax and email, but will sometimes fly out, at the customer's expense, to meet with them in person.

The best part is when his clients refer their family members and friends, whom Fred follows up with and often will get new clients. A much cleaner and more prestigious job than anything he has done so far.

Thomas Stimson

Lois's First Birthday

Sunday, May 16th
Dear My Diary,

Yesterday both Lois *and* her Grandpa Frank took their first steps…how exciting! Frank has been doing physical therapy for a long time now and is slowly getting stronger. I don't think he will ever be able to walk far, or well, but he did take some steps with a walker at his most recent therapy session on Saturday. My parents and I took photographs and video as he tottered on unsteady legs as we cheered him on. When he finished, he looked so pleased with himself, croaking out, "Damn, that felt good!" as we hugged and congratulated him.

Little Lois has been pulling herself up on chairs and low tables for some time now. After watching her Grandpa Frank take his first steps, Lois pulled herself up on his pant leg, standing up straight and as we encouraged her to walk to us…she did! We got that on the video as well! We could not believe our good luck. More cheers and hugs from everyone…including her brother. He is so proud of his baby sister!

There are many presents and envelopes of Lucky Money for her today. Frankie got a little jealous of the attention given her, but we told him that he will have a birthday soon and he will get his own presents then.

He asked "When? When I get presents?"

Fred put on a big, happy face and said "Just three months! No time at all!" like it will be tomorrow. Of course, Frankie does not know days from months so he was happy with Daddy's smiling answer and forgot all about the presents. Lois is almost the same height and weight as Frankie was at one year, recovering extremely well from her premature birth.

Parents told me that Tina is stopping by more often with Barry than without him and it is clear that they are a couple now. They take Ba and Me out sometimes for a meal or some interesting event like a concert or historical home they can tour.

They also helped parents find a good car to drive around town in. I am afraid that I do not know so much about how to buy a car in the US, but Barry has much experience doing it in England. My understanding is that he has a collection of autos back home and his charmingly flavorful accent helps a lot here in negotiations. Tina never had a car until she came to Riverton as there was no need for one in New York.

My mother gets her hair done at Thanh's shop (of course!) and is always "on the house". Me tips well and gets lots of good gossip about people she knows nothing about…but it is nice for her to spend time with other Vietnamese speakers. Ba also gets his hair cut there, but he is not so interested in making girly chit-chat like Me!

Lois got her first hair-cut last week and we saved all her little red hairs in a plastic bag. It was not easy for me to see her first hairs getting trimmed, but it was getting too long and getting into her food.

There were lots of comments and questions about her hair color and where she got it from? I am so used to it now, but it is still a surprise for many people to see an Asian with reddish, or as Barry calls it, "ginger" hair. She did not cry at all during her haircut like Frankie's first time. She was quite still and patient about it all as we fussed over how good she looks. She made a face like, "Oh my!"

Bunny's Bargain Hutch

Dear My Diary,

Ever since I introduced her to the reselling business, Bunny has been talking about having her own store and now her dream is coming true. I am so proud of how hard she has worked to get this far. Michael bought out her share of their partnership and Joe Hamilton paid off Fred for his share of Joe's business that he is selling to Bunny. She will not be a profit-sharing partner with us like the other stores we deal with, but will have the option of purchasing excess inventory from Michael as opportunities present themselves.

Bunny has made so much from Pop Boxes and saved so much of her profits, that she bought out Joe Hamilton in a private sale so he can retire to someplace warm. She put half down, and will make monthly payments after that. Old Joe is calling the loan payments his Bunny Money. How funny!

She will change the name of the store to "Bunny's Bargain Hutch". After she explained that a "hutch" is a kind of pen for rabbits, I told her that it is a cute name for the store and she smiled broadly at my compliment.

For what she paid, Bunny will get the land, a two-story building and all the inventory. The upper floor is partly storage and partly an apartment so by moving into the store, she will no longer have a rent payment and Fred can rent the house to someone else at a much higher rate than he was charging Bunny.

I asked Bunny if Joe's business had been profitable, and said Joe showed her his tax returns for the last five years and he was, as she put it, "profitable, but not getting rich". Bunny has some fresh ideas to bring in new inventory and new customers without having to leave the store too often.

Currently, there are three employees and she will keep them for now, but she thinks she can get it down to one full time and one part time once she "gets in the groove", (I love her slang!) to cut expenses. She will close on Mondays and Tuesdays as they tend to be the slowest for the shop, and will use that time to get more inventory, do shopping and laundry, make meals for the week and so forth.

Aunt Bernice: When I bought that store, I felt like I had really made something of myself. I hadn't even put up the new sign yet, but I had that power, you know? Like I knew I was going to be a success. Without Barney, I had wings and felt free to do things my own way. I was able to save up money without worrying that some jerk was going to buy a sportscar or bet big on some stupid playoff game when my back was turned.

Once I got set up, I started using some of my extra cash on Ubiddit to buy bulk lots of different things I thought would sell in the shop. On Mondays and Tuesdays, I would go to locker auctions or get things cheap or free from people on FreePost. You would not BELIEVE some of the things people just give away that I could resell within a few weeks. I worked my butt off, let me tell you!

Once a month, I would have a "Dollar Day Sale" and put out several tables full of stuff that wasn't selling so good and blow them out for a buck apiece. Lots of those customers would buy other, more expensive items and it helped keep the inventory turning over. I also spread the word that I would take donations or pay cash for items we could use and do consignments for larger, more valuable pieces. I was flexible that way and it helped generate new business and repeat customers.

It didn't take long to figure out that one of the employees I inherited was helping themselves get a pay raise. I kept finding things missing here and there but there wasn't enough in the till to justify what looked to have been sold. I told one of the cops I knew on the force about my suspicions and he came over one night with these itty, bitty cameras and a video recorder that could tape all day.

Within a week, we knew who was helping themselves to a box load or two of my stuff or cash from a sale when I was upstairs having lunch or out on an errand. I let my cop friend arrest her and she cooled her heels in county for a couple of months. After that, my receipts jumped up pretty good. For all I know, she had been stealing from Old Joe for years and he never knew it.

Kimmie came by with the kids sometimes and would ask if I need anything. By then, I was on my feet and running, but it was sweet of her to ask. And Michael called twice a month, or I called him, and we would see if there were things we could swap or sell. I liked working with him and we learned things from each other to keep on top of business without stepping on each other's toes.

Frankie: Later on, Bunny moved to Norwood, a rural township a couple of hours drive from Riverton. She found their FreePost listings were very limited and not a lot of people were buying the kinds of things she had for sale, so she changed tactics to tap into the increasingly aging population, and of those moving away from the area for better opportunities.

Aunt Bernice: By the time I moved to Norwood, I had built up a good cash reserve. I would go through the obituaries and write to the families offering to buy up unwanted things from the estate for cash or do estate sales or estate auctions for them. I did the same thing for people moving into retirement homes, offering to buy up unwanted stuff for cash by having monthly "Bring it By" days in one of their activity rooms where I gave estimates and offers for their antiques, jewelry, furniture and what not. I was able to sell a lot of the smaller nice items on Ubiddit and with my own website along with running ads in regional magazines to draw wealthy clients to my shop for nice antiques and collectables. It worked out well for years.

Dear My Diary,

Tina has been updating us about the new things happening at work. Because Bobby stepped down as the co-President after the wedding, Robbie is now President and CEO and he created a Board of Directors from employees within the company. The name of the company will not change.

Tina was offered Director of Global Development, which means she keeps doing the same job as before, but with more duties and more pay including profit sharing. Mahmood has already helped open two branch offices in nearby towns, so he will take these skills and become Director of Operations to continue their expansion of offices around the state. He will be doing a lot of travelling! And there will be four other Directors: Marketing, IT Development, Legal and Human Resources, so a total of six Directors and Robbie to make seven.

I told Fred it sounded like a lot to do, and so quickly but Fred said Bobby and Robbie have been planning and growing the company for this kind of move since even before they took over the business from Robbie's father. Both have been working for the company since their college days so the company is their "baby". They have developed a very strong and loyal base of employees so it will be easy to take the business to new levels, much like Thanh and Vo are doing with their business. Sadly, Robbie will not get to see the long-term results of their hard work.

The business has been growing faster than the two of them could manage effectively, so they are overdue for a change of direction. Tina has made a suggestion to our cousin Dot, Auntie's oldest daughter, to maybe get a position with B&R's IT department. The department is small right now, but with the addition of new branches and new technology making it easier to file federal and state taxes online, they need more experienced people for the complex changes and upgrades that need to be done. And since our families are closely tied to B&R, if Dot has the right kind of experience they need, she will be an easy pick. We will see.

Fred came home from the video store and we watched "Lost in L.A." I did not understand much of the humor and it is a silly film, BUT! I am in the deleted scenes section! I watched my scene several times to see why they might have cut me out. Fred said I was funnier than many other parts of the film, including the star. Maybe he is being kind, but I think I did a good job. I will never know, but I can keep trying! We bought the movie so I will have a record of my scene and I can use it for my portfolio, even if it was not used in the final cut.

After Mama made her name better known in the entertainment industry, her deleted scene in "Lost in L.A." was restored and she was given credit as well. That's show-biz!

Thomas Stimson

Last Visit with Bobby

June 6, 2004
Dear My Diary,

We visited Bobby today at the penthouse. There is a hospital bed in the living room, surrounded by flowers, beautiful art pieces and whatever Robbie and their friends can do to make it serene. I saw very little medical equipment and Bobby does not wish to be kept alive by machines. We brought the children and dressed extra nice. Bobby smiled to see us.

We made pleasant small talk in lieu of discussing the elephant in the room. That's an expression I recently learned. Fred chatted about how well the sales of Dissolving Debt are going and how much travelling he does now for the seminars. He will leave for Saint Paul tomorrow so that is why we came on a Sunday. I chatted about Frankie's newest cute things and how Lois has started walking.

Bobby is weak, but he told Fred how much he has valued their friendship over the whole of their lives and what a fine family he is making. He told me that Fred could not have found a better partner or a lovelier person to marry. I told Bobby he could not have found a better man to marry than Robbie and I will miss him very, very much. I will tell Frankie and Lois later about their Uncle Bobby and what a fine man he is. Fred told Bobby that he and Robbie are the brothers he wished he had.

We were all crying and happy and sad at the same time. When I hugged Bobby, it was like holding a skeleton. As we began to leave, Bobby motioned for me to come close. I leaned in and he said to me "Please…Don't beat a stranger," and made a little hitting motion with his fist. He said the last part very clearly and then gave me a wink and a little laugh. It took me back to the first time I met them, and the misunderstanding that followed.

It was his last little joke to me and the perfect thing to say. I kissed his cheek and my tears mixed with his. We made our goodbyes to Robbie. He thanked us for coming and we told him what a good job he is doing for his husband. He said he does not do it alone and there is a medical aide in the kitchen giving us privacy.

After we got in the car, Fred had to spend some time composing himself before he could drive. I offered, but Fred just needed to sit and be in his head for a bit. At home, Fred went back to the bedroom to let out his grief and I know enough to leave him alone for now.

After Ca and I put the children down for a nap, I went back to Fred and held him until he felt better. It is not fair that such a nice man should go so soon. I came to realize that Bobby had made more friends, helped more people, donated more money and been more influential in a variety of causes than most people twice his age. He will be missed by thousands, and it will be up to Robbie to carry on their legacy alone.

June 15, 2004
Dear My Diary,

Bobby fell into a long sleep yesterday and this afternoon his suffering came to an end. His family had been keeping vigil around his bed, telling stories and singing songs that he liked while the morphine kept his pain at bay. It was a very peaceful way to go. There will be no public funeral and people are asked, if they wish to make a donation, to give to the American Cancer Society, Riverton General Hospital or MFAP. I called Fred in Dayton, Ohio and let him know. Fred was in a better mood than I thought he would be, but he had had his crying time when we visited Bobby. The news left him quiet, but not so sad. I think the word is "relief". Fred feels relief that his friend will suffer no more. I do too.

Tina said the office will be closed tomorrow as a day of mourning. She and other employees will wear black armbands for the rest of the month as a sign of respect. My parents also expressed sadness for Bobby's death as they have heard much from us about Fred's closest childhood friends and daughter's employer.

Monday July 5, 2004

I had the children take naps late yesterday afternoon so they could stay awake for the fireworks at Riverton Central Park, which we thought would be fun for them. Instead, poor Lois cried and cried as it was so noisy and the fireworks frightened her with every burst and boom. We ended up leaving early while Thanh and Vo and the girls stayed to the end. Up to then, we had had a nice time with a dinner picnic at the park, pushing the babies on swings, going down slides and playing in the sand.

We also visited with Trung and his family at their food stand they set up each year for the big holidays. We bought plenty of food and drinks from them and made our chats quick as they were very busy.

I might have found a place for Trung to open the kind of shop he wants at Riverton General Hospital. It is the largest medical facility in the region and they have a food court, as opposed to a cafeteria, but we will have to apply and prove we can provide good, healthy foods at reasonable prices for the employees, patients and visitors. That should not be hard as his foods are of a very healthy kind!

We are missing Tina this holiday as she went to London for ten days to visit with Barry and his family and to see the sights. I think she has been to England once before when she was working in New York, but I can't remember for sure. I hope Barry's family likes Tina…Fred said she will be fine. "Very likable and intelligent, just like you!" Fred is always complimenting me, but I never mind it…better than the other way around.

Fred says it is serious when someone goes to meet the other person's parents. I can see Barry as a new brother for me as he is also intelligent and likeable and they make a good couple. I am keeping my fingers crossed for Tina.

July 30, 2004

The Nelsons died yesterday morning and today there was a big headline and several articles with pictures in the Riverton Review. I asked Fred how the newspaper could get so much information to write all this when the couple died only yesterday? Fred explained how media outlets keep pre-written information on hand and update it as necessary in case of some famous person dies like a president or celebrity or, in our case, an elderly couple who contributed so much to the community. The Review just updated some bits and pieces to the pre-written articles and photo layouts with their date of death, how they died and comments from the mayor and others who knew them.

The Nelsons had been in failing health the last few months and had moved into a hospice center. Nellie died first, then Peter less than six hours later. They had known each other since childhood and had recently celebrated their seventy-fifth wedding anniversary.

Such a sad and beautiful story to read. I think it is perfect that they died like this…quietly, peacefully and together, sharing everything to the last day. I read everything about them and it was all very interesting with no mention about their dealings with Barney.

I prayed for them at our altar to be together in the afterlife as they were in our world. If we are lucky, Fred and I might go the same way, but I should not think about this right now as we are still young with a whole lifetime to spend with our children.

I asked Fred what will happen to the Nelson's money since they had no children, and will Barney still be expected to repay them, even if they are gone from this Earth?

"The Nelson's have had an estate trust for a long time with several funds and foundations that operate together to invest their assets and distribute the proceeds among a variety of charitable projects like scholarships, city beautification, the children's hospital wing, among others, for a very long time to come."

As for Barney, Fred said his brother will still be "on the hook" for the money he owes them. I said, "'On the hook' makes it sound like Barney is a fish that got caught." Then I laughed because…well, he WAS! So, Barney will still have to repay the Nelsons by way of their estate trust and I am certain they will not be so charitable as to let him "off the hook" for what he owes.

August 22, 2004
Dear My Diary,

Hurrah! Japan is the first Asian country to be licensed with Fierce 5 so we all flew to Tokyo last week to film commercials. They will use many of the print ads that we use already in the US and Canada, but the Japanese have their own ideas of what they want for television and internet commercials.

In one of them, we are all race car drivers, sitting in fake cars with big helmets that only show our eyes as we pretend to drive and look this way or that and move our hands as the director instructs. From above, they show the cars with F5 on their roofs, racing around, passing other cars and all crossing the finish line at the same time. The five winners take off their helmets and shake out their long beautiful hair (yes, us!) and are handed a giant trophy while we make victory signs.

In another commercial, we are walking through a jungle in khaki shorts and safari helmets. The director said there will be some anime gorillas blocking our path and they will roar at us. We have to make big reactions to the empty air and it is fun to do, like some of the workshops I have done in drama class. Anyway, we quickly drink some F5 and roar back at the gorillas so they fall backward. In the last shot, we are sitting with the gorillas and sharing F5's like we are friends. It sounds very silly, but that's what they want.

Ca and the children came with me and I paid for them, as usual, as F5 and the ad agency will not pay for the extra people. We took a tour of Tokyo between working times and visited the shopping districts. While I work, Ca, Lois and Frankie stay at the hotel, a big, fancy one in the heart of the city, and mostly stayed in the room or wandered the hotel and nearby areas. I gave Ca my credit card to buy things she or the children might want. I did not buy very much for myself but did get some gifts for the family.

This week is our anniversary and Frankie's birthday. Fred and I gave each other a gift to take on our trip and open on August 13th. On August 14th, our F5 friends took us to the Hello Kitty Café for Frankie's birthday dinner and SUCH a fuss everyone made over him!

It was so clever how they decorated the restaurant and the foods were cute, clever and tasty, but the tables and chairs are so small for us giant women. We all just laughed and made light of the experience. The staff were so welcoming and sweet in how they treated the guests and we took lots of pictures. It was a very nice thing for my friends to do for us and even Ca couldn't stop laughing and enjoying herself.

Fred gave me a ring with a large oval Blue Topaz and it looks very good on my right middle finger. I had given Fred some new shirts to wear for his seminars. He likes wearing polo and tropical style shirts so I got two of each kind.

One thing about Fred I have started to notice…his muscles are not so big as before, but he still looks very handsome. I think I notice it more than others because I see him shirtless often and it is more noticeable than when he wears the shirts.

I am not complaining. I know parts of my body are not so firm or trim as before because of having babies and nursing, but I train hard and use higher quality underwear to keep my body the best I can look. And I know it works because Fred makes love eyes at me all the time. I suggested that he use the hotel or university gym equipment or go for walks or runs when he has time, but when he is in other cities, he is so busy with the seminars and meeting university officials that he has time for little else but sleeping…but he agreed to try. Maybe it will help him relax too.

Often, when we board our flights, the passengers in business or first class do not look pleased that we are bringing toddlers with us…their eyes say that we should be in coach. They expect lots of crying and fussiness and I don't blame them but Frankie and Lois are good little travelers, quiet and sweet most of the time. We keep their feeding and changing schedule as close to routine as we can and it makes life easier for all of us. Frankie likes to draw with the crayons and Lois enjoys looking at picture books and being read to, pointing to the things she likes.

When our flight from Tokyo had a layover in Seattle before heading to Riverton, guess who joined us? Fred! He had just finished the week at the University of Washington and arranged to fly on the same flight as us. Crystal was on the plane too, but in Coach. RU pays for coach seating and Fred pays the difference for Business Class. It was a good surprise and the children were happy to see their Daddy. Frankie told Fred some of the new Japanese words he had learned and what kind of snacks he likes now. It was so very cute.

Furious Fred

October 1, 2004
Dear My Diary,

Fred is so, so, SO MAD at me! I am afraid that what I have done will lead to a divorce…I don't know. It is all my fault and I should have seen it coming from the start. Here is what happened: The children were sleeping, I had gone shopping and everything was caught up so Ca settled in with one of my Vietnamese novels in our library. She removed the paper she had been using as a bookmark and set it on the couch next to her while she read. Fred was doing things in the office and as he walked by Ca, Fred noticed the paper. It was an envelope with the address side up. The return address is from the state prison. Fred asked Ca where the envelope had come from and she said it had been in the book she was reading. Fred gave her something else to use as a bookmark.

When I returned home, Fred was courteous but cold. Not my normal Fred. I asked him if anything is wrong and he showed me the envelope. "Have you seen this before?"

I cannot lie to Fred…not something this important, anyway. "Yes."

"Have you read it?"

"Yes."

"Did you write back?"

"No, I did not."

"Are you sure?" he persisted.

"I promise you, I did not write back to Barney…ever."

"Then why did you keep the letter?"

That is a good question, even for me. I had to think back two years ago to remember. "I felt bad that you did not open the letter and see what Barney had to say. The letter was very sad and I considered writing to him as a courtesy, to let him know his letter had been received and that he was not alone in the world.

"At first, I felt sorry for him, a small, weak man alone in prison with lots of real criminals. Then I thought back on all the bad things he said and did to me and his family and the Nelsons and everyone else. That's when I stopped feeling sorry for him and decided not to write back."

Fred maintained a soft-spoken demeanor with me all along. No threats. No yelling. But his tone had an edge like a knife. "Kimmie, if you decided not to write back, why did you keep the letter?"

"At first, I thought I might read the letter again later on, or I might write to him at Christmas or something like that. I hid the letter and then I forgot about it until now. We got busy, our family grew and the letter has sat tucked away in one of my books all this time."

I stepped forward and slipped my hands around his waist. "Please accept my apology. It was very wrong of me to have read and kept a letter that was addressed to you, only. Believe me, I have bigger and more important people and things to occupy my time than a liar and a cheat."

"Kimmie, normally I don't care if you open letters addressed to me. We are a couple and share a lot of things. That's fine. But when I threw that letter away without opening it, I had my reasons. Reasons you know full well and I don't need to explain."

Of course, I know the reasons. I feel terrible now. I dropped my hands from his waist and looked at the floor. I also feel Ca is listening nearby, wondering if she did a bad thing to me. Fred continued, "I will be honest with you. I did read the letter this time. I understand how you might have felt sorry for him. He even showed some admiration for you. But every day he spends behind bars is a day he earned all by himself." He handed me the letter. "You wanted to keep it. Here it is."

My hands did not move. "I don't want it."

He held it in front of me, quietly insistent that I take it from his fingers. Finally, I took the letter and tore it up in front of him to show I don't care about the letter or its contents and I do not want it to be something that comes between us. I turned the awful thing into confetti, dropped it in the toilet and flushed it all away.

I apologized once again, and although Fred says he understands, I am not so sure. He went into the office and closed the door. Later, he left the house and did not come back until much later. He has never been this angry with me in all our marriage. I am afraid he will divorce me.

Fred will not divorce me. He was quiet with me for most of three days, only speaking as necessary, but politely. Now Fred is back to his regular self. When I asked him if he will divorce me and should I move out? He looked surprised at my words. "Oh, Sweetheart, what happened, happened. It's over now. Let's not talk about it anymore, okay?"

He wrapped me in his arms and tried to kiss me but I turned my head away. "No divorce?" He laughed and said "Kim, it will take a far worse thing than reading a letter to make me want to divorce you."

"Then where did you go the other night after you were mad at me?"

"I met with Michael at the garage to go over sales reports and how things are going. Just business things. Nothing more than that."

"Promise?"

"Promise."

THEN we kissed! We held each other for a long time, then retired to bed and finished making up.

October 15, 2004
Dear My Diary,

I found the Japanese Fierce 5 commercials on VidLive today. They used cartoon effects in the commercials, like when we roar at the gorillas, wiggly animation lines come out of our mouths and the gorillas fall backwards into the bushes and trees and one gorilla got hit on the head with a coconut, making his eyes cross.

For the race car commercial, they edited it so our movements are choppier and more action-packed. Anyway, it was very interesting to see how different it all looked from how we filmed it. I hope F5 does well in Japan as they and Korea are the most influential countries in Asia for pop-culture trends.

Thao has put in another licensing request to Fierce 5 for our family company to be considered for a distributorship. My family often does this for newer products they have an interest in. Sometimes the requests work out and sometimes they do not, but it is one of the ways we grow our business.

I am scheduled to be in Chicago next week to make video and print ads for a line of feminine hygiene products. The advert agency says they like my looks and want to show me doing active things like running, tai chi and kung fu style high kicking. I will have no lines and just have to look strong, active and confident that the product is working for me when I do these things.

Takeela said I will get paid a flat fee plus a small amount each time the commercial is shown or used in magazines, websites, etc. It is part of a national campaign, so there will be lots of placements. It might even be used internationally!

The ad agency will provide the wardrobe and I just let them know my sizes. It is a small job, but as Takeela likes to say, "Every small job is a lead to a bigger job." Wish me luck! Now I need to learn some Tai Chi so I can look at least a little competent in front of the camera.

I make time as I can to attend acting classes and workshops at RU and River City Community Theater. I have not acted in a play yet as my schedule does not work so well to their schedule, but the community theater staff are pleased to have me in their classes because…guess why? I am considered a local celebrity!

My family is always interested to know about the new jobs I get, where I go and what I do in them. Then, when it comes out, they look for me and collect the article or ads or whatever it is. Fred says my whole family, including him and his parents, are my biggest cheerleaders for success. I do not deny, it is their interest in what I do that keeps me going.

Last week I drove with Fred to Wichita, Kansas for a DD seminar week. This is the first time I have done an out-of-town seminar and get the opportunity to see what his average week is like. It is only a few hours away and we took the children and Ca at no extra cost but for a larger room. Crystal flew as she "does not do well" on long drives and RU paid for her flight anyway. Fred gave me a twenty-minute guest spot in the seminars and I get to sign books with him as well.

It is a smoothly run operation and Crystal has her own flair in how she presents her parts. She and Fred switch back and forth and sometimes they present together. I think this helps keep the audience engaged. It reminds me of television and stage shows where the star or emcee starts alone, then a guest comes on and they have some banter, sing a song, then the guest does their own act solo, then they are back together and so forth.

Fred has already given me an outlined script to use for my twenty minutes which is the part I do about Vietnam and other third-world countries and how they use money and debt differently than we do here. My live presentation replaces the video portion for the week.

It was easy for me and I enjoyed being in front of an audience. I wish we could do this every week, but it is probably not good for the children to stay in hotels all day while their parents see them only briefly between the seminars. At least I can see for myself how it works for Fred and Crystal.

Thanh likes to tease me with a pointy tongue that Fred and Crystal might be having a love affair behind my back as they work together so much out of town. She can be like this sometimes and it is one of the traits that I do not like. I do not do the same to her even though her husband has access to many young and attractive employees and customers. I am certain that Brother Vo does not cheat as he is too scared of his wife to encourage any more wrath than he already endures.

This is the way her workers talk to each other all day…gossiping and guessing who is doing what with who. It is the petty, unproductive and hurtful behaviors of low-class people and Thanh encourages it without shame. We were not raised that way, and when I am tempted to say something snide or hurtful, I steer my mind to a peaceful place within myself and do not lower myself to her level, but keep my dignity whole.

With my own eyes, I can see that Fred and Crystal are close in the way they conduct their presentations, discuss logistics, do meet-and-greets with local university representatives and share responsibilities to make the whole visit run smoothly.

Crystal is about Maggie's age and has her own husband (retired) and grown children and grandchildren. Fred and Crystal speak in a friendly manner with each other and share some laughs and jokes, but that is all. Crystal made it a point to say she was happy that I could join them this week, along with our family, and how much Fred misses us on the road. It is perfectly clear that she is a zero threat to my marriage and I will do well to close my ears to Thanh and Vo's teasing.

Ba and Me will go home next week to help Thao and Phung during Noel and Tet seasons. My parents have had a relaxing time in their new American home. I do not see them every day but they understand my work is not on a regular schedule like most people's. Still, they are very happy to see me as a dutiful mother and wife, taking good care of the children with Ca and still able to travel and grow my new career.

At the beginning of their time here, my father was calling Vietnam almost every day and bothering Thao and Phung with details. Wisely, Me slowly changed him, giving constant reassurances that the company he built from nothing is now in good hands.

She has encouraged him to relax, go for walks with her around our city's many attractive neighborhoods and parks and visit the library where they can check out Vietnamese language books and videos.

Sometimes they go alone, sometimes with Frank and Maggie and sometimes with Ca and the children and me. I think both of them look better and healthier now, what with the walking and not worrying so much about the business. I am certain that Phung and Thao feel better not to be bothered every day by Ba, too! They all talk or email once a week or so these days and everything appears to be under control. I will miss my parents until next Spring.

Thomas Stimson

Halloween with Family

Monday, November 1st

We decided not to take our children to the hospital for our annual Halloween visit. We have been going back and forth on whether to do this or not. I worry about my babies, especially Lois, to catch something during our visit. Maybe in a few years the children can come and bring some happiness to others, but for now they are too young and susceptible. Fred, for his part, was smart enough not to fight me on this.

This year, we dressed in simple but colorful costumes of Ketchup and Mustard bottles. The costumes are soft-bodied so we can sit and move around easily in them. Fred found and made up some jokes and word plays to fit our theme for the children to laugh at. Most of them worked for the kids and made the adults groan. When that happens, Fred considers his efforts a success.

We spent two hours at the hospital handing out treats and small toys. The city cancelled the Riverton Park Halloween Party due to heavy rains, so after dinner we put the children in a Pickle costume for Lois and Frankie was a Hot Dog. So CUTE!

We visited Grandma and Grandpa for pictures and treats before heading to the mall for indoor trick-or-treating. Ca is too shy to wear a costume so she came along for the fun of it. There were SO many children and adults in costumes…even pets!

We took many pictures and met up with Vo and the twins. They are fourteen now and dressed as pirates with skirts, plastic swords and hats with skulls on them. Cam wore an eye-patch and Tam had a fake parrot on her shoulder. They make such a fussing over their little cousins and the children loved it after they understood the girls are their cousins and not strangers.

Vo asked how we like his costume, but he was not wearing a costume that we could see. Fred asked, "I'll bite. What are you dressed as?"

"A hen-peck husband!" and Vo laughed heartily at his own joke. We laughed along with him to be polite, even though I did not understand his meaning. Fred told me later what "hen-peck husband" means and now I understand. Ok. Ha ha. Still not funny, but Vo did compliment us on our costumes, so that was nice.

I asked Ca if she wants to try wearing a costume for next Halloween. She shrugged and said "Maybe." I can see she enjoys being the observer more than the observed. I am finding that I like both as do most of the entertainers I have worked with so far.

The children were fast asleep before we got home and few candies were missing from the decorated bowl we left on a porch rocker. Fred said trick-or-treating is better on dry nights than ones so wet as this. I agree! If it is dry next year, and not too cold, maybe we will take the children around the neighborhood as is the tradition.

Thanksgiving 2004

Saturday November 27, 2004

This year we had Thanksgiving Dinner at Bunny's shop/apartment. It was so much fun as Bunny has changed the layout of the shop and it looks very…how to say…organized, attractive and easy to see everything. Old Joe Hamilton kept a messy store with things scattered everywhere. He liked to explain that people enjoyed digging around looking for treasures, but I think he was just lazy.

Bunny sought out her display cases and shelving through store liquidation sales and FreePost ads, then took the time to create colorful and creative presentations of her goods. The children had so much fun exploring and calling out "Look at this!" or "Mommy! What's that?"

Bunny said it also helps her keep easy track of what is running low or what she has too much of so can make special sales or trade with Michael and other stores for things she needs. The twins chased each other around the big store until Vo yelled at them to behave. Oh, and the word "Cool!" was used more times than I can count. Now our children are saying it about anything and everything. Better "cool" than some words I hear young children say in public.

The small elevator has not worked for a long time and will be expensive for Bunny to repair, so Fred carried his father up the wide stairs where there is a big easy chair for him to relax in. Bunny lifted her skirt to show me how her legs have gotten muscular like mine from hauling boxes of goods to and from the second-floor storeroom. She is very proud of her muscles and I must say, she looks very good altogether, along with being very happy and confident with her success.

Bunny made a large turkey, tossed salad and pumpkin and apple pies. We all brought in other things for the potluck. It was the same small dinner group as last year…the perfect size for us at Thanksgiving.

During the Thanking Time, Tina announced, "This year, I am most thankful for…Barry proposing marriage to me!" She then raised her hand from her lap to show off a sparkler of a ring.

That took everyone by surprise, except Barry, who added "Luckily, she said yes…because I'd already bought the ring!" We had a good laugh and made our congratulations to them. Tina said Barry had proposed only last night as he was too shy to do it in front of us today. She kept the ring in her pocket, slipping it on as she was giving thanks.

Tina continued, "And there is one more surprise as well…"

Tam interrupted, "Are you getting a puppy?"

Cam guessed, "A kitten?"

Thanh asked hopefully, "A baby?"

Tina shook her head at each guess and looked not so happy to tell us what was on her mind. "No puppies and no kittens. Sorry girls. As for children, Barry and I have been discussing that and neither of us really want to have children, what with our careers and all."

She looked at Barry who nodded and Tina took a deep breath. "The other big announcement is…we will be moving to London next year. To live." The room went quiet for a moment.

Barry helped Tina with the rest of it. "This must be a bit of a shock, I know. Like when I told my family I was moving to America for a girl instead of another high-paying gig with a top firm. I've been offered a plum spot with Lloyd's of London and, well, my family knows people. We can get Tina set up with any number of firms and she can get dual citizenship by being married to me."

Thanh, her face darkening, was the first to speak up, and in Vietnamese, "Trinh! Why you want to go away? Why you need different job? You are director of global thing and very high in your job! You have sisters *right here!* Now you want to go away from family? Are you too good for us? What is wrong with you?!"

Tina and Barry looked shocked at her words and I felt bad for both sisters, especially having the younger sister speak so harshly to her older sister…it is not the respectful way. My American family does not know Thanh's words, but her tone and demeanor were clear.

Barry started to speak but Tina stopped him. She took a big breath to calm her emotions and spoke in English. "Em Thanh, you are right in that I am giving up a very good job with Robbie and the firm. They have been very good to me and I have learned a lot. And yes, I will be leaving my sisters and their families and my parents for the times they will stay here.

"I am not taking this action lightly. Barry and I have talked much about this. Riverton and New York have given me great experience and I will be able to use that in London. I have met Barry's family and they are very nice people. They accept me as a part of their family and, as Barry said, they are well-connected. And honestly, I miss life in big, thriving cities like New York and Saigon. London will provide us the high paying jobs we deserve and the cultural entertainments we enjoy and have difficulty finding in Riverton and Saint Louis. It is what's best for us, as a couple."

Thanh made more complaints but I stopped listening to her. I see in Tina what I experienced myself. Moving to another country for a man and starting a new life from a place where I am not so happy. I could only do one thing: I stood up and came around the table, wrapping my arms around Tina and Barry, giving them my heartfelt congratulations on their engagement and upcoming move to London.

Maggie and Fred followed my lead, and everyone else did the same but for Thanh, standing with her arms folded over her chest and Vo sitting next to her with an unhappy face, unwilling to counter Thanh's state of emotion.

I had a long talk with Tina on Friday. She knew Barry would propose to her one day as they had been discussing long-term ideas and plans for themselves. Barry is a graduate of Oxford University, as was expected from his family. They know many influential people and they tend to travel all over Europe for business and holidays.

I know this is an exciting lifestyle to Tina and she has been to London twice now to visit the city and Barry's family. Some of them will come here for an intimate American-style wedding before leaving for a much bigger, more formal wedding amongst Barry's extended family, peers and business associates.

Tina described the family as Old Money explaining "Old Money means they have country estates that we've all seen in films and television dramas. The kinds of families who not only use banks, but own them. Some of his relatives are titled as well."

"Titled?"

"Dukes, Earls, Barons. Those kinds of titles."

That really took my breath away. "Is Barry titled?"

"No. Not that he's told me anyway. And that's not why I'm marrying him. He's just a really good, honest, hardworking man who doesn't have to work, but wants to. His family does not mind that I am not British or Caucasian and I feel comfortable in their company."

I know her feelings. It is an important point for anyone joining another family, to feel that you belong. I am grateful that Fred's parents accept me 100% and they love our children too. Not every family member feels such a strong connection, like Barney within his own family or Thanh in mine. I have become much closer to Tina in the last few years and will miss her very much. I have also gotten closer to Thanh, but with her it is a mix of good and bad relations.

Of the sisters living in America, Tina is the most Western. She made herself as American as she could, short of changing her physical appearance, to fit in professionally and socially.

Thanh, on the other hand, has a husband from our homeland, so all their time is spent working, talking, eating and raising their children as though they are still in Ho Chi Minh City.

And I am in between, with an American husband and only able to speak Vietnamese with my family members, and sometimes at the Asian markets. I eat, speak and read English most of the time, but I still manage to keep many connections to my country and culture. Just not so much as Thanh and not so little as Tina.

Tina is upset with Thanh and I have not heard more since Thanh pulled her family out early from the dinner, being as angry as she was, and I do not know why. Even in Riverton, Thanh and Tina were not so close to each other, but we did see each other more. Perhaps Thanh sees our family is breaking apart? If so, I do not see it in this way.

I know Tina is bored in her off times because Riverton is an older, not so modern city and activities here are on the quiet side, especially compared to Saigon, New York and London! Tina has said that she and Barry plan to travel back to the US and Vietnam as they can, to see us and Ba and Me and Thao and Phung. They will not be leaving and ignoring us like we are nothing. Always, we are family.

I told Tina that it is sad about her going away, but I certainly understand and am very happy for her. "I can see myself in you, moving overseas for a foreign man. Fred and I have talked, and we agree that Barry is a good match for you. You are a very lucky woman and Barry is lucky to have you, too."

"It was you that helped me make this decision," Tina said. "Fred is also quite a catch for you and our family and your success inspired me to accept Barry's proposal."

"You are inspired by me?"

"Yes, it is true. Does that surprise you?"

"I am surprised that I inspire anyone to do anything except make tall woman jokes."

Tina laughed and said "You don't give yourself enough credit, Kimmie."

"Fred says the same thing to me all the time."

"Well, he's right. You should listen to us, and your heart, more often."

Tina Pham Picker: I knew the family might not be too keen on me leaving the US but I did not expect such a harsh reaction from Thanh either. She apologized later, but the sting of her words stayed with me for a long time. I think she might have felt jealous for my marrying into a wealthy family and having the freedom to pick up and go while she had businesses to run and children to raise in a town that she was never really happy living in. She never said as much, but that was always my impression of Thanh's life…quiet frustration.

Merry Bucking Christmas

Sunday, Dec 12, 2004

Last night's Merry Bucking Christmas was a fun party with even more people than before. We rented a large meeting room and had it catered at the same hotel as last year. It is more convenient and less work for us than when we try to do it ourselves.

We had considered using our new big house in Honeywood Heights, but it is not company-ready yet. We go over when we can to clean and tidy and add some furniture, decorations and other things here and there. Some walls still need repairing and some rooms need to have awful color combinations painted over.

There are many spider webs hanging in high areas that we cannot easily reach…not like Fred's childhood home where Fred and I can reach up and brush them away. Sometimes I feel like a living ladder, being able to reach so many high places. I do the same at Maggie and Frank's home, especially high shelves and corners. It was Maggie who called me a Living Ladder and now the name has stuck in my mind like a song from the radio. She meant it in a complimentary way and it is a good descriptive term.

Back to the party: the usual people were there like Robbie, the Woods sisters, some of the resale store owners, Michael and Bunny, even though she is not directly part of the Orion Group anymore, Tina and Barry, Mahmood and Nezzie and some others from B&R. Dr. Webber and his wife came by for a bit and Crystal Dahl with her husband Livingston. Crystal likes to joke that he is her "Living Dahl". I think it's a sweet term.

New attendees to the party are some of Fred's commercial real estate partners including "Make-up Stylist to the Stars" Harry Combs, a Riverton native who works mostly out of LA and New York. Also, there was Bud Weiss, owner of the beer and wine distribution warehouse, William "Wink" Martin, owner of the state's largest auto and truck dealership chain and the same man who gave Fred the deal on old car parts and finally, Dr. Gomez Adams, a popular plastic surgeon.

Tina will have a small wedding here in the Spring and has already given notice to Robbie who is looking for a replacement. There are not many highly-educated Asians living in the Midwest with the financial, language and cultural knowledge skills that Tina has. Most are shop owners, low-level employees or professionals working in non-financial areas like engineering and medicine.

Tina is helping Robbie by contacting people with her old employer who might want to live in slower-paced Riverton and former classmates and teachers from her alma mater Columbia University. Most of the coworkers Tina knew in New York died in 9/11, but she will contact the bank's HR department to see if anyone is interested in her job. We will see.

Everyone is happy that the recession is turning from a Bear back to a Bull Market and most sectors are on the rise. We expect the prices of homes to follow suit.

Dissolving Debt has sold over 100,000 copies and is now being carried by some major book retailers, along with a growing number of university bookstores.

The Woods moved out of the B&R building to a business park where clients will have free parking and more space to grow their business, allowing B&R to grow into those empty offices as well. With all the work Fred, his partners, local banks and credit unions are giving Holly and Hazel, they have added many new employees to handle all the business. I am very happy to see another set of sisters growing successful.

Fred and Crystal have done almost 200 DD seminars all over the United States and they will be taking the rest of this month off. Whew! They typically do about eight seminars in a three-day visit and sometimes one of the seminar time blocks will be used as a book signing event so there is not so much talking but lots of selling, greeting patrons and answering questions.

The numbers are very exciting, but Fred is gone so much so I have to do more things for the household. It is not easy, but we make it work and Ca is such a big help, doing much more than before with grocery shopping and taking the children out to do fun things.

Twice per month Fred and I put together a blog post for the DD website and update the calendar of where the future seminars and signings will be. The blog posts keep my English stronger and Fred appreciates my help with ideas and filler material.

The party is a good way to catch up with many people we don't get to see very often and meet some new ones. I am glad that we keep doing the Merry Bucking Christmas party as I am always learning new things about our partners and how they manage their lives.

2004 was a strong year for Fierce Five. After "A Son's Quest" came out, the demand for F5 exploded and Mama and various members of the team traveled around North America, visiting local and regional distributors in the US, Canada and Mexico, helping the company secure lucrative contracts.

Typically, the team would be at the signing of new distribution deals, promoting products, signing autographs at large grocery retailers and doing photo ops with local business leaders. Not all the F5 team members were able to be everywhere at the same time. At least two to three would be present and sometimes Rock Rollins, the Fierce Five celebrity spokesperson, would make an appearance as well. Normally that would take place in major markets like New York, Miami, Houston and Los Angeles due to his packed schedule.

Mama would go to as many as she could, sometimes taking us with her and sometimes leaving us home in the care of Aunt Ca. Each appearance meant two things to Mama…more money and more exposure. Her picture was often in the local newspapers and Chamber of Commerce newsletters as well as the Fierce 5 promotional website. She also made sure to contact the local Asian media outlets for even more exposure opportunities. The team made video and print commercials as needed at a studio in Chicago, which was centrally located to most of the team's homes.

She became popular, and even endearing, to Riverton University's Drama Department and grew adept in areas of comedy and drama through classes and workshops. Mama used humor to break the ice with strangers and make important points she was speaking on more memorable while the drama skills would be used while performing action parts or when she needed to show deeper sides of the character she was playing.

2005
The More the Merrier

January 2nd
Dear My Diary,

It has been five years since Fred and I became engaged and now the next family engagement will turn into a wedding scheduled for Sunday, February 13th. Since Valentine's is on a Monday this year, the Sunday before is a cost-effective time to get a chapel. Barry's parents and some other relatives will fly in to meet us and show their good faces as our newest family members.

It seems that, despite their wealth, or maybe because of it, Barry and his family also look for opportunities to save money. Fred is enjoying this bit of knowledge, commenting "No different from us, but for the earls and dukes. No, wait a minute. We have those. I have a cousin Earl and one of my uncles is nicknamed 'Duke'. Yeah, we *are* just like them!"

Even with all their family wealth and personal incomes, Barry and Tina have their own frugal habits. For example, they booked the venue for Sunday as it is much cheaper than Saturday, and they will not buy or rent formalwear for the wedding but use their own dress-up clothes. In England, she will rent a designer wedding dress for a fraction of the price of buying it.

Barry likes to tell stories of the Royal Family and how they spend freely of their government-provided salaries on work-related expenses, but for themselves, they often buy things on sale or at discounted prices, and Barry's family does the same thing. "It's how we've managed to hang on to our wealth during the Great War and through all the ups and downs of the economy."

Fred said, "You are my kind of guy!"

"Back at you, Mate!"

I understand now there will not be two legal weddings for Tina and Barry. The one in America will be small and official for immigration purposes and the one in England will be "for show" with hundreds of guests. It will be a faster and smoother process for Tina to get residency status in England with her husband than with her fiancé, based on the advice of their lawyers.

To me, the most important thing is that Tina has finally found someone who is a good match for her in terms of personalities, career, and lifestyle. Barry likes to drive fancy brands of cars, but only purchases used, low mileage vehicles with verifiable maintenance records and then drives them for a long time. It is like he has read our Dissolving Debt book!

Christmas with the children was so much fun! They are old enough to be excited about Santa Claus and presents and decorations. We have had snow a few times so far including Christmas when we built a snowman and threw snowballs. Frankie is potty trained now and he wanted to make "yellow snow" like the song he heard on the radio, but we discouraged this colorful Christmas wish.

We take the children to malls and shopping centers frequently here and when we travel. It is safe for walking and they all have little playgrounds. It gives them a chance to try new activities, play with other children and build their social skills, since there are not many young children in our neighborhood. Fred found some play equipment to add to our backyard to go along with the swings we have. It is a playhouse attached to a jungle gym and was mixed in with some other stuff at the garage, so he brought it home.

We all got new clothes for the holidays. Mine are from Tree Top gals, mostly, and Fred's come from specialty shops as well. I do not want him wearing used clothes for business and dressy events anymore. Sometimes they look fine, but then I notice a stretched-out collar or a small tear under the sleeve that shows his underarm hairs…ugh!

Ca is just the opposite of us, so I take her to shops with a good selection of petite and junior sizes for holiday and Spring wear. She does such a good job for us and always has big eyes at the mall, especially this time of year as everything is so dressed up. Sometimes we listen to live performances like children's choirs, piano concerts and small orchestral groups. So different from our markets in Vietnam!

Frank and Maggie took us to church for Christmas services and no one made fun of me. Many people were happy to see us and had such nice things to say. If any of them remembered my awful Easter, they never brought it up…it has been a few years, after all.

We also signed up Lois and Frankie for pre-school daycare at their grandparents' church to start on Monday. It is a very good program and will help them get used to socializing with other children. They spend too much time with adults as it is. The fee is reasonable, and the church is licensed and insured to do this, so there is much trust and confidence our children will be in good hands. We can take them out and put back in any time we need to for the times we are working out of town, on holiday and so forth.

The daycare reminds me of the orphanage we sponsor in Saigon, but of course there are no orphans here. The children will learn the alphabet and numbers, hear stories about Jesus, George Washington and other famous people, make art things, play games, have snacks and nap time. I will miss them during the day, but Ca and I can get other things done without interruptions.

We visited lots of family members and got Christmas cards from some of Barry's family, including his parents. So sweet of them! And with each piece of mail, I send a Christmas card back the next day with a family picture and good wishes for the New Year. Our family Christmas card this year has all four of us dressed in our Halloween costumes as a family portrait…too funny! Everybody loved it.

Barry's parents are James and Eileen Picker and he has two sisters and a brother, all married and with children. Barry is the oldest, but last to get married, just like Tina. His father is a "barrister", which is the British way to say "lawyer", and his mother is a housewife who is involved in many charitable organizations. They sent a picture of themselves looking tanned and athletic. They probably play tennis and golf with other wealthy people. We would probably do the same if we had competitive personalities, but I realized long ago that Fred and I are only happy competing with ourselves.

Ba and Me are busy with company work and were very pleased with how the business was run last summer while they were here visiting. I think maybe Ba is a little unhappy that it was not worse so he could be of more help, but Thao has grown up in the business, as we all did, and Phung is always looking for ways to increase productivity and profit margins. Such a good brother and son he is for our family!

Ba and Me will come for two weeks to celebrate Tet and see their eldest daughter marry at the beginning of the Lunar New Year…a lucky time to marry.

My parents will now have son-in-laws from three different continents and countries. How different from everyone else we know! Tina has already warned them not to expect grandchildren and they are not upset or disappointed but told her to be happy with her husband and successful in life. They know from other families' experiences that it is not good to demand grandbabies from children who do not want, or cannot have, children of their own. This is especially true in modern times when there is more freedom of choice than when everyone was expected to conform to societal norms.

As I finish this entry, I have an idea I am working on as a future project. When I first met with Takeela Rockett, she suggested that I use my own ideas and experiences to create stories as personal acting projects. I keep thinking about the Living Ladder comment from Maggie and have been making notes and jotting down little scenes as they pop into my head.

The character will be like myself, a very tall woman, who starts a Living Ladder business. I think it will be a romance, but how to get to the romantic part is what I am working out in my head, especially during my quiet times like in the shower or when the children are in pre-school and I am not so busy…which is not often! I feel like I have something interesting, but not sure yet. We will see.

January 18, 2005
Dear My Diary,

Fred got a letter from the state prison that Barney is being considered for early parole. Barney has asked that Fred be contacted to help him with housing and a job after he is released because the state prefers the prisoner to be with a responsible family member to reduce the chances of the parolee from going back to a life of crime.

First, Fred laughed in a cruel and bitter way, not believing Barney would ask such a thing from him. Then he said, "Oh, *hell* no! That's not going to happen. Not in a New York *minute* is that going to happen!" and other similar outbursts. I completely understand his refusal.

Fred learned from the corrections counselor that after he entered prison, Barney was beaten and raped by other prisoners because the scammer Brad Luzerk told people that Barney gave information to the police to get Brad arrested. Barney now has some brain damage from so many beatings and his behavior has changed significantly.

Because Barney is not a violent criminal and the prison system needs more room for much worse kinds of men, Barney will be released for his good behavior and the mental doctors believe he will be a good citizen if released. At least, that is how I understand everything.

The counselor asked Fred if he will consider meeting with him and Barney to make some arrangements to help get Barney back into normal life, find a job and start to repay the debts he owes. If he can get no help from his family, Barney will be put in a half-way house with a higher chance to go bad than if he has positive family support.

You might as well ask Fred to take back a dog that has bitten him many times in the past…he is NOT happy about this at all and really does not want to do it. Fred and I talked about this a lot. We don't know what the effects of the brain damage are exactly, but Barney is not in the prison hospital and has limited contact with other prisoners now. Since the prison considers Barney to be non-violent, which he is…and in Fred's words, "just a persistent asshole", he is able to return to society and be productive. But the prison system wants help from his family and none of Fred's other relatives have the income, employment opportunities or clean enough police records to meet the parole board's requirements.

I asked Fred to meet with Barney and see what he is like and make a more informed decision. I said, "I have never experienced this kind of problem in my family, but if I did, I would want to know more and make the best decision I can. But whatever you decide to do, I will accept and support it."

Fred is not sleeping well now, thinking of this and feeling pressure. He spoke with his parents about this dilemma. Maggie thinks Fred should try to help Barney if it makes sense to do so. Frank said, "Let him rot."

Kimmie: I would not say Fred and I had fights about whether to sponsor Barney or not. "Fight" is too strong a word. I prefer to think of them as "spirited discussions". Either way, Fred had no willingness to deal with Barney anymore and I didn't blame him then or now.

After all, we were busy with small children, career paths that were evolving and changing and had much too much on our respective plates. But after the things the prison officials told us, Fred learning for himself about his brother and my persuading that family should help family and I would stand beside Fred for whatever happens...your father decided to be the bigger man and take on a new responsibility.

Plans for Barney

Dear My Diary,

We visited parents and explained how Fred will help Barney with securing a job and place to live while on parole. Frank narrowed his good eye like to say, "What do you mean?" and Maggie asked us if this is a good idea?

Fred described his meeting with the prison counselor and how Barney is so much different now: more gentle, respectful and is a model prisoner as he does not talk back anymore and follows the prison rules without complaint. Then Fred met with Barney for the first time since before the arrest to see with his own eyes what the counselor had told him. "He's aged a lot in such a short time," Fred stated. "His attitude…the demeanor he gave off…was very different from his typical sour-apples self."

"Do you think this is an act by Barney to get out of prison?" his mother asked.

"I couldn't say one hundred percent that it's not," he admitted, "but the prison records indicate a long-term behavioral change that would be difficult to hide consistently. He's not that good an actor to pull something like that off without slipping up.

"They said it would be much better for everyone to get him back on his feet, be productive and provide positive role-models to keep the momentum going. Apparently, Barney asked for me personally to help with his rehabilitation and when the officials ran my record, they liked what they saw."

Then Fred went on to explain how I influenced him to help Barney. He sees how my family works together and get along so well, helping and supporting each other as we can.

Maggie smiled at me and reminded me how wonderful she thinks my family is. "I hope Barney has learned a big lesson and will be a better man than before."

Frank grunted and said carefully, "A leopard cannot change his spots."

Fred said, "Maybe not, but this leopard looks like he is tamer than before."

Frank said, "We'll see." And turned his wheelchair around to leave.

I always appreciate Fred saying nice things about me and my family. I hope he will not be sorry about my influencing him about Barney.

Fred asked his mother if she ever told Barney about his real father. Now it was Maggie's turn to make a hard face. "No, I haven't. And neither will you two!" she ordered. "Just forget I ever told you that story and leave it in the past. There's no point in bringing it up now, and it won't help what's already happened."

Later that day, I stopped at Bunny's Bargain Hutch with the children. Frankie knows how to act like a rabbit now, and when he sees his Aunt Bunny he hops around and makes his little teeth push out. Lois laughs at her brother and Bunny makes a rabbit face back at him and tousles his hair, saying in a funny voice, "How ya doin', kiddo?"

When the children settled down with some building blocks, I informed Bunny what we are doing with Barney. Her eyes got big. "Really? You are going to do that for him? After everything that happened?" After I explained much of what we told parents, she said, "So, if he's going to work with Michael, I guess that means I will have to deal with him at least sometimes, huh?"

I said, "I think so, but maybe we can avoid that if he does not visit the shop."

"Do you think he is sore at me?"

"Do you mean angry because of the divorce? Is that sore?"

I admitted that I do not know but will see if he asks or talks about Bunny after he gets out. Then I can let her know.

Bunny scoffed, "That's okay. I'm an adult. I can handle myself if Barney comes around to deliver things."

"Are you sure?"

She said with a confident smile, "Yeah, I'm a big girl!"

Lois looked up and said, "Me too!" and we both laughed at funny little Lois. All she hears and cares about is that she is a big girl like her Auntie.

Bunny gave me a hug and thanked me for stopping by to tell her this and not making it a sudden surprise. I said, "I would do the same for any of my sisters."

"You know Kim, I have always liked you from the first time I met you. Remember that day? It was your first day in America and you called me Rabbit."

We both laughed at the memory and Frankie began laughing too. "Mommy called you a Rabbit? But your name is Bunny!"

"Bummy! Bummy!" said Lois and it surprised me as this is the first time she has said Bunny's name. I gave her a hug and kiss for saying auntie's name so nicely. I gave Bunny a hug too, saying that if she wants, I will keep in touch with her about Barney.

"Oh, who cares about him? You don't have to do that," she said dismissively. Then she looked at me more directly, gave a small shrug and her lips twisted a bit, "But you can if you want to."

One of the bigger problems we see about taking care of Barney is that we are gone so much from home, with Fred doing DD seminars and my promos for Fierce 5 and other modeling jobs. We certainly do not want Barney living in any of our homes, we don't care how much he has changed. We can get him an apartment or small rental house easily enough. Most of our plans are still in the "thinking about it stage". His parole date is planned for April, if things work out, but right now, we are getting ready for Tina's wedding.

Bobby has found a person he thinks is a good fit as Tina's replacement. His name is Guong Lim but his American nickname is Gary. He is from San Francisco where his family has lived in the Chinatown District for over one-hundred years. His entire career has been in banking and primarily with the Asian community, so he knows several languages and understands the attitudes and preferences of these kinds of people. He has been looking to live somewhere with a much lower cost of living and not so crowded as the Bay Area is now.

He will not be hired as a VP as he needs to work with B&R's customers and prove himself capable. I am sure the attitudes about money between Asians of the Midwest and those of Central California have many differences that Gary will need to learn and adjust his style towards if he wishes to succeed.

The most important part is that Tina has a replacement and will get him up to speed and introduced to many of her clients…like me! But Tina can always give me good financial advice from wherever she is in the world. That's what sisters are for, right?

January 29, 2005
Dear My Diary,

    After cleaning and heating the house and buying some fresh foods I know they will like, we picked up Ba and Me from the airport and brought them home. This is their first time to be here in winter and it is very cold for them! There are several inches of snow on the ground from three days ago and so pretty, but not so pretty as when it was fresh. I laid out several pairs of long john underclothes for both of them to keep warm when they go out.

    The children are so happy to see their grandparents again, excited to tell them the many things they are learning at preschool, but after so much travelling, my parents are very tired and cannot follow Frankie's fast-paced talking, so they just smile politely saying things like "Really?" and "Wonderful!" and "That's nice."

    After a warm meal prepared by Ca, they settled in for an afternoon nap so their bodies can catch up to the local time zone and tomorrow we will meet with Tina and Barry to discuss the final details for the wedding. Fred just got back yesterday from Phoenix where daytime temperatures are in the 70's. Maybe he wishes he stayed there for the weekend too? Sounds nicer than here!

Thomas Stimson

The Final Pham Wedding

Feb 14, 2005

Dear My Diary,

We just finished lunch and my parents, Frankie and Lois are all taking a nap so I have some time to write this. We will have dinner tonight with Barry's family at an English pub downtown. It's supposed to be very authentic and is owned by a British ex-pat couple. Should be fun!

The wedding yesterday was an intimate affair with about fifty guests…mostly family and a few of Tina's coworkers including Mahmood's family and Robbie. I was not sure if Thanh and her family would attend, but they were all there and well-behaved.

I think Thanh has accepted Tina's new direction in life, or at least is keeping her true feelings to herself. The girls think the English accents are "so cool!" and try to imitate them. Most of our cousins came too with their families and Auntie is spending the winter in Saigon, but sent her best wishes and a beautiful gift that my parents brought with them. Frankie sported a cute suit and Lois wore a pretty red woolen dress with tights to keep her warm.

I am learning more about James and Eileen Picker and feel even more certain that Tina has married well. They are highly educated people with gentle manners and were very warm to everyone. They treated my parents as equals and spoke slowly and clearly, without being condescending, so my parents understood them pretty well.

The Pickers have been to America many times for business and "holiday", as they call vacations, as well as Japan, China, Singapore and Hong Kong, but never to Vietnam. My parents invited the Pickers to be their personal guests anytime they want to visit.

Two of Barry's three siblings joined the celebrations: Ian came alone as his children are in school and his wife is taking care of them while Helen was joined by her husband and two young sons. They played with Lois and Frankie and the children got along nicely.

There is a small, very lovely church outside of Riverton in the farmland district. It is white with a bell housed in a tall, pointed steeple, stained-glass windows and an organ playing richly textured music. It felt like I had stepped into a painting or a scene from an English movie. They had truly selected an old-fashioned, romantic church.

Tina wore a conservative but fashionable cream-colored dress and Barry wore a gray suit with vest and watch-chain across the front. Barry is nearly a foot taller than Tina and, with the suit, somehow looks even more towering because he is slender and the suit has pinstripes.

At the end of the ceremony, the bell was rung in celebration. It made me and the others jump as we were not expecting it…then we laughed with relief. Afterward, we enjoyed a light lunch and cake served by some of the church members. It was very different from the fancy weddings I am used to here and in Vietnam. The wedding in London will be in a "cathedral". I think a cathedral is a much larger church compared to this one in the country.

The Picker families will all be gone by Thursday night, then Barry and Tina will fly to Chicago for a three-day honeymoon. When my parents leave next week, all will be back to normal again.

I am so glad that Tina has found such a nice man for herself. Now she knows how I feel!

593

Dear My Diary,

Fred and Barney have worked out an agreement and submitted a written plan to the parole board for their approval. Here is how it will work: Barney will live at the garage with Mike and work for Fred under Mike's supervision. Fred will pay Barney the state minimum wage and after ninety days, if all is working out and Barney shows himself to be reliable and not troublesome, he will earn a commission of fifty percent of Fred's part of the net profits every quarter. Barney will live rent-free and be provided with a cell phone to be used for work. We will provide food during the first ninety days as well, then Barney will have to buy his own.

Moreover, Barney had to agree to no alcohol, illegal drugs or prescription drugs unless prescribed by a doctor. I know Barney likes to drink so I don't know if he will follow that rule so well. Also, I did not think he used recreational drugs in the past, but Bunny had informed Fred that Barney had done cocaine and marijuana while they were married. Fred knows that a lot of drugs get smuggled into prisons, but we do not know if Barney was using or not.

Barney's drivers' license has expired and will have to be renewed. He will have access to our trucks at the garage, but only under Michael's supervision, meaning Barney cannot just come and go with our vehicles as he pleases and, if he wants to buy one, he will have to do it on his own.

Barney has been permanently stripped of his license to practice law and he may not travel out of state without the court's permission during the entirety of his five-year parole. I assume that the state is afraid he will run away and make trouble somewhere else.

Fred has also negotiated that one-fourth of Barney's net wages and commissions will be garnished, which is the maximum allowed per federal rules, to repay the money his investors lost and could not get back, plus the fines that were levied. Those monies will be set aside in a special fund managed by the state to be distributed later.

The Nelsons are gone now, but their estate trust is still active for the many charities and scholarship funds they sponsor. The other investor, Nicolas Vamkros, is nearly broke now and is hoping to get some of his lost money back. It will take a long time for Barney to repay his debts and Fred will encourage Barney to voluntarily pay more than the federal minimum, which is why he will get free rent, to help him with the repayment process.

Legally, Fred can't force his brother to pay extra, but if he refuses to contribute more, Fred will simply charge him rent and use that money towards the garnishment. Either way, it will get paid down faster with Fred handling the additional money and making sure it is added to the garnishment fund.

Fred assured me that Barney understands and agrees to all the conditions. This makes us both suspicious of why he is being so cooperative and not arguing against any of the rules set out. We will both be keeping our eyes and ears open about Barney.

Meanwhile, Barney's real father will be in prison for the rest of his life due to having so many prior convictions before this scam, so none of his victims will see a dime from him.

Lastly, for the next five years Barney will make regular visits with his parole officer to show that he is making good progress, taking drug and alcohol detection tests, and will get random visits from his parole officer to be extra sure he is following the rules.

Mike is not happy about the arrangement but understands why we are doing it. For his own protection, Mike bought a safe with an electronic alarm system for his money and papers, hiding it somewhere in the cavernous garage. Better safe than sorry, and I should know. We have one built into our new home behind a secret wall panel. Not just because of Barney, but for our own protection. And the full truth? Yes, because of Barney.

Fred told Mike to keep Barney busy, but not to be hard on him. Mike is not a mean person but will need to be firm with Barney if he must and there will be plenty of other employees around as well. Mike does not want to be a babysitter, but he has to be our eyes and ears so we do not have problems with the parole office.

"And one other thing you have to know, Kimmie," Fred began.

I thought, "Uh oh. Will this be bad?"

"Legally, his name is still Bernard Bartlett, but now he wants to be called Barney, not Bernie."

I couldn't believe my ears to hear this new bit of news. "But why?"

"I'm not sure, but maybe it is a way of shaming himself and starting his life over. He made the new name to sound more professional as a lawyer. Now that he is no longer a lawyer and the Bernie Bartlett name is stained, I think he wants to get rid of his new name and change it back to his birth name. That's how I understand it, anyway."

I told Fred it will be easier for us too, as the children have only heard of him as Barney from us. So BER-nie now goes back to BAR-ney.

Saturday March 19, 2005
Dear My Diary,

We went out to dinner tonight to celebrate our belated birthdays. Fred was in Baton Rouge Louisiana this week for DD seminars at Southern University and A&M College. He said they have very beautiful campuses and good weather this time of year as it is not cold and not so hot as it will get in the summer. I explained to Fred that Baton Rouge means "red stick" in French, which, I think, is an unusual place name.

I put a shamrock necktie in Fred's suitcase as a birthday surprise and he wore it to the Thursday seminar…how sweet to do this for me! He brought home a box of Lucky Charms cereal and told me they are magically delicious! There is so much sugar in the cereal that it is not to my taste, but I said I would believe his "charm"ing claim.

He told me to open the cereal box anyway, so I did. Taped to the inside of the box top is a jade ring! I said "This is too much! You did not have to do this."

But Fred insisted, "You are very lucky to me, so do not argue against the good things that come to you."

"Okay, but it is very expensive compared to the shamrock tie."

"If it makes you feel better, you can believe the jade is colored soapstone, and then we are even."

I will wear the ring to dinner tonight at the new Irish restaurant near Bunny's shop. They feature a genuine Irish folk singing group and new dishes I have not had before. Should be fun!

This week, I have been busy designing and modeling advertising photographs with Trung Nguyen for his new Anh Hai the Sandwich Guy restaurant. Different pictures will be used for paper placemats, menus, signs and some will be saved for later use when he opens a shop at the Riverton Mall Food Court. At first, I told him that he should get a pretty model for the pictures, not me.

He said "But you are my partner, and you have a great look! When you take a bite from a Banh Mi, it is like inviting EVERYBODY to take a bite! Besides, you work cheap, right?" The way he said the last part made me laugh, so I agreed. Yes, for my business partner I will work cheap…but the more accurate word is "free". It was fun and we tried out different looks, outfits, costumes and poses. I will let Trung make the final decision on how he wants to use the pictures.

We have made the arrangements for Barney's homecoming at the garage and trying to fix things up for him as best we can. We leave for the prison one week from now and Fred will have the next week off from doing seminars so he can deal with Barney's transition.

I pray it goes well for both brothers and I pray double that I did not make a mistake in pushing Fred to agree to help Barney. If it goes badly, I will accept the blame, even though it is Fred's final decision to go through with it. He has seen Barney recently and I have not. I am not sure what to expect when we see each other for the first time in three years.

I have figured out how to move my Living Ladder character into a romantic position. So far, I feel like I have a path for the main character (me) to get to the 2nd main character (a university professor) and there will be some conflict because that is always a good thing to have in a romance story, before they find their common ground and fall in love.

Fred sees me writing in bed sometimes and I am sure I make deeply thoughtful or puzzled faces when I do not write for a time. It is in Vietnamese so he can't read over my shoulder, and it is easier to write in my own language.

When he asked me what I am writing, I told him the truth. I am hoping this story, or others I write in the future, will help me get more work in acting by doing my own story ideas and that can lead to extra money for writing and producing credits.

Fred asked if I am writing a book and I said no, just a story line that I can fill in with other ideas, characters and scenes. Maybe it will not be so specific and detailed like a book, but more like a short story or book summary.

I am getting ideas and techniques on how to do this from my acting classes and the teachers. When I think I have a good product, I will translate it into English and have Takeela review it and make suggestions. If it looks good to her, she can try to shop it around to people in the industry for possibly turning it into a film.

I think the story is different enough to be unique but with the right kind of story formula that people like to watch. I take notice of these kinds of things more often now when I watch movies and TV shows and relate them to what I learn in my classes. My eyes are much more open now to the possibilities.

Fred is impressed at my thoughts on the matter and is proud of me to make this effort, then he asked me what the story is about. I am shy to tell him the details but did say the focus is on a romance about a very tall young woman who is lonely.

"Oh, an autobiography?"

I smiled and said "Well, maybe a little."

He respects my privacy and did not ask more. I will tell him when I feel the story is more complete.

Homecoming

Saturday March 26
Dear My Diary,

Yesterday, we drove two hours to the state prison to pick up Barney. Ca stayed home to have most of a day off and just have dinner ready on our return. We brought some clothes like khaki trousers and black jeans, some medium size shirts of different styles and a pair each of loafers and athletic shoes. Nothing expensive, of course, but suitable and durable for the time being. Fred took down his sizes the last time he visited. The officials let him put on his new clothes after inspecting everything.

After signing the release papers and setting his first parole appointment, Barney and Fred came to the car. Barney looks kind of empty in the new clothes. He has lost so much weight that I barely recognized him.

The children and I got out of the car to meet him. Frankie stood up straight and said, "Hello Uncle Barney, I am your nephew Frankie," putting out his hand to shake like we practiced. Barney gave a small smile and gently shook Frankie's hand saying, "Nice to meet you, Frankie."

Lois had been staring at Barney with her thumb in her mouth, but when he looked directly at her, she turned her head into my shoulder. Barney said, "That's okay. I know kids can be like that. Give her time."

I reached out my hand and said, "It's good to see you again." I was not sure what else to say to a man who just came out of prison and was such a jerk to me in the past, but I wanted to be polite and make a new start with him.

"It is good to see you too, Kim. The children are beautiful." I thanked him for the kind words and almost felt like Barney is another man by the way he spoke.

Fred asked Barney if he was hungry to which he replied, "For anything but their food," jerking his thumb backward. We kind of laughed and got in the car. Fred drove with Barney up front and me sitting between the car-seats in the back.

We stopped at a family restaurant near the freeway and had lunch. The lack of normal chatter we have with each other at mealtimes made me feel like we had just come from a funeral. Barney was quiet, polite and did not talk much and the children were not comfortable with this stranger at our table.

They colored on the placemats and ate chicken fingers and applesauce. I know Frankie wanted to ask questions about the jail, but we had told him ahead of time that is something not to talk about unless Uncle Barney brings it up first.

Fred explained that we will go to their parents' home next and meet with Mom and Pops. Barney nodded in understanding. He ate slowly, with his eyes closed, like he wanted the food to last forever. I do not know what it is like in prison, but I think eating slowly with your eyes closed is not what they do.

On the drive back to Riverton, Fred played soft rock music and Barney mostly looked out the windows and did not say much. Suddenly, Frankie asked "Uncle Barney, are you happy to see us?"

Barney turned around and smiled at Frankie. "Yes, I am. I am very happy to see you all."

"Then why don't you talk to us?"

Barney looked a little embarrassed, so I said, "Frankie, why don't you tell Uncle Barney about what you are doing in pre-school?"

"Have you ever been to pre-school Uncle Barney?"

"Maybe, but it was a long time ago."

Then Frankie talked about his friends and the hamster they take care of and learning his ABC's and singing songs. Barney looked amused and sometimes Lois chimed in with "Me too! Me too!" It made the trip go faster and the mood lighter.

When we pulled into our driveway, Barney expressed surprise. "So, who lives in our old house?"

"We do," Fred said simply.

Fred wanted us to all go in together as we know Pops is not wanting to see Barney, but maybe with the children, Frank will have a softer reaction.

We knocked on the door and their new dog Jack is barking and jumping to greet us. Maggie opened the door and let us in. She gave Barney a big hug and kiss on the cheek before hugging and kissing the children, then us. Frank was nowhere in sight. She told Barney, "He doesn't talk very well."

Barney straightened his back and put a smile on his face, but the smile looked tired and forced and I could see he was nervous as Maggie brought Frank out from the bedroom in his electric wheelchair. He came about halfway towards us and stopped. His expression was hard, even with the children here.

"Hello, Dad."

Frank wheeled around, putting his back to us.

"I'm sorry for what I did. I want to make things…"

Frank rolled back to his room and the dog followed. The door slammed.

"…right." Barney's head slumped. "He may not talk very well, but that was loud and clear."

Frankie asked, "Why is Grandpa mad, Mommy?"

Barney said, "Because Uncle Barney was a bad boy."

Maggie shook her head in embarrassment. "I was afraid this might happen. I am so sorry, Son."

Barney shook his head. "No, I deserve it. I don't blame him."

"Fred says you are going to work for him and stay at the garage. Is that what you are going to do?"

Barney nodded, "Fred's helping me get back on my feet. I got debts to repay. I don't want to mess this up. I don't want to go back."

Maggie hugged and kissed Barney again. "See that you don't. I believe in you, Barney. We all do." Then to Fred, "Thank you for helping Barney. You are a good brother. And a good son."

We went back to our home and I put the children down for a nap. I introduced Cousin Ca to Barney and helped her finish making dinner. Fred went to his office to make some calls and Barney sat quietly watching us from the breakfast bar while drinking coffee.

I could see his eyes moving around the kitchen and dining room, seeing all our things in the house he grew up in, but his eyes looked…what? "Empty" I think is the word to describe them. Barney looked tired, thin and empty.

I must stop now. I am too tired and sad to write more. Good night, Dear My Diary.

Dear My Diary,

Back to when we were cooking dinner: The children were sleeping and Barney was quiet and thoughtful for a while, then he said to us, "Fred. Kim. I want to thank you for taking me in. I meant what I said earlier. That I don't want to mess this up. I don't want to go back to prison."

He looked at me directly and continued, "I'm really sorry for everything I said and did to you. You're nice. You're a nice lady and the kids are sweet. You didn't deserve any crap from me. I was an asshole."

Then he directed his words at Fred, "I read a lot of books in prison. I read that book you were in. The Blue Collar Millionaire. I was so blind to not see what you were doing, what you were building, what you did for the folks and what you do for the community. Bunny told me you owned the house we were living in and how you cancelled the rent after I was arrested. That was real decent of you. I'm sorry I gave you such a hard time about doing what you do. You didn't deserve it either. You did way better than I ever did…or can ever do."

Barney got quiet again, tears trickling down his cheeks. "I screwed up. I screwed up bad. I made the folks lose everything. I lost everything. And Fred, when you lost your temper and broke those handcuffs to come after me, I thought I was going to die right there. I thought sure you were going to kill me." Fred turned away from Barney to stir a pot that did not need stirring.

"You were right for me to tell the truth. I did. I did tell the truth. Everything I could. The sentence wasn't so bad as I expected. But after that…" Barney shuddered like a horse with biting flies, recalling things best left unspoken.

He sighed. "Anyway, I really want to say thank you and I'm sorry for everything. I won't let either of you, or Michael, or anyone else down again. I want to repay my debts and…and try to turn my life around."

I came around and put my hands on Barney's shoulders as Fred said "You can turn your life around if you really want to. We will help you, but you also have to help yourself. Help yourself achieve the goals you want, but also stay within the limits of the law and common courtesy and decency while you do it." Barney nodded in understanding. This is exactly the kinds of things Fred says to his DD groups and now he is telling his brother this with all his heart.

Barney looked better after getting all this off his chest. I believe he will try his best to be good, but as Fred has said many times before, "I only trust Barney as far as I can throw him."

The children woke up from their nap and came to see their Uncle Barney. Dinner was more relaxed and pleasant than I expected. The children are getting used to their new uncle and Barney appears less empty now that he had spoken his heart to us.

Again, he ate slowly, methodically, and often with his eyes closed. Frankie started to do this too, imitating his uncle, but I tapped his arm and shook my head at him. I don't think he was trying to make fun of Barney, but simply imitating something different that he sees.

At the last minute, Fred and I agreed to let Barney stay in our house this one night, not at the garage like we planned. It is too late in the day, Barney is clearly very tired and he seems genuinely contrite about his past. Moreover, the angry, nasty way he looked and spoke to people is gone from him.

We have one spare guest room for Barney to sleep in with a big soft bed…His first real bed in three years. Again, he thanked us for our kindness before retiring.

As we undressed for the night, I expressed surprise at how much Barney has changed. Fred said, "I did not share this with you before, as what happened to him was pretty rough, but according to the prison counselor…" Barney was often made a victim of bigger, stronger prisoners who would take his food when the guards were not looking. They beat Barney frequently and forced sexual acts on him, especially in the early times when he mouthed off and insulted others. He ended up in the hospital several times heavily bruised and sometimes with cuts and broken bones.

Fred thinks there might be brain damage too, but he is not sure. Maybe the brain damage made Barney gentler? Maybe he is this way because he is sorry and wants to start fresh? Will he have angry outbursts later? I have many questions and Fred does not know the answers.

"I agreed to take Barney in after the explanations from his counselor and after meeting with Barney, observing his behaviors and asking lots of questions to see what answers he would give me. For better or worse, I chose to take a chance with him. It may be a mistake, but I am willing to believe he will change."

I thought of one more thing. "Will you tell Barney about the fake handcuffs?"

Fred's eyes got big. "Oh, no! No, no and no. Not ever. And don't you dare say anything either. If he thinks I am strong enough to break steel cuffs…then he will always think twice anytime he gets an idea to make trouble. What he does not know about that day will keep everyone safer for a long time…especially Barney!"

So many secrets…

Lois: When I was thirteen, I did one of those stupid things kids do and tried to shoplift a lipstick at the urging of so-called friends. I was caught and when the store manager learned I was a Starbuckle, he called the police and refused to press charges as long as the police escorted me home and had my parents informed. I will never forget what the manager said while we were waiting for the officers to arrive: "I don't want you to turn out like your uncle."

Up to that time, we were all aware that Uncle Barney had been a lawyer, had gotten in serious trouble and spent time in prison. Barney had alluded to that fact many times, but nobody would give specifics. With my getting caught and avoiding a juvenile record, Dad had Uncle Barney come to the house that Saturday and he described to all five of us what kind of guy he was when he was younger, how he was arrested and sent to prison for multiple crimes along with how he cheated Grandma and Grandpa out of their home and business. The very home we were sitting in that day!

He described prison in some detail but not as much as we learned later…I mean, we were still kids after all. Finally, he said he was really sorry for all he had done, the people he had hurt and that he was still repaying the debts he owed to the victims, and would be doing so until the day he died.

I remember crying through a lot of his story…largely out of shame for what I did to my family and partly because of what Barney did to his own family. Later, I went back to the store, apologized to the store manager and thanked him for doing what he did. Since that day, none of us have ever spent a day in jail or been charged with anything worse than minor traffic violations.

Dear My Diary,

Ca stayed home with the children as we took Barney to the garage to meet Michael and show him around. Barney has never been to the garage since before it went out of business almost ten years ago. First, we went up to the living area with his bags. "Bags" is really not a good word. Barney brought very little home from prison. The clothes he has now came from us and what we got were a few things based on Barney guessing at his sizes. Maybe he can find better fitting clothes from things we have in inventory…and this describes a word I recently learned in acting class: Irony.

Barney looked around and said "Wow, this is…different." I thought to tell Barney that Bunny helped Fred design the living spaces, but decided that might not be a good thing to bring up. Maybe he does not want to talk about Bunny. He has not asked about her yet.

We asked Barney if he knows how to cook and he admitted not very much. We did not think so. Michael said he will make sure that Barney gets fed and hopes his cooking will be okay. Fred told Barney that one of his duties will be to learn some basic cooking from Michael and us as he needs to become more self-reliant, and Barney nodded in understanding.

Then we gave Barney the "five-dollar tour" starting from the roof and working our way down to the first floor where Michael does much of his work. We explained the different areas and how they work together efficiently. Barney kept nodding, but I am not so sure he understands everything we are saying. He will need time to train and build some skills. I remember how confusing it was for me during the first months.

We also let Barney know about the Lee family who rents all but one of our greenhouses on the roof for their produce and herb business and not to be concerned if they come over to tend and harvest their crops. We showed Barney the greenhouse we keep for ourselves and he can pick what he wants and needs for meals.

Michael went back to his work and Fred told the story of how he came to own the garage: the auction, the people who came to support Frank and Maggie, how there were no bids after Fred met the bank's minimum bid to buy it. Barney listened, but would not look directly at Fred as he told the tale. Afterward, he apologized again for the trouble he had caused.

"I just want to be clear on how I came to take back the garage for our family and the support we had from so many people. I want you to take this story, and these surroundings, and use it as a starting point for yourself. You will live here, eat here, sleep here and work here. This place will be a constant reminder of what our family's life had been, and what it has become."

Fred gave Barney a GnG gift card for $200, explaining that this is his food money for one month and every month after that it will be reloaded. That is $6.66 per day and he needs to use it with care. To make the point clearer, Fred, Barney and I will make a grocery list of what Barney wants for food this week, then we will take him to GnG and go through the store, showing his brother some tips and tricks for getting good value for his food money.

Of course, these are the same tricks Fred taught me when I first came to America…now he has to show his brother who had let his mother and Bunny shop for food in the past.

We got the groceries and Fred showed Barney how to use the gift card with the cashier. At the garage, Michael has one area of the fridge and shelves and Barney has another, to keep things separate. Michael does not drink alcohol and Barney did not try to get beer which makes me feel better for now.

Finally, Fred and Michael found some good fitting work clothes, shoes and boots they had put to the side before Barney came, so he will have what he needs to start working. Barney did not complain that they are used clothes, but they are clean and in good condition. Barney thanked us for all the time and help to get started and told Michael "Just tell me what to do and I will do it. I want to make things right."

Barney keeps saying this kind of thing over and over. I hope he means it for true. Fred and Barney made lunch together and Ca came with the children and we played until it was time to eat. I was touched, watching Fred give instructions on simple cooking steps and Barney watched and did and helped. I made sure to compliment the food and Frankie gave his uncle a "two thumbs up!" for his tasty lunch.

One part I forgot to mention about Barney at GnG: As we were shopping, a man walked by and said something to Barney I did not understand. Barney got upset and said "Hey!" to the man, who turned back and said "You got something to say?" in a not nice way.

Barney closed his mouth tight and turned away from the man who smiled and said "I didn't think so," before walking away. I asked Fred "What did the man say?" and Fred gave a little head shake like to say "Not now".

Later, I learned the man said to Barney "Wanna buy an island?"

It took a moment for the meaning to sink in, then I said "Ohhh!"

Fred commented, "The old Barney would have raised hell with the guy. The new Barney didn't. He didn't want to make a scene. I was impressed with his self-control." Maybe he was afraid to get in a fight, causing him to go back to jail. I feel sorry for Barney to get this kind of treatment from a stranger, but also proud that he kept silent and in control.

Dear My Diary,

Yesterday was Barney's first day of work with a big project to get him started. Recently, Michael bought a locker with several hundred thousand sport cards. All of them are in plastic sleeves and most look to be in very new condition. We think the person who owned the locker probably died and either his family did not know about the collection, or did not care. Either way, it is not junky stuff like we often find.

Fred and Mike are not so well versed in sports collectables and to carefully sort and appraise all these cards would take many months. But Barney has been very passionate about sports all his life and he will know far better than us who are the more popular players and teams during what years, and who is not.

Fred decided to test Barney and determine his depth of knowledge as well as his willingness to do this kind of work. Before Barney was paroled, Fred and Mike went through one box of cards and researched their value through Ubiddit and certain sports card websites, making a list of the top valued cards and putting the list away. There are about a thousand cards in the box and it took us three full days to complete the task.

They set up an area on the first floor with a big desk, lamp and computer. Fred explained what they wanted Barney to do with the box of cards and set up the research websites for him. Barney looked around and said "Are you serious?"

Fred said yes, of course, this is part of what we do. Research all the things we want to sell, determine their prices and the best way to sell them.

Barney said, "No, I mean…" and he waved his hands around the room and desk area. I think we all understood right away. He has been in prison for three years and we are putting him to work in a room with no windows. We all looked at each other and felt bad.

Fred mumbled an apology, "I wasn't thinking. You don't have to work down here." We moved everything to the living room in front of the large windows where the morning sun comes in until early afternoon. It took less than an hour to reset everything and Barney looked more at ease with the new location. Fred went over the basics again, asking Barney to make a list of the most valuable cards and their approximate values. Barney nodded and we left him alone. That was about 10 am.

Six hours later, Mike called to say Barney had completed the assignment. Fred went back and found his brother had sorted everything by years, teams, card companies and a separate pile of the most valuable cards.

Barney's list of cards and values closely matched those to what we found and took a fraction of the time. Barney said it was easy to sort out the good cards and teams and he used the internet for ones he was not completely certain about, then he kept the four websites open and averaged out what they estimated as fair value for the best cards and full team sets. Since the cards appear to have been put in their plastic sleeves as soon as they were opened, their values will be even higher as they are in excellent condition.

Mike will start photographing and listing the best individual cards on Ubiddit first, the full team sets second and the rest will be set aside and added to partial sets as more boxes are sorted.

We took Barney to our home for dinner as a way of saying "thank you" and "good job" for his first day's effort. Barney helped me make noodles and a fresh tomato sauce with vegetables (another cooking lesson).

I hate to say this, but I was nervous that Barney would do or say something rude like the last time we had a dinner with him, but Barney was very kind and interested in learning.

After dinner, Frankie and Lois climbed up in uncle's lap and he read a story book to them. I think Fred made a good decision to help Barney, but I know he is not fully trusting of his brother, especially when he becomes more comfortable outside of prison. Fred is afraid Barney will go back to making problems or creating new schemes. "Only time will tell us," I said.

Ba and Me did not go back to Vietnam after Tina's wedding. They decided to stay here to spend the time they can with sister before she goes to London. My parents are very impressed that Fred is helping his brother after so much bad blood between them. Fred is a big man in their eyes to do this thing and helping his brother get on a better path will also help Fred in his future lives.

They had never met Barney before his arrest, but we had dinner together tonight. Ba and Me were courteous to him and Barney returned their attitude in kind. Ba Frank is a different man altogether. He refused to come for dinner and said he does not want to see Barney anymore. No forgiving and no forgetting. This attitude is a kind of poison for the soul…but I can't fault Frank for his attitude, either.

The New Barney Meets the New Bunny

Monday April 11, 2005
Dear My Diary,

I was at Bunny's store when Michael came in through the back door and said hello to us. "I have a new helper I'd like you to meet," and Barney came in, glancing nervously around. Michael, of course, knows Barney is Bunny's ex-husband but he introduced them like he did to the other store owners/managers. Barney already knew that Bunny owns a store, but he did not try to ask her any questions. Maybe he is afraid of the answers.

Bunny smiled and put out her hand for him to shake, "Hello, Stranger." She said it in a soft, friendly manner. Barney shook her hand and said hello, but did not make eye contact with her. He looked painfully shy.

Barney helped Michael bring in the new inventory and take out things that are not selling well and then talked some business as Barney stood there quietly. When they finished, Bunny turned to Barney. "How have you been? Michael treating you okay?"

"Uh, I'm fine. Yeah. Mike's a good guy. Kim and Fred are helping me. I guess…I guess you know that," and Barney made a quick look to me.

"Yes, I do. Thanks for dropping the stuff off. Looks like a good load."

As they left, Bunny called out, "See you next time!"

"Okay."

And Barney was gone.

Bunny turned to me, "Was that really Barney?"

"Yes, of course."

She shook her head, "He's REALLY changed. Wow."

"So have you," I said.

Saturday April 16, 2005
Dear My Diary,

I have an empty feeling in my heart today…Tina and Barry flew to London this morning. So many of us came to see them off that we blocked foot traffic giving last minute hugs and kisses and goodbyes. There were lots of tears on both sides even though we have known this was coming for the last six months.

Last night we had a big going away party at our Honeywood Heights home. The house is finally "company ready" and this was the perfect time to use it. I thanked Tina for all her help and advice she has given me with financial issues and encouraging me to be strong and proud of myself and for her ears when I needed to talk.

She thanked me for helping her get through the bad times after nine eleven and being supportive about her move to England with Barry.

"Barry is a wonderful partner. Don't let him get away like a too big fish!"

"Don't worry, I promise to keep him hooked," she replied, pulling the corner of her mouth with a pinkie finger and making the children laugh.

My parents have been getting emotional about Tina going away again: First from Vietnam, now from America. If she gets dual citizenship, England will be her third country. None of my family has been to Europe, so if we go, traveling there will be a big adventure.

Ba and Me agree Barry is a good pick for a son-in-law and they had fun conversations with him in Mandarin. Auntie was back from Saigon and all her family came. Even Thanh made a heartfelt good-bye to her sister and I could see it was genuine. So many nice things were being said and maybe we all hoped that Tina and Barry would change their minds at the last minute and stay, but that did not happen.

We bought their cars from them to resell so it will not be a problem to transfer titles when they are in Europe. They have already shipped most of their belongings back to London and what they did not take, we will sell and transfer the remaining money.

After the party, Fred said Barry will help him revise the DD book for a British audience. No big changes need to be made but it will be tailored to the British banking, retirement, investment and tax systems to make it more accurate for their way of doing things. I think that is a wonderful thing to do, but I wonder…did Fred ask Barry to help, or did Barry offer? When I asked, Fred shrugged and said it was a little of both. That sounds like Fred!

Anyway, they are gone now and I wish them every happiness. I don't know if we will go to the wedding in London yet, but we will see. We still have to talk about it.

Dear My Diary,

Every week, Barney has to go to the Parole Office to check in and get tested for drugs. Sometimes I take him when Fred is out of town or Barney will take the bus to the office. They ask him questions about what he did this last week? Did he leave the state? Did he meet with known criminals? Did he commit any crimes? Is he still employed? Did he take any illegal drugs and etc. I think it is silly to ask these questions because if he did something he knows not to do, he can just lie and say "no".

When I told Fred my thoughts, he told me that yes, people can and do lie to their parole officers. But if they are caught lying, if the police know things the parolee has done or learn later that he did when he said he did not, then he can be sent back to jail to serve more time. Now it makes more sense, when Fred puts it in perspective.

Three times now the parole officer has been to the garage without an appointment to do a surprise check-up. Barney was not there one time as he was out collecting things for resale but other employees there told the officer what Barney was doing and the other two times they searched for weapons, drugs and required proof that he is employed. Since Barney lives where he works, and Michael is his supervisor, this part is very easy to check. So far Barney has passed everything perfectly.

May 8, 2005
Dear My Diary,

I got such a shock today. It is Sunday and Ca stayed home to cook dinner while I drove the children to the mall. When I stopped for the light, Frankie said "I see Uncle Barney!" I looked where Frankie was pointing and I saw Barney. He was on a streetcorner with a sign saying "Anything helps" and someone was giving him money from their car window. I have seen this kind of activity many times, but not from Barney!

The light turned green and I moved forward with my mind racing…do I tell Fred? Do I go back and speak directly to Barney? Do I ignore what I saw? I cannot ignore this. I simply can't.

I found a place to turn around and go back to the corner where Barney stood. The light was green at the crossroad so I made a right turn and found a place to park. Barney had looked directly at our car, so he knows I saw him too. I took the kids out of the car and we all trooped over to Barney. I don't know if I am so brave or so foolish to do this, but I know I have to say something. If there is one thing I have learned in America, it is that speaking directly is the best way to talk to others.

I put on a smile and said "Hello Barney, what are you doing?"

Barney pretended not to see us as he stared up the street with his sign. His beard was stubbled and he was wearing some old, tattered clothes I did not recognize.

"Barney, please speak to me! Why are you doing this thing?"

Still, he stared straight ahead and I started getting nervous about the way he was acting. Is he on drugs? Is this part of the brain damage Fred had talked about? Will he get violent with us?

Frankie pulled on Barney's pant leg and said "Uncle Barney? It's me, Frankie! Do you want to go to the mall with us? Please?"

Softness came into Barney's face and he looked down at his little nephew. "I can't go to the mall right now, Frankie. I'm working." Then he looked at me with sad eyes. "I have debts to repay. I have to do this."

A car stopped at the light and a man rolled down his window, "I'd be careful if I were you, lady!"

I snapped back at him, "He is my brother…leave us alone!" Frankie added "Yeah, he's my uncle too!" and the man drove off shaking his head.

"Barney, please don't do this. Come with us to the mall for lunch and watch the children play." I reached out my hand, something I have never done with Barney.

He looked at my hand, then my face. "Am I really your brother?"

"Yes, Barney, you are really my brother. Come."

Frankie said, "Yeah! Come on Uncle Barney!" and Lois said "Yeah!" before hiding her face in my shoulder.

We put his sign in the trunk and Barney came with us to the mall. We had lunch at Anh Hai the Sandwich Guy and then took the children to the big indoor play area. Frankie is very good about playing with his sister while I watch.

As they played, Barney admitting to begging on different street corners every weekend when he is not working for us, setting aside the extra money to repay his judgments. Then he told me something I have not heard from him before. "I know it's not court mandated, but I am also starting to repay my parents for what I did to them."

His words were unexpected and I came very close to crying right there. Barney has grown a heart!

I asked Barney where he got the clothes he was wearing, and of course we collect so many old clothes that he just picked things that look "poor enough". He makes $40 to $60 per day and all of it is saved to repay his debts.

I told Barney I would have to tell Fred about this and I do not think he should be doing this anymore, "But I appreciate that you are trying to make the debts go down faster."

He nodded, but did not say he would stop. I told him that Lois' second birthday is next Monday, but as Fred will be gone that day, would he like to come over Sunday afternoon for some cake and wish her a happy birthday? He finally smiled and said he would like that very much.

After the children went to sleep, I showed Fred the "Anything Helps" sign. "Do you know where I found this?" I asked.

Fred shrugged, "On the street?"

"In your brother's hands. At an intersection near the mall."

Fred shook his head and I told him everything, including Barney's wish to repay his parents.

Fred said, "Okay, I will see what I can do to convince him not to beg, but making $50 a day is pretty good money for standing on a street corner."

I told Fred, "It is not right to do this. He is not homeless. He has a job and a free place to live."

Fred pointed out that the sign says "Anything Helps". It does not say "Homeless" or "Need Food". Just "Anything Helps". "If Barney wants to keep doing this and is not harassing people and is using the extra money to pay his debts faster, then I do not see the harm in it. Remember how he used to bust my chops all the time about being a garbage man? Well, look where we are today and look where he is now."

I see what Fred means, but I do not agree that Barney should do this. Fred agreed to come up with an idea to help keep Barney from begging on the streets and still make the extra money he wants.

I told Fred that I had invited Barney to the house for cake next Sunday afternoon for Lois' birthday and I hoped that would be okay. Fred agreed that was a nice thing to do and will make Barney feel more a part of the family.

After we went to bed, I thought about what happened when I was talking to Barney and the man told me to be careful. I looked through the man's eyes at an Asian woman with two small children speaking to a skinny, homeless-looking white man in ragged clothes and the woman saying "Leave us alone! He is my brother!"

Maybe the man thinks I am crazy! The memory made me laugh and I told the story to Fred. He wrapped his arms around me and said, "That was a very kind thing you said and did for Barney today. I am sure he appreciates it."

I nodded and said "I hope so. I meant it when I said he is my brother."

Fred sighed, "Yes, like it or not, he is my brother too."

May 16, 2005
Dear My Diary,

Today is our little girl's 2nd Birthday, but we celebrated yesterday because Fred is flying to Baltimore today. We almost had a big problem yesterday, but luckily it was over before it got too messy. I will explain:

In the mid-morning, we took our family plus Cam and Tam and my parents to the zoo. The children were very excited to see the elephants, monkeys, bears and the petting zoo. The twins have almost never gone to the zoo as their parents work all week, every week, so it was a fun time for them too. We had a picnic on the big lawn where ducks, peacocks, squirrels and pigeons come to visit for any snacks they can beg from us. Frankie pee-peed on a tree before Fred could stop him…I have found that he likes to do this in our yard and Fred says lots of little boys do this, but agreed it must stop. The twins couldn't stop giggling over their cousin's casual use of the outdoor bathroom.

The girls gave Lois some pretty shorts and shirts and socks with animals on them…all very cute things to wear for spring and summer. We got home about 3pm after dropping the twins off at their house and texting Thanh and Vo to let them know. The children napped for a while, then we had a light dinner with my parents before Frank and Maggie came over with presents and a cake with Bunny arriving soon after. It was almost six when the doorbell rang and I remembered that I had invited Barney. I had not considered who would be there and what their reaction might be, but it was too late now.

He looked good in pressed khakis, a polo shirt, polished loafers and a light jacket, topped off with a fresh haircut, a hint of cologne and a wrapped gift in his hands. "Hi Kim, I'm here to see the birthday girl."

I escorted Barney into the living room and his presence was met with a variety of reactions. My parents politely smiled and waved at him. Lois and Frankie ran over and hugged his legs, so he bent down to hug them. Bunny looked amused, like "Well, well! Look who's here!" and Fred shook his hand in greeting.

Maggie stepped over and hugged her son, telling him how good he looks but Frank looked like smoke would be coming out of his ears at any second. Clearly, he was not happy to see Barney and said, "Maggie, I'm getting one of my headaches. Take me home!"

"But we just got here, and Lois hasn't opened her presents yet."

"Please stay Grandpa!" both children begged.

Frank complained again, then Maggie whispered something in his ear that made Frank go quiet and they stayed until after the cake and ice cream had been served. I don't know what she said but I can imagine it was something like "don't be an old grouch" or "don't ruin the party".

Barney brought a popular doll figure in a pink sports car. You pull the car back on the floor and let it go so the car zooms forward. Lois was thrilled with it.

I introduced Barney to my parents again and explained how Barney is working very hard at the garage with Michael, speaking in English for Barney's benefit and my parents understood enough to smile and say "Very good!" to him. I know, from my own experience with Fred, how much some nice words in front of other people can mean to someone with low self-esteem. I could tell it made Barney feel better to hear this from me.

At one point during the party, I stepped into the kitchen and saw Barney and Bunny speaking in front of the sink. Barney's hand was on the counter and her hand was on top of his. They were speaking softly so I turned back to the living room. Are they making up? Reconnecting?

Lois got lots of presents, good wishes, and hugs from everyone, including brother Frankie. He is not jealous like he was last year. Maggie spent time with her son, praising Barney on how good he is doing.

Barney still has the tired, little bit slow kind of look on his face like when he first came home from prison. I have not heard or seen him get loud, braggy or try to start an argument as he was quick to do in the past.

I spoke to Fred about this, and we believe it is a permanent part of Barney's personality and not an act as we first feared. Fred calls it a "world weary" look, like someone who has seen much of the world and life in a bad way and has grown tired of it. He was in prison for only three years, but it was enough for Barney.

Bunny offered to take Barney back to the garage and I hugged him at the door, thanking Barney for spending time with us. Lois gave her uncle and auntie a kiss on the cheek and said "thank you" with our encouragement. She is a very happy little girl and all went well. I hope Frank sees the changes in Barney as he works to rebuild his life from the first floor.

Instant Boob Job

One of the stories about Uncle Barney's early attempts at post-prison creative selling came up at a family dinner while we were in our late teens and early 20's and were considered old enough to hear it. Here is Michael's take on the incident.

Michael: We bought a going-out-of-business inventory of new clothes including boxes of athletic socks. They weren't selling well so, behind my back, Barney came up with the "Instant Boob Job" that, according to his description, was an easy-to-use non-surgical process and was guaranteed safe and effective. He had "before" and "after" photos to make his point. Twenty-five dollars for a pair of socks to stuff a bra with. Apparently, he got the idea from watching Bernice enhance her own figure.

I never learned who posed for the pictures and didn't know about this product until we got a number of bad reviews, complaints and returned merchandise demanding a refund. After discussing it with Barney, he agreed that the description was misleading and should have been more honest and clearer.

We chose to refund everyone who had bought an Instant Boob Job, whether they requested one or not. It was an expensive lesson for Barney. I don't think he intended to cheat people but was just trying to get rid of socks.

After reporting Barney to Fred, as I was obligated to do, Fred wasn't mad at his brother and came up with a twist on Barney's idea. The three of us turned The Complete Instant Boob Job Kit into a novelty sale by creating and printing tongue-in-cheek instructions with diagrams on bra-stuffing and packed three pairs of different sized socks into a cleverly designed box made by a local vendor. We patented the kit and for twenty dollars plus shipping, the sales took off to the point where we soon had to order more cases of socks through Uncle Lo's company to keep up with demand.

After a few months, due to popular demand, the low cost of making the kits and its simple premise, a number of knockoffs came to market, flooding Ubiddit and local retailers, so we updated our boxes and advertising to say "The <u>Original</u> Complete Instant Boob Job Kit". We had pretty good sales for several years before finally selling the rights to a major wholesaler.

It seems that no ideas are really new ideas. I learned later that Fred had gotten his idea from a fad of the 1970's called Pet Rocks. A small paper box with air holes, straw bedding, a rock and cleverly written instruction on the care, feeding and enjoyment of your very own pet rock. The company made millions by cleverly marketing rocks to the public.

Dear My Diary,

Fred was visiting his parents when Mom announced, "Look what I got the other day!" and showed him a gift card from GnG. "It's for $200. Do you know how I got it?"

Fred thought a moment, then it came to him. Yes, it was from Barney. He has used less than $400 from the $600 we gave him during his first three months, so instead of using the last gift card for himself, he gave it to his parents. Maggie was touched by his gesture, as we are. Barney had told me he would start repaying his parents when we spoke at the mall. I was not sure that he would, but he did and I feel better about him.

I have finished my story project and have talked to Takeela. She read it over, thinks it has some promise and will shop "Ladder Girl" around to cable channels who specialize in romance stories. I will check to see if my family in Vietnam has any connections with film makers or studios. I believe someone will be interested in working with me as I am occasionally in the VN pop culture news. But then, maybe I am hoping for too much.

I wrote the story first in Vietnamese, then rewrote it in English. Sister Bunny helped me with editing my grammar, clarifying my language and spicing up the story in spots. She likes the story and her enthusiasm gives me encouragement. Now I have two versions, one for each language. What I sent to Takeela has dialogue and much more detail, but here is the summary:

Quy is a very tall young woman living with her working-class parents. Her job is to stock shelves, in a neighborhood grocery store. She does not have a boyfriend and is alone because men are shy of being seen with her. Her parents are too poor to send her to college, so she spends much of her free time at the library, reading scientific journals, going to museums and free lectures and learning more about subjects that stimulate her intellect.

At her job, she is often asked to help customers reach products on the high shelves. One day a very small, old woman complimented Quy on being a Living Ladder. She then asked if Quy would come to her home and help dust and move things around in the higher areas. Quy accepts, does the work and is paid for her time.

Soon, other customers hear about the Living Ladder girl at the grocery store and ask her to come over for similar jobs such as rearranging knick-knacks, hanging pictures, painting walls and the like. At first, Quy just accepted whatever money or gifts of food they chose to give her, but soon she saw the opportunity to make regular extra cash on the side. She placed an ad in the local newspaper as "Living Ladder Services", what she can do and her phone number. Soon, she is working one or two appointments every day, and more on her days off.

At one of the homes, a younger man was there who had her dusting cobwebs from the ceilings and corners of his apartment. He watched her work with interest and asked a few harmless questions as she stretched and waved her feather-duster about, but mostly he just watched until she finished. He paid her and asked her to come back the same time next week.

Soon she was getting more calls from men than from women to perform a variety of tasks. At one house, the same young man was visiting the owner of the home, a middle-aged man. The owner instructed what he wanted done and she went about doing it. The two men watched TV while she was working in the main room, but whenever she looked over at them, they glanced their eyes back to the TV. Clearly, the program was not their main interest.

At one point, she went into the pantry to take spider webs down and there was a ladder in the corner. She asked the owner about the ladder, and he explained that it was old and too weak to hold his weight. Her eyes could see the ladder was not old and looked sturdy enough.

That is when she understood that the men had her come over to watch her working. When her back was turned to them, they were looking at her bottom and long legs. When she spoke to them, they had more trouble focusing on her face than on her chest. Quy updated her business model.

Now, when she gets calls from men to do Living Ladder Services, she wears close fitting shorts, tight shirts, high heels and charges a higher price for her services. As long as there is no touching or suggestions for non-ladder services, she is happy to do this. Many of the same men called often to pay her to move something from one high shelf to another or dust ceilings. Without Quy asking, the men often offer up some reason why they could not do the job themselves such as a bad back, fear of heights and other silly excuses.

One day, she gets a call from an older man in need of her services. Before asking the usual questions about price and availability, the prospective client asked Quy about how well she could read. In her culture, illiteracy was not uncommon, especially among the working classes. It was an unusual question, but she happily listed the kinds of books and journals she often read.

The client agreed to her terms so she rode her bicycle in full Living-Ladder uniform to an address in the university district where she met the customer. When he answered the door, she had to look down farther than usual as he is in a wheelchair. The office is surrounded by high shelves filled with important looking books. There is a ladder on tracks running all the way around the room.

Quy's job was to bring down specific books from a handwritten list, replace stacks of books on a cart to their proper places and to dust the shelves. He explained how the books were categorized and he watched as she carefully followed his instructions until he was satisfied enough to get back to his projects.

As she worked, her glances showed the client was absorbed by his notebooks, computer and the volumes open before him. The books were easy enough to find, well-ordered by subject, author, and title. She did the work asked of her, but he paid scant attention to her bared legs in high heels teetering precariously on the ancient wheeled ladder.

The listed books covered topics in chemistry, physics and electro-magnetism. When she was done, he asked if she can come back at the same time three days hence. She agreed, was paid, and returned as scheduled.

On her next visit, it was the same routine, retrieving books from a list, returning others back to their proper places and dusting the shelves and spines of books with a feather-duster. He worked as if she was not there, paying no attention to her activity or making small talk. He was not unfriendly but aloof and very businesslike.

One day, the Professor is having an argument on the phone with a colleague about who discovered a particular compound and when and where. When the call is finished, he is clearly upset that he did not win the argument. After some silence, Quy quietly says something like "Excuse me for overhearing your conversation, but…" and states the correct information.

He asks her how she would know such a thing…he is still upset from the call and is challenging her. She hands him a book from the office library with a post-it note marking a specific page. She says she is done for the day and must go home now. After she is gone, he opens the book to the marked page and inside is the correct answer, as Quy had given it. This opens the door of respect towards her.

One day, he explains to Quy that until recently he had had use of his legs. A motorbike accident resulted in the death of his wife and his legs too badly damaged to walk very far, let alone to climb the ladders of his office library. It is the first time he has spoken to her about something not related to the books. This will also explain his very intense manner as he is grieving for his wife and is frustrated by his disability.

Quy said she recognized some of the books in the office library because she has read them from library loans. He asks her some questions about her interest in science and she answers back with intelligent answers. He asks her to come back in three days, as always, but before she goes, he allows her to borrow any book of her choosing from the shelves.

She stops wearing the shorts and tight shirts to the university office and the professor never comments on the change. Over time, he warms up to Quy and their relationship blossoms, more from a mutual interest in science and eventually she becomes his research assistant despite having no college degree. He helps get her into college with special grants and, over time, with therapy and her encouragement, he learns to walk again. They get married and live happily ever after.

I made it as a romantic comedy, with some drama. I made Quy with a sunny disposition who is friendly and nice to everyone and is clever too. There will be many happy and funny moments, especially in the beginning, to establish her personality. She uses her attitudes to overcome the professor's short temper and very business-like attitude in the beginning and he will warm up to Quy later as the relationship develops. He will not be an old man, but maybe ten years or so older than Quy.

That is the summary. I hope someone will like it.

It took a couple of years, but the story "Ladder Girl" was turned into a script, the script into a movie and made in Vietnam by one of the larger studios with some financial backing from our family. Mom got writing and producing credits along with this being her first leading role. It was well received by audiences and won several awards an Asian and European film festivals including nominations (but no wins) for Best Film. That was enough to get Hollywood's attention. Ladder Girl was remade into an American version with the male lead played by crusty but loveable leading man Conway Twitter and Mom reprising her role as Quy with the setting in New York rather than the original Ho Chi Minh City.

Kimmie: "Ladder Girl" was my big breakout role. It was such a busy and special time for me. I worked hard putting the story together, collaborating with script writers, casting director and other producers on how to portray the characters and all the little and big parts that go into any story.

So much work, but so much reward too including cementing my relationship with Takeela Rockett and her firm. Fred was a saint for his patience with me and the children had adventures in countries their friends could never imagine. My career has had its highs and lows, but it would never have happened at all without Fred and his support and belief in me.

Tuesday July 5, 2005

Fred and Crystal are working a full week of DD seminars in Ottawa. As they do not celebrate American Independence Day in Canada, it was the first time we have celebrated July 4th without Fred. It was not so lonely as Thanh and Vo closed their shops for the holiday and we had a picnic with both sets of parents and Ca in Central Park. Michael was also closed for the day, and I did not know whether to invite Barney or not.

I decided not to and am glad I did. Bunny and Barney came to the park in the early evening and we talked for a bit. I gathered that Barney had been to her store today and helped/hung out with her as she kept the store open all day and business was good. Ahh!

As we were chatting, Duck Island was less than 100 meters away. The idiom book Fred purchased for me includes the phrase "the elephant in the room". Duck Island is the elephant in the room everybody knows about, but no one will speak of. Despite that, Barney and Bunny looked happy and relaxed, seemingly without a care in the world. Perhaps I was the only one who was thinking about Barney's purchase and the problems that hit him like a summer typhoon.

After they went on their away, I reminded my parents about the island and the role it played in Barney going to prison. They laughed and shook their heads at the irony of it all. Ba said, "If that had happened to me, I would never enter this park the rest of my life for the shame of it all."

July 2nd was Barry and Tina's wedding. After much discussing and throwing ideas around, we decided it was best not to go. They already had a wedding here and we have so many things going on this summer. Add to it, the complications involved for international travel to a place we have not been to before with small children. I'm sure it was very swanky and posh.

Tina secured a job doing research for a British investment company looking for opportunities in Asia. It is the perfect job for the skills and knowledge she already has. They will honeymoon for one week in Scotland, then Tina starts her new job. I have heard that Scotland is very pretty and I hope she likes it.

Tina and Barry married on July 2nd, 2005. Mama always regretted not going, but there were too many pressing events going on for the family to make the time and effort to be there. The pictures and videos, even today, show a fairy-tale kind of wedding, paid for by Barry's parents.

It was much more elaborate than what Tina had wanted, but the wedding was largely for the friends, business associates and society guests of the family. Tina was pretty much alone without her family in attendance, but then it was that way too when she spent years in New York going to school and later working for Asia International.

"Mama's a Badass!"

September 14, 2005
Dear My Diary,

I had such a scary moment last week that my heart still races when I think about the danger Frankie and I were in. I will explain:

Ca was at her ESL class and I took the children to the garage to pick herbs and veggies from our greenhouse. I saw a junky-looking sports car in the lot, Michael's car was gone and the big garage door was wide open. I did not think Barney had purchased a car yet and I got a funny feeling that something was not right.

I went into the glovebox and slipped on three cutter rings, blade side to my palm. Lois was asleep and Frankie sat calmly in his car seat. I make a "shush" sign to him, saying I will be right back, then I cracked open the windows and locked the car.

As I walked into the garage, I heard a threatening voice from further back. I could see a younger man, skinny with greasy black hair in a long braid. He was overly-animated, loud and using a lot of profanity. Barney was standing there quietly saying, "No, I can't do that."

My insides went cold, but I straightened my shoulders and strode with confidence back to the men, saying in my strong voice, "What's going on here?"

The man turned towards me, back to Barney, then snapped his head in a double-take, a look of surprise on his face. "Who the hell are you?"

"I asked you first…who are you? What do you want?"

"I'm just talking some business here, not that it's any of *your* business," he said with a sneer.

"You better go, Corn." Barney said.

"Shut up, jailbird," he shot back.

I drew myself up taller, "If you are here, then you are my business. This is my building and this man is my employee. Again, what is your business here?"

The man looked annoyed and told me to "F" off.

"Do you kiss your mother with that mouth?" I said, using a line I have heard Fred use on foul-mouthed individuals. "It's time for you to go."

He laughed in an odd way and said, "I'll go when I'm damn good and ready. Now just run off and leave us alone, bitch."

Now I am mad. Scared, but mad. I am several inches taller and he is unhealthily thin. I pointed back to the open door, "Go now!"

Barney mumbled "It's okay. Just go Kimmie."

"Yeah, just go Kimmie," the stranger mimicked, adding "You're awfully big for a Chink. With a big mouth to match." His eyes were glazed and bloodshot. He came towards me, hands balled into fists. "You had best get out now before I cut you down to size."

I gave him another Fred line, "That is not an option."

The drug-addict that Barney called 'Corn' swung at my head, slow and clumsy, and I pulled back easily. He got mad and took two more swings at me, a little faster and getting closer but still missing.

"Your breath stinks worse than your girly fighting style," I taunted. I am not a fighter, but I am not a coward either. Getting him madder would also make him more careless. Adrenaline surged through my body as I waited for an opening.

On Corn's next, even wilder attempt to hit me, I pushed his arm along with my left hand, stepped in and slapped his cheek hard. Spit flew from his mouth as the cutting rings dug deep, drawing three angry lines of blood like a tiger's claw. He dropped to the ground, stunned by my powerful swipe. He touched his cheek and stared uncomprehendingly at the blood. I threw Corn's words back at him, "Now, just run off and leave us alone…bitch!"

Angered, he called me a string of nasty names as Barney stared open-mouthed at the man's cuts.

Corn staggered to his feet, pulled a double-edged knife from a sheath on his belt and began circling me, waving his knife and talking in threats.

Round two. I put on my Fierce 5 face and crouched like a sumo wrestler. I do not have a plan but will defend myself the best I can.

As his back faced the big doors, I saw a little figure running toward us. Frankie! Oh my God!

"You leave my Mommy alone!"

As the angry, skinny, drugged-up man turned to face a new threat, he took his eyes off me, the knife still pointing in my direction. It was time! I stepped forward and did the scissor snap I learned for the movie, almost without thinking. Pop!

Corn screamed. I jumped on his back and dug my knees directly into his shoulder blades, pinning him to the concrete floor. Barney kicked the fallen knife and it skittered away.

"Barney, call the police! Frankie, go back to the car and lock the door!"

Frankie stared at me a moment, then ran outside as the man screamed and threatened us. His arm was bent at an odd angle, his breathing became labored but he wasn't getting up until I did.

Barney stood over us, his hands shaking. "Shut up, Corn! She was in the Viet Cong and can kill you with her bare hands!" Then he kicked Corn in the head.

I slapped Barney's leg away as he tried to launch another blow and urged him to call 911 and stay with the children. Barney ran back to my car, scooping Frankie up in his arms as he went.

I can't believe what Barney had just said…that I am a Viet Cong soldier, the enemy of South Vietnam. I was only four years old when the war ended. Then I got an idea.

I leaned over to his ear and spoke in a low voice, "Barney should not have told you that I am Viet Cong. That is a secret very few know. Since you may be dead soon, I will tell you my secret code name. It is Co Gai Xinh Dep. It means 'Deadly Tree'. I am tall, quiet and full of death."

I made a clicking sound with my tongue and pushed my middle finger deep into the bundle of muscles at the base of his neck, just below the skull. "I can shoot you now and tell police it was self-defense…" Corn had gone quiet now, "…or you can do this one thing. Do you want to know the one thing?" The man grunted as he could barely breathe with my full weight directly over his lungs. "Get a real job. Be nice to people. Stop being bad. If you threaten or try to hurt me, my family or Barney, I will kill you before you can see me. Do you understand?" The man grunted again.

By now, the police had arrived. They took statements from me and Barney and placed Corn under arrest as the EMT's tended to his broken arm, scratches and swelling ear where Barney had kicked him. Based on what I overheard, he is well-known to the police from other crimes. I learned his name is Randy Wintercorn, which is why Barney called him Corn.

The children are safe and although Barney is not in trouble with the police, I think he will be in trouble with Fred.

Barney told the police that the man was demanding money and if he did not get it, he would report to Barney's parole officer that he was selling drugs to get him sent back to prison.

Barney admitted to me that this is not the first time criminals have threatened him and he swore to me that he is clean. I learned later that it is a common kind of scam for criminals to pull on each other. Besides, I know Barney is tested regularly at the parole office and he has never failed, so I believe him.

While Ca made dinner and the children were playing on the floor, I told of what all happened in the garage. Fred looked at me with a puzzled expression and said "I know the phrase Co Gai Xinh Dep…it does not mean 'Deadly Tree'."

I was surprised at his saying this and asked "Are you sure?"

Fred looked a bit doubtful, but said "Yeah. I had Michael teach me some phrases years ago. I thought Co Gai Xinh Dep means 'Pretty Woman'."

"Ding! Ding! Ding! You are correct!" I cried out happily and kissed my Nguoi Dan Ong Dep Trai, my Handsome Man. "But he did not know that, so I acted along with what Barney told him." Then I made a clicking sound with my tongue and pointed my finger at Fred. "My deadliest weapon!"

Fred said, "You are such a badass!"

Then Frankie laughed and said "Mama's a badass!"

Frankie: We now officially have, in writing, the first time I ever called my mother a "badass". I have zero recollection of that encounter but I was only about three years old. I also don't remember anything about Uncle Barney from that period either. Too young for anything to really stick and it has been a lot of years since it all happened.

Now Barney has to go away. Not out of state, but away from Riverton. It was not a difficult decision for Fred to make, as his brother has become a risk to our family and business holdings.

Michael was not aware that Barney has been contacted by local criminals, pressuring him to hand over money or things from our business and backing up their demands with threats of violence or a return trip to prison. Barney has not caved in to anyone yet, but I am sure it has not been easy for him, either.

When we had Barney come over to discuss our decision, Bunny came with him…not just for moral support, but they have become a couple again. It wasn't easy, but we emphasized that it would be best if he can move to another part of the state and away from the local hoods, at least for a while, until things settle down and memories start to fade. At the same time, he still needs to repay his debts and we will try to do what we can to help him get employment.

Bunny spoke up and already has a plan: Her mother lives in Norwood, about two hours away, is very ill and her current husband has abandoned her. Norwood is the largest town in a rural county with no resale or consignment shops in the area.

"This is a perfect time to sell my store, move back to Norwood to care for Ma and reopen Bunny's Bargain Hutch. Barney will be my partner; the state will give us money as caretakers and I will make sure that money is paid regular to the estate administrators. Plus, it's easy to get a transfer of parole officers. I checked it out, already."

From our conversation, I got the idea that Bunny was already planning to help her mother, and this last incident was the push needed to put her plan into motion.

Fred looked pleasantly surprised as he was expecting an argument about forcing Barney to move. "Sounds like a win-win situation to me. Barney, what do you think about this idea?"

"Yeah, we've been discussing a move, but I didn't know how you would feel about it. Me up and leaving from where you could watch me and all." Barney took hold of Bunny's hand, adding "Bernice and I are getting along better now than when we were married. She's helping me with things and I want to be a better man for her."

Bunny smiled and patted his hand. "You *are* a better man!"

"I'm sorry this isn't working out like you wanted, and that I put Kim and the kids in danger," Barney said, his head lowered before looking directly at me. "But what you did was totally awesome. *Damn!*"

"Wished I had been there to see it," said Bunny. "Did you really break his arm?"

"And scarred his face for life," added Barney, with growing enthusiasm.

"Well, that went easier than I expected," Fred said with a sigh.

Bunny will drive to Norwood to find a storefront to lease ("Lots of empty buildings since the missile site closed") while Barney takes care of the Riverton store. Once that is done, she will sublet the store, pack up her inventory and move into her mother's home with Barney to start their new life.

I will fly back to Vietnam with Ba, Me, Ca and the children next month while Fred stays a temporary bachelor and keeps busy with the seminars. They are regularly booked out several months in advance now and Dissolving Debt has sold over half a million copies.

As a side business, Fred has more than fifty wealthy clients that he is helping with their debt problems. I have a hard time saying 'wealthy clients with debt problems' with a straight face, but Fred explained to me that many of them have issues with messy divorces, businesses or investments that are losing money, drug or gambling habits and family/friends using his clients as human ATMs.

Fred generally helps them over the phone, email or faxes, but sometimes he has to fly to where they are and "hold their hands" as he calls it, and look things over in person to see what can be done. Many do not want to follow Fred's guidance and insist on less painful methods that still allow them to keep up their accustomed lifestyles. Fred often complains "So many dollars and so little sense, but as long as they are paying…"

We will be gone for a full month to see everyone and I hope to speak to some film agents about Ladder Girl. I can't wait to see how things are going with the orphanage and make sure our money is spent wisely and the children are being helped as they should.

October 15, 2005
Dear My Diary,

We are days away from leaving for Vietnam and on Wednesday a woman came to our home and handed me a notice from the courthouse. I read it, but do not understand what it means so well. Since Fred is in Denver this week, I took it to Maggie who read it and told me that Randy Wintercorn is suing me for his injuries.

I panicked, "Do I have to pay?"

"You should let Fred's lawyers handle this but don't worry Kim, he attacked you and you were defending yourself. Nothing will probably come of it, but from my experience, you never know what the courts will finally decide. This guy has nothing to lose by trying to get money from you."

Yesterday, Fred looked over the notice and faxed it to one of our lawyers to handle. Maybe I will not even have to go to court!

The case was dismissed for reasons of self-defense and nothing more ever came of it. However, since Riverton is a small city, there were several times she saw Randy and his triple-scarred cheek over the years. If he saw her, she would narrow her eyes and glare at him (just to mess with his head) and he would suddenly find a reason to cross the street or look elsewhere.

Ba and Me were busy all summer buying name brand cell phones, cosmetics, PMP's and games, thong underwear, showy watches and other things popular with young people in Vietnam. Thanh and I taught my parents how to use coupons, the best places to buy clearance items and ordering bulk lots of desirable goods from Ubiddit.

Hundreds of small, profitable items can fit into one suitcase and each of us, including the children, are allowed two fifty-pound suitcases plus some carry-ons. My family will not need all that we are allowed, and Ba said we can bring just a few clothes in a carry-on for Frankie and Lois. This will free up space for resellables and he can give his grandchildren lots of new clothes and toys from their inventory. I am guessing each suitcase will hold roughly several tens of thousands in future profits. No wonder Ba is so generous with his inventory!

I know Ba and Me will put only a few clothes and personal things in a carry-on and leave everything else here. Parents will sell some things on the company website and consign others to trusted sellers in the markets for a share of the profits. The money they make from this will be used to buy another house in Riverton next year to use as a rental.

At first, I thought I still had many clothes at my parents' home that I can wear so I would not need much. Then I thought how I will most certainly be interviewed and photographed for the Asian papers and magazines. I also want to meet with entertainment managers to consider filming Ladder Girl or get work in television shows and movies.

Moreover, my clothes over there are of an older style and won't fit so well as my body has become more full-figured from making babies and lots of exercise. What I have will be fine for around the house, but not for business. Sooo, I went shopping!

Tree Top Gals has moved to a bigger storefront and all the clerks know my name. I'm a VIP! I got several outfits and dresses that flatter my figure and have bold colors and patterns to make me stand out. I need to "pop" a bit for the cameras and give the right impression to fans and business people alike.

Six people, twelve suitcases plus carry-ons and most will be full of things to sell. When I came to America, Fred and I had four suitcases and almost all of it were my things to start a new life. How funny to think about it now.

Barney and Bunny will finish moving to Norwood by the end of the month. Bunny found a storefront in a strip mall along the county highway at the edge of town. "One of the less deserted areas," as Bunny described it. They will live with her mother, help pay the bills and keep the house maintained.

Bunny understands it will be a struggle to make good income from walk-in customers, but she has lots of experience selling online and finding innovative ways to make money in this business. I believe she and Barney will make a success at best and a basic living at worst.

Maggie and Frank stay active with church and many of her siblings and older neighbors can help out so our being gone will not be a hardship for them. I think Frank is happy that Barney is going away, but Barney almost never went to see them.

Bunny told me confidentially that Maggie visits with Barney when Frank is taking a nap and Ca or someone else watches him. She is keeping up the relationship with her son and I am touched to hear this. I know she loves Barney, even with all the bad things he did to them, but he looks to be a different man. It is not fake, I am sure. No one can act so consistently for so long.

Lastly, Auntie Giang will leave Riverton soon for Vietnam. This is the third year she has spent the winter in her homeland. She intends to sell the stores soon and retire permanently to Vietnam. In fact, she is building a house in the countryside where it is quiet and she can grow flowers and herbs and be near her extended family while taking trips to Riverton in the summers to be with her American family. She will keep her home in America, just like my parents, but opposite!

October 27, 2005
Dear My Diary,

I almost forgot how warm it gets here! It is so good to see everybody…especially our newest family member! Vui is so cute, I think she takes after Me with her smile and dimples and Phung is a very good Ba. He changes diapers, makes funny faces and even gives baths! Thao and Phung have always looked happy together, but now it feels…multiplied! I think that is a good word for them: Love multiplies their happiness.

Lois and Vui are very close in age, just a few months apart, and they get along beautifully and Frankie is a good big brother around the girls. Phung and Thao are thrilled at Frankie's Vietnamese…much better than his father! It is natural because he is around me and Ca so much, and even as we try to speak more English around him, he still hears us during our casual conversations. Ca's English has greatly improved over the last three years. Phung conversed with cousin in English and is impressed.

Phung says his English is slipping a little here and there…he can't always remember the right word for what he needs sometimes. I told Phung that I have something that might help his English.

"What is it?" And I handed him a present. Like the gift he gave me just before I first left home, I gave Phung a book: his own autographed copy of Dissolving Debt. Not that he needs the information, certainly, but I thought it would be a good way to show my appreciation of how I have grown and changed.

Fred wrote "Thanks for having my back during my first visits to Vietnam. Wished I could tag along this time and catch up on the joys and headaches of fatherhood, but you know me. Work! Work! Work! Brother Fred"

And I wrote "You are our best brother and son to our parents. Thank you for sharing your knowledge of America and ideas about Fred to me. It helped me understand him better and my life could not be better. Chi Kim"

Since I am back in my old neighborhood, things are so much different. Not the neighborhood…it still looks very much the same: the same neighbors with a few new children and a few less elders; the same shops and food stalls and street sellers; the same wonderful smells of Pho and grilled pork and fried tofu with garlic.

What is different are the sounds I hear when I walk the streets: "Oi, Kimmie! You are back!" and "Chimera! I see you with Rock Rollins…Number one!" and "Pham Kim, so good to see you again! You look even more beautiful than before." And I do not hear "Cay Dua! Why you so tall?" and "Walking Bamboo! How is the weather so high in the sky?"

I wave. I greet. I introduce my children and Ca and tell people what I am doing in America. Everybody reacts with surprise to my Caucasian-looking son and red-haired Asian daughter, marveling over my son's command of our mother tongue and their good manners.

All the neighbors know about my movies and commercials or have seen me in the newspapers and magazines. I am certain that many tell friends and strangers "I know her…she is from my neighborhood. Yes, really!"

If I did not have that one recessive gene in my blood, I wonder what I would be doing now? I have thought about this since returning home and now I know the answer: I would work for my parents in the warehouses, find a nice man to marry, make healthy children and keep good relations with my sisters both near and far.

Over time, I would become a manager and help run the business when Ba and Me retire. It would not be an exciting life, and even a little boring, except for maybe taking business trips and occasional holidays to Hong Kong or Singapore or Thailand because I am Pham Lo's daughter, the businesswoman. And people would not call me names or make me feel bad for looking so different from everybody else.

But the reality is that I do have the recessive gene in my blood and I did grow very tall. I found a nice man to marry and I get to work with him in our own businesses. We have healthy children and I keep good relations with my sisters and parents.

But my life is not boring. I go places and do things and know people that I never would have thought possible, or even realistic, for someone like me. In my current life, people do not call me names, because I don't look like their version of 'normal'. I have accomplished so much in a short span of time and have earned the respect of many people whom I respect in return.

Most importantly, I am happy. Very, very happy.

The Triplets

Tuesday, November 1, 2005
Dear My Diary,

I can't believe what I did today, but I am glad I did it. I hope Fred will understand and accept what happened because what is done is done and I am not changing my mind…or my heart.

After making arrangements to bring supplies of clothes, toys, diapers, schoolbooks and new sleeping mats to the orphanage near my old home, Ca, the children and I met with the head monk and director of the orphanage. The way it looks now is sooo different from when we first saw it just three years ago. The outside is nicely painted in saffron yellow and white with a beautiful sign over the front doors.

Upon entering, the air is cool and dry, and the concrete walls are covered by rolls of foam padding in pastel and neutral colors with fun pictures everywhere painted by the local artists and creative staff members and even some of the children.

The orphans are clean with good clothes and the school rooms have proper desks and newer books and chalkboards. As the students stood up to greet us, their eyes went wide to see me before bowing in unison and greeting us as honored guests.

I introduced myself, told of my growing up nearby and having been a member of the temple for a long time. The children are about six to eight years old and I explained to them how important it is to have an education so to better find a path in life to bring them success and happiness.

"Even without parents in your life, you need to trust the monks and teachers to help you be good citizens and not to blame bad luck or being an orphan or thinking there is no way to succeed. You must believe in yourselves and encourage each other to do your best. By doing so, many good things in life will come to you.

"I never thought I would have a happy life because I was too tall and awkward to be liked by any nice man. People called me names and teased me, so I was too shy to go out. I blamed my height which is something I cannot change.

"Then I found a man who taught me to be confident and proud of my differences. His family and friends treat me as their equal and I found work that uses my height to an advantage.

"I work hard and, because of my new attitude, I have respect from others, happiness and a good life. My height, which has not changed, went from being my sour lemon to sweet lemonade by the power of confidence, self-respect and positive thinking habits about myself and others."

The children politely applauded and the monk nodded in appreciation of my words. I hope I have given them some inspiration. I told our hosts they have done good work in bringing up the quality of living for the children and this will help them feel better about themselves and create the seeds for successful adults.

The director took us to the nursery where there are many babies and toddlers. Ca set Frankie and Lois amongst them to play. At first, they were shy but very soon they were playing with the other children.

As I looked around, I found a playpen with three little girls, about six months old. They were dressed differently from each other, but they shared the same features. It was too obvious, but I asked "Are they sisters?"

"Yes, identical sisters."

I picked one up and cradled her in my arms. She stared back at me with interest. I asked their age but the monks do not know exactly. They were left at the temple as very small babies about seven months ago so they are eight months, or a little less.

I asked if they have any physical or mental problems like from drug addiction or a strong illness? I was assured that the sisters are in good health and, like all the children, get vaccines and regular check-ups by visiting doctors and nurses.

"What is your plan for these sisters? Will they be adopted together?"

The head monk and director looked at each other briefly and the director explained that when people adopt, especially foreigners, they tend to want only one baby, sometimes two if they are siblings, but almost never will people adopt more than two. Cost is a big reason…the cost for adoption, and then to raise so many children at once.

I sang a bit to the baby and I saw a band on her wrist. Trang. I made some baby talk to Trang and picked up another. Her name is Lang and she cried a bit about being picked up. I checked her diaper but there was no rash. Perhaps it is because I am a stranger. The third girl is Sang. The names rhyme and sound musical. Trang, Lang and Sang. One of the workers said the girls have a very sweet nature and are easy to care for.

I asked the head monk and director that if they cannot find someone to take all three at once, will they stay here all their childhood? The director shook his head and told me what I thought might happen: If someone wants one of the babies, they will be separated. It is not a policy to keep siblings together if one can find a home. "It is better to have three different families adopt, than none at all."

My heart sank. I explained what I had read regarding this kind of twin/triplet separation and how it does more harm than good to their mental health. "Does not the fact that the children spend eight months in the most intimate confines of the womb, then spend every hour after that, asleep and awake, with each other, feeding off each other's company and energy and then one day…poof! The bond is broken and they never see each other again. It causes a kind of hole or missing piece in their soul. Don't you think that if they are born together, they should be raised together?"

The director agreed. "It would be ideal if that can happen. If they are adopted out before the age of four, they will not remember their siblings and it won't make a difference."

I began to tell the director that studies show this is not true at all, especially of multiple birth children, but I could see my words will not change her mind. I asked them to reconsider this way of releasing the children but they shrugged and said it can't be helped. There are so many children to feed and teach, and with over 25,000 orphans in Vietnam, the older the child, the harder they are to place.

Also, there are the many costs of adoption with various fees for Vietnam and the governments of the adopting family, inspections of the home, police, medical and financial records must be pulled for all the adopting family members and etc. The cost for just one child can run $25-$35k to adopt. If someone wishes to adopt all three, then they will be happy to do it, of course, but it is a rare event and not likely to happen.

The head monk said "Certainly it would be better to have siblings stay together, and even better if the children have parents and other family present in their lives. Since they do not, it is better they were brought to the orphanage than killed or discarded like trash as happens to some. Not everyone can have the same life many of us had." I know he is right about this. Of course.

I look at my son and daughter playing happily with the other children. Ca is playing with them too. My children have all they can want and will never lack for food or clothes or love. I look at the three girls in front of me. I am sorry that my body cannot have another child, but that does not mean I cannot take care of another. I pick up Sang and tickle her tummy. She wiggles in happiness. I hold her hair to my nose and smell the smell only babies have.

Frankie hugged my leg suddenly and, looking up, he asked "Who that, Me?"

I brought the little girl down to my son's level and said "This is your new little sister. Say hello to Sang."

"Hello Sang! I'm Frankie!" He says it like he expects Sang to answer back.

I point to the girls in the playpen. "And that's Trang and Lang. They will be your new sisters too!"

"They are?"

"Yes, my son, they are."

I laid Sang back down with her sisters, stood to my full height, pulled my shoulders back like Fred taught me and said "I will not let these girls be separated. How do we begin the adoption paperwork?"

The Director asked me if I wanted to speak to my husband about this first?

I smiled when I told him, "I do not need to speak to my husband. I already know what he will say. He will say, 'The more, the merrier!'"

Lois: This is the end of the last notebook I found. I asked Mama if there are any other notebooks and she told me that the next notebook had gotten lost in her travels and by then she was getting busier with acting work, adoption requirements to be met, her suddenly much larger family and expanding business ventures.

Mama told us "The diary was like a friend to me. Someone to talk to as I had few close friends in either country. I was also able to go back to it from time to time as a reference for different events in our lives. But as our lives got busier, I had less time to write and once I lost the last notebook, I decided the writing of the diary had run its course. I simply put that part of my life away and concentrated on growing what we had started. That included you five!"

When Mama called Dad from Vietnam and told that she was going to be a mother again, she couched it to sound like she was pregnant, without actually saying it. He was worried, of course, for her health and that of the baby after what had happened with me. And worried too, as to whose baby it was since Dad had had a vasectomy soon after I was born. When Mama had her fun and explained about her decision to adopt triplet girls and that yes, she was not joking or making fun with him now, he laughed and said "Kimmie, you never cease to amaze me. Well, the more the merrier!"

As for Sang, Trang and Lang, it took less than eighteen months to get all the adoption paperwork and interviews done. It helped a great deal that our mother and her family were sponsors of the orphanage and both our parents had spotless records on every level, thereby cutting the normal two to three year processing period by half. By then, our sisters were just over two years old and Mama had already become an American citizen with the blue passport to prove it. They arrived in the US on March 17th, 2007, our parents' birthday, to a whole new family and future.

The End

Acknowledgements

Thanks to Trung Ly and Kenny Nguyen who helped me determine Kimmie's colorful and appropriate nickname along with sharing Vietnamese-related trivia that I was able to use to throughout this novel.

Thanks to the late Geoff Edwards' brilliant suggestion of giving this diary-based story more depth by sprinkling additional voices throughout with related anecdotes, back stories and teasers.
You are missed.

About the Author

Thomas Stimson is a native of Washington State who has found his writing voice with 'fish out of water stories' where the primary character(s) make their way through unfamiliar, and sometimes dangerous, situations in a humorous fashion.

Under the pen-name Charles Thomas, he has also published the SweetSips series of liqueur-making recipe books which can be found on Amazon along with his novels.

His first published works are a historical novella set in Spain and Central America in the time of Columbus "The Jackass" (2020) and a mystery set in 1960's Eastern Europe "The Secret of Linden Court (2023).

In the works are a rollicking comedy set in Italy, "The Prince of Nothing" scheduled for the Spring of 2025 and "A Bitter Ending in Sugar Land" involving a Sikh engineer's desperate attempts to repay family obligations after he secures a plum job in Texas (Fall of 2025)

Impending retirement and lots of imagination are the impetus to write and share his stories at this stage of his life.

Other Titles by Thomas Stimson

The Jackass

The Secret of Linden Court

The Prince of Nothing (2025)

A Bitter Ending in Sugar Land (2025)

"An American in the Cotswolds"
(NIWA Anthology *Guests*)

"Grass Valley"
(NIWA Anthology *Illusion*)

"1492"
(NIWA Anthology *Journey*)

Titles under Charles Thomas

SweetSips –
Wining and Dining with Homemade Liqueurs

SummerTime SweetSips –
Homemade Liqueurs for Summertime Entertaining

SweetSips for the HoliDays –
Homemade Liqueurs for Holiday Entertaining